GREAT TALES
OF
MADNESS &
THE MACABRE

GREAT TALES
■ OF ■
MADNESS &
THE MACABRE

Compiled by
Charles Ardai

Introduction by
Lawrence Block

Galahad Books  New York

Published in 1990 by

Galahad Books
A division of LDAP, Inc.
166 Fifth Avenue
New York, NY 10010

Galahad Books is a registered trademark of LDAP, Inc.

Published by arrangement with Davis Publications, Inc.

Library of Congress Catalog Card Number: 89-81788

ISBN: 0-88365-750-3

Printed in the United States of America.

ACKNOWLEDGMENTS

Grateful acknowledgment is made to the following for permission to reprint their copyrighted material:

The Living Dead by Robert Bloch, copyright © 1967 by Davis Publications, Inc., reprinted by permission of Scott Meredith Literary Agency, Inc.; *The Dive People* by Avram Davidson, copyright © 1958 by Davis Publications, Inc., reprinted by permission of the author; *Graffiti* by Stanley Ellin, copyright © 1983 by Davis Publications, Inc., reprinted by permission of Curtis Brown Ltd.; *The Marked Man* by David Ely, copyright © 1979 by Davis Publications, Inc., reprinted by permission of Roberta Pryor, Inc.; *Something Evil in the House* by Celia Fremlin, copyright © 1968 by Celia Fremlin, reprinted by permission of the author; *The Wedding Gig* by Stephen King, copyright © 1980 by Davis Publications, Inc., reprinted by permission of Kirby McCauley, Inc.; *Report on a Broken Bridge* by Dennis O'Neil, copyright © 1971 by Davis Publications, Inc., reprinted by permission of the author; *Placebo* by Andrew Vachss, copyright © 1989 by Davis Publications, Inc., reprinted by permission of Cohen, Glickstein & Lurie; all first appeared in *Ellery Queen's Mystery Magazine*.

Sometimes They Bite by Lawrence Block, copyright © 1976 by Davis Publications, Inc., reprinted by permission of the author; *Three Men in a Tub* by Lemuel Cork, copyright © 1989 by Davis Publications, Inc., reprinted by permission of the author; *Flicks* by Bill Crenshaw, copyright © 1988 by Davis Publications, Inc., reprinted by permission of the author; *Killer in the House* by James R. Petrin, copyright © 1988 by Davis Publications, Inc., reprinted by permission of the author; all first appeared in *Alfred Hitchcock Mystery Magazine*.

The Dim Rumble by Isaac Asimov, copyright © 1982 by Davis Publications, Inc., reprinted by permission of the author; *The Beast from One-Quarter Fathom* by George Alec Effinger, copyright © 1985 by Davis Publications, Inc., reprinted by permission of the author; *Deathbinder* by Alexander Jablokov, copyright © 1988, reprinted by permission of the author; *Trinity* by Nancy Kress, copyright © 1984 by Davis Publications, Inc., reprinted by permis-

CONTENTS

Putting this book together has been a most peculiar labor of love. The stories you are about to read are ones which have haunted me for years. These are not tales you will soon forget . . . If they bring you the chills and the wicked thoughts that they have brought me, then they have done their job and I have done mine.

This volume would never have existed without the participation of certain people whose efforts I would like to acknowledge here: Cynthia Manson, who got me started and who shepherded the project through its many stages; Kathy Roche, the best editor an editor could have; Froggy MacIntyre, Greg Cox and Mark Munro for their patience, ideas, and help; and all the authors of the tales that follow for showing us unflinchingly the many faces of fear.

Finally, I dedicate this volume to the two people who have contributed the most to my own madness: Larry Block and Alix Florio.

— Charles Ardai
October, 1989

Introduction

LAWRENCE BLOCK

In the fall of 1975 I was alone, and traveling. I had left New York, reduced my worldly goods to what would fit in the back of a rusted-out Ford station wagon, and was on my way to Los Angeles. It took me nine months to get there, but then I was in no particular hurry.

I spent the month of September in Rodanthe, on North Carolina's Outer Banks. I had started work on a novel which would turn out to be *Ariel*, the story of an adopted child in Charleston, South Carolina, who may or may not have murdered her baby brother in his crib. The book was not going well, and what I was mostly concentrating on was fishing. There was a pier sticking out into the ocean and you could fish off it all day and night. I literally lived that month on what I hauled out of the ocean, occasionally varying my fare by driving over to the bay side of the island and catching eels. I had a great recipe for eels. They came out tasting like chicken fricassee, except eelier.

And I started writing short stories. I wrote one called *Click!*, about a jaded hunter who tries to hunt with a camera instead, and it turns out that he can't, and that it's human beings he hunts, not animals. I wrote another called *Funny You Should Ask*, about a young hitch-hiker who wonders where recycled jeans come from, since nobody ever throws them out; he learns to his chagrin that they are the byproduct of a firm involved in processing unwary young people into pet food.

And then I wrote *Sometimes They Bite*, which appears in this volume.

I sent it off to my agent, as I had done with the others. After he read it he called a friend of mine. "Have you heard from Larry lately?" he wanted to know.

"I think he's in North Carolina," my friend said.

"I know where he is," my agent said. "I wondered if you'd heard from him. He's been writing these short stories."

"And?"

"And I have a feeling he's been alone too long," my agent said.

I think he was probably right. And, if there is a common denominator in the stories you will find in this collection, I suspect it is that they were all written by people who have been alone too long. They might not have been geographically remote, as I was, and they might not have been deprived of the company of others, as I also was. But I have a feeling they were too much alone in the recesses of their own minds, too much in touch with their own madness, too often face to face with their own demons. As I was.

It is this turning inward, this view of the hidden and frequently unsettling chambers of the self, that generates the ideas from which such stories spring. "Where do you get your ideas?" some readers ask—when they read anything, but especially when they read stories like these. We get them as oysters get pearls, by carefully wrapping the stuff of our innards around the sharp grains of sand that cause us pain.

I am writing these lines in Virginia, where I am briefly in residence at a colony, a sort of refuge for artists and composers and writers. My wife Lynne is here as well, making art, and we are in the good company of twenty fellow artists. A few weeks ago, however, I put aside a novel and began writing short stories, and some of them look for all the world to be the work of a man who has been alone too long.

And today we wait in the path of Hurricane Hugo. The sky is light one minute and dark the next. The trees are already being whipped by high winds, and the air is warm and dense and choked with menace.

Awful and *wonderful* once meant the same thing. This weather is awful and wonderful. Storms like Hugo are dangerous beyond description, and the sane part of me hopes this one will miss us, or strike us only a glancing blow.

Another part of me, the part that's been alone too long, yearns for the full fury of the storm.

These stories are awful and wonderful. May you enjoy weather such as this across your own inner landscape as you read them.

—Lawrence Block

"There is a pleasure sure
In being mad which none but madmen know."

— John Dryden

Deathbinder

ALEXANDER JABLOKOV

The El station platform was empty, and the winter Chicago Sunday afternoon had turned into night. Stanley Paterson paused at the turnstile and rubbed his nose doubtfully. The overhead lamps cast circular pools of light on the gouged surface of the platform, but this made Stanley feel obvious, rather than safe. He hunched his shoulders inside his wool topcoat, puffed out his cheeks, and shuffled along the platform, looking down the tracks in the direction of the expected train. His mind was still full of the financial affairs of a medium-sized Des Moines metals trading company which was slated for acquisition. It was a big project, worth working weekends for, so, aside from the inside of his condominium, the inside of his office, and the inside of various El trains, he no longer knew what anything looked like. Winter had somehow arrived without an intervening autumn. He'd been to Oak St. Beach once, near the end of the summer, he remembered. Or had that been last year?

The wind blew dried leaves past him; delicately curved, ribbed, and textured leaves. He felt himself among them, heavy and gross, and thought about going on a diet. It was tough when you worked as hard as he did, he thought, excusing himself. It was hell on your eating habits. Today he'd eaten—what? He couldn't remember. The coat slapped his legs. The skin by his nose was oily, there was an itch under his right shoulder blade, and he was hungry. He wondered what he could put in the microwave when he got home. What did he have left in the freezer? Chinese? Chicken Kiev? Hell, he'd see when he got there. High above him floated the lighted windows of the city, rank upon rank, like cherubim.

The turnstile clattered. Stanley tried to tell himself that it was ridiculous to feel afraid, even in the dark, alone on the platform, but succeeded only in feeling afraid and ridiculous, both. He leaned forward, looking again for the train, trying to pull it into the station by the force of his gaze, but the tracks remained empty. He glanced towards the turnstile. A man stood there, a shadow. He didn't look like a big man, and his race was not obvious, but he wore a hat, which looked like leather. Respectable people did not wear hats, Stanley felt. Particularly not leather ones. It looked too silly. The man turned and, with slow, confident steps, walked towards Stanley.

Stanley thought about running, but didn't. It would have made him feel like a fool. He rocked back on his heels, hands in his pockets, and ignored the other. He tried to project an air of quiet authority. The platform on the other side of the tracks was completely empty.

He never saw it, but he felt the knife press, sharp, against his side, just above the right kidney. There was, somehow, no doubt whatsoever about what it was.

"Your money."

"Excuse me? I—"

"Your money."

The knife cut through the expensive fabric of his coat and grazed his flesh. Stanley felt a surge of annoyance at the wanton damage. Spontaneously, unthinkingly, like a tripped mousetrap, Stanley cried out and hit the man in the face with a balled fist, remembering only at the last second not to put his thumb inside his fingers. It was like striking out in sleep, but he did not awaken, as he usually did, sweat-soaked and tangled in sheets. Instead, the dark cold night remained around him, and as the man stumbled back, Stanley grappled with him, and tried to get his hands around his throat. He really was a small man, much smaller than he had expected, and he couldn't remember why he had been so frightened of him. The knife blade twisted, and Stanley felt it penetrate flesh. A scream cut the night. There was suddenly a warm glow in Stanley's belly, which spread up through his chest. He felt dizzy, and flung his suddenly weightless assailant across the platform, seeing him whirl tiny, tiny away, joining the leaves in their dance, then vanishing back through the turnstile, which clattered again. Blackness loomed overhead like a tidal wave and blotted out the lights of the windows. The dark heaviness knocked Stanley down on to the platform, and he heard a wailing sound, like sirens, or a baby crying. He rested on the platform, which had become as soft as a woman's breast. It was late, he was tired, and the train did not seem to want to come, so he decided to take a well-deserved nap.

The scream of the nurse, who had come in to check Margaret's pulse, but found, when she pulled back the blankets, that her patient had turned into a mass of giant black bats which burst up from the rumpled sheets to fill the bedroom with the fleshy beating of their wings, became the shrill ring of the telephone. Matthew Harmon woke up with a shock, jerked the cord until the phone fell on the bed, and cradled the receiver under his ear.

"Dr. Harmon," the voice on the phone said. A simple, flat statement, as if someone had decided to call in the middle of the night to wake him up and reassure him about his identity. Harmon felt a surge of irritation, and knew he was once again alive. He reached up and turned on the bedside lamp, which cast a pool of light over the bed. He did not look at the other half of the bed, but he could hear Margaret's labored breathing there. She muttered something like "Phone, Matt . . . phone," then choked, as if having a heart seizure. There were no bats, at least.

"Yes?" he said. "What is it?" His throat hurt again, and his voice was husky.

A pause. "I was asked to make this call. Against my better judgment . . . it's information I don't think you should have. But," a deep sigh, "it seems that we have one of what you call . . . abandoned souls. That is what you call them, isn't it?" Another pause, longer than the first. "This is stupid. I wonder why I called you."

"That makes two of us." The voice on the line was contemptuous, but uncomfortably so, ill at ease despite its advantage of identity and wakefulness. It was a familiar voice, from somewhere in the past, one of so many familiar voices, voices of medical students, interns, residents, nurses, fellow doctors, researchers, all ranged through over forty years of memory, some respectful, some exasperated, some angry. He ran his hand over his scalp and thought about that tone of defensive contempt. "Orphaned. Not abandoned. Though that will do just as well." Given the subject of the call, it had to be someone at an Intensive Care Unit, probably at a city hospital. Possibly connected with a trauma center. That narrowed things . . . got it. "Masterman," he said. "Eugene Colin Masterman. Johns Hopkins Medical School, class of '75. You're at Pres St. Luke's now. I hope that you are finally clear on the difference between afferent and efferent nerves. I remember you had trouble with the distinction, back in my neuroanatomy class at Hopkins. Just remember: SAME, sensory afferent, motor efferent. It's not hard. But, as you said, you didn't decide to call me. Leibig, chief of your ICU, told you to. How is Karl?"

"Dr. Leibig is well," Masterman said sulkily. "Aside from the inevitable effects of age. He has a renal dysfunction, and seems to have developed a vestibular disorder which keeps him off his feet. He will be retiring next year."

"A pity," Harmon said. "A good man. And three years younger than I am, as I'm sure I don't have to remind you. Well, Eugene, why don't you tell me the story?" Masterman, he recalled, hated being called Eugene.

Masterman gave it to him, chapter and verse, in offensively superfluous detail. Patient's name: Paterson, Stanley Andrew. Patient's social security number. Patient's place of employment, a management consulting firm in the Loop. Locations of stab wounds, fractures, lacerations. Patient's blood type and rejection spectrum. Units of blood transfused, in the ambulance, in the Emergency Room, in the ICU, divided into whole blood and plasma. Names of the ambulance crew. Name of admitting doctor. Name of duty nurse. All surname first, then first name and middle initial.

"Who was his first grade teacher?" Harmon said.

"What—Dr. Harmon, I did not want to make this call, understand that. I did so at the specific request of Dr. Leibig."

"Who also wonders if I am crazy. But he did it for old time's sake, bless him. Eugene, if, as it seems, you are not enjoying this call, perhaps you should make an effort to be more . . . pithy."

"Paterson suffered a cardiac arrest at, let's see, 1:08 AM. We attempted to restart several times with a defibrillator, but were finally forced to open the chest and apply a pacemaker. We have also attached a ventilator. His condition is now stable."

"Life is not stable," Harmon said, but thought, "The stupid bastards." Would they never learn? Didn't they understand the consequences? *Doctors.* Clever technicians who thought themselves scientists. "Brain waves?"

"Well . . . minimal."

"Minimal, Eugene? Where did he die?"

"He isn't dead. We have him on life support."

"Don't play games with me! Where was he murdered?"

"At the Adams St. El station, at Adams and Wabash. The northbound platform." He paused, then the words spilled out. "Listen, Harmon, you can't go on doing this, talking about ghosts and goblins and all sorts of idiocy about the spirits of the unburied dead. This isn't the Middle Ages, for crissakes. We're doctors, we know better, we've learned. We *know* how things work now. Have you forgotten everything? You can't just let people under your care die to protect their souls. That's crazy, absolute lunacy. I don't know how I let Leibig talk me into this, he knows you're crazy too, and the patient's *not* dead, he's alive, and if I have anything to say about it he'll stay that way, and I won't pull the plug because of some idiotic theory you have about ghosts. And I do so know the difference between afferent and efferent. Afferent nerves—"

"Never mind, Dr. Masterman," Harmon said wearily. "At this hour, I'm not sure I remember myself. Get back to your patients. Thank you for your call." He hung the receiver up gently.

After a moment to gather his strength, he pulled his legs out from under the comforter and forced them down to the cold floor. As they had grown thinner, the hair on them, now white, seemed to have grown thicker. He pulled the silk pajamas down so that he could not see his shins. The virtues of youth, he thought, too often become the sins of age. He had once been slim, and was now skinny. His nose, once aquiline, was a beak, and his high, noble forehead had extended itself clear over the top of his head.

These late night phone calls always made him think of Margaret, as she had been. He remembered her, before their marriage, as a young redhead in a no-nonsense gray suit with a ridiculous floppy bow tie, and later, in one of his shirts, much too long for her and tight in the chest, as she raised her arms in mock dismay at the number of his books she was expected to fit into their tiny apartment, and, finally, as a prematurely old woman gasping her life out in the bed next to him. None of it had been her fault, but it had been she who had suffered.

He dialed the phone. It was answered on the first ring. "Sphinx and Eye of Truth Bookstore, Dexter Warhoff, Owner and Sole Proprietor. We're closed now, really, but we open at—"

"Dexter," Harmon said. "Sorry to bother you. It looks like we have another one."

"Professor!" Dexter said with delight. "No bother at all. I was just playing with some stuff out of the Kabbalah. Kind of fun, but nothing that won't wait. Where is this one? Oh, never mind, let it be a surprise. Usual place, in an hour? I'll call him and get him ready. Oh boy."

Harmon restrained a sigh. He could picture Dexter, plump and bulging in a shirt of plum or burgundy, with his bright blue eyes and greasy hair, behind the front desk at the Sphinx and Eye of Truth Bookstore, where he spent most of his waking hours, of which he apparently had many, scribbling in a paperback copy of *The Prophecies of Nostradamus* with a pencil stub or, as tonight, rearranging Hebrew letters to make anagrams of the Name of God.

The store itself was a neat little place on the Near North Side, with colorful throw pillows on the floor and the scent of jasmine incense in the air. It carried books on every imaginable topic relating to the occult and the supernatural, from Madame Blavatsky to Ancient Astronauts, from Edgar Cayce to the Loch Ness Monster, from Tarot cards to ESP. It had been almost impossible for Harmon to go there, but go there he did, finally, after exhausting every other resource, to accept a cup of camomile tea from Dexter's dirty-fingernailed hands and learn what he reluctantly came to understand to be the truth.

"Yes, Dexter. St. Mary's, as usual."

"Right. See ya."

Harmon hung up. He'd searched and searched, down every avenue, but he was well and truly stuck. When it came to the precise and ticklish business of the exorcism and binding of the spirits of the uneasy dead, there was no better assistant alive than Dexter Warhoff.

A train finally pulled into the station. It was lit up golden from inside, like a lantern. The doors slid open, puffing warm air. Stanley thought about getting up and going into the train. He could get home that way. But he remembered how uncomfortable the seats were on the train, and what a long, cold walk he had from the station to his condo, so he just remained where he was, where the ground was soft and warm. After waiting for a long moment, the train shut its doors and whooshed off, up along the shining metal tracks as they arched into the sky, to vanish among the stars and the windows of the apartment buildings, which now floated free in the darkness, like balloons let loose by children.

Once he was alone again, Stanley found himself standing, not knowing how he had come to be so. The wind from Lake Michigan had cleared the sky, and a half moon lit the towers of the city. The city was alive; he could hear the soughing of its breath, the thrumming of its heart, and the murmuration of its countless vessels. Without thinking about it, he swung over the railing and slid down the girders of the El station to the waiting earth. The city spread out before him, Stanley Paterson ambled abroad.

After some time, the wind carried to him the aroma of roasting lamb, with cumin and garlic. He turned into it, like a salmon swimming upstream, and soon stood among the cracked plaster columns and fishing nets of a Greek restaurant. A blue flame burst up in the dimness, and Stanley moved towards it. A waiter in a white sailor's shirt served a man and a woman saganaki, fried kasseri cheese flamed with brandy.

Stanley could taste the tartness of the cheese and the tang of the brandy as they both ate, and feel the crunch of the outside and the yielding softness of the inside. He could taste the wine too, the bitterly resinous heaviness of retsina.

They looked at each other. She was young, wearing a cotton dress with a bold, colorful pattern, and made a face at the taste of the wine. The man, who had ordered it, was older, in gray tweed, and grinned back at her. Stanley hovered over the two of them like a freezing man over a fire. However, as he drew close, something changed between them. They had been friends for a long time, at the law office where they both worked, but this was their first romantic evening together. She had finally made the suggestion, and now, as she looked at him, instead of thoughts of romance, her mind wandered to the coy calculations already becoming old to her, of getting to his apartment, giggling, of excusing herself at just the right moment to insert her diaphragm, of her mock exuberant gesture of tossing her panties over the foot of the bed at the moment he finally succeeded in getting her completely undressed, of how to act innocent while letting him know that she wasn't. The older man's shoulders stiffened, and he wished, too late, that he had resisted her, resisted the urge to turn her from a friend into yet another prematurely sophisticated young woman, wished that he could stop for a moment to think and breathe, in the midst of his headlong pursuit of the Other. The saganaki grew cold as they examined, silently, the plastic grapes that dangled in the arbor above their heads. Stanley moved back, and found himself on the street again.

Music came to him from somewhere far above. He slid up the smooth walls of an apartment building until he reached it. The glass of the window pushed against his face like the yielding surface of a soap bubble, and, then, suddenly, he was inside.

A woman with a mass of curly gray hair and an improbably long neck sat at the grand piano, her head cocked at the sheet music as she played, while a younger woman with lustrous black hair and kohl-darkened eyes sat straight-backed on a stool with an oboe. The music, Stanley knew, though he had never heard it before, was Schumann's *Romances for Oboe and Piano*, and they played it with the ease of long mutual familiarity. Their only audience was a fuzzy cat of uncertain breed who sat on a footstool and stared into the fire in the fireplace.

Stanley felt the notes dance through him, and sensed the blissful self-forgetfulness of the musicians. He wanted desperately to share in it, and moved to join them. The oboist suddenly thought about the fact that, no matter how well she played, and how much she practiced, she would never play well enough to perform with the Chicago Symphony, or any orchestra, ever, and the love of her life would always remain a hobby, a pastime. The pianist's throat constricted, and suddenly she feared the complexity of the instrument before her, knowing that she was inadequate to the task, as she was to all tasks of any importance, that no one would ever approve of her, and that she was old. The instruments went completely out of sync, as if the performers were in separate rooms with soundproof walls between them, and the music crashed into cacophony. The cat stood up, bristling, stared right at Stanley, and hissed. The pianist tapped one note over and over with her forefinger. The oboist started to cut another reed, even though she had two already cut. Stanely passed back out through the window.

He left the residential towers and wandered the streets of three-story brownstone apartment buildings. He felt warm, soapy water on his skin, and drifted through the wide crack under an ill-fitting door.

The bathroom was warm and steamy, heated by the glow of a gas burner in one wall. A plump woman in a flower print dress, with short dark hair, washed a child in that most marvelous of bathing devices, a large, freestanding claw-foot bathtub. The little girl in the tub had just had her hair washed, and it was slicked to her head like a mannikin's. She stared intently down into the soapy water like a cat catching fish.

"Point to your mouth, Sally. Your mouth." Sally obediently put her finger in her mouth. "Point to your nose." She put her finger in her nose. "Very good, Sally. Can you point to your ear? Your ear, Sally." After a moment's thought, the little girl put her finger in her ear. "Where is your chin?" Sally, tiring of the game, and having decided which she liked best, stuck her finger back up her nose and stared at her mother. Her mother laughed, delighted at this mutiny. "Silly goose." She poured water over the girl's head. Sally closed her eyes and made a "brrr" noise with her lips. "Time to get out, Sally." The little girl stood up, and her mother pulled the plug. Sally waved as the water and soap bubbles swirled down the drain and said, "Ba-*bye*. Ba-*bye*." Her mother pulled her from the tub and wrapped her in a huge towel, in which she vanished completely.

The feel of the terry cloth on his skin, and the warm, strawberry scent of the mother covered Stanley like a benediction. He stretched forward, as the mother rubbed her daughter's hair with the towel until it stood out in all directions. The mother's happiness vanished, and she felt herself trapped, compelled, every moment of her life now given over to the care of a selfish and capricious creature, no time to even think about getting any work done on the one poem she'd been working on since she left high school to get married, her life predetermined now until she grew old and was left alone. She rubbed too vigorously with the towel and Sally, smothered and manipulated by forces she could not control, or even understand, began to shriek. "Quiet, Sally. Quiet, *damn it*."

Stanley remembered the platform. What was he doing in here? He had a train to catch, he had to get home. He could not even imagine how he had managed to stray. He turned and hurried off to the El station.

The two of them walked down the street together, Harmon with a long, measured stride, and Dexter with the peculiar mincing waddle he was compelled to use because of the width of his thighs. Harmon wore a long, thick overcoat and a karakul hat, but the cold still struck deep into his bones. He wore a scarf to protect his throat, which was always the most sensitive. He remembered a time, surely not that long ago, when he had enjoyed the winter, when it had made him feel alive. He and Margaret had spent weekends in Wisconsin, cross-country skiing, and making grotesque snowmen. No longer. Dexter wore a red windbreaker that made him look like a tomato, and a Minnesota Vikings cap with horns on it. As he walked, he juggled little beanbags in an elaborate fountain. He had a number of similar skills—such as rolling a silver dollar across the back of his knuckles, like George Raft, and making origami animals—all of which annoyed Harmon because he had never learned to do things like that. He thought about the image the two of them presented, and snorted, amused at himself for feeling embarrassed.

"Father Toomey looked a little bummed out," Dexter said. "I think we woke him up."

"Dexter, it's three-thirty in the morning. Not everyone sits up all night reading books on the Kabbalah."

"Yeah, I guess. Anyway, he cheered up after we talked about the horoscope reading I'm doing for him. There's a lot of real interesting stuff in it."

"An ordained Catholic priest is having you do his *horoscope*?"

Dexter looked surprised. "Sure. Why not?"

Why not indeed? Harmon hefted his ancient black leather bag. The instruments it contained had been blessed by Father Toomey, and sprinkled with holy water from the font at St. Mary's. Harmon, in the precisely rigorous theological way that devout atheists have, doubted the efficacy of a blessing from a priest so far sunk in superstition that he had his horoscope done, and performed holy offices for a purpose so blatantly demonic, but he had to admit that it always seemed to do the job. When he handed the sleepy, slightly inebriated priest the speculum, the wand, the silver nails, the censer, the compass, and the rest of the instruments of his new trade, they were nothing but dead metal, but when he took them in his hands after the blessing, they vibrated with suppressed energy. The touch of such half-living things was odious to him, essential though they were. It disturbed him that such things worked. As quickly as he could, he wrapped them in their coverings of virgin lamb hide, inscribed with Latin prayers and Babylonian symbols, and placed them, in correct order, into his bag. That bag had once held his stethoscope, patella reflex hammer, thermometer, hypodermics, laryngoscope, and the rest of his medical instruments, and though he had not touched any of them in years, it had pained him to remove them so that the bag could be used for its new purpose.

"You know, Professor, the other day I was reading an interesting book about the gods of ancient Atlantis—"

"Oh, Dexter," Harmon said irritably. "You don't really believe all these things, do you?"

Dexter grinned at him, yellow-toothed. "Why not? You believe in *ghosts*, don't you?"

Dexter's one unanswerable argument. "I believe in them, Dexter, only because I am forced to, not because I like it. That's the difference between us. It would be terrible to *like* the idea that ghosts exist."

"Boy, did you fight it," Dexter said with a chuckle. "You sat with me for an hour, talking about Mary Baker Eddy. Then you shut up. I asked you what was wrong. 'A ghost,' you said. 'I've got to get rid of a ghost.' Took you three cups of tea to say that. You don't even like camomile tea, do you?"

"It served."

"It sure did. You remember that first time, don't you? I'll never forget it. We hardly knew what we were doing, like two kids playing with dynamite. I had pretended I knew more about it than I did, you know."

"I know." They often talked about the first ghost. They never talked about the second.

"I thought I could handle it, but it almost swallowed me and you had to save my ass. Quite a talent you have there. Strongest I've ever heard of. You should be proud."

"I feel precisely as proud as I would if I discovered that I had an innate genius for chicken stealing."

Dexter laughed, head thrown back. He had a lot of fillings in his back teeth. "Gee, that's pretty funny. But anyway, this Kabbalah stuff is real interesting. . . ."

Harmon suffered himself to be subjected to a rambling, overly detailed lecture on medieval Jewish mysticism, until, much too soon, they were at the El station.

Dexter craned his head back and looked up at the dark girders of the station, his face suddenly serious. "I feel him up there. He's a heavy one. Strong. He didn't live enough, when he had the chance. Those are always the worst. Too many trapped desires. Good luck to you. Oh . . . wait. They lock these things when the trains stop running, and we're not exactly authorized." He reached into his pocket and pulled out a little black pouch, which, when opened, revealed a line of shiny lock-picking tools.

"I used to pick locks at school," Dexter said. "Just for fun. I never stole anything. Figuring out the locks was the good part. Schools don't have very good locks. Most students just break in the windows." He walked up to the heavy metal mesh door at the base of the stairs, and had it opened about as quickly as he could have with a key. He sighed, disappointed. "The CTA doesn't either. I don't even know why they bother. Well, now it's time. Good luck." They paused and he shook Harmon's hand, as he always did, with a simple solemnity.

Nothing to say, Harmon turned and started up towards the El station.

They *were* always the worst. "The people who want to live forever are always the ones who can't find anything to do on a rainy Sunday afternoon," as Dr. Kaltenbrunner, the head of Radiology at Mt. Tabor Hospital, had once said. Dr. K was never bored, and certainly never boring, enjoyed seventeenth-century English poetry, and died of an aneurism three months before Harmon encountered his first ghost. Died and stayed dead. Harmon always thought he could have used his help. Thomas Browne and John Donne would have understood ghosts better than Harmon could, which was funny, because there hadn't *been* enough ghosts in the seventeenth century to be worth worrying about.

Some doctors managed to stay away from ER duty, and it was mostly the young ones—who needed to be taught, by having their noses rubbed in it, about the mixture of fragility and resilience that is the human body—who took the duty there, particularly at night. In his time, Harmon had seen a seventy-year-old lady some anonymous madman had pushed in front of an onrushing El train recover and live, with only a limp in her left leg to show for it, and a DePaul University linebacker DOA from a fractured skull caused by a fall in the shower in the men's locker room.

As Harmon climbed the clattering metal stairs up to the deserted El platform, he remembered the first one. It was always that way with him. He was never able to see the Duomo of Florence without remembering the first time he and Margaret had seen it, from the window of their pensione. There were some words he could not read without remembering the classroom in which he learned them, and whether it had been sunny that day. It meant there were some things he never lost, that he always had Margaret with him in Florence. And it meant that he could never deal with a ghost without remembering the terror of the first one.

He had been working night duty, late, when they brought in a bloody stretcher. It had been quiet for about an hour, in that strange irregular rhythm that Emergency Rooms have, crowded most of the time, but sometimes almost empty. A pedestrian had been hit by a truck while crossing the street. There was a lot of bleeding, mostly internal, and a torn lung filled with blood, a hemothorax. His breathing was audible, a slow dragging gurgle, the sound a straw makes sucking at the bottom of a glass of Coke when the glass is almost empty. Harmon managed to stop much of the bleeding, but by that time the man was in shock. Then the heart went into ventricular fibrillation. Harmon put the paddles on and defibrillated it. When the heart stopped altogether, he put the patient on a pacemaker and an external ventilator. The autopsy subsequently showed substantial damage to the brainstem, as well as complete kidney failure. Every measure Harmon took, as it turned out, was useless, but he managed to keep the patient alive an extra hour, before everything stopped at once, in the ICU.

A day or so later, the nurse on duty came to him with a problem. Rosemary was a redhead, cute, and reminded him of Margaret when she was young, so he was a little fonder of her than he should have been, particularly since Margaret had been sick. The nurse wasn't flirting now, however. She was frightened. She kept hearing someone drinking out of a straw, she said, in a corner of the ER, only there wasn't anyone there. She was afraid she was losing her mind, which can happen to you after too many gunshot wounds, suicides, and drug overdoses. Harmon told her, in what he told himself was a fatherly way, that it was probably something like air in the pipes, which he called an "embolism," a medical usage which delighted her. She teased him about it.

Harmon remembered being vaguely pleased about that, while he searched around and listened. He didn't hear anything. It was late, and he finally climbed up on a gurney and went to sleep, as some of the other doctors did when things weren't busy. He'd never done it before, and why he did it was something he could not remember, though everything about the incident, from the freckles around Rosemary's nose to the scheduling roster for that night's medical staff, was abnormally clear in his mind, the way memories of things that happened only yesterday never were. When he woke up, he heard it. A slow dragging gurgle. He listened with his eyes closed, heart pounding. Then it stopped.

"Hey, have you seen my car?" a voice said. "It's a blue car, a Cutlass, though I guess it's too dark here to see the color. I know I parked it near here, but I just can't find it."

Harmon slowly opened his eyes. Standing in front of him was a fat man in a business suit, holding a briefcase. He wasn't bloody, and his face was not pasty white, but Harmon recognized him. It was the man who had died the night before.

"Look, I have to get home to Berwyn. My wife will be going nuts. She expected me home hours ago. Have you seen the damn car? It's a Cutlass, blue. Not a good car, God knows, and it needs work, but I gotta get home."

Harmon had met the wife, when she identified the body. She had, indeed, expected him hours ago.

"Jeez, I don't know what I could have done with it."

Harmon was a logical man, and a practical man, and he hadn't until that moment realized that those two characteristics could be in conflict. What he saw before him was indubitably a ghost, and as a practical man he had to accept that. He also knew, as a logical man, that ghosts did not, indeed could not, exist. This neat conundrum, however, did not occur to him until somewhat later, because the next time the dead man said, "Do you think you could help me find my car? I gotta get home," he launched himself from the gurney, smashing it back into the wall, bolted from the ER, and did not stop running until he was sitting at the desk in his little office on the fifth floor, shaking desperately and trying not to scream.

The El platform was windswept and utterly empty. Harmon walked slowly across its torn asphalt until he came to the spot where it had happened. The police had cleaned up the blood, and erased the chalk outline, that curious symbol of the vanished soul used by police photographers as a record of the body, so morning commuters would not be unpleasantly surprised by the cold official evidence of violent death. He didn't have to see it. He could feel it, like standing in the autopsy room and knowing that someone had left the door to the cold room where the bodies were kept open because you could feel the cold formaldehyde-and-decay scented air seeping along the floor.

He didn't know why he had this particular sense, or ability, or whatever. To himself he compared it to someone with perfect pitch and rhythm who nevertheless dislikes music, someone who could play Bach's *Goldberg Variations* through perfectly after hearing the piece only once, and yet hate every single note. It was a vicious curse. He set his black bag down, opened it, and began to remove his instruments.

To start, Harmon had, cautiously, cautiously, sounded out his colleagues on the subject of ghosts. He'd read too many books where seemingly reasonable men lost all of their social graces when confronted by the inexplicable and started jabbering and making ridiculous accusations, frightening and embarrassing their friends. So, in a theoretical manner, he asked about ghosts. To his surprise, instead of being suspicious, people either calmly said they didn't believe in them, or, the majority, had one or more anecdotes about things like the ghost of a child in an old house dropping a ball down the stairs or a hitchhiking girl in a white dress who would only appear to men driving alone and then would vanish from the car. Others had stories about candles being snuffed out in perfectly still rooms, or dreams about dying relatives, or any number of irrelevant mystical experiences. No one, when pressed, would admit to having actually seen anything like a real, demonstrably dead man walking and talking and looking for a blue Cutlass. A man who persisted, week after week, in trying to get Harmon to help him find the damn thing. Harmon transferred from the ER. Rosemary thought it was something personal, because she'd asked him to her house for dinner, and they rarely spoke after that.

He told Margaret, however, as much of it as he could. It gave her something to think about, as she lay there in bed and gasped, waiting for the end. She wondered, of course, if the strain of her illness had not made her husband lose what few marbles he had left, as she put it, but she only said this because both of them knew Harmon was coolly sane. It interested her that some people could hear ghosts, but that Harmon could see them and talk to them. She, like Dexter, used the word "gift."

In good scholar's style, Harmon did research, in the dusty, abandoned stacks of the witchcraft and folklore sections of Northwestern,

the University of Chicago, and the University of Illinois, Circle
Campus. He even had a friend let him into the private collections of
the Field Museum of Natural History. He learned about lemures, the
Roman spirits of the dead, about the hauntings of abandoned pavil-
ions by sardonic Chinese ghosts, and about the Amityville Horror. It
was all just . . . literature. Stories. Tales to tell at midnight. Not a
single one of them had the ring of truth to it, and Harmon was by this
time intimately familiar with the true behavior of ghosts.

Everyone was very good to him about Margaret, and about what
he did to himself as a result, though no one understood the real
reason for it. It got to be too much, in the apartment, in the hospital,
and he finally started to say things that concerned people. They
didn't think he was crazy, just "under stress," that ubiquitous modern
disease, which excuses almost anything. Then, someone at the Field
Museum mentioned, with the air of an ordinarily respectable man
selling someone some particularly vile pornography, that Dexter
Warhoff, of the Sphinx and Eye of Truth Bookstore, might have
some materials not available in the museum collection. It was ru-
mored that Dexter possessed a bizarrely variant scroll of the Egyptian *Book of the Dead*, as well as several Mayan codexes not collected in the *Popul Vuh* or the *Dresden Codex*, though no one was
quite sure. Harmon had come to the conclusion that using ordinary
reason in his new circumstances was using Occam's Razor while
shaving in a fun house mirror. Common sense was a normally useful
instrument turned dangerous in the wrong situation. So he went to
Dexter's store, drank his sour tea, and talked with him. Dexter
scratched his head with elaborate thoughtfulness, then took Harmon
upstairs, where he lived, to a mess with a kitchen full of dirty dishes,
and brought him into a room piled with newspaper clippings, elabo-
rately color coded, in five different languages, as well as sheets of
articles transcribed from newspapers in forty languages more.

"You poor guy," Dexter said sadly. "That's a terrible way to find
out about what's hidden. I can see that it was terrible. But I must say,
I've been wondering about a few things. You've got the key there, I
think, with this life support stuff. Look at this." He showed Harmon
a French translation of a photocopied Russian *samizdat* document
from the Crimea. It described ghosts haunting a medical center at an
exclusive Yalta sanatorium. The tone was slightly metaphorical, but,
for the first time, Harmon read things that confirmed his own expe-

rience. Dexter showed him an article from the house newspaper of a medical center in Bombay, an excerpt from the unpublished reminiscences of a surgeon in Denmark, and a study of night terrors in senile dementia cases in a Yorkshire nursing home, from *Lancet*. The accounts were similar. "There's almost nothing before the 1930s, very few up to about 1960, and a fair number from the 70s and 80s."

"Life support," Harmon said, when he was done reading. "Artificial life support is responsible."

"Now, Professor, let's not jump to conclusions. . . ." But Harmon could see that Dexter agreed with him and, for some strange reason, that pleased him.

"When the body is kept alive by artificial means, for however long, when it should be dead and starting to rot, the soul, which normally is swept away somewhere—heaven, hell, oblivion, the Elysian Fields, it doesn't matter—is held back in this world, tied to its still-breathing body. And, being held back, it falls in love with life again." Harmon found himself saying it again, alone on the platform. It had seemed immediately obvious to him, though it was not really an "explanation" of the sort a scientist would require. It was, however, more than sufficient for a doctor of medicine, whose standards are different. A doctor only cares about what works, without much attention to why.

None of his colleagues had understood, though. He had gotten a little cranky on the subject, ultimately, he had to admit that, but he felt like someone in the eighteenth century campaigning against blood letting. He had always known that doctors were, by and large, merely skilled fools, so he quickly stopped, but not before acquiring a certain reputation.

He drew his chalk circle on the rough surface of the platform, using the brass compass. Using a knife with a triangular blade, he scraped some material from within the circle. No matter how well the police had cleaned, it would contain some substance, most likely the membranes of red blood cells, that had belonged to the dead man. He melted beeswax over a small alcohol lamp whose flame kept going out, then mixed in the scraped up blood. He dropped a linen wick into a mold of cold worked bronze and poured the wax in. While he waited for the candle to harden, he arranged the speculum, the silver nails, and the brass hammer so that he could reach them quickly. It was strange that most of the techniques they used had their roots in earlier centuries, when ghosts were the extremely rare results of accidental comas or overdoses of toxic drugs. People had had more time then to worry about such things, and some of their methods were surprisingly effective, though Dexter and Harmon had refined them. He set the candle in the center of the circle, lit it, and called Stanley Paterson's name.

The train still had not come. What was wrong? Why had there been no notification by the CTA? Stanley stood on the platform and shivered, wondering why he had wandered away, and why he had come back. Where was the damn train? Beneath his feet he could see a circle of chalk, and a half-melted candle, but he didn't think about them. Had he daydreamed right past the train, with those thoughts of musicians and mothers? Had the trains stopped for the night?

There was a rumble, and lights appeared down the tracks. They blinded him, for he had been long in darkness, and he stumbled forward with his eyes shut. He felt around for a seat. It seemed like he'd been waiting forever.

"It's a cold night, isn't it, Stanley?" a man's voice said, close by.

"Wha—?" Stanley jerked his head around and examined the brightly lit train car. It was empty. Then he saw that the man was sitting next to him, a tall old man with sad brown eyes. He was wearing a furry hat. "What are you talking about? How do you know my name?" Not waiting for an answer, he turned and pressed his nose against the glass of the window. A form lay there on the platform, sprawled on its back. It wore a long black overcoat. A large pool of blood, black in the lights of the station, had gathered near it, looking like the mouth of a pit.

"Stanley," the man said, his voice patient. "You have to understand a few things. I don't suppose it's strictly necessary, but it makes me feel less . . . cruel."

The train pulled into the next station. Out on the platform lay a dead man with a black coat. Three white-clad men burst onto the platform and ran towards it with a stretcher. The train pulled out of the station. "I don't care how you feel," Stanley said.

The man snorted. "I deserve that, I suppose. But you must understand, the dead cannot mix with the living. It just cannot be. We had a dead man in our Emergency Room once. He wouldn't go away. He tried to be part of everything. A ward birthday party turned gloomy because he tried to join it, and the patient whose birthday it was sickened and died within the week. He tried to participate in the close professional friendship of a pair of nurses, built up over long years of night duty and family pain, and they had fights, serious fights, and stopped ever speaking to each other. The gardener, whose joy in his plants he tried to share, grew to hate the roses he took care of, and in the spring they bloomed late and sickly. I've always liked roses. Life is hell with ghosts around, Stanley. Believe me, I know all about it." He had put the roses last, he noticed, as if they were more important than people. How much like a doctor he still was. . . .

Stanley watched as the white-clad men strapped the man in the black coat into the stretcher and rushed off, one of them holding an IV bottle over his head. The train pulled out of the station. "I—you don't understand, you don't understand at all." Stanley found himself shaken with sobs. How could he explain? As a child he'd wanted to play a musical instrument, like his sister, who played the piano, or even Frank, his next door neighbor, who played the trumpet in the school band. He'd tried the piano, the saxophone, the cello. None had lasted longer than two years, and he never practiced, despite his mother's entreaties. As an adult he'd tried the recorder, the guitar, and failed again. Yet, this very night, he'd felt what it was like to play Schumann on a piano and an oboe, and feel the music growing out of the intersection of spirit and instrument. He'd felt what it was like to be alive. "I know what to *do* now, don't you see. I realize what I was doing wrong, how I was wasting everything. Now I know!"

"So now, at last, you know." The man shook his head sadly, and held a flat, polished bronze mirror in front of Stanley's face. Stanley looked into the speculum, but saw nothing but roiled darkness, like an endless hole to nowhere. He felt weak. "Lie down, Mr. Paterson," Harmon said softly. "You don't look at all well. You should lie down."

Somehow they had come to be standing on the same damn platform again, as if the train had gone absolutely nowhere at all. The unnatural blankness of the mirror had indeed made him feel dizzy, so Stanley lay down. The platform was hard and cold on his back now. Nothing made sense anymore. He watched the stars spin overhead. Or was it just the lights of the apartment buildings?

"You can't leave me here," he said. "Not just when I've figured it out."

"Shut up," Harmon said, savagely. "It's too late." He drove a long silver nail into Stanley's right wrist. Stanley felt it go in, cold, but it didn't hurt. "You're dead." He drove another nail through Stanley's foot, tinking on the head with a little hammer. "That first one, in the ER. He almost killed *us*, he was so strong. But we bound him, finally, once we'd figured out what to do. If I went back there now, I would hear him, talking to himself, as if he'd just woken up from a nap and was still sleepy. I hear you everywhere, where I have bound you, on street corners, in hallways, in alleys. In beds." Harmon found himself crying, tears wetting his cheeks, as if he were the one Stanley Paterson was supposed to be feeling sorry for. Stanley Paterson, who would have only the understanding that he was dead, not alive, to keep him for all eternity. "Don't worry, Stanley. Life is hateful."

"No!" Stanley cried. "I want to live!" He reached up with his free hand and grabbed Harmon by the throat.

Harmon felt like he was being buried alive, but not buried in clean earth. He was being buried, instead, in the churned-over, corrupted earth of an ancient cemetery, full of human teeth and writhing worms. It pushed, damp and greasy, against his face. The smell was unbearable. Darkness swelled before him, and he almost let go.

The darkness drained away, and the platform reappeared. Dexter stood over him, his tongue sticking out slightly between his lips. He held the speculum over Stanley's face, forcing him back. Dexter's clothes flapped, and he leaned forward, as if into a heavy, foul wind. "Quick, Professor," he choked. "He's a strong one, like I said." Harmon tapped the fourth nail into Stanley's left wrist.

"I want to live!" Stanley said, quieter now.

Harmon said nothing. Dexter held the fifth nail for him, and he drove it through Stanley's chest. "There. Now you will remain still." He rested back on his heels, breathing heavily. How like a doctor, he thought. He could eliminate the symptom, but not cure the disease. Those ghosts, no longer disturbing the living, would lie where he had nailed them until Judgment Day. And there was nothing he could do to help them. He sat there for a long time, until he felt Dexter's hand on his shoulder. He looked up into that kindly, ugly face, then back at the platform, where five silver dots glittered in the overhead lights.

"That was a bad one, Professor."

"They're all bad."

"It's worse if they never lived before they died. They want it then, all the more." Dexter packed the instruments away. Then he rubbed the tension out of Harmon's back, taking the feel of death up into himself. Dexter, with his credulous beliefs in anything and every-thing, absurd in his Minnesota Vikings cap with the horns. Without him, Harmon could not have kept moving for even a day.

Harmon thought about going home. Margaret would be there, as she always was, on the side of the bed where the blankets were flat and undisturbed. He hadn't acted in time, when she had her final, fatal heart attack. He had waited, and doubted his own conclusions, and let them put her on life support for three days, in the cardiac ICU, before he decided it was hopeless, and let them pull the plug on her. By then, of course, it had been much too late. He should simply have let her die there, next to him. But how could he have done that? Whenever he changed the sheets, he could see the rounded heads of the five silver nails driven into the mattress, to keep her fixed where she died.

She had loved life, but she had wanted to stay with him . . . always. So he had laid down on the bed with her and felt her cold embrace. For a doctor with a good knowledge of anatomy his suicide attempt had been shockingly bad. Slitting your own throat is rarely success-ful. It's too imprecise. They had found him, and healed him, recon-structing his throat. Modern medicine could do miracles. When he was well enough, though still bandaged, he went and found Dexter. They took care of the man in the ER, and then Margaret. She had cried and pleaded when the nails went in. But she had loved life, so it wasn't as hard as it could have been, though Harmon could not imagine how it could have been any harder.

When he came back, she would ask him, sleepily, how it had gone. She always sounded like she was about to fall asleep, but she never did. She never would.

"Let's go," Dexter said. "It'll be good to get back to bed. I gotta open the store in three hours. Jeez."

"Yes, Dexter," Harmon said. "It will be good to get to bed."

The Marked Man

DAVID ELY

It was early evening when he entered the Park. He headed for the darkest part, away from the lamps that lighted the pathways. He didn't see any other strollers, but he hurried all the same, not wanting to take chances.

When he reached the shelter of the first trees, he stopped and looked back toward the drive, even though he knew the car was no longer there. They had driven off as soon as they'd let him out. He'd been clapped on the shoulder—like the jump sign in a plane—and one of them had said, "Good luck, Major," and then he'd stepped out, with the weight of his flying suit dragging on him.

Good luck, Major. If he did have luck, those would be the last words anyone would address to him for four weeks.

He pulled back, startled. Someone had run past him, right past him, no more than a yard away—a man or boy running hard but with light steps in the direction of Fifth Avenue.

The Major squatted; his breath came quick, his pulse beat high. That had shaken him, whatever it had been—some college kid training for track, or some fellow running for the hell of it, or maybe a purse snatcher, and in that case there might be police on the way. The police were the ones he feared the most. The Agency had cleared things with the Commissioner, and the captains of the nearest precincts had been informed, as a safeguard against publicity in the event he got caught, but of course the ordinary officer didn't know. Just one flash of a patrolman's torch could put an end to the project.

He had to avoid the lights. He'd had no idea there would be so many, not only the lamps along the pathways but also the automobile headlights on the drive that crossed the Park, and the big hotels and apartment buildings along its boundaries.

He kept moving through the trees, trying to shore up his confidence by physical activity. This first night would be the hard one. He knew that. If he managed this one, and the day to come, he'd probably be all right. He'd have to pick a hiding place that was far from where people normally went—away from the zoo, the lake, and the playing fields. He'd rather be caught by a policeman than by kids playing ball. If one of them got a glimpse of him, they'd all come shouting and pointing. He imagined a grotesque chase—a gang of boys pursuing a man made clumsy by the pilot's suit. They'd be yelling: *His head, his head. Look at his head.*

The head—that was the Agency's guarantee of his honesty. He couldn't cheat, not with that head. When they'd told him about it, he hadn't objected. He knew they were right. The project psychologist had talked to him for a long time about it. The object was to measure the psychological stress on a man hiding in the midst of a hostile population. If they could do that, then they could build a rescue program that made sense for the one pilot in twenty who'd been shot down but not captured, and had managed to hide somewhere—in a field, a bomb-blasted ruin, an abandoned apartment, anywhere he could find.

"You'll be that twentieth pilot, Major," the psychologist had told him. "You'll make it to the Park. Then you'll have to hide until you're rescued. But remember, you're a marked man. You're isolated from the people around you by the one thing you can't change—you can't speak the language. Well, for the purposes of this test, we can simulate almost anything but that. Nothing would prevent you from hiding that flying suit and swiping the pants off some Park tramp if you had to. Then you could just stroll over to the nearest bench to spend a quiet day reading the papers with nobody the wiser, and if some policeman came up to you, you could pass the time of day with him just as nicely as you pleased.

"Oh, we know you have no such intention, Major. We know you're determined to play this thing straight. But we also know that when a man is in a stress situation, even if it's a simulated situation, he may do things he wouldn't normally do. So you understand that we've got to protect the project. We've got to give you a handicap that's roughly the equivalent of loss of language. We've got to make you conspicuous in a way that's beyond your control."

And so they'd shaved his head and stained it green, a clear fresh green, green as new-grown grass.

The Major found a crevice between two boulders at the base of a small ridge. It was just wide enough for him to squeeze his body through. He worked for several hours in there with his entrenching tool hollowing out a cavity in the earth. He had stripped off his pilot's suit and laid it on the ground to hold the dirt he dug out. When he had a load, he gathered up the suit in his arms and carried it off, shaking it, so that the dirt was distributed over a wide area. Then from one of his pockets he took a small can—dog-repellent—and sprayed his entrance carefully.

The spring night was chill, but at least it wasn't raining. On a wet night he'd have left muddy prints and tracks all over. He was lucky, too, that it was mid-week, for there'd be fewer people in the Park during the day. It was the weekends that brought the crowds, and by the weekend he'd have his place improved or would have found a better one.

The night was ending. Dawn was on its way. He watched the sky lighten, and the trees and shrubs take shape. The cold mist was drifting where the ground was low. In the distance the skyscrapers blazed with red fire as the sun struck their crowns. He edged out of the crevice to examine the entrance one last time. There were no traces of his work. The grass was flattened where he had laid the flying suit, but it would rise again, and besides, the Park was full of places where kids had played and couples had spread blankets.

Then he saw his entrenching tool lying on open ground ten feet away. He crawled over and grabbed it, scuttled back, wedged himself through and inside, and lay there, breathing hard. That was worse than carelessness, he thought. The psychologist had warned him that he'd be his own worst enemy, that there'd be times when his fear would make traps for him, that there'd be a weakness in him that couldn't take the strain. He cursed himself, and spat in the dirt. Suppose he hadn't seen that tool and had left it there? Typical, he thought bitterly. He'd always forgotten something; he'd always fallen short. He'd tried to qualify for the space program, but he'd been rejected. He hadn't quite been up to the standards.

But the project psychologist hadn't made it either, had he? The psychologist had been nosed out by psychologists who had just a little bit more on the ball. Yes, the Major thought, he and the psychologist were leftovers. They hadn't made the space team. They weren't quite good enough.

And maybe the project wasn't any better than they were. He had wondered about it already. True, it didn't look bad on paper. But suppose a man could survive undetected in the middle of Manhattan for four weeks—would that really produce much useful information for survival-and-rescue planning? Or was it just a flashy stunt dreamed up by some Operations lieutenant bucking for promotion?

Well, it wasn't his job to criticize the project. He was supposed to make it work—and he wasn't starting off very well. He hadn't made that hole long enough. He couldn't stretch out full length. Already his legs were cramping. He began massaging them. Weariness came on him, and hunger. He hadn't eaten since afternoon. He opened a can of rations, and ate with his fingers, then buried the can in the earth beside him, and put the sleeping mask on his face—it covered the mouth to muffle snoring—and settled back to wait out the day.

By nightfall he was in agony. His legs tormented him. He felt stifled by the mask. He kept falling into a dangerous kind of sleep where he twisted like an animal trying to burrow deeper, or maybe to burrow out into the air and sunlight, his traitor hands trying to rip off the mask, his legs threatening at any moment to go into a full screaming cramp.

The entire population of New York came, it seemed, to climb on his boulders and sit on the ridge above him. He heard voices, footsteps, shouts, laughter. At times unseen feet sent dirt sifting down. He cursed those who came. He feared them, he hated them. Yes, it was a definite reaction. He ought to remember to tell the psychologist. He could imagine what these people were from their voices—stupid kids and nagging mothers, and old men full of nastiness, and younger ones who had no business lounging around parks during the day. He was their prisoner. The least of them might find him, and turn him out to sunlight, like a mole. He clasped his knees tighter, and rocked his body to and fro, grinding his teeth to keep from crying out in pain and rage.

When darkness came, he stretched out at last, his head and shoulders thrust out of the hole and into the narrow space between the boulders. He slept until midnight, and woke in panic when the moon sent its light slicing through the crevice to fall on his upturned face.

Then he worked, digging to make his burrow longer. After that he crawled about the area outside picking up candy wrappers, cigarette butts, and sandwich bags—why, he didn't know. Perhaps to wipe out every trace of the people who had tormented him all day.

He forced himself to walk off through the trees. He needed to stay away from his refuge until dawn. The psychologist had warned him he'd be tempted to keep too close to it for the safety it offered, until finally he might surrender to a compulsion to remain in it night and day.

He knew he would have to be careful. He was under unusual pressure: a man alone, fearing every hint of human presence—every voice, every movement, every sound—fearing the light of day most of all. True, it was a simulated situation. He could end it any time he chose. But that would be humiliating to his pride, and hurtful to his career. And he was a volunteer. He'd asked for it.

From one of his pockets he took a radio no larger than a pack of cigarettes. He could transmit three simple signals. The first meant: *I am here.* He sat at the base of a tree, holding the radio, studying the shadows that stretched toward the glow of the lamps along the pathways. At five-minute intervals he repeated: *I am here, I am here.* Somewhere someone was listening. He was in contact with another human being. But then he reasoned that the Agency would be unlikely to pay a technician to sit up night after night simply to monitor his signals. They'd have a machine record them. And the machine would answer him—yes, there it was, a return signal, barely audible.

The return signal meant: *We hear you.* He was heard, then, but only by a machine, and it wouldn't be until morning that they'd check to be sure their man in the Park had called in.

He wondered if the green head had been talked about. Probably. It was too ludicrous for the Houston people to keep quiet about. "Remember that gung-ho major who didn't make the space program? Well, guess where he is now. And guess what color his head is . . . That's right, I said his *head.*"

He signaled again—*I am here*—just to hear the machine whisper back: *We hear you, we hear you.* Four weeks of this. They said they'd need that much time in a real situation, first to alert the nearest undercover agent that a flyer was down, and then to allow the agent to track down the signal, and finally, to work out a plan of escape.

He sent his second signal, a variation of the first. It meant: *I receive you.* And the machine dutifully replied: *We receive each other.* That was all. A few pulses through the ether, back and forth, meaningless to an enemy monitoring system, and then one day the *we hear you* would become more frequent, indicating that the agent was coming for him.

There was a third signal. *Emergency*. Which would mean he was sick or caught or couldn't stand it any more and was giving up.

I am here.

I receive you.

Emergency.

This was his vocabulary. This was all he had, he thought. He was just a green-headed man in a dirt-caked flying suit, sitting in a city park at night, talking without words to a machine he'd never see.

As the days went by, he deepened his burrow, made it more comfortable, more secure, better camouflaged. By night he explored the Park, studying each unknown reach of ground with care before venturing onto it. Whenever he passed the zoo, the animals sensed him, and stirred. It occurred to him that he was like them, in a way—a creature caged, and troubled by the scent of man.

Sometimes he saw others at night. He hid from them, drawing back in the deepest shadows. He had known he wouldn't be alone. The Agency people had told him he'd find himself among the scourings of New York—the weird ones, the oddballs, the misfits, the crazy men, all roaming the Park, hunting one another down. Well, he could take care of himself. He could handle two or three of them with judo and the knife. Besides, anybody who got a look at his head would run, for he was weirder than any of them, and more alone. Except that he would have just four weeks of it, and they were trapped for life. That was a difference; quite a difference.

They were frightened; so was he. They were hungry—and he'd be hungry, too. He didn't have enough rations for four weeks. The people at Houston had explained that they wanted him to live off the land—in part, anyway. That meant he would have to rummage through trash baskets looking for apple cores and sandwich leavings. If he had to, he could graze on grass, wild onions, daisies, and chew the bark of saplings. With care he might be able to stretch his rations. He had spent nine days in the Park already. There were nineteen to go, then. He could calculate how much he could allow himself to eat each day.

But of course a downed pilot wouldn't know how long he'd have to hold out. And therefore he, the Major, shouldn't know, either. Surely the Agency people had thought of that. Surely they had planned something to simulate the uncertainties of a real situation.

The Major thought about that. It worried him. He wondered if the Agency people intended to lengthen the test. That must be it. Nobody would come for him on that twenty-eighth night. They'd make him sweat for a few more days, maybe as long as a week.

Or they would trick him in another way. Perhaps they had filled some of the ration cans with water, or sand. It could be that. He would go along half starving himself to maintain food discipline—and then he'd find two or three useless cans.

He hefted each can, and shook it near his ear, but there was no way of telling what was inside. He'd have to wait. He couldn't open the cans early.

They would know that these doubts would occur to him. They would know he'd worry about them. They had planned it that way. It was part of the test. The tension, the strain. On top of the loneliness, on top of the fear. They had lied to him—lied for the good of the project, of course. But it was a dirty business, lying. You told the truth to your friends. That was the rule, wasn't it? It was the enemy you lied to.

The sounding of a siren deep in the city came echoing across the Park. He glanced uneasily around in the darkness, hearing something in that distant mechanical cry that made him want to speak out—to curse, to pray, anything—just to hear his own voice. But he was afraid to speak aloud; he was afraid.

He had premonitions of deep hunger. His limbs and eyes would ache. Sometimes he would drift in the delirium of fatigue. He worried about remembering things. When he filled his canteen at the lake, had he put in the purifier? Fear nagged at his senses, sharpening some, dulling others. He lost the exact count of his days—was it sixteen, seventeen?—but he had a greater awareness of the shape and touch of things.

He lived in the dark. He never saw the sun. By day he lay in his hole, sweating in the thick air, listening drowsily to the voices of people he could not see. He dreamed of capture, of death. When night came, he crept out, his body stiff, his bones aching, to face the dangers of the darkness.

One night he saw an old man shuffling along a path some thirty yards away, and he knew what would happen even before it occurred, as though it had taken place already in his dreams. Two figures rushed out of the dark; the old man fell at once to the ground beneath their blows. They tore at his clothing, searching for something of value. The Major crouched where he was, his knife open in his hand, but he was unable to intervene. He could not jeopardize the project.

Besides, the robbers moved with the swiftness of young men. He might not be equal to them, weakened as he was. They found nothing, and in their fury they kicked their victim, and stamped on his face before they ran off. The old man might be dead or dying, and yet the Major could do nothing, and so he turned away, in a rage that he had been the one to see that attack, impotent as he was, when those who might have helped were sleeping in comfort far away—the ones for whom the Park had been created, for whom it was patrolled and kept clean, and for whose amusement the zoo beasts were caged. The body would be found in the morning, and removed. They would not know about it. The incident was too common to warrant more than a line or two in the newspapers. At noon people would be walking over the very spot.

He saw other things on other nights—a dog stoned to death; a woman raped; a cripple beaten with his own crutch; a tramp sleeping in newspapers set afire and sent dancing, dressed in flames.

His anger left him. He watched as an animal might watch, ready at any moment to retreat and hide. The daytime people had lost the attributes of humankind. They were only voices, and footsteps. He could no longer imagine their faces. The ones who appeared at night were little more than shadows; still, they seemed more real to him. He thought about them often, wondering if any of these miserable, ferocious outcasts inhabited the Park as he did, hiding by day, prowling by night. He wasn't sure; he couldn't tell. But he wanted to believe there were at least a few. It made him feel less alone.

There were heavy rains for several days. His shelter was a morass. He himself was smeared with mud. His hands were blackened now. He thought that perhaps his face, too, had changed color, for the filth and dirt of the Park had been ground into his skin. He could feel his new-grown hair and beard stubble, and he wondered what he might look like, but he could not form a satisfactory picture in his mind.

He thought the full period had elapsed, but he wasn't sure. In any case, he had mastered the test; he had survived. But his achievement wasn't much. He had got through a few weeks. Those others—the night people of the Park—they had survived years. And in all that time no one had come to save them. No one had sought to arrange their escape.

He picked up his radio, and sent the signal. *I am here, I am here.* And the answer came back as always: *We hear you, we hear you.* But now he wondered—did they really hear him, were they listening?

For a time he was ill. He didn't know for how long. He lay in his burrow shivering with fever day and night. He had difficulty remembering why he was there, and pondered the matter, puzzled, until the answer came to him—oh, yes, the project. But it seemed to him that the project was not reason enough for him to be buried this way, alone and suffering and sick. There must be another, more important reason. He could not think what it might be.

His fever slackened, but he remained hidden. He did not care to leave his refuge. The project people might be searching for him, he realized. They would come at night with dogs and flares. But if they couldn't find him? If he'd hidden himself too well? Perhaps this time he had done that absolutely first-rate piece of work he had been struggling to do all his life—and it would be the end of him. How the Agency men would grumble. How annoyed with him they'd be. They might suspect that he had sabotaged the project on purpose, vanishing into the earth like that.

Or maybe they wouldn't come at all. Maybe they wouldn't search. They hadn't looked for the others—the other men who lived underground. They hadn't cared about them. Perhaps he, too, would be abandoned.

He crawled to the lake. He was too weak to stand. At the water's edge he plunged his head down and drank at the reflected lights of the buildings as though by drinking he could extinguish them. He drank the foulness of the water that had already put poison in him, but the lights remained on the surface, and when he roiled the water in his hand, the lights raced back and forth, dancing, shaking, as if quivering with laughter.

The days were hot now, the nights humid. There was the odor of decay everywhere. The rain slid down like grease. There was no grass to eat; it had been trodden away. The bark of the young trees was denied him, for somehow he had lost his knife. He scraped with his fingernails at the saplings, pulled weeds from the earth, leaves from the shrubs.

It was clear to him now that he had misinterpreted the meaning of the test. The object wasn't survival. A man who wants to survive doesn't hide in the earth, doesn't make himself sick with loneliness and fear—no, no, a man who does that has been betrayed into doing it. *Good luck, Major.* They had sent him off to get rid of him. He wasn't quite good enough for their needs, and so they shoved him out with a Judas touch to bury himself among the other outcasts for the sake of the project, which was death.

He was expected to die. He knew that now. They did not really believe, did they, that a man shot out of the sky could be rescued? The risks were too great. No agent—if there were any agents—could be asked to undertake them. Rather, their intention was to prevent a pilot from surrendering by persuading him that all he had to do was find a hiding place and wait for a rescue that had never even been considered. It would be death that came instead.

The radio was the cleverest part of the trick. A desperate man would believe its lies right up to the end, but there was no one listening, not even a machine, for surely it was the radio itself that produced those answering responses, as if they came from far away: *We hear you.* That was the ultimate betayal, to kill a man with hope.

He was to die, like those others who lived underground, the hopeless ones, too weak to strike out at the enemies who had promised to save them but didn't come, who gave them short rations and told them to eat grass, who'd shorn their heads to humiliate them into hiding. And the poor crippled fools, they had accepted all that, just as he had. They had been eager to make the project work—and if the daytime laughter overhead sometimes drove them to violence, all they were capable of doing was to maim and to kill one another.

The project was death. They were all to die. Very well, he thought, but let them die in the sight of their executioners, let them die in the open air, beneath the sun.

He left his refuge at noon, when the Park was crowded. The sun was blinding. At first he could hardly see the people among whom he staggered, his arms outstretched, feeling his way. He gestured impatiently at trees, bushes, rocks; he shouted for the others to come out

of hiding, too. He went tottering about looking for them, commanding them to appear.

The crowds gathered to follow him, warily and at some distance
until they saw how weak he was. He fell sometimes, and crawled, rose
again to his feet and lurched forward, crying out a summons that
went unanswered.

People came nearer; they circled around him. Boys ran up close,
hooting. Women held their babies high, so they, too, could see, the
young men jogged over from the playing fields, anxious to look at the
green-headed man crusted with dried mud, the madman in rags,
the zany, the fool howling in their midst—yes, all were eager to have
a good look at him before the police arrived to bundle him away.

The Ones Who Turn Invisible

F. GWYNPLAINE MACINTYRE

"There's a panhandler over on Vesey Street who's got only one arm," Wendy told me, when she came back to the Commodities Exchange. "He's got two hands, but only one arm."

I had a deskful of spec sheets to check before I could send the prospectus roughs over to Legal, and I didn't particularly want to talk about deformed panhandlers, but just to be polite I asked: "You mean, his hand grows right out of his shoulder, with no arm attached to it?"

"No; his hands are where they ought to be, but there's an arm missing," she said. "I can't figure out how he does it. Go have a look at him."

Well, I had better things to do with my life than go looking at drug addicts on street corners, so I got back to work and forgot all about it. Until the next morning.

The next day I was cabbing it down to work from my loft in TriBeCa, and the damned cab-driver got gridlocked over on the Chambers Street extension, and I don't need that hassle, so I got out and walked even though it was starting to snow. There was a bum in the middle of the sidewalk—blocking pedestrians, of course—trying to wangle spare change from the passing suckers. He was a real scuzz-case: probably a druggie, I decided; he needs the money for his crack habit. Well, *some* of us have honest jobs to go to, so I side-stepped the guy, and I would have kept walking, until I suddenly noticed his hands.

The bum was waving his left arm around in its ragged coat-sleeve, as if he was conducting a phantom orchestra inside his head, that no one else could hear. His right hand was holding the sucker-pot: a crumpled cardboard coffee cup with cardboard handles. One of the handles was torn halfway off; it kept flapping around loose when the bum waved the cup. He had a few coins in the cup; he kept rattling it around in people's faces as they passed him, and once in a while some sucker was chump-brained enough to toss him some spare change. Just your typical average druggie, right? He certainly *smelled* like the standard-model panhandler, and looked like it, too . . . except that a detail was missing.

He had no right arm. His right hand—the hand with the cup in it— was dangling in mid-air just an arm's length from his shoulder, exactly where it would have been if he'd *had* a right arm. But his arm was gone. I watched the disembodied hand move up and down, rattling the cup, shoving itself at people. The guy's hand behaved exactly as if it was leashed to him by an invisible arm . . . except that there *wasn't* an arm. I could see the snowflakes drifting down through the space where his arm should be. But no arm. Other people walking past the druggie would glance at him, drop a coin in the cup, and then hurry on past him. Sometimes they just hurried past, ignoring him altogether. I was surprised, at first, that no one but me in this hurrying crowd had noticed that the druggie had a discon- nected hand. Then I realized: nobody pays much attention to street people. Especially when it's snowing.

Back in prep school I used to impress girls with card tricks, and making coins disappear. Of course I outgrew that Houdini stuff later on—no *time* for it, in Harvard Business School—but just the same I wanted to find out how this guy did his trick with the vanishing arm. Most street magicians really suck, but *this* guy could have been playing Vegas, even with only one trick up his invisible sleeve.

I grabbed one of the singles from my money-clip, and held it up where the druggie could see it, but far enough away so that he couldn't snatch it—unless that floating hand of his had a seven-foot reach. "That's a pretty good trick with the hand, there," I said to him. "How do you *do* it?"

He saw the dollar, and made a grab for it, but I kept it just out of his reach. "Lemme get a dollah, Mister," he protested. "Ain't hurtin' you none." His armless hand, like a fluttering bird in mid-air, shook and rattled the cup. "Ain't playin' roun' wit'chall. Jus' wanna get somethin' to eat."

"Sure thing, buddy." I kept the dollar away from him; with my other hand I reached out and sawed the air where his invisible arm had to be, expecting to feel my hand touch an invisible scuzzy coat-sleeve.

Damn it, his arm *wasn't there*. I figured he had to be some kind of amputee; maybe one of the medical schools was developing some weird new artificial hand, and field-testing it on this guy. But I couldn't see the wires connecting his wrist to his shoulder, or the threads that would keep his hand suspended in mid-air. I felt around again. There *weren't* any wires.

"Lemme get a dollah, Mister," he repeated. "Jus' tryin' get m'self straighten' out."

Well, to Hell with this. I wasn't going to stand around in the gutter, talking to refugees from Bellevue where one of my clients might see me. I shoved the dollar back in my pocket, and threw the guy a quarter. It was snowing pretty bad now; by the time I got to the Exchange the market had already opened. Trading was heavy all morning, and by the time Wendy and I got to P.J.'s for lunch I'd forgotten all about the scuzz-bum.

Heading home, I actually managed to find a cab going up the West Side, even though the snow was coming down worse than ever. When we got a block north of City Hall the driver started honking at something. I looked out; some damned bag-lady with nothing better to do was blocking traffic: she was right in the middle of the street, wearing a raggedy skirt, standing next to the car in front of us and cursing at the driver.

"Hey, I've got to get home," I told the cabbie. "Can you get past this car ahead of us?"

The cabbie must have been the last remaining hack-driver in Manhattan who could actually speak English. "She's blocking the road, pal," he told me, and gestured at the bag-lady. "You want I should run her over?"

Well, screw this. "I've got to go home, guy," I said. "Run her over."

The cabbie's cigar looked like it was surgically attached to his face, but he gulped so hard he almost swallowed it. "You don't mean that, mister."

"Go ahead," I insisted. "She'll get out of your way fast enough when she sees you mean business. *Try* running her over; I guarantee she'll get out of the way."

The cab-driver leaned on his horn again. He kept honking, but the crazy old bitch wouldn't move. Then I got a look at her legs.

The bag-lady's left leg was gone. Her left *foot* was there, but someplace north of the ankle and south of the skirt-line her leg did a vanishing act. I saw *air* where her knee should have been. She was stomping up and down in the middle of Broadway and Warren Street just as if she had two good legs. But one leg was invisible. Then I remembered the druggie I'd seen, with the hand.

I tapped on the cab-driver's partition. "You see anything strange about that bag-lady?" I asked him.

He shrugged. "She's a bag-lady, mister."

"Her legs. Look at her legs."

The cabbie shrugged again. "I got a wife in Brooklyn and a girl friend out by Rego Park. Why should I start looking at some bag-lady's legs?"

The traffic wasn't moving. I paid the driver exactly what was on the meter, told him what he could do with it, and got out. The bag-lady saw me and started cursing, so I gave her the finger. She started chasing me. Like an idiot, I ran. A block away, I stopped to look back.

She was still coming after me. There was nothing but air connecting her left foot to her body, but she could run like a linebacker. Then I saw her left foot disappear *while I was looking at it*, but she kept running. I ducked behind a Korean fruit-and-vegetable stand; she went right past me and started cursing out somebody else. Nobody noticed, except for me, that the shrieking bag-woman was minus a leg.

"I saw that bum you were talking about," I told Wendy at work the next day. "The guy with the levitating hand." We still had a few minutes before the Tokyo prices came in, so I told her about the one-legged bag-lady who ran through the streets.

I'd expected Wendy to laugh at me, but she nodded. "They're all over the place, Brett," she said. "This morning I saw a wino with no neck."

"*Lots* of winos have no neck," I told her.

"I mean his head was just floating a couple of inches above his shoulders, with no neck in between. Disconnected. He saw me staring at him, and he started cursing."

I looked at Wendy, and didn't say anything.

"Do you think they're disappearing, Brett?" she asked me.

"Eh?" I was watching the London commodities quotations coming in on Wendy's computer monitor; long rows of electronic numbers dancing down the green-glowing screen.

"The street people," Wendy was saying. "Do you think they're all fading away, a little bit at a time? And where are all the missing pieces *going*?"

I shrugged. "So far nobody in New York City's noticed it, except you and me." I tapped the glass screen on Wendy's monitor. "Maybe the radiation from these monitors could be screwing up our eyes. I'll see my doctor about it."

Wendy nodded again. "Maybe *that's* it, Brett." Then the bell rang for trading to start, and we didn't have any more time to think about disappearing bag-ladies.

I started paying more attention to street people after that. Most of them seemed physically complete when I took a good look at them, but once in a while some wino would sneak past the edge of my vision, and his legs would be invisible from the knees down, or something. Nobody else seemed to notice.

Next Saturday I was partying, and I met some guys I knew from Shearson over at Wendy's apartment. "Any of you guys seen any strange-looking bag-ladies lately?" I asked them, realizing how dumb it sounded as soon as I said it.

Pete started laughing; he'd always laughed like a dork when we'd been at Choate together, and he *still* laughed like a dork. "Brett, *all* bag-ladies look strange," he said, and kept laughing till I wanted to strangle him.

"I mean abnormal," I said. "Heads disconnected from their bodies, invisible legs, and so on."

Larry gave me a funny look. "I'd say you've been doing too many lines of bad coke, Brett."

"I'm serious," I told him.

"So am I."

Pete kept up his dork-laugh like a dip-shit buffoon, and started making some joke about me being the world's leading authority on invisible bag-ladies. I considered taking a poke at him, but I didn't want to make a scene in Wendy's place, so I just grabbed my coat. "Later, guys."

I was still mad when I got to the elevator. Somebody was following me. She was Wendy's room-mate: Jacintha, I think her name was. Some screwy actress; I didn't know her very well. She got into the elevator with me. "I heard you talking to those other guys . . ." she started to say.

I didn't need to hear any more jokes. "Look, I. . ."

"Brett, I've seen them too." Her eyes got big; she suddenly looked scared. "The other day a panhandler came walking towards me, *with no head.* He didn't speak; he just rattled his cup, and I could see the hole in his neck where his head should have been. I thought that I was going crazy, but now *you're* seeing them too. Brett, what's happening to all the street people?"

"How should *I* know?" I said. "They've been a nuisance for years. Everybody's been wishing they'd go *someplace else.* Maybe they finally took the hint, and they're going away . . . one piece at a time."

"Yes, but where are they *going?*"

"That's not *my* problem," I told her.

"Brett, how can you *say* that?" she asked me. "The homeless are *everybody's* problem."

The elevator reached the street floor. I stepped into the lobby. "So they're everybody's problem?" I said to Jacintha. "That's funny, lady. I don't see *you* inviting any drug addicts or bag-ladies to come live in *your* high-rise apartment, so don't lay any guilt trips on me. If some jerk gets evicted because he fed the rent money to his drug-habit, it's *his* fault he has to sleep on subway gratings. It sure as hell isn't *my* fault. I pay my taxes; let New York City find some place to put the street people. If they can't do it, then I'm paying taxes for nothing."

I pushed my way past Jacintha through the lobby, and into the street.

The next day I brunched it at P.J.'s with Rooney, my connection at the *Wall Street Journal.* "Have you noticed lately," I asked, when Rooney ordered a pitcher of beer, "that all the street bums are turning into jigsaw puzzles?"

Rooney laughed as he reached for the beer. "So you've noticed that too, hey? Damnedest thing. Been happening all over Manhattan."

"Then you *have* seen it? Why the hell hasn't your paper run an article about it?"

Rooney glanced at me, and cocked one massive eyebrow. "We're a financial paper, Brett; we don't give much ink to Believe-It-or-Not stuff." He drained his glass, and refilled it. "A friend of mine, over at the *Post,* thought this jigsaw-wino stuff might be worth a few inches . . ."

"Then why didn't he print it?" I asked.

"Well, that's the screwy part." Rooney held his beer glass up to the light for a moment, regarding it silently. The bastard knew he had me in suspense. Then he said: "My friend took his story about invisible street people to his editor, and the editor told him he was crazy. Claimed there aren't as many homeless people in New York as there used to be, and that to *his* knowledge *none* of them were doing fade-aways on the installment-plan. Or pulling vanishing acts. Further-more," Rooney finished his drink, "according to this particular edi-tor, there have been entirely too many plight-of-the-homeless articles printed lately: vastly out of proportion to the actual problem, which is very minor indeed. Or so this editor said."

Come to think of it, I *had* seen fewer street people lately. The only reason I'd noticed them at all was because every tenth or eleventh wino, every sixteenth bag-lady, was turning slightly invisible around the edges. The rest of them were still business as usual.

"You want to know what *I* think?" Rooney asked.

"Spill it."

"Well, it stands to reason that these Vanishers must *know* why they're vanishing, right? Otherwise, as soon as a wino's hand or a bag-lady's foot disappeared, they'd go screaming for help all the way to the detox ward. But they *accept* the Vanishing. They may be doing it to *themselves* somehow. *Deliberately.*"

I hadn't thought of that before. "But *why?*"

Rooney shrugged his eyebrows. "There's such a thing as hobo fraternities, and secret societies of gypsies, and so on," he told me. "These street-bums, they're more organized than we suspect they are. They'll be forming a union next. My guess is, the street-ones are doing their slow-motion fade-outs on purpose, to get attention. To pay us back for ignoring them all these years."

"Okay, but *how* are they turning invisible?"

Rooney flagged down the bar-maid so he could reorder. "That's not my department. At my paper, I don't work the Science Desk. But five'll get you ten: the Vanishers are doing it deliberately."

Rooney's explanation made as much sense as any other theory I could think of, so I thanked him, paid my end of the tab, and headed for work.

There was a raggedy street-man in Washington Square Park, banging wooden drumsticks against the sidewalk. He looked per-

fectly coherent except for the fact that every few seconds he'd bend at
the waist, give a rat-a-tat-tat to the pavement with these greasy-
looking sticks he was carrying, and then straighten up again.

The left side of his face was missing.

I waited until he stopped drumming for a while, and then I walked
over, looking him squarely in the eye. The right eye. When I looked
at the place where his left eye should have been I could see Washington Square Arch, twenty feet in back of him. The whole side of his
head had vanished. "Uh, you got a second, buddy?" I asked, feeling
faintly ridiculous.

The expression on his half-face looked rational enough. "What's
goin' down, friend?" he wanted to know.

"Is this some kind of conspiracy, or something?" I asked him. I
held out a dollar, to show I was friendly; he made no attempt to take
it. "All you streeters, the abandoned ones: are you trying to get
attention with this disappearing stuff?"

The sidewalk drummer shook his head. "Don't know what you're
talkin' about, friend." The hell of it was he didn't seem the least bit
concerned that fifty percent of his skull had gone bye-bye. "Just don't
know what you're talkin'."

I was getting impatient. By now I was thoroughly convinced that
these damned street people *knew* what was happening to their bodies—maybe even caused it intentionally somehow—but they'd sworn
some kind of street-oath agreeing never to discuss it with outsiders
like me. Well, I could break that. "You trying to get *back* at us? Is
that it?" I asked the drummer. "Is this your way to *make* us notice
you?"

He turned his back on me, and kept drumming the curb. "I don't
know where you're from, man."

"Look, I'll give you this dollar if . . ."

"Don't want your dollar." He bent over again, rat-a-tatting the
cement, perfectly blissful. "Just want to perform."

"Okay. Let me see you perform." I took out another dollar.
"Here's two bucks. Let me see you touch your left ear."

The street drummer stood up, turned, and faced me. He shifted
both his drumsticks to his right hand, and then raised his left hand. I
looked straight at the spot where his left ear *should* have been,
expecting all the missing parts of his face to reappear when he
touched them.

His left hand reached up, and invaded the space where half his head had gone AWOL. His hand closed around a phantom ear, and then . . . his hand vanished, clear up to the wrist. Then his arm began to fade. All the flesh on the right side of his face disappeared; I could see the naked facial muscles, and the blood vessels underneath where his skin should have been. Then the veins and muscle-tissue vanished, and the skull beneath them started to confront me.

I turned and ran. Behind me, I could hear the drummer laughing.

For a week or so, it got worse. I couldn't go anywhere—to a restaurant, to a party, to my job at the brokerage house—without somebody saying *"Hey, how about those bag-ladies? Weird, huh? Has anybody noticed?"* And then somebody else would change the subject. After a while nobody would talk about the Vanishers any-more—nobody knew what caused the Vanishing, and it didn't seem to be contagious; people with jobs and homes to go to showed no sign of catching the invisibility plague, or whatever it was. The new rule was: Don't talk about the homeless. Don't write about the home-less. They're vanishing, but we're not supposed to notice. Change the subject.

I *did* notice, though, that the problem of the homeless was resolv-ing itself. There *were* fewer street people lately, as my friend Rooney had said. What I found hard to take was the incompleteness of the street-ones who remained. The plague of invisibles had started with an arm missing here, or a leg over there. *Now* it was getting worse. A pair of swollen legs with cracked veins and broken shoes came walking past me in the street one day; from crotch-upwards, there was nobody there. One night I turned a corner suddenly, and almost bumped into just a *head*, that went ambling right past me. I nearly shit when *that* happened. The head didn't float; it sort of rocked back and forth in mid-air, the way a drunkard walks. But the head had no body. One day outside the Stock Exchange I saw a pair of female hands, with no body attached to them, creeping along like little frightened spiders on the rim of a litter-basket. One hand was clutch-ing a broken shopping-bag. The other hand dipped into the litter-basket, and retrieved an especially precious piece of garbage. It care-fully placed this in the shopping-bag, and then went back for more plunder. One night somebody tapped my shoulder from behind; I turned, and saw a disembodied hand beside me, rattling a cup. I

shouted something and ran, but the flying hand kept up with me. I
flung some money at it, and when the hand stopped to pick up the
coins I escaped . . .

A week went by, and there was nothing left of the street people at
all now, except for *the faces*. I would pass them on the corners, and
hear them pleading for handouts, or moaning obscenities. There were
no floating arms or disembodied legs now; only faces. Soon the faces
themselves began to subdivide. One night a festering mouth came
towards me on Houston Street, and followed me for seven blocks,
whispering curses. Near a street-lamp, outside the Waverly movie-
house in Greenwich Village, a single eye suspended in mid-air watched
me walk past, and winked obscenely when I glanced at it. I was
networking with two commodities traders at South Street Seaport
one day; we got to talking shop, and then I noticed that an extra ear
was listening. I threw a newspaper at it and the ear flitted away from
us, bat-like.

Eventually the blessed day arrived when all the Vanishers were
absent. There were no street people in the city at all now: no druggies,
no alkies, no bag-ladies, no bums. "I think I know where they went,"
Wendy told me one night, on our way over to my condominium loft.
"There's another universe, next door. It's just like Earth, but with
more room for people. A planet that *wants* them. So all the homeless
from Earth have moved to a place where they're happy."

"That's the craziest thing I ever heard," I told her, and instantly
blew my chances for getting laid that night. The next day at work I
tried to apologize. "Maybe you were right about those street people,"
I said to Wendy.

"Street people?" she asked, looking at me funny.

"The ones who lived in the street . . ." I began.

"Brett, why would anyone live in the street? Who would *want* to?
There's room enough in Manhattan for everyone who can afford it.
And there's cheaper housing in Brooklyn. Why would *anyone* live in
the street?"

I changed the subject. Later, I got to a phone and called up
Rooney, and Pete, and some others, and asked them all a direct
question: had they seen any street people lately?

Everyone thought I was kidding: *"People living in the street? You
mean, like the alligators that live in the sewers? This is a joke, right?"*
They'd *never* seen any homeless people, they assured me. They

very much doubted that anyone, anywhere, had ever been homeless; it had certainly never happened in *New York*, the Big Apple, for Chrissakes. The concept of having no place to live seemed totally alien to everyone I asked. I finally got Rooney to admit that maybe somebody somewhere had been homeless *once*, an isolated incident, but he certainly couldn't remember the details. Might be on file in the newspaper morgue someplace. He'd forgotten all about it.

So did everybody else.

So did I.

For a while.

Business fell off on the Exchange, and our brokerage house got swallowed in a megamerger. After the take-over, I had trouble justifying some of my commissions to the new board of directors, and my condo's expenses were getting too high, and finally everything got to be too much of a hassle, so I just said screw this. After pulling down six figures a year for the past five years I had some money put away; I sold my loft, and moved to New England. I bought a cabin up in Maine, near Casco Bay. I deserved to take it easy for a while, after all . . . and if *that* got boring, I could try writing a novel.

The recession had hit Maine pretty badly. The sawmills were closed, there were some factory lay-offs; in the township I moved into, there was a bill going through to raise taxes to pay for a rehabilitation center for the laid-off workers who had nothing to do all day except sit around drinking. And then it wasn't just drunks: suddenly a lot of the younger laid-off workers, or the kids of the older folks, started doing drugs. Some bastard broke into my cabin one night when I wasn't home, and stole my VCR and some cash. The local sheriff, when I told him about it, replied that crime was up all over the area.

"You're from New York, aren't you?" he asked. "I heard you folks down there had this problem for years, and then finally somebody did something about it. We could use a slice of that action up here."

"I don't know what you're talking about," said my voice. I could hear the words coming out of my mouth, automatically, and for some reason the truth of what I said seemed so obvious that I didn't feel any need to think about it. "New York is the Big Apple. A cultural paradise. There's no unemployment there. No crime, no homeless people. Never *have* been. I certainly don't *remember* any."

"That so?" the sheriff asked me. "Well, if New York is so piss-wonderful, then why did you leave?"

Well, why *did* I leave? I couldn't remember *that* either.

So I came back to New York City.

The Arrivals terminal at Kennedy Airport was full of vagrants. At least three different people tried to steal some of my luggage. The waiting lounge was choked with ragged women nursing filthy children. Emissaries of various dubious religions milled around, shaking cans under my face, pleading for donations. The street was worse. I hailed a cab, but some bastard made off with one of my suitcases before I could stop him.

I'd booked ahead with a hotel. When I got there, the whole street for a three-block radius around the place was absolutely sardine-packed with druggies, and drunks, and scabrous-looking prostitutes, and thieves. I heard gunshots at least twice. I couldn't see any police cars at all. "Where are all the police?" I asked the cab-driver.

"Don't need any," he told me.

I got out in front of the hotel, and fought my way through a crawling mass of clutching whimpering humanity, all begging pleading threatening for money drugs a cigarette a drink food *food* **FOOD**. The twenty-foot walk from the curb to the entrance of the hotel was the hardest trip I ever took. Fortunately there were armed security guards in the lobby of the hotel, although one of them looked like *he* belonged in the street with the druggies. The other rent-a-cops didn't seem much healthier; they looked like they were barely one step above the screaming beggars in the street, and one step below normal people.

I was surprised to see Wendy waiting for me in the hotel lobby; I'd phoned and told her I was coming, but when she didn't meet my flight I'd just assumed she didn't care about me any more.

"Where did all these people come from?" I asked, shaking a few clots of filth off my sleeve, where one of the street people had grabbed me. "Where do they live? Where do they go at night? *Do they live in the street?*"

"There *are* no people in the street, Brett," Wendy told me. "Isn't it wonderful? Every once in a while I seem to recall that there *used* to be a few homeless people, but they all disappeared one day. *Everybody* knows that. Don't you remember?"

"There *are* no homeless," said the desk clerk, and the bell captain, and the guests in the lobby. The security guards mumbled something, and wouldn't look me in the eye, but the others spoke loud: "There *are* no homeless. Not here. Not in New York." Wendy nodded, and reached for my hand.

I looked at her, and then I looked beyond her out the window at the thousands of hungering homeless in the street. For a moment all the shrieking pleading hungry ones flickered away, and the streets were deserted . . . then they suddenly winked back into existence, and it seemed to me that now there were twice as many as before. Then the hordes of the unwanted all vanished again, and instantly returned in greater numbers: screaming thousands—doubling, doubling. All the legions of discarded who had always been there, who had multiplied in my absence, who had never disappeared at all while the rest of us, in order to survive, had evolved the ability to *unsee* them, *unhear* them, *unhappen* them, denying their existence. I looked at Wendy, and I looked at all the city. And then at last I understood.

Ever After

SUSAN PALWICK

"Velvet," she says, pushing back her sleep-tousled hair. "I want green velvet this time, with lace around the neck and wrists. Cream lace—not white—and sea-green velvet. Can you do that?"

"Of course." She's getting vain, this one; vain and a little bossy. The wonder has worn off. All for the best. Soon now, very soon, I'll have to tell her the truth.

She bends, here in the dark kitchen, to peer at the back of her mother's prized copper kettle. It's just after dusk, and by the light of the lantern I'm holding a vague reflection flickers and dances on the metal. She scowls. "Can't you get me a real mirror? That ought to be simple enough."

I remember when the light I brought filled her with awe. Wasting good fuel, just to see yourself by! "No mirrors. I clothe you only in seeming, not in fact. You know that."

"Ah." She waves a hand, airily. She's proud of her hands: delicate and pale and long-fingered, a noblewoman's hands; all the years before I came she protected them against the harsh work of her mother's kitchen. "Yes, the prince. I have to marry a prince, so I can have his jewels for my own. Will it be this time, do you think?"

"There will be no princes at this dance, Caitlin. You are practicing for princes."

"Hah! And when I'm good enough at last, will you let me wear glass slippers?"

"Nonsense. You might break them during a gavotte, and cut yourself." She knew the story before I found her; they always do. It enters their blood as soon as they can follow speech, and lodges in their hearts like the promise of spring. All poor mothers tell their daughters this story, as they sit together in dark kitchens, scrubbing pots and trying to save their hands for the day when the tale becomes real. I often wonder if that first young woman was one of ours, but the facts don't matter. Like all good stories, this one is true.

"Princess Caitlin," she says dreamily. "That will be very fine. Oh, how they will envy me! It's begun already, in just the little time since you've made me beautiful. Ugly old Lady Alison—did you see her giving me the evil eye, at the last ball? Just because my skin is smooth and hers wrinkled, and I a newcomer?"

"Yes," I tell her. I am wary of Lady Alison, who looks too hard and says too little. Lady Alison is dangerous.

"Jealousy," Caitlin says complacently. "I'd be jealous, if I looked like she does."

"You are very lovely," I say, and it is true. With her blue eyes and raven hair, and those hands, she could have caught the eye of many princes on her own. Except, of course, that without me they never would have seen her.

Laughing, she sits to let me plait her hair. "So serious! You never smile at me. Do magic folks never smile? Aren't you proud of me?"

"Very proud," I say, parting the thick cascade and beginning to braid it. She smells like smoke and the thin, sour stew which simmers on the hearth, but at the dance tonight she will be scented with all the flowers of summer.

"Will you smile and laugh when I have my jewels and land? I shall give you riches, then."

So soon, I think, and my breath catches. So soon she offers me gifts, and forgets the woman who bore her, who now lies snoring in the other room. All for the best; and yet I am visited by something very like pity. "No wife has riches but from her lord, Caitlin. Not in this kingdom."

"I shall have riches of my own, when I am married," she says grandly; and then, her face clouding as if she regrets having forgotten, "My mother will be rich too, then. She'll like you, when we're rich. Godmother, why doesn't she like you now?"

"Because I am stealing you away from her. She has never been invited to a ball. And because I am beautiful, and she isn't any more."

What I have said is true enough, as always; and, as always, I find myself wondering if there is more than that. No matter. If Caitlin's mother suspects, she says nothing. I am the only chance she and her daughter have to approach nobility, and for the sake of that dream she has tolerated my presence, and Caitlin's odd new moods, and the schedule which keeps the girl away from work to keep her fresh for dances.

Caitlin bends her head, and the shining braids slip through my fingers like water. "She'll come to the castle whenever she wants to, when I'm married to a prince. We'll make her beautiful too, then. I'll buy her clothing and paint for her face."

"There are years of toil on her, Caitlin. Lady Alison is your mother's age, and all her riches can't make her lovely again."

"Oh, but Lady Alison's mean. That makes you ugly." Caitlin dismisses her enemy with the ignorance of youth. Lady Alison is no meaner than anyone, but she has borne illnesses and childlessness and the unfaithfulness of her rich lord. Her young nephew will fall in love with Caitlin tonight—a match Lord Gregory suggested, I suspect, precisely because Alison will oppose it.

Caitlin's hair is done, piled in coiled, lustrous plaits. "Do you have the invitation? Where did I put it?"

"On the table, next to the onions."

She nods, crosses the room, snatches up the thick piece of paper and fans herself with it. I remember her first invitation, only six dances ago, her eagerness and innocence and purity, the wide eyes and wonder. *I? I have been invited to the ball?* She refused to let go of the invitation then; afraid it might vanish as suddenly as it had come, she carried it with her for hours. They are always at their most beautiful that first time, when they believe most fully in the story and are most awe-stricken at having been chosen to play the heroine. No glamour we give them can ever match that first glow.

"Clothe me," Caitlin commands now, standing with her eyes closed in the middle of the kitchen, and I put the glamour on her and her grubby kitchen-gown is transformed by desire and shadow into sea-green velvet and cream lace. She smiles. She opens her eyes, which gleam with joy and the giddiness of transformation. She has taken easily to that rush; she craves it. Already she has forsaken dreams of love for dreams of power.

"I'm hungry," she says. "I want to eat before the dance. What was that soup you gave me last night? You must have put wine in it, because it made me drunk. I want more of that."

"No food before you dance," I tell her. "You don't want to look fat, do you?"

No chance of that, for this girl who has starved in a meager kitchen all her life; but at the thought of dancing she forgets her hunger and takes a few light steps in anticipation of the music. "Let me stay longer this time—please. Just an hour or two. I never get tired any more."

"Midnight," I tell her flatly. It won't do to change that part of the story until she knows everything.

So we go to the dance, in a battered carriage made resplendent not by any glamour of mine but by Caitlin's belief in her own beauty. This, too, she has learned easily; already the spells are more hers than mine, although she doesn't yet realize it.

At the gates, Caitlin hands the invitation to the footman. She has grown to relish this moment, the thrill of bending him to her will with a piece of paper, of forcing him to admit someone he suspects—quite rightly—doesn't belong here. It is very important that she learn to play this game. Later she will learn to win her own invitations, to cajole the powerful into admitting her where, without their permission, she cannot go at all.

Only tonight it is less simple. The footman glances at the envelope, frowns, says, "I'm sorry, but I can't admit you."

"Can't admit us?" Caitlin summons the proper frosty indignation, and so I let her keep talking. She needs to learn this, too. "Can't admit us, with a handwritten note from Lord Gregory?"

"Just so, mistress. Lady Alison has instructed—"

"Lady Alison didn't issue the invitation."

The footman coughs, shuffles his feet. "Just so. I have the very strictest instructions—"

"What does Lord Gregory instruct?"

"Lord Gregory has not—"

"Lord Gregory wrote the invitation. Lord Gregory wants us here. If Lord Gregory learned we were denied it would go badly for you, footman."

He looks up at us; he looks miserable. "Just so," he says, sounding wretched.

"I shall speak to her for you," I tell him, and Caitlin smiles at me and we are through the gates, passing ornate gardens and high, neat hedges. I lean back in my seat, shaking. Lady Alison is very dangerous, but she has made a blunder. The servant could not possibly refuse her husband's invitation; all she has done is to warn us. "Be very careful tonight," I say to Caitlin. "Avoid her."

"I'd like to scratch her eyes out! How dare she, that jealous old—"

"Avoid her, Caitlin! I'll deal with her. I don't want to see you anywhere near her."

She subsides. Already we can hear music from the great hall, and her eyes brighten as she taps time to the beat.

The people at the dance are the ones who are always at dances; by now, all of them know her. She excites the men and unnerves the women, and where she passes she leaves a trail of uncomfortable silence, followed by hushed whispers. I strain to hear what they are saying, but catch only the usual comments about her youth, her beauty, her low birth.

"Is she someone's illegitimate child, do you think?"

"A concubine, surely."

"She'll never enter a convent, not that one."

"Scheming husband-hunter, and may she find one soon. I don't want her taking mine."

The usual. I catch sight of Lady Alison sitting across the wide room. She studies us with narrowed eyes. One arthritic hand, covered with jeweled rings, taps purposefully on her knee. She sees me watching her and meets my gaze without flinching. She crosses herself.

I look away, wishing we hadn't come here. What does she intend to do? I wonder how much she has learned simply by observation, and how much Gregory let slip. I scan the room again and spot him, in a corner, nursing a chalice of wine. He is watching Caitlin as intently as his wife did, but with a different expression.

And someone else is watching Caitlin, among the many people who glance at her and then warily away: Randolph, Gregory's young nephew, who is tall and well-formed and pleasant of face. Caitlin looks to me for confirmation and I nod. She smiles at Randolph—that artful smile there has never been need to teach—and he extends a hand to invite her to dance.

I watch them for a moment, studying how she looks up at him, the angle of her head, the flutter of her lashes. She started with the smile, and I gave her the rest. She has learned her skills well.

"So," someone says behind me, "she's growing accustomed to these late nights."

I turn. Lady Alison stands there, unlovely and shrunken, having crossed the room with improbable speed. "Almost as used to them as you," she says.

I bow my head, carefully acquiescent. "Or you yourself. Those who would dance in these halls must learn to do without sleep."

"Some sleep during the day." Her mouth twitches. "I am Randolph's aunt, mistress. While he stays within these walls his care lies in my keeping, even as the care of the girl lies in yours. I will safeguard him however I must."

I laugh, the throaty chuckle which thrills Gregory, but my amusement is as much an act as Caitlin's flirtatiousness. "Against dancing with pretty young women?"

"Against being alone with those who would entrap him with his own ignorance. He knows much too little of the world; he places more faith in fairy tales than in history, and neither I nor the Church have been able to persuade him to believe in evil. I pray you, by our Lord in heaven and his holy saints, leave this house."

"So you requested at the gates." Her piety nauseates me, as she no doubt intended, and I keep my voice steady only with some effort. "The Lord of this castle is Lord Gregory, Lady Alison, by whose invitation we are here and in whose hospitality we will remain."

She grimaces. "I have some small power of my own, although it does not extend to choosing my guests. Pray chaperone your charge."

"No need. They are only dancing." I glance at Caitlin and Randolph, who gaze at each other as raptly as if no one else were in the room. Randolph's face is silly and soft; Caitlin's, when I catch a glimpse of it, is soft and ardent. I frown, suddenly uneasy; that look is a bit too sudden and far too unguarded, and may be more than artifice.

Lady Alison snorts. "Both will want more than dancing presently, I warrant, although they will want different things. Chaperone her—or I will do it for you, less kindly."

With that she turns and vanishes into the crowd. I turn back to the young couple, thinking that a chaperone would indeed be wise to-night; but the players have struck up a minuet, and Caitlin and Randolph glide gracefully through steps as intricate and measured as any court intrigue. The dance itself will keep them safe, for a little while.

Instead I make my way to Gregory, slowly, drifting around knots of people as if I am only surveying the crowd. Alison has positioned herself to watch Caitlin and Randolph, who dip and twirl through the steps of the dance; I hope she won't notice me talking to her husband.

"She is very beautiful," says Gregory softly when I reach his side. "Even lovelier than you, my dear. What a charming couple they make. I would give much to be Randolph, for a few measures of this dance."

He thinks he can make me jealous. Were this any other ball I might pretend he had succeeded, but I have no time for games tonight. "Gregory, Alison tried to have us barred at the gate. And she just threatened me."

He smiles. "That was foolish of her. Also futile."

"Granted," I say, although I suspect Lady Alison has resources of which neither of us are aware. Most wives of the nobility do: faithful servants, devoted priests, networks of spies in kitchens and corridors.

Gregory reaches out to touch my cheek; I draw away from him, uneasy. Everyone here suspects I am his mistress, but there is little sense in giving them public proof. He laughs gently. "You need not be afraid of her. She loves the boy and wishes only to keep him cloistered in a chapel, with his head buried in scripture. I tell her that is no sport for a young man and certainly no education for a titled lord, who must learn how to resist the blandishments of far more experienced women. So he and our little Caitlin will be merry, and take their lessons from each other, with no one the worse for it. See how they dance together!"

They dance as I have taught Caitlin she should dance with princes: lingering over the steps, fingertips touching, lips parted and eyes bright. Alison watches them, looking worried, and I cannot help but feel the same way. Caitlin is too obvious, too oblivious; she has grown innocent again, in a mere hour. I remember what Alison said about history, and fairy tales; if Caitlin and Randolph both believe themselves in that same old story, things will go harshly for all of us.

"Let them be happy together," Gregory says softly. "They have need of happiness, both of them—Randolph with his father surely dying, and the complexities of power about to bewilder him, and Caitlin soon to learn her true nature. You cannot keep it from her much longer, Juliana. She has changed too much. Let them be happy, for this one night; and let their elders, for once, abandon care and profit from their example."

He reaches for my hand again, drawing me closer to him, refusing to let go. His eyes are as bright as Randolph's; he has had rather too much wine. "Profit from recklessness?" I ask, wrenching my fingers from his fist. Alison has looked away from her nephew and watches us now, expressionless. I hear murmurs around us; a young courtier in purple satin and green hose raises an eyebrow.

"This is my castle," Gregory says. "My halls and land, my musicians, my servants and clerics and nobles; my wife. No one can hurt you here, Juliana."

"No one save you, my lord. Kindly retain your good sense—"

"My invitation." His voice holds little kindness now. "My invitation allowed you entrance, as it has many other times; I provide you with splendor, and fine nourishment, and a training ground for the girl, and I am glad to do so. I am no slave of Alison's priests, Juliana; I know full well that you are not evil."

"Kindly be more quiet and discreet, my lord!" The courtier is carefully ignoring us now, evidently fascinated with a bunch of grapes. Caitlin and Randolph, transfixed by each other, sway in the last steps of the minuet.

Gregory continues in the same tone, "Of late you have paid far more attention to Caitlin than to me. Even noblemen are human, and can be hurt. Let the young have their pleasures tonight, and let me have mine."

I lower my own voice, since he refuses to lower his. "What, in the middle of the ballroom? That would be a fine entertainment for your guests! I will come to you tomorrow—"

"Tonight," he says, into the sudden silence of the dance's end. "Come to me tonight, in the usual chamber—"

"It is a poor lord who leaves his guests untended," I tell him sharply, "and a poor teacher who abandons her student. You will excuse me."

He reaches for me again, but I slip past his hands and go to find Caitlin, wending my way around gaudily-dressed lords and ladies and squires, catching snippets of gossip and conversation.

"Did you see them dancing—"

"So the venison disagreed with me, but thank goodness it was only a trifling ailment—"

"Penelope's violet silk! I said, my dear, I simply must have the pattern and wherever did you find that seamstress—"

"Gregory's brother in failing health, and the young heir staying here? No uncle can be trusted that far. The boy had best have a quick dagger and watch his back, is what I say."

That comment hurries my steps. Gregory's brother is an obscure duke, but he is a duke nonetheless, and Gregory is next in line of succession after Randolph. If Randolph is in danger, and Caitlin with him—

I have been a fool. We should not have come here, and we must leave. I scan the colorful crowd more anxiously than ever for Caitlin, but my fears are groundless; she has found me first, and rushes towards me, radiant. "Oh, godmother—"

"Caitlin! My dear, listen: you must stay by me—"

But she hasn't heard me. "Godmother, he's so sweet and kind, so sad with his father ill and yet trying to be merry—did you see how he danced? Why does it have to be a prince I love? I don't care if he's not a prince, truly I don't, and just five days ago I scorned that other gawky fellow for not having a title, but he wasn't nearly as nice—"

"Caitlin!" Yes, we most assuredly must leave. I lower my voice and take her by the elbow. "Listen to me: many men are nice. If you want a nice man you may marry a blacksmith. I am not training you to be a mere duchess."

She grows haughty now. "Duchess sounds quite well enough to me. Lord Gregory is no king."

Were we in private I would slap her for that. "No, he isn't, but he is a grown man and come into his limited power, and so he is still more useful to us than Randolph. Caitlin, we must leave now—"

"No! We can't leave; it's nowhere near midnight. I don't want to leave. You can't make me."

"I can strip you of your finery right here."

"Randolph wouldn't care."

"Everyone else would, and he is outnumbered."

"Randolph picks his own companions—"

"Randolph," I say, losing all patience, "still picks his pimples. He is a fine young man, Caitlin, but he is young nonetheless. My dear, many more things are happening here tonight than your little romance. I am your magic godmother, and on some subjects you must trust me. We are leaving."

"I won't leave," she says, raising her chin. "I'll stay here until after midnight. I don't care if you turn me into a toad; Randolph will save me, and make me a duchess."

"Princesses are safer," I tell her grimly, not at all sure it's even true. On the far side of the room I see the courtier in the green hose talking intently to Lady Alison, and a chill cuts through me. Well, he cannot have heard much which isn't general rumor, and soon we will be in the carriage, and away from all this.

"Caitlin!" Randolph hurries up to us, as welcoming and guileless as some friendly dog. "Why did you leave me? I didn't know where you'd gone. Will you dance with me again? Here, some wine if you don't mind sharing, I thought you'd be thirsty—"

She takes the goblet and sips, laughing. "Of course I'll dance with you."

I frown at Caitlin and clear my throat. "I regret that she cannot, my lord—"

"This is my godmother Juliana," Caitlin cuts in, taking another sip of wine and giving Randolph a dazzling smile, "who worries over-much about propriety and thinks people will gossip if I dance with you too often."

"And so they shall," he says, bowing and kissing my hand, "because everyone gossips about beauty." He straightens and smiles down at me, still holding my hand. His cheeks are flushed and his fingers very warm; I can feel the faint, steady throb of his pulse against my skin. What could Caitlin do but melt, in such heat?

"Randolph!" Two voices, one cry; Alison and Gregory approach us from opposite directions, the sea of guests parting before them.

Alison, breathless, reaches us a moment before her husband does. "Randolph, my love—the players are going to give us another slow tune, at my request. You'll dance with your crippled old aunt, won't you?"

He bows; he can hardly refuse her. Gregory, standing next to Caitlin, says smoothly, "And I will have the honor of dancing with the young lady, with her kind godmother's assent."

It isn't a petition. I briefly consider feigning illness, but such a ruse would shake Caitlin's faith in my power and give Gregory the excuse to protest that I must stay here, spend the night and be made comfortable in his household's care.

Instead I station myself next to a pillar to watch the dancers. Alison's lips move as Randolph guides her carefully around the floor. I see her press a small pouch into his hand; he smiles indulgently and puts it in a pocket.

She is warning him away from Caitlin, then. This dance is maddeningly slow, and far too long; I crane my neck to find Caitlin and

Gregory, only to realize that they are about to sweep past me. "Yes, I prefer roses to all other blooms," Caitlin says lightly. (That too is artifice; she preferred forget-me-nots until I taught her otherwise.)

So at least one of these conversations is insignificant, and Caitlin safe. Alison and Randolph, meanwhile, glare at each other; she is trying to give him something on a chain, and he is refusing it. They pass me, but say nothing; Caitlin and Gregory go by again a moment later. "Left left right, left left right," he tells her, before they are past my hearing, "it is a pleasing pattern and very fashionable; you must try it."

A new court dance, no doubt. This old one ends at last and I dart for Caitlin, only to be halted by a group of rowdy acrobats who have just burst into the hall. "Your pleasure!" they cry, doing flips and twists in front of me as the crowd laughs and gathers to watch them. "Your entertainment, your dancing hearts!" I try to go around them, but find myself blocked by a motley-clad clown juggling pewter goblets. "Hey! We'll make you merry, at the generous lord's invitation we'll woo you, we'll win you—"

You'll distract us, I think—but from what? I manage to circle the juggler, but there is no sign of Caitlin or Randolph. Gregory seems likewise to have disappeared.

Alison is all too evident, however. "Where are they? What have you done with them?" She stands in front of me, her hands clenched on the fine silk of her skirt. "I turned away from Randolph for a mere moment to answer a servant's question, and when I looked back he was gone—"

"My lady, I was standing on the side. You no doubt saw me. I am honestly eager to honor your wishes and be gone, and I dislike this confusion as much as you do."

"I know you," she says, trembling, her voice very low. "I know you for what you are. I told Randolph but he would not believe me, and Gregory fairly revels in dissolution. I would unmask you in this hall and send town criers to spread the truth about you, save that my good lord would be set upon by decent Christian folk were it known he had trafficked with such a creature."

And your household destroyed and all your riches plundered, I think; yes, the poor welcome such pretexts. You do well to maintain silence, Alison, since it buys your own safety.

But I dare not admit to what she knows. "I am but a woman as yourself, my lady, and I share your concern for Randolph and the girl—"

"Nonsense. They are both charming young people who dance superbly." Gregory has reappeared, affable and urbane; he seems more relaxed than he has all evening, and I trust him less.

So does Alison, by the look of her. "And where have you hidden our two paragons of sprightliness, my lord?"

"I? I have not hidden them anywhere. Doubtless they have stolen away and found some quiet corner to themselves. The young will do such things. Alison, my sweet, you look fatigued—"

"And the old, when they get a chance. No: I am not going to retire conveniently and leave you alone with this creature. I value your soul far more than that."

"Although not my body," Gregory says, raising an eyebrow. "Well, then, shall we dance, all three? With linked hands in a circle, like children? Shall we sit and discuss the crops, or have a hand of cards? What would you, my lovelies?"

Alison takes his hand. "Let us go find our nephew."

He sighs heavily and rolls his eyes, but he allows himself to be led away. I am glad to be rid of them; now I can search on my own and make a hasty exit. The conversation with Alison worries me. She is too cautious to destroy us here, but she may well try to have us followed into the countryside.

So I make my way through corridors, through courtyards, peering into corners and behind pillars, climbing winding staircases and descending them, until I am lost and can no longer hear the music from the great hall. I meet other furtive lovers, dim shapes embracing in shadows, but none are Randolph and Caitlin. When I have exhausted every passageway I can find I remember Caitlin and Gregory's discussion of roses and hurry outside, through a doorway I have never seen before, but the moonlit gardens yield nothing. The sky tells me that it is midnight: Caitlin will be rejoicing at having eluded me.

Wherever she is. These halls and grounds are too vast; I could wander all night and still not find her by dawn. Gregory knows where she is: I am convinced he does, convinced he arranged the couple's disappearance. He may have done so to force me into keeping the tryst with him. That would be very like him; he would be thrilled by my seeking him out while his guests gossip and dance in the great hall. Gregory delights in private indiscretions at public events.

So I will play his game this once, although it angers me, and lie with him, and be artful and cajoling. I go back inside and follow hallways I know to Gregory's chambers, glancing behind me to be sure I am not seen.

The small chapel where Lady Alison takes her devotions lies along the same path, and as I pass it I hear moans of pain. I stop, listening, wary of a trap—but the noise comes again, and the agony sounds genuine: a thin, childish whimpering clearly made by a woman.

Caitlin? I remember Alison's threats, and my vision blackens for a moment. I slip into the room, hiding in shadows, tensed to leap. If Alison led the girl here—

Alison is indeed here, but Caitlin is not with her. Doubled over in front of the altar, Gregory's wife gasps for breath and clutches her side; her face is sweaty, gray, the pupils dilated. She sees me and recoils, making her habitual sign of the cross; her hand is trembling, but her voice remains steady. "So. Didn't you find them, either?"

"My lady Alison, what—"

"He called it a quick poison," she says, her face contorting with pain, "but I am stronger than he thinks, or the potion weaker. I was tired—my leg . . . we came here; it was close. I asked him to pray with me, and he repented very prettily. 'I will bring some wine,' he said, 'and we will both drink to my salvation.' Two cups he brought, and I took the one he gave me . . . I thought him saved, and relief dulled my wits. 'Mulled wine,' he said, 'I ground the spices for you myself,' and so he did, no doubt. Pray none other taste them."

So much speech has visibly drained her; shaken, I help her into a chair. What motive could Gregory have for killing his wife? Her powers of observation were an asset to him, though he rarely heeded them, and he couldn't have felt constrained by his marriage vows; he never honored them while she was alive.

"It is well I believe in the justice of God," she says. "No one will punish him here in the world. They will pretend I ate bad meat, or had an attack of bile."

"Be silent and save your strength," I tell her, but she talks anyway, crying now, fumbling to wipe her face through spasms.

"He tired of me because I am old. He grew tired of a wife who said her prayers, and loved other people's children although she could have none of her own. No doubt he will install you by his side now, since you are made of darkness and steal the daughters of simple folk."

Gregory knows far better than to make me his formal consort, whatever Alison thinks. "We choose daughters only when one of us has been killed, Lady Alison. We wish no more than anyone does— to continue, and to be safe."

"I will continue in heaven," she says, and then cries out, a thin keening which whistles between her teeth. She no longer sounds human.

I kneel beside her, uncertain she will be able to understand my words. This does not look like a quick-acting potion, whatever Gregory said; it will possibly take her hours to die, and she will likely be mad before then. "I cannot save you, my lady, but I can make your end swift and painless."

"I need no mercy from such as you!"

"You must take mercy where you can get it. Who else will help you?"

She moans and then subsides, trembling. "I have not been shriven. He could have allowed me that."

"But he did not. Perhaps you will be called a saint someday, and this declared your martyrdom; for now, the only last rites you will be offered are mine."

She crosses herself again, but this time it is clearly an effort for her to lift her hand. "A true death?"

"A true death," I say gently. "We do not perpetuate pain."

Her lips draw back from her teeth. "Be merciful, then; and when you go to your assignation, tell Gregory he harms himself far worse than he has harmed me."

It is quick and painless, as I promised, but I am shaking when I finish, and the thought of seeing Gregory fills me with dread. I will have to pretend not to know that he has murdered his wife; I will have to be charming, and seductive, and disguise my concern for my own safety and Caitlin's so I can trick her whereabouts out of him.

I knock on his door and hear the soft "Enter." Even here I need an invitation, to enter this chamber where Gregory will be sprawled on the bed, peeling an apple or trimming his fingernails, his clothing already unfastened.

Tonight the room is unlit. I see someone sitting next to the window, silhouetted in moonlight; only as my eyes adjust to the dimness do I realize that Gregory has not kept our appointment. A priest waits in his place, surrounded by crucifixes and bottles of holy water and plaster statues of saints. On the bed where I have lain so often is something long and sharp which I force myself not to look at too closely.

"Hello," he says, as the door thuds shut behind me. I should have turned and run, but it is too late now; I have frozen at the sight of the priest, as they say animals do in unexpected light. In the hallway I hear heavy footsteps—the corridor is guarded, then.

The priest holds an open Bible; he glances down at it, and then, with a grimace of distaste, sideways at the bed. "No, lady, it won't come to that. You needn't look so frightened."

I say nothing. I tell myself I must think clearly, and be very quick, but I cannot think at all. We are warned about these small rooms, these implements. All the warnings I have heard have done me no good.

"There's the window," he explains. "You could get out that way if you had to. That is how I shall tell them you escaped, when they question me." He gestures at his cheek, and I see a thin, cruel scar running from forehead to jaw. "When I was still a child, my father took me poaching for boar on our lord's estate. It was my first hunt. It taught me not to corner frightened beasts, especially when they have young. Sit down, lady. Don't be afraid."

I sit, cautiously and without hope, and he closes the book with a soft sound of sighing parchment. "You are afraid, of course; well you should be. Lord Gregory has trapped you, for reasons he says involve piety but doubtless have more to do with politics; Lady Alison has been weaving her own schemes to destroy you, and the Church has declared you incapable of redemption. You have been quite unanimously consigned to the stake. Which is—" he smiles "—why I am here. Do you believe in God, my dear? Do your kind believe in miracles?"

When I don't answer he smiles again and goes on easily, as if we were chatting downstairs at the dance, "You should. It is a kind of miracle that has brought you to me. I have prayed for this since I was very young, and now I am old and my prayer has been answered. I was scarcely more than a boy when I entered the religious life, and for many years I was miserable, but now I see that this is why it happened."

He laughs, quite kindly. His kindness terrifies me. I fear he is mad. "I came from a poor family," he says. "I was the youngest son, and so, naturally, I became a priest. The Church cannot get sons the normal way, so it takes other people's and leaves the best young men to breed more souls. You and I are not, you see, so very different."

He leans back in his chair. "There were ten other children in my family. Four died. The littlest and weakest was my youngest sister, who was visited one day by a very beautiful woman who made her lovely, and took her to parties, and then took her away. I never got to say good-bye to my sister—her name was Sofia—and I never got to tell her that, although I knew what she had become, I still loved her. I thought she would be coming back, you see."

He leans forward earnestly, and his chair makes a scraping sound. "I have always prayed for a way to reach her. The Church tells me to destroy you, but I do not believe God wants you destroyed—because He has sent you to me, who thinks of you only with pity and gratitude and love. I am glad my little sister was made beautiful. If you know her, Sofia with green eyes and yellow hair, tell her Thomas loves her, eh? Tell her I am doubtless a heretic, for forgiving her what she is. Tell her I think of her every day when I take the Holy Communion. Will you do that for me?"

I stare at him, wondering if the watchers in the hallway can distinguish words through the thick wooden door.

He sighs. "So suspicious! Yes, of course you will. You will deliver my message, and I'll say you confounded me by magic and escaped through the window. Eh?"

"They'll kill you," I tell him. The calmness of my voice shocks me. I am angry now: not at Lord Gregory who betrayed me, not at Lady Alison, who was likewise betrayed and died believing me about to lie with her husband, but with this meandering holy man who prattles of miracles and ignores his own safety. "The ones set to guard the door. They'll say you must have been possessed by demons, to let me escape."

He nods and pats his book. "We will quite probably both be killed. Lady Alison means to set watchers on the roads."

So he doesn't know. "Lady Alison is dead. Gregory poisoned her."

He pales and bows his head for a moment. "Ah. It is certainly political, then, and no one is safe tonight. I have bought you only a very little time; you had best use it. Now go: gather your charge and flee, and God be with you both. I shall chant exorcisms and hold them off, eh? Go on: use the window."

I use the window. I dislike changing shape and do so only in moments of extreme danger; it requires too much energy, and the consequent hunger can make one reckless.

I have made myself an owl, not the normal choice but a good one; I need acute vision, and a form which won't arouse suspicion in alert watchers. From this height I can see the entire estate: the castle, the surrounding land, gardens and pathways and fountains—and something else I never knew about, and could not have recognized from the ground.

The high hedges lining the road to the castle form, in one section, the side of a maze, one of those ornate topiary follies which pass in and out of botanical fashion. In the center of it is a small rose garden with a white fountain; on the edge of the fountain sit two foreshortened figures, very close to one another. Just outside the center enclosure, in a cul-de-sac which anyone exiting the maze must pass, another figure stands hidden.

Left left right. Gregory wasn't explaining a new dance at all: he was telling Caitlin how to reach the rose garden, the secret place where she and Randolph hid while Alison and I searched so frantically. Doubtless he went with his wife to keep her from the spot; with Alison's bad leg, and the maze this far from the castle, it wouldn't have been difficult.

I land a few feet behind him and return to myself again. Hunger and hatred enhance my strength, already greater than his. He isn't expecting an approach from behind; I knock him flat, his weapons and charms scattering in darkness, and have his arms pinned behind his back before he can cry out. "I am not dead," I say very quietly into his ear, "but your wife is, and soon you will be."

He whimpers and struggles, but I give his arm an extra twist and he subsides, panting. "Why, Gregory? What was all of this for? So you could spy on them murmuring poetry to one another? Surely not that. Tell me!"

"So I can be a duke."

"By your wife's death?"

"By the boy's."

"How?" I answer sharply, thinking of Randolph and Caitlin sharing the same goblet. "How did you mean to kill him? More poison?"

"She will kill him," he says softly, "because she is aroused, and does not yet know her own appetites or how to control them. Is it not so, my lady?"

My own hunger is a red throbbing behind my eyes. "No, my lord. Caitlin is no murder weapon: she does not yet know what she is or where her hungers come from. She can no more feed on her own than a kitten can, who depends on the mother cat to bring food and teach it how to eat."

"You shall teach her with my puling nephew, I warrant."

"No, my lord Gregory. I shall not. I shall not teach her with you either, more's the pity; we mangle as we learn, just as kittens do—and as kittens do, she will practice on little animals as long as they will sustain her. I should like to see you mangled, my lord."

Instead I break his neck, cleanly, as I broke Alison's. Afterwards, the body still warm, I feed fully; it would be more satisfying were he still alive, but he shall have no more pleasure. Feeding me aroused him as coupling seldom did; he begged to do it more often, and now I am glad I refused. As terrible as he was, he would have been worse as one of us.

When I am finished I lick my fingers clean, wipe my face as best I can, and drag the body back into the cul-de-sac, where it will not be immediately visible. Shaking, I hide the most obvious and dangerous of Gregory's weapons and step into the rose garden.

Caitlin, glowing in moonlight, sits on the edge of the fountain, as I saw her from the air. Randolph is handing her a white rose, which he has evidently just picked: there is blood on his hands where the thorns have scratched him. She takes the rose from him and bends to kiss his fingers, the tip of her tongue flicking towards the wounds.

"Caitlin!" She turns, startled, and lets go of Randolph's hands. "Caitlin, we must leave now."

"No," she says, her eyes very bright. "No. It is already after midnight, and you see—nothing horrid has happened."

"We must leave," I tell her firmly. "Come along."

"But I can come back?" she says, laughing, and then to Randolph, "I'll come back. Soon, I promise you. The next dance, or before that even. Godmother, promise I can come back—"

"Come along, Caitlin! Randolph, we bid you goodnight—"

"May I see you out of the maze, my ladies?"

I think of the watchers on the road, the watchers who may have been set on the maze by now. I wish I could warn him, teach him of the world in an instant. Disguise yourself, Randolph; leave this place as quickly as you can, and steal down swift and secret roads to your father's bedside.

But I cannot yet speak freely in front of Caitlin, and we have time only to save ourselves. Perhaps the maze will protect him, for a little while. "Thank you, my lord, but we know the way. Pray you stay here and think kindly of us; my magic is aided by good wishes."

"Then you shall have them in abundance, whatever my aunt says."

Caitlin comes at last, dragging and prattling. On my own I would escape with shape-changing, but Caitlin doesn't have those skills yet, and were I to tell her of our danger now she would panic and become unmanageable. So I lead her, right right left, right right left, through interminable turns.

But we meet no one else in the maze, and when at last we step into open air there are no priests waiting in ambush. Music still sounds faintly from the castle; the host and hostess have not yet been missed, and the good father must still be muttering incantations in his chamber.

And so we reach the carriage safely; I deposit Caitlin inside and instruct the driver to take us to one of the spots I have prepared for such emergencies. We should be there well before sun-up. I can only hope Lady Alison's watchers have grown tired or afraid, and left off their vigil; there is no way to be sure. I listen for hoofbeats on the road behind us and hear nothing. Perhaps, this time, we have been lucky.

Caitlin doesn't know what I saw, there in the rose garden. She babbles about it in the carriage. "We went into the garden, in the moonlight—he kissed me and held my hands, because he said they were cold. His were so warm! He told me I was beautiful; he said he loved me. And he picked roses for me, and he bled where the thorns had pricked him. He bled for me, godmother—oh, this is the one! This is my prince. How could I not love him?"

I remain silent. She doesn't yet know what she loves. At length she says, "Why aren't we home yet? It's taking so long. I'm hungry. I never had any dinner."

"We aren't going home," I tell her, lighting my lantern and pulling down the shades which cover the carriage's windows. "We have been discovered, Caitlin. It is quite possible we are being followed. I am taking you somewhere safe. There will be food there."

"Discovered?" She laughs. "What have they discovered? That I am poor? That I love Randolph? What could they do to me? He will protect me; he said so. He will marry me."

This is the moment I must tell her. For all the times I have done this, it never hurts any less. "Caitlin, listen to me. You shall never marry Prince Randolph, or anyone else. It was never meant that you should. I am sorry you have to hear this now. I had wanted you to learn some gentler way." She stares at me, bewildered, and, sadly, I smile at her—that expression she has teased me about, asked me for, wondered why I withhold; and when she sees it she understands. The pale eyes go wide, the beautiful hands go to her throat; she backs away from me, crossing herself as if in imitation of Lady Alison.

"Away," she tells me, trembling. "I exorcise thee, demon. In vain dost thou boast of this deed—"

I think of kind Thomas, chanting valiantly in an empty stone chamber as men at arms wait outside the door. "Keep your charms, Caitlin. They'll do you no good. Don't you understand, child? Why do you think everyone has begun to look at you so oddly; why do you think I wouldn't give you a mirror? What do you think was in the soup I gave you?"

The hands go to her mouth now, to the small sharp teeth. She cries out, understanding everything at once—her odd lassitude after the first few balls, the blood I took from her to cure it, her changing hours and changing thirsts—and, as always, this moment of birth rends whatever I have left of a heart. Because for a moment the young creature sitting in front of me is not the apprentice hunter I have made her, but the innocent young girl who stood holding that first invitation to the ball, her heart in her eyes. *I? I have been invited?* I force myself not to turn away as Caitlin cries out, "You tricked me! The story wasn't true!"

She tears at her face with shapely nails, and ribbons of flesh follow her fingers. "You can't weep anymore," I tell her. I would weep for her, if I could. "You can't bleed, either. You're past that. Don't disfigure yourself."

"The story was a lie! None of it was true, ever—"

I make my voice as cold as iron. "The story was perfectly true, Caitlin. You were simply never told all of it before."

"It wasn't supposed to end like this!" All the tears she can't shed are in her voice. "In the story the girl falls in love and marries the prince and—everyone knows that! You lied to me! This isn't the right ending!"

"It's the only ending! The only one there is—Caitlin, surely you see that. Living women have no more protection than we do here. They feed off their men, as we do, and they require permission to enter houses and go to dances, as we do, and they depend on spells of seeming. There is only one difference: you will never, ever look like Lady Alison. You will never look like your mother. You have escaped that."

She stares at me and shrinks against the side of the carriage, holding her hands in front of her—her precious hands which Prince Randolph held, kissed, warmed with his own life. "I love him," she says defiantly. "I love him and he loves me. That part of it is true—"

"You loved his bleeding hands, Caitlin. If I hadn't interrupted, you would have fed from them, and known then, and hated him for it. And he would have hated you, for allowing him to speak of love when all along you had been precisely what his aunt warned him against."

Her mouth quivers. She hates me for having seen, and for telling her the truth. She doesn't understand our danger; she doesn't know how the woman she has scorned all these weeks died, or how close she came to dying herself.

Gregory was a clever man; the plot was a clean one. To sacrifice Randolph to Caitlin, and kill Caitlin as she tried to escape the maze; Gregory would have mourned his nephew in the proper public manner, and been declared a hero for murdering one fiend in person as the other was destroyed in the castle. Any gossip about his own soul would have been effectively stilled; perhaps he had been seduced, but surely he was pure again, to summon the righteousness to kill the beasts?

Oh yes, clever. Alison would have known the truth, and would never have accepted a title won by Randolph's murder. Alison could have ruined the entire plan, but it is easy enough to silence wives.

"Can I pray?" Caitlin demands of me, as we rattle towards daybreak. "If I can't shed tears or blood, if I can't love, can I still pray?"

"We can pray," I tell her gently, thinking again of Thomas who spared me, of those tenuous bonds between the living and the dead. "We must pray, foremost, that someone hear us. Caitlin, it's the same. The same story, with that one difference."

She trembles, huddling against the side of the carriage, her eyes closed. When at last she speaks, her voice is stunned. "I'll never see my mother again."

"I am your mother now." What are mothers and daughters, if not women who share blood?

She whimpers in her throat then, and I stroke her hair. At last she says, "I'll never grow old."

"You will grow as old as the hills," I tell her, putting my arm around her as one comforts a child who has woken from a nightmare, "but you will never be ugly. You will always be as beautiful as you are now, as beautiful as I am. Your hair and nails will grow and I will trim them for you, to keep them lovely, and you will go to every dance, and wear different gowns to all of them."

She blinks and plucks aimlessly at the poor fabric of her dress, once again a kitchen smock. "I'll never be ugly?"

"Never," I say. "You'll never change." We cannot cry or bleed or age; there are so many things we cannot do. But for her, now, it is a comfort.

She hugs herself, shivering, and I sit beside her and hold her, rocking her towards the certain sleep which will come with dawn. It would be better if Randolph were here, with his human warmth, but at least she doesn't have to be alone. I remember my own shock and despair, although they happened longer ago than anyone who is not one of us can remember; I too tried to pray, and afterwards was thankful that my own godmother had stayed with me.

After a while Caitlin's breathing evens, and I am grateful that she hasn't said, as so many of them do, *Now I will never die.*

We shelter our young, as the mortal mothers shelter theirs—those human women who of necessity are as predatory as we, and as dependent on the invitation to feed—and so there are some truths I have not told her. She will learn them soon enough.

She is more beautiful than Lady Alison or her mother, but no less vulnerable. Her very beauty contains the certainty of her destruction. There is no law protecting women in this kingdom, where wives can be poisoned in their own halls and their murderers never punished. Still less are there laws protecting us.

I have told her she will not grow ugly, but I have not said what a curse beauty can be, how time after time she will be forced to flee the rumors of her perpetual loveliness and all that it implies. Men will arrive to feed her and kiss her and bring her roses; but for all the centuries of gentle princes swearing love, there will inevitably be someone—jealous wife or jaded lord, peasant or priest—who has heard the whispers and believed, and who will come to her resting place, in the light hours when she cannot move, bearing a hammer and a wooden stake.

The Living Dead

ROBERT BLOCH

All day long he rested, while the guns thundered in the village below. Then, in the slanting shadows of the late afternoon, the rumbling echoes faded into the distance and he knew it was over. The American advance had crossed the river. They were gone at last, and it was safe once more.

Above the village, in the crumbling ruins of the great chateau atop the wooded hillside, Count Barsac emerged from the crypt.

The Count was tall and thin—cadaverously thin, in a manner most hideously appropriate. His face and hands had a waxen pallor; his hair was dark, but not as dark as his eyes and the hollows beneath them. His cloak was black, and the sole touch of color about his person was the vivid redness of his lips when they curled in a smile.

He was smiling now, in the twilight, for it was time to play the game.

The name of the game was Death, and the Count had played it many times.

He had played it in Paris on the stage of the Grand Guignol; his name had been plain Eric Karon then, but still he'd won a certain renown for his interpretation of bizarre roles. Then the war had come, and with it, his opportunity.

Long before the Germans took Paris, he'd joined their Underground, working long and well. As an actor he'd been invaluable.

And this, of course, was his ultimate reward—to play the supreme role, not on the stage, but in real life. To play without the artifice of spotlights, in true darkness; this was the actor's dream come true. He had even helped to fashion the plot.

"Simplicity itself," he told his German superiors. "Chateau Barsac has been deserted since the Revolution. None of the peasants from the village dare to venture near it, even in daylight, because of the legend. It is said, you see, that the last Count Barsac was a vampire."

And so it was arranged. The short-wave transmitter had been set up in the large crypt beneath the chateau, with three skilled operators in attendance, working in shifts. And he, "Count Barsac," in charge

83

of the entire operation, as guardian angel. Rather, as guardian demon.

"There is a graveyard on the hillside below," he informed them. "A humble resting place for poor and ignorant people. It contains a single imposing crypt—the ancestral tomb of the Barsacs. We shall open that crypt, remove the remains of the last Count, and allow the villagers to discover that the coffin is empty. They will never dare come near the spot or the chateau again, because this will prove that the legend is true—Count Barsac is a vampire, and walks once more."

The question came then. "What if there are skeptics? What if someone does not believe?"

And he had his answer ready. "They will believe. For at night I shall walk—I, Count Barsac."

After they saw him in the makeup, wearing the black cloak, there were no more questions. The role was his.

The role was his, and he'd played it well. The Count nodded to himself as he climbed the stairs and entered the roofless foyer of the chateau, where only a configuration of cobwebs veiled the radiance of the rising moon.

Now, of course, the curtain must come down. If the American advance had swept past the village below, it was time to make one's bow and exit. And that too had been well arranged.

During the German withdrawal another advantageous use had been made of the tomb in the graveyard. A cache of Air Marshal Goering's art treasures now rested safely and undisturbed within the crypt. A truck had been placed in the chateau. Even now, the three wireless operators would be playing new parts—driving the truck down the hillside to the tomb, placing the objets d'art in it.

By the time the Count arrived there, everything would be packed. They would then don the stolen American Army uniforms, carry the forged identifications and permits, drive through the lines across the river, and rejoin the German forces at a predesignated spot. Nothing had been left to chance. Some day, when he wrote his memoirs—

But there was no time to consider that now. The Count glanced up through the gaping aperture in the ruined roof. The moon was high. It was time to leave.

In a way he hated to go. Where others saw only dust and cobwebs he saw a stage—the setting of his finest performance. Playing a vampire's role had not addicted him to the taste of blood—but as an actor he enjoyed the taste of triumph. And he had triumphed here.

"Parting is such sweet sorrow." Shakespeare's line. Shakespeare, who had written of ghosts and witches, of bloody apparitions. Because Shakespeare knew that his audiences, the stupid masses, believed in such things—just as they still believed today. A great actor could always make them believe.

The Count moved into the shadowy darkness outside the entrance of the chateau. He started down the pathway toward the beckoning trees.

It was here, amid the trees, that he had come upon Raymond, one evening weeks ago. Raymond had been his most appreciative audience—a stern, dignified, white-haired elderly man, mayor of the village of Barsac. But there had been nothing dignified about the old fool when he'd caught sight of the Count looming up before him out of the night. He'd screamed like a woman and run.

Probably Raymond had been prowling around, intent on poaching, but all that had been forgotten after his encounter in the woods. The mayor was the one to thank for spreading the rumors that the Count was again abroad. He and Clodez, the oafish miller, had then led an armed band to the graveyard and entered the Barsac tomb. What a fright they got when they discovered the Count's coffin open and empty!

The coffin had contained only dust that had been scattered to the winds, but they could not know that. Nor could they know about what had happened to Suzanne.

The Count was passing the banks of the small stream now. Here, on another evening, he'd found the girl—Raymond's daughter, as luck would have it—in an embrace with young Antoine LeFevre, her lover. Antoine's shattered leg had invalided him out of the army, but he ran like a deer when he glimpsed the cloaked and grinning Count. Suzanne had been left behind and that was unfortunate, because it was necessary to dispose of her. Her body had been buried in the woods, beneath great stones, and there was no question of discovery; still, it was a regrettable incident.

In the end, however, everything was for the best. Now silly superstitious Raymond was doubly convinced that the vampire walked. He had seen the creature himself, had seen the empty tomb and the open coffin; his own daughter had disappeared. At his command none dared venture near the graveyard, the woods, or the chateau beyond.

Poor Raymond! He was not even a mayor any more—his village had been destroyed in the bombardment. Just an ignorant, broken old man, mumbling his idiotic nonsense about the "living dead."

The Count smiled and walked on, his cloak fluttering in the breeze, casting a batlike shadow on the pathway before him. He could see the graveyard now, the tilted tombstones rising from the earth like leprous fingers rotting in the moonlight. His smile faded; he did not like such thoughts. Perhaps the greatest tribute to his talent as an actor lay in his actual aversion to death, to darkness and what lurked in the night. He hated the sight of blood, had developed within himself an almost claustrophobic dread of the confinement of the crypt.

Yes, it had been a great role, but he was thankful it was ending. It would be good to play the man once more, and cast off the creature he had created.

As he approached the crypt he saw the truck waiting in the shadows. The entrance to the tomb was open, but no sounds issued from it. That meant his colleagues had completed their task of loading and were ready to go. All that remained now was to change his clothing, remove the makeup, and depart.

The Count moved to the darkened truck. And then—

Then they were upon him, and he felt the tines of the pitchfork bite into his back, and as the flash of lanterns dazzled his eyes he heard the stern command. "Don't move!"

He didn't move. He could only stare as they surrounded him— Antoine, Clodez, Raymond, and the others, a dozen peasants from the village. A dozen armed peasants, glaring at him in mingled rage and fear, holding him at bay.

But how could they dare?

The American Corporal stepped forward. That was the answer, of course—the American Corporal and another man in uniform, armed with a sniper's rifle. They were responsible. He didn't even have to see the riddled corpses of the three short-wave operators piled in the back of the truck to understand what had happened. They'd stumbled on his men while they worked, shot them down, then summoned the villagers.

Now they were jabbering questions at him, in English, of course.

He understood English, but he knew better than to reply. "Who are you? Were these men working under your orders? Where were you going with this truck?"

The Count smiled and shook his head. After a while they stopped, as he knew they would.

The Corporal turned to his companion. "Okay," he said. "Let's go." The other man nodded and climbed into the cab of the truck as the motor coughed into life. The Corporal moved to join him, then turned to Raymond.

"We're taking this across the river," he said. "Hang onto our friend, here—they'll be sending a guard detail for him within an hour."

Raymond nodded.

The truck drove off into the darkness.

And it *was* dark now—the moon had vanished behind a cloud. The Count's smile vanished, too, as he glanced around at his captors. A rabble of stupid clods, surly and ignorant. But armed. No chance of escaping. And they kept staring at him, and mumbling.

"Take him into the tomb."

It was Raymond who spoke, and they obeyed, prodding their captive forward with pitchforks. That was when the Count recognized the first faint ray of hope. For they prodded him most gingerly, no man coming close, and when he glared at them their eyes dropped.

They were putting him in the crypt because they were afraid of him. Now that the Americans were gone, they feared him once more—feared his presence and his power. After all, in their eyes he was a vampire—he might turn into a bat and vanish entirely. So they wanted him in the tomb for safekeeping.

The Count shrugged, smiled his most sinister smile, and bared his teeth. They shrank back as he entered the doorway. He turned, and on impulse, furled his cape. It was an instinctive final gesture, in keeping with his role—and it provoked the appropriate response. They moaned, and old Raymond crossed himself. It was better, in a way, than any applause.

In the darkness of the crypt the Count permitted himself to relax a trifle. He was offstage now. A pity he'd not been able to make his exit the way he'd planned, but such were the fortunes of war. Soon he'd be taken to the American headquarters and interrogated. Undoubtedly there would be some unpleasant moments, but the worst that could befall him was a few months in a prison camp. And even the Americans must bow to him in appreciation when they heard the story of his masterful deception.

It was dark in the crypt, and musty. The Count moved about restlessly. His knee grazed the edge of the empty coffin set on a trestle in the tomb. He shuddered involuntarily, loosening his cape at the throat. It would be good to remove it, good to be out of here, good to shed the role of vampire forever. He'd played it well, but now he was anxious to be gone.

There was a mumbling audible from outside, mingled with another and less identifiable noise—a scraping sound. The Count moved to the closed door of the crypt and listened intently; but now there was only silence.

What were the fools doing out there? He wished the Americans would hurry back. It was too hot in here. And why the sudden silence?

Perhaps they'd gone.

Yes. That was it. The Americans had told them to wait and guard him, but they were afraid. They really believed he was a vampire— old Raymond had convinced them of that. So they'd run off. They'd run off, and he was free, he could escape now—

So the Count opened the door.

And he saw them then, saw them standing and waiting, old Raymond staring sternly for a moment before he moved forward. He was holding something in his hand, and the Count recognized it, remembering the scraping sound that he'd heard.

It was a long wooden stake with a sharp point.

Then he opened his mouth to scream, telling them it was only a trick, he was no vampire, they were a pack of superstitious fools—

But all the while they bore him back into the crypt, lifting him up and thrusting him into the open coffin, holding him there as the grim-faced Raymond raised the pointed stake above his heart.

It was only when the stake came down that he realized there's such a thing as playing a role too well.

Report on a Broken Bridge

DENNIS O'NEIL

It wasn't love or money that drove Otis Belding to his very thorough suicide: it was something bigger, lots bigger, and knowing about it is pushing me toward a premature demise, too.

You know, boss, we might have guessed the *why* of his death if we'd bothered to think about who he was, where he came from, and especially what he'd accomplished. I'd already completed my investigation by the time I got round to looking at the movies that kid happened to be taking when Belding made his spectacular exit; but as soon as I saw them I knew my guesses were correct. I sniffed an apocalypse.

You're now reading this night letter and you'll never see the prints I've forwarded to the New York office, so I'll give you a preview. Here's what the kid's camera caught:

Background: the Bridge Research complex. Foreground: a lake, placid, dotted with tiny ripples, deep-blue near the shore and powder-blue in the center. In the far distance: the Ozark Mountains. Above: more blue, streaked with wisps of white. And around, everywhere: deep-green—leaves that look heavy enough to use as anchors.

Enter Belding, in a sleek shiny aluminum dinghy, rowing to the middle of the water—rowing despite a hefty outboard perched on the stern. (At this point the kid changed to a telescopic lens.) Belding carefully cuts off the end of a long brown cigar, places the gold cigar clipper and severed tip in the pocket of his shirt, puts fire to the cigar with a gold lighter. Draws, exhales, slowly gazes up, down. Then he cautiously edges to the bow and sits on top of the wooden keg: the boat lists, and he has a few bad moments getting balanced. He does, though, and after another long look at the scenery he reaches down with his cigar and calmly touches a fuse stuck in the keg's lid.

He sits quietly and I'm pretty sure he's smiling. Sits relaxed as a stone, peacefully smoking. There is a hard red flash and the camera shakes violently, and searches randomly, glimpsing a small army of frogs leaping like dervishes, and then focuses on where Belding had been. He isn't, not any more. There is only a widening circle of dirty gray in the powder-blue, and a cloudlet of bluish haze crowning a roiling column.

It reminds me of the climax of an arty foreign flick—the kind that beats you over the head with Profound Symbolism and in which the director uses the H-bomb mushroom the way a comic strip uses exclamation points.

My favorite headline was on page three of the *Daily News*, amid human-interest drivel about our Indian Summer heat wave. You remember: *Boy Wonder Multimillionaire Ends With a Bang.*

Before the ink was dry on that little paradigm of class journalism you had me and my hangover in your office. The air-conditioning was on the blink—again!—and your bald pate was sweat-shiny enough to use as a shaving mirror. You looked like you'd been moldering in a rain forest for a couple of centuries, and coherency was not your strong trait, not that morning. I understood from your sputtering that Otis had done himself in, that the Board had panicked, and that unless we could demonstrate that our late president had shuffled off for reasons unconnected with the affairs of Bridge Enterprises, Inc., our stock certificates would soon be worth something less than bus transfers. I concurred, and hied away to shoot the trouble.

By noon I was aboard an Eastern jet out of Newark, grimly contemplating the early market report in the first edition of the *Post:* Bridge Enterprises was selling at 31½, down 7 in the first two hours of trading. My wallet ached: I own 300 shares myself.

I picked up a St. Louis paper while waiting for my rent-a-car at Lambert Field: at the day's closing we were selling at 29.

I drove southwest wondering why nobody touts the beauty of that part of the country. There's nothing out here so awesome as the Grand Canyon or as numbingly spectacular as the Rockies, but nonetheless the geography is lovely—soft-edged hills and quiet valleys and lush forests. That land, west of St. Louis, is feminine America, loving and open: maybe if I'd ever found a human equivalent I wouldn't be typing this with a Beretta in my lap.

Ugliness begins about five miles north of Belding's birthplace, a town called Feeley that used to be small and isn't now because our company built a lead-refining plant close by. Along came Bridge

Enterprises and zapped 75 acres of trees and bulldozed 75 acres of grass and filled a stream with pulped garbage, bringing population and prosperity. Belding's gift to his childhood. Swell gift. The stink is so powerful it must have seeped into the soil; the sky is the color of sooty canvas; the buildings are as shocking as tarantulas on a love-seat. Up there in our air-conditioned, pastel-hued headquarters we just don't realize how gruesome the nitty-gritty is.

Feeley itself can't have changed much. Basically it's one square containing a post office, a bar with liquor store attached, an I.G.A. supermarket, a funeral parlor, and a gas station. Sundry other businesses and a scattering of houses border the square, and more are abuilding. I patronized the liquor store, obtained a fifth of my favorite, and the information that one Hap Elsenmeyer had once been Otis Belding's boyhood buddy. I went to see old buddy Hap, owner of the gas station.

Detective fiction is full of scenes in which the amiable private eye loosens the tonsils of suspicious locals with a dram of the barley. No lie, boss. Elsenmeyer is obviously a man familiar with a bottle. I had to merely hint, to sort of wave the bottle nonchalantly. Old Hap told an adolescent to mind the pumps and we retired to his office.

He produced cracked china mugs with the panache of a carny conjuror producing bunnies, and I poured. The room was pleasantly old-fashioned—even had an overhead fan that sort of sloshed the humidity around—and the pungent smell of petroleum was a relief from the lead fumes outside. We opined on the heat, agreed it sure was fierce for November, and nitter-nattered our way to talking about Otis.

I won't attempt to transcribe Elsenmeyer's dialect in all its drawly splendor. You'll have to be satisfied with the bones of the story he told me.

Otis Belding's real-life Horatio Alger saga began with a hook and a worm. The lad was a pure genius at finding fishing holes. From age six on he had hunches where they'd be biting on any given morning, and the hunches were always dead-center. That was a useful talent for him, giving him a tot of social acceptance and putting food in his belly. Came fishing time his schoolmates forgave him his pa, the town ne'er-do-well, and his ma, the town crazy. During the winter Otis starved and was taunted; summers, he ate fresh fish and was grudgingly respected. Elsenmeyer once asked Otis how he could be so gol-ding *certain*, and Otis said he didn't know, he just had these *feelings*.

He was, in effect, orphaned at the age of ten. His father expired in a ditch one winter night and the authorities carted his mother off to the county mental hospital, where she died some years later. An aunt did a perfectly rotten job of guardianship. Mostly, Otis lived alone in a shack near the site of the future refinery, getting to school now and again, somehow surviving the cold months. Age eleven, he discovered games and took his first hesitant steps toward the Dow Jones Index and a cask of high-grade blasting powder.

A bunch of the good old boys used to meet in the back room of the tavern evenings for cards. Friendly poker, two-bit limit. Otis took to hanging around, probably to escape the cold of the shack. I'm guessing now, but I think he must have swiped some money from his aunt's purse one day and wangled himself a seat at the table. Played smart, according to Elsenmeyer—real smart. Uncanny smart. Walked away with enough dollars to stand beers for the bunch, root beer for himself. Kept out a stake, though, and sat in the following session, and every session thereafter, and won more than he could have made in a whole summer's field laboring. The boys were mildly amazed but, I gather, tolerant. Otis became a pet topic of Feeley conversation.

A trucker named Batson J. Frink ended Otis's poker career. Frink pushed a tractor-trailer rig for a Kansas City outfit and often joined the game when he was passing through. Nobody much liked Frink, but nobody told him, because he was big and mean. He was also a sore loser. He lost heavily to Otis on July 4, 1951—Elsenmeyer remembers the date exactly—and didn't enjoy it, not one bit.

He waited for Otis outside the bar while Otis was buying drinks, caught the boy, dragged him behind the building, and beat him mercilessly. Elsenmeyer was a witness; he tells it with a connoisseur's glee—how the trucker punched Otis to blood and bruises, broke a rib, kicked out teeth. Finally Frink was too tired to continue. He paused to catch his breath—and heard his death pronounced.

Sitting against the rear wall, Otis looked up through swollen eyelids and said, "You're going to die tonight." Just those five words, spoken with absolute conviction. Frink must have been shaken by them, because he went to his rig and drove off.

I checked with the Highway Patrol. The official report confirms Hap Elsenmeyer's story. Between 9:00 and 9:15 on the night of July 4, 1951 a tractor-trailer driven by Batson J. Frink was rounding a steep curve eight miles south of Feeley. The load in the trailer apparently shifted, causing the rig to topple off the road, down into a gulley, and explode. The cargo of magnesium ingots caught fire. Frink's body was never recovered.

Leaving Feeley, I had my first intimations that our late leader had been a hint spooky. Then I thought, no, it was only a coincidence. Sure.

The data you supplied led me next to East St. Louis. The records there showed that Belding had resided in a boardinghouse near the Obear Nestor bottle factory, which is not any urban gem of a neighborhood, believe you me. A Mrs. McNally was, and is, the landlady. Picture the dark side of the moon and see McNally—a walking crater, this senior citizen, and easily 90% malice. The remaining 10% praises the memory of Otis Belding.

"A *good* boy," she insisted. "Best boy I ever knew."

To prove the assertion she pointed to a plaster Virgin set on a doily on a shelf in the parlor. "Bought me that with his first big winnings, Otis did," Mrs. McNally crowed. "Ain't it lovely?"

You bet, Mrs. McNally, I agreed. Now about those winnings—?

Belding's co-boarder had been a man named Lewis Thalier, a wine jockey and doer of odd jobs at a racetrack, Cahokia Downs. Thalier, it seems, had been a big noise in the twenties. The usual weepy history: he'd lost everything in the '29 crash, cocooned himself inside the grape, and never really emerged. Until young Otis appeared, that is.

In the beginning Otis developed his gambling talent—studied the horse forms Thalier brought home and had the wino place bets for him. Thalier noticed that the lad won consistently, and he began making duplicate bets. Thalier prospered, as did his youthful mentor. After a particularly spectacular afternoon with the ponies Thalier fueled himself with champagne—no more California port for *this* ex-tycoon—and reminisced, aloud and at length. Dug forth from his trunk a sheaf of gaudy stock certificates, displayed them to Otis, and discoursed regarding the market.

Otis was interested, and how. He exhausted Thalier's lore and the next morning got an armful of books from the public library. He spent days poring over the books and the financial sections of local papers and, when he learned of its existence, *The Wall Street Journal*. Then he bought Thalier a new suit and embarked on his second and penultimate career.

"The other boarders' eyes plain bugged when they see old Lewis and Otis come out on the porch looking like a bandbox," Mrs. McNally croaked warmly. "They go over the bridge downtown and come back with a big envelope. They spread a bunch of papers on the kitchen floor and look at them like they was gold or something. 'We gonna be rich,' Lewis says. Young Otis, he nods his head yes."

Belding stayed at Mrs. McNally's for nine years. Thalier resurrected dormant expertise in food, drink, music, and in the midst of that slum they lived lavishly. Each Wednesday Thalier obediently guided a spanking limousine across the bridge and returned bearing a fresh envelope and the grandest largess that St. Louis could provide—records, clothes, prime steaks, bonded bourbon.

"Boarders was green with envy," Mrs. McNally solemnly assured me.

Let it be noted that Belding's appetites extended beyond his stomach, as is normal, and as the gossip columnists have frequently observed. With whom is not relevant, and anyway, you'll have a chance to leer further on in this narrative.

Belding terminated the slum idyll on his twenty-first birthday. He and Thalier drove across the Eads Bridge for the last time, saw a lawyer, signed papers, and returned to the boardinghouse. At the curb Belding took the wheel, said goodbye to Thalier, and went away without bothering to collect the belongings from his room. Thalier was official owner of $100,000 worth of blue-chip securities; Belding held for himself $600,000 worth of wildly speculative issues.

Thalier's income kept him happily juiced for his remaining half decade: his liver had the privilege of succumbing to only the finest French and Italian vintages.

Our accounting department will confirm that Mrs. McNally still receives a check for $400 every month—more than the old witch deserves.

I won't bore you with my pursuit of the Belding success saga. What you're getting, boss, is pure poetry; if you want prosaic details send another lackey for them. Suffice to say, for a week I relearned what we both vividly know. If you've forgotten any of it read the clippings from *Time, Fortune, Forbes, The Wall Street Journal,* et al.

Boy Wonder Belding could do no financial wrong: he got rich, richer, damn near richest. Two weeks before the beginning of the great computer boom he bought the software outfit. Two weeks prior to the McDonnell-Douglas merger he bought McDonnell. Two weeks before the Apollo contracts were awarded he bought Texas Instruments. And two weeks before the start of the TV season that made camp as obsolete as button hooks he unloaded that corny television show. The list goes on and on, like a list of Howard Hughes's fondest dreams.

I'm an investigator, an expert snoop, so I snooped, thoroughly and relentlessly; through the pads in Malibu, Newport, and Acapulco; the permanent suite in Las Vegas; the yacht; and I disproved to my complete satisfaction the hoary notion that the wealthy can't be happy. Listen, he was *happy*. Young, healthy, handsome, and able to buy spares of anything—a regular bouncing bundle of sybaritic joy was Otis Belding. Until last September.

In 1966 he formed Bridge Enterprises and unleashed on the world the hokey motto that graces our letterheads: *Building Bridges to the Future*. Otis Belding believed those words, I think. He was cut from a fairly idealistic cloth; he was maybe that rare mass entrepreneur who actually saw himself and his affairs as a force for progress. Sure, he engineered dirty deals, but he was unique in *admitting* them, and he had an excuse. You remember the speech he delivered at the convention of the National Association of Manufacturers—the lines quoted in all the press releases: "I regret having harmed a few relatively innocent parties. I harmed them in order to insure a brighter tomorrow for their children."

Horrible speech. Honest sentiment, though. Bear it in mind while I take you to upstate New York.

I won't give you my impressions of our Hudson River plant: you've already been treated to my description of the Feeley refinery, right? Well, the Hudson facility isn't quite as bad, not quite. A lot of money was spent on landscape cosmetics.

The manager, Tyrone Thomas, gave me the grand tour. He's a proud fellow. He speaks of extracting detergent phosphates from raw chemicals like a frat brother boasting a conquest. I understood maybe one-tenth of his rap. We finished the tour at the wide grass terrace between the plant and the river. Looking out over the Hudson, with the industrial labyrinth at my back, I could almost forget where I was, except that I felt the vibration of drainage pumps through my shoe soles and saw the churning of the water where the pipes empty into it.

"You can see for yourself this is the finest facility of its kind in the world," Thomas was saying. "Per diem gross is forty tons. We hope to up that the coming fiscal period."

"Very impressive," I said. "Was Mr. Belding pleased?"

"Pleased as punch. Gave me a bonus, promised another."

"No problems?"

"None worth talking about. We had some trouble with the radicals at the beginning, but Mr. Belding handled it all right."

"Radicals?"

Thomas smiled wearily. "Not the card-carrying sort. The dupes. At least, I think they're dupes."

I asked, "Who exactly are they?"

"The crowd from the university. They did a lot of picketing when we first went into operation. Men with the beards and the hair, girls with the signs and the beads—the whole shebang. It got on the TV news shows."

"They have something against phosphates?"

"They have something against progress," Thomas said righteously. "Darn fools. Claimed we were ruining the environment. That's a pile of you-know-what. Look around, judge for yourself. This land was going to waste before Bridge moved in. Nothing here but chipmunks. We pumped millions into the local economy, put five thousand men to work, going to take another two thousand if we get a go-ahead on the new wing. I ask you, is that *ruining*?"

"Did Mr. Belding do anything about the protests?"

"Oh, sure. He met with 'em on four or five separate occasions. He was a heck of a sight more patient than I'd've been in his position. He volunteered to put in the sod we're standing on and the drainage network underground. Cost a bundle, but they weren't satisfied. They said we're killing fish. Imagine. All that fuss over some fish. Heck-fire, I'd've offered to buy 'em a carload of fish to shut 'em up. Finally Mr. Belding promised to finance a research laboratory and that got rid of the pests."

And it got rid of me, too. I left Thomas to his phosphates and tucked myself into a motel for the night. You're getting nowhere, I told myself sternly, and myself agreed. My notebook and tape recorder were jammed with information, true, but I'd discovered no tidbits absent from *Who's Who*.

The only thing I had learned was that Otis Belding never—*never*—made a financial mistake. I'd always assumed he must have committed a blunder or two along the way, even as you and I. He hadn't. Not one blunder. He'd cast his mortal remains to the lake breeze with a perfect financial record and although his tranquillity had been infinitesimally marred by the Hudson protests, they shouldn't have upset him much, considering that they clued him to the sweetest tax dodge-cum-public relations coup a multimillionaire could wish for. Compared to the Bridge Research Center, Carnegie's libraries were so many sandboxes: the intellectuals applauded, the I.R.S. condoned, and the Silent Majority didn't hear about it, as usual. In short, the Center is another monotonous success.

As I was leaving the motel the next morning you phoned and told me that the corporate fortunes were improving—we were selling over 30 again—and you said I should stay with the investigation another twenty-four hours, prepare a document to exhibit in the annual stockholders' booklet—show the Bridge Family that their officers *care*—and bring my expense account home. We'd gone through the motions and that was sufficient. You said.

As it happened, I *did* nail the reason for the suicide within a day, but if I hadn't I would have hung with the case regardless. Suddenly you didn't seem so almighty impressive, boss; suddenly your wrath held no terrors for me. Nor the loss of my job, either. Conclusion: subconsciously, I had the answer. Or I was on the edge of an inkling—no, in this context, better call it a premonition.

I had two more people to see. Dr. Harold Seabrook, head of the Research Center, would be in Europe until Thursday, his secretary told me long distance. So that left Miss X—Belding's mistress. I'd known about her, of course, as had you and most of the guys in the executive suite. Otis Belding's bucolic lady was the worst kept secret in the company. As acting chief of security I'd made it my business to obtain her name and address; more, I'd run a somewhat-more-detailed-routine check on her—wouldn't do to have Belding victimized by an adventuress, I rationalized. I needn't have worried. Sandra Burkholt is nobody's *femme fatale*.

Frankly I was curious. What manner of woman, I wondered, would cause a man like Belding to abandon his string of pneumatic starlets, theatrical *grandes dames*, and society sweethearts? Because abandon them he did—lopped them off like diseased limbs last summer, about the time he established the Research Center. My field personnel said *la Burkholt* was 32, single, living alone in a small isolated house not far from the Center, and the mother of an illegitimate son. Belding probably met her in November 1968, while she was employed as a typist at the Feeley refinery. It's possible he'd known her earlier, during his miserable childhood.

I arrived at her house at dusk on Wednesday. There was a sports car in the driveway: no other signs of prosperity. On the contrary. A bent rusty tricycle lay on the walk; the grass needed cutting; the house itself needed shingles and paint. Hardly a magnate's love nest.

She answered my knock and led me into the living room. The inside was a perfect reflection of the exterior: shabby furniture, cracked linoleum floor, peeling wallpaper. And Sandra completed the motif. She isn't homely: there are lingering phantoms of an artful feline girl in her bold glance, in her quick sensuous smile. But she's worn. The red hair is stringy and faded, the skin rough, the figure sagging. Had Belding liked his women pitiable? Was it really love?

Feeling strangely like an archeologist prowling an ancient temple, I followed Sandra to the bedroom they had shared and viewed Belding's artifacts: a medium-priced portable phonograph, a mixed collection of records, and the books and magazines he'd read himself to sleep with. Three sorts of reading matter, divided into separate piles. Books on extrasensory perception, ranging from inexpensive paperbacks to footnotey tomes to science-fiction novels. Stuff on ecology of approximately the same range, including a complete set of Sierra Club publications and a series of pamphlets from Barry Commoner's group at Washington University. And history books, mostly comprehensive texts. I paged through them, to no avail: Belding had not been an underliner.

We went into the kitchen. I unobtrusively turned on my tape recorder while Sandra concocted lemonade. That's right, boss— lemonade. As remarked, Miss Burkholt is not a *femme fatale*.

"I'll have to ask you to hold down your voice," the tape recorder echoes Sandra as I write. "My boy is sick in the next room there. Generally he's healthy as a horse. Must be one of those viruses."

Me: "I hope he feels better."

Sandra: "Thank you."

Me (hesitantly): "Did you know Mr. Belding well?"

Sandra: "'Course. Not long, but well as can be. We were lovers."

Me (embarrassed): "Forgive me for asking—but did he buy you gifts? Did he have an arrangement with you?"

Sandra (chuckling, bless her): "You mean was I a kept woman? No, sir. Oh, he bought little presents for the house and for my boy. He brought me a mixmaster once, was I think the biggest thing. He never gave me money and I didn't ask for any. Didn't expect any. It was purely a man-woman thing with us. I liked him. I believe he liked me. I'll miss my Otis."

Me: "Did you notice any recent change in his behavior?"

Sandra: "He was always—well, odd. Funny, he could be touching you and somehow not be there at all, like he'd left his body behind. Oh, yes, there was one present Otis brought on his last visit I forgot about. He said something strange—"

She was interrupted by a thump from behind the wall. We rushed into the boy's cubbyhole. The child was lying in a tangle of quilt beside the bed, breathing in harsh rattling gasps. He was drenched with sweat, his skin wax-white. He wasn't suffering from virus: the kid was dying.

"We'd better get him to a hospital," I said.

Sandra wrapped him in the quilt and carried him to my car. I pegged the speedometer needle at 70 most of the distance to the local clinic. The decrepit general practitioner there diagnosed a ruptured appendix and confessed he had no facilities for treating acute peritonitis. I knew a clinic that did—coincidentally, the best medical setup in that area is at the Bridge refinery in Feeley. I got on the phone, chartered a private plane, and alerted one of those bright young specialists the company boasts of recruiting that Sandra and her son were on the way.

At the airfield I gave her my card and asked her to call the office if she or the boy needed anything. She promised she would.

Not being tired yet, I drove into the Ozark foothills, toward the Center. I surrendered to bizarre reflections—bizarre for me, anyway. Not since I'd been an altar boy waiting scared in the musty closeness of the confessional had I contemplated eternity. Maybe it was the country. If there are ghosts, they lurk in those hills, flash briefly, mockingly in headlight glare, and rattle forebodingly in leaves. Or maybe it was simple shame, an attempt to excuse my lack of professionalism. I hadn't seen Sandra earlier, during the Feeley phase of the inquiry, and that oversight had been wasteful, costly. But if I *had*, then I wouldn't have been there to bully medicos and pilots, and the boy might not have got the attention he needed. I entertained the notion that I served a benevolent destiny. Fate? Predestination? Whose will was my master? Certainly not Belding's.

Bridge Enterprises can be proud of its Research Center. Architecturally it's the best we have: instead of the usual eyesore, the building is dignified—predominantly vertical lines harmonizing with the surrounding pines. I parked in the visitor's lot and admired the flood-lit scene a bit. A guard demanded to know who I was. Then, miraculously transformed by my credentials, he hefted my bag and escorted me to the VIP quarters. Nice digs. Pastel and Danish plastic modern. Home away from . . .

A shaft of sunlight across my face woke me. I put on my most expensive lightweight suit and a white-on-white shirt-tie combo—to impress the scientific yokel with my Manhattan class.

Huh-*uh*. I doubt that Dr. Harold Seabrook *can* be impressed. He's a large chunk of dour impatience—six-six, big-bellied, features drawn as though his jowls were weighted. He doesn't speak: he spews.

We met in the lounge. As we talked he traced tiny precise geometrics on the formica table top in a spilling of iced tea.

"I can give you five minutes," he said brusquely.

I was annoyed. I'm a bigger corporate cheese than Seabrook. "You've got somewhere to go?" I asked.

"I've got to see about saving the human race from itself," he replied, managing not to sound corny. "I won't do it prattling with you."

"Funny," I mused sarcastically. "I read your job description. It said 'ecologist,' not 'messiah.'"

"No difference," he snapped.

Having nary a comeback to that I asked, "What exactly are you doing with the company's money? What's the project?"

He raised a brow. "At the moment? We're seeking a way to reduce the so-called 'greenhouse effect.'"

"You're messing with flowers?"

His tone put me back in knee pants and a dunce cap: I was the Second Grade's biggest dumbo, he the exasperated teacher. He said,

"You've noticed the weather? Not enough heat is escaping into space. Pollutants have formed a curtain that traps short-wave radiation near the ground, and the temperature is rising to—"

I interrupted, "I don't need a pee-aitch-dee to tell me it's a hell of a hot November. I'm sure you geniuses will dope out the damnedest refrigerator in twenty years and we'll give you either a gold watch or a Nobel Prize, take your choice."

"Many of my colleagues would agree with you," he said with unexpected gentleness. "I do not, and neither did Otis Belding. He had a theory that a critical point will come in our poisoning of Earth, and when it does the planet will simply stop living—*stop*. All the life-support systems will disintegrate at once, and that will be the end. Finish. No more. We may have a few days, or a few hours, to regret our stupidity."

"That doesn't sound like it makes a lot of sense, Doc."

"I didn't think so either, at first. But I was reasoning conventionally. Then I pursued a line of research that Otis suggested and—" His voice changed: the gentleness was gone. "You've wasted enough of my time."

He pulled a folded memo sheet from his yellow-stained lab jacket. "Otis said I was to give you this."

My name was scrawled on it, in Belding's handwriting.

"Hold it, Doc," I said. "I never *met* Otis Belding. He didn't even know I exist. You want me to believe he addressed a note to me personally before he died and left it with you? No way."

"Facts are facts," he said, getting up. "Excuse me."

He was gone, that fast, leaving another protest snagged in my throat and a zero limned in cold tea on the table. Vowing to humble him later, I opened the note. It read:

"There's nothing to be done. It is too late. See model in my office."
Signed: Otis Belding.

I obtained the key to his private office from the receptionist, climbed to the top floor, and entered. The room was barren as a Trappist cell—furnishings consisted solely of an army cot and a metal stand on top of which was a scale model of the Eads Bridge. The model was broken. Someone had hit it and broken it in half. It was a bridge that went nowhere.

There was a question yet to be answered. I used a phone in the lobby to call Sandra.

"How's your son?" I asked.

"He's doing nicely. That nice Dr. Benedict said he caught it in time. I want to thank you."

"My pleasure. Sandra, you remember what you were saying? About a present Otis bought?"

"That was the funniest he ever did. It was a gun—a pistol. I still have it, though Lord knows what I'll ever do with a gun. He gave it to me and said, 'If you love your son you'll do him this favor.' I suppose he was joking."

"Could be. 'Bye, Sandra."

I strolled outside and ambled across the sweep of lawn, down to the lake. No hurry, not any more, for me, for you, for anyone. Because it's obvious why Otis Belding killed himself. He had a genius for prophecy, remember? I figure he had premonitions about the future—premonitions that slowly grew to convictions until, two weeks before an event, they became certainties. Once he became aware of something, he could predict its course. He became aware of ecology, he saw the "critical point" coming; he saw his future—our future—and sought refuge with a simple woman and her son, and failing to find comfort he chose to die.

Exactly thirteen days ago he chose to die.

I know how he felt. Like a man standing on a broken bridge.

I have my gun, and I've always hated being the last one out.

So—goodbye, boss.

The Beast From One-Quarter Fathom

GEORGE ALEC EFFINGER

How they loved it when they saw Finster come into the store! He never paid any attention to the cute, furry animals that were placed cleverly near the cash register to tempt the kids and their moms: the gerbils, the baby ferrets, the Angora bunnies, the white mice twitching their pink noses, the hamsters. No, Finster walked right on by. He walked by the birds, too, the outrageously expensive macaws and the cheerful finches twittered in vain, as if they didn't deserve a crumb of his attention. The puppies—good grief, you'd think Finster's mother had been terrified by some puppy during her pregnancy, because he treated every dog, large or small, winsome or snarly, as if it had nothing on its obtuse canine mind but injuring Finster. One morning about a year ago, a little girl not more than eight years old shoved a baby beagle she'd fallen in love with into Finster's face; Finster had a powerful urge to slap down the puppy first and the little girl second, but he controlled himself. He just shoved the girl aside, knocking her into a tidily arranged pyramid of birdseed boxes. Kittens held no allure for Finster, either. Playful, big-eyed, mischievous kittens always grew up into cats, and Finster despised cats as much as he hated dogs. He smiled as he considered this thought; kittens didn't *always* turn into cats: not if you had the strength of your convictions.

No, when he burst his way into Critters R Us, he maintained his rather military bearing and unswerving, penetrating gaze as he stormed toward the rear of the shop, where the fish tanks were. Then, at last, Finster relaxed a little. His face even allowed itself something like a smile. Finster had no use for things with wings or fur or feet. Finster was a fish man, wholly and entirely a fish man. His family had always been fish people.

He'd gotten his first fish from his father. Finster was raising black mollies and swordtails in a ten-gallon freshwater tank while he was still in grade school. They reproduced profligately, and he was able to trade the bumper crops of infant mollies for packages of fish food. As it happened, just about everything Finster would ever learn about sex he learned from his tropical fish. He could tell that there were boy mollies and girl mollies; one kind chased the other kind; the second kind mostly didn't want to be bothered; and yet every once in a while the first kind would trap the second kind in a corner or against a decorative sunken treasure chest, and four weeks later there'd be three or four dozen new black mollies in the world. This conformed in a general way with much of what Finster overheard about sex from his young school friends. His adolescent fantasies often centered around trapping the incendiary Sandra Bartkus against a huge decorative sunken treasure chest.

The owner of Critters R Us, a tall, thin, anxious man named Les Moss, came around the counter to meet Finster. Moss talked to everyone as if they'd all been born hard of hearing. He zeroed in on Finster with a ravenous shopkeeper's sonar. Finster was a prize customer. Finster left lots of money in this particular store's cash register. "Looking for anything special today, Mr. Finster?" cried Moss.

Finster did not slow his pace or glance at Moss. "Maybe," he said thoughtfully. "I think just maybe."

"We got in a large shipment last night," shouted Moss, following slightly behind Finster like an eager little dog. "Some unusual tropicals, lovely fish, rare ones. They'd look marvelous with your—"

Finster had made his decision. He stopped suddenly, and Moss almost bumped into him. Finster turned with a look of determination on his face. "Mr. Moss," he announced, "I think it's time I tried setting up a saltwater tank."

Moss almost fainted dead away. This sale was going to be big bucks. "Naturally," he said in his softest shout.

"People have told me for years that saltwater tanks are too much bother," said Finster. "You have to monitor the pH and the salinity and all of that, and the fish are expensive and delicate. My freshwater tanks are doing fine—I've cut the death rate almost in half in the last couple of months. Yet I feel the need of a new challenge. I think I'd like to take a stab at saltwater."

"No problem, no problem at all. It's not all *that* difficult. Once you get the tank set up, it practically runs itself. We have people—" Moss paused; he had been about say "even stupider than you," but he caught himself—"people much less experienced than you who have beautiful setups that afford them hours of enjoyment and pleasure. I've seen people sit and watch their tanks all evening, for hours. Fish are peaceful. Fish are relaxing. Fish are—"

"These are the same idiots who stare at their radios, waiting for the video problems to clear up," said Finster acidly. Although he spent a lot of money in Moss's store, he didn't necessarily think that Moss himself was the final authority on submarine subjects. Whenever he thought of Moss, he pictured a fawning, obsequious salesman, always rubbing his hands together greedily like some caricature out of Dickens. Actually, Moss didn't rub his hands together, but he still managed to convey an unctuous and avaricious image. There were other things about Moss that Finster didn't like. For one, Moss himself took charge of feeding the large, ugly, brutish fish in the three tanks at the end of the left-hand row of freshwater fish. Feeding the fish was a menial job, and the other employees were each responsible for a section of tanks. Moss wouldn't permit anyone to feed the fish in the three end tanks, though. Finster didn't know what the fish were called—he didn't really want to know. There was only one fish in each tank, but it was big and mean. Moss fed them live goldfish. Moss tossed a wriggling goldfish into one of the tanks; it was gone, swallowed whole in an instant. Moss grinned and plopped another goldfish. Finster was disgusted by the obscene pleasure Moss took from it. Finster said something about the poor goldfish, about how unfair it was that some lucky goldfish end up in little round bowls as prizes at carnivals, and others end up gobbled down by their malignant cousins. And these big, hungry things didn't have the least bit of color or elegance about them.

"Don't start fretting about the goldfish," said Moss, flipping another one in a high arc into the second tank. Finster was sure that the famished black fish gulped it before the goldfish even broke the water's surface. "Some fish are meant to be eaten by other fish. You know about that, that's the law of nature. It's a fact of life. The ocean is a jungle, Mr. Finster."

The ocean is a jungle, thought Finster. Now there was a brilliant observation if ever he heard one. Moss was probably a fascist, too, and didn't even know it. Finster understood all about the law of nature; what he objected to was Moss's repellent glee. It was as if Moss were sacrificing sanctified virgins or putting Marine recruits through basic training. They were jobs that had to be done, but you didn't have to revel in them. Finster himself had a reverence for life, just as Albert Schweitzer had had a reverence for life. Finster felt he shared several noble qualities with Albert Schweitzer. They both liked Bach, for example.

And Finster was beginning to suspect that Moss didn't have so much knowledge about the care of fish as he pretended. The last time Finster consulted him about sick fish—the freshwater fish were *always* getting sick, by ones and twos or by the whole tankful in a general plague—Moss advised him in such a patently absurd way that Finster was certain for the first time that the shopowner was bluffing.

"My two sunset gouramis just hang in one place and rock back and forth," Finster had said worriedly.

"Any white spots on them? Clamped fins? Signs of fin or tail rot, or patches of missing scales? Anything like that?" asked Moss.

"No, I checked for everything I could think of. They look perfectly healthy, except they just hang there, rocking back and forth."

"Ah," said Moss, a wise expression creeping slowly across his face, "it must be Gourami Rocking Disease."

"Never heard of that one."

"It has some long Latin name," said Moss, shrugging. "I don't know all that technical stuff, I'm a self-made man. Experience and careful observation have taught me all I know." Moss tapped his shrewd old skull a few times. "Gourami Rocking Disease, that's what it sounds like to me." That was a nice touch, admitting that he didn't know absolutely everything. It almost persuaded Finster that Moss wasn't faking from the getgo.

"Gourami Rocking Disease," said Finster slowly. "What do I do for it?" Moss stocked a whole aisle full of medicines, tonics, and water treatments, and surely one of them would save Finster's ailing gouramis.

"I just don't know," said Moss, shaking his head sadly. "It still baffles the experts. Try dumping in some of this stuff for parasites. Let me know if it works." Gourami Rocking Disease. It reminded Finster of the rocker panel cotter pins the older guys had told him to fetch back in auto shop in high school; they laughed at him over that one for weeks. Anyway, he bought the medicine. "Try this," said Moss, "and if they don't get better, maybe you should move them to a drier climate. Like Arizona." The medicine stopped their rocking in less than a day, however. Both gouramis—along with two cardinal tetras, a rasbora, and Finster's pet upside-down catfish—sank to the bottom of the tank, never stirred again, and quickly turned all white and fuzzy. *Muerto*, folks. Finster had had to change half the water in that tank to be sure none of the other fish would suffer the same fate.

After that incident, Finster hated Moss's guts and was suspicious of his word on anything that had to do with tropical fish. Nevertheless, Moss's shop was the most complete and most convenient in town. A couple of the other employees were also hobbyists and sometimes gave Finster genuine help, if Finster could get to them before Moss cut in with his phony smile and his clangorous greeting.

Once Finster made the decision to buy a saltwater tank, his life turned onto an unalterable course. He could not know this, naturally; yet for the brief remainder of his life, he would refer to this time as Finster's Herculean Labors. Finster was like that; he was kind of a jerk, if you want to know the truth, pretty much the same sort of jerk that Moss was.

The First Labor, thought Finster, was getting past Moss and out of the store with what he needed. "I guess when it's all set up," he said, "it will be more interesting and colorful than the freshwater tanks."

"Look around you," said Moss proudly. The marine tanks were filled with spectacular specimens: bright flags of blue; swift, startling scraps of yellow; splashes of every hue imaginable. Even the creatures that just sat there—the sea anemones, for example—came in flaming red or luminous green. The freshwater fish and plants seemed drab by comparison. The variety and beauty of the saltwater creatures captivated Finster. How would he ever be able to choose among them? He wanted them all. How sad to be limited to just a few, as if he'd walked into a secret cave massed with uncountable tons of treasure, gold and jewels, and he was able to steal away with but one poor pocketful.

"So buy a bigger tank," suggested Moss.

Finster had never owned anything but ten-gallon tanks, but the saltwater fish demanded more room to show off their individual glories. He looked around at the display tanks. Some of them were immense. There were twenty-nine-gallon and thirty-gallon tanks, varying slightly in their dimensions. Finster saw tanks of fifty, sixty, ninety—there was even one display tank setup of two hundred twenty gallons. A human family of four could have lived in that tank, except for all the water. Finster imagined them with their noses lifted up like turtles, desperately raised into the air space between the bubbles and the tank's lid. He shook his head grimly; so many people led wretched lives all around the world, yet here large, showy butterfly and triggerfishes were dining daintily in a costly imitation of a coral reef. There were moral dilemmas everywhere, you couldn't avoid them. "Yes," said Finster, "I'll go with the twenty-nine-gallon."

"A truly excellent choice. Not too large, not too small," said Moss. He was being obsequious again. "You'll need a stand, too. We have these nice black iron stands or these handsome handcrafted wooden ones."

"I have a stand left over at home," said Finster. "I moved my second ten-gallon tank into the bedroom, on the dresser. I use it as a nursery now for the baby mollies and swordtails. I can use the old stand."

Moss gave a tart laugh. "Do you have any idea how much twenty-nine gallons of water *weighs*?" he asked. "*Do* you? I'd *like* to see you put the big tank on your old ten-gallon stand and fill it up. *That* would be a laugh. You'd end up ankle-deep in saltwater in your living room. That would serve you just right, wouldn't it? Trying to save a buck here and a buck there. Look, Mr. Finster, take my advice: either you go about this the right way, or you just forget it. That's what I tell *all* my customers. I couldn't care less about the sales, the money means nothing to me. I just want to make sure all my fishes find good, caring, happy homes. *God-fearing* homes. Fish have rights, too, you know. I'm sorry if this causes you a moment of painful self-evaluation, but you ought to have considered it before you came in here."

Finster was chastened. "You're right about all of that," he said glumly. He bought an appropriate iron stand. Then he let Moss choose for him a hinged cover with a fluorescent light, an under-gravel filter, a good pump, tubing and valves, boxes of Minute Sea salt, and a hydrometer. Finster voiced no further objections. Moss gave a quick look around to see if he'd left anything out, and decided that he hadn't. "This should start you out just fine, Mr. Finster. Pick out your gravel over there. Let me know if you have any problems." He turned to one of his employees. "Debbie," he said, "ring up all this stuff for Mr. Finster, will you?" Then, with the thrill of the chase at an end, Moss began to stalk a couple of new customers who'd just come into his store.

"Will this be all?" asked Debbie.

"No," said Finster, "I'd like to get a few fish, too." Finster pointed out a modest selection and Debbie netted them out of their display tanks. She filled plastic bags with tank water, plopped one creature in each bag, and twist-tied it closed.

"They'll be all right like this for hours," she said.

"Great," said Finster. He selected a few bags of pale pink gravel and carried them to the counter. He also bought a can of flake food for the fish and a special preparation for the invertebrates. Then he looked at his beautiful new acquisitions. He'd settled on a pink-tipped Haitian sea anemone; a red-and-white banded coral shrimp; a jet black fish with three white spots, called a domino damsel (Finster immediately named the domino "Fats"); a brilliant blue damsel; a pair of bright orange and white clownfish; and a "live rock," which was just a hunk of rock from some seabed encrusted with many different creatures: tiny anemones, tiny featherduster tubeworms, minute copepods and bristleworms that would seed the tank and provide variety in the diet of the larger animals.

The total of his purchases, after he threw in a guidebook to marine invertebrates and another book on saltwater fish, came to nearly four hundred dollars. Finster trembled just a little as he wrote out the check. It was a lot of money to spend at one time on a hobby, some items of which were by nature perishable. Yet he felt a swelling elation as he and another employee carried the equipment and the bags of living things to his car.

Finster's Second Labor: He chose a place in the living room for the stand, across from the couch, where most people would have had a television. He carefully rested the tank on top. He laid the filter on the bottom, covered it with gravel, and connected it with the tubing and valves to the pump. Then he put the hinged cover on the tank and plugged both it and the pump into the nearest wall socket. The pump was forcing air bubbles to stream out of the tubes in the back corners. "The earth was without form and void, and darkness was upon the face of the deep," said Finster, smiling. He switched on the fluorescent lamp. "Let there be light!"

He filled three five-gallon buckets with tap water and lugged them into the living room. Then he read the directions on the box of

Minute Sea. The box pictured a Melvillian seafaring man, patch over one eye and harpoon in one hand. What was this ancient mariner planning to do? Harpoon a crummy little three-inch clownfish? Finster was easily irked by commercial art.

Combined with ordinary tap water, the Minute Sea became a chemical solution almost identical to seawater, and even healthier for both fish and invertebrates. Finster measured out portions and dumped them into the buckets. He raised the hinged cover; then he lifted a heavy bucket and poured the saltwater into the tank. He emptied the other two buckets and repeated the operation, until the tank was filled almost to the top. "Let the waters under the heavens be gathered together into one place," he murmured. He tested salinity with the hydrometer and was satisfied that it fell in the proper range. He checked the temperature: perfect.

He was all set to let his new roommates into their new home. He let a little tank water into their bags every few minutes until they'd acclimated to the tank's conditions; then he set them all free. "Let the waters bring forth swarms of living creatures," he said, and he placed the live rock in a decorative position near the back.

Almost immediately, a little hermit crab emerged from the rock, followed by a sandy brown creature that Finster couldn't identify. It was about the size of a child's hand. Finster looked forward to tracking it down in the reference book. He wanted to know absolutely everything about his creatures: what they liked to eat, how they reproduced, how he could tell if they were happy.

Finster stepped back from the tank and sat on the couch. He watched the brightly colored creatures darting around their little world. The clownfish and the damsels swam curiously back and forth. The coral shrimp floated gently to the bottom and began poking along on the gravel for bits of food. The anemone tumbled foolishly until it hit bottom upside-down, and stood there for a while on its tentacles, its cream-colored foot wavering uselessly in the gentle current. The hermit crab and the unknown thing crawled along, taking the measure of their new environment. "Behold," Finster whispered, "it was very good." He watched them for a long time.

The next morning, after Finster turned on the freshwater tanks' lights and fed the fish, he hurried excitedly to the new tank. The sight that awaited him made him shiver. The anemone had withdrawn its tentacles and fallen over on its side; it looked like it had turned itself inside-out. Finster opened the cover and prodded the animal; it did not respond. The coral shrimp lay on its side, also, and just floated away inertly when Finster touched it. The blue damsel hung head down, obviously dead, in a back corner. The domino drifted sideways on the surface with the bubbling water. One clownfish was dead, stuck between the filter tube and the tank glass; the other clownfish rested on the gravel, breathing with difficulty and jerking spasmodically, only minutes from death. The hermit crab was dead, too, and the live rock was no longer live. The unidentified brown invertebrate was still alive, but its color had changed to a dark chocolate and it was curled up in a tight spiral.

Finster stared at the tank with a mixture of sadness, anger, and helplessness. He hadn't had the animals long, but he had already become fond of them. He knew that he had done something wrong. He knew that he had killed them.

Moss wasn't in the store when Finster arrived, so he went to Debbie, the attractive and knowledgeable assistant manager. He told her what had happened. "That was nearly a hundred dollars' worth of fish I just flushed down the toilet," he said.

Debbie looked at him for a moment and blinked. "You were just setting up that tank yesterday?"

"Of course."

"I thought you already had another saltwater tank. If I'd known you were just setting it up, I wouldn't have sold you the fish."

"What did I do wrong?" said Finster, sighing. She made him review the whole process, step by step.

"Chloramines," she said at last. "You didn't dechlorinate the water."

Finster was outraged. "I know enough to dechlorinate water," he cried. "I assumed that Minute Sea stuff had a dechlorinator in it."

Debbie shook her head. "There are several brands of salt, and none of them has a dechlorinator. Now listen. If it was just chlorine, it would evaporate in a few days by itself; but the city uses chloramines, and they'll stay in the water forever unless you add some of this." She handed him a plastic bottle. "The directions are the same for fresh and saltwater tanks."

Finster nodded dejectedly. The want of a tiny quantity of sodium thiosulfate had cost him dearly. "The only thing that didn't die was some kind of invertebrate that came with the live rock. I couldn't find a picture of anything like it in my book."

Debbie squinted at him a little. "What's it look like?"

"About yea big, brown, with four legs or tentacles reaching forward. It's got some kind of cartilaginous hump with a deep cleft in it. There are a lot of pairs of legs on each side, and it rounds off in back to a bulgy, shapeless sac. This morning it was all twisted up on the bottom."

Debbie grimaced. "Sounds ugly."

Finster felt suddenly defensive. "Well, *I* like him. Do you know what it is?"

She shook her head. She looked at two of her co-workers. "Max?"

Max shrugged. "Sounds ugly to me, too."

"Curled up in a spiral?" asked Rudy, the other employee. Finster nodded. "It's a sea pen."

"Oh," said Finster. He'd read all about sea pens when he got home.

Finster's Third Labor: A few days later, confident of the absence now of chloramines in the tank water, Finster spent fifty dollars for fish and invertebrates, different ones than the first time. The next morning, they, too, were dead, all but the brown tentacled thing. Finster didn't know what it was, but it absolutely was *not* a sea pen. Sea pens are a kind of soft coral, related to the anemones. The mystery animal's legs and cartilage put it higher in the animal kingdom.

Finster returned to the store. "Your pH is much too low," Debbie told him. He learned that he had the wrong kind of gravel; he bought bags of crushed oyster shell to keep the water slightly alkaline. Taking out all the pink gravel and replacing it with the crushed shell would be a long, tedious, boring job.

"By the way," he said, "it wasn't a sea pen."

Rudy turned up his hands; was he expected to know every lousy invertebrate that swimmeth or creepeth?

Max called Moss out of his office. "Les," said Max, "do you know what this is?" Finster made a quick sketch of the thing.

"How big?" asked Moss. Finster showed him. "It's a sea hare. Very definitely."

"Oh," said Finster.

Finster's Fourth Labor: He wasn't about to spend another fifty dollars on fish until he was certain it was safe. He spent two dollars and thirty cents on a small white Florida anemone, and four fifty for a common black-and-white striped damsel. "It's a shame you can't spend more today, Mr. Finster," said Moss, with a wide smile that almost seemed to ooze oil from the ends. "Special sale, all this week. Prices slashed. Everything must go, to the bare walls. There'll never be a sale like this again. We're wheeling and dealing. If you can find anyone who can beat our—"

"That will be six eighty and tax, out of ten," said Finster, handing the money to Debbie. Moss's expression changed so quickly it looked like a bad splice in a home movie. He spun on his heel and stalked away, offended, bored, or possibly just out of habit. "It's not a sea hare, either," Finster called after him. Moss paid no attention.

"No?" said Debbie. She was getting very curious herself.

"Sea hares are molluscs, and this thing looks like some kind of arthropod to me. The legs, I mean."

Debbie took a pink comb out of her hair, brushed her hair back, and replaced the comb. "Yeah, but," she said. "There are some fish that walk around on the bottom with 'legs.' They're actually just the first few spines of their ventral fins, modified by evolution."

"I've looked through every book in the library."

Debbie brightened. "I know somebody at school who set up an exhibit at the Toth Aquarium. You'd like him. He likes to sit around all day and all night classifying dead specimens. He specializes in marine invertebrates. I'll give him a call."

"Terrific," said Finster, and he took his puny little fish and his puny little anemone and went home.

Finster's Fourth Labor: The anemone and the damselfish did not die. Not immediately. Well, after a week, the brown invertebrate caught hold of the damsel somehow and was shoving it somewhere between its tentacles, toward a wide horizontal opening at the front of the cleft. There were pale structures in the opening—too small for Finster to see clearly—bristles, smaller tentacles, teeth? It took the animal about five minutes to swallow the small fish. Finster realized that he had his first piece of real information: the brown thing was carnivorous. He got a notebook and turned to a blank page, where he wrote OBSERVATIONS CONCERNING THE BEHAVIOR OF CREATURE X, FOR THE PURPOSES OF MAKING A TENTA- TIVE IDENTIFICATION. He underlined that, skipped a space, then wrote Carnivorous. On the next line he wrote Brown. Then it occurred to him that perhaps, just perhaps, he had in his own tank an animal completely unknown to science. He may have discovered an entirely new species. . . .

Enigmatis finsteri.

He liked that so much, he didn't even mind losing the damsel. He'd keep Creature X well-fed with shrimp from his freezer; then it probably wouldn't attack the other residents of the tank. And there were going to be lots more, now that he was rather certain the water was at last conditioned. He celebrated by buying a royal gramma, a neon goby, two more clownfish and a yellow carpet anemone for them to hide in, another coral shrimp, a purple sea urchin, three six-inch featherduster tubeworms, a graceful sailfin tang, a red pistol shrimp that burrowed beneath the decorative rocks, two three-striped damsels, a bright red flame scallop, a little brown starfish, a sea slug, a pearl-scale butterflyfish, and a mandarin that shimmered in swirls of red, blue, and green.

Debbie's friend, Fred the marine biologist, came by several days later to inspect Creature X. Fred was a tall, gaunt young man with very short red hair and a bushy red beard. He stood in the hallway uncomfortably until Finster remembered to invite him in. Fred was impressed by the tank. "That's some collection you have there," he said.

"Thank you," said Finster. "I like to think so. All those fish, all those friendly colors zipping around, I try to grasp their wholeness as a community, if you know what I mean. But they won't hold still long enough."

"What I mean, Mr. Finster," said Fred, coughing apologetically into his fist, "is that in a tank this size, you have a certain amount of bacteria in the substrate that breaks down the waste products from the fish and the invertebrates. If you have too many fish, the bacteria can't keep up, and you start building up dangerous levels of ammonia. If you're over-feeding them, the extra food just adds to the problem. You could lose that whole population almost overnight."

Finster's face paled. "What should I do?" he asked.

"You can test for ammonia. If the level's too high, you replace the water. You know what a bitch that is. The general rule is one inch of fish or less for every gallon."

Finster's pale face reddened. "That's only twenty-nine inches of fish! You're asking me to get rid of almost everything in there!"

Fred shrugged. "Okay, maybe the two clownfish and a couple of small damsels or gobies, maybe the tang until it grows too big. It's your tank, Mr. Finster, but it's *their* funeral."

Finster swallowed hard. "So what do you think of Creature X?"

Fred gave an amused little laugh. "Can't tell you, Mr. Finster. I've never seen anything like that before. It doesn't exist, there's no such thing."

"But look at it! It's—"

"It's just caught your neon goby. See the way the goby's sort of stuck to that tentacle? I'll bet your creature has stinging cells, like an anemone. Nematocysts. It paralyzes the prey, then draws it to its mouth. Look, that's just what it's doing."

"Well, what *is* it?"

Fred shrugged again. "I can't tell you a damn thing, Mr. Finster. It has a gut like a coelenterate, tentacles like an anemone, legs like a crab, skin like an echinoderm, a proto-skeleton, and probably dual Holley carbs, four on the floor, mag wheels, and fuzzy dice hanging from its rear-view mirror. It's some nifty little predator, Mr. Finster. I'd actually like to study it. I'd like that a lot."

"You mean, take it with you?" Finster was horrified by the very thought. He saw his name disappearing from the article in *Scientific American*, replaced by the name of this Fred guy.

"Not really. I study these animals all day, I don't want to see them at home. I won't have anything in my house that needs to be fed or cleaned up after. I wouldn't want to keep it at the university, either. The undergraduates are always confusing nitrates and nitrites or dosing sick fish with quadruple the right amount of copper sulfate, thinking it will make them better faster. Maybe you'd allow me to drop around to observe your little discovery now and then."

"Certainly," said Finster, greatly relieved. He thought that he might not mind sharing credit, if Fred actually wrote the paper.

The last thing Fred said as he left was, "I'd try to take back some of those fish, see if the store will give you a credit slip."

"I will," said Finster, "first thing Monday." Two fish had already died by that evening, before Finster even went to bed. More died Saturday, still more on Sunday, and on Monday morning there were only six living things in the tank: three featherdusters, the starfish, one of the three-striped damsels, and Creature X, which was just finishing off a breakfast of the other striped damsel.

"You know," Debbie remarked later, "the only thing that's come through all these disasters of yours has been that strange invertebrate."

"*Enigmatis finsteri*. It survived the chloramines, it survived the low pH, and now it's surviving the ammonia build-up." Finster sighed. He had a sort of paternal pride in the thing. When he got home, everything else in the tank was dead, except Creature X. Two hundred dollars' worth of fish and invertebrates. Plus tax.

Finster's Fifth Labor: Now time passes . . . days go by . . . weeks go by . . . two, three, four months go by. You can see the pages of the calendar tearing off, tumbling down in quick succession, superimposed over the twenty-nine gallon tank. Finster had learned much the hard way, yet he still had a few things left to discover. He kept the population in the tank under control; he monitored the water quality; and soon, as Moss had predicted, the tank stabilized. Everything was fine in Finster's saltwater world, as it was in Finster's freshwater world. He had jotted many notes on Creature X, but neither Fred nor anyone else had been able to classify the animal. Well, Creature X wasn't going anywhere—that was very apparent. Creature X was the healthiest, most robust animal in any of Finster's tanks. Indeed, Finster had to spend more time and money satisfying its appetite than he did for all the other saltwater animals combined. Finster could study it at his leisure.

During these last idyllic months, Finster learned quite a lot about Creature X. He watched it crawl along the bottom in search of prey, but he discovered that it could climb the glass, as well. With its four long specialized legs or tentacles, it could grab unwitting fish swimming too near. Its brown color changed: when the light was off, it became a dark shadow on the tank's bottom. In the morning, when Finster clicked on the fluorescent light, Creature X gradually assumed a mottled sandy color. Creature X grew considerably during these weeks, until it was nearly ten inches long. Finster considered getting it a separate tank; it was too large and too voracious to keep with the peaceful, defenseless fish he had collected.

There had been no more disasters, though it had been a near thing. Debbie warned him just in time to prevent Finster from buying a beautiful but perpetually hungry variety of triggerfish. It looked like a thing a Cubist might have painted, with its oddly placed eyes and mouth and its colorful, angular markings. It was a Humu-Humu-

Nuku-Nuku-A-Puaa, but everybody just called it a Picasso trigger. "It looks great now," said Debbie, "but when it gets a little bigger, it'll eat everything in your tank. You'll end up with the Picasso at one end of the tank and Creature X at the other, staring each other down."

"Might be an interesting matchup," suggested Moss. Finster gave him a quick, disdainful look. As Finster turned away to choose another fish, he heard Moss say to Debbie, "Don't tell customers things like that. Just sell the fish." Finster knew Debbie would ignore the order; she had too much integrity. She seemed to be the only person in the shop who knew her caudal fin from a hole in the ground. Finster had fantasies of inviting her home to see Creature X for herself. He assumed, however, that because she was so lovely, she had schools of other boyfriends. She might laugh airily in his face at his invitation.

Later she saved him from making a second bad selection. "Here's another general rule," she told him. "If you have a cheap fish bigger than an expensive fish, the cheap fish will eat the expensive fish. If you have a cheap fish and an expensive fish of the same size, the cheap fish will again eat the expensive fish. If the expensive fish is bigger, it may eat the cheap fish, but it will probably die the next day. This raggedy brown sargassum costs about eight bucks, but it'll take your honey of a fifty-dollar flame angel to the mat in about four minutes. This three-dollar arrow crab is neat to look at, but it'll sneak up on your forty-dollar Indian fire shrimp and there won't be enough left of the shrimp to float to the surface."

"Don't tell him that!" said Moss. Since Finster's saltwater fish had stopped dying so dependably, Moss had seen his weekly sales total drop alarmingly. He was getting desperate. Both Debbie and Finster turned to look at him, but neither said anything. Finster believed that Moss was not a well man.

Finster bought neither the sargassum nor the arrow crab. As a matter of fact, Finster never bought another fish again. When he returned home, he served supper to his tanked-up friends. It took a while, but at last he realized that Creature X was missing. It couldn't have been hiding; there wasn't anywhere for such a big animal to hide. Now this was a real puzzle. The only explanation that seemed likely was that nature had taken its course. None of the fish or invertebrates stood a chance against Creature X one-on-one, but possibly they had ganged up on it in self-defense. It was a grievous blow. The steady march of science had been given a serious setback.

Finster was right. Nature *had* taken its course. Finster was wrong. Creature X was not dead.

Finster's Sixth Labor: Now, of course, a purist might complain that Finster was a trifle presumptuous to compare his hobbyist's tribulations to those of Hercules. After all, Hercules had to face twelve of them, and Finster only six. The important point to remember is that Hercules survived his Labors, while Finster did not. It is further cogent to remark that Hercules was the son of Zeus, and therefore half-immortal. Finster was as certain as one can be about these things that no divinity of any sort had been involved in his own lineage for at least four generations.

It was a beautiful morning in the middle of October. It was the time of year when Finster always began to feel just a little melancholy, in a gratifying way. Nostalgia seemed to rule him. He rose from his bed thinking of his youth, his drear and vanished youth. He sighed heavily as he opened the medicine cabinet to get his razor. He noticed nothing unusual at first, reaching automatically for the instrument and turning his head rather slowly to look. His hand stopped frozen in mid-air. Just above the second shelf, between a twelve-year-old prescription bottle and the English Leather, curled into a tight coffee-colored spiral, was Creature X. Finster was stunned for a few seconds; it had been weeks since he'd even thought about Creature X. He looked closer: no, it wasn't Creature X, after all. It was a miniature version of Creature X, smaller than a bar of soap. It was a newborn or hatchling.

Hypotheses raced through his mind. How could this small marine invertebrate be in Finster's bathroom? How could it be alive out of the saltwater? What had happened to its parent?

The answer to the last question Finster never learned. He guessed, however, that Creature X had climbed the tank's glass and forced the lid open. It had certainly been large and powerful enough to do that. Then, like certain amphibians, it had left Finster's miniature sea to procreate on dry land. Perhaps, having passed on its heritage of genetic information, Creature X perished immediately. Or else, Finster thought uncomfortably, it was still alive in the apartment. Somewhere. He wasn't crazy about the thought of stepping on it barefoot in the dark some night.

Finster got a fine mesh net from his aquarium supplies and scraped the stubborn young X off the wall of the medicine cabinet. The ugly thing began to uncurl, and Finster hurried with it into his living room. He opened the lid of the saltwater tank and dumped the X in. It sank quickly to the bottom, twitched a few times, and died. Finster had made another vital observation: only the older X was able to survive in the saltwater. He felt a pang of sorrow over killing, however accidentally, this infant X. It might have been fascinating to watch it develop. He made an entry of the event in his notebook, and then went back to the bathroom to shave.

That night, after dining alone in his favorite Italian restaurant, Finster returned home to find two more young Xs, one part way up the refrigerator and the other attached to a leg of the dresser in the bedroom. He was at a loss to know what to do. He tried another experiment, plopping one of them into a tank of freshwater. The result was the same; the X drowned. Finster flushed it down the toilet, then put the second X in a small goldfish bowl that had been long unused. As a precaution, he put a square of glass over the bowl. He was fortunate that, after all, he did have one young X to study.

The next morning was not so pleasant. It was murky and drizzling, and the first hint of winter was in the low, grim sky. Finster received an immediate shock: he saw three young Xs in the bedroom, and another in the hall. In the bathroom there were four more. He walked around his apartment taking inventory. The total came to twenty-eight. That was too many. The creatures had stepped over that fine line between scientific puzzle and common nuisance. Finster decided to call his pest control man and see what he might suggest. The X in the goldfish bowl was all he needed or wanted. Perhaps Moss would buy some of the others; it was worth asking. He finished dressing and had all twenty-eight scooped up and bagged in a few minutes. He drove to the pet shop. It was Debbie's day off, so unfortunately he had to deal with Moss himself. Moss was not in a spending mood. Finster let the baby Xs loose on the pavement outside Critters R Us. "Run," he urged them, "be free. You are responsible now for your own salvation. The world promises nothing more to any of us."

The following morning came after a night of troubled dreams. He woke to the pins-and-needles sensation you get when you've slept with an arm trapped under your body. "I'm going to hate this in a minute," Finster said to himself. He tried to flex the tingling arm, but he couldn't. He tried to roll over. He couldn't; both legs were tingling to the hip. He tried to reach over with the other hand and physically pull his sleeping arm free, but he couldn't. All four limbs were paralyzed.

He could raise his head a little. When he realized what he was watching, he knew he had made a tremendous scientific discovery. He would become famous for this. His body was almost blanketed by young Creature Xs, clinging to his legs and arms or crawling toward his chest. That explained the tingling, he thought. They had stung him with . . . he groped for Fred's word . . . with their nematocysts. There were so many of them that their cumulative poison had rendered him almost helpless. Well, he thought, I've got to do something about this. He exerted all his strength in an effort to roll over and out of bed. He moved nowhere. He wrenched his neck painfully, but otherwise there was no result at all.

"I think they've got you," came a voice from the foot of the bed.

Finster's mind was beginning to spin. He felt dreamy and numb. He tried to focus on the unknown speaker. It seemed to be an old man, dressed in a flowing white garment. Finster wondered how the man kept it on; it just seemed to loop here and wrap there. It was none of Finster's business. The old man wore a golden laurel wreath on his brow. He smiled gently at Finster. "Who . . . who are you?" Finster asked in a croaking voice.

"I am—"

"I know. I know who you are. You're Linnaeus. I remember seeing your picture. You're Carl von Linné, the Father of Taxonomy."

Linnaeus (1707–1778) smiled again, but said nothing.

"You've always been one of my heroes," murmured Finster. "You devised the modern system of classifying animals and plants."

"Yes, one of the most tedious, boring, dull, and exacting sciences in the world. There are many who know my name, but few who do me so much honor."

"I want to learn everything I can about taxonomy. If only I knew more. I hoped the discovery of *Enigmatis finsteri* would bring me money and the time to study. I could open my own aquarium and pet shop; I have a name all picked out: Beastworld. If I had—"

"Peace, sir," said Linnaeus. "I have come to offer you everything you could hope for. I have come to take you with me."

"Take me? Where?" asked Finster. He felt no fear at all, conversing with this specter. Finster's mind was whirling and his eyelids began to droop. One of the hungry Xs was stretching toward his throat.

"Where you'll have nothing to do all day but make endless lists of insect species, and sort immense collections of identical shells, and tally infinite columns of figures, and take an eternity of redundant measurements of spiders and thistles and lapwings and euglena and all manner of dead living things."

"Why," whispered Finster, "it sounds like Heaven."

Linnaeus, the great Swedish scientist, held forth his hand. "And so it is, Butchie."

Butchie, thought Finster, no one's called me that . . .

His dream, spun out of the invertebrates' toxin, faded. The creature on Finster's throat found the carotid artery and, after a little effort, began to drink.

Was It a Dream?

GUY DE MAUPASSANT

I had loved her madly!

Why does one love? Why does one love? How queer it is to see only one being in the world, to have only one thought in one's mind, only one desire in the heart and only one name on the lips—a name which comes up continually, rising, like the water in a spring, from the depths of the soul to the lips, a name which one repeats over and over again, which one whispers ceaselessly, everywhere, like a prayer.

I am going to tell you our story, for love only has one, which is always the same. I met her and lived on her tendernesses, on her caresses, in her arms, in her dresses, on her words, so completely wrapped up, bound and absorbed in everything which came from her that I no longer cared whether it was day or night, or whether I was dead or alive, on this old earth of ours.

And then she died. How? I do not know; I no longer know anything. But one evening she came home wet, for it was raining heavily, and the next day she coughed, and she coughed for about a week and took to her bed. What happened I do not remember now, but doctors came, wrote and went away. Medicines were brought, and some women made her drink them. Her hands were hot, her forehead was burning, and her eyes bright and sad. When I spoke to her she answered me, but I do not remember what we said. I have forgotten everything, everything, everything! She died, and I remember very well her slight, feeble sigh. The nurse said: "Ah!" and I understood; I understood!

I knew nothing more, nothing. I saw a priest who said: "Your mistress?" And it seemed to me as if he were insulting her. As she was dead, no one had the right to say that any longer, and I turned him out. Another came who was very kind and tender, and I shed tears when he spoke to me about her.

They consulted me about the funeral, but I do not remember anything they said, though I recollect the coffin and the sound of the hammer when they nailed her down in it. Oh! God, God!

She was buried! Buried! She! In that hole! Some people came—

female friends. I made my escape and ran away. I ran and then walked through the streets, went home and then started the next day on a journey.

Yesterday, I returned to Paris, and when I saw my room again— our room, our bed, our furniture, everything that remains of the life of a human being after death—I was seized by such a violent attack of fresh grief that I felt like opening the window and throwing myself out into the street. I could not remain any longer among these things, between these walls which had enclosed and sheltered her, which retained a thousand atoms of her, of her skin and of her breath, in their imperceptible crevices. I took up my hat to make my escape, and just as I reached the door I passed the large glass in the hall, which she had put there so that she might look at herself every day from head to foot as she went out, to see if her appearance looked well and was correct and pretty from her little boots to her bonnet.

I stopped short in front of that looking glass in which she had so often been reflected—so often, so often, that it must have retained her reflection. I was standing there trembling with my eyes fixed on the glass—on that flat, profound, empty glass—which had contained her entirely and had possessed her as much as I, as my passionate looks had. I felt as if I loved that glass. I touched it; it was cold. Oh, the recollection! Sorrowful mirror, burning mirror, horrible mirror, to make men suffer such torments! Happy is the man whose heart forgets everything that it has contained, everything that has passed before it, everything that has looked at itself in it or has been reflected in its affection, in its love! How I suffer!

I went out without knowing it, without wishing it, and toward the cemetery. I found her simple grave, a white marble cross, with these few words:

She loved, was loved and died.

She is there below, decayed! How horrible! I sobbed with my forehead on the ground, and I stopped there for a long time, a long time. Then I saw that it was getting dark and a strange, mad wish, the wish of a despairing lover, seized me. I wished to pass the night, the last night, in weeping on her grave. But I should be seen and driven out. How was I to manage? I was cunning and got up and began to roam about in that city of the dead. I walked and walked. How small this city is in comparison with the other, the city in which we live. And yet how much more numerous the dead are than the living. We want high houses, wide streets and much room for the four generations who see the daylight at the same time, drink water from the spring and wine from the vines and eat bread from the plains.

And for all the generations of the dead, for all that ladder of humanity that has descended down to us, there is scarcely anything, scarcely anything! The earth takes them back and oblivion effaces them. Adieu!

At the end of the cemetery I suddenly perceived that I was in its oldest part, where those who had been dead a long time are mingling with the soil, where the crosses themselves are decayed, where possibly newcomers will be put tomorrow. It is full of untended roses, of strong and dark cypress trees, a sad and beautiful garden, nourished on human flesh.

I was alone, perfectly alone. So I crouched in a green tree and hid myself there completely amid the thick and somber branches. I waited, clinging to the stem like a man does to a plank.

When it was quite dark I left my refuge and began to walk softly, slowly, inaudibly, through that ground full of dead people. I wandered about for a long time but could not find her tomb again. I went on with extended arms, knocking against the tombs with my hands, my feet, my knees, my chest, even with my head, without being able to find her. I groped about like a blind man finding his way; I felt the stones, the crosses, the iron railings, the metal wreaths and the wreaths of faded flowers! I read the names with my fingers, by passing them over the letters. What a night! What a night! I could not find her again!

There was no moon. What a night! I was frightened, horribly frightened in these narrow paths between two rows of graves. Graves! Graves! Graves! Nothing but graves! On my right, on my left, in front of me, around me, everywhere there were graves! I sat down on one of them, for I could not walk any longer; my knees were so weak I could hear my heart beat. And I heard something else as well. What? A confused, nameless voice. Was the noise in my head, in the impenetrable night or beneath the mysterious earth, the earth sown with human corpses? I looked all around me, but I cannot say how long I remained there; I was paralyzed with terror, cold with fright, ready to shout out, ready to die.

Suddenly it seemed to me that the slab of marble on which I was sitting was moving. Certainly it was moving, as if it were being raised. With a bound I sprang onto the neighboring tomb, and I saw, yes, I distinctly saw the stone which I had just quitted rise upright. Then the dead person appeared, a naked skeleton, pushing the stone back with its bent back. I saw it quite clearly, although the night was so dark. On the cross I could read:

Here lies Jacques Olivant, who died at the age of fifty-one. He loved his family, was kind and honorable and died in the grace of the Lord.

The dead man also read what was inscribed on the tombstone; then he picked up a stone off the path, a little, pointed stone, and began to scrape the letters carefully. He slowly effaced them, and with the hollows of his eyes he looked at the places where they had been engraved. Then with the tip of the bone that had been his forefinger he wrote in luminous letters, like those lines which boys trace on walls with the tip of a lucifer match:

Here reposes Jacques Olivant who died at the age of fifty-one. He hastened his father's death by his unkindness, as he wished to inherit his fortune; he tortured his wife, tormented his children, deceived his neighbors, robbed everyone he could and died wretched.

When he had finished writing, the dead man stood motionless, looking at his work. On turning around I saw that all the graves were open, that all the dead bodies had emerged from them and that all had effaced the lines inscribed on the gravestones by their relations, substituting the truth instead. And I saw that all had been the tormentors of their neighbors—malicious, dishonest, hypocrites, liars, rogues, calumniators, envious; that they had stolen, deceived, performed every disgraceful, every abominable action, these good fathers, these faithful wives, these devoted sons, these chaste daughters, these honest tradesmen, these men and women who were called irreproachable. They were all writing at the same time, on the threshold of their eternal abode, the truth, the terrible and the holy truth of which everybody was ignorant, or pretended to be ignorant, while they were alive.

I thought that *she* also must have written something on her tombstone and now, running without any fear among the half-open coffins, among the corpses and skeletons, I went toward her, sure that I should find her immediately. I recognized her at once without seeing her face, which was covered by the winding sheet, and on the marble cross where shortly before I had read:

She loved, was loved and died.

I now saw:

Having gone out in the rain one day to deceive her lover, she caught cold and died.

It appears that they found me at daybreak, lying on the grave, unconscious.

The Madonna of the Wolves

SOMTOW SUCHARITKUL

"Excuse me. Might I respectfully inquire . . . are you . . . might you possibly be . . . Mademoiselle Martinique?"

"Sir, this is the ladies' waiting room. I trust that you will recognize the impropriety of your presence amongst these unescorted ladies, and that you will retire a few paces beyond the entrance and state your request without the forwardness you have just exhibited."

"I say. Awfully sorry, I'm sure."

Overhearing this conversation and her own name, Speranza Martinique looked up from her Bible. A corpulent woman, whose feathery hat ill suited her belligerent demeanor, was having an altercation with a bearded gentleman in morning dress. Perhaps this was the messenger that his lordship's secretary had mentioned in his letter to her. She rose and tugged at the fat woman's sleeve. "Your pardon, madam, but I think the gentleman is looking for me."

The woman turned on her with a look of sheer disdain. She shuddered, and her unnatural plumage shuddered with her. "A railway station waiting room is hardly the place for a furtive encounter," she said. "I find the fact that you seek to disguise your unnatural intentions behind a *Bible* most revolting."

Mildly, Speranza said to the aggravating woman: "Look to the mote in your own eye, madam; it is the best way, I have found, of alleviating the harm that a prolonged meditation on the world's evils can afflict upon a lady's refined sensibilities."

"I never!" the fat woman said, as Speranza swept past her and accosted the bearded gentleman, who was waiting by the entrance. She could see that he was amused by their exchange; but seeing her approach, he suppressed his laughter and was all gravity.

"Mademoiselle," he began in atrocious French, pulling a sealed paper from his waistcoat pocket, "j'ai l'honneur de vous présenter cette lettre écrite par—"

"Heavens!" the fat woman remarked, eavesdropping at the door.

"I should have known. A Frenchwoman. What an unprincipled lot, those frogs!"

"Only half French, actually," Speranza said, "and half Italian. Oh, sir, do let's continue this conversation elsewhere! Certain people are becoming most tiresome! Surely the crowds that are gathered here will render a chaperone unnecessary."

"I say, you speak English awfully well, what."

"I do," Speranza said, "and if it is not too forward of me, might I ask that we use English from now on? I think my command of that tongue might be a little . . ." She tried to say it tactfully, but could not; so she changed the subject slightly. "I was, after all, the governess of the son of Lord Slatterthwaite, the Hon. Michael Bridgewater, before he was unfortunately taken from us—"

"Consumption, I understand," said the messenger, shaking his head. "But I have neglected to introduce myself. My name is Cornelius Quaid. I represent . . . a certain party, whose name I am not presently at liberty to divulge."

"Lord Slatterthwaite assured me that this party's credentials are impeccable. I will take him at his word, Mr. Quaid. And where is the boy?"

"Soft, soft, Mademoiselle Martinique. All in good time. First let me go over the plans with you. Here is the letter I spoke of; it will allow you and the lad safe passage to your destination. Attached to it is a banker's note which, you will find, will cover any emergency you may encounter; I trust you will not abuse it. The traveling papers, tickets, itineraries, and other paraphernalia are here as well. You depart in a little over an hour. Your things are at the left luggage office, I presume? I shall have my man see to them. Furthermore—" he reached into a capacious trouser pocket and pulled out a small purse "—I have been authorized to give you a small advance." Speranza was very grateful for this, for her dismissal from Lord Slatterthwaite's service, though no fault of hers, would have left her destitute, had it not been for this rather mysterious new development. "Count it at your leisure, mademoiselle. You will find that it contains one hundred guineas in gold. The rest, you may be sure, will be forthcoming upon the safe delivery of the boy to a certain Dr. Szymanowski, in Vienna."

"I will take your word on it, Mr. Quaid," Speranza said, tucking the purse into an inside pocket of her coat. Where was the child? His lordship had told her that her new duties would involve escorting a young lad across Europe, for which, he said, she was eminently suited; for not only was she trained in the care of children, but she was well acquainted not only with French, English, and Italian, but had a smattering of the many languages of the Austro-Hungarian Empire. There was no more information about the boy, however, and Speranza was anxious to learn all she could. She was regretting having left the relative warmth of the ladies' waiting room. Victoria Station, imposing though it was, was not well heated; and she could see, clinging to the hair of beggars and urchins and to the hats and overcoats of those who could afford them, evidence of the snowstorm that was raging without. It was a veritable bedlam here: flower girls, newspaper vendors, old women hawking steak and kidney pies, and of course the passengers themselves. Rich and poor, they shuffled about, their expressions bearing that self-imposed bleakness which Speranza found all too common amongst the English.

"The boy?" she said at last.

"Ah yes, the boy." For the first time, a look of trepidation seemed to cross the face of Cornelius Quaid. Was the boy ill? Consumptive, perhaps, and capable of spreading the disease? But Speranza had remained at poor little Michael's bedside day and night for many weeks. Surely, if she were going to catch it, she would have done so already.

She said, "Sir, I am not afraid of catching a disease. I take it that disease is at issue here, since you desire me to deliver him to this doctor. A specialist, I assume? I assure you I will take the greatest pains to—"

"Mademoiselle, the boy's affliction is not physical. It is of the soul."

"Ah, one of the newfangled *dementiae*?" Speranza was aware that certain research was being done into the dark recesses of the mind; but of course such subjects were not within the boundaries of decent discourse.

"No, I mean the soul, mademoiselle, not the mind."

She stiffened a little at this, for the fat lady had been unwittingly right in one thing; the Bible that Speranza Martinique carried upon her person was a purely cosmetic device. For Speranza suffered constantly from thoughts that, she felt, should correctly be suppressed; her severe dress and her Bible were intended to deflect the suspicions of strangers, who she was certain could see into her very soul did she not stand constant guard against discovery.

"The boy is possessed," Mr. Quaid said in profound earnest. "Sometimes, when the moon is full . . ."

"Tush, Mr. Quaid! This is the nineteenth century; we don't believe such superstitions any more, do we?" she said, a little uncomfortably, shivering a little, thinking to herself: I have every right to shiver, do I not? It is the dead of winter, and these beastly English do enjoy the cold so. "Let us just say that the boy is . . . ill."

"Very well, then. I am no expert on the young. But I will tell you this. The boy's parents are dead. They were killed under most unpleasant circumstances. I wasn't made privy to the details, but there was . . ." he lowered his voice, and Speranza had to strain to hear him, "devil worship. Heathen rites. Mutilation, I believe. Terrible, terrible!"

"If so, then the boy's distress is perfectly understandable. Possession, indeed! Grief, confusion, perhaps a misunderstanding of the nature of good and evil . . . nothing that proper, attentive care won't heal," Speranza said. She did not add—though she almost blurted it out—that she found the English notion of loving care most astonishing, consisting as it did of little more than an assiduous application of the birch to the behind. Ah, where do they get their love of flagellation from? she mused.

"Well," Mr. Quaid said, interrupting her reverie, "it is time you met your charge."

He gestured. So imperious was his gesture that the crowd seemed to part. Two men came forward; they appeared to be footmen from some well-established household. The boy was between them. The shame of it, Speranza thought, having him escorted like a prisoner! After all he has suffered!

"Come, Johnny," said Mr. Quaid. "This is Mademoiselle Martinique, who will assume the responsibility for your welfare until you are safely in the hands of Dr. Szymanowski."

He makes him sound like a sacrificial animal, Speranza thought. And she looked at the boy who walked towards her with his eyes downcast. She had expected a rich, pampered-looking child; but Johnny wore clothes that, had they not recently been cleaned, might have come from a poorhouse; his coat, she noticed with her practiced eye, had been clumsily mended. He was blond and blue-eyed; his hair was clipped short; only prisoners and denizens of lunatic asylums had their hair that short, because they had sold it to wigmakers. She wondered where Johnny had been living before his nameless benefactor found him. And no more than seven years old! Or perhaps he was small for his age, improperly fed. He came closer but continued to stare steadfastly at the ground. His face, she noticed, was scarred in a dozen places. He had clearly been mistreated. Those English! she thought bitterly, remembering that even in the final stages of his consumption the Hon. Michael Bridgewater had occasionally been subjected to the rod.

And to the fresh air, she remembered. That fresh air that they love so much here, freezing though it might be. She was sure that the fresh air had driven little Michael to his death. She was determined that no such thing would happen to this Johnny. Already she felt a fierce protectiveness towards him.

"Johnny Kindred," Cornelius Quaid said, "you are to obey your new guardian in all ways. Understood?"

"Yes, sir," the boy mumbled.

"You make shake Mademoiselle Martinique's hand. Bow smartly. There. Now say, 'How do you do, Mademoiselle Martinique.'"

Speranza grew impatient. "Mr. Quaid, I trust you will allow me to exercise my particular speciality now." She turned to the child and took his hand. It was shaking with terror. She gripped it affirmatively, reassuringly. "You may call me Speranza," she said to him. "And you needn't shake my hand. You may kiss me on the cheek, if you like."

Mr. Quaid rolled his eyes disapprovingly.

"Speranza," the boy said, looking at her for the first time.

She did not wait for Mr. Quaid to harangue her. Without further ado, still grasping the boy's hand, she steered him towards the platform. Soon they would reach the sea. Soon they would cross the English Channel and reach a land where men did not hesitate to show their feelings.

Already she had begun to love the child they had entrusted to her care. Already she was determined to heal his anguish. Affliction of the soul indeed, the poor boy! Speranza believed that love could cure most every illness. And though she was a woman possessed of many accomplishments, it was love that was her greatest talent.

On the train from London, on the ferry across the Channel, the boy said nothing at all. In France he merely asked for food and drink at the appropriate times. Their benefactor had bought them second class tickets; Speranza was glad of that, for she had had occasion to travel by third class, and she knew that it would be crowded and cold and crammed to bursting with unpleasant characters.

When they crossed the German border, the two old priests who had been occupying their compartment left, and she and the boy had it to themselves. His mood lightened a little. There was not much to watch but fields and fields of snow, and now and then a country station with an ornate, wrought-iron sign and a bench or two. Speranza decided that the best tactic would be to wait; when the boy was ready, he would doubtless begin to talk. He was afraid of everything; she already knew that, for whenever she tried to touch him, he flinched violently away from her as though she were on fire.

A few kilometers into Germany, the boy asked her, "Have you any games, Mademoiselle?"

At last, she thought, he is giving me an opening. Another part of her reflected: Yet I must not become too attached to him; he is mine for only a few more days. And in the back of her mind she saw Michael Bridgewater's pathetically small coffin being lowered into the ground. That too had been in the snow.

"Speranza," she said to him, reminding him that they were to be companions, not opponents. She opened a valise which Quaid's people had provided, labeled *Entertainments*; it contained, she saw, a pack of cards, a backgammon set, and a snakes and ladders board. "Shall we play this?" she said, pulling it out and setting it down in the middle seat, between them. Steadily the fields of snow unreeled. The game was not printed on cardboard, but handpainted on a silken surface. The snakes were very realistically depicted. There was a velvet pouch with a pair of ivory dice and a tortoiseshell die-cup.

The boy nodded.

"Good, Johnny," she said. She wished she could pat his cheek, but knew that he would flinch again. Instead she handed him the dice.

He threw a 3 and eagerly moved his counter three squares. There was a ladder, and he clambered up to the third row. Speranza threw a 5, and was stuck on the bottom. They played for a few minutes, until Speranza encountered her first snake and slid back down almost to square one. Johnny laughed.

Then he said, "Those snakes, they're just like a man's prick, aren't they, Speranza?"

Speranza did not quite believe she had heard him say that. She was flustered for a moment, then said, "Why, where did you learn a word like that from, Johnny?"

"Jonas taught me."

"And who might Jonas be?" Speranza asked, intrigued. Clearly the boy's upbringing had had almost nothing to commend it.

The boy said nothing; he had a guilty look, and Speranza felt that to probe further would perhaps be inopportune. They went on playing. Johnny's counter hit a snake and slid. He cackled. "Right through to the snake's bleeding arsehole!" he said. His voice seemed different; harsher, more grownup.

"Johnny, I am a rather unorthodox woman, but even I find your language a trifle indecent," she said mildly.

"Fuck you!" Johnny said. He looked her straight in the eye. There was anger in those eyes, blazing, unconscionable anger. "Fuck, fuck, fuck, fuck, fuck!"

"Johnny!"

He started to cry. "I'm sorry," he sobbed, "I'm sorry, sorry, sorry. Jonas told me to do it, it wasn't me, honestly it wasn't." He crumpled into her arms, dashing the snakes and ladders board to the floor. Seeing how much he needed affection made Speranza hug him tightly to her. But as he buried his face in her breast she heard him growl, she *felt* his growl reverberate against the squeezing of her corsets. It was like the purring of a cat, but far more vehement, far more menacing. She thought: I cannot be afraid of him; he is only a child, a poor hurt child, and she clasped him to her bosom, struggling not to disclose her anxiety.

They crossed the Rhine. At Karlsruhe, they waited for several hours; part of the train was detached and sent north, and they were to be joined by another segment that had come up from Basle. Thinking to give the boy some exercise, Speranza took him for a walk, up and down the platform. Although the station was canopied, there was some snow and slush on the cars and on the tracks, and many of the passengers milling around outside had snow in their hair and on their coats. The car that joined theirs was elaborate, and bore on its sides the crest of some aristocratic family. Of course, Speranza thought, we have to wait for those high-and-mighty types.

"Let's go and see!" Johnny said. There was nothing in him now of the obscene, deep-voiced child that had emerged earlier. He was all innocence. She was convinced now that his problem was some kind of division within his soul, some combat between the forces of light and darkness. Taking his hand, she took him up to the carriage.

Heavy drapes prevented one from seeing inside. The car seemed dilapidated, and the coat-of-arms had not been painted lately; beneath it was the legend:

von Bächl-Wölfing

in the *fraktur* script which Speranza found difficult to read. The arms themselves were fairly ordinary looking. Two silver wolf's heads glared at each other across a crimson field. Argent, she reminded herself, and gules. Little Michael had always been very particular about heraldry. But then he had been the son of a peer of the realm. As she mused on her former life as the young aristocrat's governess, she saw that Johnny had stepped up very close to the track, that he was shaking his fist at the coat-of-arms . . . that the same menacing growl was issuing from his throat.

Then, to her alarm, Johnny pulled down his trousers and urinated onto the side of the train.

"Johnny, you must stop!"

"I am Jonas!" He turned; their eyes met once; she saw that his eyes were slitty-golden . . . like the eyes of a wild animal! Terrified, she started to follow him, but he growled and sprinted to the front of the train, across the track, clambered up to the other side of the platform. She called after him. Then she started to run after him.

I'll have to take a short cut, she thought. She dived into the train. An old peasant woman with two hens in a basket looked up at her. She tried to open the door on the other side, but it would not come open.

She pressed her face against the window, called his name again. He was urinating again, on the track, on the steps into the train, and shouting, "This is my place I'll not run in your pack I'm me I'm me leave me alone alone alone!"

"Help me," Speranza whispered. "If you please, though I can't speak your language . . . au secours, j'ai perdu mon enfant. . . ."

Some of the others in the carriage were looking out, too. A burly man said to her, "Is' es Ihr Kind dort aufm Gleis?"

She nodded, not understanding. The man began shouting, and an official in uniform came and opened the door. Speranza and some of the others leapt down onto the side of the track.

"I'll not run in it I'll not I'll not!" Johnny screamed, spraying them with piss.

"Was sagt er denn?" The strange man caught the boy and held him tight as he wriggled. "Beruhe dich," he said softly to him, and stroked him gently on the neck and head. Johnny grew still.

"Thank you." Speranza reached out to take him from the man. He was curled up in fetal position, sucking his thumb. His clothes and his face and arms were stained and foul-smelling; it was an unfamiliar odor, as though his urine were somehow not quite human.

In the compartment, she filled a jug with water, moistened a towel, and began to swab his face. He did not stir. A whistle sounded, and the train began to ease itself away from the station. The odor was pungent, choking. But Speranza had cleaned and washed little Michael every day in the last weeks of his consumption, and her stomach was not easily turned. The boy seemed to be fast asleep. She did not want to embarrass him. She took off his coat and laid him on it. Very gently she began to undo his back and front collar-stud and to pull his shirt over his head, and to unbutton his braces so that she could unfasten his trousers. The shirt tore as it came away. The backs of the child's hands were covered with fine, shiny hair. His back was unusually hairy, too; when she started to wipe it it gleamed like sealskin. There were welts and scars all over him; she knew from this that he had been beaten, probably habitually, since many of the marks were white and smooth. She wrung out the cloth, soaked it in water again, and cleansed him as best she could. Though she tried to look away, she could not help seeing his tiny penis, quite erect above a tuft of silverwhite hair. She did not think little Michael had had hair down there. This boy definitely had some minor physical abnormalities as well as his obvious emotional ones.

The sun began to set behind distant white hills. She managed to get him into a nightgown that had been starched stiff; clearly it had never been used before, like all the other clothes in the trunk that Quaid's men had loaded onto the train. The sharpness of the fabric must have disturbed him. He opened his eyes and said, "Tell me a story, please, Speranza. Then I'll be fast asleep and Jonas won't come, he never comes when I'm asleep."

She was going to ask him about Jonas, but she was afraid her questioning might bring more strange behavior; so she merely said, easing back into the padded seat and allowing him to lie with his head against the lace and black satin of her skirts, "What story would you like? A story about a prince in a castle? A beautiful princess? A dragon, perhaps? Or would that be too frightening?"

"I want Little Red Riding Hood," he said in a small voice. "But make Little Red Riding Hood a boy."

She tried not to show how startled she was at his request. She felt a strange indecency about what he had asked, though she could not put into words why it would feel that way. She did not look at him while she spoke; she watched the fields go by, the snow slowly blooded by the setting sun. "Once upon a time there was a girl—"

"A boy."

"—named Little Red Riding Hood who lived by the edge of the forest." When she reached the part about the wolf dressed in the grandmother's clothing, the boy clung to her in terror, but that terror was also something a little bit like lust . . . she had always known that children are not pure and innocent, as the English liked to believe. But the idea that the boy was enjoying her discomfiture, actually, in some inchoate way, taking advantage of her person . . . and yet, she could tell already, he loved her. So she went on: "And the wolf said, 'The better to eat you with, my darling boy.' And ate the little boy up. In one gulp. And then the hunters—"

"That's enough. They just put the hunters in so little children won't be frightened. But you and I know the truth, don't we?"

"The truth?"

"The hunters don't care. And even if the boy was still alive inside the wolf, then the hunters' rifles would just rip them both apart anyway, wouldn't they, Speranza?"

"It's only a story," she said. The sexual tension had passed away; perhaps, Speranza thought, it was just in herself, she had imagined it; how could a seven-year-old boy, even a profoundly disturbed one, manipulate me in this fashion?

"It's not a story, Speranza. Believe me. And if you can't quite make yourself believe me, maybe you'll talk to Jonas one day." And he drifted into sleep, lulled by the repetitive clanging, and she covered him and sat thinking for a long time. She had forgotten, after all the day's commotion, that they had missed the early session in the dining car.

There was a knock at the door.

"Darf ich herein, bitte?" A slimy voice; the sort of man used to toadying; not the kind of voice she expected for a railway official. Her heart beat faster.

"Je m'excuse," she said in French, "je ne comprends pas l'allemand." Then she added in English, "Please, sir, I have no German."

She unlatched the door of the compartment.

It was a man in evening dress, very stiff and proper, bearing a silver tray. "May it please you, Fräulein Martinique," he said, "my master would very much enjoy the pleasure of your company at dinner, now that the boy is asleep."

"How does he know—"

"He felt it, gnädiges Fräulein. In his heart."

"Sir, I do not think it is quite proper for a man to invite a woman to whom he has not been properly introduced—"

The steward, or butler, or whoever it was, handed her the little platter. There was a calling card on it, printed on rag paper, with a gold border. It contained only the name:

Graf Hartmut von Bächl-Wölfing

Speranza knew that the word *Graf* meant Count or Earl or some such title. What did this man know about her and the boy? How could he have felt the boy's waking and sleeping? And why did Johnny try to urinate all over the Count's railway carriage? She was afraid of what this might be leading to. She felt a premonition of something . . . unnatural. Perhaps even supernatural. But Speranza was not superstitious, and curiosity vanquished her fear.

The Count's servant was waiting for her reply.

"I will be glad to come," she said, "if you will send someone to watch the child while I dine; and perhaps the Count's cook could prepare some small tidbit for me to bring back to him. Poor Johnny is worn out, but he hasn't had his supper, and I think he may wake up hungry in the middle of the night."

The servant paused, perhaps translating her comments to himself; the train clattered as it negotiated a curve. "Yes, gnädiges Fräulein," he said at last.

"Now leave me so that I can dress. If I am to meet a Count, I ought perhaps to try not to look so shabby," she said, feeling suddenly frail.

When the man departed, Speranza looked through her trunk and found little to wear; she changed into a somewhat cleaner black dress, tried to tidy her hair, and threw over the drab costume a rabbitfur pelisse. She did have a few articles of jewelry; she selected a silver necklace studded with cabochon amethysts. A little ostentatious, perhaps? But it was all she had. She looked at her reflection against the glass and the snow. Perhaps, she thought, I could be more attractive. In the window I seem to be a governess, only a governess . . . but I have dark dreams for a governess, dark and daring thoughts.

Presently a serving maid, perhaps fourteen, in a uniform came, curtseyed, said, "Für den Knaben." Speranza assumed she had come to watch the boy, and left; the manservant was waiting to conduct her down the corridor. A moment of intense cold as the footman helped her across the precarious coupling between the two cars, and then it was warm again, stiflingly warm, inside the domain of the Count von Bächl-Wölfing.

The first thing she felt was gloom. The curtains were tightly drawn, and the only light was from a gold candelabrum in the middle of a table of dark Italian marble. The candles were black. The servant showed her to a fauteuil, overplump, dusty, dark velvet; a second servant poured wine into a crystal goblet. Were it not for the ceaseless motion of the train, she would have thought herself in a sumptuous, if somewhat ill-kept, apartment in Mayfair.

The servant, seeming to address the empty room, said, "Euer Gnade, das französische Fräulein, das Ihr eingeladen habt." He bowed.

"Welcome," said a voice: liquid, deep, suggestive, even, of some hidden eroticism. At first she saw only eyes; the eyes glittered. Strangely, they reminded her of Johnny's eyes, when he had undergone that eerie metamorphosis into his other, demented self; clear, yellow, like polished topazes. Now she saw the face they were set in: a lean face, a man clearly middleaged yet somehow also youthful. His hair, balding, was silver save for a dark streak above his left temple. His upper lip sported the barest hint of a mustache.

He said, "Ou est-que vous préférez que je vous parle en français, peut-être?" His pronunciation was impeccable.

"It doesn't matter," Speranza said, "what we speak. But perhaps you can explain to me . . . oh, so many things . . . who are you, why do you seem to know so much about the child and me."

"I am but a pilgrim," von Bächl-Wölfing said, "I journey to the same shrine as you, my dear Mademoiselle Martinique—or perhaps you will permit me the liberty of addressing you as Speranza. Your name means *hope*, and without hope our cause is doomed, alas."

"Your cause?"

The Count moved closer to her, and seated himself in a leather armchair. "Ah yes. We are all going to see Dr. Szymanowski, are we not?"

"I am to deliver the boy to him."

He sighed; she felt an almost unbearable sadness in him, though she could not tell why. It was as if his emotions were borne on the dust in the air of the carriage, as though she could smell his melancholy. "And after?" he said.

"I do not know, sir. Perhaps I shall return to my family in Aix-en-Provence." A maid was serving a fish course; the Count nibbled distractedly, but Speranza was more hungry than she had thought. "Something your servant said . . . that you *felt* that Johnny had gone to sleep . . . in your heart. What did that mean?"

"We have a secret language."

"But you did not even see him."

The Count wrinkled his nose. "I most certainly smelt him, mademoiselle! Still that odor lingers in the air . . . ah, but you cannot smell it. Some of us are more . . . deprived . . . than others."

"If you are referring to Johnny's unfortunate . . . accident . . ."

"It was no accident!" the Count said, laughing. "But he has much to learn. A youngling cannot usurp the territory of a leader merely by baptizing his environment with piss! Ah, but you are shocked at my language; I forgot, you have been in England for a long while. Seriously, mademoiselle, the boy knows only instinct at the moment; soon he will combine that instinct with intelligence. To be able to help mold his mind, so malleable, yet so filled with all that separates our kind from—"

"I have no idea, Count, what you are talking about."

"I apologize. I begin to ramble when the moon waxes. It makes up for the times when I am robbed of the power of human discourse."

Why, Speranza thought, he is as mad as the boy is! Who was this Dr. Szymanowski? Surely the purveyor of a lunatic asylum. And they were going to use Johnny. Experiments, perhaps. Speranza had read *Frankenstein*. She knew what scientists could be like. She wondered whether the young serving girl who was alone with the boy was really—

"She knows nothing," said Count von Bächl-Wölfing.

"You read minds, Count?"

"No. But I *am* observant," he said softly. "I know, for example, that though you appear to me in the guise of a prim, severe governess, that is merely a shield behind which hides a woman of passion, a woman who can take agonizing risks; a dangerous woman, a woman fascinated by what other women shy away from; a woman capable of profound, consuming love."

Speranza's heart began to pound. "Count, I am perhaps a more modern woman than many of my occupation; but I hardly think the first few moments of a meeting, even when the difference in rank between us is so great, is a suitable time for—"

"You are quite wrong, Speranza. I do desire you, but . . . some things one can perforce live without. The boy is important, though. He is a new thing, you see, a wholly new kind of creature. But I see you do not understand me." He sighed; again she seemed to sense that perfume of dolorousness in the air. "It is all so unfair of me . . . but believe me, I would not say these things about you without having first ordered a thorough investigation into your character."

"My character is unassailable!" Speranza said, feeling terribly vulnerable, for the Count had ripped away the mask, so painstakingly assumed, and exposed it for the flimsy self-delusion that it was. "How dare you pry into my life, how dare you have me brought here! I think that under the circumstances I should depart immediately."

"Of course. But before that there is something I ought perhaps to tell you."

"We have nothing to say to each other—"

"Except, Mademoiselle Martinique, that I happen to be your employer."

"You! Who communicated with Lord Slatterthwaite—who sent Cornelius Quaid to Victoria Station—" She was trembling now; she felt as lost and bewildered as poor mad Johnny Kindred, who did not know if he was one person or two.

The Count merely smiled, and offered her another glass of wine.

Speranza had left the Count's private coach as soon as she could. She had found the child awake, picking at the light supper which had been brought in for him: a little pâté, a bowl of soup, a loaf of black bread, a goblet of hot spiced wine. The maid, seeing her approach so soon after she had left to join von Bächl-Wölfing, curtseyed and departed, smirking . . . or was Speranza only imagining the worst?

"You stink of him," the boy said. It was the other one. The one with the tongue of a guttersnipe. "You reek of him, he's bursting with animal spunk, he's been wanking all over your cunny, did you let him get inside?" Speranza did not attempt to respond, but waited for the fit to end. At last Johnny Kindred emerged long enough to say, "I'm glad you're back; stay with me always." And then he fell asleep in her arms.

The night passed uneasily. Moving, the train seemed to breathe. She was in the belly of a serpent, slithering over the snow, towards . . . towards . . . she could not tell. She blew out the lamp, eased the boy onto his back on the seat opposite hers, and stared at the passing snowscape. Dark firs, silvered by the moon, stretched as far as she could see. Cold, dappled, the light streamed into the compartment. She tried not to think of the Count von Bächl-Wölfing. But her dreams were of being pursued by him through the dank forest, the stench of earth and wolf-piss burning her nostrils, the wind sharp and ice-cold . . . in the dream she remembered thinking that they had left the German forests behind, that this was some quite alien forest of leviathan trees and unfamiliar animals, a forest in some strange new world.

In the morning the same servant appeared with an invitation to breakfast. "You should bring the child," the man said. She looked at Johnny. He seemed contrite; he offered no resistance as she dressed him from the clothes they found in the trunk. For herself she again selected dark colors; again she wore the silver necklace, although she was afraid he would think poorly of her for wearing the same jewelry two days in a row. Then she castigated herself for her foolishness. The Count was immeasurably wealthy, and, more to the point, far above her station; she was only a governess, and of dubious legitimacy at that!

The curtains in the Count's car were still closed. She could not help noticing the smell; she recognized it from last night's dream. The boy began to growl. "Quiet, Johnny, quiet," she said softly. Some daylight seeped in between the closed draperies; dust swam in the rays. She could see the Count's back; he was seated at a writing desk, paying them no heed. She took in details she had missed before; the car was partitioned by a curtain of heavy purple velvet bearing the wolf-crest; perhaps there was a sleeping area behind. Suddenly she was afraid the boy would start pissing on all the priceless furniture. But his growling seemed more for show; soon he became withdrawn, fidgety, his eyes following a dust-mote as it circled.

The Count moved, shrugged perhaps; abruptly the divider drew open, and music played from the adjoining section, soft-pedaled chords on a piano. After a few bars, a clear, sweet tenor voice joined in with a plaintive melody in the minor key. Sunlight streamed in.

The boy's attention was drawn immediately to the music. At last, for the first time, he smiled.

"Schubert," Speranza said, for the song cycle *Winterreise* had not been unknown in the Slatterthwaite household, though His Lordship had sung it in his cousin's stilted English translation, with little Michael pounding unmercifully on the family Broadwood. She had not known it could be so beautiful.

The Count said: "'*Fremd bin ich eingezogen, fremd zieh ich wieder aus.*' Do you know what it means, Speranza? It means, 'I came here a stranger; a stranger I depart.' How true. Look, the boy understands it instinctively. He is no longer annoyed with me."

He clapped his hands. The music stopped; the boy's smile faded. "Shall we have breakfast now?" He got up and beckoned them to follow; as he crossed the partition, he nodded and the music resumed almost in midnote. She took Johnny by the hand and led him. As they passed the desk where von Bächl-Wölfing had been sitting, she saw that he had been writing a letter in English. She had already read the salutation—"My dear Vanderbilt"—before realizing her appalling breach of manners. Of course she would never normally have contemplated scrutinizing another's correspondence; it only showed how powerful an effect the Count had had on her. She resolved to be more prim, more severe in her demeanor. She would not step one inch over the line of propriety—not one inch!

They had a pleasant enough breakfast of pheasant pâté, egg-and-bacon pies, and toast and marmalade. Coffee was served in blue-and-white Delft demitasses. She admired the china. She admired the cutlery, whose ivory handles were carved in the shape of lean wolves, each one with tiny topaz eyes. Throughout the meal the Count said little. He stared at the boy. The boy stared back. They spoke without words. She became aware that she was babbling, trying to fill an uncomfortable silence with chatter. She stopped abruptly. The music filled the air. Schubert's song cycle dealt with beauty and desolation. And so it was here. The windows had been opened a crack, driving out the musky animal odor. The train moved out of the forest, past frozen lakes and somnolent villages. There were mountains in the distance. In a few hours they would enter the empire of Austria-Hungary, teeming with exotic peoples and dissonant languages. She sipped her coffee, which was flavored with nutmeg and topped with whipped cream, and watched the wordless communion of the deranged boy and the worldly aristocrat.

At last the Count said, "You seem to have made quite an impression on the boy, Speranza. He loves you very much, you know. You have a certain magic with children . . . and even, I may add, with the middleaged."

He smiled disarmingly. She blushed like a schoolgirl even as she forced herself to purse her lips and respond with unyielding decorum. "You are pleased to flatter me, Count," she said.

"You shall call me Hartmut," he said expansively.

"I would not make such a presumption," Speranza said. Her pulse quickened. She steadied her hand by meticulously buttering a slice of toast and applying the pâté to it, patting it into place and making firm, precise ridges with the pâté-knife. Before she could finish, he had reached across the table and was grasping her hand firmly. His hand was hairy and slick with sweat. She felt as though her hand had been plunged into a furnace. Quickly she snatched it away. The Count smiled with his lips, with the contours of his face; but his eyes betrayed an untouchable sadness.

"What are you thinking? That you should touch that sadness?" How strange, she thought, that he could read her mind so accurately. "Ah, but you have not yet learnt the impossibility of the task you set yourself. You are young, so terribly young. Can *you* cage the beast within, Speranza, even though you are fully human?"

"Sir, you are forward."

"It is because you wish it."

There was danger here, though the compartment was awash with light. Speranza decided that she might as well be direct. "Why, Count von Bächl-Wölfing, have you had us brought here? Why do you keep hinting of mysteries? There is an air that you affect, a feeling almost of some supernatural being. I do not think that it is merely the result of your high birth, if I do not overstep—"

"Everything you have imagined, mademoiselle, is true."

But she had not yet imagined . . . the boy was growling again. He was toying with his food. He leapt onto the table on all fours. The Count turned to him. In a second his face seemed transformed. He snarled once. The boy slid sullenly back into his seat. The Count's face returned to normal. Speranza studied him for some clue as to its metamorphosis, but saw nothing.

"What did you do to make him stop?" she asked him.

"We have a way with each other."

"To return to this subject . . . why are we playing at these guessing games, Count? I am a modern woman, and not fond of mysteries."

"I am a werewolf."

They rode on, not speaking, for some moments. The train clattered harshly against the Schubert melodies. Her rational mind told her that the Count was once more entertaining some elaborate fantasy to which she was not privy. Once more she considered the notion that he might be as mad as little Johnny. But another part of her had already seized on the statement. She could not deny that it was intriguing. Though she hardly dared admit it to herself, she even found the idea glamorous.

"Noch was Kaffee, gnädiges Fräulein?" the manservant said, smoothly gliding into position on her right. She nodded absently and he poured.

"I hear no reaction, mademoiselle, to what must constitute a most singular revelation." Was he laughing at her? But no, he seemed all seriousness. "Perhaps I should go on about wolf's bane, about nocturnal metamorphoses under the full moon, about silver bullets, and so on. But you will only say, 'I am a modern woman,' and dismiss with that specious argument the accumulated knowledge of millennia. Let me suggest, instead, that you ask the boy. He knew at once. He knows now. By the way, he's a werewolf, too."

She turned to Johnny. She knew at once that the boy believed at least part of what the Count was saying. But there was something not quite right about Johnny's place in this scheme. "Perhaps you, Count, are suffering from some dementia that convinces you that you are . . . other than human," she said. "But Johnny's troubles are far less simple."

"True," said the Count. "How quickly you have divined, mademoiselle, the dilemma that is at the very heart of my involvement with him!" He did not seem to want to expand on the subject, and turned his attention instead to a snuffbox which his manservant had brought him on a silver tray.

She was bursting with curiosity and frustration. Instead she asked him, "And Dr. Szymanowski? Who is he?"

"A visionary, my dear mademoiselle! Whereas I . . . I merely pay the bills. By the way, what is your opinion of America?"

Taken aback by his change of subject, she said, "Why, very little, Count! That is, I know that it is a wild country of savages who are ruled by renegades scarcely less savage than the *Indiens peaux-rouges* themselves."

The Count laughed. "Ah, a wild country. Perhaps you will understand why it calls to the wildness within us. In humans, but especially in us, who are—humor me at least for the moment—not entirely human. It cries to us across the very sea." Almost as an afterthought, he added, "I have been making a number of investments there. They are, I think, shrewd ones."

Speranza had the distinct impression that he was attempting, in a roundabout manner, to answer her questions; at the same time he was testing her, daring her to reveal the darkness inside herself. There was also something in him of a small boy with a secret . . . the frog in the waistcoat pocket . . . the Latin book coded with obscene messages in invisible ink . . . he wanted to know if he could trust her with the truth, but the truth excited him so much that he could hardly contain himself from spilling everything. Even the sadness in his eyes seemed to have lifted a little. This in him she could understand, for she well knew the minds of children.

She had an idea. "But the cutlery . . . is it not silver? And if it is true that you are indeed what you claim to be . . . is not silver a substance that might cause you distress?"

"My dear Speranza, heft my spoons and forks in your dainty hands! Are they not of unwonted heaviness? I have no cutlery on my dining table that is not purest platinum." He grinned, as though to say, "I was ready for that one; ask something a little more tricky."

"And the full moon. . . ."

"Will soon be upon us. Oh, don't worry, my dear Mademoiselle Martinique. You will be quite safe, as long as you observe certain conditions which I will spell out to you before moonrise. Ah, I see that you are skeptical, are you not? You think little of these extravagant claims?"

"Only, Count, that you are possessed of a powerful imagination." She felt uncomfortable, since both man and boy were staring intently at her, so she continued, "Oh, come, sir! Here we are sitting amidst brilliant sunshine, doing nothing more supernatural than eating a pheasant pâté; how can you expect your ghost stories to have their full effect?"

"Ghost stories! Is that what you think they are?"

"Is it not what they are?"

"You mistake me, Speranza. I do not believe in ghosts. Nor spirits, nor demons, nor any of the trappings of damnation. How can I allow myself to believe in such things? I would fall prey to the utmost despair, for in the Christian hegemony in which we find ourselves, such as I dare hope for no salvation, no redemption from the everlasting fire; we are damned already, damned without hope, damned before we are ever judged! Quindi, Speranza, quindi bramo la speranza!"

He spoke to her in her mother's tongue, the tongue of gentleness and warmth; she felt as though he had violated her final, innermost hiding place. She did not yield, but continued in English, to her the coldest of languages: "And why, Count von Bächl-Wölfing, why is it that you so ardently yearn for hope?"

"But I forget myself." The Count's passion had been but fleeting; now he was all correctness. "I apologize for inflicting my religious torment on you, mademoiselle; I trust you have not been too disturbed by my words?"

"On the contrary, the fault is mine," Speranza said automatically, thinking nothing of the kind. "I should perhaps be going now?"

The sun hung low over the snow.

Johnny sat with his nose pressed against the pane.

"What do you think?" he asked her suddenly. "Shall we trust him? Shall we run with him in the cold cold forest?"

"I don't know what you mean."

"You're going to go to him tonight, aren't you? He'll invite you. Maybe he won't, but you'll find some excuse. Because you're dying from curiosity. You want to know if it's true. And you want to fuck him."

"Johnny, I really must insist—" But she knew that all he said was true. He understood her so well, this lunatic.

"My language. I can't help it, though, I'm possessed by demons, you see. Everyone says so."

"Johnny, there aren't any demons. Even the Count says so."

"I don't want to be this way."

"You don't have to be, Johnny, because I'm going to help you, I'm going to pull you out of this sickness of yours somehow."

"Will you love me, Speranza?"

"Of course I will."

"Then you must fuck me, too, mustn't you?" The words no longer offended her; she knew it was part of his illness. Somehow these things had become terribly confused for him. How could she blame him? Even she was confused, and she was a sane woman, was she not? She tried to pry him from the window, thinking to comfort him; he resisted at first, but then threw himself into her arms with a hunger that was like anger, and it frightened her, how so much passionate anguish could come in so frail a package; and as she hugged him she heard him wailing, with a desperate concern for her and for his own future, "When you go to see him tonight, you have to wear the silver necklace, don't ever take it off whatever he says don't you ever ever *ever* take it off!"

The inner world of Johnny Kindred was like a forest; not the picturebook forest of fairytales, but a forest of gnarled trees knotted with rage, of writhing vines, of earth pungent with piss and putrescence, of clammy darkness. At the very center of the forest there was a clearing. The circle was the center of the world, and it was bathed in perpetual, pallid moonlight. When you stood in the circle of light, you could see the outside world, you could hear, touch, smell. You controlled the body. But you always had to fend off the others. Especially Jonas.

And when you were tired, they gathered, surrounding the circle, thirsting for the light. Waiting to touch the world outside.

Waiting to use the body.

Right now the circle was empty. The body slept.

"Let me through," Johnny said faintly.

The darkness seethed. Vines shifted. And always the wolves howled. There were unformed persons in the depths of the forest, their strength growing. Johnny could smell them. He could smell Jonas most of all. Jonas hanging head downward from a tree. Jonas laughing, the drool glistening on his canines. Calling his name: "Johnny, Johnny, you silly boy, you're just a fucking figment, you're just a dream."

"Let me through—" He had to step into the light before the body weakened. Because the moon would be rising soon.

"Through? You don't even exist. I'm the owner of this body, and you're just a little thing I made up once to amuse myself. Get back, get back. Into the dark, do you hear? Or I'll send for—"

"No!"

"Our father."

"Our father in Hell," Johnny whispered.

"In Hell." He could see Jonas more clearly now. The other boy was swinging back and forth, back and forth. He looked like one of the cards in their mother's tarot deck . . . The Hanged Man. "Fuck you! Why did you have to think of our mother, simple Johnny? Do you want to go back to the madhouse? Perhaps you have fond memories of your mudlarking days, my little mad brother?"

"I forgot. That you can read my mind." The thought of their mother could still hurt Jonas. Johnny tried to think of her again, but he saw only a great blackness. Jonas had been at work, striking out any bits of the past that displeased him, tossing them aside like the offal that lined the banks of the Thames, like the rubbish piled up against the walls of their old home. Jonas used to bully him all the time at the home. Whenever the beatings started he would push Johnny out into the clearing so that Johnny would feel all the pain. Even though it was always Jonas who had done wrong. "Get out of my mind!" Johnny screamed, despairing.

"Our mind. No. My mind. It's *my* mind, you're in *my* mind. Why can't you be more like me? I'm not a snivelling, snotty-nosed boy who's afraid of the truth. Our mother never could face the truth, could she? You're weak, like *her*, weak, weak, weak!"

Johnny started to run. The mud clung to his toes. Brambles slithered around his ankles. Thorns sliced into his arms, opening up fresh wounds. The clearing didn't get any nearer. He leapt over rotted logs and mossy stones. He had to reach it first, he had to. Dread seeped into him. He knew that Jonas was swinging from tree to tree, his animal eyes piercing the dark. There it was! He was at the edge now, all he had to do was step inside—

He fell! Twigs and leaves flurried. He was at the bottom of a pit. He breathed uneasily. His hand collided with something hard. Pale light leaked in from the clearing. He saw who was in the trap with him . . . a skeleton, chained to the earthen walls with silver that glinted in the light, cold, cold.

"Let me *out*—"

Jonas stood above him: "The body is mine," he said slowly, triumphantly. Johnny could see that he had already begun to change. The snout was bursting from flaps of human skin . . . the eyes were narrowing, changing color.

Desperate, Johnny beat against the wall of his prison. And Jonas cackled. His laughter was already transforming itself into an inhuman howling.

Speranza watched the boy as he slept. The moon was rising. She had half believed the Count's insane suggestion that the boy would now transform into a wolf . . . but he lay peacefully, his eyes closed, curled up on a woollen blanket.

Speranza watched the moon. She knew she would soon go to him. Since crossing the Austro-Hungarian border she had felt dread and desire in equal measure. They were moving into a thick forest. Bare trees, their branches weighed down with icicles, obscured the moon. The train rattled and sighed and seemed almost to breathe. She steadied herself and watched the trees go by. Soon, she thought, I will lose the child . . . I will be free of these madmen. What then? Obscurity in Aix-en-Provence?

The boy stirred. He moaned. Beneath closed eyelids, his eyes moved feverishly. She touched his hand. Recoiled. The hand was burning. Burning! It must be a fever, she thought. And remembered little Michael's consumption once more. Gingerly she touched his forehead. It was drenched with sweat. She shook him. He would not waken. "Johnny," she whispered, "Johnny."

He moaned.

"Johnny!" Why am I panicking? she thought. This dread is quite unreasonable . . . I must cool his brow.

She opened the door of the compartment. The servant girl who had looked after Johnny before was sleeping in the corridor. She awoke instantly. "I am sent . . . by the Count, gnädiges Fräulein."

The Count. . . .

"Has he done something to the boy?" Thoughts of cruel scientific experiments . . . potions in the food . . . mesmerism . . . "Fetch some water. Quickly."

"Jawohl, gnädiges Fräulein." The maid hurried down the narrow walkway. Speranza watched her disappear. Wind from an open window whipped at her and left sprinkles of snow on her black dress. She was still wearing the necklace of silver and amethysts.

She expected the maid to return any moment. Time passed. A powerful odor was wafting into the corridor . . . the reek of animal urine. She heard a trickling sound from within the compartment. The poor child, she thought. He is wetting himself. She went back in.

She looked at him in the moonlight. His nightshirt was stained. The urine was running onto the floor of the compartment. His eyes were darting back and forth beneath squeezed lids. His whole body was slick with sweat. She held a handkerchief over her nose, but still the stench was suffocating. Where was the maid? Could they not understand that the boy was sick? She went out into the corridor once more. The cold blasted her. The dread came again, teasing at her thoughts. The maid, she thought, the maid. . . .

"At last!" she cried, seeing the girl come back. She was clutching something in her arms . . . a small bottle and a book . . . a Bible, Speranza saw. "I sent you to get water!"

"Holy water," the maid whispered. The terror in her face was unmistakable.

"What's the matter with you?" said Speranza angrily. "Come inside and help me with the child." She went back into the compartment and put her arm under the boy's neck to lift him into a sitting position. The boy was limp, lifeless-seeming.

The maid stood at the door.

"Come and help me—"

The girl made the sign of the cross and looked down at the floor. The train rocked and clattered. The girl held out the holy water and the Bible—

"This is nonsense, purest nonsense!" Speranza cried. "Superstition and nonsense! This Count of yours has you all under the diabolical influence of his mad illusions . . . you must calm yourself, girl." How much did the servant understand?

"Ich habe Angst, gnädiges Fräulein."

"Stop chattering and—" She tried to seize the bottle from the girl. It smashed against the seat and broke. Still the boy slept. "You can see quite clearly that the boy is not a werewolf," Speranza said, trying to keep calm. "Stay with him. I'm going to bring the Count. We'll settle this matter once and for all. Stay with the boy, do you understand?"

The girl had thrown herself against the wall and was sobbing passionately. "What's the *matter* with you?" Speranza said. She was losing all patience now. It was one thing to take charge of a child for a few days . . . quite another to be made to cope with an entire trainload of madmen. The maid's hysteria grated on her ears. She could endure it no longer. She stalked out into the corridor and slammed the door of the compartment.

In that moment Jonas leapt into the clearing, seized control of the body, forced open the child's tired eyes, which glowed like fire in the light of the moon.

And howled.

Speranza felt the dread again. It must be the wind, she thought, the desolate relentless wind. It was howling down the hallway. The walls were damp, and snow glistened on the threadbare carpet.

She had to see him. She had to unmask his terrible deception, had to allay this dread that gnawed at her and would not release her . . . she made her way to the end of the corridor, stumbling as the train lurched. She opened the door.

The wind came, whistling, abrasive. She grasped a handhold. There was no one to help her step over the coupling mechanism, which groaned and clanked between the two cars. An animal's cry sounded above the pounding of the train and the clanging of the couplers. The forest stretched in every direction. They were moving downhill. She took a deep breath and skipped across, feeling frantically for a railing. The howling came again. So close . . . it almost seemed to be coming from the train itself and not the forest.

She peered into the Count's private car. Black drapes shrouded the window. "Let me in!" she cried, banging on the glass with her fists.

Abruptly the door opened. She fell into utter darkness.

She heard the door slam. She could see nothing. The air was close and foul. Even the clerestory windows had been covered up. "Count . . ." she whispered.

"You came."

His voice was changed. There was a rasp to it. She stood near the doorway. She could see nothing, nothing at all.

"Come closer, Speranza. Do not be afraid. The utter darkness does tend to impede the transformation a little. You see, I do have your interests at heart."

She hesitated. The stench filled her nostrils. Its fetor masked a more subtle odor, an odor that was strangely exciting. She backed against the door. The train's motion made her tingle. She was sweating. Still she saw nothing. But she could hear him breathing . . .

"You're driving the boy mad," she whispered. "Though it's true that I am being paid, I ought perhaps to dissociate myself from—"

"You did not come here to discuss business, Speranza. Am I wrong?"

The smell was seeping into her . . . she felt a retching at the back of her throat . . . and a stirring, a dark stirring beneath her petticoats . . . "No, Count—" she said softly, at last admitting her shameful desire to herself.

"Only the king wolf mates," said the Count, "and he takes for his consort a female from another tribe. . . . ."

Something furry had reached up her skirts. It touched her thigh. It was searing hot. She whimpered. The hand stroked her, burned her . . . moved inexorably up towards her private parts . . . it caressed them now, and she cried out in pain, but there was pleasure behind the pain, and the warmth burst through her body as it shuddered, as it vibrated with the downhill movement of the train . . . "You must not . . . you ought not to . . ." she said . . . she felt something moist teasing at the lips of her vagina, and she felt her inner moisture mingling with sweat and saliva . . . I must resist him, she thought, I would be ruined . . . yet she made no move to escape, for the fire was racing in her nerves and veins. . . .

The hands roved, brutal now. Something lacerated her thighs . . . she moaned at the sharp pain . . . were they claws or hands? My imagination is running wild, she thought. The madness is infecting me. The cloth was tearing now. She felt hot blood spurting. "No," she said, trying to tear herself away, "no, don't hurt me." The Count did not answer her with words but with a growl that resonated against her sexual organs. She tried to inch away, but the hands gripped her thighs tighter. She could see nothing, nothing at all, but the railway car smelled of musk and mud and rotten leaves, the air was dank and clogged with the smells of rutting and animal piss . . . at last she managed to free herself. She groped along the wall . . . the wall was clammy, like a earthy embankment . . . her feet were sliding in damp soil. . . .

I'm dreaming! she thought. It's because of the darkness. I'm starting to imagine things—

Her hand touched something soft now. Curtains. I have to let in the light, she thought. She tugged at the velvet. A sliver of moonlight lanced the darkness and—

The Count's voice, barely human, "You should not have—not the light—I will change now—change—"

The curtain fell away and the moonlight streamed in across glittering fields of snow. . . .

The Count . . . his face . . . his nose had elongated into a snout. Even as she watched he was changing. Bristles sprouting on his cheeks. His teeth were lengthening, his mouth widening into the foaming jaws of an animal. The eyes . . . bright yellow now, slitty, implacable. His hands, already covered with hair, were shrinking into paws. With a snarl the Count fell down on all fours. His teeth were slick with drool. The stench intensified. Her gorge rose. She tasted vomit in the back of her throat. Then the wolf leapt.

She was thrown back. She fell down into the patch of moonlight. The beast was ripping away her dress now. It still desires me, she thought. The wolf's spit sprayed her face and ran down her neck. She tried to beat it back but it straddled her now, about to sink its teeth into her throat—

It touched the silver necklace—

And recoiled, howling! Speranza scrambled to her feet. The wolf watched her warily. Where its snout had touched the necklace, there was a burn mark . . . an impression of the silver links in the chain. The wolf whined and growled. There was a smell of charred fur. Her heart beat fast. The trickling drool scalded her neck, her exposed breasts.

She found the door, flung it open, ran, clambered across to the next car, entered. As she slammed the door shut, she heard an anguished howling over the cacophony of steam and iron.

For a long moment she stood. The howling died away, or was drowned by the clatter of the train. She stood, her arms crossed over the front of her tattered chemise, the chill air numbing the places where the wolf's touch had seared her.

She touched the silver necklace. It was cool to her fingers. She thought: impossible, it's all impossible.

Could it have been done with conjurer's tricks? With pails of animal dung, with suggestive disguises, preying on a mind already primed to expect a supernatural metamorphosis? Moonlight streamed into the corridor. They were emerging from the forest now. There were mountains in the distance. In the middle distance was a church, enveloped in snow, its spire catching the cold light and softly glittering.

She thought of Johnny.

Whatever the Count was, he was trying to make Johnny into one, too. Perhaps it was all some inhuman scientific experiment . . . or some kind of devil-worship. Had Cornelius Quaid not spoken of mutilations and atrocities? The poor child!

I must steal him away, she thought. I cannot suffer him to remain here, succored by lunatics, a lamb amongst wolves!

Perhaps they had done something to him already. . . .

She opened the door of the compartment.

Wind gusted in her face. The window had been smashed. The floor, the seats, were blanketed in snow. "Where is he?" she said.

She could not see the young maidservant. Only something lying on one of the seats, covered in a blanket. Much of the car was in shadow; perhaps the maid was lurking in a corner, ashamed of something she had done to the boy! But Speranza did not want to contemplate it. . . .

"Where is the boy?" Speranza said.

There was no answer.

"Where is he? He was entrusted to your care!"

Still there was no response.

"I have had enough of these enigmas!" Speranza said. Anger and frustration deluged her. She strode into the compartment, meaning to slap the servant's face.

Slowly the blanket slid away. Beneath it was a small boy, naked, disconsolately sobbing. There was blood everywhere; the seat looked as though it had been painted with it. It was clear that the maid had tumbled to her death—that is, if she had not been dead *before* she was cast out.

"Johnny!" She was too shocked to feel revulsion at first.

Slowly the boy's cries ceased. Slowly he lifted his head up. His mouth, his cheeks were smeared with blood, black in the silver moonlight. His hair was matted with it. He said, "I tried to stop Jonas from coming. I *tried*, Speranza. Oh, I didn't want you to know, I threw her out of the window, but I didn't have enough time . . . Oh, Speranza, it's hopeless, I'm never going to be like you and the other humans."

Speranza remembered what the Count von Bächl-Wölfing had said to her also: "Therefore, Speranza, I long for hope." She knew she could not abandon the boy now. Even though he had killed. It was a sickness, a terrible sickness. She swallowed her dread and allowed him to come to her arms. "Oh, Johnny, you must have hope!" she cried out.

"Yes, I must, mustn't I?" said the child. And he wept bitterly, as though the world were ending, the tears mingling with coagulating blood.

Speranza did not sleep at all that night. She held the child firmly to her bosom, and allowed him to sob until he was quite spent. Little Johnny trembled in her arms, and behind the clatter of the train and the wind whistling through the broken window pane she could hear a faint and plaintive howling from von Bächl-Wölfing's private car. She dared not close her eyes; no, she told herself, I cannot, not until I am sure that the moon has set behind those snowy mountains.

It was cold, unconscionably cold; but a feverish heat arose from the boy's body, and now and then he seemed different, his arms dangling at a strange angle, his nose oddly distended, his cheeks covered with silvery down. Each time she thought he had somehow transformed himself she would look away, her heart pounding; but when she looked back he was always a little child again. And she thought: I am mad, I am imagining everything. After some hours there came a dank odor of putrescence from the bloodstained seat. Speranza resolutely faced the shattered window, letting the fresh chill wind mask the faint stench of decay.

"There are no monsters," she whispered to herself over and over. "Only bad dreams."

And they reached Vienna the next morning, and drove to the Spiegelgasse in a carriage with an impressive-looking footman as their guide.

On the left, twin staircases led to a baroque façade. There was a long line of carriages along the side of the street. Some were the ordinary station carriages; others were private, and blazoned with various emblems and insignia. One was an imported American Concord, and it was this one that bore the von Bächl-Wölfing arms. People were dismounting from their carriages and being escorted up the steps by footmen. The air was cloudy with horses' breath and rank with their manure; two brawny lads in uniform were sweeping dung off the snowy pavement, chattering to each other in some Slavic dialect.

"This is the residence of Dr. Szymanowski?" Speranza asked.

"Oh, no!" Johnny piped up. "This is the town house of that Count, the one who frightens me so."

"There is nothing to be afraid of. He is a very generous man."

For a moment Speranza panicked, thinking that the boy would once more attempt to baptize the Count's dwelling with urine. But there was no invasion from the mysterious Jonas, and the boy was nothing if not angelic—almost alarmingly so, Speranza thought.

The guide spoke. "Dr. Szymanowski comes from a little town in Poland—Oswieçim—Auschwitz, we call it in German—and the Count has graciously allowed him the use of an apartment in the town house, along with some basement space for his experiments. He's a harmless old fool, the doctor. Quite round the bend, I'm afraid. He is an expert, you know, in the . . . ah . . . in the mating patterns of wolves."

Speranza watched as the Count's guests ascended the steps. Each seemed more outlandish than the last. There was a turbaned gentleman now, whose silken garments, stitched with jewels, almost blinded her with their colors: turquoise, shocking pink, lemon, and pea-green. There was a ragged, stooped old woman who looked just like one of those operatic gipsy fortune tellers. There were elegantly dressed men, in top hats and opera cloaks, and there were those whose origins seemed less than aristocratic; but all were accorded equal deference by the Count's retainers.

They entered through the tradesmen's door, concealed from the street by the twin ornamental balustrades of the grand façade.

A kind of soirée was in progress; she and Johnny stood beside the grand doorway of the ballroom and listened to the chatter, the laughter, the strains of a string quartet. Was it her imagination, or was there mixed into that laughter a sound like wild wolves' howling? She beckoned to Johnny and, gripping his hand, stepped out into a vast ballroom, lit by glittering chandeliers, filled with guests in opulent clothes, decorated with marble statues and unicorn tapestries and pastoral paintings, permeated with the faint but insistent odor of canine piss. . . .

Johnny clutched her hand tightly as they stood beside the doorway. In her severe black dress, wearing the single strand of silver around her neck, Speranza had never felt more out of place. The guests paid her no regard at all; most were deep in conversation with one another, and a few stood next to the dais beside the French windows at one end of the ballroom, where the string quartet was performing, the four musicians immaculately dressed in tails, starched wing collars, hunched over their music stands. The French windows were shuttered, admitting neither fresh air nor evening light, and although the hall was spacious, the air was dank and close.

An old man in a dinner jacket stood aloof from the others. From the whispered remarks she overheard, she knew it must be Dr. Szymanowski—the man who, according to the Count, was the architect of some grand scheme that would transform the lives of all werewolves. . . .

She stood, a little embarrassed, not quite certain what she was expected to do. Presently one of the guests—the richly attired Indian whom she had seen enter the town house—accosted her. "Mademoiselle," he said, and continued in heavily accented German, "Sie sind also auch beim Lykanthropenverein—"

"I have no German," she said with a smile.

"Oh, I am jolly glad," he said. "It is good to be encountering a fellow subject of her Britannic Majesty, isn't it?" He surveyed her haughtily, twirling one end of his moustache as he spoke, and extending to her, with his other hand, an open snuffbox made of gold and inlaid with amethysts, emeralds, and mother-of-pearl. "You will perhaps be caring for snuff?" When she demurred, he clapped his hands and a little Negro boy, costumed in an embroidered silk tunic stitched in gold thread, sidled up to him and took the snuffbox from his hands. "Perhaps you will be preferring a cigarette? I know that amongst you people cigarettes are considered more becoming in a woman than the more vulgar incarnations of tobacco. But where we are going, cigarettes are very costly, so I understand."

"We are going—" She noticed that Johnny was sniffing the air and glancing shiftily from side to side, and held on to him even more tightly. "I am not quite sure what you mean."

"Ah, but let us not be speaking of the stark, pioneering future! Let us revel in our past while we may. I will jolly well be missing my homeland. You are, from your manner of dressing, an Englishwoman, isn't it?"

"I'm French actually. But I have lived in England. And this boy, who has at present been entrusted to my care, is English, as he will tell you himself."

"Nevertheless—for we cannot all be fortunate enough to be born beneath that destiny-laden Britannic star—I salute you, madam." He bowed deeply to her, and the peacock plumes that adorned his turban quivered. Johnny reached out and tried to touch them, and laughed when they tickled his fingers. "And, young sahib, I salute you most humbly. I am called Shri Chandraputra Dhar, and was once Lord High Astrologer to the Nawab of Bhaktibhumi, before I was sent away in disgrace and shame, for reasons which no doubt you will already have guessed."

"I'm sure I don't know what you mean," Speranza said. They all seemed to assume that she was one of them, that she knew their secrets. Were they all mad?

The young Negro page reappeared as if by magic with a tray, some glasses of champagne and a small dish of caviar, and Chandraputra idly ran his finger through the boy's curls. "I no longer serve the Nawab, but his Grace the Count is being kind enough to allow me a position in his household, for which I am being most humbly and abjectly grateful. But you are doubtless understanding me when I say that blood is thicker than water, especially that blood that runs in the

veins of those who walk between the two worlds. You will of course
know this from your own experience, Miss . . ."

"Martinique," Speranza said. His talk of blood disturbed her. She
remembered her dream of the river of blood. The air seemed thicker
now, as though the ballroom somehow had been transported to the
edge of a dark forest. "And the boy's name is—"

"James," the boy said distinctly. His manner of speaking was quite
different from any she had heard him use before: refined, almost
haughty, like that of a servant in a highborn household. "My name is
James Karney, if you please, sir."

"Oh, nonsense, child!" Speranza said in exasperation. "Do excuse
my charge, Mr. Chandraputra . . . we are both very tired from our
journey across Europe, and young Johnny Kindred is very much
given to make-believe—"

"Ah! He is the one with many names!" said Shri Chandraputra.
"Now I understand everything." To Speranza's amazement, the Indian fell on his knees before the child and gazed upon him with a
humility that would have seemed comical were it not so full of
earnest. He rose, grasped Speranza's hand fervently, and stooped to
kiss it. His nose felt curiously cold against her hand, almost like a
dog's. "You, madam, you, you . . . all our company is honoring you
. . . you, *you* are, in all truth, the very Madonna of the Wolves
incarnate! Ah, Countess, to have given birth to the one who will be a
bridge between our two races . . . permit me to be the first to
worship. Boy! Boy! Champagne, mountains of caviar! Or shall I be
fetching the gold, the frankincense, the myrrh?"

"Surely, sir, you are making fun of me," Speranza said, laughing
out loud at last, for the fellow was making an astonishing spectacle of
himself. "This is no Christ, but a poor, half-crazed young child who
cries out for affection; and I am no madonna but a mere governess in
the Count's employ."

"Then you are not having the privilege of being the child's
mother?" said Shri Chandraputra, raising one eyebrow skeptically.

"No," she said, "I am afraid that honor is not mine," and started to
turn away.

She was not comfortable in his presence. But he was standing in
between her and the doorway into the inner parlor. Since she could
not retreat, she steeled herself and dived into the throng, seizing a
glass of champagne from a passing footman as she did so. She saw

the Indian whispering into the ear of another guest and pointing to her. A couple who had been waltzing stopped and stared with naked curiosity. Speranza turned and saw others pointing, tittering. The music was abruptly cut off as one of the guests rushed over to tell the latest gossip to the quartet players. Frantically she looked down at her dress, wondering whether she had accidentally exposed some part of her person.

For a few seconds there was no sound at all, and the guests stood stock-still, their jewels glittering, their eyes narrowed, like predators preparing to pounce.

The smell intensified. Sweet-sour fragrance of rotting leaves. A dank forest. The rutting of wild beasts.

Then she heard a whisper somewhere in the crowd: "Der Mond steht in einer halbe Stunde auf." And the others nodded to each other and slowly backed away from her. And glanced warily at each other, taking each other's measure, like fellow beasts of prey. And the Indian astrologer growled at her . . . growled, like an angry hound!

"Der Mond steht auf . . ."

Moonrise . . . in half an hour!

"A dance!" A woman in an embroidered gown stretched out her delicate arms and languorously shrilled: "A dance, my dears, before we all turn into ravening beasts!"

The string quartet, joined by a pianist, burst into a rhapsodic waltz, and all around Speranza guests formed couples and swept out to the center of the ballroom.

"Speranza, Speranza, I'm frightened!" Where was the voice coming from? She thought she saw the boy, scuttling behind a tall man who was doffing his hat to a petite old woman wrapped in a voluminous shawl. She made off in the man's direction, and he turned to her, smiling, his arm outstretched to invite her to the dance, and his teeth were white, and knife-sharp, and glistening with drool. . . .

"Speranza!" It was coming from somewhere else . . . from behind her. The music welled up, and with it the mingled smells of lust and terror. . . .

Where is the child? she thought. I must find the child, I must protect him from these madmen!

There he was, talking to Dr. Szymanowski . . . were her eyes deluding her, or was the professor's face becoming longer, his nose more snoutlike, his eyes more narrow and inhuman? His smile had become a canine leer, and the tufts of hair pushing up through his bald scalp—

No! She rushed to the boy's side and grasped his hand. His palm was bristly, hot. She pulled him from the professor's side. "We've got to get away from these people," she said. "Come on, Johnny. Please."
I mustn't let my dread show, mustn't startle the child, mustn't provoke the monster inside him—

"I've killed Johnny forever, I'm with my own people now!" The boy's voice was deep and rasping. Dr. Szymanowski snarled at her, and she saw saliva running down his chin, which was sprouting dark hairs, and she held on to Johnny and elbowed her way through the guests as they danced frantically to the accelerating music, the jewelled gowns and the chandeliers whirled, she lashed out with her free hand and sent champagne glasses crashing onto the Persian carpet with its design of wolves chasing each other's tails in an infinite spiral—

"Speranza, I'm afraid—" Johnny's tiny voice was interrupted by the voice of the other. "Get back inside! It's not your turn anymore. Get back inside and let me kill the bitch!'

"Johnny!"

Shri Chandraputra Dhar had torn off his turban now and had dropped down on all fours. He was sloughing his face. He howled as though racked by the pain of childbirth. Pieces of flayed skin hung from his neck, his palms. Blood gushed from his eyes like tears. His nails were lengthening, his hands shrivelling into paws. Speranza could not move, though her heart was pounding, for there was in his transformation a fierce, alien beauty.

The woman in the elegant gown screeched, "Oh, how tedious, my dears . . . it's that hotblooded oriental nature . . . even with the moon shut out he's off and howling. Oh, someone see to him before he sets everybody else off—" Her words trailed off into inchoate screaming, and fangs jutted from her moist, painted lips, and hairs were poking through her porcelain complexion—

Speranza ran, dragging the boy behind her.

Two footmen guarded the double oak doors that led to the vestibule. They bowed and let her through. The doors slammed shut behind them. Speranza was shaking. The boy wrested himself free of her grip and looked at her.

"Why are you taking me away from them?" he said softly. "I

understand their language a little, I think. And I belong to them somehow." It was the voice of Johnny Kindred once again: always afraid, always a little child.

From behind the massive doors came howling, snarling, screeching, growling, to the accompaniment of passionate music. The vestibule was dark. A single candelabrum, at the foot of a sweeping staircase, flickered forlornly. The walls were hung with purple velvet drapes, and the floor was richly carpeted, siphoning away the faint sound of their footsteps.

And Speranza was at a loss to answer him. There was fear here; there was a palpable, brooding evil; and yet she too had felt the allure of darkness. She dared not remain, and yet . . . she thought of the times when, helping the Hon. Michael Bridgewater with his Latin verbs, or pouring tea at one of Lord Slatterthwaite's interminable garden parties, she had fallen into a reverie of thoughts too dark, too sensual to allow of public expression. Even then she had dreamed of being touched, in the midst of a primal forest, by a creature barely human, and of succumbing to a shuddering delight that was laced with pain and death. And she had thought to herself: I am vile, I am utterly without shame, to let such lewd thoughts surface in myself. She knew that it would be best to take the child away forever. But the abyss at whose edge they both stood called out to them.

So she did not respond; she merely held the child close to herself. He seemed dazed. He moved, scratching her arms and drawing blood. She stared at his fingernails in the half-light. They had lengthened and crooked themselves into the shape of claws. But his face had not changed.

"We'll go away from here," Speranza said. "If you're away from these people, you'll not become one of them."

"Could it be so simple?" said the boy.

Ahead was the massive front entrance she had earlier seen from the outside; the doors, inlaid with ivory and gilt, were shadowed, and she saw only glimpses of the sylvan scene depicted on them.

The doorknobs were the paws of wolves that faced each other in a contest of wills; in the meager light their eyes, which were cabochon topazes set into the wood, glowed with an intense ferocity. She backed away, still carrying the child in her arms.

Behind her: laughter, music, the howling of wolves.

Gingerly she touched the doorknob, turned it—

The portals swung open! Footmen stood on either side. And, framed in the doorway, tall, dark against the driving snow, his cloak billowing in the wind, stood the man she most dreaded: the man who had brought her to the brink of darkness, and who had awakened in her such unconscionable desires. . . .

"Speranza," he said. "I see you have decided to remain with us."

"Your guests—they are—they are changing—becoming wild animals—"

"Tush! Could they not wait for moonrise? Do they have so little self-discipline? They will destroy all that I have worked for! I begin to regret that I called together this gathering of the Lykanthropenverein."

"Lykan—" She had heard the word spoken many times now; it was one of those Germanic portmanteau words, and she had paid it little regard. But now she looked at him questioningly, and he responded:

"The Society of Werewolves, my dear Speranza. Of which I find myself, by right of single combat, the Herr Präsident. Oh, it was stupid of me to arrange for the meeting at the Vienna residence . . . we could be seen, we could be noticed . . . far better to have the gathering at my estates in Wallachia . . . it was a silly gesture on my part, to encourage such openness, such ostentation!" The Count sighed. "But . . . you were on your way out, were you not, Mademoiselle Martinique?"

She summoned up her last reserves of defiance. "I cannot allow you or Dr. Szymanowski to take charge of this child, Count von Bächl-Wölfing. I apologize for my failure to perform my duties, and I shall attempt to repay your generous stipend when I have obtained some other employment—"

"Have you consulted the child?"

"No . . . but of course he doesn't want to stay here! He's a frightened little boy, a lamb amongst wolves. He needs tenderness and warmth, not your mad professor's bestial experiments!"

"Ask him."

"I don't need to ask him . . . I can see the terror in his eyes, I can tell by the way he clings to my side."

"Ask him!"

He clapped his hands. The doors slammed shut, and the footmen, holding their kerosene lamps aloft, entered and stood on either side of the Count. She heard a voice shriek out from the ballroom within:

"Only one more minute until the fatal hour—only one more minute until moonrise!"

The boy extricated himself from Speranza's arms. In the lamplight he cast a huge double shadow against the velvet drapes. He shrank away from the Count; and yet there was in his eyes a certain awe, a certain love.

"Oh, Speranza, don't ask me to choose between you. Oh, Speranza, I do love you, but I have to stay, don't you see? I know that now." As he spoke the reek of canine urine became suddenly more powerful, choking her almost. And the boy spoke again, in the deep voice of Jonas: "He is my father."

"You see?" said von Bächl-Wölfing. "The child knows instinctively. Instinctively! He is my son, conceived on an English harlot in Whitechapel, raised in a madhouse, but my blood runs true—he has the eyes of the wolf, the senses, the memory; he knows me for what I am. And, since he has learnt to call me father, I acknowledge him, I embrace him as mine."

"You can't mean—" Speranza began, trying to shield Johnny from him with her arms. But the boy himself pushed her brusquely aside. His eyes glowed now. The feral odor became more rank, more suffocating.

The Count spread his arms wide to receive the child. With halting steps the boy came forward. Through the stained glass moon above the door, Speranza could see the rising of the real moon, pale and haloed by the icy air. The Count's cloak flapped as the wind gusted around it.

The boy stood close to the Count now, dwarfed. The Count enfolded him in the cloak. Speranza cried out the boy's name, but her voice was lost in the wind's howling and the cacophony from the ballroom. . . .

The Count looked longingly into her eyes. His gaze mesmerized her; she could not move. There was in it a kind of love. The Count advanced toward her, and already his lips were being wrenched apart as the wolf's jaw began extruding itself from within. As she stood transfixed, he began to court her in Italian: "Come sei bella, fanciulla; come sei bella, o mia Speranza." The voice was harsh, guttural, a travesty of her native tongue . . . yet the wolf was wooing her, trying to make love to her. Her blood raced. Her skin tingled. A hand reached out to her from under the cloak: a twisted, furry hand. A claw grazed her cheek. She closed her eyes, shuddering, desiring yet loathing him. Her cheek burned where his paw had touched it. She did not retreat from him, for he held the child captive still, and she told herself that to effect the child's rescue from this brutish destiny must be a sacred task for which she must sacrifice what small chastity she could lay claim to. She met his gaze with defiance.

"I'll save him yet . . . somehow. . . ."

"Will you, my Madonna of the Wolves? I have a fancy to make you one of us this very moment. A bite from me should suffice. Or else I could force you to drink the dew that has formed in one of my footprints; we keep phials of such precious fluids in this house for just such an occasion. Or perhaps you would care to wear the sacred pelt of my ancestors, which being worn can be cast off only by death?"

"I could never become one of you."

His paw continued to stroke her cheek, drawing blood now. She shook her head, loosening the silver necklace from beneath her collar. The Count recoiled. His voice was barely human: "Consider yourself fortunate, mademoiselle, that you are wearing the necklace! The servants will show you to your room! You are safe until the next full moon!"

His forehead was flattening now, his brow creasing and uncreasing as bristles began to shoot out from folds of skin. He howled, and a uniformed servant emerged from an antechamber, lantern in hand.

"If the gnädiges Fräulein would care to follow me," he said, bowing deeply.

She hesitated. She was about to protest when the Count cast aside his cloak and she saw the wolf cub leap from his arms, and she knew that Johnny was beyond help, that night at least. In the morning she would see what could be done with him. She could not abandon the boy now, never, never.

From her little room—a garret, more or less—in the attic of the von Bächl-Wölfing town house, Speranza was able to see the street below and the private park, for the snow had abated a little and the moon was full. From below there came howling: not the cacophony she had witnessed in the ballroom, but something far more purposeful. First came a single note, drawn out, with an almost metallic resonance. Then another joined in, on another pitch, stridently dissonant with the first; then came a third and a fourth, each adding a note to the disharmony. The window rattled. Her very bones seemed to feel the vibration.

The howling crescendoed. The floor trembled against her feet. The chair she sat in was shaking. And suddenly it was over. She heard a slamming sound, and she saw the wolves pouring out into the street. They streamed past the row of parked carriages. She was glad none of the horses had been left outside.

When they howled they had seemed hundreds, but now she saw there were only perhaps twenty. They stood, still as statues, for a few moments, in the middle of the alley, their breath steaming up the air. Snow flecked their pelts. Their leader's fur was black and streaked with silver just as the Count's hair was . . . and beside him stood a young pup, the very one she had seen leaping out of the Count's opera cloak . . . and behind them other wolves. Even from this far up she could see how their eyes glowed. The moon was low, and the wolves cast giant shadows across the wrought iron angel gates of the park. The leader shook the snow from his fur and looked from side to side. Then they moved. Sinuously, with an alien grace, almost as one. A sharp bark from their leader and they began to trot down the Spiegelgasse. Quite silently, for the deep snow muffled the patter of their paws. At the corner, the wolves turned and vanished behind a stone wall.

She watched a while longer. But at length she was overcome by an intense weariness, and went to her bed. Her sleep was fitful, for she dreamt of the forest, and the river, and the lupine lover waiting for her at its source.

The wolfling sniffed the chill air and shook the snow out of his pelt. At last he had quelled the rebellion in his soul . . . at last he was as he was meant to be: proud, ferocious, one with the darkness. He was unsteady on his feet at first. But he imitated his father's gait and soon fell into its liquid rhythm.

The wolves moved silently. Now and then the wolfling's father paused to mark his scent, arrogantly lifting his leg to urinate on some memorable spot: a stone, a brick wall, the wheel of a cart. They spoke a language of the dark: now and then with a whine or a bark, more often with a quick motion of the head or a quiver of a nostril or a glance.

"My son," said the leader with his eyes, as the pack slipped into the shadow of another alley. "My son. How much I rejoice that I have found you . . . and that you are truly one of us, able to change . . ."

"Why did you not seek me out before?" the wolfling cried out with a shrug and a circular motion of his paws.

"Because," said his father, lashing the snow with his tail, "I was afraid. Your mother was not one of us."

"My mother. . . ."

There was another voice within the wolfling's mind, a voice that seemed to cry out: No, I am not one of these . . . I am a child, a human.

Whose was this inner voice? The young wolf followed his father, faster now, darting from shadow to shadow. The voice distressed him. It did not belong here. It was good to be this way. Good to paw the ground and sniff the air. The air was vivid: he could smell the blood of distant prey, racing, already sensing death. The inner voice spoke again, saying, This vision is bleak, gray, colorless . . . but the wolfling did not understand what the voice meant, for his eyes could not see color, only infinite gradations of light and shadow. And the possessor of the inner voice could not seem to grasp the richness of sound and scent he was experiencing, but continually bemoaned the absence of this thing he called color.

He pushed the voice further back into his mind. It was a useless thing, a vestige of some past existence. He followed his father. The pack had split up now. There were the two of them, hunting as father and son.

Hunting! For the pit of his stomach burned with an all-consuming hunger. Not only for fresh, warm meat, but for the act of killing. . . .

Abruptly his father stopped, cocked his head. The wind had dropped. The snow fell straight down. Footsteps, human footsteps. He smelled blood: sluggish blood, tainted with the sour smell of wine. "Come, my son," his father said with an imperious bark. "We will celebrate together, you and I, the mystery of life and death. The quarry is nigh."

He saw nothing. They did not move. The smell came closer. There was a shape to the smell, a two-legged shape. He stood beside his father, tense, waiting. A second shape, much smaller, beside the first. What were they doing in the cold, in the dark? His father growled . . . a faint, ominous sound, like a distant earth tremor.

The snow thinned and the young wolf saw more. The quarry was on the steps of a church. There was a woman and a child, perhaps four or five years old. A half-empty bottle lay next to them. There was a small puddle of wine on the snow. They were shivering, huddled together under a man's greatcoat.

The woman was muttering to herself in some Slavic tongue, and rocking the child back and forth. She wore a woolen shawl; beneath it he could see wisps of gray hair. She had a drawn, pinched face. The child was sullen, distracted. He could not smell what sex the child was; it was too young.

"They are street people," said the wolfling's father. "They have strayed from the herd. They have sought the desolation of the cold and dark. They belong to us."

And loped up the steps, his jaws wide open, while his son followed closely behind.

At first the woman did not even seem to notice. The wolf circled her several times. Then he pounced.

She let go of the child. The child began to whine. Its scrawny shoulders showed through the torn nightshirt. It began to clamber up the steps towards her. The wine bottle rolled away, chiming as it hit each step. The wolfling watched his father and the woman. For a few seconds they gazed at each other, neither of them moving, oblivious to the bawling of the child. In those moments it seemed almost as though they were exchanging vows, each choosing the other as partner in the ritual of death.

Then his father leapt. He tore out her throat with his jaws. There was an eerie whistling as the wind left her. The child, crying, was pummeling at the wolf's side with its fists, but the wolf ignored it. The woman's shawl, pinned between her torso and the steps, fluttered in the wind.

The wolfling smelled the child's fear. It maddened him. He rushed at the child. The child's eyes widened. It backed away, up the steps. Then it turned and began to run. The wolfling followed. The child's blood smelled warmer than the woman's.

There was a door at the top of the steps. The child pounded at it with tiny fists. It did not budge. The wolfling jumped up, clawing at the nightshirt, gouging out great gashes in the child's chest and arms. Suddenly the door gave way. A rusty bolt, perhaps. The child ran inside. Through the rips in the nightshirt the wolfling saw its tiny vulva, and knew its gender for the first time.

He smelled incense. And dust. And sweet fragrance of over-varnished rotting wood. In the distance there was an altar. A painted stone Pietà stood guard in the antechapel. There were candles everywhere.

The girl ran. He followed the sound of her footsteps, shoeless on the stone floor. She was hiding somewhere among the pews. She was panting. He could smell her exhaustion, her desperation. It was only a matter of time. He felt his heart pounding. He heard her heartbeat too, and paused to pinpoint it.

There! He scurried down the aisle. She was under the altar. He ripped the altarcloth with his jaws and found her huddled, clasping a leg of the altar, sobbing. Roughly he threw her down, hulking over her, teasing her face with his tongue and the edges of his teeth, urinating on her to show his possession. And gazed at her, as he had seen his father gaze into the eyes of the woman.

He saw her fear. And behind her fear he saw something else, too . . . a kind of invitation . . . the dark side of desire. He sensed that what they were doing together, hunter and quarry, was a sacred thing, a dance of life and death. The girl trembled. Pain racked her body. He spoke to her in the language of the forest, asking her forgiveness; and she answered in the same language, the language that men believe they have forgotten until such moments as these, giving him permission to take her life.

He was about to tear her apart when a long shadow fell across them both. He looked up and saw his father. Blood dripped from his jaws. There was a trail of blood from the antechapel all the way up the nave. His eyes glowed. His breath clouded the musty air.

"Now," said his father. "Kill. Feel the joy. Feel the spurting blood. Bathe in its warmth."

"I feel no joy," the wolfling said, "only a strange solemnity. I feel a kind of kinship with her."

"Good! You understand the law of the forest well, my son! Men see us as unreasoning, ravening beasts, but that is not all we are. We are not simply Satan's children. There are some of us to whom the killing is nothing more than the exercise of lust. Perhaps most of our little society are like that. But with you it is something more. Good.

You are truly my son. To lead the Lykanthropenverein you must be more than a crazed creature of death . . . you must also feel a certain love for your victims. Now kill quickly. Shock her nervous system so that she will no longer feel pain."

The wolfling bent over the girl, ready to despatch her. Then he heard the inner voice: "Get away! Go back into the darkness! I want the body!" There were several other voices, too. Voices of humans. There was a mutiny going on inside his mind! The other personalities were seizing control! He struggled. But he was losing his grip. The girl was fighting him. And there was something going wrong with the vibrant layers of scents and fragrances around him . . . he was losing his sense of smell . . . the shapes were shifting too, darkening, becoming fringed with garish *colors.* . . .

Johnny Kindred snapped into consciousness beneath an altar inside a huge church, with a little girl in his arms. Her eyes widened. She began jabbering away in a foreign language. She pointed. There was a black wolf in the church. Staring at the two of them. Its fur was matted with bright red blood. Blood and drool dribbled from its teeth, which glistened golden in the candlelight.

"Jonas won't harm you," Johnny said to the girl. "I've sent him away."

The wolf growled. Johnny felt that he could almost understand what he was saying. If Jonas were nearby he could translate, but Jonas was being held down by the others. He was not being allowed to go anywhere near the clearing.

"The big bad wolf won't harm you," Johnny said, stroking the girl's curly hair, "he's . . . my father."

At dawn she drifted into sleep. And dreamed.

There was a forest. She ran among thick trees. She wore no corsets, no confining garments. Her hair was long and free to fly in the hot wind. She was naked but she felt no guilt because she was clothed in darkness. The air reeked of a woman's menses. Her feet were bare. They trod the soft earth. Moist leaves clung to her soles. Twigs lacerated her arms, her thighs, but the pain was a joyous pain, like the pangs of a lascivious passion. Worms crawled along her toes and tickled them and made her laugh. She laughed and her laughter became an animal's howling.

The primal atmosphere put her in mind of a witches' sabbath, or perhaps one of those bacchanalian orgies of the ancient Greeks, with the wild women who used to dance around and tear wild animals to pieces with their bare hands.

A brief memory surfaced: she was helping young Michael Bridgewater with his Euripides one day, only to come across passages which she could not in all decency translate . . . at least not into English, for in that language things that could be made to sound elevated in Italian or French were rendered intolerably crude. It was this enforced crudity, she had reflected at the time, that gave the English their preoccupation with prurience. And then they had lowered young Michael into the ground and it seemed as though it had not stopped snowing, as though she'd never escape the snow, not even by fleeing across half Europe. . . .

Here there was no snow.

No snow at all. There was moisture that dripped from the branches overhead, that oozed out of the earth, that was wrung out of the very air. The ground was slippery. She slid, glided almost, cried out with childish delight as the very earth seemed to carry her along. And always came that pungent scent of menstrual blood.

Light broke over leaves streaked with black and silver. Moonlight over a stream. She sat at the edge, bathing her feet. The water warm, like fresh blood . . . the ground trembling a little, with the regularity of a heartbeat . . . and she heard the cry of a wolf, distant, mournful. The sound was both repulsive and somehow alluring. She knew it might well be a love song, if she could but understand its language. . . .

And in the dream she knew, as by a profound inspiration, that the howling came from the water's source. The beast was waiting for her upstream. And that she was drawn to the beast as the beast was drawn to her. . . .

And when she awoke she saw the Count von Bächl-Wölfing standing at the foot of her bed, and the boy beside him, clutching his cloak, as the rays of dawn broke through the high window.

The Count said: "Speranza, these are the last days of the old world. You know why we have gathered here. Dr. Szymanowski's grand scheme is this: in the spring we, the werewolves, will travel to America. There is wilderness there. There is ample food—thousands upon thousands of acres of land untouched by civilization, where only the savages live, and they will be our quarry. We will build our own kingdom, our private paradise. We will hunt by night and by day we will sing songs. America will be our utopia and you will be its queen, my Madonna of the Wolves."

She had sworn to herself that she would never leave the child. Now she understood at last all that that meant. She had been chosen. Beneath her black dresses and austere demeanor, she too harbored a beast within. A passion that could only be slaked by darkest love.

"The boy has no mother now," said von Bächl-Wölfing. "And he has come to love you."

"And I him," she said.

"We must guard him well. He is a completely new kind of child— he is very special—the first link between my kind and your kind. You understand that, don't you?"

"It is a pity about his mother. . . ." He did not look at her, and she got the impression that he was remembering some past unpleasantness. "Some of the wolves think of him as a savior, a redeemer. Because he is a link between the two species—proof that we are of man, and man is of us. That's the real reason I want to go to the New World. A new world for a new idea—a new world for a new kind of being—a bridge between the natural and the supernatural, between the divine and the animal within us."

She took the child to her bosom, and embraced the Count, whose cloak enveloped the three of them, and said, "I will."

Only the king wolf mates, and he takes for his consort a female from outside his tribe. . . .

Placebo

ANDREW VACHSS

I know how to fix things. I know how they work. When they don't work like they're supposed to, I know how to make them right.

I don't always get it right the first time, but I keep working until I do.

I've been a lot of places. Some of them pretty bad—some of them where I didn't want to be.

I did a lot of things in my life in some of those places. In the bad places, I did some bad things.

I paid a lot for what I know, but I don't talk about it. Talking doesn't get things fixed.

People call me a lot of different things now. Janitor. Custodian. Repairman. Lots of names for the same thing.

I live in the basement. I take care of the whole building. Something gets broke, they call me. I'm always here.

I live by myself. A dog lives with me. A big Doberman. I heard a noise behind my building one night—it sounded like a kid crying. I found the Doberman. He was a puppy then. Some freak was carving him up for the fun of it. Blood all over the place. I took care of the freak, then I brought the puppy down to my basement and fixed him up. I know all about knife wounds.

The freak cut his throat pretty deep. When the stitches came out, he was okay, but he can't bark. He still works, though.

I don't mix much with the people. They pay me to fix things—I fix things. I don't try and fix things for the whole world. I don't care about the whole world. Just what's mine. I just care about doing my work.

People ask me to fix all kinds of things—not just the boiler or a stopped-up toilet. One of the gangs in the neighborhood used to hang out in front of my building, give the people a hard time, scare them, break into the mailboxes, petty stuff like that. I went upstairs and talked to the gang. I had the dog with me. The gang went away. I don't know where they went. It doesn't matter.

Mrs. Barnes lives in the building. She has a kid, Tommy. He's a sweet-natured boy, maybe ten years old. Tommy's a little slow in the head, goes to a special school and all. Other kids in the building used to bother him. I fixed that.

Maybe that's why Mrs. Barnes told me about the monsters. Tommy was waking up in the night screaming. He told his mother monsters lived in the room and they came after him when he went to sleep.

I told her she should talk to someone who knows how to fix what's wrong with the kid. She told me he had somebody. A therapist at his special school—an older guy. Dr. English. Mrs. Barnes couldn't say enough about this guy. He was like a father to the boy, she said. Took him places, bought him stuff. A real distinguished-looking man. She showed me a picture of him standing next to Tommy. He had his hand on the boy's shoulder.

The boy comes down to the basement himself. Mostly after school. The dog likes him. Tommy watches me do my work. Never says much, just pats the dog and hands me a tool once in a while. One day he told me about the monsters himself. Asked me to fix it. I thought about it. Finally I told him I could do it.

I went up to his room. Nice big room, painted a pretty blue color. Faces out the back of the building. Lots of light comes in his window. There's a fire escape right off the window. Tommy tells me he likes to sit out there on nice days and watch the other kids play down below. It's only on the second floor, so he can see them good.

I checked the room for monsters. He told me they only came at night. I told him I could fix it but it would take me a few days. The boy was real happy. You could see it.

I did some reading, and I thought I had it all figured out. The monsters were in his head. I made a machine in the basement—just a metal box with a row of lights on the top and a toggle switch. I showed him how to turn it on. The lights flashed in a random sequence. The boy stared at it for a long time.

I told him this was a machine for monsters. As long as the machine was turned on, monsters couldn't come in his room. I never saw a kid smile like he did.

His mother tried to slip me a few bucks when I was leaving. I didn't take it. I never do. Fixing things is my job.

She winked at me, said she'd tell Dr. English about my machine. Maybe he'd use it for all his kids. I told her I only fixed things in my building.

I saw the boy every day after that. He stopped being scared. His mother told me she had a talk with Dr. English. He told her the machine I made was a placebo, and Tommy would always need therapy.

I go to the library a lot to learn more about how things work. I looked up "placebo" in the big dictionary they have there. It means a fake, but a fake that somebody believes in. Like giving a sugar pill to a guy in a lot of pain and telling him it's morphine. It doesn't really work by itself—it's all in your mind.

One night Tommy woke up screaming and he didn't stop. His mother rang my buzzer and I went up to the apartment. The kid was shaking all over, covered with sweat.

He saw me. He said my machine didn't work any more.

He wasn't mad at me, but he said he couldn't go back to sleep. Ever.

Some guys in white jackets came in an ambulance. They took the boy away. I saw him in the hospital the next day. They gave him something to sleep the night before and he looked dopey.

The day after that he said he wasn't afraid any more. The pills worked. No monsters came in the night. But he said he could never go home. He asked if I could build him a stronger machine.

I told him I'd work on it.

His mother said she called Dr. English at the special school, but they said he was out for a few days. Hurt himself on a ski trip or something. She couldn't wait to tell Dr. English about the special medicine they were giving the boy and ask if it was all right with him.

I called the school. Said I was with the State Disability Commission. The lady who answered told me Dr. English was at home, recuperating from a broken arm. I got her to tell me his full name, got her to talk. I know how things work.

She told me they were lucky to have Dr. English. He used to work at some school way up north—in Toronto, Canada—but he left because he hated the cold weather.

I thought about it a long time. Broken arm. Ski trip. Cold weather.

The librarian knows me. She says I'm her best customer because I never check books out. I always read them right there. I never write stuff down—I keep it in my head.

I asked the librarian some questions and she showed me how to use the newspaper index. I checked all the Toronto papers until I found it. A big scandal at a special school for slow kids. Some of the staff were indicted. Dr. English was one of the people they questioned, but he was never charged with anything. Four of the staff people went to prison. A few more were acquitted. Dr. English, he resigned.

Dr. English was listed in the phonebook. He lives in a real nice neighborhood.

I waited a couple of more days, working it all out in my head.

Mrs. Barnes told me Dr. English was coming back to the school next week. She was going to talk to him about Tommy, maybe get him to do some of his therapy in the hospital until the boy was ready to come home.

I told Tommy I knew how to stop the monsters for sure now. I told him I was building a new machine—I'd have it ready for him next week. I told him when he got home I wanted him to walk the dog for me. Out in the back where the other kids played. I told him I'd teach him how.

Tommy really liked that. He said he'd try and come home if I was sure the new machine would work. I gave him my word.

I'm working on the new machine in my basement now. I put a hard rubber ball into a vise and clamped it tight. I drilled a tiny hole right through the center. Then I threaded it with a strand of piano wire until about six inches poked through the end. I knotted it real carefully and pulled back against the knot with all my strength. It held. I did the same thing with another ball the same way. Now I have a three-foot piece of piano wire anchored with a little rubber ball at each end. The rubber balls fit perfectly, one in each hand.

I know how to fix things.

When it gets dark tonight, I'll show Dr. English a machine that works.

The Man at the Window

CHARLES GORDON

When I was growing up, I had dreams, and they all went the same: there was a man waiting on my balcony, a man with a shotgun in his hands. In the morning, I'd get out of bed, pull the venetian blinds up and there he'd be. His gun would be aimed dead center on my face, and I wouldn't move, and he wouldn't scowl or laugh like a killer in the movies, but he'd pull the trigger and the last sound I'd hear would be my window smashing into a thousand bits.

The worst part of it was that I'd have this dream and then I'd wake up, and there would the blinds, and I'd have to pull them up. And I knew better, but I'd think, who knows? Maybe this time he's there. So I'd stop breathing and listen carefully, and I'd never hear anything, but I'd think, these are storm windows, maybe I *wouldn't* hear him.

So I'd swallow my heart and pull the blinds up as quickly as I could. Inevitably, the balcony was there and the man with the shotgun wasn't. Maybe a pigeon, maybe some fog, but that was it. And I'd say to myself, Charlie, you're a fool.

The next night, I'd have my dream again.

Then there were half-open doors . . . they held even more terror for me than covered windows did. You see, you never know who's behind a half-open door. In my mind it was always a man in a black overcoat and a black hat with a long, black brim and he had a black, black knife raised over his head. This man was waiting for me, behind my bedroom door, behind my kitchen door, behind my bathroom door, in my closet—I mean he wasn't really, but how could I be sure?

I'd have visions of this man, and in my visions he'd step from behind the door as soon as I walked into a room, and then his black, black knife would turn red.

So I spent my youth entering rooms gingerly, snatching at doors and jumping back, my pulse racing, my body tense, and all the while wanting desperately to be free of these spectres who terrified me in my own home.

177

The killer at the window and the man behind the half-open doors dogged my every step, through elementary school, through junior high, through high school; when I moved out they came with me. And when I started living alone, their ranks multiplied—where once I had found sanctuary in closing my eyes and swaddling myself tight in my comforter, I now imagined hordes descending on me as soon as my eyelids fell.

And closed eyes are as bad as covered windows and half-open doors combined! You close your eyes, and you don't know what's going on out there; even if you're locked tight in your own room, lying in your own bed, you close your eyes and you might as well be lying on the street in the Bowery. Who's to say something didn't crawl out from under your bed the instant you closed your eyes? All it takes to find out is for you to open your eyes again, but if there really is something there, you don't *want* to open your eyes. And then you open your eyes, and nothing's there, but the next time you're not sure again . . .

It's the sceptic's demon. Surely there is no man lurking behind my doors; why would there be? How could he get in? Has there ever been one? No. And a man with a shotgun hovering outside my window— impossible, for now I live five stories up and have no balcony. But can I be sure? I can't, not absolutely, not without looking. And if I can't be sure, then I might be wrong, just possibly. It is this miserable possibility which has kept me a slave to my fears all my life. Once the sceptic's demon has been loosed, it cannot be bottled again.

People who haven't thought about it can't understand. It's a lunatic position, I grant you; but that doesn't mean it can't be taken seriously. How I wish it couldn't!

All the logic in the world can't change my mind; it doesn't help that I know it's crazy. So I ask you to open your mind, that you may look upon my hell, learn from my demons.

The first step is to discard the sweet security of logic. Follow my lead. I will not steer you wrong.

Consider the parable of King Luis. When King Luis was deposed, the new king placed him before the door of the royal dungeon, explaining that the dungeon consisted of nine rooms connected in a straight line, and that in one of those rooms he had placed a monster which would snap King Luis up and devour him in an instant.

Further, the usurper insisted, the attack would come when it was not expected.

King Luis reasoned as follows: if he entered the dungeon and went through the first eight rooms without finding the monster, he'd know for sure that it waited for him in the last room. And if he knew the monster was there, the attack would not be unexpected. Therefore, King Luis concluded, the beast could not be in the last room.

But then he thought further. Suppose the monster could not be in the ninth room, and King Luis were to travel through the first seven rooms without seeing it—then he would know for sure that the beast was in the eighth room, the only one left. Again, this would not allow for an unexpected attack; therefore, the beast could not be in the eighth room either.

In this manner, King Luis determined that the monster wasn't in the seventh room, or the sixth, or the fifth, or the fourth, third, second or first. That is, he proved that there could be no monster in the dungeon at all, because wherever it would be, he'd expect it. With this knowledge lightening his heart, he entered the first room of the dungeon. The monster was there. It snapped King Luis up and devoured him in an instant.

And sure enough, he hadn't expected the attack at all.

The point is, logic is good in its place, but it makes a terrible shield. Could King Luis have cried to his monster, "You can't exist!" More to the point, would it have done any good?

Don't you see? You can tell me I'm wrong, but you can't prove it. And even if you could, it would all be words, words, words: no match for adrenaline in a hollow heart, quavering limbs, insides turned to stone. You tell me I'm wrong and I just want to cry because I can't believe you, because what if, just what if *you're* the one who's wrong? What if?

They proved that heat is a liquid; they proved that man can't fly; they proved that man couldn't survive a trip to the moon. Wrong each time. They've proved any number of wrong things throughout history. Why couldn't you be wrong this time?

The questions echo back and forth in my head, louder and louder, why, *why*, why, *why*, whywhywhywhywhy! And: mightn't it be the case. . . ? And: isn't it *possible*. . . .?

I've got to get it out of me, but I can't, because there are blinds to be raised, and doors to be opened, and he's out there, damn it, I can *feel* him out there; I'll lift the blinds and he'll be there; but he's not there, not there, not there, maybe he's behind me (*you're a fool, Charlie!*), maybe he's there with a knife, with a gun (*a damn fool, Charlie!*) with a black, black knife with a knife knife knife knife knife knife knife—

Relief.

And then came relief.

Cool water trickling, smooth pebbles in a riverbed, deep breaths, lying back on a hill, a new dream. Relief.

Freedom.

How? I fought back. I bought life with death. Follow me.

Thirty-fourth Street, twenty minutes past midnight. Walking to clear my head after an especially bad day. I had stayed in bed, awake, sweating into my sheets, for fifteen hours.

Terrified, whimpering.

I finally had enough, got up, took a subway to Herald Square. Stayed in the middle of any crowd I could find: Macy's, Nedick's, Roy Rogers's. Don't ask me why crowds make me feel safe; the stranger next to me is more likely to be my killer than a phantom at my window. But fear isn't always rational. You should realize that by now.

The subway home. After midnight. Deserted.

The Ninety-sixth Street station, silent after the train pulled out and empty as a nightmare. The token booth twenty feet away, the stairs thirty, the street thirty feet more. Then home, thank God, then home. I closed my eyes, steeled myself with a vision of my bed, my desk, my television, nothing to fear.

But the fear hit like never before. My arms started shaking, my knees buckled, my breath ran out of my chest and I had to suck it back in ragged mouthfuls. *Why?* My mind raced through the image-apartment I'd called up: doors locked, all my lamps turned on, venetian blinds up, no killer outside my window. What was terrifying me now?

The image-apartment vanished in answer to my question, and I was left with darkness.

What had I done? I was alone in a subway station after midnight, and I had closed my eyes. Why did I do it? Why? I tried to open my eyes, but fear kept them clamped shut.

Damn it!

I'm alone, I told myself. Alone. There's no one here. Open your eyes, Charlie, and you'll see there's no one here.

But what if there is?

There isn't.

But what if there is?

I opened my eyes.

There was.

He was young, maybe seventeen, maybe less, but he was as tall as I was, and he was right in front of me. My heart puckered up tight and for an instant I was frozen, then I screamed and lunged at him.

I pressed the heels of my hands against his breast and half shoved, half hurled him over the lip of the subway platform. He toppled and fell, arms and legs flailing uselessly.

When he crashed onto the tracks he began screaming. One of his legs was twisted beneath him, probably broken. From deep within the subway tunnel came the wind of an approaching train, then the rumble, and he tried to drag himself off the tracks.

Then he shouted to me for help, stretched his arm out toward me, begged me to pull him out. I picked up some garbage from the platform and threw it down at him: foil wrappers, a torn cellophane bag, cigarette butts. I pelted him with whatever I could find. And just before the train tore into him he cried out, "*Why?*", and that night I slept well for the first time I can remember.

Relief.

Blessed purgation, like a splash of water from a porcelain basin.

I woke up, faced the blinds, and I *knew* the man at my window wasn't there. I had killed him the night before.

The morning news called him Roderigo Sanchez, age fifteen, pushed under a subway car by an unknown assailant some time before one o'clock. His crying mother said he was a good boy. His neighbors said it was a tragedy, you just didn't feel safe in the city any more.

An investigation pending, back to you in the studio, Jim; we'll have the five-day forecast for you after these messages. I turned off the television.

Safe in the city? I felt safe. Never felt safer.

I went down for breakfast, ate french toast with bacon at a luncheonette on Madison Avenue. And you know something? Food tastes better when you don't have to swallow it through a mouthful of fear. I suspect you'd have to have lived my life to appreciate it—all of a sudden, you're free to taste your food, to savor it, and even the meanest, starchiest crumb tastes luxurious.

For four days I sampled heaven, ate, breathed and bathed in the incomparable pleasure of an ordinary life.

On the fifth day, something inside me woke up and decided that I'd been having it too good. It put ideas in my mind. I tried to resist them, but I couldn't. This is what I thought:

Roderigo Sanchez was not the man I'd been afraid of for twenty-seven years. He couldn't be; he was only fifteen years old. Even if he had been, and I'd gotten rid of him, that didn't mean there was no one else for me to be afraid of. After all, I had been afraid of the man at the window and the man behind the half-open doors at the same time. Getting rid of one didn't mean I'd gotten rid of the other.

In short, whatever threat there ever had been still existed.

As I thought this, I felt myself fall. I turned to face my window and was struck rigid with fear. The blinds were down. Why couldn't there be a man there, a man with a shotgun and the will to use it? It was possible . . . possible . . . *always* possible . . .

The possibilities exploded inside my head, battered me from within, tore me to shreds and left me crying on the floor by my bed.

I couldn't stay home. The pain was unbearable.

The subway took me to Herald Square again. This time I brought a sharp knife, from Macy's.

When I went home the pain was bearable.

The headlines screamed at me, and I screamed back.

I didn't want to do it! I had to do it! I swear to God, I didn't want to, but *it hurt so much*!

Three fewer people who might lurk outside my window. That much less weight pressing me down. Because what it comes to in the end is probability. It is extremely unlikely at any given time that a killer is waiting for me at my window, but the fewer people there are, the *less* likely it becomes. Until there's no one left, the probability won't be zero—but every dead man makes the probability that much lower.

Fair? Don't ask me about 'fair'! Is it fair that I should be tortured as I am? I want to be free again, I want the luxury I tasted, the happiness everyone else has without thinking about it! Is that so much to ask?

Today, when my eyes are open I strain to keep them from closing, and when they are closed I have to fight to open them again. Tomorrow I'll go uptown with my knife, and the day after I'll have bought myself a little peace, a little, little peace. And then I'll have to do it again.

I can see already, it will never end.

Now it's your turn. You have all the information before you. Time to make your decision.

Am I mad? Am I merely a pathological, sadistic monster? Or do you understand me? I am not asking for sympathy, only comprehension. Can you look on me now and ask why I do what I do?

Better, perhaps, to ask yourselves why you *don't* do what I do.

Soon they will catch up with me. New York is a big place, but with the entire police force out looking, it's only a question of time. If they catch me on the street, I have my knife; if at home, I'll go out the window. Otherwise they'd send me to prison, where I'd really have something to be scared of. Or to an asylum.

Never.

Which is why I'm putting down these notes, because when they do catch me I'm not going to stay around to tell you all this in person. You hate me, I understand that; I hate all of you, too. But open your minds, let my demon in, please, please understand me.

The funny thing is, all this time you're saying 'he's crazy,' 'who could really believe the stuff he's saying?' But the fact of the matter is, my nightmares came true, every last one of them. Only thing is, a window's got two sides.

Every time I raise my blinds, there's a killer at the window.

Yanqui Doodle

JAMES TIPTREE, JR.

Of course they have to visit a hospital. To show they care. But which hospital? Not a big base hospital, but not a front-line station either—Congressional Armed Service Committee members are too precious to go where real iron is flying. Not to mention the value of the half-dozen generals escorting the fact-finding tour of the Bodéguan front.

A perfect hospital is found. The town of San Izquierda, just inside the Bodéguan border, has finally been liberated by American troops after the Libras had nibbled at it several times, and each time been run out by the Guévaristas. After the sixth loss the GIs were sent in to take it conclusively—what was left of it. Now the front has rolled forward twenty-five or fifty kilometers—depending on whose maps you used—and a big mansion formerly owned by one of the dictator's pals has been converted into an Intermediate Rehab Unit. The patients are a mix of GIs who would go back on duty, with some whose condition was bad enough to invalid them back to base, or even home.

So now the cavalcade is driving toward San Izzy, trying to make time. This is the last event of the Senators' day, and they've been delayed at Hona Base. There was an obstacle course demonstration by U.S. field instructors, and a parade of Libra troops in training, and speeches. That caused the trouble; even General Sternhagen has been moved to say more than a few words.

Senator Biller, the ranking Committee member, sits in the rear of the stretch Mercedes with two American flags on the fenders. Behind him come two new '98 Caddies with the rest of the Committee and some more generals, similarly beflagged. All the other escort vehicles bear twin flags, one American, the other the official Libra flag, which had been somewhat hastily designed and is not everywhere recognized with confidence.

The Senator sits between General Schehl and the interpreter. She is a neat and sultry-looking young lady, whose grasp of such fundamental phrases as "founding fathers" is, Senator Biller feels, a trifle shaky. He is wishing he could give her a short course in American— er, United States—history.

He is also musing on the Libra troops he had spoken with after their parade. The Freedom Fighters. The average Freedom Fighter had a distressing tendency to look like a fifteen-year-old Hispanic delinquent embracing an M-30.

"What did the Guévaristas do to you?" he had asked one youth. "Why are you here?"

The youth looks at the ground, then into space. "Guéyas very bad," he says to the interpreter, who amplifies, "Much oppression."

Biller persists. "What did they do to you? How did they oppress you?"

The boy says something cryptic. "They wanted to recruit him for the Army," the interpreter explains.

"But you're in the Army now," Biller says against his better judgment.

"Gué army very bad!" The interpreter smiles ravishingly. "Here is more better."

Looking around at Hona's substantial barracks, the lad's new uniform and boots, the slight but perceptible bulge under his belt, Senator Biller can believe it.

The boy adds something, scuffing his toe.

"Only he is worried about his Mama," the interpreter goes on. This is something Biller can relate to. He pats the boy's shoulder comfortingly and smiles.

"He is afraid she will sell his motorcycle," the interpreter finishes.

Several Libras are listening to the exchange. Senator Biller looks round at their young faces and tells them what fine young men they are, what a good thing they are doing evicting Marxist-Leninism and saving their country for Democracy—all of which the interpreter seems to shorten unduly.

Then there is a bark, and all come smartly to attention, faces blank. The senator moves on.

Meanwhile his colleagues, some of whom could speak Spanish, were likewise mingling with the troops, forming invaluable first-hand impressions of the state of the minds and hearts of the people to whose aid their country had sent her armed might and the blood of her sons. Afterwards Senator Moverman exclaimed, "Fine brave boys! To think they'd be fighting Soviet gunships bare-handed if we hadn't sent them aid!"

Another legislator inquired as to whether they had captured many Cubans. A look of intense wariness came over his informants' faces. "Fidelistas very bad. Very bad soldier." It turned out that they meant "very dangerous."

"Where are they? Can we see some of the Cubans you captured?"

There was a quick confab, and somebody said "Fidelisto!" and laughed in a private way that gave Senator Biller grave qualms about the Geneva Conventions. A traitorous thought crossed his mind, about other boy-men in other uniforms, sent abroad to die for Soviet geopolitik. He shrugged it away. War is evil. Lying down under communist tyranny is worse.

It was at this point that old Senator Longmast had indicated his desire to address the assembled Libra and U.S. troops, and got into his brief explanation of What They Were Fighting For that so terminally delayed them. When he was reminded that they had a hospital to visit, he said "We owe it to them," and went on.

Now the party is trying to make up lost time on the San Izquierda road, which features a plethora of potholes and other obstacles. At the moment they have come onto a herd of scraggly cattle trapped between the steep banks of the mountain road.

The cars stop, the party gets out to stretch. Below them is a superb view of San Izquierda in the evening sun, nestled around its almost-intact cathedral. Shadowy mountain ridges, forested by pines, stretch away on either hand. Senator Biller reaches for his camera, as do others.

They are at a small crossroad. On the other road a rusty country bus has also stopped, is letting out people. The scene is very peaceful. Tropical birds are making exotic evening sounds. There is only the far-off rumble of heavy trucks on another road; a convoy, probably.

Beside the Senator there looms up what seems to be a self-propelled great load of sticks. It turns out to be on the head of a small old woman. Biller reflects that only weeks ago she and the town had been under the iron boots of the Guévaristas. He catches her curious eyes on him and grins broadly, saying "Libertad!"

"Si! Si!" Her face lights up with a toothy grin. Life is good; only that morning she had sold her twelve-year-old daughter to three *Yanquis* for pesos four hundred, about twenty dollars.

Senator Biller steels himself against the impulse to tell his driver to help her with her load. (They're used to it, this is the way they live.) He turns to his snapshots of the town below.

Ahead, the cattle are dispersing. The party is getting back into their cars. On the side road the bus has started up, too.

"See—Hospital!" the driver throws back over his shoulder, waving at a large building set in a garden just in view several kilometers ahead and below.

In that same hospital, Pfc. Donald Still had come back to life some two weeks before. The last thing he remembered was hearing his patrol leader yell and finding himself falling with an unbelievable pain on the inside of his thigh. He also remembered thinking that the path behind the ridge they were following was a natural site for mines, but he was too exhilarated to object. They were in hot pursuit of a bunch of Gués who were running and dodging just behind the spine of the ridge. The trees cleared out ahead. Don popped another BZ, looking forward to getting himself some good bursts.

Now he was flat on his back, feeling terrible, with a heavy wrapped-up leg. Steel rails on the bed. Above him afternoon sun filtered through ornate windows in a high dome. Mostly silence all around, no shots, no footsteps running. This was no battle-aid station. The choppers must have carried them all the way back to wherever this was. He felt that a lot of time had passed here: dreams of struggles, dreams of himself shouting.

His mouth and eyes were painfully dry, his head hurt, he felt weak and fluttery inside, and his leg ached horribly. Automatically he reached for a Maintenance pill. But his pill kit wasn't there. He was in hospital pjs, no pockets, no pills, nada.

"Hey! Hello!"

A dizzyingly beautiful girl's face swam in front of him. No, on second look she wasn't so gorgeous, only cute and very clean.

"Where am I? What's with my leg?"

She produced a clipboard. "You're in San Izquierda Intermediate Rehab Fifteen. Your leg is okay, you'll be walking tomorrow when the cast comes off. You were lucky, you just lost a lot of blood." She smiled meaningfully. "*Very* lucky."

"I need an M."

"Oh-oh." She frowned. "Wel-l-l. Tomorrow you start detox."

"But this is still today!" He tried to smile over sudden panic.

"Wel-l-l. You're just making it harder for yourself."

"But it's today. You said. *Please*."

Without saying anything she turned away and came back with the precious yellow tab. He managed to clutch it and dry-swallowed. She tut-tutted at him.

"We've got to stop that pill-seeking behavior, soldier," she said cutely.

In spite of himself he grinned at her, or rather at the blessed tide of relief that would come through his veins in a minute.

"Make the most of it, soldier," she told him and went away.

He loathed people who called him "soldier" but he wasn't about to antagonize his supply. The M was working already, he could feel the first faint glow, the all-rightness, stealing over him. Without Ms, who could make this war? Nobody he knew of.

"Hey, what happened to the others? To my unit?" He asked when she passed by later. "Jack Errin, Benjy?"

"Your friends? I'm afraid I don't know. You were brought in alone. I did hear you were an only survivor. I'm afraid your friends were casualties, soldier. Or maybe they weren't badly hurt."

Friends, he thought. Yes, he'd liked Jack in a far-off sort of way, and Benjy was a good guy. But didn't she know that in this war you don't have pals? When you're on Ms you don't need 'em, when you're on BZs you don't remember the word.

"What do you mean about detox tomorrow? What are they going to do to me?"

"Because you're going home, soldier. *Home*—I told you you were lucky. Why do you think you're in an Intermediate Unit?"

He had no idea.

"Because we can't let you boys go home full of that awful stuff, can we? So you have to get two–three weeks of detox. It won't be so bad. Think about going home."

He lay back, his head spinning. Through his body the gentle glow of the M was taking away all worries. Tomorrow was a long way off.

But think about going home? He didn't particularly want to. Home wasn't much since Geri had split. But to tell the truth he could hardly remember her. It had been one of those draft-notice marriages anyway, and so far as he knew he hadn't left a child. Her letters had been short and almost illegible, starting with a hot sort of personal pornography, and ending last fall with "I guess we better think this all over" one. She'd been staying with his folks in San Diego. Not much of a life for her. He guessed she was really divorcing his mother. He chuckled to himself.

So now where should he go? Back to San D. first, then he'd see. Something would turn up. No point in worrying now. In fact, he couldn't worry if he tried.

He remembered the week they had first issued the Ms. What a change. All the guys who were muttering about going AWOL just quit. They'd often wondered what was in them. Not cocaine, nothing he'd ever heard of. Miracles of modern science.

No, wait—the first things they issued were the BZs. He'd been given some specially, when someone had noticed him firing his M-18 in the air instead of at the Gués in front of them. What the hell, a lot of the others were doing that, too. The boys they killed had been so young, and they shot so badly. He'd expected the Commie Gués to be ten feet high and mean. Not baby-faced twelve-year olds. Of course those same twelve-year olds had been laying mines that blew unlucky grunts apart, but . . . but . . . looking straight at one and blowing his guts out was somehow different. They ran away fast enough, wasn't that what counted?

But the Army saw things differently. Kill! Kill! His training . . . so he found himself being given some red capsules and instructed to take one when he was in a shooting situation. BZs . . . Battle Zones . . . they had removed all his reservations about blowing anybody away, made it exhilarating. In fact, they had removed all his reservations about anything. But luckily your memory of what you'd done behind BZs wasn't too good. They had swept through several little hamlets, putting the flamers to it all, and there were flash-memories of other things. Patch-views of female flesh, lots of screaming, and one that bothered him a lot—he didn't want to think about that now.

So then had come the green Sleeper tabs, and after that there weren't any more dreams. Trouble was, men started nodding over their rifles on patrol. So then there was the general issue of Ms For Maintenance. It made an ideal combo.

But detox? Detox before going home? Nobody had said a word to them about that. He'd always assumed they had some other magic potion, that there'd be some kind of gentle end. Well, it would all be okay. It had to, he thought, drifting off. Nobody'd do anything so brutal.

He woke up with somebody pushing a tray at him. "Soft diet."

Trying to eat the stuff he didn't feel so good. The M was wearing off. Probably they hadn't given him enough while he'd been here, his blood levels were low.

A different nurse was on duty, an older, dark-haired woman. She brought him an M when asked, without comment.

"You're starting detox tomorrow, you know," she told him. But she seemed nicer, more like she was worried for him.

"What's so big about that? Is it bad?"

"Well-l-l . . . you've been on this stuff how long? A year?"

"Around that."

"We're just starting to get long-timers like you."

"What happens?" he persisted.

She frowned. "Detoxification is always hard. You have to get your body making the chemicals again itself. The only way is to go cold; tapering off is like cutting a dog's tail off an inch at a time to be kind. But some people take it like a breeze. Most do. Hold the thought."

He wasn't worried. But still he wondered. "I thought they'd have something for us. I mean, they put us on it."

"You mean you were ordered to take the stuff?"

"Oh, no . . . but strongly suggested. Because . . . because there were things. . . ." He wanted to stop talking and enjoy the M's good feeling.

"Well, there is Slobactin. That helps. You'll be given some."

"Thank you," he said dreamily. She went away.

He lay back, looking vaguely around. The room seemed to have been part of a mansion—a ballroom, maybe. Only a few other beds were in here—too far spaced to talk. A bed was rolled in with a lot of fuss going on around it—a new arrival fresh from the operating room, he made out. This was some kind of way-station. By craning his head he could see metal-grilled doorways, apparently leading into corridors the Army had built on. Two muscular-looking male techs or orderlies sat behind desks, keeping an eye on things. It was very peaceful; the first time in a long time he had heard no firing.

Bedtime came, and the cute little blonde nurse came in to douse the lights and distribute pills. The yellow-and-pink cap she gave him was all wrong.

"Nurse, I want my Army sleep pill. My ND." ND was for No Dreams.

"This is just as effective," she said serenely.

He doubted it strongly. "I want my regular ND. I'm entitled to it, it's still today."

"You're not entitled to any particular medication, soldier. You're entitled to have us make you well, that's what we're doing."

Her voice had a nasty edge, her smile was pure plastic.

"But it's not fair! The NDs are for—for special reasons." He couldn't tell her about the dreams. "—Please. Can I have mine tonight? It's still today."

"You have your sleeping pill. Now calm down and go to sleep, you're disturbing the other patients."

"I'll keep everybody awake if you don't give me the right one!"

"Don't try it, soldier." She smiled toward the grille where the two big orderlies were watching him alertly. She went away.

He lay back, fuming. He'd meant that the dreams made him yell. Well, they'd find out.

"You get on *her* shit list, you dead," said the soldier in the next bed, separated from him by a tiled plant-stand.

"But she said—"

"You dead," the man repeated.

To his surprise, he did drift off, and dreamt only innocuous fantasies about his old dog.

He woke in the night, feeling a knife grinding him under his ribs. His old ulcer pain. He'd almost forgotten, he hadn't had that since his first ND-tab. And there was another trouble, an itch under his leg-cast. A roach or something must have somehow got under it and was struggling about. He banged at it futilely, and finally called.

Miss Plastic approached with a flashlight.

"Shshsh! What is it, soldier?"

"My ulcer hurts. I need some antacid."

She made a note on the clipboard. "I'll tell the doctor about it. Maybe he'll prescribe you some in the morning."

"In the morning? Christ, I need it right now, I feel like my stomach's boring through.

"Sorry, I can't prescribe medication. But I'll have the doctor look at you first thing, I promise." Cutie-doll smile.

"But antacid isn't a prescription drug, a medication! Christ, you can buy Maalox or Mylanta over the counter by the gallon. You must have some here. I *hurt.*"

"Anything other than your meals is a medication, soldier." She turned the flash off.

"Wait! Do you mean this shit?"

"Don't swear at me."

"Well, wait one minute—there's bugs under my bandage. A bug. I can feel it crawling around."

Expertly she slipped back the sheet and explored the top of the cast with the light.

"No bugs. You calm down, the bugs will go away."

"But I can feel them! They itch! Can't you at least cut that stuff so I can scratch? You said it comes off tomorrow." No use, he could see that. "Isn't there something you could squirt under it? Some bug killer?" He asked weakly.

"Sorry, soldier. There are no insects, nothing, under that bandage. It's all in your head. Now, are we going to be good and go to sleep— or are you going to cause trouble? There are men here a lot sicker than you are, you know."

He looked up at her in the dim light, living proof that a cute girl five feet three inches high could be a monster.

"If you'd give me my ND I could sleep. It's not yet tomorrow!" His voice was high with anguish. She didn't reply, just clicked the flash off and went away.

He saw her checking the inhabitants of the other beds on her way out. Two men came awake at this, screamed briefly and thrashed about. Doesn't she know being wakened like that could be bad news in the combat zone, doesn't she know *anything*?

"Take it easy, soldier," he heard her say. Then she was gone.

He lay back and felt the supposedly non-existent bug scratching like mad. One bastard's legs were in the tender place back of his knee. Goddamn. He made a determined effort to break the cast on the bedrails, got nowhere. Then he recalled something.

In a story he'd read, "insects" like this were a feature of going off drugs cold turkey. Victims were driven crazy, tore themselves bloody.

The dopers' DTs. Was *this* what detoxification was going to be like? Oh, Christ, oh Christ.

He tried to relax, but there was no more possibility of sleep. And his ulcer was really hurting now, gnawing deep. Going without antacids could be dangerous, his old doc had said. Your stomach could perforate. He almost hoped his would, that would be a lesson for Miss Plastic. Medications! . . . God, he could see the inside of a US drugstore, all those good things laid out ready to your hand. Mylanta, Maalox, Alternagel, Tums—in his civilian days he'd been a good customer for all that. But the ND-tabs had stopped the pain. He'd have to get hold of more the minute he was turned loose. But what if they only issued them in the combat zone? Well, he'd get back there by hook or crook. Back to combat? Why not? If he was comfortable and could sleep there. How long would this damn detox take? Two, three weeks had they said? Could he endure it?

He rolled, rolled, tossed, trying to find a position where the pain was better and the bugs were quieter. . . . Some time toward morning he must have lost consciousness.

Detox started officially right after breakfast, when two strange orderlies descended on his bed, checked the rails, and starting rolling him toward one of the closed-off corridors. He'd been enjoying a nap at last, almost didn't wake up in time to size up his surroundings. As they relocked the grille he sat up and saw that he was in a wing the Army must have added on—plain plywood walls, low ceilings, all the way down, with doors opening off each side, to a blank wall at the far end. First came a second grille, strong steelwork, and polished in the middle as though hundreds of hands had gripped it. As they went through, he saw that the first door bore a hand-lettered sign: Quiet Room. The door had a small wire-reinforced glass window in it. And there was sound coming from it—a faint, pallid mewling or keening, like an animal far away. Then they were passing closed, featureless doors, 205, 207. At 209 the orderlies stopped, opened up and pushed him in.

Room 209 was about four meters square, with a screened, barred, frosted window. There was a bed already in it. The orderlies wrestled it around to take out.

Don said, "They told me I was going to walk today. They're supposed to take the cast off. Where's the doctor?"

"Don't know anything about that," one of them grunted, opening the door.

He started to panic. It seemed to him that once he was shut in here they would just forget him, let him starve and die, immobilized in the heavy cast.

"Where's a *doctor*? Would you tell them I need a doctor? I have ulcers, see," he added idiotically to their backs as they went out. The door closed.

At that he dragged himself up and by tremendous effort managed to get one leg over the guard-rails. Then he saw that the reason the cast was so immovable was that somebody had strapped it to the bed-rails, top and bottom. Must have been done when he dozed off. By straining to his limit he got the top buckle undone, but no way could he reach his ankle. Panting, he lay back. His hands were shaking like leaves in a wind.

"I'm not functioning," he thought. God how he needed an M. Was it possible that only ten days ago he had been a competent combat-ant, leaping up mountainsides?

He looked around. The room contained a straight chair, a small set of drawers on wheels, and a lidless toilet. No means of calling for help.

That gave him an idea. Legitimate need.

He called tentatively, "Nurse!" No response, nothing. There was nobody out there. He raised his voice as loud as he could. "Nurse! Nurse! Nurse! *Help*!"

Almost instantly there were footsteps and the door opened. Miss Plastic.

"Nurse, I have to go to the can. Why isn't this cast off? You said I'd walk today. Where's the doctor? Does he know about my ulcer?"

She stared at him unsmiling. "We don't holler like that, soldier. It upsets other patients. You have to think of the others here."

"Well, how can I get help?"

"Someone looks in every fifteen minutes, around the clock. You can tell them what you need."

They went through the bedpan routine; she restrapped the buckle he'd opened and departed.

The morning dragged on. As she'd said, every quarter-hour the door opened and a face looked in. Often it was the dark-haired nurse, but he didn't bother her except to ask once if the cast would really be removed. "Yes. Soon, now. Doctor is making rounds."

The invisible insects had quieted down to where he could forget them, but in their place came a growing horde of aches and discomforts, everywhere. Bruises he dimly remembered from combat time hurt. Was all this what the Ms had been hiding from him? He groaned, trying to get comfortable. Did they even *have* a doctor in this crazy place?

At noon came the doctor, and with him Miss Plastic, carrying his lunch. She put the tray down on the bureau, out of his reach. The doctor was old, about Don's father's age. He was a grunter. He tackled the cast with an electric saw. Miss Plastic kept having to hand him things; it did Don good to see her obeying orders, sweet as peaches.

"You were very lucky, son, (grunt) very lucky. Hm'm. I think I'll take these stitches out now, but (grunt) no walking for three days, hear?"

"I can get to the toilet, can't I?"

"Hm'm'm. Very well, yes, to the toilet—but *only* there and back, understand? Mm'm. Meals in bed."

"Yes sir."

"And nurse, you keep an eye on him to see he stays put."

"We always do, sir."

"That's right (grunt). We put a pin in that bone, son, so you won't have a short leg. We don't want it wiggling around (grunt), we want it to heal tight. Keep it just as quiet as you can."

"Yes sir."

"M'm'm . . . Say, that looks good. Mind if I steal a bite?"

Without waiting for a reply the doctor plucked a small something off the tray, nodded, and went out. As they were leaving, Don called, "Nurse, I can't reach my lunch."

"Someone will be right in."

He lay and watched it getting cold. Food here was godawful enough when hot. In desperation, he crawled up on his good knee and then got that leg to the ground and leaned just far enough to grab the tray and pull it across himself as he collapsed. God, he was weak!

Just as he got settled the door opened and a strange red-headed nurse came in.

"My, we *are* impatient, aren't we?"

"I didn't step on the leg," he said defensively.

"Good." She looked at him seriously. "You'll have to live the rest of your life with whatever you do to yourself now. The doctor went to a lot of trouble. Follow his orders."

Somehow this got through to him. The nurse was someone in authority, he felt. He realized he'd been acting childishly. Long ago he'd been known for his patience and good temper. What had happened to him? Was all this the drugs? Or the effect of being without them? He no longer felt at all hungry, now that he'd gotten the tray. In fact he felt sick. And he was trembling and sweating.

"Nurse, I feel pretty terrible. They said you had something that helps. May I have some? Something bactin, I think."

"Slobactin. Yes, you'll be getting some with your regular medication."

"And I forgot to tell the doctor, I have ulcers. They've been acting up. Can I have some antacid?"

She made a note on her clipboard. "Yes, I'll tell the doctor as soon as he comes off rounds."

She was straightening his bedclothes. As she patted the undersheet she suddenly frowned disapprovingly, but said nothing more before departing.

He fell into a sweaty sleep, forgetting his lunch, from which he was wakened by a man saying "Roll. Roll over here."

"Huh?"

It was one of the two big orderlies. He was dumping something into the bed, something heavy that felt both cold and warm.

"Roll over to the edge so I can spread this."

Groggily he complied, finally made out that the man was working a rubber sheet onto the mattress under the regular sheet. When he rolled back the bed felt clammy and hard on his bruises.

As the man left, Don began to feel scared. Did these precautions mean that he was going to be sick in some ghastly uncontrolled way? Well, he was starting to feel much more nauseated. And, goddamn, nothing to york into here, except the untouched lunch tray with its weak white plastic flatware. The orderly had put it back on top of him. He hoped it wouldn't come to that, tried deep breathing that hurt his ribs.

At the next door check he asked for a sick-basin, and to have the tray taken away. It was little Miss Plastic. She checked the uneaten food.

"It's starting, eh, soldier? You're slow—you must have been on that stuff a long time."

"A year."

"My, my . . . Soldier, how *could* you do that to your body?"

How could he begin to tell her, assuming she really wanted to know? Instead he asked her a question.

"Nurse, have you ever had ulcers?"

She laughed. Then she said with a smug little lift of her chin. "I've never used a day of sick-leave in my life." The implication was strong: those people who got sick did it to themselves.

"Try it sometime," he said through suddenly chattering teeth.

"No thanks!" Merrily she exited, taking the tray but forgetting his basin.

That afternoon was bad. The itching started again, and he scratched his arms bloody. Miss Plastic caught the blood on the sheet, looked at his nails, and clucked. "Marie hasn't been here."

Shortly an orderly came in, leading a small mestiza girl in a pink smock.

"Manicure time."

The girl grabbed his hand in a surprisingly firm small grip, and was already cutting. Cutting right down to the quick, he saw. When he protested, the man came and stood over him. "Routine procedure, fella." Don subsided, and the orderly produced a movie magazine and sat in the chair. The cutting went quickly; Don realized he would be helpless to ease himself, and tried to save out one finger. "No, no!" Marie said.

"Yes! Leave it, please."

The orderly put down his magazine and loomed over him again. "I said it's routine procedure. She does them all. Every one . . . You want to make trouble, fella?"

Looking up at him, Don decided he didn't. The girl finished with a filing job, and then, to his amazement, pulled back the sheet and tackled his toenails with a dog-clipper.

"Oh, no!"

"Oh, yes!" she said mockingly. The orderly watched impassively as she began, then returned to his gaudy magazine. "You could infect yourself fella," he observed.

When the job was finished Don felt like a declawed cat, or a defanged wolf. God, the lengths they went to render him helpless!

And more. Just after they left, Miss Plastic came in with a mestizo porter carrying what Don recognized with wonder as his duffelbag from main camp. One of the Army's eerie efficiencies. The duffel was plonked down and the little nurse swiftly opened it and started to unpack it onto the floor. Searching. His hunting knife went first into a big plastic bag she had. Then his cigarettes, and then she opened his shaving roll.

"You can keep these." She pulled out toothpaste and brush, and then resealed the kit and dumped it into her bag.

"Hey, are you going to take that away? I need those things."

"No metal or glass," she said firmly. "No liquids. And no heavy plastic."

Don was a fairly neat packer; he had put a clean uniform and his fresh laundry into plastic bags. Those got dumped, and the bags confiscated.

"Why those?"

"No bags. Patients have been known to try to do themselves harm."

"With a *baggie*?"

She didn't answer. He guessed she meant you could smother yourself with one. Ugh—what a way to go. A tremor of fear ran down him. Did people here really get that desperate?

"That reminds me—where's my watch?"

"At the desk. With your dog-tags. You get them back when you leave."

He felt nakeder than ever, but nausea was rising in him again and he couldn't protest. This time she brought him a basin, and watched him as he retched up liquid. Then she crammed his remaining stuff back into the eviscerated duffel, zipped it up and left with her bag of booty.

He lay back, sweating and shaking. There was a peculiar sourceless pain in his legs; no position eased it. The itching started again, and rubbing with his denuded fingers only made it worse. Finally in desperation he managed to get out of bed and grab his toothbrush from the window sill. Scratching with that gave him some help, but it soon became bloody and he knew if somebody saw that it would be taken away. There was no water in his room other than the can, so he sucked the toothbrush clean, sick with disgust at the taste of his own blood.

The endless hours passed so; finally came medication-time. With the vitamin-like pills came two small brownish tablets—the drug-deprival medicine?—and a tiny paper cup containing Maalox. So Redhead hadn't forgotten. He gulped it hungrily, and took the pills, dreaming of the beautiful yellow M-tabs he needed so.

Dinner came and went untasted, and then the night settled in. To his exasperation, they wouldn't switch off the ceiling light. He tossed and turned, finally ending with the small pillow over his eyes.

And then the deprivation really started on him. The random pains that had bothered him turned ten times worse, savage stabbings in his arms, legs, guts. His head throbbed. His mouth and eyes were painfully dry. And the skin-itch he had thought intolerable migrated into the interior of his joints, where he couldn't get at it. He had visions of armies of rustling termites marching with their little tickling legs, through his capillaries, and finally into the marrow of his bones. The only relief was to jerk the joint, but then it came back worse a moment later, so he had to jerk again. He tried to relax, but there was no respite from the beastly internal tickling and no hope of sleep. The light glared down on him, he was twisted and contorted and jerking in a pool of sweat, the rubber under him sticking everywhere. There was an interval he didn't remember clearly, which brought the two orderlies in to put him back to bed. At another point the heat was so bad that he got out and grabbed up the chair to push it through the screen and break the glass of the closed window. His weakness was appalling; but even so he managed a strong jab with the chair-legs. But this was no ordinary screen; the chair bounced back on him without leaving a dent in the wire. Weeping with frustration he tried again, with the same result, and finally staggered back into the bed to shiver and sweat. His nose itched and ran unceasingly. Nothing to wipe it on but his pajamas.

Only one part of the night he remembered: toward morning he must have fallen into a doze, and the nightmares began. The worst was a static image of the inside of a hut. A woman lay on the floor by his feet; he didn't want to look at her. But in front of his eyes a cloudy red-and-tan bundle hung in midair. He particularly didn't want to look at this; it seemed to him that if he saw it clearly he would die. He jerked himself awake, trembling and quivering all over his body.

Daylight brought some relief, but not much. He was weeping continuously now and retching. He had given up trying to keep himself clean; the bed was sodden. His bones had turned to termite-ridden Jello, and the pains gnawed and jabbed him. Once he thought that the worst was over, but soon the excruciating bone-deep tickling began again, and he lay jerking helplessly, unable to rest.

Time passed in a torture-ridden blur. Strange people looked in on him, spoke meaninglessly and did unhelpful things. Several times he became aware that he was raving and shouting, but had no idea what he said, or to whom. Medications came, and he promptly threw them up. Meals came and went; sometimes he upset the tray in his bed.

The vomiting began to give way to uncontrollable diarrhea. At first he tried to get out of bed and make it to the can, but he was so weak that soon he failed and lay in his filth on the floor until the next room-check.

The windows darkened, and night brought with it all symptoms intensified. At one point he became aware that his wrists and ankles were tied to the bed-rails, and roared in protest until his dry throat gave out. There was an IV stand by the bed; a face scolded him for tearing the needle out.

Only toward morning did he fall into an exhausted doze, and the nightmares came again. He was with the patrol, rushing a bunch of Gués. The man next to him fell, screaming. He was holding a flamer to a thatched roof, the roof caught and roared up. And always there was the terrifying static scene of the interior of the hut, and the supine woman. By now he made out that she was wounded in the belly. He tried not to look at the ambiguous bundle hanging before his eyes, but it had more details; a bright point was sticking up from it, and something ran up to it from below. Also it moved and cried. He woke screaming to see the windows lightening, and experience the strange momentary relief that dawn seemed to bring.

Days and nights, how many he didn't know, passed so. The IV apparatus came again, and the tying up. He was too weak to protest.

Finally came the afternoon when he realized that the horrible internal tickling had given way to plain pain, which was far more bearable. When medication came next he was able to keep it down, and to drink a glass of water, which stayed down too. But his mood had changed; from anger and bewilderment he was in the grip of a terrible bleakness and despair. Every train of thought ended in horror and death. His body might be somewhat detoxified now, he thought, but his mind was not. If this was reality, he desperately needed the magic tabs which would keep it at a distance. Images of them floated in his mind; his need was so great that he had hallucinations they were somewhere in his room—surely in his duffelbag. Three times he crawled out of bed and searched, finding, of course, nothing. He wept. Behind the tears, an iron resolve formed; he would get hold of some somehow, get back on the regime which made life bearable, even pleasant. The tabs were everywhere at the front, distributed freely. That was where he belonged, not home. What was home compared to that relief?

That night he fell into a really deep sleep, and with it came a jumble of new nightmares. Himself firing directly into the face of a little mestizo boy, watching the boy's head explode. The platoon awakened at night by a rush of Gués toward the ammo cache. And again, that static hut interior, where he was standing by the wounded woman. He saw her wounds clearly now; her whole belly was opened, and skin and fat folded back from emptiness like a heavy fruit-rind. She writhed feebly. Knife-work, that. And, inexorably, the amorphous bundle before his face cleared, became—Oh, no!—a bleeding newborn baby, skewered on a long machete blade. The lower part of the blade was clear now, there was a hand gripping the handle. Whose hand? Not his—Oh yes, *his*, he could feel the balance shift as its gruesome burden wriggled, moved its legs. A desperate squalling sound came from it.

He tore himself awake by sheer willpower, lay gasping as the windows paled. And in the growing light he knew—this was no nightmare, this was a memory. *He had done that thing.* He had gutted the parturient woman, skewered her baby on his knife. What came next he did not know—the deed itself was quite enough. Under the Battle-Zone tablets he had become a savage beast, seeing the enemy everywhere, even in the unborn. *He* had done this. And god knew what else. The sleeper-tabs had kept it from breaking through. God, how he needed one!

As day grew, a kind of sanity came back to him. For the first time in days he could think. He thought about what life would be like, remembering his deed. Impossible. His soul was one huge flinch. He could not help hearing the cries, seeing more details, smelling the stink of guts. No. He wanted only surcease, wanted to die.

To die—taking these horrors with him, forever finished. Yes. Every hour he remained alive he would be tortured by those scenes in his mind, by the utter shame and sickening remorse. Afraid of what else he might remember. He couldn't go on like this. To go home, bearing this living memory in him like a cancer? Never. He would die here, he would manage somehow.

The resolve seemed to ease him a little. But when he drifted to sleep again, the memory came back, and with it the brief touch of bloody little hands pawing at him, as he drove the machete in. He screamed and woke.

Some time later the little blonde nurse stuck her head in. "You're better!" she observed brightly. "All right, today you get corridor privileges. Up and out!"

He could barely make it; she had to assist him and let him lean along the wall crab-fashion as she took him out in the corridor. He blinked; he had forgotten that the world held more than that room of torment.

"You better practice so you can make meal-times. You'll get your meals up in the day-room now, no more service in bed." Somehow they had arrived at the grille ending the corridor. He held on and peered through it blearily.

"They unlock this when meals are served," she told him. "Someone will call you."

The mention of meals set him retching again, but nothing came out. She came along as he crab-walked back to Number 209. "Practice!" she repeated cheerily. When they got back inside he struggled for the can, but failed to make it. When the spasm was over, Miss Plastic helped him back to bed. From somewhere she had produced a mop.

"This is the last time. From now on you'll be expected to keep your room clean. The mop can stay in the corner here for awhile." Expertly she wrung it out in the can, washed her hands in the tank, and flushed. It came to him that the scene had been repeated over and over before this.

He didn't see how he could make that trip again, let alone eat anything, but at chow time the biggest orderly stuck his head in and ordered him out. He staggered into the corridor, found it filled with what seemed hundreds of people. The man coming out of 207 was bandaged all over his head and shoulders, only three black holes showing for eyes and mouth. Bemused, Don fumbled along the wall with the crowd to the open grille, found a big dolly stacked with trays. A man beside him said, "Look for your name." Seeing Don's helplessness, he asked, "What's your name?"

"Still."

"Smith?"

"No . . . Still."

The stranger pounced on a shelf. "Here it is: Take it and sit down at that table and eat, or they'll take it away."

"Thanks."

Shakily Don carried the tray over to an empty seat. Soup had sploshed all over. In spite of his illness, he managed to hoist a bowl of it and drink some. Surprisingly, it tasted good. He finished it. On all the trays the flatware was the same wobbly white plastic, like a cheap airline's. No metal.

When he got up to go, someone pulled his sleeve.

"Take your tray back or they'll get your ass."

"Oh, thanks." He hoisted up the iron-heavy tray, grateful for the strange camaraderie of this hell-hole. These others had been subject to Miss Plastic and her bully-boys, they knew the drill. He noticed a couple of men who kept rhythmically jerking their knees, tapping their feet. He knew what they were feeling—that ghastly unstoppable tickle. Did it ever go away for good?

When he got back to Number 209 the nice dark-haired nurse was making up his bed with clean sheets.

"Oh, thank you." He collapsed in the chair.

"And here are some clean pjs." He realized he'd been going around in sweaty shit-stained ones. God, he must stink.

"You can get clean ones any time from the laundry room. It's opposite the showers, down by the dayroom."

"Showers?"

"That's right. But you have to tell the nurse you're going in."

"Great. Thank you . . . The trouble is, I'm so weak. *Weak*. I can't believe only a few days ago I was in combat."

"That's the effect of amphetamine withdrawal, honey. You have to pay a price for being Superman for awhile."

"How long does it last?"

"Until you exercise it away. That's the only cure, keeping active."

"But it seems to be worse every day. Weaker and weaker. I'm afraid I'll die here."

"Don't say that, honey. Nobody ever died from detox and they never will. You'll just get healthier and healthier." Earnestly looking at him, she went on. "You're perfectly safe here. Don't be afraid."

Something in her tone struck him. You don't talk about dying here, he thought. They're afraid of suicides. That's what she means by safe. I can't get away. He chuckled painfully. "Safe" to him meant something quite different; well-secured perimeters, safety from Guévarista attack.

"Where are the Gués now? I don't know anything."

"The war's going well, I hear. The front's quite a ways farther than when you came in."

"I've got to get back."

"Oh, no you don't. The war's over for you, honey!" She bundled up the old sheets and prepared to leave.

"Thank you very much," he called after her. But a qualm had smitten him in the pit of the stomach. *She meant it*. No more, for him, the easy world of combat with the little yellow pill-cases full. What would he do at home? Roam the night streets, looking for black-market Ms? No way. He had to get back. Back at the front was everything he needed, including the neat way to die.

Depression and nausea washed over him deeper as he got into bed. The images of the dying woman, the tortured baby came again. He couldn't go on like this. Couldn't. Hatred of himself was like a poisonous fog in his head. It lasted all afternoon.

That night when he got to the tray-dolly he found that someone had made a mistake. A real metal knife lay gleaming on the tray that held butter and catsup, just above his own.

Nobody was watching. It was the work of an instant to get that beautiful knife into his pajama leg, stuck into the bandage.

He made himself pretend to eat, to wait until others were leaving. Then he hobbled back to 209 with his prize. Relief. The way out. But that would be at night; where to hide it meanwhile?

He found the perfect place—a loose piece of molding in the upper window edge. All but the very end slid neatly inside. Then he took it out again—it was much too dull, it needed sharpening. The window-screen might do.

Between room-checks he honed it carefully. It took a decent edge. He tested it on his wrist, leaving a thin red line that oozed a red drop at one end. Okay. He put the knife back in its hidey-hole and lay in the bed, studying his wrists and memorizing where the best cuts would be . . . A peaceful death, bleeding. You jut got cold. Pity he couldn't hang his arms over the edge of the bed to drain, but room-checkers would spot that. They wouldn't spot blood under him in the bed until much too late. . . . He'd have to cut deep, get the arteries flowing well. That would hurt—but not so much as the stuff in his head. *That* would never hurt him again.

Some commotion was going on in the corridor, but he took no notice. Not his concern. Never again, his concern. . . . The noise was from the next room, where the bandaged man was. Someone had told Don that he was a cook, burned by a stove-fire. He was due for a lot of plastic surgery after detox. Now he seemed to be just outside Don's door, yelling at someone. "Leave my room alone!" It didn't seem to do any good. Doors banged.

Presently Don's own door opened, and Miss Plastic marched in, followed by the two big blond orderlies. Don had named them in his mind, *Hans und Klaus.*

"Get up and sit in the chair, please."

"Chair? Why?"

"Just get up and let us at your bed. This is routine."

As he went to the chair, Hans intercepted him and gave him a quick but efficient body-search, patting all down his pajama legs. Then he seized Don's hand and turned it over and grunted. He held it out to show the nurse the cut wrist. She nodded, grimly. The search intensified.

Klaus was stripping the bed thoroughly. Sheets, rubber, pillow-case, all went on the floor. Then he expertly flipped over the mattress to expose the springs and searched all around the bottom and the bed-rails.

Don had got it by now. They were looking for the knife. *His* precious knife. Thank god he had resisted his first impulse to hide it under the spring-bars.

Klaus had been circling the room, checking the baseboards. When he came to the set of drawers, he and the nurse took it apart, looking at the bottoms of every drawer, the bottom of the chest. Then he turned to check thoroughly around the toilet and in the tank, while Miss Plastic put the drawers back in. Hans was heaping bedding and pillow on the bed.

"Now sit on the bed, please." Dumbly he obeyed. They went over the chair. Then Klaus and Hans went back to the baseboards, while the nurse dumped out his duffelbag.

Hans was circling the room now, looking higher and higher. A quick probe of the door jamb, the electric outlet—and then he was at the window. Don sat rigid, not daring to breathe or look, while Hans' hands ran around the lower sills. Klaus was stuffing his things back into the duffel. Miss Plastic had gone to the door, frowning and tapping her foot.

"All right." They seemed about to leave. Don's heart thudded with relief—but suddenly Hans turned back and ran his hand along the top of the window molding. Oh, no!—A rustle, and, damn it, god damn it—he was drawing out the knife from its hiding place, looking at it curiously, testing the edge Don had put on it.

Miss Plastic and Klaus were advancing on him with a canvas thing.

"Just slip your arms in here."

"What is it?"

"A tux," Hans said, and giggled. They had his hands drawn half-way down the sleeves before he could react. But when his hands found no cuffs, he realized what it was—they were putting a strait-jacket on him!

"No! *No!*"

"Come on soldier, relax. You're due for a night in the Quiet Room."

"What? I haven't done anything, you can't—"

Much too late he started to struggle. He was on the bed now, face down, with Hans on top of him and Klaus tightening the long straitjacket sleeves around his body. He kicked, kicked, could connect with nothing. Then Klaus was kneeling on his legs, pulling up a heavy zipper.

In seconds he was being hustled out into the corridor, helpless. Even so, his training enabled him to swing them, to get one hearty kick aimed at Klaus' crotch. But at the last minute he held it—he couldn't win here, god knew what nasty revenges they would wreak on him if he broke Klaus' balls.

His first impressions of the Quiet Room were heat, and the stink of disinfectant. There was no window, only the small heavy glass insert in the door. There was a can with no seat. A bare mattress lay on the floor skew-wise. That was all.

They dumped him on the mattress, and then came the final indignity—they pulled off his pajama pants. He was protesting and crying out, and he could hear how his voice sounded muted. The Quiet

Room was efficiently soundproofed. The faint keening he had heard near here might have been someone yelling his lungs out.

"How long? How long?" he beseeched.

"We'll see," said Miss Plastic crisply, and they marched out. The door slammed to with a heavy thud.

He got up behind them, to press his face against the glass in the door. It was one-way. Behind his own reflection he could make out only the blur of a ceiling light. In despair, he let himself fall back on the mattress. But there was no relaxing—under the straitjacket the invisible insects were starting their scratching again.

That night he could not, would not remember.

He tried things, nearly breaking his teeth. He located a rough edge on the toilet and backed up to it, sawing the canvas against it. But he accomplished only the smoothing of the metal edge, the damn jacket wasn't normal canvas but some super-stuff. He spent an hour leaning against the door with his face to the glass. Once a head loomed up outside. He shouted "Help!" with all his might. The head went away.

The diarrhea came back, he tried to make the can but fouled himself. The insect-itching was beyond belief, he could not lie down but paced, paced, paced the tiny hot room.

Finally weakness felled him, he crawled to the mattress and lay curled in a crazy ball, jerking. And on, hour after torment-filled hour . . .

Sometime during the eternity the door opened and the dark-haired nurse came in. She had a glass of water for him, and a cool wet cloth with which she mopped his face. He felt unbelievably good.

"How . . . longer?"

She frowned. "Soon, now. I'll speak to somebody."

"What is this . . . bad-cop-good-cop routine?"

She didn't get it, just shook her head No.

"Look, I'm not yelling . . . any more . . . I'll be . . . good."

Gently she said, "Here's something a patient told me, he said it helps. Find some place on your body that doesn't hurt—maybe your left ear, maybe a hand, your tongue, maybe. Anything that isn't hurting—you concentrate on that. Think *only* about this place that isn't hurting. *Think* about it. I was told it really helps."

She went away.

He tried her recommendation. Maybe it helped.

When the light in the door-window was changing, Hans and Klaus came in. They boosted him up and untied the jacket. His arms were so stiff he could barely pull them free.

All dirty and naked as he was, he was led back through the empty corridor and pushed onto the bed. He was careful to say nothing, not to resist in any way. He had done some thinking.

The point was, to get out of here. Ending his life here was just plain impossible, they'd convinced him of that. He was terminally "safe," all right.

So he had to get out their way. He had to go along. Grin, pretend to be getting better, stand everything. No asking even for Maalox. No arguing about gradual detoxification. Even smile at Miss Plastic . . .

Could he do it? Oh, Christ, Oh Christ, for even a quarter of an M-tab! He was so weak, so weak. Could he do all that cold, keep it up?

He had to.

After all, they thought he was headed home, they couldn't keep him here forever. And he guessed they were overcrowded—there'd been a lot of beds visible through the grille, in the big domed room he'd woken up in. Probably they were eager to mark him "cured" and get shut of him. Probably they were eager to see that their savage system worked, that he was successfully "detoxed."

He smiled grimly lying in his dirt and shame. He'd be playing to an audience that wanted to believe.

So he tried. Almost falling, with weakness, he carried his trays to the table, made himself eat, spoke friendly to the guys beside him, and didn't tell anybody when he got back to his room and threw it all up. The world spinning around him with dizziness, he paced the corridor, swinging his arms. "For exercise." The dark-haired nurse smiled at him. When Miss Plastic stuck her head in on her fifteen-minute checks, he made himself smile and greet her. Once he even apologized for giving her so much trouble. She smiled and said, "That's what we're here for, soldier." In his mind's eye he held a picture of what she'd be here for if he had a chance, and grinned back. He made a try at keeping his room clean, used the mop when a check was due.

But the trouble was, he wasn't getting any better, inside. The nights were hells of nightmare memories. And he grew not stronger but weaker, the weakness was like an iron yoke on his shoulders, and every effort left him dizzy and gasping. He hid this as well as he could, blaming his occasional falls on the loose hospital slippers. One day he made it to the showers, and nearly drowned himself fainting in the stall. He found the linen-room and clean pajamas, but it took him half an hour to get them on, leaning against the shelves, the room almost blacked out. Weaker day by day.

What was the plan—that his body must relearn to make the substances, as somebody had told him? What if his body wouldn't, what if he was too far gone? He didn't know much about his internal workings, nor care, but he did know that individuals varied greatly. What if he were the one who didn't recover, whose adrenaline gland or whatever had died? He felt he was running on a shrinking energy-supply, like an exhausted battery, each day less. He became genuinely frightened that he couldn't keep up the deception, that he would be stuck here with his unbearable memories forever.

But, miraculously, it worked. They *were* overcrowded in the detox wing. In less than a week he found himself ordered to move again, this time to a corridor with chairs in it, with open access to the space between the grilles, the "dayroom." At the far end of the corridor were normal double doors, giving onto a green gardeny-looking place. His room was no bigger; but he had a table, and the window, though screened, had clear glass and curtains. He went to it, looked out on a wall and a tangled garden. And the glass could be opened by a screw-handle through the screens! He made his trembling arms turn them wide, sank down on the chair to pant in the fresh air. Oh, god! For a moment he actually felt better.

On his second day there he was given "Grounds privilege." Hans came and unlocked the end doors and pointed out the path around the untended garden. "Take walks! Three a day." He went back in.

For a few minutes he couldn't believe it. Air! Openness! He buried his face in an overblown big red rose flower. Perfume of wine, perfume of freedom.

Tentatively, slowly, he walked out along the path. An eight-foot chain-wire fence topped by triple barbed wire ran beside him. Nothing he could climb. The fence enclosed the garden and a piece of wild country with trees just outside it.

Just then a twinge of dysentery struck him. He pushed through the garden hedge toward a small grove of pines. They'd run the fence outside this. He could see why—the grove was edged with a shoulder-high growth of thorn-bushes. He fought his way through these to a tiny clearing in the center. Here he stopped, warned by a familiar smell. It took him an instant to locate the cause, under the blanket of pine-needles.

For sure, the fencing team hadn't bothered to check out this grove. A dead GI lay among the needles, his M-30 by his outstretched hand. The hand was almost gone to bone; the body was weirdly shrunken and desiccated under its shell of body-armor. He must have been killed when they finally took San Izquierda. But Don stopped not to think of this—with a strangled cry he flung himself down beside the dead man, his hand clawing at the inside pocket of the rigid vest.

And—oh, god in heaven!—it was there!

Incredulous, he drew out the small yellow case, opened it with fingers all but out of control. It was—full! Oh, precious, precious— he stared at the rows of Ms, the slot of BZs, the line of Sleepers. Here, in his hand. Carefully, carefully, he drew out an M and closed the box, before swallowing it. What incredible luck, come to save him just as he was at his last strength!

Then his body made its needs felt again, and he hastily dropped his pants. Squatting there, he saw that the dead man had been on the same mission—his armor pants were down. Somebody had seen him, or was waiting there, the corpse's lowest parts were blown away, gray fragments of pelvis sticking out of the long-dead meat. Big black tarry puddle, mess, so old that the flies were almost gone. Death finished up quickly down here. But leaving him the priceless pack in his hands, the first faint glow stealing through his veins.

Where to hide it?

Under his leg bandage. Then he rose and made his way carefully back to the path, around to the door. On his way he noticed that the big link fence had a set of gates, chained and padlocked.

He knocked on the glass, and Hans presently let him back in, locking up behind him.

"Great walk," he babbled at Hans. "Makes you feel better already."

In his room he took careful thought. Here they didn't do the fifteen-minute check, but no telling when someone would come in. Finally he took the pills out of the case, and hid them by ones and twos, in the hems of the curtain, under the edge of the electric outlet, in a crack around the back of the can, and other nooks. He wouldn't forget where they were, not he! At supper-time he slipped the empty box, twisted out of recognition, into the waste-can that came with the trays.

Dinner that night was a time of glory. The weakness had faded to a mild fatigue, all pains were gone; the M was affecting him the way it used to, giving a rosy glow of alertness, all trouble far away. He talked to people, asked them questions and listened to the answers, even helped one of the zombies from the detox corridor to find his tray. The man grunted at him; looking closely at his eyes, Don saw the redness left by BZs not quite gone. His arm was in a heavy sling, sticking out from his side. "It'll get better," Don told him gently. "You just have to put up with the shit." The man grunted again.

Seeing Miss Plastic, Don saluted her cheerfully and told her that the garden walk had really set him up. Better be careful, he warned himself. I'm acting drunk. He toned down his grin.

She frowned. "If you're going to be going outside, soldier, you'd better wear some clothes."

"Clothes?"

"In the laundry room you'll find fatigues. That's what they're there for."

Better and better. On his way back to his room he collected a set that seemed to have all its buttons and parts. The laundry here was done by rock-crusher, he thought merrily, glowing with all-rightness.

That night he had his Sleeper, and slept for the first time, sweetly, without dreams. Whatever the war had brought was far away and somebody else's story.

His last thought was that he must be systematic, ration the pills. They had to get him back to the front. He knew now that he was hooked; with the tabs he was normal, without them he was a sick shadow. And the front was where they were. It wouldn't be hard to break away and head there; not many people went AWOL *to* the fighting. And with a little fast talking, any unit would take him in.

The next days passed like floating flowers. Again and again he had to caution himself not to act too euphoric, but no one seemed to see anything odd. Even the dark-haired nurse accepted his story of what the garden and the flowers had done for him, and smiled tenderly.

Then came the morning when everybody but he seemed to know he'd be leaving the next day, with four or five other guys who had been detoxed.

That afternoon he found out something else, too. Had he miscalculated or forgotten? Whichever, he could locate no more Ms. Search as he would, there were none. The NDs and the BZs were okay, but no Maintenance. What the hell, he'd been without before, he could make it.

But as the hours dragged by and the insects began to show up again, his resolve weakened. He fingered a red BZ. They were supposed to be for when you were in actual contact with the enemy. But here, far from the front, what could they do to him? He couldn't recall any bad effects, except a burst of strength. . . .

A nonexistent termite column crawled under his waistband, he writhed to scratch it. A minute later he had to do it again. Oh, god, not this . . . if he watched himself carefully, didn't let anyone look too closely at his eyes, it'd be all right.

He popped the BZ.

. . . As he'd thought, nothing happened except that he felt more alert and the bugs faded out. Colors seemed lighter and brighter, too. Hell, BZs are only some kind of super pep-pill, he thought. But he'd gotten sloppy; he was standing right in front of the window, where any stranger could look in and see him. Perfect target. He backed away, pulling the curtains to.

His mind drifted to his last day of combat. Hill Number thirteen-forty-seven, that's what they were taking. Down here they called mountains "hills." The front was well ahead of there by now, people said. But where was the enemy now?

He glanced worriedly around, opened a chink in the curtains and peered out. Nothing moving out there. Nothing in the corridor, either. Or, wait—his ears seemed to have sharpened—there were some footsteps up at the far end in the dayroom. Little tapping steps.

As he listened, they grew clearer, sharper. Heading his way now!

And he could catch a faint jangling sound. Aha, that would be the big key-ring Miss Plastic wore on her wrist.

Enemy sounds, coming along the wall. Coming for him?

Automatically he flexed his hands, fingered the callus on the outer edges of his palms. Had they grown soft? Did someone think they could take him, now? He sidled to the door, listening hard.

The footsteps were alone.

The little blonde nurse came on duty early again that afternoon. She takes extra duty a lot, partly because there is nothing to do in San Izquierda, but mostly because of a nagging sense of responsibility. Twice, coming back, she has found doors open that should have been locked. People were so sloppy. Right now, for instance, both the orderlies are out on lunch break together, quite contrary to orders. She looks round the dayroom; no hard cases here. But are the garden doors locked? The orderlies have grown specially careless about that, now that so many patients have Grounds privilege.

She decides to check them before she does the detox ward check.

She straps on her official key-ring, and starts down the empty corridor, tap-tap-tap.

As she passes one of the last doors, it opens silently and a shadowy face looks out, right into hers.

To cover her start, she smiles brightly and starts to say, "Hello, soldier."

They are the last sounds she ever utters.

She never knew what struck her throat, smashing the delicate larynx and crushing her vocal cords. She had no idea that the human hand could strike such a blow as the Army's sentry chop, no idea that she could be rendered voiceless before she had a chance to scream.

Bent over with pain, she feels herself being dragged into the room. Her clothes are being yanked up. She beats futilely at inhumanly strong hands. A voice says thickly, "You know I'm going to kill you afterwards?"

And then a smashing blow hits her face, breaking teeth, and another.

"You won't be a cute corpse."

The orderly he called Hans had given him the idea with his bed-search. Now Don heaves up the mattress, and flattens the little corpse on the sagging springs. No blood on him, no blood anywhere. He pulls the mattress back—there's scarcely a discernible mound. To disguise it he makes up the bed tight and neat. Anyone looking in would see a nice clean empty room, soldier.

Now to fix up a few little things, collect his pills and go. He has taken charge of the key-ring first thing; there were two padlock-type keys on it.

The corridor is empty, Hans and Klaus are nowhere to be seen. The garden door is locked, but the first key he tries opens it smoothly. He slips out, locks up behind him. In a moment he is forcing his way into the little pine-grove.

Nothing has changed, except a few more pine-needles on the corpse's face. His first thought had been the gun and ammo—but wait, he'll need ident. He grabs the dead man's dog-tags. Its chain slices through the poor hollow shell of neck. Isidore West—he is Isidore West now. Isidore for San Izzy. West hadn't been carrying any papers, only a crumpled snapshot of a girl. Well, he'll be welcome wherever he turns up.

Maybe the body-armor would be a good idea too. Reluctantly he slides the dead man out of his jerkin, but can't bring himself to touch the fouled breeches. He shakes a big black beetle out of the vest, and gets it on under his fatigues, the usual way. Ammo belts on top.

Okay, now out the gate, the M-30 stuck into the loose fatigue legs. At the last minute he picks up two grenades West had been carrying, and hooks them on his belt.

The second key opens the fence-gate padlock, and he exits neatly before anyone comes out to the garden. Good; he doesn't want any more hassles, although he now has a neat place to stow any bodies. He resnaps the chain and lock behind him.

Outside is a gravel road. A sign points to San Izquierda, it carries a silhouette of a bus. Good. Transport is what he needs, and GIs can ride free on buses.

But he wishes he had a map. The front must be somewhere to the north—he can identify that by the sun—but where and how far? He recalls the company's maps, with their neatly-drawn lines and estimates of Gué position and strength, even his own company marked in. Somewhere up in the States men are sitting in peaceful rooms, drawing such lines. Numbering hills. Moving little tin soldiers over the terrain, as word comes to them.

He is one little soldier out of place, but the map-makers won't know that. He and Isidore West.

Chuffing behind him. He whirls, but it is only the San Izquierda bus, on its way out from the town. It stops beside him, right on cue, and a girl gets out. For a flash, he thinks it's the girl who chopped his nails. But no matter now; he hops in and hobbles back down the aisle, still concealing his gun. The BZ feels like it's running low. He sits down on the back seat, fishes out another and swallows.

The bus holds only a few passengers; three women with babies, a few very old women and men, two or three children, baskets of chickens, and a pig with a rope on its hinder legs.

He waits till the hospital is well behind them before slipping out the gun. It needs cleaning badly, but it's functional. Cradling it in one arm, he makes his way up to the driver.

"Where are the Guévaristas now?" he asks in his painful Spanish.

"Nada, nada," the driver seems amused.

"But where is the fighting?" Don persists. "I am lost." As he says it he realizes he's saying he has perished, so he tries again. "*Me equivo-cado*—I've made a mistake. *Dondé*—where are they? *Mis amigos* are there. I must go to my friends."

"Ah!" The driver gestures grandly ahead. "*Al norte*—far, *muy lejos*, very far."

"Ah," he says in his turn, "*Gracias.* I go with you to the north. I do not want to go back to San Izquierda."

"*Si.*"

He turns and heads back to his seat, nearly falling over the pig.

At the next stop an old woman with chickens gets off and a boy on crutches swings himself on. He is minus one foot, the leg ends in a dirty sock strapped up. He looks a very young sixteen. As he sits down Don sees that he is wearing Gué uniform pants under his smock, and his one boot is Gué combat issue. A wounded veteran, apparently, left behind when the front moved on. The boy casts him a sharp look, then turns his head away.

Don flinches, takes out another BZ. But it doesn't work fast enough to prevent him from thinking of those easy-living men up home in their war-rooms, drawing lines on maps, moving their tin soldiers.

The bus keeps chuffing northward, now and then stopping to let people off. Going home after a day in San Izquierda. Here and there in the woods are tucked little Maya-style *casitas*, each with its tiny corn-and-melon-and-bean plot. Almost all have a papaya tree lean-ing close to the roof.

The bus passes a hamlet. Here almost all the houses have been burned and gutted, but two old men get off. The boy with one foot is still aboard, talking to a middle-aged woman. His tone sounds angry.

Don can't help staring at him, feeling adrenalin pump a little. Had this lad been one of those who had ambushed B Company, back before Hill thirteen-forty-seven? A lot of his comrades bought it then. It was well inside Bodégua, but no one knew how far. The border was mushy here, it supposedly followed a mountain ridge that divided and divided again. *It's their country*, a voice had kept saying in Don's head. Just as the pants that boy was wearing were the official uniform of their army. However unsavory their government, it was theirs. Not his, to invade and shoot up their sons. But this was the *enemy*, a limb of International Atheist Red Communism. He didn't look much like the enemy, or a limb of anything now.

The boy laughs sharply at something the woman is saying, and turns to glance at Don. "*Yanqui*," he says under his breath, or seems to say—the bus is making so much noise it's hard to be sure. "*Yanqui* assassin." He looks hard at Don, meeting his eyes, then suddenly seems to see something that changes his mood. He slumps in his seat, saying something to the woman. She gathers her baskets, gets off at the next stop.

It comes to Don that his eyes must be reddening from the BZs and the boy had seen that and knew that Don was a berserker. They know about BZs, all right.

The bus has turned off the main road, and seems to be circling back toward San Izquierda. He'll have to get off and start looking for a ride north.

Suddenly the boy cocks his head to listen. The bus stops, and Don can hear it too now—the heavy rumble of six-by-sixes. In a moment it comes in sight on the road they'd left—a long convoy of camouflage-painted trucks and weapons-carriers. American soldiers were crowded in the trucks, hanging their legs out over the tailgates. That would be replacements and supplies headed for the front. That's the kind of ride he wants to catch. And that must be the main road to the front, too. He'll get out here and go back and wait.

Just as he's making his way up to the doors, there comes another sound. The crippled boy gives a peculiar whistle. Then Don hears it—under the convoy's noise and the bus's engine is a steady slapping beat—a chopper. Probably guarding the convoy. But wait a minute—the sound isn't right. He twists to stare out the back window and catches a glimpse.

No mistaking—the ugly square end of a Krasny 16, guns sticking out. A Gué fireship, out after the convoy.

Meanwhile guns have opened up ahead, from something he can't see. The fireship slides neatly sideways, out of sight over the ridge. All sounds cease.

For a second Don has a double flash; BZs sometimes do that to you. It's so peaceful here, in an ordinary bus on a quiet country road, the pines rustling in the soft wind. He feels disastrously out of place.

And then the sun flashes on copter blades beyond the ridge, and there's the racket of guns and thuds out of view to the right. The people in the bus come to life in a general stampede for the doors. They know a bus could be a target, they'd rather take their chances by ones and twos in the brush. The pig screams.

But the driver resists. He shouts "San Izquierda! San Izquierda!" and the bus starts fast. People are pounding on the doors, yelling at him to stop. Don is beside him now, he grabs the emergency brake, but it has no effect. He gets his foot down on the brake, the driver pushes him and tries to punch him away. Don punches back. The bus wobbles to a stop, the doors open, and people pour out, including the boy on crutches. At the last minute, the driver yells something and dives for the door after them, leaving Don alone in the bus.

Panting, he sits down in the driver's seat to consider. Now he really has transport—he can turn this thing around and follow the convoy till the gas gives out.

There's a crossroad just ahead. But as he looks, it fills up, first with cattle, then with a bunch of civilian-looking cars, obviously waiting for the cows to clear. Clean, expensive-looking cars with fender flags on them. Even the escort jeeps are shiny clean, with little flags too. Obviously it's some kind of high-level party touring here. They seem unaware of the Gué fireship behind him. Senior-looking civilians, shining generals, and a woman, have gotten out, are staring around at the scenery, looking at San Izquierda which must be right below them. To Don's amazement, several of the men produce cameras and start to take photos. *Tourists*, by God, Don thinks.

And then corrects himself. These aren't tourists—these are, these are some of the easy-living men he'd dreamed of, the ones sitting in front of big terrain maps, drawing lines, while their aides move little soldiers and flags around.

Without thinking, he has popped another BZ.

Without thinking, he has started the bus. Automatically, he unhooks the two grenades and arms them. Meticulously, he breaks out the front window with his gun-butt, then reverses the gun to point out.

The men ahead are getting into their cars, all bunched together. Good.

A raging fury he has never experienced roars through his body. Do those men know, can they guess, that the little figures they move around are real live men and boys, boys who bleed?

The front, the Guévaristas, fade far away. His foot slams down on the accelerator, the old bus churns forward. Faster, faster yet. Don is half-crouched now, his rifle through the empty windshield. Standing on the gas, steering with one elbow, he takes aim. Faster yet the bus surges forward, dead toward them. The grenades tick. The first burst comes from his rifle, finding targets. Then another. Screams.

—And Don Still, standing on the gas on his glory ride, fires, fires, fires—his enemy in his sights at last.

An Inhabitant of Carcosa

AMBROSE BIERCE

For there be divers sorts of death—some wherein the body remaineth; and in some it vanisheth quite away with the spirit. This commonly occurreth only in solitude (such is God's will) and, none seeing the end, we say that man is lost, or gone on a long journey—which indeed he hath; but sometimes it hath happened in the sight of many, as abundant testimony showeth. In one kind of death the spirit also dieth, and this it hath been known to do while yet the body was in vigor for many years. Sometimes, as is veritably attested, it dieth with the body, but after a season is raised up again in that place where the body did decay.

Pondering these words of Hali (whom God rest) and questioning their full meaning, as one who, having an intimation, yet doubts if there be not something behind, other than that which he has discerned, I noted not whither I had strayed until a sudden chill wind striking my face revived in me a sense of my surroundings. I observed with astonishment that everything seemed unfamiliar. On every side of me stretched a bleak and desolate expanse of plain, covered with a tall undergrowth of sere grass, which rustled and whistled in the autumn wind with heaven knows what mysterious and disquieting suggestion. Protruded at long intervals above it stood strangely shaped and somber-colored rocks, which seemed to have an understanding with one another and to exchange looks of uncomfortable significance, as if they had reared their heads to watch the issue of some foreseen event. A few blasted trees here and there appeared as leaders in this malevolent conspiracy of silent expectation.

The day, I thought, must be far advanced, though the sun was invisible; and although sensible that the air was raw and chill my consciousness of that fact was rather mental than physical—I had no feeling of discomfort. Over all the dismal landscape a canopy of low, lead-colored clouds hung like a visible curse. In all this there were a menace and a portent—a hint of evil, an intimation of doom. Bird, beast, or insect there was none. The wind sighed in the bare branches of the dead trees and the gray grass bent to whisper its dread secret to the earth; but no other sound nor motion broke the awful repose of that dismal place.

I observed in the herbage a number of weather-worn stones, evidently shaped with tools. They were broken, covered with moss and half sunken in the earth. Some lay prostrate, some leaned at various angles, none was vertical. They were obviously headstones of graves, though the graves themselves no longer existed as either mounds or depressions; the years had levelled all. Scattered here and there, more massive blocks showed where some pompous tomb or ambitious monument had once flung its feeble defiance at oblivion. So old seemed these relics, these vestiges of vanity and memorials of affection and piety, so battered and worn and stained—so neglected, deserted, forgotten the place, that I could not help thinking myself the discoverer of the burial ground of a prehistoric race of men whose very name was long extinct.

Filled with these reflections, I was for some time heedless of the sequence of my own experiences, but soon I thought, "How came I hither?" A moment's reflection seemed to make this all clear and explain at the same time, though in a disquieting way, the singular character with which my fancy had invested all that I saw or heard. I was ill. I remembered now that I had been prostrated by a sudden fever, and that my family had told me that in my periods of delirium I had constantly cried out for liberty and air, and had been held in bed to prevent my escape out-of-doors. Now I had eluded the vigilance of my attendants and had wandered hither to—to where? I could not conjecture. Clearly I was at a considerable distance from the city where I dwelt—the ancient and famous city of Carcosa.

No signs of human life were anywhere visible nor audible; no rising smoke, no watchdog's bark, no lowing of cattle, no shouts of children at play—nothing but that dismal burial place with its air of mystery and dread, due to my own disordered brain. Was I not becoming again delirious, there beyond human aid? Was it not indeed *all* an illusion of my madness? I called aloud the names of my wives and sons, reached out my hands in search of theirs, even as I walked among the crumbling stones and in the withered grass.

A noise behind me caused me to turn about. A wild animal—a lynx—was approaching. The thought came to me: if I break down here in the desert—if the fever returns and I fail, this beast will be at my throat. I sprang toward it, shouting. It trotted tranquilly by within a hand's breadth of me and disappeared behind a rock.

A moment later a man's head appeared to rise out of the ground a short distance away. He was ascending the farther slope of a low hill whose crest was hardly to be distinguished from the general level. His whole figure soon came into view against the background of gray cloud. He was half naked, half clad in skins. His hair was unkempt, his beard long and ragged. In one hand he carried a bow and arrow; the other held a blazing torch with a long trail of black smoke. He walked slowly and with caution, as if he feared falling into some open grave concealed by the tall grass. This strange apparition surprised but did not alarm, and taking such a course as to intercept him I met him almost face to face, accosting him with the familiar salutation, "God keep you."

He gave no heed, nor did he arrest his pace.

"Good stranger," I continued, "I am ill and lost. Direct me, I beseech you, to Carcosa."

The man broke into a barbarous chant in an unknown tongue, passing on and away.

An owl on the branch of a decayed tree hooted dismally and was answered by another in the distance. Looking upward, I saw through a sudden rift in the clouds Aldebaran and the Hyades! In all this there was a hint of night—the lynx, the man with the torch, the owl. Yet I saw—I saw even the stars in absence of the darkness. I saw, but was apparently not seen or heard. Under what awful spell did I exist?

I seated myself at the root of a great tree, seriously to consider what it were best to do. That I was mad I could no longer doubt, yet recognized a ground of doubt in the conviction. Of fever I had no trace. I had, withal, a sense of exhilaration and vigor altogether unknown to me—a feeling of mental and physical exaltation. My senses seemed all alert; I could feel the air as a ponderous substance; I could hear the silence.

A great root of the giant tree against whose trunk I leaned as I sat held enclosed in its grasp a slab of stone, a part of which protruded into a recess formed by another root. The stone was thus partly protected from the weather, though greatly decomposed. Its edges were worn round, its corners eaten away, its surface deeply furrowed and scaled. Glittering particles of mica were visible in the earth about it—vestiges of its decomposition. This stone had apparently marked the grave out of which the tree had sprung ages ago. The tree's exacting roots had robbed the grave and made the stone a prisoner.

A sudden wind pushed some dry leaves and twigs from the uppermost face of the stone; I saw the low-relief letters of an inscription and bent to read it. God in heaven! *my* name in full!—the date of *my* birth!—the date of *my* death!

A level shaft of light illuminated the whole side of the tree as I sprang to my feet in terror. The sun was rising in the rosy east. I stood between the tree and his broad red disk—no shadow darkened the trunk!

A chorus of howling wolves saluted the dawn. I now saw them sitting on their haunches, singly and in groups, on the summits of irregular mounds and tumuli filling a half of my desert prospect and extending to the horizon. And then I knew that these were the ruins of the ancient and famous city of Carcosa.

Such are the facts imparted to the medium Bayrolles by the spirit Hoseib Alar Robardin.

Real Time

LAWRENCE WATT-EVANS

Someone was tampering with time again; I could feel it, in my head and in my gut, that sick, queasy sensation of unreality.

I put my head down and gulped air, waiting for the discomfort to pass, but it only got worse.

This was a bad one. Someone was tampering with something serious. This wasn't just someone reading tomorrow's papers and playing the stock market, this was *serious*. Someone was trying to change history.

I couldn't allow that. Not only might his tampering interfere with my own past, change my whole life, possibly even wipe me out of existence, but I'd be shirking my job. I couldn't do that.

Not that anyone would know. They must think I'm dead. I haven't been contacted in years now, not since I was stranded in this century. They must think I was lost when my machine and my partner vanished in the flux.

But I'm not dead, and I had a job to do. With help from headquarters or without, with a partner or without, even with my machine or without, I had a job to do, a reality to preserve, a whole world to safeguard. I knew my duty. I *know* my duty. The past can't take tampering.

They might send someone else, but they might not. The tampering might have already changed things too much. They might not spot it in time. Or they might simply not have the manpower. Time travel lets you use your manpower efficiently, with one hundred percent efficiency, putting it anywhere you need it instantly, but that's not enough when you have all of the past to guard, everything from the dawn of time to the present—not *this* present, the *real* present— you'd need a million men to guard it all, and they've always had trouble recruiting. The temptations are too great. The dangers are too great. Look at me, stuck here in the past, for the dangers—and as for the temptations, look at what I have to do. People trying to *change* everything, trying to benefit themselves at the cost of reality itself—they need men they can *trust*, men like me, and there can never be enough of us.

I sat up straight again and I looked at the mirror behind the bar and I knew what I had to do. I had to stop the tampering. Just as I had stopped it before, three—no, four—four times now.

They might send someone else, but they might not, and I couldn't take that chance.

I had to find the tamperer myself, and deal with him. If I couldn't find him directly, if he wasn't in this time period but later, then I might need to tamper with time myself, to change *his* past without hurting *mine*.

That's tricky, but I've done it.

I slid off the stool and stood up, gulped the rest of my drink, and laid a bill on the bar—five dollars in the currency of the day. I shrugged, straightening my coat, and I stepped out into the cool of a summer night.

Insects sang somewhere, strange insects extinct before I was born, and the streetlights pooled pale gray across the black sidewalks. I turned my head slowly, feeling the flux, feeling the shape of the time-stream, of my reality.

Downtown was firm, solid, still rooted in the past and the present and secure in the future. Facing in the opposite direction I felt my gut twist. I crossed the empty street to my car.

I drove out the avenues, ignoring the highways; I can't feel as well on the highways, they're too far out of the city's life-flow.

I went north, then east, and the nausea gripped me tighter with every block. It became a gnawing pain in my belly as the world shimmered and shifted around me, an unstable reality. I stopped the car by the side of the street and forced the pain down, forced my perception of the world to steady itself.

When I was ready to go on I leaned over and checked in the glove compartment. No gloves—the name was already an anachronism even in this time period. But my gun was there. Not my service weapon; that's an anachronism, too advanced. I don't dare use it. The knowledge of its existence could be dangerous. No, I had bought a gun here, in this era.

I pulled it out and put it in my coat pocket. The weight of it, that hard metal tugging at my side, felt oddly comforting.

I had a knife, too. I was dealing with primitives, with savages, not with civilized people. These final decades of the twentieth century, with their brushfire wars and nuclear arms races, were a jungle, even in the great cities of North America. I had a knife, a good one, with a six-inch blade I had sharpened myself.

Armed, I drove on, and two blocks later I had to leave the avenue, turn onto the quiet side-streets, tree-lined and peaceful.

Somewhere, in that peace, someone was working to destroy my home, my life, my *self*.

I turned again, and felt the queasiness and pain leap within me, and I knew I was very close.

I stopped the car and got out, the gun in my pocket and my hand on the gun, my other hand holding the knife.

One house had a light in the window; the homes on either side were dark. I scanned, and I knew that that light was it, the center of the unreality—maybe not the tamperer himself, but something, a focus for the disturbance of the flow of history.

Perhaps it was an ancestor of the tamperer; I had encountered that before.

I walked up the front path and rang the bell.

I braced myself, the knife in one hand, the gun in the other.

The porch light came on, and the door started to open. I threw myself against it.

It burst in, and I went through it, and I was standing in a hallway. A man in his forties was staring at me, holding his wrist where the door had slammed into it as it pulled out of his grip. There had been no chainbolt; my violence had, perhaps, been more than was necessary.

I couldn't take risks, though. I pointed the gun at his face and squeezed the trigger.

The thing made a report like the end of the world, and the man fell, blood and tissue sprayed across the wall behind him.

A woman screamed from a nearby doorway, and I pointed the gun at her, unsure.

The pain was still there. It came from the woman. I pulled the trigger again.

She fell, blood red on her blouse, and I looked down at her as the pain faded, as stability returned.

I was *real* again.

If the man were her husband, perhaps she was destined to remarry, or to be unfaithful—*she* would have been the tamperer's ancestor, but *he* might not have been. The twisting of time had stopped only when the woman fell.

I regretted shooting him, then, but I had had no choice. Any delay might have been fatal. The life of an individual is precious, but not as precious as history itself.

A twinge ran through my stomach; perhaps only an after-effect, but I had to be certain. I knelt, and went quickly to work with my knife.

When I was done, there could be no doubt that the two were dead, and that neither could ever have children.

Finished, I turned and fled, before the fumbling police of this era could interfere.

I knew the papers would report it the next day as the work of a lunatic, of a deranged thief who panicked before he could take anything, or of someone killing for perverted pleasure. I didn't worry about that.

I had saved history again.

I wish there were another way, though.

Sometimes I have nightmares about what I do, sometimes I dream that I've made a mistake, killed the wrong person, that I stranded myself here. What if it wasn't a mechanical failure that sent the machine into flux, what if I changed my own past and did that to myself?

I have those nightmares sometimes.

Worse, though, the very worst nightmares, are the ones where I dream that I never changed the past at all, that I never lived in any time but this one, that I grew up here, alone, through an unhappy childhood and a miserable adolescence and a sorry adulthood—that I never traveled in time, that it's all in my mind, that I killed those people for nothing.

That's the worst of all, and I wake up from that one sweating, ready to scream.

Thank God it's not true.

Killer in the House

JAS. R. PETRIN

"You *will* be all right, won't you, Nanny?"

'Course I will. Go out, and have fun, and leave me at home with a killer!

Nanny sat in her wheelchair, silent, angry, swathed in her blanket, watching her granddaughter Gwen fuss in and out of the bathroom, the bedroom, putting on her clothes, her scent, and her face, while her husband Will leaned his head in at the door and called with annoyance, "The car's warmed up and running, the Arabs are getting rich, are we going to the damn restaurant or not?"

"I'm *coming*, can't you give me a minute's peace? I've only got to put on my coat and see if Nanny needs anything."

Gwen came stumping across the living room, shaking the floor, and bent over Nanny. She smelled like a harlot's picnic. She was a good girl, though, Gwen was, more considerate of Nanny than her sister Liz had ever been. Considerate and caring, but none too bright. She was a stupid, and so was her husband. They were both stupids.

"Nanny," Gwen whispered, "we're leaving now. You know I'll worry about you the whole time we're gone. We may go to a movie after din-din, we may not. I don't know. But if we're late, you mustn't worry. Louie will be along. I made him promise to skip the bar at the Red Lantern tonight, to come home early and fix your dinner. So you'll only be alone for an hour or so. Now tell me, darling, if there's anything you want before we go."

She was studying Nanny's lips, and Nanny's eyes swam from the scent of her perfume.

There's lots I want, Nanny thought. *I want you to stay right here and not charge off and leave me alone with that murdering Louie, and I want Will to go on out to that freezer Louie brought here with him when he moved in and crowbar that lock open and get your frozen-stiff sister Liz out of it and thaw her out and bury her proper and Christian, and I want Louie dragged out of here by a policeman, kicking, and a rope got around him, and him hung up high until he's dead, dead, dead!*

But when a stroke comes along and hits you like a runaway wagon the way it had Nanny last fall, you were lucky if you could still draw breath.

She could feel Gwen's eyes on her face. Out in the driveway Will was revving up the Dodge like he was part of a getaway. Which maybe he was. A getaway from Nanny.

Nanny struggled to shape the words on her lips.

Killer, she mouthed, *in the house! Look . . . the freezer*!

Gwen straightened, puffing out her fat cheeks and laughing.

"Oh, Nanny, don't start up with *that* again."

"Don't start up with what?" It was Will poking his head in on a blast of winter air.

"I think she's going on about Louie's freezer again. You know how it upsets her. She thinks he's got Lizzie Mae's body inside it. I wish you'd make him open it and give Nanny a look inside so as to set her mind at rest."

Will sighed a long weary breath and rolled his eyes in his best God-give-me-strength expression.

"Look. You know I talked to Louie, and you know I explained it all to Nanny a dozen times. He keeps the freezer locked so those kids you babysit don't go trapping themselves in it and suffocating; he keeps it running so it doesn't get to smelling all skunky inside; and she doesn't need to look in it anyways because, like I told her another dozen times, me and Louie seen Liz at the mall. I seen her myself with my own two eyes, walking large as life through the Easton Mall. Now if all that don't satisfy her, nothing will. Can we go now?"

Gwen's eyes flashed with sudden annoyance.

"I wish you'd stop talking in front of Nanny like she wasn't even here. It wouldn't hurt Louie to let her have a little peek. It wouldn't hurt anybody one bit." She bent over Nanny again, with a look of concern. "There's nothing for you to worry about, darling, every-thing's fine. You'll see."

She kissed Nanny's forehead—lightly, so as not to smear her lipstick. Then the big door banged and they were gone.

Nanny would have stamped her foot in frustration if it were possible. Nothing to worry about!

Everything's fine, is it? But you haven't see Louie kneeling by his freezer, reaching down into it and speaking softly and crying. No you haven't, have you?

Leaving her alone with a killer! Did they think Nanny shouldn't have fears, simply because her welfare was entirely in their hands? Neither of them had ever awakened in the night with eyes stretched wide as sealer rings, sweating, wanting to scream, run, turn over and cry out to someone, but only able to lie there with one's body wrapped around one like a steel clamp and silently shriek into the dark.

A killer in the house!

Being paralyzed, she'd learned fear, all right. Fear such as she'd never known before in her life. Fear of fire. Fear of being at the mercy of some cruel person—like a killer.

And even, because it was always present, the fear of falling.

Except for the killer, that was the worst. Even sitting quietly here at home in her chair held a terror that made her head reel. Falling out of her chair was a horrifying notion. The nightmare of it woke her every night. The slow weightless launch into space and the floor hurtling up to smash her. It was the old childhood dream of falling, falling, falling, and not being able to raise an arm to save yourself. She shuddered.

And now they'd invited a killer to stay.

Louie.

With his freezer.

The cold they'd let in was making the oil stove groan; it whirred its fan in the corner and creaked its joints at her. She wished she had thought to ask Gwen to turn it up a notch or two; she wished she could just reach out herself and give the dial a damn good twist.

But she'd have to lift her arm to do that, and it was all she could do to lift her fingers. She lifted a finger now to the little control wand on her chair, and the motor hummed and crept her across the kitchen. It hesitated before it went; the switch wanted cleaning again. She stopped a few feet from the stove and let the heat soak into her.

Her eyes were still bleary from that horrid perfume Gwen had been wafting around. She blinked once, twice to clear them; it was an awful thing to be unable to rub your eyes when you wanted to. Her eyesight had always been good. She could read the chrome letters on the stove that spelled CHAMPION, she could read the spine of the telephone book on the stand by the back doorway, she could read the name ARCTIC through the partly opened door on the . . .

FREEZER!

It was visible there in the open doorway, hulking, one hard angular white shoulder in the dark.

Louie's freezer.

The one with Lizzie Mae's body locked inside it like a frozen pork roast.

Damn it, Gwen, you could at least have thought to close that door before you went off to enjoy yourself. Nanny moved her finger to hum the motor to turn the wheelchair away and not look.

And Louie saying he had seen Liz at the mall. What rubbish. Did he think he could fool Nanny with a comment like that? Liz couldn't be in two places at the same time and she sure as heck hadn't clambered out of that freezer, what with its being locked and all, and her lying at the bottom of it stabbed or shot or strangled, with a glaze of ice over her and her lips all blue. And Will, who had backed Louie up, had only caught a glimpse from the barbershop window where he had sat breathing with the rest of the men, all of them lathered up like mad dogs, watching the women's legs go by. It wasn't as if he'd actually *spoken* to her.

But Will, listening to Louie, thought he'd seen Liz, and so neither he nor Gwen would consider the real truth. They weren't surprised at Liz's staying away; it was just like her to cut them out. They assigned no blame for the marriage breakup, and they let Louie go smiling on. They liked him. Thought he was the cat's whiskers. It was only Nanny who had seen him, when Gwen and Will were gone for groceries and he thought she was asleep, kneeling over that open freezer like a monk, bowing and talking into the frost and sobbing.

Louie was a clothing salesman, or had been. Best in the business, he liked to brag. He'd made his managers jealous, on account of, with his commissions, he made more money than they did. Or so he said.

Nanny had never warmed to him.

She hadn't liked him from the day three years ago when Liz had waltzed him in the door, hanging all over him, announcing to a shocked silence that she was marrying him the very next day. Liz had always been impulsive like that. Taking up with any half-cracked lunatic that came smiling out of the sun. She'd found three husbands that way before Louie came along, and though all three of them had been stupids, Louie had been the only one who had struck Nanny as being totally . . .

BAD!

So Nanny had done some phoning—she wasn't all seized up then—and found out some very curious things from her friend Emma Parker in Youngerville. *They'd* had a fellow just like Louie working in their clothing store—Casey's on Third Street—and he had been simply the *strangest* man! Folks had seen him on warm evenings, parked on Lover's Lookout—which was the hill over the river where the young folks liked to go—and he had a different girl with him every single time. One night a blonde, next night a redhead—always somebody different. The gossip had gone round about it, and the next thing anybody knew, he'd got the sack from Casey's and had left town. Folks had pried away at Casey with crowbars for weeks, but he wouldn't say a word about it. Said he wouldn't bring disgrace on his store.

That same night, after the phone call, Nanny had waked up screaming because she had looked on death in a dream. And the next few times she saw Louie, she saw death following one step behind him, or peeking around him, or standing next to him and holding his arm like a bride. That dream was prophetic.

He'd killed Liz, all right. Nanny had seen it coming from the first. And now here was the proof, if anybody would bother to look. In the back room. Under lock and key. In the freezer.

Of course she'd tried to warn Liz, but Liz had only turned all huffy and cold and gone for her coat, wanting to leave right away. Then she'd begun staying away altogether, which was that Louie's doing for sure, whispering evil in her ear.

Right about then the stroke had hit Nanny, and that had been Louie's doing, too, just as sure as sheep dip. He'd hexed her. Who else had the evil to do it, after all?

Oh, Louie was trouble, all right, and nothing but. In the end, Nanny had been proved right.

Just take that night Liz had phoned. She must have been crying up a storm, Gwen was so sympathetic with her. And later Nanny had overheard Gwen telling Will about it:

". . . lost his job at the store."

"How come?"

"She wouldn't say exactly. But they caught him redhanded at something . . . something pretty bad. Louie wouldn't talk about it, so she phoned the manager and he told her what it was. She was ashamed to tell me too much, but I think it was because he wouldn't leave the female customers alone. Liz said she'd always had her suspicions about that, and now she was going to leave him . . ."

So things hadn't worked out too well down at the clothing store. And after Louie's bragging how he'd been too good for all those other stores, too—he'd worked in half a dozen. It told Nanny a lot. He hadn't been victimized by jealous managers at all. It was just the old wandering fingers problem.

And suddenly Liz had stopped phoning. Just like that, no more calls. Very suspicious. Nobody saw hide nor hair of either one of them until Louie showed up at the door with his battered suitcase and his freezer. And wasn't *that* just the darnedest thing? A freezer! Most men would have brought their TV or their liquor cabinet, but here comes Louie with a freezer.

He'd explained with his easy smile that he and Liz had broken up, that Liz didn't want to be bothered with it, and he'd brought it because it was the only thing in the house they owned free and clear. And if anybody believed *that* story, they'd buy a raffle ticket with the World Trade Center as first prize.

He hadn't fooled Nanny. Not one bit.

And now here they were. All of them under the same roof. Liz in her frozen sleep; Gwen, foolish Gwen, suspecting nothing; Will, who liked having a man in the house to talk sports with; and Nanny in her chair.

And Louie.

Hating her. No, *despising* her!

He made no secret of *that*, either.

Only a week ago there had been just the two of them in the living room, watching TV, Louie seated on the end of the couch, cursing her under his breath. Oh, he was quiet and cute about it, speaking feather soft so that Gwen shouldn't hear in the kitchen, keeping his murdering hands in his lap, his murderous eyes on the television, barely moving his lips.

"Nanny, Nanny, Nanny, hard old Nanny, mean old Nanny, Nanny the witch." He'd gone on like that for twenty minutes. Oh, he was confident with her so seized up from the stroke he'd hexed on her.

Nanny closed her eyes, tried not to think of the freezer in the dark in the room behind the wall. After a while she rested.

What woke her was a thump at the door.

Somebody cursing, fumbling, laughing.

Louie was home, and tight as a tick. So he had stopped at the Lantern, after all. Nanny felt her pulse pick up a beat from somewhere, then settle itself again.

Louie was home.

Louie the killer.

And no Gwen.

Nanny waited in her chair by the stove, and at that moment the blower shut off, sighing to a stop and impressing her with the silence of the house when Louie wasn't around. Sober or drunk, he had a loud way about him. Too friendly when sober, laughing too harshly and smiling too broadly and always standing one step too close to you; and too stupid when drunk, playing the clown, telling rude jokes and mimicking famous people to turn those around him purple with laughter.

There was a crash from the steps outside, and a loud groan. A tinkle of broken glass.

He didn't fool Nanny, though.

Nanny could see the real Louie behind the smokescreen of jokes and laughter. She had known a lot of Louies in her time. He was a type. The sort you got a glimpse of sometimes when a fresh wind gusted the smoke away, and you were always strangely shocked to see just what you'd expected, like a glimpse of hard white bone in a deep red wound.

You learned a thing or two in eighty-two years.

Now she heard the jangle of keys at the lock. Louie seemed in awful shape. He was fumbling around out there badly. Despite what Gwen had said, he must have started earlier than usual today down at the Lantern, and run into some generous friends, too.

Then the door crashed open, and there stood Louie, smiling.

"Hello—Nanny!"

He swayed in the doorway, more concerned with holding himself up than in shutting out winter with the door. He had brought two cases of beer home with him, one tucked up high under his arm, the other clutched tight in his fingers and now just a boxful of broken glass, dribbling suds and amber stains over Gwen's polished linoleum.

He made one false attempt, then another, and finally managed to set the two cases down, handling even the broken one gently, as if he hoped it held something that might yet be salvaged. He fumbled his parka off, dropped it by the fridge, and, finally sensing the chill from the open door, closed it hard by falling backwards against it.

"I said *hello*, Nanny!"

He rattled a chrome chair out from the table, arranged it with extraordinary precision, and then dropped into it, letting out one of the loudest belches Nanny had ever heard.

You wouldn't dare act like this if Gwen and Will were here. You're like every other drunk I've ever seen, with a kind of radar that lets you go on fooling certain people. All the rest, you don't want to fool. Them you want to impress with how nasty you can be. But I can see through you like a glass coffin lid, mister, see your grinning death's head face getting ready to pop out at me. Oh, I know you!

Nanny was feeling the heat of the stove now. She wanted to back away a little but was afraid to draw attention to herself. If she could somehow remain inconspicuous for the next while, maybe Gwen and Will would come crunching in out of the snow, shaking off the night and filling the room with loud talk about the movie. As Gwen had promised earlier, everything would be all right.

Louie fumbled in his shirt for cigarettes. He didn't notice that he'd already put them on the table. He gave up with a flourish of disgust, leaned forward and hooked the undamaged beer case with his finger, dragged it to him across the floor. He popped the case open with one hand—even in his drunkenness it was a polished motion—opened a bottle, took a long swallow, then groped again and finally found a cigarette.

He looked at Nanny.

"S'how the hell are ya?"

Nanny found herself wondering how she could appease him, knowing in her heart at the same time that appeasement was not possible. And even if it was, there was little she could do in her condition.

"Come here, Nanny, an' have a beer."

Her fingers fluttered at the controller. She was afraid to try it, afraid not to.

"Come *on*, Nanny!"

He swayed up out of his seat, leaning towards her with a list to one side. Then he was at the back of her chair, gripping the handles, pushing her up to the table. He was not gentle; he collided her with a table leg.

He giggled.

"Sorrysorrysorry! I'm sorry, Nanny. Don't tell Gwen on me, Nanny."

He sat down and faced her. She could smell the stink on him now, the acrid smoky bar, the heavy overripe scent of beer. He had mussed his hair somehow and it jutted from one side of his head like a wig that had slipped. He sucked on his bottle, then his cigarette, and put his head on one side, questioningly.

"You like tellin' Gwen things about me, don't you, Nanny? Why d'you do it? Ain't I always been friendly to you, Nanny? Don't I try to ch—cheer you up? Huh?"

He studied her down the length of his cigarette with his careful drunken eyes. She didn't like it. There was a menace in his tone, a hardening towards her with those last few words.

"Tellin' Gwen madeup stories about me. Not nice, Nanny, not nice."

And I'll have even more to tell her after tonight, you pig.

"You never liked me, Nanny."

Darn right, I never liked you. I saw you for what you were the day Liz dragged you in here out of some barroom garbage can.

"You worked real hard, Nanny, turnin' Liz against me. Got what you wanted, too. Bust us up. Did a good job on us, Nanny, a real good wrecking job."

Not as good as I should have done. Or it'd be you out there in that freezer, and her in here talking to me.

Louie went to suck at his bottle, found it empty, and rapped it down hard on the table. He probed into the case at his feet and fished out two more bottles.

"Le's have a drink together, Nanny. An' a long talk. You and me should've had a long talk years ago. Here, this is for you—you like beer, dontcha?"

He pushed the bottle across the table. She wondered if in his drunkenness he had forgotten that she didn't have the use of her hands. He was watching her and smiling as if he were the most agreeable man God had ever put breath into. His head was propped up with the hand that held his cigarette clipped between two nicotine-stained fingers. He smoked steadily, taking a lungful, then regurgitating the smoke and dribbling it out of his mouth in curds of solid white, which he then swallowed up again. It was a wonder to Nanny that it didn't make him sick. Maybe it would yet.

"How come you doan like me, Nanny?"

Because you're evil.

"What's so wrong with me, anyway?"

You're a destroyer, a breaker-down of things, you're a killer.

"I tried t'make you like me, Nanny. Tried real hard for Liz. But you wouldn' let me, wouldn' give me a chance. An' Liz blamed *me* for that, Nanny. Me. S'at fair?"

Suddenly his heavy hand crashed down to make the table jump.

"*You answer me!*"

She flinched. He must have noticed.

Then he was calm again. Almost wheedling.

"Le's be friends, Nanny, okay? Le's be *good* friends. Bottoms up!" He drank, then watched her, waiting, blinking. He giggled. "Oops! Forgot, Nanny. Forgot your bum arm. Ole war wound, right? Here, lemme help you."

He picked up her bottle, loomed in at her, reaching, pressed it to her lips, tipped it forward. She took some of the bitter fluid into her mouth, gagged, and felt the rest of it splash down her chin, onto her blouse and her blanket.

Louie pulled the bottle away.

"Sorry, Nanny, sorrysorrysorry. *Sorry*! You doan drink fast, do you? You're a lady. A real lady." He frowned. "Liz was a real lady, too, jus' like her Nanny. Oh, I could have my pick of any girls, take 'em out any time I want. But Liz was special. Better than the others. I loved her. Yup. You doan b'lieve that, do you?" His face clouded. "You *never* believe me, Nanny. Liz tole me once you said I was—a *liar*!"

Again he gave the table a heavy smack.

Nanny cringed inside at his Jekyll and Hyde transformations. From calm discussion to sudden rage. She found herself hating him with every atom of her being. She had always despised drunks, and she despised this one with a special passion. This was the drunk who had ruined the life of her granddaugther Liz. The drunk who had finally killed Liz in some intoxicated rage and sealed her up in a freezer. The hate made her paralysis even more intolerable. She wished she were once again a healthy woman who could leap up and strike at this disgusting brute; or a man, a strong man, who could take him by the neck and squeeze and squeeze . . .

I hate you oh how I hate you, you drunken pig. I'd do anything to punish you for what you did to my Liz. I hope there's ghosts, and I hope I'm one real soon because even ghosts can do more in this world than a paralyzed old woman, and I'll come back to you then, cold and cadaverous and moldering, and I'll put my rotting hands on you and—

"Wanna see Liz, Nanny?"

She blinked.

He was gulping curds of smoke again and watching her with a brewing anticipation. She wondered if she had heard him right.

"Wanna see her, Nanny, or not?" He cackled. "You're pleased t'hear that, arncha? *I* know what you been tellin' Gwen. Proves you were right, doan it? Proves they should've listened to you, Nanny. You knew best. You knew nobody could walk out on ole Louie." He emptied his beer down his throat, opened another one and scowled. "But later, Nanny. Yes, I think later. Then you can see her. Okay? Drink first. You'll need it. She ain't as pretty as she used to be."

He laughed. Again he pushed the bottle at her, forcing open her mouth, pouring in the beer until she choked. He yanked it away so roughly this time that he pulled her false teeth askew. "Ooops," he said, giggling. "Sorry!" And stuck his fingers into her mouth to set them right again.

Nanny sat and glared at him. How terrible impotence was. It gripped you like a constricting snake and crushed the dignity out of you.

"You know," Louie said, "I was dancin' down at the Lantern tonight. I like dancin'. So did Liz. How 'bout you? Wanna dance, Nanny? Cut the old rug? Shake a tail feather?"

He was halfway to his feet when he fell back with a simpering grin.

"I fergot, Nanny. You doan dance so good now. Your legs doan work so hot." He took some beer, began laughing in the middle of a swallow, snorted it up his nose and coughed horribly.

He put his cigarette back in his mouth; it waggled as he spoke.

"An' your arms, too, huh, Nanny? An' your neck, an' your back, an' your feet, an' your hands—oh, you're in *awful* shape, aincha?

Your whole damn bod is shot. If only you could wheel on down to the graveyard and dig yourself up a few spare parts, eh, Nanny?"

He collapsed in his chair, convulsed with laughter.

Go ahead. Laugh away. Laugh till you choke on your own rotten tongue. Then I'll do the laughing. In my mind. At your funeral while they're wheeling you down to the graveyard.

He tossed his head as if to shake the laughter away.

"I wanna dance. I'm a dancin' fool, Nanny! Me an' Liz use to dance alla time. You can do it, Nanny. I'll lead."

He pulled himself up by the edge of the table. Two bottles went crashing against the wall, scattering dark brown splinters of glass. He chortled. "Dead soldiers, Nanny." Then he had caught hold of the wheelchair from behind and was rolling her back and forth and around the room, and singing his own accompaniment.

It was a heavy chair, what with the battery and motor; he used it partly as a support for his lurching, unsteady body. Around and around he trundled her, hooting. She felt giddy. She closed her eyes; that was worse; she opened them again. The room ran liquidly around her in watercolors. The stove came and went, came and went. Louie howled in her ear. "ROUN' AN' ROUN' AN' ROUN' SHE GOES. WHERE SHE STOPS, NOBODY *KNOWS* . . ."

And he threw Nanny away.

The chair shot out and across, flying, soaring over the floor, through the room, and fetched slam-*bang!* into the stove.

The chimney pipes shuddered and dropped a dusting of soot. The stove jerked back three inches. Nanny felt herself lifted up, floating on and outward, the hot metal stove looming, halting, then receding again as she fell back into her chair, her nostrils filled with the stink of scorching steel.

She thanked God for Gwen's care in tucking her feet well back under the blanket. If not for that her toes would surely have been crushed.

She could not see Louie with her chair facing the stove. The heat beat against her face and trembled the little gray hairs that stuck out over her eyes. Behind her Louie groaned with laughter, creaked with it. In a moment or two his grunting subsided and she heard the snap of another beer being opened. The heat was terrible, she could scarcely breathe. She yanked the chair control level angrily back and, to her surprise, the chair responded instantly and rolled her backwards.

She stopped in the center of the room. She tried to get the chair to turn but the control level had gone dead on her again. She sighed with frustration, and a nervous convulsion shook her violently.

She could only sit.

Hoping for Gwen.

Hating Louie.

Behind her, the sound of a cigarette pack being opened, the soft pop of the breaking seal, a crinkle of paper, a whisper of foil. The hiss and flare of a match.

"By God, you're a damn good dancer, Nanny."

Go to hell, Louie. Light another match. Set yourself on fire.

An acrid scent of sulphur reached her nose.

"A *damn* good dancer, Nanny. You mus've taught Liz everythin' she knew. Oh, she was a dancer. We had a good time, Nanny, till you bust us up. Real mean of you. You turned her against me an' I never done nothin' to you. Mean. Mean as winter. Tha's you, Nanny. It's your fault me an' her had to go our ways."

Liz didn't go anywhere. You killed her.

"Now she's got nothin'. I got nothin' . . ."

Oh yes you have. You've still got her. You've got her poor dead body out there in the back room, all frost and freezer burn and snowflakes on her eyes. Wrapped up in towels, maybe, or sheets. Like an Egyptian.

"You're hard, Nanny, hard."

Yes. I'm hard. I've had to be. But I'm not like you. Not a killer.

"You're like all those mean people I used to work for. You got no compassion for a man. You got a heart of . . . of *ice.* Black ice."

Louie was beginning to wander in his thoughts. Beginning to mumble. Nanny was having trouble understanding him.

"You're old, Nanny. Used up. Got only dust in you now. Dust and ice. Ever seen dust and ice mixed together, Nanny? Like a frozen chunk of midnight. Tha's what meanness looks like, Nanny. If we opened you up now with a knife an' looked inside you, tha's what we'd see. Old black ice." She heard him scraping at his cartons for more beer. A clink of glass. "Old things, Nanny, ought to be thrown away. Heaved down the basement an' tossed on a shelf to keep the dust off it. S'all you're good for now, Nanny. That an' breakin up families."

There were more scuffling cardboard sounds, the chinking of tumbled glass.

Then a roar.

"*NANNY!*"

She shut her eyes. *Oh, God, what's got at him now, don't let him start flinging me round again, I'll throw up if he does, I'll faint, I'll die, oh please don't let him start in on me again!*

"NANNY, WHY'D YOU GO AN' BUST MY BEER?"

A chair crashed to the floor. Louie came around from the side into her view, breathing raggedly, and towered over her, enormous, dark, full of hurt and poison.

"WHY'D YOU DO IT, NANNY?"

I didn't break it, you stupid, stupid, stupid! Aren't I sitting paralyzed in a wheelchair? Didn't you drop it yourself when you came in? Think, you stupid, think, think!

He leaned even closer, wrinkling his face with disgust and hatred. He was only inches away now, as if he were trying to peer, not just into her eyes, but to something in behind them, her most secret thoughts.

He said, very coldly, his voice like a long sliver of ice that sank into her slowly. "I doan wanna drink with you no more, Nanny. No. I don't. You get mean when you drink, Nanny."

He pulled away then, trying to find his balance.

"An' you're even meaner when you *don't* drink, Nanny."

Leave me alone. Get your horrid stinking face away from me. Don't you dare preach to me about meanness!

"I can be mean, too, Nanny. Real mean. S'at what you want? S'at why you bust up me and Liz? To make me mean—like you?"

Go away!

"Why don't you say something, Nanny?"

BECAUSE I CAN'T! I CAN'T! I WANT TO, BUT I CAN'T!

He put on an expression of mock concern.

"Your eyes, Nanny. They're gettin' all red. You're cryin' inside of that old head, arncha, Nanny?—just the way Liz used to cry after you'd tell her some mean thing about me. Show me some tears now, Nanny. Show me some tears for what you done to me an Liz."

LEAVE ME ALONE! OH, PLEASE, PLEASE, GWEN, COME HOME AND HELP ME NOW . . . !

"*I'll* get tears out of you, Nanny. Tears for me and Liz." He straightened up, overbalanced and staggered to one side a step. "Soon as I find somethin' in this house to drink." He tottered away,

opening drawers, cabinets, peering into corners bleary-eyed. "Mus'
be somethin' here. Will, he'll unnerstand when I tell him how you
broke my beer. 'Cause of your meanness." He chortled. "I'm gonna
have one more drink an' then I'm gonna *fix* you, Nanny."

*You can't drink anything more. You mustn't. Oh dear God in
heaven, don't let him find anything more to drink!*

He swung her chair rudely to face the wall.

"Doan peek, Nanny."

Nanny looked down at her body, inert and immovable, something
separate from herself, remote as a carving. Oh! the things this same
body had done years before: like winning the sack race at the Sunday
school picnic; and outclimbing the boys on the tree behind Mason's
store. And even now she felt the tremendous churning life within it,
the rushing and the hurrying of blood in her veins, the quivering
nerves that screamed at her *run, run, run,* the terrors exploding in her
brain like flash cards, visions of Louie beating her, holding lit cigarettes against her flesh, tipping her out of her chair—

Falling!

Oh, that was the worst!

The falling dream come to life. Full color and immediate. The
floor starting toward her slowly, now lifting, now rising, faster,
faster, now speeding, hurtling, rocketing at her while her arms planed
useless at her sides.

Bang!

It was Louie slamming a cupboard door. He'd found something. A
bottle. A quick new thrust of fear stabbed through her.

"Gin, Nanny. Only gin. I hate gin, Nanny, but it's better'n after-
shave—better'n Aqua Velva." He cackled at his own wit like some
evil warlock; she heard him guzzle a large gulp of gin straight from
the bottle, then cough. "And now I'm gonna fix you up a surprise."

Nanny closed her eyes, squeezed them lock-shut tight against the
world. The worst had happened. She had prayed he would not find
anything to drink, not find anything more to fuel the hatred and
violence in him. Gin—straight gin. It was like dashing raw alcohol
over naked flame. Surely God had deserted her.

There were muffled thumps behind her, and the creaking of floor-
boards. She heard him grunt, then let out a long low chortle of
wicked mirth.

"Just goin' to the sandbox, Nanny. Doan go away."

He shambled away down the hall, past the living room, to the back of the house. A pause. Silence followed by a harsh scrape. A door opening, closing. The flush of the toilet. Then footsteps returning.

He was coming back towards her, staggering. She kept her eyes screwed shut. He was coming, he was here! He turned her chair out into the room so that she could see what he was about. He winked, then moved off again in his uneven drunken tread. She peeked out of herself to see what he was about.

He had crossed the kitchen towards the back room doorway, the entrance to the room where he kept his freezer locked tight. But he didn't enter. He stopped. He bent over, down on one knee, reaching.

What in heaven's name—?

He was lifting the cellar trapdoor. He was throwing back the lid. It yawned like a mouth.

Now he was up and teetering over the black cavern in the floor, swaying dangerously, doing a breath-catching float out over the opening, then lurching safely back to Nanny's side, fumbling in his pocket, clutching, withdrawing.

He dropped a flat steel key into her lap.

"You been wantin' a look into my freezer, Nanny. Well, there it is, waitin'. All you got to do is get to it." He laughed. "'Course, I din want to make it too easy. No fun then, Nanny. So all you got to do is get over to that trap an' drop it down somehow an' roll on in there an' have yourself a look. Simple." He bent crookedly like a kindly uncle offering a gift, and gusted his sour breath into her face. "If you make it past the trap," he whispered, "I'll even help you with the padlock."

He giggled away, pleased with himself, and fell into a chair.

The cellar trap opened sideways and to the right, like the cover of an enormous book. A chain held it upright, almost vertical. It only needed a nudge to send it crashing shut again. She wanted so badly to look into that freezer; already Nanny found herself wondering if there wasn't some way she could manage it. And there was! The way she closed her own bedroom door. She could hook one front wheel behind the door, and turn sharp left to bring the door slamming down. It was dangerous. She could easily fall—fall into the cellar. But here was the freezer key, here, right in her lap. And out there was the freezer, with Liz beckoning, Liz waiting, Liz calling silently out to her . . . She had to *try*.

She thrust out her fingers to tilt the control switch to roll her forward. Nothing. She flicked at the switch again and again. Dead.

Louie cackled. He drank some more gin.

"S'matter? Outta gas? Dead batt'ry?" He squeaked with laughter, then arched his eyebrows. "Wanna boost?"

That sent a chill of terror through her. The idea of this stumbling drunk wheeling her toward that hole in the floor was too horrifying to imagine. Her fingers danced at the switch. She had to move. Had to—

The motor whirred, rolling her forward.

Louie, already halfway to his feet, collapsed again. He clapped his hands. "Go, Nanny, go! Yeehah!"

The chair hummed Nanny across the kitchen, toward the yawning gulf in the floor. Three feet from the edge of the hole it stopped. Without even wanting to she had let go of the switch. Her nerve had given out. She wanted to continue, wanted to get out to the back room and see her Liz, her Liz, her lonely Liz, but she was brought up sharp by her own fear. Her fear of falling. That fear kept her from Liz as surely as Louie's padlock had done before. In her mind, she wept.

"Nanny! What's wrong now? Damn batt'ry again? I'll help you, Nanny, I'll help . . ."

He was standing now, grinning broadly, holding the gin bottle, swaying forward, catching himself, leaning back again, like a monstrous puppet worked by an uncertain hand on loose strings. A puppet baby taking its first steps. —Look, Ma, no hands!

Stay away, Nanny screamed in her mind, *stay away from me! Don't touch me, don't push me into that hole. Oh, Gwen, come home! Come home!*

Louie took a step towards her, then another, and another.

Gwen, HELP ME!

Louie stretched out his hand for her, and stretching, lost his balance completely, tried to correct for it, leaned back, twirled around and crashed to the floor on his skinny rear end. He sat there a moment, looking back at her stunned. *Maybe he won't get up. Maybe he—*

But he *was* getting up, struggling to his feet and laughing, holding out the gin bottle. "I d'in break it, Nanny. I di'n break it!"

He began rolling her forward.

"Here we go loop-de-loop, Nanny, here we go loop-de-lie . . ."

The cellar door gaped under her wheels like a hungry maw. Two more feet, one . . .

Over the edge!

She closed her eyes. She was falling. It was just the way it had been in her dream. A slow haunting terrifying plunge into a black nothingness. A long trip through forever before the final stunning blow. An age . . .

Nothing.

She opened her eyes.

Louie was reeling around the room like an airplane out of control, laughing fit to bust. The chair was grounded above the hole. Her right front wheel was dangling magically over the abyss. Her left front wheel was caught on the side lip of the hole. If she trembled, breathed, anything, she was going to fall straight in.

"Whooo!" Louie crowed, staggering, going down, kneeling, the bottle swinging out in his hand, catching and reflecting the light. "Whooo!" Then he caught himself up, gasped, and hooted. "Nanny. What happened? Got a flat? Wanna shove?" He came at her again, this time on his knees, his face beet-red with the humor of it all.

NO! Nanny shrieked silently, *GET BACK! STAY—AWAY—FROM—ME!*

She willed him to stop, flung all the strength of her mind at him. And it worked.

He did stop.

And then he fell.

He didn't have far to go, being on his knees already, and he passed out cleanly as he came knee-boning up to her, his face diving by her in a perfect blurred pink arc, his head booming off the sheet metal corner of the stove and hitting the floor with a dull vegetable sound.

This time he didn't move.

First, Nanny told herself, *got to get away from this hole.*

She feathered the control switch timidly, trembling it back and to the left. Once, three times, five times. Then it caught. The motor hummed. It reversed her clear of the hole.

Louie lay still, his head projecting out past the stove.

His thrusting Adam's apple only a foot from her rear wheel.

A surge of triumph flashed through Nanny and carried her away. Here was her enemy at her mercy! *Not so helpless now, am I?* she gloated. She touched the control switch. The motor hummed. She stopped, and from the corner of her eye she saw Louie's neck under her big rear wheel, his larynx bulging like a rope, his throat pulsing with each surge of his heart. All she had to do now was . . .

She hesitated. It was too easy. He was so vulnerable lying there. *But what about Liz? Didn't my Liz have a right to enjoy her life, too? It hadn't been too difficult to kill her, had it? Not for a big, strong man like you. Hadn't she been vulnerable? And an execution was something different from a murder, oh yes, something quite different.*

Her fingers toyed with the control lever. She watched them in amazement. Her right hand, the only part of her body she'd had any real control over for months, now seemed to have taken on a will of its own. Like a spectator, she watched, as if from a great distance, the fingers having their own way, tightening, tightening . . .

Then Louie's hand closed powerfully on the spokes of her wheel, his one eye flew open, and he grinned.

"Boo!" he said.

She shrieked in silent terror.

Louie clambered to his feet, kicked the trapdoor shut with a crash and a musty wind, and rolled her into the back room. Softly cackling he undid the lock, then paused with his hand on the lid of the freezer. He whispered:

"You ready for this, Nanny? Hope so! It's a horrible sight. A killer."

The lid flew back.

Nanny looked in.

Gentle vapors. Icy crusts. The freezer was empty.

The room spun crazily around her, grew larger, shrank away, went black, then blindingly bright. Louie went tramping away, whooping laughter, panting and wheezing with it, crashing into things. He dragged his parka around his shoulders, fumbled at the doorknob and staggered out into the night. She heard his car start, the crunch of tires on snow as he rolled away.

When Will and Gwen got home, they found Nanny parked inches away from the old stove, which was roaring away against the gale that had got its start at the North Pole, gathered power and speed on a journey to bring it leaping in at Nanny through the door Louie hadn't bothered to close. They shut the door with a huge slam, stood for a moment blinking stupidly at the broken glass, spilled beer, overturned chairs, stove knocked askew on its fireproof pad. Will ran his fingers through his hair; his face was the color of ashes. Then Gwen was at Nanny's side in a rush, kneeling, clasping Nanny's hand, fussing and full of quick, questioning words, gripping Nanny's fingers tight, her gaze darting from Nanny to the mess in the room and back again.

"Oh, I'm so sorry, so sorry, Nanny, I'll never go off and leave you like that again, never." She looked at Will toeing a sodden beer case with the tip of his shoe. "It was Louie, wasn't it? Oh, God! And he *promised* he'd take care of you." Her voice went suddenly vicious. "I'll never let him set foot in this house again! I won't! I'll throw him out—Will, *you'll* throw him out!" She was starting to cry. "Nanny, I don't know what to say, I'm just—"

She stopped. Swallowed. Stared.

Will was mumbling away to himself: "Must've been in one of his moods. Nothing *she* could do. She must've just sat here, scared out of her wits . . ."

But Gwen stared past him. Stared into the back room with a feeling of numb bewilderment. Will turned to gaze with her into the back room shadows, at the long white waiting freezer with its lid thrown back. They then went slowly together to stand with linked hands and peer into the frosted emptiness. They turned then and looked at Nanny. Put their heads together, buzzed.

Gwen said sternly, "This freezer is empty, Nanny!"

Will stooped over her.

"Nanny, tell the truth, did you start in on him? That's it, isn't it? You made him understand your . . . your accusations. He got angry and raged around. Broke things. Then he gave you what you wanted—let you see into the freezer. That's what happened, isn't it, Nanny?" His voice was as firm and stern as his face. "I guess when he cools down and comes back, you'll owe him an apology, won't you?"

Gwen was glancing around the room, eyes angry with tears.

"Oh, this *mess*! This awful *mess*!"

Gwen and Will both shook their heads. They'd had enough.

And so had Nanny. Her trembling fingers clutched at her control lever, and the chair obediently responded, whispered her off to her room with a silk swiftness of rubber tires on linoleum. She whirred past the living room where the shadows sat slumped in the chairs, along the twilight hall to the back of the house, turned into her room, spun expertly, and caught the door with her right footrest to send it slamming shut.

The drapes were still undrawn, the night pushing in through the glass and filling the room with itself. An otherwise empty room. Like Nanny's heart. Empty yet tidy, with all the emptiness in its place.

You're too old. Too old and too foolish. A stupid. There's no place for you here any more. You caused trouble tonight. You drove Louie and Liz apart with your whisperings. You're a misery, you leave trails of miserableness behind you, it rubs off you onto other people. . . .

You're responsible for everything that's happened between those two young people.

Gwen came into the room so briskly the edge of the door clunked into Nanny's chair. She swooped in on a flood of dim electric light from the hall. She put firm hands on Nanny, hands that Nanny knew had been cleaning up the mess, impatient, sudden hands. Hands that said by their movements that they'd be better occupied somewhere else. Gwen lifted Nanny in a brisk Victorian Nurse dead lift, stretched her on the bed, tumbled her quickly out of her clothes and into her nightie, rolled her under the quilt, kissed her with hard, dry lips.

"Now you just go right to sleep. We'll have a good talk about this in the morning." She paused at the door. "I hope you're satisfied. I don't know *how* I'm going to deal with Will and Louie after this."

The door closed.

All right, then. Be in a snit. Don't even ask me if I have to go to the bathroom. Blame me for everything. I don't mind. I know it's my fault. You can punish me, dump me into this old cold bed.

And it *was* a cold bed. Colder than it ought to be . . .

That's what guilt does to a person. Stops their circulation. Bed, get colder. I deserve it.

And it did. A numbing cold was creeping out of the bedding in waves. Also a frosty, cloying damp which gradually became a long slim bulk under the quilt only inches away. And then she knew she was not alone in her bed.

Not alone at all.

She remembered those few moments earlier when she had sat in the corner and listened to Louie's heavy footsteps in the hall.

There was, after all, something much worse than falling.

She began her silent screams.

Sometimes They Bite

LAWRENCE BLOCK

Mowbray had been fishing the lake for better than two hours before he encountered the heavyset man. The lake was supposed to be full of largemouth bass and that was what he was after. He was using spinning gear, working a variety of plugs and spoons and jigs and plastic worms in all of the spots where a lunker largemouth was likely to be biding his time. He was a good fisherman, adept at dropping his lure right where he wanted it, just alongside a weedbed or at the edge of subsurface structure. And the lures he was using were ideal for late fall bass. He had everything going for him, he thought, but a fish on the end of his line.

He would fish a particular spot for awhile, then move off to his right a little ways, as much for something to do as because he honestly expected the bass to be more cooperative in another location. He was gradually working his way around the western rim of the lake when he stepped from behind some brush into a clearing and saw the other man no more than a dozen yards away.

The man was tall, several inches taller than Mowbray, very broad in the shoulders and trim in the hips and at the waist. He wore a fairly new pair of blue jeans and a poplin windbreaker over a navy flannel shirt. His boots looked to be identical to Mowbray's, and Mowbray guessed they'd been purchased from the same mail order outfit in Maine. His gear was a baitcasting outfit, and Mowbray followed his line out with his eyes and saw a red bobber sitting on the water's surface some thirty yards out.

The man's chestnut hair was just barely touched with gray. He had a neatly trimmed mustache and the shadowy beard of someone who had arisen early in the morning. The skin on his hands and face suggested he spent much of his time out of doors. He was certainly around Mowbray's age, which was forty-four, but he was in much better shape than Mowbray was, in better shape, truth to tell, then Mowbray had ever been. Mowbray at once admired and envied him.

The man had nodded at Mowbray's approach, and Mowbray

nodded in return, not speaking first because he was the invader. Then the man said, "Afternoon. Having any luck?"

"Not a nibble."

"Been fishing long?"

"A couple of hours," Mowbray said. "Must have worked my way halfway around the lake, as much to keep moving as anything else. If there's largemouth in the whole lake you couldn't prove it by me."

The man chuckled. "Oh, there's bass here, all right. It's a fine lake for bass, and a whole lot of other fish as well."

"Maybe I'm using the wrong lures."

The big man shook his head. "Doubtful. They'll bite anything when their dander is up. I think a largemouth would hit a shoelace if he was in the mood, and when he's sulky he wouldn't take your bait if you threw it in the water with no hook or line attached to it. That's just the way they are. Sometimes they bite and sometimes they don't."

"That's the truth." Mowbray nodded in the direction of the floating red bobber. "I don't suppose you're after bass yourself?"

"Not rigged up like this. No, I've been trying to get myself a couple of crappies." He pointed over his shoulder with his thumb, indicating where a campfire was laid. "I've got the skillet and the oil, I've got the meal to roll 'em in, and I've got the fire all laid just waiting for the match. Now all I need is the fish."

"No luck?"

"No more than you're having."

"Which isn't a whole lot," Mowbray said. "You from around here?"

"No. Been through here a good many times, however. I've fished this lake now and again and had good luck more often than not."

"Well," Mowbray said. The man's company was invigorating, but there was a strict code of etiquette governing meetings of this nature. "I think I'll head on around the next bend. It's probably pointless but I'd like to get a plug in the water."

"You never can tell if it's pointless, can you? Any minute the wind can shift or the temperature can drop a few degrees and the fish can change their behavior completely. That's what keeps us coming out here year after year, I'd say. The wonderful unpredictability of the whole affair. Say, don't go and take a hike on my account."

"Are you sure?"

The big man nodded, hitched at his trousers. "You can wet a line here as good as further down the bank. Your casting for bass won't make a lot of difference as to whether or not a crappie or a sunnie takes to the shiner on my hook. And, to tell you the truth, I'd be just as glad for the company."

"So would I," Mowbray said, gratefully. "If you're sure you don't mind."

"I wouldn't have said boo if I did."

Mowbray set his aluminum tackle box on the ground, knelt beside it, and rigged his line. He tied on a spoon plug, then got to his feet and dug out a pack of cigarettes from the breast pocket of his corduroy shirt. He said, "Smoke?"

"Gave 'em up a while back. But thanks all the same."

Mowbray smoked his cigarette about halfway down, then dropped the butt and ground it underfoot. He stepped to the water's edge, took a minute or so to read the surface of the lake, then cast his plug a good distance out. For the next fifteen minutes or so the two men fished in companionable silence. Mowbray had no strikes but expected none and was resigned to it. He was enjoying himself just the same.

"Nibble," the big man announced. A minute or two went by and he began reeling in. "And a nibble's the extent of it," he said. "I'd better check and see if he left me anything."

The minnow had been bitten neatly in two. The big man had hooked him through the lips and now his tail was missing. His fingers very deft, the man slipped the shiner off the hook and substituted a live one from his bait pail. Seconds later the new minnow was in the water and the red bobber floated on the surface.

"I wonder what did that," Mowbray said.

"Hard to say. Crawdad, most likely. Something ornery."

"I was thinking that a nibble was a good sign, might mean the fish were going to start playing along with us. But if it's just a crawdad I don't suppose it means very much."

"I wouldn't think so."

"I was wondering," Mowbray said. "You'd think if there's bass in this lake you'd be after them instead of crappies."

"I suppose most people would figure that way."

"None of my business, of course."

"Oh, that's all right. Hardly a sensitive subject. Happens I like the taste of little panfish better than the larger fish. I'm not a sport fisherman at heart, I'm afraid. I get a kick out of catching 'em, but my main interest is how they're going to taste when I've fried 'em up in the pan. A meat fisherman is what they call my kind, and the sporting fraternity mostly says the phrase with a certain amount of contempt." He exposed large white teeth in a sudden grin. "If they fished as often as I do, they'd probably lose some of their taste for the sporting aspect of it. I fish more days than I don't, you see. I retired ten years ago, had a retail business and sold it not too long after my wife died. We were never able to have any children so there was just myself and I wound up with enough capital to keep me without working if I didn't mind living simply. And I not only don't mind, I prefer it."

"You're young to be retired."

"I'm fifty-five. I was forty-five when I retired, which may be on the young side, but I was ready for it."

"You look at least ten years younger than you are."

"If that's a fact, I guess retirement agrees with me. Anyway, all I really do is travel around and fish for my supper. And I'd rather catch small fish. I did the other kind of fishing and tired of it in no time at all. The way I see it, I never want to catch more fish than I intend to eat. If I kill something, it goes in that copper skillet over there. Or else I shouldn't have killed it in the first place."

Mowbray was silent for a moment, unsure what to say. Finally he said, "Well, I guess I just haven't evolved to that stage yet. I have to admit I still get a kick out of fishing, whether I eat what I catch or not. I usually eat them but that's not the most important part of it to me. But then I don't go out every other day like yourself. A couple times a year is as much as I can manage."

"Look at us talking," the man said, "and here you're not catching bass while I'm busy not catching crappie. We might as well announce that we're fishing for whales for all the difference it makes."

A little while later Mowbray retrieved his line and changed lures again, then lit another cigarette. The sun was almost gone. It had vanished behind the tree line and was probably close to the horizon by now. The air was definitely growing cooler. Another hour or so would be the extent of his fishing for the day. Then it would be time to head back to the motel and some cocktails and a steak and baked potato at the restaurant down the road. And then an evening of bourbon and water in front of the motel room's television set, lying on the bed with his feet up and the glass at his elbow and a cigarette burning in the ashtray.

The whole picture was so attractive that he was almost willing to skip the last hour's fishing. But the pleasure of the first sip of the first martini would lose nothing for being deferred an hour, and the pleasure of the big man's company was worth another hour of his time.

Then, a little while later, the big man said, "I have an unusual question to ask you."

"Ask away."

"Have you ever killed a man?"

It *was* an unusual question, and Mowbray took a few extra seconds to think it over. "Well," he said at length, "I guess I have. The odds are pretty good that I have."

"You killed someone without knowing it?"

"That must have sounded odd. You see, I was in the artillery in Korea. Heavy weapons. We never saw what we were shooting at and never knew just what our shells were doing. I was in action for better than a year, stuffing shells down the throat of one big mother of a gun, and I'd hate to think that in all that time we never hit what we aimed at. So I must have killed men, but I don't suppose that's what you're driving at."

"I mean up close. And not in the service, that's a different proposition entirely."

"Never."

"I was in the service myself. An earlier war than yours, and I was on a supply ship and never heard a shot fired in anger. But about four years ago I killed a man." His hand dropped briefly to the sheath knife at his belt. "With this."

Mowbray didn't know what to say. He busied himself taking up the slack in his line and waited for the man to continue.

"I was fishing," the big man said. "All by myself, which is my usual custom. Saltwater though, not fresh like this. I was over in North Carolina on the Outer Banks. Know the place?" Mowbray shook his head. "A chain of barrier islands a good distance out from the mainland. Very remote. Damn fine fishing and not much else. A lot of people fish off the piers or go out on boats, but I was surfcasting. You can do about as well that way as often as not, and that way I figured to build a fire right there on the beach and cook my catch and eat it on the spot. I'd gathered up the driftwood and laid the fire before I wet a line, same as I did today. That's my usual custom. I had done the same thing the day before and I caught myself half a dozen Norfolk spot in no time at all, almost before I could properly say I'd been out fishing. But this particular day I didn't have any luck at all in three hours, which shows that saltwater fish are as unpredictable as the freshwater kind. You done much saltwater fishing?"

"Hardly any."

"I enjoy it about as much as freshwater, and I enjoyed that day on the Banks even without getting a nibble. The sun was warm and there was a light breeze blowing off the ocean and you couldn't have asked for a better day. The next best thing to fishing and catching fish is fishing and not catching 'em, which is a thought we can both console ourselves with after today's run of luck."

"I'll have to remember that one."

"Well, I was having a good enough time even if it looked as though I'd wind up buying my dinner, and then I sensed a fellow coming up behind me. He must have come over the dunes because he was never in my field of vision. I knew he was there, just an instinct I suppose, and I sent my eyes as far around as they'd go without moving my head, and he wasn't in sight." The big man paused, sighed. "You know," he said, "if the offer still holds, I believe I'll have one of those cigarettes of yours after all."

"You're welcome to one," Mowbray said, "but I hate to start you off on the habit again. Are you sure you want one?"

The wide grin came again. "I quit smoking about the same time I quit work. I may have had a dozen cigarettes since then, spaced over the ten year span. Not enough to call a habit.

"Then I can't feel guilty about it." Mowbray shook the pack until a cigarette popped up, then extended it to his companion. After the man had helped himself Mowbray took one as well, and lit them both with his lighter.

"Nothing like an interval of a year or so between cigarettes to improve their taste," the big man said. He inhaled a lungful of smoke, pursed his lips to expel it in a stream. "I'll tell you," he said, "I really want to tell you this story if you don't mind hearing it. It's one I don't tell often, but I feel a need to get it out from time to time. It may not leave you thinking very highly of me but we're strangers, never saw each other before and as likely will never see each other again. Do you mind listening?"

Mowbray was fascinated and admitted as much.

"Well, there I was knowing I had someone standing behind me. And certain he was up to no good, because no one comes up behind you quiet like that and stands there out of sight with the intention of doing you a favor. I was holding onto my rod, and before I turned around I propped it in the sand with the butt end down, the way people will do when they're fishing on a beach. Then I waited a minute, and then I turned around as if not expecting to find anyone there, and there he was, of course.

"He was a young fellow, probably no more than twenty-five. But he wasn't a hippie. No beard, and his hair was no longer than yours or mine. It did look greasy, though, and he didn't look too clean in general. Wore a light blue t-shirt and a pair of white duck pants. Funny how I remember what he wore but I can see him clear as day in my mind. Thin lips, sort of a wedge shaped head, eyes that didn't line up quite right with each other, as though they had minds of their own. Some active pimples and the scars of old ones. He wasn't a prize.

"He had a gun in his hand. What you'd call a belly gun, a little .32-calibre Smith & Wesson with a two-inch barrel. Not good for a single damned thing but killing men at close range, which I'd say is all he ever wanted it for. Of course I didn't know the make or calibre at the time. I'm not much for guns myself.

"He must have been standing less than two yards away from me. I wouldn't say it took too much instinct to have known he was there, not as close as he was."

The man drew deeply on the cigarette. His eyes narrowed in recollection, and Mowbray saw a short vertical line appear running from the middle of his forehead almost to the bridge of his nose. Then he blew out smoke and his face relaxed and the line was gone.

"Well, we were all alone on that beach," the man continued. "No one within sight in either direction, no boats in close offshore, no one around to lend a helping hand. Just this young fellow with a gun in his hand and me with my own hands empty. I began to regret sticking the rod in the sand. I'd done it to have both hands free, but now I thought it might be useful to swing at him and try whipping the gun out of his hand.

"He said, 'All right, old man. Take your wallet out of your pocket nice and easy.' He was a Northerner, going by his accent, but the younger people don't have too much of an accent wherever they're from. Television, I suppose, is the cause of it. Makes the whole world smaller.

"Now I looked at those eyes, and at the way he was holding that gun, and I knew he wasn't going to take the wallet and wave bye-bye at me. He was going to kill me. In fact, if I hadn't turned around when I did he might well have shot me in the back. Unless he was the sort who liked to watch a person's face when he did it. There are people like that, I understand."

Mowbray felt a chill. The man's voice was so matter-of-fact, while his words were the stuff nightmares are made of.

"Well, I went into my pocket with my left hand. There was no wallet there. It was in the glove compartment of my car, parked off the road in back of the sand dunes. But I reached in my pocket to keep his eyes on my left hand, and then I brought the hand out empty and went for the gun with it, and at the same time I was bringing my knife out of the sheath with my right hand. I dropped my shoulder and came in low, and either I must have moved quick or all the drugs he'd taken over the years had slowed him some, because I swung that gun hand of his up and sent the gun sailing, and at the same time I got my knife into him and laid him wide open."

He drew the knife from its sheath. It was a filleting knife, with a natural wood handle and a thin slightly curved blade about seven inches long. "This was the knife," he said. "It's a Rapala, made in Finland, and you can't beat it for being stainless steel and yet taking and holding an edge. I use it for filleting and everything else connected with fishing. But you've probably got one just like it yourself."

Mowbray shook his head. "I use a folding knife," he said.

"You ought to get one of these. Can't beat 'em. And they're handy when company comes calling, believe me. I'll tell you, I opened this youngster up the way you open a fish to clean him. Came in low in the abdomen and swept up clear to the bottom of the rib cage, and you'd have thought you were cutting butter as easy as it was." He slid the knife easily back into its sheath.

Mowbray felt a chill. The other man had finished his cigarette, and Mowbray put out his own and immediately selected a fresh one from his pack. He started to return the pack to his pocket, then thought to offer it to the other man.

"Not just now. Try me in nine or ten months, though."

"I'll do that."

The man grinned his wide grin. Then his face went quickly serious. "Well, that young fellow fell down," he said. "Fell right on his back and lay there all opened up. He was moaning and bleeding and I don't know what else. I don't recall his words, his speech was disjointed, but what he wanted was for me to get him to a doctor.

"Now the nearest doctor was in Manteo. I happened to know this, and I was near Rodanthe which is a good twenty miles from Manteo if not more. I saw how he was cut and I couldn't imagine him living through a half hour ride in a car. In fact if there'd been a doctor six feet away from us I seriously doubt he could have done the boy any good. I'm no doctor myself, but I have to say it was pretty clear to me that boy was dying.

"And if I tried to get him to a doctor I'd be ruining the interior of my car for all practical purposes and making a lot of trouble for myself in the bargain. I didn't expect anybody would seriously try to pin a murder charge on me. It stood to reason that fellow had a criminal record that would reach clear to the mainland and back, and I've never had worse than a traffic ticket and few enough of those. And the gun had his prints on it and none of my own. But I'd have to answer a few million questions, and hang around for at least a week and doubtless longer for a coroner's inquest, and it all amounted to a lot of aggravation for no purpose, since he was dying anyway.

"And I'll tell you something else. It wouldn't have been worth the trouble even to save him, because what in the world was he but a robbing murdering snake? Why, if they stitched him up he'd be on the street again as soon as he was healthy and he'd kill someone else in no appreciable time at all. No, I didn't mind the idea of him dying." His eyes engaged Mowbray's. "What would you have done?"

Mowbray thought about it. "I don't know," he said. "I honestly can't say. Same as you, probably."

"He was in horrible pain. I saw him lying there, and I looked around again to assure myself we were alone, and we were. I thought that I could grab my pole and frying pan and my few other bits of gear and be in my car in two or three minutes, not leaving a thing behind that could be traced to me. I'd camped out the night before in a tent and sleeping bag and wasn't registered in any motel or campground. In other words, I could be away from the Outer Banks entirely in half an hour, with nothing to connect me to the area, much less to the man on the sand. I hadn't even bought gas with a credit card. I was free and clear if I just got up and left. All I had to do was leave this young fellow to a horribly slow and painful death." His eyes locked with Mowbray's again, with an intensity that was difficult to bear. "Or," he said, his voice lower and softer, "or I could make things easier for him."

"Oh."

"Yes. And that's just what I did. I took and slipped the knife right into his heart. He went instantly. The life slipped right out of his eyes and the tension out of his face and he was gone. And that made it murder."

"Yes, of course."

"Of course," the man echoed. "It might have been an act of mercy, but legally it transformed an act of self defense into an unquestionable act of criminal homicide." He breathed deeply. "Think I was wrong to do it?"

"No," Mowbray said.

"Do the same thing yourself?"

"I honestly don't know. I hope I would, if the alternative was leaving him to suffer."

"Well, it's what *I* did. So I've not only killed a man, I've literally murdered a man. I left him under about a foot of sand at the edge of the dunes. I don't know when the body was discovered. I'm sure it didn't take too long. Those sands shift back and forth all the time. There was no identification on him, but the police could have labelled him from his prints, because an upstanding young man like him would surely have had his prints on file. Nothing on his person at all except for about fifty dollars in cash, which destroys the theory that he was robbing me in order to provide himself with that night's dinner." His face relaxed in a half smile. "I took the money," he said. "Didn't see as he had any need for it, and I doubted he had much of a real claim to it, as far as that goes."

"So you not only killed a man but made a profit on it."

"I did at that. Well, I left the Banks that evening. Drove on inland a good distance, put up for the night in a motel just outside of Fayetteville. I never did look back, never did find out if and when they found him. It'd be on the books as an unsolved homicide if they did. Oh, and I took his gun and flung it halfway to Bermuda. And he didn't have a car for me to worry about. I suppose he thumbed a ride, or came on foot, or else he parked too far away to matter." Another smile. "Now you know my secret," he said.

"Maybe you ought to leave out place names," Mowbray said.

"Why do that?"

"You don't want to give that much information to a stranger."

"You may be right, but I can only tell a story in my own way. I know what's going through your mind right now."

"You do?"

"Want me to tell you? You're wondering if what I told you is true or not. You figure if it happened I probably wouldn't tell you, and yet it sounds pretty believable in itself. And you halfway hope it's the truth and halfway hope it isn't. Am I close?"

"Very close," Mowbray admitted.

"Well, I'll tell you something that'll tip the balance. You'll really want to believe it's all a pack of lies." He lowered his eyes. "The fact of the matter is you'll lose any respect you may have had for me when you hear the next."

"Then why tell me?"

"Because I feel the need."

"I don't know if I want to hear this," Mowbray said.

"I want you to. No fish and it's getting dark and you're probably anxious to get back to wherever you're staying and have a drink and a meal. Well, this won't take long." He had been reeling in his line. Now the operation was concluded, and he set the rod deliberately on the grass at his feet. Straightening up, he said, "I told you before about my attitude toward fish. Not killing what I'm not going to eat. And there this young man was, all laid open, internal organs exposed—"

"Stop."

"I don't know what you'd call it, curiosity or compulsion or some primitive streak. I couldn't say. But what I did, I cut off a small piece of his liver before I buried him. Then after he was under the sand I lit my cookfire and—well, no need to go into detail."

Thank God for that, Mowbray thought. For small favors. He looked at his hands. The left one was trembling. The right, the one gripping his spinning rod, was white at the knuckles, and the tips of his fingers ached from gripping the butt of the rod so tightly.

"Murder, cannibalism, and robbing the dead. That's quite a string for a man who never got worse than a traffic ticket. And all three in considerably less than an hour."

"Please," Mowbray said. His voice was thin and high pitched. "Please don't tell me any more."

"Nothing more to tell."

Mowbray took a deep breath, held it. This man was either lying or telling the truth, Mowbray thought, and in either case he was quite obviously an extremely unusual person. At the very least.

"You shouldn't tell that story to strangers," he said after a moment. "True or false, you shouldn't tell it."

"I now and then feel the need."

"Of course, it's all to the good that I *am* a stranger. After all, I don't know anything about you, not even your name."

"It's Tolliver."

"Or where you live, or—"

"Wallace P. Tolliver. I was in the retail hardware business in Oak Falls, Missouri. That's not far from Joplin."

"Don't tell me anything more," Mowbray said desperately. "I wish you hadn't told me what you did."

"I had to," the big man said. The smile flashed again. "I've told that story three times before today. You're the fourth man ever to hear it."

Mowbray said nothing.

"Three times. Always to strangers who happen to turn up while I'm fishing. Always on long lazy afternoons, those afternoons when the fish just don't bite no matter what you do."

Mowbray began to do several things. He began to step backward, and he began to release his tight hold on his fishing rod, and he began to extend his left arm protectively in front of him.

But the filleting knife had already cleared its sheath.

Three Men in a Tub

LEMUEL CORK

"You know what's going to happen," Cap'n Andy said. "One of us is going to get eaten."

The three men looked at each other.

"Which one?" John asked at last.

"Not me," Cap'n Andy said. "I'm the Cap'n."

"It ain't gonna be me," said the Bosun. "I'm the Bosun."

Cap'n Andy and the Bosun stared at John. He looked from one set of hungry eyes to the other. "No," John said. Then again, more firmly: "No." He hadn't the strength, after four weeks at sea, to resist a third time. But he shook his head as forcefully as he was able. After a few minutes, he got his voice back. "Oh, no, you don't," he said, and fell silent.

"So what do you think?" Cap'n Andy asked the Bosun. "Cut his throat for supper tonight? You still got your knife, don't you?"

The Bosun felt around his dessicated body until he found the long bulge of his knife in the pocket of what had once been a natty white uniform. "Yup," he said. He licked his chapped lips with his dry tongue.

"Then it's settled," Cap'n Andy said. "Tonight we dine like kings."

Panic returned some of John's strength to him. "You can't do it," he said. "It isn't fair. I'm the one who rowed us this far!" He was, too, which was why he was twice as tired, twice as hungry, and twice as thirsty as Cap'n Andy and the Bosun combined.

"You rowed us this far." Cap'n Andy waved his hand over the side of the boat. The water receded evenly in every direction around them. There was no land in sight, that went without saying; but since they had left the wreck of the *Tractatus* behind, they hadn't seen anything but water—and each other. No birds, no planes, no islands on the horizon, nothing. "You rowed us this far. Look around you, boy. We're in the middle of nowhere, going nowhere. That we can do without you."

"But you *told* me to row!" John insisted.

"Sure I did," Cap'n Andy said. "Had to keep you occupied somehow. Now I'm telling you to lay down your life for your fellow crewmen. Don't tell me you'd disobey your Cap'n?"

"No, sir."

"Like I said, then. It's settled."

"No, sir," John said. "I mean, yes, but . . ."

"What *do* you mean, boy?"

John's sixteen-year-old face was a mixed canvas of agony, confusion, and sunburn. "I mean yes, I would disobey you. I would. What's the worst you could do to me?"

"Kill ya," said the Bosun, licking his lips again.

"You're set to do that anyway," John said.

"Yes," said Cap'n Andy, "but our way you die with honor."

"Honor be damned," John said miserably. "I'm not going to let you eat me."

"You're not going to let us? There are two of us. We're bigger than you are." Cap'n Andy pointed at the Bosun. "He's got a knife. Doesn't look to me like you've a lot of choice."

That's exactly how it looked to John, too, though he didn't want to say so.

"Yeah," he said. "Okay. Maybe so." John looked at the Bosun, always a knife-edge of a man; now his tattered uniform hung off him like a coat off a coat-hanger. And Cap'n Andy, who had been so robustly, administratively fat! His drained, wasted skin now hung about him like . . . well, like the Bosun's uniform hung on the Bosun. "Yeah, well, okay, but—"

John was floundering and he knew it.

"But what?" Cap'n Andy asked.

"But then what?" John said, snatching at a new argument. "What do you do next? I mean, let's suppose you kill me and eat me—which is not for a minute to suggest that I think it's a good idea—but let's suppose. Then what? You've eaten, that'll give you a few more days, but how are you going to get anywhere? Who's going to row you? Look at you! Neither of you has the strength to row. That means you'll just drift until you get real hungry again, and then one of you will have to eat the other."

Cap'n Andy and the Bosun considered this, sizing each other up. "And *then* what?" John continued. "Then there's one of you left to die out here all alone. What good is that?"

After a moment's thought, the Bosun pulled his knife out. "Ah still think we should eat ya," he said, unfolding the blade.

Cap'n Andy nodded at John. "'After we eat you, we *will* have the strength to row. That's the idea." Cap'n Andy looked at the Bosun, who nodded agreement.

John took a deep breath and let it out slowly. *Well,* he thought, *if we don't do something we'll* all *die, and soon. And there are worse ways to go. There must be. Even if none come to mind right away.* He swallowed heavily.

"Alright," John said. "But promise me you'll make sure I'm dead before you start carving me up?"

"Of course, son," Cap'n Andy's face shone beatifically. The Bosun just looked as ravenous as ever.

"One other thing," John said. "Let me do it myself."

"Out of the question," Cap'n Andy said, the angelic glow fleeing his face. "I don't trust you, boy. You'd throw the knife overboard."

"No," John said with a sigh of the utterest resignation. "I won't. What would be the use? There'd still be two of you, and you'd still kill me. Please, Cap'n, at least I would die by my own hand, and you could tell my parents—"

"Alright, alright," Cap'n Andy said. "Bosun, give him the knife."

The Bosun extended the knife, handle first. John took it and threw it overboard.

Cap'n Andy stared at him with a unique look of despairing rage that, in all of human experience, can only be mustered up after weeks of starvation and exposure to the elements in a wooden rowboat in the middle of the Atlantic Ocean. The Bosun just looked as ravenous as ever.

"You little fool," Cap'n Andy said. "You little goddamn fool."

"I said," John said, regaining his confidence, "I am not going to let you eat me."

"You shouldna done that," the Bosun said. "That was m'knife." He stood up in the boat. "That was *m'knife*. Ah'm hungry!" The Bosun tried to grab John by the lapels of his jacket, which would have worked better if John's jacket had had lapels. After struggling for a while in vain the Bosun made to slap John across the face, but Cap'n Andy tugged his first mate back to their side of the boat.

"We shoulda cut ya up the first day out," the Bosun said, but he sat down.

"We're going to eat, boy." Cap'n Andy lurched to his feet and moved between John and the Bosun. He made a show of smoothing John's jacket. "We're going to eat, boy, or we're going to die. Maybe we're going to eat fish, but for that we need bait. Or maybe we're not going to eat fish, in which case we'll eat you—" Cap'n Andy raised a finger to silence John's interruption, which he knew was coming "—there is no other choice."

"There is another choice," John said. "We could eat you. Or him."

"I'm the Bosun," the Bosun said.

Cap'n Andy laughed softly, uncomfortably. "And I'm the Cap'n. Don't you see?"

"I don't see why any of us has to die, is what I see," John said. "Look at it this way. You kill me, and with this heat I'll spoil in a day. Tops. You'll be lucky if I last a whole day. You're right, we have to eat. Maybe you're even right, we have to eat each other. But we don't have to kill each other to do it."

"How else is there?" Cap'n Andy said.

"Suppose we each cut off a toe." John could hardly believe he was offering to dismember himself. "A toe—we make tourniquets, and we each cut off a toe. We can use them for bait, catch fish. Couldn't we do that?"

"Nope," the Bosun said.

"Why not?" John asked.

"Ya threw m'knife overboard."

But Cap'n Andy was interested. The other two could tell because his eyes got real narrow and then shut altogether. John and the Bosun waited in silence for the Cap'n's eyes to open again.

Eventually, they did. "That's some idea you've got there, boy," Cap'n Andy said. John nodded a *yessir* nod. "What can we do for tourniquets?"

John glanced around the boat. "We can tear strips from our clothing. And three pieces of wood . . . maybe we could take up one of the seats, break it into three pieces." He looked Cap'n Andy in the eye. "What do you think?"

"Beats dying," Cap'n Andy said. "Better than nothing."

The Bosun tapped Cap'n Andy on the shoulder.

"Yes?"

"He threw m'knife overboard," the Bosun said.

"So?"

"So what'll we do for a knife?"

"We'll make do, man," Cap'n Andy said. "We'll make do."

The lifeboat was rather too narrow for the arrangement they had in mind, but the three men made the best triangle they could. Six-feet-plus of Bosun lay along the long axis, curved slightly at the waist; John and Cap'n Andy filled in the other two sides. Each man had his trousers torn off at the knees, and the cloth they had gained in this manner was cinched around their calves and twisted into place with rough blocks of seat-wood.

They had given enough time for the blood to leave and for numbness to set in. Now they lay mouth to foot, mouth to foot, mouth to foot. Cap'n Andy went over the agreement one last time: they would each bite off a single toe, biting down simultaneously. The toe would be the smallest toe on either foot, biter's choice. The toes would be spat out and used to bait fishing lines. If necessary, the process would be repeated.

John tried to suppress his dry heaves, but he couldn't. *What if I can't do it?* he asked himself. He glanced back at the Bosun, who already had John's left foot clamped between his teeth. *What if he can't do it?*

"Fellows," Cap'n Andy said, "men of the *Tractatus*, we are survivors and survivors we shall always be. We undertake now a truly distasteful measure, but a measure which speaks volumes about our unity and our ability to cooperate. Captain and cabin boy, officer and recruit, we are now one. The import of—"

The Bosun spat John's foot out to interrupt. "C'n we eat already?"

Cap'n Andy stiffened. "Yes, Bosun, in a minute." The Bosun nudged John's foot back into position while Cap'n Andy went on. ". . . our Father, who art in heaven, we thank you now for the bounty we are about to receive."

"Amen," John said through a mouthful of toes.

"Amen," said Cap'n Andy. "On the third beat, men." He pounded on the boat with his fist. "One . . . two . . ." On the third beat they bit down.

Some beneficent deity must have been passing by, for at that instant they were blessed with jaw strength equal to the task and pain so extraordinary that none of them remained conscious to feel it.

* * *

When John came to, he had nine toes and a throbbing pain where the tenth had been. Cap'n Andy and the Bosun were already conscious. The latter was smiling and picking his teeth with something small and white. The former was staring mournfully at the grayish-pink lump before him. The Bosun had a similar lump lying at his feet. John sat up and looked around. He couldn't see his lump anywhere.

"Boy," Cap'n Andy said, "we have to tell you something."

The images connected in John's fevered brain. "He ate my toe!"

The Bosun spat his toothpick to the floor of the boat. On closer examination, it turned out to be a well-gnawed bone. "Yup."

John turned to his Cap'n for justice. "He ate my toe!"

"Yes, he certainly did." Cap'n Andy shook his head. "He certainly did."

John thought for a moment. "Well, then I get his. It's only fair."

A look of feral territoriality leapt into the Bosun's eyes. He grabbed up his toe and clamped it tight in his fist. "No ya don't."

"Cap'n," John said, "make him give me the toe."

"John, listen . . ."

"No, why should he get two? Make him give it to me!"

"Bosun," Cap'n Andy said, "the toe."

The Bosun shook his head fiercely. Cap'n Andy lunged for the Bosun, making the boat lurch, but the Bosun yanked his fist away. He popped the toe in his mouth and, with a little effort, swallowed it whole.

"Did you see what he did?" John demanded. "Did you see that?"

Cap'n Andy sat back and shrugged. With the violation of his body, a lot of the Cap'n spirit had left him. He waved away John's complaint. "Look, boy, you'll get extra from the first few fish we catch, okay?"

Once again, it didn't look like John had any choice. He wanted to say no, that bastard owes me a toe, and he'd better cough one up, you'll pardon the expression. What he said instead was, "Yes, sir."

Cap'n Andy slapped his hands down beside him. "Good. One happy family. That's us." He muttered this over and over as he fashioned a fishing line out of his toe, his sleeve, and the bone the Bosun had tossed away. "Line, hook and bait," he said. "Line, hook and bait."

"Ah'm hungry," the Bosun said again.

"Get him," John said. "He's hungry. He ate two toes and he's hungry!"

"Please, John," Cap'n Andy said as he cast the line over the side. "Shh. You'll scare the fish."

Now, whether it was because John shouted, or because the bait was none too appetizing, or because the fish in the Atlantic are just plain *smarter* than your average fish, maybe we'll never know; but for whatever reason, they didn't get a bite all day. Each time Cap'n Andy drew the line out of the water, there was nothing at the end of it. This went on until just before dark, when he checked and there *really* was nothing there, just the sopping cloth. The toe was gone.

Cap'n Andy was of the opinion that a fish had snuck it away. John was of the opinion that it had slipped off the hook and sunk to the bottom. The Bosun didn't voice an opinion, he just looked as ravenous as ever.

What was clear to all three was that more bait was needed, so they tightened the knots, lay in position once more, and bit the bullet.

This time there was less blood, and they didn't pass out. John kept a careful watch over his toe, holding it in his lap and trying to stay awake through the night. Some time before dawn he did fall asleep, but his toe was there when he woke up.

All three of them baited fishing lines, and all three waited through the day without a bite. This time, however, the toes were still there at day's end, which meant that they could all eat. It was their first meal since the hardtack and dried fish had run out after their first week at sea.

Cap'n Andy said grace and cried a little, told his crew to chew each bite twenty-seven times for good luck. They gnawed away at the bones until late into the evening, and then cast them over the side.

The next day they went through the same ritual, but by the day after that they had given up on the fish and just ate the toes right away. And two days later, they each had to start in on the next foot.

By then John noticed that their legs were turning black and beginning to give off a powerful stink. The others didn't believe him right away, but soon it became too evident to deny.

Rather than waste meat which could mean the difference between life and death, they stepped up their program. Now they bit off as much as they could, and ate as much of it as hadn't already gone bad.

The Bosun started to fill out a little, but Cap'n Andy deflated steadily; and John grew to look painfully gaunt. He still rowed when he could, until he could no longer. Somehow they never got any closer to land.

One morning he thought he saw a boat, and he shouted out, "Cap'n Andy! Look!" Cap'n Andy looked and so did the Bosun.

"Why, it's an island," Cap'n Andy said. "We've found land! And look, there are women dancing on the shore."

The Bosun leaned over the side. "It's a steak," he said, looking in another direction entirely. "A big steak." John had to hold him at the waist to keep him from leaping out of the boat.

John decided that he probably hadn't seen a boat after all.

And that's the story, fellas and femmes, the sad-but-true tale of three men cast upon the bosom of Mother Nature. There's one more piece I've left off, but maybe it's best if I tell it, 'cause I bet you want to know what happened to the boys.

Only sometimes people don't believe it.

They kept eating each other, see, bite by bite, trying to stay alive. And whenever he could, Johnny would row them a little bit further, though without a direction to aim the boat it was probably worse than useless.

But it was inevitable that one day they'd see land, that they'd run aground somewhere. As it happened, they drifted into port, soft as anything, at São Luis de Maranhão. Early in the morning, so the piers were empty, and the sun was just starting to burn through the clouds.

So there was this boat, and you could hear voices coming from it, but for all the world it looked like the boat was empty. When it came knocking up against the pier, though, you could see that it wasn't. The seats had all been torn up, and they lay in pieces in the bottom of the boat, along with the oars. And in the middle of this mess there were three heads—just heads, nothing else, no necks even.

They were still, like you'd expect them to be, for a second. Then the smallest one, the youngest one, said real loud, "We did it!"

And the other two started to laugh.

That's when they told me their story. You see, they had managed to *cheat* Mother Nature, something no one had ever done before and that no one's done since.

Naturally, I ran for my camera, but as I came back I heard the most awful sound in the world. I can't describe it exactly, but I knew what it meant—and sure enough, when I got to the boat, they had eaten each other up. There was nothing left but a pile of white shiny teeth.

I don't know why people don't believe it. I've got the boat right here to prove it. What's more, I've got the teeth.

That's right, friends, the teeth: the teeth that allowed them to survive, the teeth of the men who beat Mother Nature at her own game. Now in an hour or so you'll all be going out in your boats, and God willing you'll all come back tonight—but if you don't, don't you think you ought to have one of these teeth with you?

That's right, step right up.

The Wedding Gig

STEPHEN KING

In the year 1927 we were playing jazz in a speakeasy just south of Morgan, Illinois, which is 70 miles from Chicago. It was real hick country, not another big town for 20 miles in any direction. But there were a lot of plowboys with a hankering for something stronger than Moxie after a hot day in the field, and a lot of young bucks out duding it up with their drugstore buddies. There were also some married men (you know them, friend, they might as well be wearing signs) coming far out of their way to be where no one would recognize them while they cut a rug with their not-quite-legit lassies.

That was when jazz was jazz, not noise. We had a five-man combination—drums, clarinet, trombone, piano, and trumpet—and we were pretty good. That was still three years before we made our first records and four years before talkies.

We were playing *Bamboo Bay* when this big fellow walked in, wearing a white suit and smoking a pipe with more squiggles in it than a French horn. The whole band was a little drunk but the crowd was positively blind and everyone was having a high old time. There hadn't been a single fight all night. All of us were sweating rivers and Tommy Englander, the guy who ran the place, kept sending up rye. Englander was a good fellow to work for, and he liked our sound.

The guy in the white suit sat down at the bar and I forgot him. We finished up the set with *Aunt Hagar's Blues*, which was what passed for racy out in the boondocks back then, and got a good round of applause. Manny had a big grin on his face as he put his horn down, and I clapped him on the back as we left the bandstand. There was a lonely-looking girl in a green evening dress that had been giving me the eye all night. She was a redhead, and I've always been partial to those. I got a signal from her eyes and the tilt of her head, so I started threading my way through the crowd to get to her.

Halfway there the man in the white suit stepped in front of me. Up close he looked tough, with bristly back hair and the flat, oddly shiny eyes that some deepsea fish have. There was something familiar about him.

"Want to talk to you outside," he said.

The redhead was looking away. She seemed disappointed.

"It can wait," I said. "Let me by."

"My name is Scollay. Mike Scollay."

I knew the name. Mike Scollay was a small-time racketeer from Chicago who made his money running booze in from Canada. His picture had been in the paper a few times. The last time had been when another little Caesar tried to gun him down.

"You're pretty far from Chicago," I said.

"I brought some friends. Let's go outside."

The redhead looked over and I pointed to Scollay and shrugged. She sniffed and turned her back.

"You queered that," I said.

"Bimbos like that are a penny the bushel in Chi," he said. "Outside."

We went out. The air was cool on my skin after the smoky close atmosphere of the club, sweet with fresh-cut alfalfa grass. The stars were out, soft and flickering. The hoods were out too, but they didn't look a bit soft, and the only things flickering on them were their cigarettes.

"I've got some money for you," Scollay said.

"I haven't done anything for you."

"You're going to. It's two C's. Split it up with the band or hold back a hundred for yourself."

"What is it?"

"A gig," he said. "My sis is getting married. I want you to play for the reception. She likes Dixieland. Two of my boys say you play good Dixieland."

I told you Englander was good to work for. He was paying eighty a week split five ways, four hours a night. This guy was offering well over twice that for one gig.

"It's from five to eight, next Friday," Scollay said. "At the Grover Street Hall in Chi."

"It's too much," I said. "How come?"

"There's two reasons," Scollay said. He puffed on his pipe. It looked out of place in that yegg's face. He should have had a Lucky dangling from his mouth, or a Sweet Caporal. The pipe made him look sad and funny.

"First," he said, "maybe you heard the Greek tried to rub me out."

"I saw your picture in the paper," I said. "You were the guy trying to crawl into the sidewalk."

"Smart guy," he growled, but with no real force. "I'm getting too big for him. The Greek is getting old and he still thinks small. He ought to be back in the old country, drinking olive oil and looking at the Pacific."

"It's the Aegean," I said.

"An ocean's an ocean," he said. "Anyway, the Greek is still out to get me."

"In other words, you're paying two hundred because our last number might be arranged for Enfield rifle accompaniment."

Anger flashed on his face, and something else—sorrow? "I got the best protection money can buy. If anyone funny sticks his nose in, he won't get a chance to sniff twice."

"What's the other thing?"

Softly he said, "My sister's marrying an Italian."

"A good Catholic like you," I sneered softly.

The anger flashed again, white-hot, and I thought I'd pushed it too far. "A good *mick*! I'm a good mick, sonny, and you better not forget it!" To that he added, almost too low to be heard, "Even if I did lose most of my hair, it was red."

I started to say something, but he didn't give me the chance. He swung me around and pressed his face down until our noses almost touched. I never saw such anger and humiliation and rage and determination in a man's face. You never see that on a white face these days, the love-hate pressure of a man's race. But it was there then, and I saw it that night.

"She's fat," he breathed. "A lot of people have been laughing at me when my back is turned. They don't do it when I can see them, though. I'll tell you that, Mr. Cornet Player. Because maybe this little twerp was all she could get. But you're not gonna laugh at her and nobody else is either because you're gonna play too loud. No one is going to laugh at my sis."

I didn't know what to say. I didn't know why he told me or even why he thought a Dixieland band was his answer, but I didn't want to argue with him. You wouldn't have wanted to, either, funny clothes and pipe or not.

"We don't laugh at people when we play our gigs," I said. "Makes it too hard to pucker."

That relieved the tension. He laughed a short barking laugh. "You be there at five, ready to play. Grover Street Hall. I'll pay your expenses both ways."

I felt railroaded into the decision, but it was too late now. Scollay was already striding away, and one of his paid companions was holding open the back door of a Packard coupe.

They drove away. I stayed out a while longer and had a smoke. The evening was soft and fine and Scollay seemed more and more like something I might have dreamed. I was just wishing we could bring the bandstand out to the parking lot and play when Biff tapped me on the shoulder.

"Time," he said.

"Okay."

We went back in. The redhead had picked up some salt-and-pepper sailor who looked twice her age. I don't know what a member of the U.S. Navy was doing in central Illinois, but as far as I was concerned, he could have her if her taste was that bad.

I didn't feel so hot. The rye had gone to my head, and Scollay seemed a lot more real in here, where the fumes of what his kind sold were strong enough to float on.

"We had a request for *Camptown Races,*" Charlie said.

"Forget it," I said curtly. "None of that now."

I could see Billy-Boy stiffen just as he was sitting down to the piano, and then his face was smooth again. I could have kicked myself around the block.

"I'm sorry, Billy," I told him. "I haven't been myself tonight."

"Sure," he said, but there was no big smile and I knew he felt bad. He knew what I had started to say.

I told them about the gig during our next break, being square with them about the money and how Scollay was a hood (although I didn't tell them there was another hood out to get him). I also told them that Scollay's sister was fat but nobody was to even crack a smile about it. I told them Scollay was sensitive.

It seemed to me that Billy-Boy Williams flinched again at that, but you couldn't tell it from his face. It would be easier to tell what a walnut was thinking by reading the wrinkles on the shell. Billy-Boy was the best ragtime piano player we ever had and we were all sorry about the little ways it got taken out on him as we traveled from one place to another—the Jim Crow car south of the Mason-Dixon line, the balcony at the movies, the different hotel room in some towns—but what could I do? In those days you lived with those differences.

We turned up at Grover Street on Friday at four o'clock just to make sure we'd have plenty of time to set up. We drove up from Morgan in a special Ford truck that Biff and Manny and I had put together. The back end was all enclosed, and there were two cots bolted to the floor. We even had an electric hotplate that ran off the battery, and the band's name was painted on the outside.

The day was just right—a ham-and-egg summer day if you ever saw one, with little white angel clouds floating over the fields. But it was hot and gritty in Chicago, full of the hustle and bustle you could get out of touch with in a place like Morgan. When we got there my clothes were sticking to my body and I needed to visit the comfort station. I could have used a shot of Tommy Englander's rye, too.

The hall was a big wooden building, sort of affiliated with the church where Scollay's sis was getting married, I guess. You know the kind of joint I mean—Ladies' Robert Browning Society on Tuesdays and Thursdays, Bingo on Wednesdays, and a sociable for the kids on Friday or Saturday night.

We trooped up the walk, each of us carrying his instrument in one hand and some part of Biff's drum-kit in the other. A thin lady with no breastworks to speak of was directing traffic inside. Two sweating men were hanging crepe paper. There was a bandstand at the front of the hall, and over it was a pair of pink-paper wedding bells and some tinsel lettering which said *BEST ALWAYS MAUREEN AND RICO.*

Maureen and Rico. Damned if I couldn't see why Scollay was so upset. Maureen and Rico. Now wasn't that a combination!

The thin lady saw us and swooped down to our end of the hall. She looked like she had a lot to say, so I beat her to the punch. "We're the band," I said.

"The band?" She blinked at our instruments distrustfully. "Oh. I was hoping you were the caterers."

I smiled as if caterers always carried snare drums and trombone cases.

"You can—" she began, but just then a tough-looking boy of about 19 strolled over. A cigarette was dangling from the left corner of his mouth, but so far as I could see, it wasn't doing a thing for his image except making his left eye water.

"Open that stuff up," he said.

Charlie and Biff looked at me and I just shrugged. We opened our cases and he looked at the horns. Seeing nothing that looked lethal, he wandered back to his corner and sat down on a folding chair.

"You can set your things up right away," she went on, as if there had been no interruption. "There's a piano in the other room. I'll have my men wheel it in when we're done putting up our decorations."

Biff was already lugging his drum-kit up onto the little stage.

"I thought you were the caterers," she said to me in a distraught way. "Mr. Scollay ordered a wedding cake and there are hors d'oeuvres and roasts of beef and—"

"They'll be here, ma'am," I said. "They get payment on delivery."

"—capons and roasts of pork and Mr. Scollay will be furious if—" She saw one of her men pausing to light a cigarette just below a dangling streamer and screamed, *"HENRY!"* The man jumped as if he had been shot, and I escaped to the bandstand.

We were all set up by a quarter to five. Charlie, the trombone player, was wah-wahing away into a mute and Biff was loosening up his wrists. The caterers had arrived at 4:20 and Miss Gibson (that was her name; she made a business out of such affairs) almost threw herself on them.

Four long tables had been set up and covered with white linen, and four black women in caps and aprons were setting places. The cake had been wheeled into the middle of the room for everyone to gasp over. It was six layers high, with a little bride and groom on top.

I walked outside to have a smoke and just about halfway through it I heard them coming, tooting away and making a general racket. When I saw the lead vehicle coming around the corner of the block below the church, I snubbed my smoke and went back inside.

"They're coming," I told Miss Gibson.

She went white as a sheet. That lady should have picked a different profession. "The tomato juice!" she screamed. "Bring in the tomato juice!"

I went back up to the bandstand and we got ready. We had played quite a few gigs like this before—what band hasn't?—and when the doors opened, we swung into a ragtime version of *The Wedding March* that I had arranged myself. Most receptions we played for loved it.

Everybody clapped and yelled and then started gassing among themselves, but I could tell by the way some of them were tapping their feet that we were getting through. We were on—it was going to be a good gig.

But I have to admit that I almost blew the whole number when the groom and the blushing bride walked in. Scollay, dressed in a morning-coat and a ruffled shirt and striped trousers, shot me a hard look, and don't think I didn't see it. The rest of the band kept a poker face too, and we didn't miss a note. Lucky for us. The wedding party, which looked as if it were made up almost entirely of Scollay's goons and their molls, were wise already. They had to be, if they'd been at the church. But I'd only heard faint rumblings, you might say.

You've heard about Jack Sprat and his wife. Well, this was a hundred times worse. Scollay's sister had the red hair he was losing, and it was long and curly. But not that pretty auburn shade you may be imagining. It was as bright as a carrot and as kinky as a bedspring. She looked just awful. And had Scollay said she was fat? Brother, that was like saying you can buy a few things in Macy's. The woman was a dinosaur—350 if she was a pound. It had all gone to her bosom and hips and thighs like it does on fat girls, making her flesh grotesque and frightening. Some fat girls have pathetically pretty faces, but Scollay's sis didn't even have that. Her eyes were too close together, her mouth was too big, and her ears stuck out. Even thin, she'd have been as ugly as the serpent in the garden.

That alone wouldn't have made anybody laugh, unless they were stupid or just poison-mean. It was when you added the groom, Rico, to the combination that you wanted to laugh until you cried.

He could have put on a top hat and stood in the top half of her shadow. He was about five three and must have weighed all of 90 pounds soaking wet. He was skinny as a rail, and his complexion was darkly olive. When he grinned around nervously, his teeth looked like a picket fence in a slum neighborhood.

We just kept right on playing.

Scollay roared, "The bride and the groom! May they always be happy!"

Everyone shouted their approval and applauded. We finished our number with a flourish, and that brought another round. Scollay's sister Maureen smiled nervously. Rico simpered.

For a while everyone just walked around, eating cheese and cold cuts on crackers and drinking Scollay's best bootleg Scotch. I had three shots myself between numbers, and it was pretty smooth.

Scollay began to look a little happier, too—I imagine he was sampling his own wares pretty freely.

He dropped by the bandstand once and said, "You guys play pretty good." Coming from a music lover like him, I reckoned that was a real compliment.

Just before everyone sat down to the meal, Maureen came up herself. She was even uglier up close, and her white gown (there must have been enough white satin to cover three beds) didn't help her at all. She asked us if we could play *Roses of Picardy* like Red Nichols and His Five Pennies, because it was her very favorite song. Fat and ugly or not, she was very sweet about it, not a bit hoity-toity like some of the two-bitters that had been dropping by. We played it, but not very well. Still, she gave us a sweet smile that was almost enough to make her pretty, and she applauded when it was done.

They sat down to the meal around 6:15, and Miss Gibson's hired help rolled in the chow. They fell to it like a bunch of animals, which was not entirely surprising, and kept drinking it up all the time. I couldn't help noticing the way Maureen was eating, though. She made the rest of them look like old ladies in a roadside tearoom. She had no more time for sweet smiles or listening to *Roses of Picardy*. That lady didn't need a knife and a fork. She needed a steam shovel. It was sad to watch her. And Rico (you could just see his chin over the edge of the table where the bride's party was sitting) just kept handing her things, never changing that nervous simper.

We took a twenty-minute break while the cake-cutting ceremony was going on and Miss Gibson herself fed us out in the back part of the hall. It was hot as blazes with the cook stove on, and none of us was too hungry. Manny and Biff had brought some pastry boxes though, and were stuffing in slabs of roast beef and roast pork every time Miss Gibson turned her back.

By the time we returned to the bandstand, the drinking had begun in earnest. Tough-looking guys staggered around with silly grins on their mugs or stood in corners haggling over racing forms. Some couples wanted to Charleston, so we played *Aunt Hagar's Blues* (those goons ate it up) and *I'm Gonna Charleston Back to Charleston* and some other jazzy numbers like that. The molls rocked around the floor, flashing their rolled hose and sounding as shrill as macaws. It was almost completely dark outside, and millers and moths had come in through the open windows and were flitting around the light fixtures. And as the song says, the band played on. The bride and groom stood on the sidelines—neither of them seemed interested in slipping away early—almost completely neglected. Even Scollay seemed to have forgotten them. He was pretty drunk.

It was almost 8:00 when the little fellow crept in. I spotted him immediately because he was sober and dressed better than the rest of them. And he looked scared. He looked like a near-sighted cat in a dog pound. He walked up to Scollay, who was talking with some floozie right by the bandstand, and tapped him on the shoulder. Scollay wheeled around, and I heard every word they said.

"Who the hell are you?" Scollay asked rudely.

"My name is Katzenos," the fellow said, and his eyes rolled whitely. "I come from the Greek."

Motion on the floor came to a dead stop. We kept on playing though, you bet. Jacket buttons were freed, and hands stole out of sight. I saw Manny looking nervous. Hell, I wasn't so calm myself.

"Is that right?" Scollay said ominously.

The guy burst out, "I din't want to come, Mr. Scollay—the Greek, he has my wife. He say he kill her if I doan' give you his message!"

"What message?" Scollay asked. His face was like a thundercloud.

"He say—" The guy paused with an agonized expression. His throat worked like the words were physical, and caught in there. "He say to tell you your sister is one fat pig. He say . . . he say . . ." His eyes rolled wildly at Scollay's expression. I shot a look at Maureen. She looked as if she had been slapped. "He say she's tired of going to bed alone. He say—you bought her a husband."

Maureen gave a great strangled cry and ran out, weeping. The floor shook. Rico pattered after her, his face bewildered and unhappy.

But Scollay was the frightening one. His face had grown so red it was purple and I half expected his brains to just blow out his ears. I saw the same look of mad agony. Maybe he was just a cheap hood, but I felt sorry for him. You would have, too.

When he spoke his voice was very quiet.

"Is there more?"

The little Greek wrung his hands with anguish. "Please doan' kill me, Mr. Scollay. My wife—the Greek, he got my wife! I doan' want to say these thing. He got my wife, my woman! He—"

"I won't hurt you," Scollay said, quieter still. "Tell me the rest."

"He say the whole town is laughing at you."

There was dead silence for a second. We had stopped playing. Then Scollay turned his eyes to the ceiling. Both his hands were shaking and held out clenched in front of him. He was holding them in fists so tight that it seemed his hamstrings ran all the way up his arms.

"All right!" He screamed. *"ALL RIGHT!"*

And he ran for the door. Two of his men tried to stop him, to tell him it was suicide, just what the Greek wanted, but Scollay was like a crazy man. He knocked them down and rushed out into the black summer night.

In the dead quiet that followed, all I could hear was the little man's tortured breathing and somewhere out back, the soft sobbing of the fat bride.

Just about then the young kid who had braced us when we came in uttered a curse and made for the door.

Before he could get there, automobile tires screeched on the pavement down the block and a car engine roared.

"It's him!" The kid screamed from the doorway. "Get down, boss! Get down!"

The next second we heard gunshots—maybe as many as ten, mixed calibres, close together. The car howled away. I could see all I wanted to reflected in that kid's horrified face.

Now that the danger was over, all the goons rushed out. The door to the back of the hall banged open and Maureen ran through again, everything jiggling. Her face was even more puffy, now with tears as well as weight. Rico came in her wake like a bewildered valet. They went out the door.

Miss Gibson appeared in the empty hall, her eyes wide. The man who had brought the message to Scollay had powdered.

"What happened?" Miss Gibson asked.

"I think Mr. Scollay just got rubbed out," Biff said. He looked green.

Miss Gibson stared at him for a moment and then just fainted dead away. I felt a little like fainting myself.

Just then, from outside, came the most anguished scream I have ever heard, then or since. You didn't have to go and peek to know who was tearing her heart out in that street, keening over her dead brother even while the cops and news photographers were on their way.

"Let's get out of here," I muttered. "Quick."

We had it packed in before five minutes had passed. Some of the goons came back, but they were too drunk and too scared to notice the likes of us.

We went out the back, each of us carrying part of Biff's drum-kit. Quite a parade we must have made, walking up the street, for anyone who saw us. I led the way, with my horn case tucked under my arm and a cymbal in each hand. When we got to the truck we threw everything in, willy-nilly, and hauled our butts out of there. We averaged 45 miles an hour going back to Morgan, back roads or not, and Scollay's goons must not have bothered to tip the cops to us, because we never heard from them.

We never got the 200 bucks, either.

She came into Tommy Englander's speak about ten days later, a fat girl in a black mourning dress. It didn't look any better than the white satin.

Englander must have known who she was (her picture had been in the Chicago papers, next to Scollay's) because he showed her to a table himself and shushed a couple of drunks at the bar who were sniggering.

I felt really bad for her, like I feel for Billy-Boy sometimes. It's tough to be on the outside. And she had been very sweet, the little I had talked to her.

When the break came, I went over.

"I'm sorry about your brother," I said, feeling awkward and hot in the face. "I know he really cared for you—"

"I might as well have fired those guns myself," she said. She was looking at her hands, which were really her best feature, small and well formed. She had a musician's fingers. "Everything that little man said was true."

"That's not so," I said uncomfortably, not knowing if it was so or not. I was sorry I'd come over, she talked so strangely. As if she were all alone, and crazy.

"I'm not going to divorce him, though," she went on. "I'd kill myself first."

"Don't talk that way," I said.

"Haven't you ever wanted to kill yourself?" she asked, looking up at me passionately. "Doesn't it make you feel like that when people use you and then laugh about it? Do you know what it feels like to eat and eat and hate yourself and then eat more? Do you know what it feels like to kill your own brother because you're *fat*?"

People were turning to look, and the drunks were sniggering again.

"I'm sorry," she whispered.

I wanted to talk to her, to tell her I was sorry too. I wanted to tell her something that would make her feel better, but I couldn't think of a single thing.

So I just said, "I have to go. The next set—"

"Of course," she said softly. "Of course you do. Or they'll start to laugh at *you*. But why I came was—will you play *Roses of Picardy*? I thought you played it very nice at the reception. Will you?"

"Sure," I said. "Glad to."

And we did. But she left halfway through the number. And since it was sort of schmaltzy for a place like Englander's, we swung into a ragtime version of *The Varsity Drag*, which always tore them up. I drank too much the rest of the evening and by closing time I had forgotten all about it, almost.

Leaving for the night, it came to me that I should have told her that life goes on. That's what you say when someone's loved one dies. But, thinking about it, I was glad I hadn't. Maybe that's what she was afraid of.

Of course now everyone knows about Maureen Romano and her husband Rico, who survives her as the taxpayer's guest in the Illinois State Penitentiary. How she took over Scollay's two-bit organization and worked it into a Prohibition empire that rivaled Capone's. How she wiped out the Greek and two other North Side gang leaders, swallowing their operations. Rico, the bewildered valet, became her first lieutenant and was supposedly responsible for a dozen gangland hits himself.

I followed her exploits from the West Coast, where we were making some pretty successful records. Without Billy-Boy, though. He formed a band of his own after we left Englander's, an all-black Dixieland band, and they did real well down south. It was just as well. Lots of places wouldn't even audition us with a Negro in the group.

But I was telling you about Maureen. She made great news copy, not just because she was shrewd, but because she was a big operator in more ways than one. When she died of a heart attack in 1933, the papers said she weighed 500 pounds, but I doubt that. No one gets that big, do they?

Anyway, her funeral made the front pages—more than anyone could say for Scollay, who never got anyplace past page 4 in his whole miserable career. It took ten pallbearers to carry her coffin. There was a picture of that coffin in one of the tabloids. It was a horrible thing.

Rico wasn't bright enough to hold things together by himself, and he fell for assault with intent to kill the very next year.

I've never been able to get her out of my mind, or the agonized, hangdog way Scollay had looked that first night when he talked about her.

It's all very strange. I can't feel too sorry for her, looking back. Fat people can always stop eating. Poor guys like Billy-Boy Williams can only stop breathing. I still don't see any way I could have helped either of them, but I do feel sort of bad every now and then. Probably because I'm not so young as I once was. That's all it is, isn't it? Isn't it?

Flicks

BILL CRENSHAW

He knew it wasn't a question of if his beeper would go off.

This time Devin Corley was home, his apartment, had just opened a beer, turned on the TV, stretched out on the couch. He phoned in. Dispatcher said Majestic Theater, across town. He started the VCR, took a last pull at the beer, gave the cat fresh water, got a quick shower. Then he left. Speed was not of the essence.

He knew what he'd find. A body; Ray Tasco, his partner, taking statements, popping his gum, looking amused and surprised at once; Maggie Epps with her wedge face and her black forensic kit, diagramming the scene, scooping nameless little forensic glops into baggies; Joe Franks in a safari shirt, slung with cameras, smiling like always, always smiling, always angry. He'd give Corley grief about being away from his desk again, or being late. Corley had been away from his desk a lot. He was always late.

At the Majestic there were two uniforms in the men's john. The room was done in men's room tile, blue and white, smelled of urine, wet tobacco, stale drains, pine. Trash can on side, brown paper towels spilling out, balled up, dark with water, some with red smears. Floor around sinks wet, scattered splashes and small pools. Hints of blood in wet footprints running back and forth across the tile. In near stall somebody retching. The uniform watching the somebody was pointedly not looking at him.

"What we got?" Corley asked the uniforms.

"Got a slashing, lieutenant," said the older uniform, twenty-six maybe, Lopez maybe. Corley glanced down at the name-tag. Lopez. The younger uniform looked green at the gills. Corley didn't know him, knew he wouldn't be green long, not this kind of green. Lots of greens in Homicide, green like Greengills, green like a two-day corpse, green like Corley, like old copper.

"In here?" Corley asked.

Lopez snapped his head back. "In the first theater."

Corley moved to the stall. Lopez moved beside him. Greengills went to the sink and splashed water on his face.

"Who we got?" said Corley.

"Pickpocket, he says. Says he just lifted the guy's wallet. Says he didn't know he was dead."

The pickpocket turned around, face pasty, hair matted. "I didn't know, man," he said, whiney, rocking. "Jesus, I didn't know. That was blood, oh god, that was blood, man, and I didn't even feel it. My hands . . ." He grabbed for the john again. Corley turned away.

"Any of that blood his?" he asked.

"Don't think so."

The wallet was on the stainless steel shelf over the sinks. It was smeared with bloody fingerprints. Corley took out a silver pen and flipped the wallet open. "Find it in the trash can?"

"Yessir," said the younger uniform, wiping the water from his face, looking at Corley in the mirror.

"Money still in it? Credit cards?"

"Yessir."

The driver's license showed a fifty-five-year-old business type, droopy eyes, saggy chin, looking above the camera, trying to decide if he should smile for this official picture. Bussey, Tyrone Otis. Toccoa Falls, Georgia.

The pickpocket told Corley that he'd like seen this chubby dude asleep at the end of his row, which he'd seen him before with a big wad of cash in his wallet at the candy counter and seen him put the wallet inside his coat and not in his pants. Near the end of the flick when he got to the guy he kind of tripped and caught himself on the guy's seat and said sorry, excuse me, while lifting his wallet real neat, and he dropped the wallet into his popcorn box and headed right for the john to ditch the wallet and just stroll out with the plastic and the cash, but in the john his hands were bloody and the guy's wallet and his shoes, and then he heard screaming in the lobby and he ditched the wallet and tried to wash the blood off but there was too much, the more he looked, the more he saw, and somebody came in and went out, so he tried to hide. He didn't know what was happening, but he knew it was real bad.

There was a spritzing noise and thin, piney mist settled into the stall and spotted Corley's glasses. Corley tore off a little square of toilet paper and smeared the spots around on the lenses. He had the pickpocket arrested on robbery and on suspicion of murder, but he knew he wasn't the killer.

"Victim here alone?" asked Corley.

"As far as we know," said Lopez.

"Convention, maybe. Is Tasco here? Do you know Sergeant Tasco?"

Joe Franks leaned into the restroom, cameras swinging at his neck. "Hey, Corley, you in on this or not? The meat wagon's waiting. Come show me what you want."

Corley smiled. "You know what I want."

"Yeah, show me anyway so if you don't get it all, you don't blame me. Where've you been?"

"You shoot in here?"

"Yeah, I shot in here." He sounded impatient.

"You get the footprints?"

"Yeah, I got the footprints."

"Get the towels and the sink?"

"Yeah, the towels, the sink, and the stall, and the punk, and I even got a closeup of his puke, okay?"

"See, Joe," said Corley, smiling again, "you know exactly what I want."

"I hate working with you, Corley," said Franks as Corley pushed past him.

In the theater Maggie Epps was sitting on the aisle across from the body, sketchpad on her knees. "Glad you could make it, Devin," she said.

Corley fished for a snappy comeback, couldn't hook anything he hadn't said a hundred times before, said hello.

Franks showed Corley the angles he had shot. Corley asked for a couple more. The flashes illuminated the body like lightning, burned distorted images into Corley's retina.

Tasco came in, talking to somebody, squinting over his notebook. "Ray, you got the manager there?" Corley called.

"I'm the owner," the man said.

"Think you could give us some more light?"

"This is as bright as it gets, officer. This is a movie theater."

Corley turned back around. Franks snorted.

Mr. T. O. Bussey sat on the aisle in the high-backed chair, sagging left, head forward, eyes opened. Blood covered everything from his tie on down, had run under the seats toward the screen. People had tracked it back toward the lobby, footprints growing fainter up the aisle.

"You shoot that?" asked Corley.

Franks nodded. "Probably thought they were walking through cola."

Corley bent over Mr. Bussey. He put a hand on the forehead and raised the head an inch or two so that he could see the wound. "You see this?"

"Yeah. Want a shot?"

"Can I lift his head, Maggie?"

"Just watch where you plant your big feet," she said.

Corley stood behind Mr. Bussey, put his hands above the ears, and raised the head face forward, chin up. He turned his eyes away from the flashes.

"What did he get?" said Corley.

"Everything," said Maggie. "Jugular, carotid, trachea, carotid, jugular. Something real sharp. This guy never made a sound, never felt a thing. Maybe a hand in his hair jerking his head back. Nothing after that."

"From behind?" Corley lowered the head back to where he had found it.

"Left to right, curving up. You got your man in the john?"

"Don't think so. Too much blood on his shoes. He walked out in front, not behind."

"So what have you got?"

"Headache."

Maggie smiled. "It's going to get worse."

Corley smiled back. "It always does."

Corley made Greengills help bag the body. He could say that he was helping the kid get used to it, that it didn't get any better, that as bodies went this one wasn't bad, but he wasn't sure he had done it as a favor. He was afraid he'd done it to be mean.

They spent half an hour looking for the weapon. Corley didn't expect to find anything. They didn't.

He had a videotape unit brought over and sent Lopez and Green-gills into the other theaters to block the parking lot exits and send the audiences through the lobby.

The owner pulled him aside and protested. Corley told him that the killer might be in another theater. The owner said something about losing the last *Deathdancer* audience and not needing any publicity hurting ticket sales and being as much a victim as that poor man. "I own nine screens in this town," he said, dragging his hand over his jaw. "I'm not responsible for this. Let's keep the profile low, okay?" There was nothing Corley could say, so he said nothing, and the owner bristled and said he had friends in this town. "I'll speak to your superior about this, Officer . . . ?"

"Corley," he said, walking away. "That's l-e-y."

The other movies ended and the audiences pushed into the lobby. Corley had them videotaped as they bunched and swayed toward the street. Two more uniforms arrived and he started them searching the other theaters for the weapon.

He left Tasco in charge and went to the station and hung around the darkroom while Franks did his printing and bitched about wasting his talent on corpses and about Corley's always wanting more shots and more prints than anybody else. Corley didn't bother to tell Franks again that it was his own fault, that Franks was the one who always waxed eloquent over his third beer and said that the camera always lied, that the image distorted as much as it revealed, that photographs were fictions. He had convinced Corley, so Corley always wanted more and more pictures, each to balance others, to offer new angles, so that reality became a sort of compromise, an average. Corley didn't say any of that again. He made the right noises at the right times, like he did when Franks said how he was going to quit as soon as he finished putting his portfolio together, as soon as he got a show somewhere.

Maybe Franks really was working on a project. Maybe he should be a real photographer. Corley didn't know. He knew Franks about as well as he could, down to a certain level, no further. He imagined that Franks knew him in about the same way. It wasn't the kind of thing they talked about.

Corley lifted a dripping print out of the fixer. "Why'd you become a cop anyway?" he said.

Franks took the print from him and put it back. It was hard to read Franks's eyes in the red light. "You're asking that like you thought there were real answers," Franks said.

Corley took the prints to his desk and did what paperwork he could. He worked until the sky got gray. By the time he stopped for doughnuts on the way home, the first edition of the *News* was in the stands. It didn't have the murder.

He thought sometimes there were real answers instead of just the same patterns and ways to deal with patterns and levels beyond which you couldn't go. He thought sometimes that there was a way to get to the next level. He thought sometimes he'd quit, do insurance fraud, something. He thought maybe he hated his job, but he didn't know that either. He had thought there was something essential about working Homicide, essential in the sense of dealing with the essences of things, a job that butted as close to the raw edge of reality as he was likely to get, and how would he do insurance after that? But whatever kind of essence he was seeing, it was mute, images beyond articulation. None of it made any sense, and he was bone-marrow tired.

The landing at his apartment was dim, and as he slid his key into the second lock, he could see the peephole darken in the apartment next door. Half past five in the morning and Gianelli was already up and prowling. Corley stood an extra second in the rectangle of light from his apartment so that Gianelli could see who he was, whoever the hell Gianelli was besides a name on a mailbox downstairs, an eye at the peephole, the sounds of pacing footsteps, of a TV. Corley's cat sniffed at the flecks of dried blood on his shoes.

Corley tossed the paper and Franks's pictures on the desk, opened a can of smelly catfood, had a couple of doughnuts and some milk. Then he rewound the tape in the VCR and stretched out on the couch to watch the program that the call to the theater had interrupted. It was a cop show. At the station they laughed at cop shows. Things made sense in cop shows. He fell asleep before the first commercial.

Corley woke up with the cat in his face again. He got a hand under its middle and flicked it away, watched it twist in the air, land on all fours, sit and stretch, lick its paws. It wasn't even his cat. The apartment had come with the cat and a wall of corky tile covered with pictures of the previous occupant. The super hadn't bothered to take them down. "Throw 'em away if you want," he'd said. "What do I care?" She was pale and blonde. An actress who never made it, maybe. A model. A photographer. Corley wondered what kind of person would leave a cat and a wall covered with her own image. He still had the pictures in a box somewhere. He used the cork as a dart board, to pin up grocery lists and phone numbers. After eight months he was getting used to the cat, except when it tried to lie in his face, which it always did when he fell asleep on the couch. One of these times he was going to toss it out of the window, down to the street. Four floors down, it didn't matter if it landed on its feet or not.

He looked at his watch. Only nine thirty, but he knew he wouldn't get back to sleep. He might as well go in.

He stopped for doughnuts and coffee and the second edition. Big headline. HORROR FLICK HORROR. *Blood flowed on the screen and in the aisles last night at the Majestic Theater* . . . Great copy, he thought, great murder for the papers. Stupid murder in a stupid place. Not robbery. Not a hit, not on some salesman from upstate Georgia. Tasco would say somebody boozed, whacked, dusted. Corley didn't think so. This one was weird. There was something going on here, something interesting, a new level, maybe, something new. He sat for a long time thinking.

It was going on eleven by the time he dropped the paper on his desk.

"My kids love those things," said Tasco.

"What things?"

Tasco pointed to the headline. "Horror flicks."

Corley looked at the paper. The story was covered in green felt tip pen with questions about the case, with ideas, with an almost unrecognizable sketch of the scene. Corley didn't remember doodling.

There was a tapping of knuckle on glass. Captain Hupmann motioned them into his office.

"Finally," said Tasco.

"How long you been waiting?" said Corley.

"Too long."

"Sorry." He knew the captain had been waiting for him, had made Tasco wait on him, too.

"Just go easy, okay?" Tasco said.

The captain shut the door and turned to Corley. "So where are we on this one?"

Tasco looked at Corley. Corley shrugged.

The captain started to snap something but Tasco flipped open his notebook. "Family notified," he said. "Victim in town for sales convention, goes to same convention every year, never takes wife.

Concession girl remembers him because he talked funny, had an accent she meant, and he made her put extra butter on his popcorn twice and called her ma'am. Nobody else remembers him. Staying at the Plaza, single room, no roommate. They don't take roll at the meetings, so we don't know if he's been to any or if he's been seeing the sights." Tasco looked up, popping his gum, then looked at Corley.

"I think we've got a nut," said Corley. "Random. Maybe a one-shot, maybe a serial."

The captain raised his eyebrows in mock surprise. "Are we taking an interest in our work again?"

Corley shifted his weight.

"A nut," said the captain. "Ray?"

Tasco shrugged. "Seems reasonable, but we're not married to it. Might be a user flipped out by the flick."

The captain turned back to Corley. "Why did he pick Bussey?"

Corley could picture Bussey at the convention, anonymous in the city and the crowd, free to cuss and stay out late if he wanted, hit the bars and the ladies, drink too much and smoke big cigars. But Mr. Bussey hadn't gone that far. He'd just gone to a movie he wouldn't be caught dead in at home.

"He sat in the wrong place," said Corley. "He was on the aisle. Quick exit."

"What quick exit? This is a theater, for chrissakes. This is public. You don't do a random in public." The captain drew his lips together. "Where do you want to go with this?" he asked finally, looking more at Tasco than Corley.

Corley looked at Tasco before answering. He hadn't told Tasco anything. "We want to talk to the pickpocket again, the employees again. We've got some names from the audience, the paper had some more. We want them to see the tapes, see if they recognize somebody coming out of the other theaters. Ray wants to do more with Mr. Bussey's movements, see if there's some connection we don't know about."

"Okay," said the captain. "You've both got plenty of other work, but you can keep this one warm for a couple of days. Check the gangs. Maybe something there, initiation ritual, something. If it's some kind of hit, or if it's a user, it won't go far."

"I think it's a serial," said Corley.

"You mean you hope it's a serial," said the captain. "Otherwise you're not going to get him. That it?"

"Yessir," said Tasco.

"Oh, and Corley," the captain said as Corley was halfway through the door, "welcome back. Back to stay?"

They followed up with the employees and what members of the audience they could find, asked if they'd known anybody else in the theater, seen anything unusual, remembered someone walking around near the end of the movie. They showed them pictures of the pickpocket and Mr. Bussey's driver's license, the tapes of the other audiences, asked if anyone looked familiar.

Corley tried to make himself ask the questions as if they were new, as if he'd never even thought of them before. Same questions, same answers, and if you didn't listen because it all seemed the same, you missed something. Tasco always asked the questions right and was somehow not dulled by the routine, by the everlasting sameness. Tasco hunkered down and did his job, would see the waste and the stupidity of it all, say, "Jeez, why do they do that, we got to get the SOB that did this, aren't people horrible." Tasco's saving grace was that he didn't think about it. Corley didn't mean that in a mean way. It was a quality he envied, maybe even admired. Welcome back, back to stay? Sometimes he wondered why he didn't just walk away from it all.

They got Maggie to draw a seating chart and they put little pins in the squares, red for Mr. Bussey, yellow for the people they questioned, blue in seats that yellows remembered being occupied. The media played the story and boosted ratings and circulation, and more people from the audience came forward, and others who claimed to have been there but who Tasco said were probably on Mars at the time. The number of pins increased, but that was all.

"They sat all around him," said Corley, "and they didn't see anything."

"So who in this city ever sees anything?"

"Yeah, well, they should have seen something. Maybe they were watching the movie. Maybe we should see it."

They used their shields to get into the seven o'clock show. The ticket girl told them that the crowd was down, especially in *Death-*

dancer. Tasco bought a big tub of popcorn and two cokes, and they sat in the middle about halfway to the screen.

The horror flicks that had scared Corley as a kid played with the dark, the uncertain, the unknown, where you might not even see the killer clearly, where you were never sure if the clicking in the night outside was the antenna wire slapping in the wind or the sound of the giant crabs moving. One thing might be another, and there was no way to tell, and you never really knew if you were safe.

But this wasn't the same. Here the only unknowns were when the next kid was going to get it and how gross it would be. A series of bright red brutalities, each more bizarre than the last, more grotesque, more unreal. Corley couldn't take it seriously. But maybe the audience could. Unless they were cops or medics, maybe this was what it was like. Corley started watching them.

They were mostly under forty, sat in couples or groups, boys close to the screen or all the way to the wall and the corners, girls in the middle, turning their heads away and looking sideways; dates close, touching, copping feels; marrieds a married distance apart. They all talked and laughed too loud. On the screen the killer stalked the victim and the audience got quiet and focused on the movie. Corley could feel muscles stiffen, tension build as the sequence drew the moment out, the moment you knew would come, was coming, came, and they screamed at the killing, and after the killing sank back spent, then started laughing nervously, talking, wisecracking at the screen, at each other. Corley watched three boys sneak up behind a row of girls and grab at their throats, the girls shrieking, leaping, the boys collapsing in laughter. A girl chanted, "Esther wet her panties," and the whole audience broke up. On the screen, the killer started stalking his next victim and the cycle began again.

"What do you think?" asked Corley, lighting a cigarette as soon as they hit the lobby. People in line for the next show stared at their faces as if trying to see if they would be scared or bored or disgusted. Corley thought they all looked hopeful somehow.

Tasco shrugged, placid as ever. "It was a horror flick."

"Was it any good?"

"Who can tell? You'll have to ask my kids."

The summer wind was warm and filled with exhaust fumes.

"You wanta come up for a beer or something?" Corley asked.

Tasco looked at his watch. "Nah, better get back. Evelyn. See you tomorrow."

Corley thought about rephrasing it, asking if he wanted to stop in for a beer somewhere, but Tasco had already made his excuse. Used to be they'd have a beer once or twice a week before Tasco started his thirty minute drive back to Evelyn and the kids and the postage-stamp yard he was so proud of, but that was before Corley had moved across town, out of his decent apartment, with the courtyard and the pool, into what he lived in now. Tasco had been to the new place once only. He'd looked around and popped his gum and looked surprised and amused and inhaled his beer and left. Corley was relieved that Tasco hadn't asked him why he'd moved. He asked himself the same thing.

After he fed the cat, Corley put on the tape of the audience leaving the other screens. At first they ignored the camera, looked away, pretended not to see it, nudged a companion, pointed discreetly. Some made faces and more people saw it, and more made faces or shot birds or mouthed, "Hi, Mom," or walked straight at the camera so that their faces filled the pictures, stuck hands or popcorn boxes in front of the lens, waved, mugged, danced, pretended to strip, to moon the camera, to kiss Corley through the TV screen.

They had taped three audiences. They acted about the same.

Before he went to bed, Corley posted the newspaper articles and Franks's pictures on the cork wall, with a shot of Mr. Bussey in the center.

The heat woke him. He lay sweating, disoriented, fingers knotted in sheets. The night light threw a yellow oval on the wall opposite, gave the room a focus, showed him right where he was. He hated the panic that came from not being sure. He took three or four deep, slow breaths.

He hadn't always had the night light. He hadn't always strapped an extra gun to his leg or carried two speedloaders in his coat pockets every time he went out. He hadn't always spent so much time in his apartment, in front of the TV, in bed. He tried not to think about it. He tried not to think.

It was too early to be up, too late to go back to sleep, too hot to stay in the apartment. He could make coffee and go to the roof before the sun hit the tar, could catch the breeze off the river, let the cat stalk pigeons.

While the coffee dripped he sat on the couch and looked at the pictures on the wall. In the central picture Mr. Bussey sat with head up and eyes open, like he was watching the movie, the wound like a big smile. Death in black and white. Not like the deaths in the movie. Real was more . . . something. Casual. Anticlimactic. Prosaic. Unaccompanied by soundtrack. Maybe Bussey wasn't really dead. Maybe it was just special effects. In the picture his hands held Mr. Bussey's head just above the ears. He wiped his palms on his shorts.

Mr. Gianelli's peephole darkened as Corley shut his door and the cat slid up the stairs. He was halfway to the landing when the door opened the width of the chain and Gianelli's face pressed into the crack, cheeks bulging around the wood. Over his shoulder a room was lit by a television's multi-colored glow.

"I know what you're doing, young man," Gianelli called in a rasping voice.

"Sorry if I woke you," Corley said, kept climbing, smiled. Maybe thirty-eight seemed young to Gianelli.

"You leave my antenna alone," Gianelli said. "The one on the chimney. I been seventeen years in this building. I got rights. You hear me, young man? Next time my picture goes I'm calling a cop." He slammed his door and it echoed in the stairwell like a gunshot.

Corley beat Tasco to work.

"Whoa," said Franks on his way to the coffee pot. "On time and everything. You must have figured it out."

"Figured what out?" said Corley.

Franks smiled. "That you won't get fired for being late. You want out, you got to quit."

"So who wants out?"

"Who doesn't?"

Tasco had never said anything about Corley's being late. When Tasco came in, he didn't say anything about Corley's being early.

Another homicide came in and they spent the morning and most of the afternoon down by the river and the warehouses, Tasco and Corley and Maggie and Joe and the smells of creosote and fish and gasoline. Some punk had taken a twelve-gauge to the gut, sawed-off,

Maggie said, because of the spread and the powder burns, another drug hit as the new champions of free enterprise tried to corner the market. It wasn't going to get solved unless somebody rolled over. A crowd gathered at the yellow police line ribbons. Lopez and Greengills came in for crowd control. The paramedics bitched about hauling corpses. Greengills didn't seem to be bothered by the body.

It was late when they got back to the station.

"I'm going to the movie," said Corley. "I'm going to take our pickpocket. Want to come?"

"What for?"

"Like you said, maybe something in the movie freaked this guy. Maybe we can find something."

"I don't think we're going to get anywhere on this one."

"So you want to come, or not?" Tasco said no.

The pickpocket didn't want to go either. "My treat," Corley told him, not smiling.

Corley sat in Mr. Bussey's seat and told the pickpocket to reconstruct exactly what he had done, when he had done it. He got popcorn and grape soda like Bussey, put the empties into the next seat like Bussey, concentrated on the movie, tried not to see the pickpocket in the corner of his eye, tried to ignore the feeling that his back was to the door, tried to control his breathing. He hated this, hated the dark, the people around him, the long empty aisle on his left, he felt full of energy demanding use, fought to sit still. Finally on the screen the killer reached for the last survivor and the background music shrieked, and Corley slumped left and lowered his head and sat, and on the screen the girl fought off the killer, and they rescued her just in time, and they killed the killer and comforted the girl, and they discovered that the killer wasn't dead and had escaped, and then Corley felt the pickpocket fall across him, heard his "Sorry," felt the wallet slide out of his coat only because he was waiting for it. He sat slumped over while the audience filed out, giggling or groaning or silent. He sat until a nervous usher shook him and asked him to wake up.

He found the pickpocket throwing up in the men's room.

"We're just going to leave this open for a while," said the captain. "Put the river thing on warm."

Tasco nodded, popping his gum. Corley said nothing.

"Problem, Devin?"

"I'd like to stay on this a while."

"Got something to sell? New leads? Anything?"

Corley shook his head. "Not really."

"Okay, then."

They went back to their desks.

"Learn anything last night?" asked Tasco.

Corley shrugged, remembering the dark, palpable and pressing; the icy air pushing into his lungs as he sat and waited, the effort to exhale; trying to concentrate on the movie, on what might have snapped somebody; and after, trying to help the pickpocket out of the stall, embarrassed for him now, and sorry, and the pickpocket twisting his elbow out of Corley's grip and tearing in half the twenty that Corley had stuffed into his shirt pocket, bloody money maybe, something, he wouldn't have it. "Not much," he said. "Bussey must have gotten it in that last sequence, like we thought."

"Funny, isn't it, all that stuff up there on the screen, and out in the audience some dude flicks out a blade and that's that."

"Yeah," said Corley. "That's that."

Corley found himself at a movie again that night, a horror flick near the university. He sat on the aisle, last row, back to the wall. The movie looked the same as the other, felt the same, same rhythms, same victims, same bright gore. The audience was younger, more the age of the characters on the screen, and louder, maybe, but still much the same as the others, shouting at the screen, groaning, cracking jokes, laughing in the wrong places, trying to scare each other, strange responses, inappropriate somehow. They had come for the audience as much as the movie. They had come to be in a group.

He found himself the next night in another movie, on the aisle, last row, back to the wall, fingering the speedloader in his pocket, trying to remember why he was wasting his time there.

Near the end of the show, he saw a silhouette down front rise and edge toward the aisle, stop, and his guts iced as he saw it reach out its left hand and pull back someone's head, heard a scream, saw it slash across the throat with its right hand and turn and run up the aisle for the exit, coming right for him, too perfect. He braced, tightening his grips on the armrests, fought to sit, sit, as the silhouette ran toward him, then he stuck out a leg and the man went down hard and Corley was on him with his knee in the back and his gun behind the right ear.

He yelled for an ambulance, ordered the man to open his fist. The man was slow. Corley brought a gun butt down on the back of his hand. The fingers opened, and something bright rolled onto the carpet. Corley stared at it for a few seconds before he saw it was a tube of lipstick.

"It's only a game, man," said a voice above him, quavering. Corley looked up. The owner of the voice was pointing with a shaking finger to the bright red lipstick slash along his throat. "Only a game."

Corley cuffed them to each other and took them in. He was not gentle with them.

The papers had fun with the story. "Off-duty Detective Nabs Lipstick Slasher," said one headline. Corley posted the stories on the corkboard.

They gave him a hard time when he got to work, asked if he'd been wounded, if the stain would come out, warned him about the chapstick chopper. He didn't let it get to him.

What got to him was how much fun the slasher and his victim had. He tried to tell Tasco about it. He'd almost lost it, he said. He'd been shaking with rage, wanted to push them around, run them in hard, give them a dose of the fear of God, but it didn't sink in. They just kept replaying it all the way into the station.

"You really didn't know for sure, did you?" the slasher had asked.

"Thought I was *gone*," said the victim. "For a second there I thought this was it." He laid his head back on the seat, his face suddenly blue fading to black as the unit passed under a street light. "Oh, wow," he said.

"Shut up," Corley had snarled. "Just shut the hell up." They had gone silent, then looked at each other and giggled.

"Drugs," said Tasco.

"They weren't looped. It was like they were, but they weren't. This guy, the victim—for all he knew it was the killer. He was scared shitless, Ray, and he loved it."

Tasco shrugged. "It's a cheap high. Love that rush, maybe. Or maybe it's like they're in the flick. Makes 'em movie stars. Everybody wants to be a movie star. Put a Walkman on your head and your *life's* a fucking movie."

"I just wish I knew what the hell was going on." Corley rocked back in his chair. "I'm going to a movie tonight. Want to come?"

Tasco stared at Corley for a second or two. "This on your own time?"

"You want to come, or not?"

"The river's on warm, remember? We're not going to get this one. It was a one shot." He paused a second. "You okay?"

Corley rocked forward. "What the hell is that supposed to mean?"

"It's not supposed to mean anything. I only wanted . . ."

"All I did was ask if you wanted to go to a flick."

"Keep your voice down. Jesus. For six months you've been a walking burnout. I've been like partnered with a zombie . . ."

"I do my job, nobody can say I don't do my job."

". . . now suddenly you're doing overtime. I'm your partner. I just want to know if you're okay, that's all."

"I'm fine," Corley snapped.

"Okay, great. I'm just asking."

Corley got up and crossed the squad room and refilled his coffee cup and sat back down. He took a sip, burned his tongue. "Yeah, well," he said, "thanks for asking. You want to come?"

Tasco shook his head. "It's going to be a long day without that."

It was a long day, but Corley made the nine o'clock at the Majestic. The ticket girl let him in on his shield again, said the numbers were up, really up. The lobby was crowded, people two deep at the candy counter, clumped around video games, whooping over electronic explosions as someone blasted something on the screen. There were no seats left at the back or on the aisle, and Corley had to sit between two people. He kept his elbows off the armrests. During the movie the audience seemed more tense, everybody wide-eyed and alert, but he caught himself with knotted muscles more than once and thought the tension maybe was in him.

The lipstick game spread like bad news, and every night Corley ran in one or two slashers for questioning, and for anger, because it wasn't a game when he saw a head snap back or heard a scream, wasn't a game when the man moving down his row or running up the aisle might have a razor tucked in his fist. The games got elaborate, became contests with teams, slashers and victims alternating roles and tallying points in the lobby between shows. Sometimes someone would slash a stranger, and Corley broke up the fights at first, but later didn't bother, didn't waste time or risk injury for a pair of idiots. He went to movies every night that week, and every night he saw more people than the night before, and felt more alert and tense, and left more exhausted. His ulcer flared like sulphur; he was smoking again.

On Friday night near the end of the movie his beeper went off and half the audience screamed and jumped and clutched in their seats, then sank back as a wave of relief swept over them and they gave themselves to laughter and curses and groans and chatter, ignoring the movie.

Corley phoned in from the lobby. They had found a body after the last show at the Astro. He had been slashed.

Corley was strangely pleased.

"Could be some frigging copycat," said Tasco the next day, yawning.

Corley wasn't sleepy. "No way," he said. "Exactly the same."

"The paper had the details."

"It's the same guy, Ray."

"Okay, okay," said Tasco, palms up. "Same guy."

The routine began again, interviews, hunting up the audience, blue and yellow pins, lack of a good witness. Tasco asked where they'd sat, what they'd seen, who they'd known. Corley asked them why they'd gone, whether they'd liked it, if they went to horror flicks often, if they'd played the assassin games. They didn't know how to answer him. He made them uncomfortable, sometimes angry, and they addressed their answers to Tasco, who looked amused and popped his gum and wrote it all down.

Corley posted the new pictures on the corkboard, and the articles and the editorials, and the movie ads. Various groups blasted the lipstick game, called for theaters to quit showing horror movies, called for theaters to close completely. Corley's theater owner wrote a guest editorial calling on readers not to be made prisoners by one maniac, not to give in to the creatures of the night. The Moviola ads promised armed guards; the Majestic dared people to come to the late show. The corkboard was covered by the end of the week, a vast montage filling the wall behind the blank television.

Tasco went with him to the movies now. There were lines at every ticket window, longer lines every night. The Moviola's security guards roamed the lobby and aisles; the Majestic installed airport metal detectors at the door; the Astro frisked its patrons, who laughed nervously, or cracked wise like Cagney or Bogart, and the guards made a big production when they found tubes of lipstick, asked if they had a license, were told it was for protection only or that they were collectors or with the FBI. They were all having a great time. The ticket girl said they gave her the creeps.

"That's two of us," Corley said.

Corley and Tasco sat on opposite sides of the theater, on the aisle, backs to the wall, linked with lapel mikes and earphones. Fewer and fewer played the lipstick game, but the audiences seemed electric and intense; Corley felt sharp and coiled, felt he could see everything, felt he was waiting for something.

After the movies, when he came home drained and sagged down on the couch, Corley found himself staring at the wall, at the picture of T. O. Bussey looking out at him from the aisle seat, his hands holding up the head, and he felt like he didn't know anything at all.

Corley turned off his electric razor and turned up the radio. An early morning DJ was interviewing a psychiatrist about the slasher. Corley knew he'd give the standard whacko profile, a quiet, polite, boy-next-door type who repressed sex and hated daddy, and that everybody who knew him would be surprised and say what a nice guy he was and how they could hardly believe it. He got his notebook to write it down so he could quote it to Tasco.

"Said he was 'quiet, withdrawn, suffers repressed sexuality and sexual expression, experiences intense emotional build-up and achieves orgasm at climax of movie and murder, cycle of build-up and release, release of life, fluids, satisfaction.'" He flipped the note-book shut.

"Jeez, I hate that," said Tasco. "I hate the hell out of that. That doesn't mean squat. That's just words. Who is he, gets paid to say crap like that? He doesn't know anything."

"I want to talk to this guy," said Corley. "I just want to sit down and talk to him, you know? I just want to buy him a drink or something and ask him what the hell is going on."

"You mean the shrink?" Tasco was squinting.

"Our guy," said Corley. "The slasher."

Tasco didn't say anything.

"He knows something," said Corley.

Tasco looked angry again. "He doesn't know anything. What are you talking about?"

Corley tried to say what he meant, couldn't find it, couldn't make it concrete. Why was it so important to get this guy, see him, find out what he looked like, why he did it, not why, exactly, but how, maybe, how in the sense of giving people a chance to maybe have their throats cut, and having them line up like it was a raffle? What would that tell him about what was driving him off the street, what kept drawing him back down, why he was carrying an extra piece, what kept him in that lousy apartment in the middle of all of this tar and pavement when he could just walk away? What did he want?

"He knows something about people," Corley said finally.

Tasco waved his hand like he was fanning flies. "What could he know? He's just a sicko . . ."

"Come on, Ray, we've seen sickoes. They don't slash in public, not like this."

Anger was in both voices now.

"Maybe they do. Maybe he just wanted to see if he could. Ever think of that? Maybe it's the thrill of offing somebody in front of a live audience. Maybe that's all."

"Yeah, that's all, and all those people out there know he's out there, too, and they can't stay away. Why can't they stay away, Tasco?"

"We can't just keep going to movies, Devin. We got lives, you know."

"We're not going to get him unless we get him in the act."

"That's just stupid. That won't happen. That's a stupid thing to say."

"Watch it, sergeant."

"Oh, kiss it, Corley. Jesus."

They were silent again, avoiding each other's eyes.

"I just want to bust this guy," said Corley.

"Yeah, well," said Tasco, looking out of the window, "what I want is to go home, see my wife and kids, maybe watch a ball game." He looked back to Corley. "So, we going out again tonight or what?"

They went again that night and the next night and the next. They always sat on the aisle at opposite ends of the last row so that they could cover both rear exits. Tasco would sit through only one show; Corley sat through both. He felt better when Tasco was at the other end, when he could hear him clear his throat, or mutter something to himself, or even snore when he nodded off as he sometimes did, which amazed Corley. Corley stayed braced in his seat.

When Tasco left, Corley felt naked on the aisle, so he'd move in one seat and drape a raincoat across the aisle seat so it looked occupied, so no one would sit there. The nine o'clock show was usually a sell-out, the audience filling every seat and pressing in on him, a single vague mass in the dark at a horror flick, hiding a man with a razor, maybe even inviting him, desiring him, seeking him. After five nights Corley was ragged and jumpy.

"I'm going to sit in the projection booth," he told Tasco. "Better view."

Tasco shrugged. "End of the week and that's it, okay?"

"We'll see."

"That's got to be it, Devin."

The booth gave Corley a broader view, and gave him distance, height, a thick glass wall. At first he felt conspicuous whenever a pale face lifted his way as the audience waited for the movie to start. The manager showed him how to override the automatics and turn up the house lights, otherwise hands off. The projector looked like a giant Tommy gun sighted on the screen through a little rectangle outlined on the glass in masking tape. He had expected something more sophisticated.

Tasco was just out of sight below him, left aisle, last row, back to the wall. Through his earphone, Corley could hear the audience from Tasco's lapel mike, a general murmur, a burst of high-pitched laughter, the crying of a baby who shouldn't even be there. Corley wiped his glasses on his tie. Hundreds of people out there, could be any one of them, and what the hell were the rest of them doing out there, and what the hell was he doing up here?

The lights dimmed and the projector lit up, commercials, previews, the main feature. A little out-of-focus movie danced in the rectangle on the glass, blobs of color and movement bleeding out onto the masking tape; the soundtrack was thin and tinny from the booth speaker and just half a beat behind in the earphone, disconcerting. Beyond the glass, on exhibition, the audience stirred and rippled; beyond them the huge and distorted images filled the screen. He watched, and when someone stood and moved toward the aisle, he warned Tasco and felt adrenaline heat arms and legs and the figure reached the aisle and turned and walked toward restroom or candy counter, and Corley tried to relax again. It was easier to relax up here, above it all.

The movie dragged on. Corley found by staring at a central point in the audience and unfocusing his eyes, he could see all movement instantly, and everybody was moving, scratching ears and noses and scalps, lifting hands to mouths to cover coughs or to feed, rocking, putting arms around dates, leaning forward, leaning back, covering eyes with fingers. Again he saw the patterns emerge around the on-screen killings, movements ebbing as the killing neared, freezing at the death itself, melting after, and flowing across the audience again, strong and choppy, then quieter and smooth. He had to concentrate, breathe slowly and carefully, to keep himself from narrowing his vision, focusing on one person. He didn't see the movie.

A flicker in the corner of his eye, flick of light on steel. He swung eyes right, locked on movement, saw the head pulled back, the blade flicker again, realized it was happening, that he hadn't seen the killer move down the row because he was sitting right behind his victim, it was happening now, all the way across the theater from Tasco. He radioed Tasco as he turned for the stairs and punched the lights, heard Tasco yell for the man to stop, knew they were too late for the victim, but they had him now, they had him now, they had him now. He took the stairs three at a time, slipped, skidded down arms flailing, wrenched his shoulder as he tried to break the fall, then on his feet and bursting through the door behind the concession stand, drawing his pistol as he ran, putting out his left arm and vaulting over the counter, popcorn and patron flying. He stopped in front of the double doors, pistol leveled, waiting for the maniac to run into his arms.

Nobody came. Corley crouched, frozen, pistol extended in two hands, and in his left ear the theater, voices and screams and music, and Tasco maybe, Tasco shouting something, and still nobody came. He moved forward, gun still extended, and jerked open a door with his left hand.

Lights still brightening, movie running, and the screams and shouts and music in the earphone echoed, echoed in his right ear and for an instant he lost where he was. Then he heard Tasco calling him in his earphone and saw him trying to hammer his way into a knot of people below the screen, the rest of the audience in their seats, watching the movie or those down front attacking the slasher.

Corley ran down the aisle, yelling for Tasco. The earphone went dead and Tasco was gone. Corley reached the mass, started pulling people out of his way, stepping on them, pushing. Some pushed back and turned on him, and he knocked one down and another man grabbed him, and he hit the man in the face, and backed toward the wall, gun leveled. The man changed his mind, backed away. Corley called Tasco, heard nothing through the earphone. He tried to elbow his way in the crowd, started clubbing with both hands around the pistol, fighting the urge to just start pulling the trigger and have done with it. A huge man turned and started to swing; Corley watched the fist come around in slow motion, easily deflected the blow, put a knee in the solar plexus, watched the man fall like a great tree, cuffed him across the jaw as he went down, felt that he could count the pores in the potato nose. They were right beneath the speakers, the music pounding his bones. He reached for the next one in his way.

He heard a shot, saw Tasco cornered by four or five, his gun pointed toward the ceiling but lowering. The next one wouldn't be a warning shot and those guys knew it and they weren't backing off. Corley tried to shout above the music, raised his pistol and fired toward the ceiling, fired again, heard Tasco's gun answer, fired a third time, and the crowd started breaking at the edges, some hurt, some bloody. Corley tried to hold them back, grabbed at one who twisted away, and they pushed past, ignoring him, laughing or shouting, and the others were leaving their seats now, mixing with them, and some in their seats were applauding and cheering.

There were people lying all around them, some groaning, some bleeding. The slasher's victim sprawled across an aisle seat, throat opened to the stars painted on the ceiling. "Help me, Jesus," someone was saying over and over. "Jesus, help me." He heard someone calling his name, saying something. It was Tasco.

"I couldn't stop them," Tasco was saying. Corley looked down. They had used the slasher's blade, and whatever else was handy. The slasher's features were unrecognizable, the head almost severed from the body. A sudden fury flashed through Corley, and he kicked the person lying nearest to him. "Couldn't stop them," Tasco repeated, his voice trembling.

"Is this him, do you think?" asked Corley.

Tasco didn't say anything.

"Maybe Maggie can tell us," said Corley. "Maybe the M.E." He could hear the desperation in his voice.

"It could be anybody," said Tasco.

When he used the phone in the ticket office to call it all in, he heard people demanding a refund because they hadn't gotten to see the end of the movie.

Corley didn't get home until late the next afternoon. He'd made it through the last eighteen hours by thinking about the crummy little apartment high above the street, with the couch and the double locks and the television. He heard the cat yowling before he even put the key in the first lock.

He fed the cat and opened a beer, and turned on his television, but the pictures were wrong, fuzzy, filled with snow. He tried to fix the image, but nothing worked, and he grew angry. Finally he checked the roof and found his antenna bent over.

"Gianelli," he shouted, pounding, standing to one side of the door, seeing an image of Gianelli spinning in slow motion toward pavement four floors down. "Come out of there, Gianelli." No answer. He spread the name out, kicking on the door once for each syllable. "*Gi-a-nel-li*!"

"You go away now," came a voice from inside. "You go away. I'm calling the cops."

"I *am* a cop," Corley shouted, dragging out his shield and holding it to the peephole.

"You go away now," Gianelli said after a moment of silence.

Corley gave the door one last kick.

He tried to salvage the antenna, but Gianelli had done a job on it, twisting the crosspieces, cutting the wires into a dozen pieces.

Before he went to sleep, he took down the pictures and clippings about Mr. Bussey, and he dug around until he found the pictures of the previous occupant, and he pinned them all up. He crossed the room and sat on the couch to look at them. They were all black and white, blonde and pale eyes, and he wondered if she had walked away from whatever brought her here. He thought she was very beautiful. But who could tell from pictures?

He locked the doors and cut on the night light.

The Leopard Man's Story

JACK LONDON

He had a dreamy, faraway look in his eyes, and his sad, insistent voice, gentle-spoken as a maid's, seemed the placid embodiment of some deep-seated melancholy. He was the Leopard Man, but he did not look it. His business in life, whereby he lived, was to appear in a cage of performing leopards before vast audiences, and to thrill those audiences by certain exhibitions of nerve for which his employers rewarded him on a scale commensurate with the thrills he produced.

As I say, he did not look it. He was narrow-hipped, narrow-shouldered, and anemic, while he seemed not so much oppressed by gloom as by a sweet and gentle sadness, the weight of which was as sweetly and gently borne. For an hour I had been trying to get a story out of him, but he appeared to lack imagination. To him there was no romance in his gorgeous career, no deeds of daring, no thrills—nothing but a gray sameness and infinite boredom.

Lions? Oh, yes! he had fought with them. It was nothing. All you had to do was stay sober. Anybody could whip a lion to a standstill with an ordinary stick. He had fought one for half an hour once. Just hit him on the nose every time he rushed, and when he got artful and rushed with his head down, why, the thing to do was to stick out your leg. When he grabbed at the leg you drew it back and and hit him on the nose again. That was all.

With the faraway look in his eyes and his soft flow of words he showed me his scars. There were many of them, and one recent one where a tigress had reached for his shoulder had gone down to the bone. I could see the neatly mended rents in the coat he had on. His right arm, from the elbow down, looked as though it had gone through a threshing machine, such was the ravage wrought by claws and fangs. But it was nothing, he said, only the old wounds bothered him somewhat when the rainy weather came on.

Suddenly his face brightened with a recollection, for he was really as anxious to give me a story as I was to get it.

"I suppose you've heard of the lion tamer who was hated by another man?" he asked.

He paused and looked pensively at a sick lion in the cage opposite.

"Got the toothache," he explained. "Well, the lion tamer's big play to the audience was putting his head in a lion's mouth. The man who hated him attended every performance in the hope sometime of seeing that lion crunch down. He followed the circus about all over the country. The years went by and he grew old, and the lion tamer grew old, and the lion grew old. And at last one day, sitting in a front seat, he saw what he had waited for. The lion crunched down, and there wasn't any need to call a doctor."

The Leopard Man glanced casually over his fingernails in a manner which would have been critical had it not been so sad.

"Now that's what I call patience," he continued, "and it's my style. But it was not the style of a fellow I knew. He was a little, thin, sawed-off, sword-swallowing and juggling Frenchman. De Ville, he called himself, and he had a nice wife. She did trapeze work and used to dive from under the roof into a net, turning over once on the way as nice as you please.

"De Ville had a quick temper, as quick as his hand, and his hand was as quick as the paw of a tiger. One day, because the ringmaster called him a frog eater, or something like that and maybe a little worse, he shoved him against the soft pine background he used in his knife-throwing act, so quick the ringmaster didn't have time to think, and there, before the audience, de Ville kept the air on fire with his knives, sinking them into the wood all around the ringmaster so close that they passed through his clothes and most of them bit into his skin.

"The clowns had to pull the knives out to get him loose, for he was pinned fast. So the word went around to watch out for de Ville, and no one dared be more than barely civil to his wife. And she was a sly bit of baggage, too, only all hands were afraid of de Ville.

"But there was one man, Wallace, who was afraid of nothing. He was the lion tamer, and he had the selfsame trick of putting his head into the lion's mouth. He'd put it into the mouths of any of them, though he preferred Augustus, a big, good-natured beast who could always be depended upon.

"As I was saying, Wallace—'King' Wallace we called him—was afraid of nothing alive or dead. He was a king and no mistake. I've seen him drunk, and on a wager go into the cage of a lion that had turned nasty, and without a stick beat him to a finish. Just did it with his fist on the nose.

"Madame de Ville—"

At an uproar behind us the Leopard Man turned quietly around. It was a divided cage, and a monkey, poking through the bars and around the partition, had had its paw seized by a big gray wolf that was trying to pull off the paw by main strength. The arm seemed stretching out longer and longer like a thick elastic, and the unfortunate monkey's mates were raising a terrible din. No keeper was at hand, so the Leopard Man stepped over a couple of paces, dealt the wolf a sharp blow on the nose with the light cane he carried, and returned with a sadly apologetic smile to take up his unfinished sentence as though there had been no interruption.

"—looked at King Wallace and King Wallace looked at her, while de Ville looked black. We warned Wallace, but it was no use. He laughed at us, as he laughed at de Ville one day when he shoved de Ville's head into a bucket of paste because he wanted to fight.

"De Ville was in a pretty mess—I helped to scrape him off; but he was cool as a cucumber and made no threats at all. But I saw a glitter in his eyes which I had seen often in the eyes of wild beasts, and I went out of my way to give Wallace a final warning. He laughed, but he did not look so much in Madame de Ville's direction after that.

"Several months passed by. Nothing had happened and I was beginning to think that it was a scare over nothing. We were West by that time, showing in 'Frisco. It was during the afternoon performance, and the big tent was filled with women and children, when I went looking for Red Denny, the head canvasman, who had walked off with my pocket-knife.

"Passing by one of the dressing tents I glanced in through a hole in the canvas to see if I could locate him. He wasn't there, but directly in front of me was King Wallace, in tights, waiting for his turn to go on with his cage of performing lions. He was watching with much amusement a quarrel between a couple of trapeze artists. All the rest of the people in the dressing tent were watching the same thing, with the exception of de Ville, whom I noticed staring at Wallace with undisguised hatred. Wallace and the rest were all too busy following the quarrel to notice this or what followed.

"But I saw it through the hole in the canvas. De Ville drew his handkerchief from his pocket, made as though to mop the sweat from his face with it—it was a hot day—and at the same time walked past Wallace's back. He never stopped, but with a flirt of the handkerchief kept right on to the doorway, where he turned his head, while passing out, and shot a swift look back. The look troubled me at the time, for not only did I see hatred in it, but I saw triumph as well.

"'De Ville will bear watching,' I said to myself, and I really breathed easier when I saw him go out the entrance to the circus grounds and board an electric car for downtown. A few minutes later I was in the big tent, where I had overhauled Red Denny. King Wallace was doing his turn and holding the audience spellbound. He was in a particularly vicious mood, and he kept the lions stirred up till they were all snarling—that is, all of them except old Augustus, and he was just too fat and lazy and old to get stirred up over anything.

"Finally Wallace cracked the old lion's knees with his whip and got him into position. Old Augustus, blinking good-naturedly, opened his mouth and in popped Wallace's head. Then the jaws came together, *crunch*, just like that."

The Leopard Man smiled in a sweetly wistful fashion, and the faraway look came into his eyes.

"And that was the end of King Wallace," he went on in his sad, low voice. "After the excitement cooled down I watched my chance and bent over and smelled Wallace's head. Then I sneezed."

"It . . . it was . . . ?" I queried with halting eagerness.

"Snuff—that de Ville dropped on his hair in the dressing tent. Old Augustus never meant to do it. He only sneezed."

Something Evil in the House

CELIA FREMLIN

Looking back, I find it very hard to say just when it was that I first began to feel anxious about my niece, Linda. No, anxious is not quite the right word, for of course I have been anxious about her many times during the ten years she has been in my care. You see, she has never been a robust girl, and when she first came to live with me, a nervous, delicate child of twelve, she seemed so frail that I really wondered sometimes if she would survive to grow up.

However, I am happy to say that she grew stronger as the years passed, and I flatter myself that by gentle, common-sense handling and abundant affection I have turned her into as strong and healthy a young woman as she could ever have hoped to be. Stronger, I am sure, (though perhaps I shouldn't say this) than she would have been if my poor sister Angela had lived to bring her up.

No, it was not anxiety about Linda's health that has troubled me during the past weeks; nor was it simply a natural anxiety about the wisdom of her engagement to John Barrow. He seemed a pleasant enough young man, with his freckled, snub-nosed face and ginger hair. Though I have to admit I didn't really take to him myself—he made me uneasy in some way I can't describe. But I would not dream of allowing any prejudice of mine to stand in the way of the young couple—there is nothing I detest more than this sort of interference by the older generation.

All the same, I must face the fact that it was only after I heard of their engagement that I began to experience any qualms about Linda—those first tremors of a fear that was to grow and grow until it became an icy terror that never left me, day or night.

I think it was in September that I first became aware of my uneasiness—a gusty September evening with autumn in the wind, in the trees, everywhere. I was cycling up the long gentle hill from the village after a particularly wearisome and inconclusive committee meeting of the Women's Institute. I was tired, so tired that before I reached the turning into our lane I found myself getting off my bicycle to push it up the remainder of the slope—a thing I have never done before.

For in spite of my 54 years I am a strong woman, and a busy one. I cycle everywhere, in all weathers, and it is rare indeed for me to feel tired. Certainly the gentle incline between the village and our house had never troubled me before. But tonight, somehow, the bicycle might have been made of lead—I felt as if I had cycled fifteen miles instead of the bare one and a half from the village; and when I turned into the dripping lane, and the evening became almost night under the overhanging trees, I became aware not only of tiredness, but of an indefinable foreboding. The dampness and the autumn dusk seemed to have crept into my very soul, bringing their darkness with them.

Well, I am not a fanciful woman. I soon pulled myself together when I reached home, switched on the lights, and made myself a cup of tea. Strong and sweet it was, the way I always like it. Linda often laughs at me about my tea—she likes hers so thin and weak that I sometimes wonder why she bothers to pour the water into the teapot at all, instead of straight from the kettle to her cup!

So there I sat, the comfortable old kitchen chair drawn up to the glowing stove, and I waited for the warmth and the sweet tea to work their familiar magic. But somehow, this evening, they failed. Perhaps I was really *too* tired; or perhaps it was the annoyance of noticing from the kitchen clock that it was already after eight. As I have told you, I am a busy woman, and to find that the tiresome meeting must have taken a good two hours longer than usual *was* provoking, especially as I had planned to spend a long evening working on the Girls' Brigade accounts.

Whatever it may have been, somehow I couldn't relax. The stove crackled merrily, the tea was delicious, yet I sat, still tense and uneasy, as if waiting for something.

And then, somehow, I must have gone to sleep, quite suddenly, because the next thing I knew I was dreaming. Quite a simple, ordinary sort of dream it will seem to you—nothing alarming, nothing even unusual in it, and yet you will have to take my word for it that it had all the quality of a nightmare.

I dreamed that I was watching Linda at work in the new house. I should explain that for the past few months Linda has not been living here with me, but in lodgings in the little town where she works, about six miles from here. It is easier for her to get to and from her office, and also it means that she and John can spend their evenings working at the new house they have been lucky enough to get in the Estate on the outskirts of the town. The house is not quite finished yet, and they are doing all the decorating themselves—I believe John is putting up shelves and cupboards and all kinds of clever fittings. I am telling you this so that you will see that there was nothing intrinsically nightmarish about the setting of my dream—on the contrary, the little place must have been full of happiness and bustling activity—the most unlikely background for a nightmare that you could possibly imagine.

Well, in my dream I was there with them. Not with them in any active sense, you understand, but hovering in that disembodied way one does in dreams—an observer, not an actor on the scene. Somewhere near the top of the stairs I seemed to be, and looking down I could see Linda through the door of one of the empty little rooms. It was late afternoon in my dream, and the pale rainy light gleamed on her flaxen-pale hair making it look almost metallic—a sort of shining gray. She had her back to me, and she seemed absorbed in painting the far wall of the room—I heard that suck-sucking noise of the paint brush with extraordinary vividness.

And as I watched her I began to feel afraid. She looked so tiny and thin, and unprotected; her fair, childlike head seemed poised so precariously on her white neck—even her absorption in the painting seemed in my dream to add somehow to her peril. I opened my mouth to warn her—to warn her of I know not what—but I could make no sound, as is the way of dreams.

It was then that the whole thing slipped into a nightmare. I tried to scream, to run, I struggled in vain to wake up—and as the nightmare mounted I became aware of footsteps, coming nearer and nearer through the empty house.

"It's only John!" I told myself in the dream, but even as the words formed themselves in my brain I knew that I had touched the very core of my terror. This man whose every glance and movement had always filled me with uneasiness—already the light from some upstairs room was casting his shadow, huge and hideous, across the landing—

I struggled like a thing demented to break the paralysis of nightmare. And then, somehow, I was running, running, running . . .

I woke up sick and shaking, the sweat pouring down my face. For a moment I thought a great hammering on the door had awakened me, but then I realized that it was only the beating of my heart, thundering and pounding so that it seemed to shake the room.

Well, I have told you before that I am a strong woman, not given to nerves and fancies. Linda is the one who suffers from that sort of thing, not me. Time and again in her childhood I had to go to her in the night and soothe her off to sleep again after some wild dream. But for *me*, a grown woman, who never in her life has feared anyone or run away from anything—for *me* to wake up weak and shaking like a baby from some childish nightmare! I shook it off angrily, got out of my chair and fetched my papers, and as far as I can remember, worked on the Girls' Brigade accounts far into the night.

I thought no more about it until, perhaps a week later, the same thing happened again. The same sort of rainy evening, the same coming home unusually tired—and then the same dream. Well, not quite the same. This time Linda wasn't painting; she was on hands and knees, staining the floor or something of the sort. And there were no footsteps. This time nothing happened at all; only there was a sense of evil, of brooding hatred, which seemed to fill the little house. Somehow I felt it to be focused on the little figure kneeling in its gaily patterned work-apron. The hatred seemed to thicken round her—I could feel giant waves of it converging on her, mounting silently, silkily, till they hung poised above her head in ghastly, silent strength. Again I tried to scream a warning; again no sound came; and again I woke, weak and trembling, in my chair.

This time I was really worried. The tie between Linda and me is very close—closer, I think, than the tie between Linda and her mother could ever have been. Common-sense sort of person though I am, I could not help wondering whether these dreams were not some kind of warning. Should I call her, and ask if everything was all right?

I scolded myself for the very idea! I mustn't give way to such foolish, hysterical fancies—I have always prided myself on letting Linda lead her own life, and not smothering her with possessive anxiety as her mother would have surely done.

Stop! I mustn't keep speaking of Linda's mother like this—of Angela, my own sister. Angela has been dead many years now, and whatever wrong I may have suffered from her once has all been forgotten and forgiven years ago—I am not a woman to harbor grievances. But, of course, all this business of Linda's approaching marriage was bound to bring it back to me in a way. I couldn't help remembering that I, too, was once preparing a little house for my marriage, that Richard had once looked into my eyes as John now looks into Linda's.

Well, I suppose most old maids have some ancient, and usually boring, love story hidden somewhere in their pasts, and I don't think mine will interest you much—it doesn't even interest me after all these years, so I will tell it as briefly as I can.

When I fell in love with Richard I was already 28, tall and angular, and a schoolteacher in the bargain. So it seemed to me a miracle that he, so handsome, so gay and charming, should love me in return and ask me to marry him. Our only difficulty was that my parents were both dead and I was the sole support of my younger sister, Angela. We talked it over, and decided to wait a year, until Angela had left school and could support herself.

But at the end of the year it appeared that Angela had set her heart on a musical career. Tearfully she begged me to see her through her first two years at college; after that, she was sure she could fend for herself.

Well, Richard was difficult this time, and I suppose one can hardly blame him. He accused me of caring more for my sister than for him, of making myself a doormat, and much else that I forget. But at last it was agreed to wait the two years, and meantime to work and save for a home together.

And work and save we did. By the end of the two years we had bought a little house, and we spent our evenings decorating and putting finishing touches to it, just as Linda and John are doing now.

Then came another blow. Angela failed in her exams. Again I was caught up in the old conflict; Richard angry and obstinate, Angela tearful and beseeching me to give her one more chance, for only six months this time. Once again I agreed, stipulating that this time would really be the last. To my surprise, after his first outburst, Richard became quite reasonable about it; and soon after that he was sent away on a series of business trips, so that we saw much less of each other.

Then, one afternoon at the end of May, not long before the six months were up, something happened. I was sitting on the lawn correcting papers when Angela came out of the house and walked slowly toward me. I remember noticing how sweetly pretty she looked with her flaxen hair and big blue eyes—just like Linda's now. The spring sunshine seemed to light up the delicacy of her too-pale skin, making it seem rare and lovely. She sat down on the grass beside me without speaking, and something in her silence made me lay down my pen.

"What is it, Angela?" I said. "Is anything the matter?"

She looked up at me then, her blue eyes full of childish defiance, and a sort of pride.

"Yes," she said. "I'm going to have a baby." She paused, looking me full in the face. "Richard's baby."

I didn't say anything. I don't even remember feeling anything. Even then, I suppose, I was a strong-minded person, who did not allow her feelings to run away with her. Angela was still talking.

"And it's no use blaming *us*, Madge," she was saying. "What do you expect, after you've kept him dangling all these years?"

I remember the papers in front of me, dazzling-white in the May sunshine. One of the children had written "Nappoleon"—like that, with two p's—over and over again in her theme. There must have been half a dozen of them just on the one page. I felt I would go mad if I had to go on looking at them, so I took my pen and crossed them out, one after another, in red ink. Even to this day I have a foolish feeling that I would go mad if I ever saw "Nappoleon" spelled like that again.

I felt as if a long time had passed, and Angela must have got up and gone away ages ago; but no, there she was, still talking.

"Well, *you* may not care, Madge," she was saying. "I don't suppose you'd stop correcting your old papers if the world blew up. But what about *me*? What am I to *do*?"

"Do?" I said gently. "Why, Richard must marry you, of course. I'll talk to him myself."

Well, they were married, and Linda was born, a delicate, sickly little thing, weighing barely five pounds. Angela, too, was poorly. She had been terribly nervous and ill during her pregnancy and took a long time to recover; and it was tacitly agreed that there should be no more children. A pity, because I knew Richard would have liked a large family. Strange how I, a strong, healthy woman who could have raised half a dozen children without turning a hair, should have been denied the chance, while poor sickly Angela . . .

Ah, well, that is life. And I suppose my maternal feelings were largely satisfied by caring for delicate little Linda—it seemed only natural that when first her father and then Angela died the little orphan should come and live with me. And indeed I loved her dearly. She was my poor sister's child as well as Richard's, and my only fear has been that I may love her too deeply, too possessively, and so cramp her freedom.

Perhaps this fear is unfounded. Anyway, it was this that prevented me from lifting the telephone receiver then and there on that rainy September night, dialing her number, and asking if all was well. If I had done so, would it have made any difference in what followed? Could I have checked the march of tragedy, then and there, when I woke from that second dream?

I didn't know. I still don't know. All I know is that as I sat there in the silent room, listening to the rain beating against my windows out of the night, my fears somehow became clearer—came into focus, as it were. I knew now, with absolute certainty, that what I feared had something to do with Linda's forthcoming marriage, her marriage to John Barlow.

But what could it be? What *could* I be afraid of? He was such a pleasant, ordinary young man, from a respected local family; he had a good job; he loved Linda deeply. Well, he seemed to. And yet, as I thought about it, as I remembered the uneasiness I always felt in his presence, it occurred to me that this uneasiness—this anxiety for Linda's safety—was always at its height when he made some gesture of affection toward her—a light caress, perhaps—a quick, intimate glance across a crowded room . . .

Common sense. Common sense has been my ally throughout life, and I called in its aid now.

"There is nothing wrong!" I said aloud. "There is nothing wrong with this young man!"

And then I went to bed.

It must have been nearly three weeks later when I had the dream again. I had seen Linda in the meantime and she seemed as well and happy as I have ever known her. The only cloud on her horizon was that for the next fortnight John would be working late, and so they wouldn't be able to spend the evenings painting and carpentering together in the new house.

"But I'll go on by myself, Auntie," she assured me. "I want to start on the woodwork in that front room tonight. Pale green, we thought, to go with the pale yellow . . ." She chattered on, happily and gaily, seeming to make nonsense of my fears.

"It sounds lovely, dear," I said. "Don't knock yourself out, though, working too hard."

For Linda *does* get tired easily. In spite of the thirty years' difference in our age I can always outpace her on our long rambles over the hill, and arrive home fresh and vigorous while she is sometimes quite white with exhaustion.

"No, Auntie, don't worry," she said, standing on tiptoe to kiss me—she is such a little thing; "I won't get tired. I'm so happy I don't think I'll ever get tired again!"

Reassuring enough, you'd have thought. And yet, somehow, it didn't reassure me. Her very happiness—even the irrelevant fact that John would be working late—seemed somehow to add to the intangible peril I could feel gathering round her.

And three nights later I dreamed the dream again.

This time she was alone in the little house. I don't know how I knew it with such certainty in the dream, but I did—her aloneness seemed to fill the unfurnished rooms with echoes. *She* seemed nervous, too. She was no longer painting with the absorbed concentration of my previous dreams, but jerkily, uncertainly. She kept starting, turning round, listening; and I, hovering somewhere on the stairs as before, seemed to be listening too.

Listening for what? For the fear which I knew was creeping like fog into the little house? Or for something more?

"It's a dream!" I tried to scream, with soundless lips. "Don't be afraid, Linda, it's only a dream! I've had it before, I'll wake up soon! It's all right, I'm waking right now, I can hear the banging—"

I started awake in my chair, bolt upright, deafened by the now familiar thumping of my heart.

But was it my heart? Could that imperious knocking, which shook the house, be merely my heart? The knocking became interspersed with a frantic ringing of the bell. This was no dream.

I staggered to my feet and somehow got down the passage to the front door and flung it open. There in the rainy night was Linda, wild and white and disheveled, flinging herself into my arms.

"Oh, Auntie, Auntie, I thought you were out—asleep—I couldn't make you hear—I rang and rang . . ."

I soothed her as best I could. I took her into the kitchen and made her a cup of the weak thin tea she loves, and heard her story.

And after all it wasn't much of a story. Just that she had gone to the new house as usual after work, and had settled down to painting the front room. For a while, she said, she had worked quite happily, and then suddenly she had heard a sound—a shuffling sound—so faint that she might almost have imagined it.

"And that was all, really, Auntie," she said, looking up at me, shamefaced. "But somehow it frightened me so. I ought to have gone and looked round the house, but I didn't dare. I tried to go on working, but from then on there was such an awful feeling—I can't describe it—as if there was something evil in the house, something close behind me, waiting to get its hands round my throat. Oh, Auntie, I know it sounds silly. It's the kind of thing I used to dream when I was a little girl. Do you remember?"

Indeed I did remember. I took her on my lap and soothed her now just as I had done then, when she was a little sobbing girl, awake and frightened in the depth of the night.

And then I told her she must go home.

"Auntie!" she protested. "But, Auntie, can't I stay here with you for the night? That's why I came. I *must* stay!"

But I was adamant. I can't tell you why, but some instinct warned me that, come what may, she must not stay here tonight. Whatever fear or danger might be elsewhere, they could never be as great as they would be here, in this house, tonight.

So I made her go home to her lodgings in the town. I couldn't explain it to her, or even to myself. In vain she protested that the last bus had gone, that her old room here was ready for her. But I was inflexible. I rang up a taxi, and as it disappeared with her round the corner of the lane, casting a weird radiance behind it, I heaved a great sigh of relief, as if a great task had been accomplished—as if I had just dragged her to shore out of a dark and stormy sea.

The next morning I found that my instinct had not been without foundation. There *had* been danger lurking round my house the night before. For when I went to get my bicycle to go and help about the Mothers' Outing, I found it in its usual place in the shed, but the tires and mudguard were spattered with a kind of thick yellow clay. There is no clay like that anywhere between here and the village. Where could it have come from? Who had been riding my bicycle through unfamiliar mud in the rain and wind last night? Who had put it back silently in the shed, and as silently gone away?

As I stood there, bewildered and shaken, the telephone rang indoors. It was Linda, and she sounded tense, distraught.

"Auntie, will you do something for me? Will you come with me to the house tonight and stay there while I do the painting and—sort of keep watch for me? I expect you'll think it's silly, but I *know* there was somebody there last night—and I'm frightened. Will you come, Auntie?"

There could be only one answer. I got through my day's work as fast as I could and by six o'clock I was waiting for Linda on the steps of her office. As we hurried through the darkening streets Linda was apologetic.

"I know it's awfully silly, Auntie, but John's still working late, and he doesn't even know if he'll finish in time to come and fetch me. I feel scared there without him. And the upstairs lights won't go on again—John hasn't had time to see the electrician about it yet—and it's so dark and lonely. Do you think someone really *was* there last night, Auntie?"

I didn't tell her about the mud on my bicycle. There seemed no point in alarming her further. Besides, what was there to tell? There was no reason to suppose it had any connection—

"Watch out, Auntie, it's terribly muddy along this bit where the builders have been."

I stared down at the thick yellow clay already clinging heavily to my shoes; and straight in front of us, among a cluster of partially finished red-brick houses, stood Linda's future home. It stared at us with its little empty windows out of the October dusk. A light breeze rose, but stirred nothing in that wilderness of mud, raw brickwork, and scaffolding. Linda and I hesitated, looked at each other.

"Come on," I said, and a minute later we were in the empty house.

We arranged that she should settle down to her painting in the downstairs front room just as if she were alone, and I was to sit on the stairs, near the top, where I could command a view of both upstairs and down. If anyone should come in, by either the front or back door, I should see them before they could reach Linda.

I was very quiet as I sat there in the darkness. The light streamed out of the downstairs room where Linda was working, and I could see her through the open door, with her back to me, just as she had been in my dream. How like poor Angela she was, with her pale hair and her white, fragile neck! She was working steadily now, absorbed, confident—reassured, I suppose, by my presence in the house.

As I sat there, I could feel the stair behind me pressing a little into my spine—a strangely familiar pressure. My whole pose indeed seemed familiar—every muscle seemed to fall into place, as if by long practice, as I sat there, half leaning against the banisters, staring down into the glare of light.

And then, suddenly, I knew. I knew who had cycled in black hatred through the rainy darkness and the yellow mud. I knew who had waited here, night after night, watching Linda as a cat watches a mouse. I knew what horror was closing in even now on this poor fragile child, on this sickly, puny brat who had kept *my* lovely, sturdy children from coming into the world—the sons and daughters *I* could have given Richard, tall and strong—the children he should have had—the children *I* could have borne him.

I was creeping downstairs now, on tiptoe, in my stockinged feet, with a light, almost prancing movement, yet silent as a shadow. I could see my hands clutching in front of me like a lobster's claws, itching for the feel of her white neck.

At the foot of the stairs now—at the door of the room—and still she worked on, her back to me, oblivious.

I tried to cry out, to warn her. "She's coming, Linda!" I tried to scream: "I can see her hands clawing behind you!" But no sound came from my drawn-back lips, no sound from my swift light feet.

Then, just as in my dream, there were footsteps through the house, quick and loud, a man's footsteps, hurrying, running, rushing— rushing to save Linda, to save us both.

How the Wind Spoke
at Madaket

LUCIUS SHEPARD

1

Softly at dawn rustling dead leaves in the roof gutters, ticking the wires of the television antenna against the shingled wall, seething through the beach grasses, shifting the bare twigs of a hawthorn to claw at the toolshed door, playfully flipping a peg off the clothesline, snuffling the garbage and tattering the plastic bags, creating a thousand nervous flutters, a thousand more shivery whispers, then building, keening in the window cracks and rattling the panes, smacking down a sheet of plyboard that has been leaning against the woodpile, swelling to a pour off the open sea, its howl articulated by throats of narrow streets and teeth of vacant houses, until you begin to imagine a huge invisible animal throwing back its head and roaring, and the cottage is creaking like the timbers of an old ship . . .

2

Waking at first light, Peter Ramey lay abed a while and listened to the wind; then, steeling himself against the cold, he threw off the covers, hurriedly pulled on jeans, tennis shoes, and a flannel shirt, and went into the front room to kindle a fire in the wood stove. Outside, the trees were silhouetted by a backdrop of slate clouds, but the sky wasn't yet bright enough to cast the shadow of the window frame across the picnic-style table beneath it; the other furniture—three chewed-up wicker chairs and a sofa bunk—hunched in their dark corners. The tinder caught, and soon the fire was snapping inside the stove. Still cold, Peter beat his arms against his shoulders and hopped from one foot to another, setting dishes and drawers to rattling. He was a pale, heavyset man of thirty-three, with ragged black hair and beard, so tall that he had to duck through the doors of the cottage; and because of his size he had never really settled into the

320

place: he felt like a tramp who had appropriated a child's abandoned treehouse in which to spend the winter.

The kitchen was an alcove off the front room, and after easing the chill, his face stinging with heat, he lit the gas stove and started breakfast. He cut a hole in a slice of bread, laid it in the frying pan, then cracked an egg and poured it into the hole (usually he just opened cans and cereal boxes or heated frozen food, but Sara Tappinger, his current lover, had taught him to fix eggs this way, and it made him feel like a competent bachelor to keep up the practice). He shoveled down the egg and bread standing at the kitchen window, watching the gray-shingled houses across the street melt from the darkness, shadowy clumps resolving into thickets of bayberry and sheep's laurel, a picket-line of Japanese pines beyond them. The wind had dropped and it looked as if the clouds were going to hang around, which was fine by Peter. Since renting the cottage in Madaket eight months before, he had learned that he thrived on bleakness, that the blustery, overcast days nourished his imagination. He had finished one novel here, and he planned to stay until the second was done. And maybe a third. What the hell? There wasn't much point in returning to California. He turned on the water to do the dishes, but the thought of LA had soured him on being competent. Screw it! Let the ants breed. He pulled on a sweater, stuffed a notebook in his pocket, and stepped out into the cold.

As if it had been waiting for him, a blast of wind came swerving around the corner of the cottage and numbed his face. He tucked his chin onto his chest and set out walking, turning left on Tennessee Avenue and heading toward Smith Point, past more gray-shingled houses with quarterboards bearing cutesy names above their doors: names like Sea Shanty and Tooth Acres (the vacation home of a New Jersey dentist). When he had arrived on Nantucket he'd been amused by the fact that almost every structure on the island, even the Sears Roebuck store, had gray shingles, and he had written his ex-wife a long, humorous, let's-be-friends letter telling about the shingles, about all the odd characters and quirkiness of the place. His ex-wife had not answered, and Peter couldn't blame her, not after what he had done. Solitude was the reason he gave for having moved to Madaket, but while this was superficially true, it would have been more accurate to say that he had been fleeing the ruins of his life. He had been idling along, content with his marriage, churning out scripts for a PBS children's show, when he had fallen obsessively in love with another woman, herself married. Plans and promises had been made, as a result of which he had left his wife; but then, in a sudden reversal of form, the woman—who had never expressed any sentiment other than boredom and resentment concerning her husband—had decided to honor her vows, leaving Peter alone and feeling both a damned fool and a villain. Desperate, he had fought for her, failed, tried to hate her, failed, and finally, hoping a change of geography would provoke a change of heart—hers or his—he had come to Madaket. That had been in September, directly after the exodus of the summer tourists; it was now May, and though the cold weather still lingered, the tourists were beginning to filter back. But no hearts had changed.

Twenty minutes of brisk walking brought him to the top of a dune overlooking Smith Point, a jut of sand extending a hundred yards or so into the water, with three small islands strung out beyond it; the nearest of these had been separated from the point during a hurricane, and had it still been attached, it—in conjunction with Eel Point, some three-quarters of a mile distant—would have given the western end of the island the shape of a crab's claw. Far out at sea a ray of sunlight pierced the overcast and dazzled the water beneath to such brilliance that it looked like a laving of fresh white paint. Seagulls made curving flights overhead, hovered and dropped scallops onto the gravelly shingle to break the shells, then swooped down to pluck the meat. Sad-vowelled gusts of wind sprayed a fine grit through the air.

Peter sat in the lee of a dune, choosing a spot from which he could see the ocean between stalks of the pale green beach grass, and opened his notebook. The words HOW THE WIND SPOKE AT MADAKET were printed on the inside cover. He had no illusions that the publishers would keep the title; they would change it to *The Keening* or *The Huffing and Puffing*, package it with a garish cover and stick it next to *Love's Tormenting Itch* by Wanda LaFontaine on the grocery store racks. But none of that mattered as long as the words were good, and they were, though it hadn't gone well at first, not until he had started walking each morning to Smith Point and writing long-hand. Then everything had snapped into focus. He had realized that it was *his* story he wanted to tell—the woman, his loneliness, his psychic flashes, the resolution of his character—all wrapped in the eerie metaphor of the wind; the writing had flowed so easily that it seemed the wind was collaborating on the book, whispering in his ear and guiding his hand across the page. He flipped the pages and noticed a paragraph that was a bit too formal, that he should break up and seed throughout the story:

"Sadler had spent much of his life in Los Angeles, where the sounds of nature were obscured, and to his mind the constancy of the wind was Nantucket's most remarkable feature. Morning, noon and night it flowed across the island, giving him a sense of being a bottom-dweller in an ocean of air, buffeted by currents that sprang from exotic quarters of the globe. He was a lonely soul, and the wind served to articulate his loneliness, to point up the immensity of the world in which he had become isolated; over the months he had come to feel an affinity with it, to consider it a fellow-traveler through emptiness and time. He half-believed its vague, speechlike utterances to be exactly that—an oracular voice whose powers of speech were not yet fully developed—and from listening to them he derived an impression of impending strangeness. He did not discount the impression, because as far back as he could recall he had received similar ones, and most had been borne out by reality. It was no great prophetic gift, no foreshadowings of earthquakes or assassinations; rather, it was a low-grade psychic ability: flashes of vision often accompanied by queasiness and headaches. Sometimes he could touch an object and know something about its owner, sometimes he would glimpse the shape of an upcoming event. But these premonitions were never clear enough to do him any good, to prevent broken arms or—as he had lately discovered—emotional disaster. Still, he hearkened to them. And now he thought the wind might actually be trying to tell him something of his future, of a new factor about to complicate his existence, for whenever he staked himself out on the dune at Smith Point he would feel . . ."

Gooseflesh pebbling his skin, nausea, an eddying sensation behind his forehead as if his thoughts were spinning out of control. Peter rested his head on his knees and took deep breaths until the spell had abated. It was happening more and more often, and while it was most likely a product of suggestibility, a side-effect of writing such a personal story, he couldn't shake the notion that he had become involved in some Twilight Zone irony, that the story was coming true as he wrote it. He hoped not: it wasn't going to be a very pleasant story. When the last of his nausea had passed, he took out a blue felt-tip, turned to a clean page and began to detail the unpleasantness.

Two hours and fifteen pages later, hands stiff with cold, he heard a voice hailing him. Sara Tappinger was struggling up the side of the dune from the blacktop, slipping in the soft sand. She was, he thought with a degree of self-satisfaction, a damned pretty woman. Thirtyish; long auburn hair and nice cheekbones; endowed with what one of Peter's islander acquaintances called "big chest problems." That same acquaintance had congratulated him for having scored with Sara, saying that she'd blue-balled half the men on the island after her divorce, and wasn't he the lucky son of a bitch. Peter supposed he *was*: Sara was witty, bright, independent (she ran the local Montessori school), and they were compatible in every way. Yet it was not a towering passion. It was friendly, comfortable, and this Peter found alarming. Although being with her only glossed over his loneliness, he had come to depend on the relationship, and he was concerned that this signalled an overall reduction of his expectations, and that this in turn signalled the onset of middle-age, a state for which he was unprepared.

"Hi," she said, flinging herself down beside him and planting a kiss on his cheek. "Wanna play?"

"Why aren't you in school?"

"It's Friday. I told you, remember? Parent-teacher conferences." She took his hand. "You're cold as ice! How long have you been here?"

"Couple of hours."

"You're insane." She laughed, delighted by his insanity. "I was watching you for a bit before I called. With your hair flying about, you looked like a mad Bolshevik hatching a plot."

"Actually," he said, adopting a Russian accent, "I come here to make contact with our submarines."

"Oh? What's up? An invasion?"

"Not exactly. You see, in Russia we have many shortages. Grain, high technology, blue jeans. But the Russian soul can fly above such hardships. There is, however, a shortage of one commodity that we must solve immediately, and this is why I have lured you here."

She pretended bewilderment. "You need school administrators?"

"No, no. It is more serious. I believe the American word for it is
. . ." He caught her by the shoulders and pushed her down on the
sand, pinning her beneath him. "Poontang. We cannot do without."

Her smile faltered, then faded to a look of rapt anticipation. He
kissed her. Through her coat he felt the softness of her breasts. The
wind ruffled his hair, and he had the idea that it was leaning over his
shoulder, spying on them; he broke off the kiss. He was queasy again.
Dizzy.

"You're sweating," she said, dabbing at his brow with a gloved
hand. "Is this one of those spells?"

He nodded and lay back against the dune.

"What do you see?" She continued to pat his brow dry, a concerned frown etching delicate lines at the corners of her mouth.

"Nothing," he said.

But he did see something. Something glinting behind a cloudy
surface. Something that attracted him yet frightened him at the same
time. Something he knew would soon fall to his hand.

Though nobody realized it at the time, the first sign of trouble was
the disappearance of Ellen Borchard, age thirteen, on the evening of
Tuesday, May nineteenth—an event Peter had written into his book
just prior to Sara's visit on Friday morning; but it didn't really begin
for him until Friday night while drinking at the Atlantic Cafe in the
village of Nantucket. He had gone there with Sara for dinner, and since
the restaurant section was filled to capacity, they had opted for drinks
and sandwiches at the bar. They had hardly settled on their stools when
Jerry Highsmith—a blond young man who conducted bicycle tours of
the island (". . . the self-proclaimed Hunk of Hunks," was Sara's
description of him)—latched onto Peter; he was a regular at the cafe
and an aspiring writer, and he took every opportunity to get Peter's
advice. As always Peter offered encouragement, but he secretly felt that
anyone who liked to do their drinking at the Atlantic could have little
to say to the reading public: it was a typical New England tourist trap,
decorated with brass barometers and old life preservers, and it catered
to the young summer crowd, many of whom—evident by their Bahama
tans—were packed around the bar. Soon Jerry moved off in pursuit of
a redhead with a honeysuckle drawl, a member of his latest tour group,
and his stool was taken by Mills Lindstrom, a retired fisherman and a
neighbor of Peter's.

"Damn wind out there's sharp enough to carve bone," said Mills by way of a greeting, and ordered a whiskey. He was a big red-faced man stuffed into overalls and a Levi jacket; white curls spilled from under his cap, and a lacing of broken blood vessels webbed his cheeks. The lacing was more prominent than usual, because Mills had a load on.

"What are you doing here?" Peter was surprised that Mills would set foot in the cafe; it was his conviction that tourism was a deadly pollution, and places like the Atlantic were its mutant growths.

"Took the boat out today. First time in two months." Mills knocked back half his whiskey. "Thought I might set a few lines, but then I run into that thing off Smith Point. Didn't feel like fishin' anymore." He emptied his glass and signalled for a refill. "Carl Keating told me it was formin' out there a while back. Guess it slipped my mind."

"What thing?" asked Peter.

Mills sipped at his second whiskey. "Off-shore pollution aggregate," he said grimly. "That's the fancy name, but basically it's a garbage dump. Must be pretty near a kilometer square of water covered in garbage. Oil slick, plastic bottles, driftwood. They collect at slack points in the tides, but not usually so close to land. This one ain't more'n fifteen miles off the point."

Peter was intrigued. "You're talking about something like the Sargasso Sea, right?"

"Spose so. 'Cept these ain't so big and there ain't no seaweed."

"Are they permanent?"

"This one's new, the one off Smith Point. But there's one about thirty miles off the Vineyard that's been there for some years. Big storm'll break it up, but it'll always come back." Mills patted his pockets, trying unsuccessfully to find his pipe. "Ocean's gettin' like a stagnant pond. Gettin' to where a man throws in a line and more'n likely he'll come up with an ol' boot 'stead of a fish. I 'member twenty years ago when the mackerel was runnin', there'd be so many fish the water would look black for miles. Now you spot a patch of dark water and you know some damn tanker's taken a shit!"

Sara, who had been talking to a friend, put her arm around Peter's shoulder and asked what was up; after Peter had explained she gave a dramatic shudder and said, "It sounds spooky to me." She affected a sepulchral tone. "Strange magnetic zones that lure sailors to their dooms."

"Spooky!" Mills scoffed. "You got better sense than that, Sara. Spooky!" The more he considered the comment, the madder he became. He stood and made a flailing gesture that spilled the drink of a tanned college-age kid behind him; he ignored the kid's complaint and glared at Sara. "Maybe you think this place is spooky. It's the same damn thing! A garbage dump! 'Cept here the garbage walks and talks"—he turned his glare on the kid—"and thinks it owns the goddamn world!"

"Shit," said Peter, watching Mills shoulder his way through the crowd. "I was going to ask him to take me to see it."

"Ask him tomorrow," said Sara. "Though I don't know why you'd want to see it." She grinned and held up her hands to ward off his explanation. "Sorry. I should realize that anyone who'll spend all day staring at seagulls would find a square kilometer of garbage downright erotic."

He made a grab for her breasts. "I'll show you erotic!"

She laughed and caught his hand and—her mood suddenly altered—brushed the knuckles against his lips. "Show me later," she said.

They had a few more drinks, talked about Peter's work, about Sara's, and discussed the idea of taking a weekend together in New York. Peter began to acquire a glow. It was partly the drinks, yet he realized that Sara, too, was responsible. Though there had been other women since he had left his wife, he had scarcely noticed them; he had tried to be honest with them, had explained that he was in love with someone else, but he had learned that this was simply a sly form of dishonesty, that when you went to bed with someone—no matter how frank you had been as to your emotional state—they would refuse to believe there was any impediment to commitment that their love could not overcome; and so, in effect, he had used those women. But he did notice Sara, he did appreciate her, and he had not told her about the woman back in LA: once he had thought this a lie, but now he was beginning to suspect it was a sign that the passion was over. He had been in love for such a long time with a woman absent from him that perhaps he had grown to believe absence was a precondition for intensity, and perhaps it was causing him to overlook the birth of a far more realistic yet equally intense passion closer at hand. He studied Sara's face as she rambled on about New York. Beautiful. The kind of beauty that sneaks up on you, that you assumed was mere prettiness. But then, noticing her mouth was a bit too full, you decided that she was interestingly pretty; and then, noticing the energy of the face, how her eyes widened when she talked, how expressive her mouth was, you were led feature by feature to a perception of her beauty. Oh, he noticed her all right. The trouble was that during those months of loneliness (*Months? Christ, it had been over a year!*) he had become distanced from his emotions; he had set up surveillance systems inside his soul, and every time he started to twitch one way or the other, instead of completing the action he analyzed it and thus aborted it. He doubted he would ever be able to lose himself again.

Sara glanced questioningly at someone behind him. Hugh Weldon, the chief of police. He nodded at them and settled onto the stool. "Sara," he said, "Mr. Ramey. Glad I caught you."

Weldon always struck Peter as the archetypal New Englander. Gaunt; weatherbeaten; dour. His basic expression was so bleak you assumed his gray crewcut to have been an act of penance. He was in his fifties but had a habit of sucking at his teeth that made him seem ten years older. Usually Peter found him amusing; however, on this occasion he experienced nausea and a sense of unease, feelings he recognized as the onset of a premonitory spell.

After exchanging pleasantries with Sara, Weldon turned to Peter. "Don't want you to go takin' this wrong, Mr. Ramey. But I got to ask where you were last Tuesday evenin' 'round six o'clock."

The feelings were growing stronger, evolving with a sluggish panic that roiled inside Peter like the effects of a bad drug. "Tuesday," he said. "That's when the Borchard girl disappeared."

"My God, Hugh," said Sara testily. "What is this? Roust out the bearded stranger every time somebody's kid runs away? You know damn well that's what Ellen did. I'd run away myself if Ethan Borchard was my father."

"Mebbe." Weldon favored Peter with a neutral stare. "Did you happen to see Ellen last Tuesday, Mr. Ramey?"

"I was home," said Peter, barely able to speak. Sweat was popping out on his forehead, all over his body, and he knew he must look as guilty as hell; but that didn't matter, because he could almost see what was going to happen. He was sitting somewhere, and just out of reach below him something glinted.

"Then you musta seen her," said Weldon. "'Cordin' to witnesses she was mopin' 'round your woodpile for pretty near an hour. Wearin' bright yellow. Be hard to miss that."

"No," said Peter. He was reaching for that glint, and he knew it was going to be bad in any case, very bad, but it would be even worse if he touched it and he couldn't stop himself.

"Now that don't make sense," said Weldon from a long way off. "That cottage of yours is so small, it 'pears to me a man would just naturally catch sight of somethin' like a girl standin' by his woodpile while he was movin' 'round. Six o'clock's dinnertime for most folks, and you got a nice view of the woodpile out your kitchen window."

"I didn't see her." The spell was starting to fade, and Peter was terribly dizzy.

"Don't see how that's possible." Weldon sucked at his teeth, and the glutinous sound caused Peter's stomach to do a slow flip-flop.

"You ever stop to think, Hugh," said Sara angrily, "that maybe he was otherwise occupied?"

"You know somethin', Sara, why don't you say it plain?"

"I was with him last Tuesday. He was moving around, all right, but he wasn't looking out any window. Is that plain enough?"

Weldon sucked at his teeth again. "I 'spect it is. You sure 'bout this?"

Sara gave a sarcastic laugh. "Wanna see my hickey?"

"No reason to be snitty, Sara. I ain't doin' this for pleasure." Weldon heaved to his feet and gazed down at Peter. "You lookin' a bit peaked, Mr. Ramey. Hope it ain't somethin' you ate." He held the stare a moment longer, then pushed off through the crowd.

"God, Peter!" Sara cupped his face in her hands. "You look awful!"

"Dizzy," he said, fumbling for his wallet; he tossed some bills on the counter. "C'mon, I need some air."

With Sara guiding him, he made it through the front door and leaned on the hood of a parked car, head down, gulping in the cold air. Her arm around his shoulders was a good weight that helped steady him, and after a few seconds he began to feel stronger, able to lift his head. The street—with its cobblestones and newly budded trees and old-fashioned lamp posts and tiny shops—looked like a

prop for a model railroad. Wind prowled the sidewalks, spinning
paper cups and fluttering awnings. A strong gust shivered him and
brought a flashback of dizziness and vision. Once more he was
reaching down toward that glint, only this time it was very close, so
close that its energies were tingling his fingertips, pulling at him, and
if he could just stretch out his hand another inch or two . . . Dizziness
overwhelmed him. He caught himself on the hood of the car; his arm
gave way, and he slumped forward, feeling the cold metal against his
cheek. Sara was calling to someone, asking for help, and he wanted
to reassure her, to say he'd be all right in a minute, but the words
clogged in his throat and he continued lying there, watching the
world tip and spin, until someone with arms stronger than Sara's
lifted him and said, "Hey, man! You better stop hittin' the sauce or I
might be tempted to snake your ol' lady."

Streetlight angled a rectangle of yellow glare across the foot of
Sara's bed, illuminating her stockinged legs and half of Peter's bulk
beneath the covers. She lit a cigarette, then—exasperated at having
given into the habit again—she stubbed it out, turned on her side and
lay watching the rise and fall of Peter's chest. Dead to the world.
Why, she wondered, was she such a sucker for the damaged ones?
She laughed at herself; she knew the answer. She wanted to be the
one to make them forget whatever had hurt them, usually another
woman. A combination Florence Nightingale and sex therapist, that
was her, and she could never resist a new challenge. Though Peter
had not talked about it, she could tell some LA ghost owned half his
heart. He had all the symptoms. Sudden silences, distracted stares,
the way he jumped for the mailbox as soon as the postman came and
yet was always disappointed by what he had received. She believed
that she owned the other half of his heart, but whenever he started to
go with it, to forget the past and immerse himself in the here and
now, the ghost would rear up and he'd create a little distance. His
approach to lovemaking, for instance. He'd come on soft and gentle,
and then, just as they were on the verge of a new level of intimacy,
he'd draw back, crack a joke or do something rough—like tackling
her on the beach that morning—and she would feel cheap and
sluttish. Sometimes she thought that the thing to do would be to tell
him to get the hell out of her life, to come back and see her when his

head was clear. But she knew she wouldn't. He owned more than half her heart.

She eased off the bed, careful not to wake him, and slipped out of her clothes. A branch scraped the window, startling her, and she held her blouse up to cover her breasts. Oh, right! A Peeping Tom at a third-floor window. In New York, maybe, but not in Nantucket. She tossed the blouse into the laundry hamper and caught sight of herself in the full-length mirror affixed to the closet door. In the dim light the reflection looked elongated and unfamiliar, and she had a feeling that Peter's ghost woman was watching her from across the continent, from another mirror. She could almost make her out. Tall, long-legged, a mournful expression. Sara didn't need to see her to know the woman had been sad: it was the sad ones who were the real heartbreakers, and the men whose hearts they had broken were like fossil records of what the women were. They offered their sadness to be cured, yet it wasn't a cure they wanted, only another reason for sadness, a spicy bit to mix in with the stew they had been stirring all their lives. Sara moved closer to the mirror, and the illusion of the other woman was replaced by the conformation of her own body. "That's what I'm going to do to you, lady," she whispered. "Blot you out." The words sounded empty.

She turned back the bedspread and slid in beside Peter. He made a muffled noise, and she saw gleams of the streetlights in his eyes. "Sorry about earlier," he said.

"No problem," she said brightly. "I got Bob Frazier and Jerry Highsmith to help bring you home. Do you remember?"

"Vaguely. I'm surprised Jerry could tear himself away from his redhead. Sweet Ginger!" He lifted his arm so Sara could burrow in against his shoulder. "I guess your reputation's ruined."

"I don't know about that, but it's certainly getting more exotic all the time."

He laughed.

"Peter?" she said.

"Yeah?"

"I'm worried about these spells of yours. That's what this was, wasn't it?"

"Yeah." He was silent a moment. "I'm worried, too. I've been having them two and three times a day, and that's never happened before. But there's nothing I can do except try not to think about them."

"Can you see what's going to happen?"

"Not really, and there's no point in trying to figure it out. I can't ever use what I see. It just happens, whatever's going to, and then I understand that *that* was what the premonition was about. It's a pretty worthless gift."

Sara snuggled closer, throwing her leg across his hip. "Why don't we go over to the Cape tomorrow?"

"I was going to check out Mills' garbage dump."

"Okay. We can do that in the morning and still catch the three o'clock boat. It might be good for you to get off the island for a day or so."

"All right. Maybe that's not such a bad idea."

Sara shifted her leg and realized that he was erect. She eased her hand beneath the covers to touch him, and he turned so as to allow her better access. His breath quickened and he kissed her—gentle, treasuring kisses on her lips, her throat, her eyes—and his hips moved in counterpoint to the rhythm of her hand, slowly at first, becoming insistent, convulsive, until he was prodding against her thigh and she had to take her hand away and let him slip between her legs, opening her. Her thoughts were dissolving into a medium of urgency, her consciousness being reduced to an awareness of heat and shadows. But when he lifted himself above her, that brief separation broke the spell, and she could suddenly hear the fretful sounds of the wind, could see the particulars of his face and the light fixture on the ceiling behind him. His features seemed to sharpen, to grow alert, and he opened his mouth to speak. She put a finger to his lips, *Please, Peter! No jokes. This is serious.* She beamed the thoughts at him, and maybe they sank in. His face slackened, and as she guided him into place he moaned, a despairing sound such as a ghost might make at the end of its earthly term; and then she was clawing at him, driving him deeper inside, and talking to him, not words, just breathy noises, sighs and whispers, but having meanings that he would understand.

3

That same night while Peter and Sara were asleep, Sally McColl was driving her jeep along the blacktop that led to Smith Point. She was drunk and not giving a good goddamn where she wandered, steering in a never-ending S, sending the lights veering across low gorsey hills and gnarled hawthorns. With one hand she kept a choke-hold on a pint of cherry brandy, her third of the evening. 'Sconset Sally, they called her. Crazy Sally. Seventy-four years old and still able to shell scallops and row better than most men on the island. Wrapped in a couple of Salvation Army dresses, two moth-eaten sweaters, a tweed jacket gone at the elbows, and generally looking like a bag lady from hell. Brambles of white hair sticking out from under a battered fisherman's hat. Static fizzled on the radio, and Sally accompanied it with mutters, curses, and fitful bursts of song, all things that echoed the jumble of her thoughts. She parked near the spot where the blacktop gave out, staggered from the jeep and stumped through the soft sand to the top of a dune. There she swayed for a moment, dizzied by the pour of wind and the sweep of darkness broken only by a few stars on the horizon. "Whoo-ooh!" she screeched; the wind sucked up her yell and added it to its sound. She lurched forward, slipped and went rolling down the face of the dune. Sand adhering to her tongue, spitting, she sat up and found that somehow she'd managed to hold onto the bottle, that the cap was still on even though she hadn't screwed it tight. A flicker of paranoia set her to jerking her head from side-to-side. She didn't want anybody spying on her, spreading more stories about old drunk Sally. The ones they told were bad enough. Half were lies, and the rest were slanted to make her seem loopy . . . like the one about how she'd bought herself a mail-order husband and he'd run off after two weeks, stowed away on a boat, scared to death of her, and she had come riding on horseback through Nantucket, hoping to bring him home. A swarthy little bump of a man, Eye-talian, no English, and he hadn't known shit from shortcake in bed. Better to do yourself than fool with a pimple like him. All she'd wanted had been the goddamn trousers she'd dressed him in, and the tale-tellers had cast her as a desperate woman. Bastards! Buncha goddamn . . .

Sally's train of thought pulled into a tunnel, and she sat staring blankly at the dark. Damn cold, it was, and windy a bit as well. She took a swig of brandy; when it hit bottom she felt ten degrees warmer. Another swig put her legs under her, and she started walking along the beach away from the point, searching for a nice lonesome spot where nobody was likely to happen by. That was what she wanted. Just to sit and spit and feel the night on her skin. You couldn't hardly find such a place nowadays, what with all the summer trash floating in from the mainland, the Gucci-Pucci sissies and the little swish-tailed chick-women eager to bend over and butter their behinds for the first five-hundred-dollar suit that showed interest, probably some fat boy junior executive who couldn't get it up and would marry 'em just for the privilege of being humiliated every night . . . That train of thought went spiraling off, and Sally spiraled after it. She sat down with a thump. She gave out with a cackle, liked the sound of it, and cackled louder. She sipped at the brandy, wishing that she had brought another bottle, letting her thoughts subside into a crackle of half-formed images and memories that seemed to have been urged upon her by the thrashings and skitterings of the wind. As her eyes adjusted, she made out a couple of houses lumped against the lesser blackness of the sky. Vacant summer places. No, wait! Those were them whatchamacallems. Condominiums. What had that Ramey boy said about 'em? Iniums with a condom slipped over each. Prophylactic lives. He was a good boy, that Peter. The first person she'd met with the gift for dog's years, and it was strong in him, stronger than her gift, which wasn't good for much except for guessing the weather, and she was so old now that her bones could do that just as well. He'd told her how some people in California had blown up condominiums to protect the beauty of their coastline, and it had struck her as a fine idea. The thought of condominiums ringing the island caused her to tear up, and with a burst of drunken nostalgia she remembered what a wonder the sea had been when she was a girl. Clean, pure, rife with spirits. She'd been able to sense those spirits . . .

Battering and crunching from somewhere off in the dunes. She staggered to her feet, cocking an ear. More sounds of breakage. She headed toward them, toward the condominiums. Might be some kids vandalizing the place. If so, she'd cheer 'em on. But as she climbed to the top of the nearest dune, the sounds died away. Then the wind picked up, not howling or roaring, but with a weird ululation, almost a melody, as if it were pouring through the holes of an enormous flute.

The back of Sally's neck prickled, and a cold slimy worm of fear wriggled the length of her spine. She was close enough to the condominiums to see their rooflines against the sky, but she could see nothing else. There was only the eerie music of the wind, repeating the same passage of five notes over and over. Then it, too, died. Sally took a slug of brandy, screwed up her courage, and started walking again; the beach grass swayed and tickled her hands, and the tickling spread gooseflesh up her arms. About twenty feet from the first condominium she stopped, her heartbeat ragged. Fear was turning the brandy to a sour mess in her stomach. What was there to be afraid of, she asked herself. The wind? Shit! She had another slug of brandy and went forward. It was so dark she had to grope her way along the wall, and she was startled to find a hole smack in the middle of it. Bigger than a damn door, it was. Edged by broken boards and ripped shingles. Like a giant fist had smashed it through. Her mouth was cottony, but she stepped inside. She rummaged in her pockets, dug out a box of kitchen matches, lit one and cupped it with her hands until it burned steadily. The room was unfurnished, just carpeting and telephone fixtures and paint-spattered newspapers and rags. Sliding glass doors were inset into the opposite wall, but most of the glass had been blown out, crunching under her feet; as she drew near, an icicle-shaped piece hanging from the frame caught the glow of the match and for a second was etched on the dark like a fiery tooth. The match scorched her fingers. She dropped it and lit another and moved into the next room. More holes and heaviness in the air, as if the house were holding its breath. Nerves, she thought. God-damn old-woman nerves. Maybe it *had* been kids, drunk and ramming a car into the walls. A breeze eeled from somewhere and puffed out the match. She lit a third one. The breeze extinguished it, too, and she realized that kids hadn't been responsible for the damage, because the breeze didn't blow away this time: it fluttered around her, lifting her dress, her hair, twining about her legs, patting and frisking her all over, and in the breeze was a feeling, a knowledge, that turned her bones to splinters of black ice. Something had come from the sea, some evil thing with the wind for a body had smashed holes in the walls to play its foul, spine-chilling music, and it was surrounding her, toying with her, getting ready to whirl her off to hell and gone. It had a clammy, bitter smell, and that smell clung to her skin every-where it touched.

Sally backed into the first room, wanting to scream but only able to manage a feeble squawk. The wind flowed after her, lifting the newspapers and flapping them at her like crinkly white bats, matting them against her face and chest. Then she screamed. She dove for the hole in the wall and flung herself into a frenzied, heart-busting run, stumbling, falling, scrambling to her feet and waving her arms and yelling. Behind her, the wind gushed from the house, roaring, and she imagined it shaping itself into a towering figure, a black demon who was laughing at her, letting her think she might make it before swooping down and tearing her apart. She rolled down the face of the last dune, and, her breath sobbing, clawed at the door handle of the jeep; she jiggled the key in the ignition, prayed until the engine turned over, and then, gears grinding, swerved off along the Nantucket road.

She was halfway to 'Sconset before she grew calm enough to think what to do, and the first thing she decided was to drive straight to Nantucket and tell Hugh Weldon. Though God only knew what *he'd* do. Or what he'd say. That scrawny flint of a man! Like as not he'd laugh in her face and be off to share the latest 'Sconset Sally story with his cronies. No, she told herself. There weren't going to be anymore stories about ol' Sally drunk as the moon and seeing ghosts and raving about the wind. They wouldn't believe her, so let 'em think kids had done it. A little sun of gleeful viciousness rose in her thoughts, burning away the shadows of her fear and heating her blood even quicker than would a jolt of cherry brandy. Let it happen, whatever was going to happen, and *then* she'd tell her story, *then* she'd say I would have told you sooner, but you would have called me crazy. Oh, no! She wouldn't be the butt of their jokes this time. Let 'em find out for themselves that some new devil had come from the sea.

4

Mills Lindstrom's boat was a Boston whaler, about twenty feet of blue squarish hull with a couple of bucket seats, a control pylon, and a fifty-five horsepower outboard racketing behind. Sara had to sit on Peter's lap, and while he wouldn't have minded that in any case, in this case he appreciated the extra warmth. Though it was calm, the sea rolling in long swells, heavy clouds and a cold front had settled over the island; farther out the sun was breaking through, but all around them crumbling banks of whitish mist hung close to the water. The gloom couldn't dampen Peter's mood, however; he was anticipating a pleasant weekend with Sara and gave hardly a thought to their destination, carrying on a steady stream of chatter. Mills, on the other hand, was brooding and taciturn, and when they came in sight of the off-shore pollution aggregate, a dirty brown stain spreading for hundreds of yards across the water, he pulled his pipe from beneath his rain gear and set to chomping the stem, as if to restrain impassioned speech.

Peter borrowed Mills' binoculars and peered ahead. The surface of the aggregate was pocked by thousands of white objects; at this distance they looked like bones sticking up from thin soil. Streamers of mist were woven across it, and the edge was shifting sluggishly, an obscene cap sliding over the dome of a swell. It was a no-man's land, an ugly blot, and as they drew near, its ugliness increased. The most common of the white objects were Clorox bottles such as fishermen used to mark the spread of their nets; there were also a great many fluorescent tubes, other plastic debris, torn pieces of netting, and driftwood, all mired in a pale brown jelly of decayed oil products. It was a Golgotha of the inorganic world, a plain of ultimate spiritual malaise, of entropy triumphant, and perhaps, thought Peter, the entire earth would one day come to resemble it. The briny, bitter stench made his skin crawl.

"God," said Sara as they began cruising along the edge; she opened her mouth to say more but couldn't find the words.

"I see why you felt like drinking last night," said Peter to Mills, who just shook his head and grunted.

"Can we go into it?" asked Sara.

"All them torn nets'll foul the propeller." Mills stared at her askance. "Ain't it bad enough from out here?"

"We can tip up the motor and row in," Peter suggested. "Come on, Mills. It'll be like landing on the moon."

And, indeed, as they rowed into the aggregate, cutting through the pale brown stuff, Peter felt that they had crossed some intangible border into uncharted territory. The air seemed heavier, full of suppressed energy, and the silence seemed deeper; the only sound was the slosh of the oars. Mills had told Peter that the thing would have roughly a spiral shape, due to the actions of opposing currents, and that intensified his feeling of having entered the unknown; he pictured them as characters in a fantasy novel, creeping across a great device inlaid on the floor of an abandoned temple. Debris bobbed against the hull. The brown glop had the consistency of Jello that hadn't set properly, and when Peter dipped his hand into it, beads accumulated on his fingers. Some of the textures on the surface had a horrid, almost organic beauty: bleached, wormlike tendrils of netting mired in the slick, reminding Peter of some animal's diseased spoor; larval chips of wood matted on a bed of glistening cellophane; a blue plastic lid bearing a girl's sunbonneted face embedded in a spaghetti of styrofoam strips. They would point out such oddities to each other, but nobody was eager to talk. The desolation of the aggregate was oppressive, and not even a ray of sunlight fingering the boat, as if a searchlight were keeping track of them from the real world, not even that could dispel the gloom. Then, about two hundred yards in, Peter saw something shiny inside an opaque plastic container, reached down and picked it up.

The instant he brought it on board he realized that this was the object about which he had experienced the premonition, and he had the urge to throw it back; but he felt such a powerful attraction to it that instead he removed the lid and lifted out a pair of silver combs, the sort Spanish women wear in their hair. Touching them, he had a vivid mental image of a young woman's face; a pale, drawn face that might have been beautiful but was starved-thin and worn by sorrows. Gabriela. The name seeped into his consciousness the way a paw-track frozen in the ground melts up from beneath the snow during a thaw. Gabriela Pa . . . Pasco . . . Pascual. His finger traced the design etched on the combs, and every curlicue conveyed a sense of her personality. Sadness, loneliness, and—most of all—terror. She'd been afraid for a very long time. Sara asked to see the combs, took them, and his ghostly impression of Gabriela Pascual's life flew apart like a creature of foam, leaving him disoriented.

"They're beautiful," said Sara. "And they must be really old."

"Looks like Mexican work," said Mills. "Hmph. What we got here?" He stretched out his oar, trying to snag something; he hauled the oar back in and Sara lifted the thing from the blade: a rag showing yellow streaks through its coating of slick.

"It's a blouse." Sara turned it in her hands, her nose wrinkling at having to touch the slick; she stopped turning it and stared at Peter. "Oh, God! It's Ellen Borchard's."

Peter took it from her. Beneath the manufacturer's label was Ellen Borchard's name tag. He closed his eyes, hoping to read some impression as he had with the silver combs. Nothing. His gift had deserted him. But he had a bad feeling that he knew exactly what had happened to the girl.

"Better take that to Hugh Weldon," said Mills. "Might . . ." He broke off and stared out over the aggregate.

At first Peter didn't see what had caught Mills' eye; then he noticed that a wind had sprung up. A most peculiar wind. It was moving slowly around the boat about fifty feet away, its path evident by the agitation of the debris over which it passed; it whispered and sighed, and with a sucking noise a couple of Clorox bottles popped out of the slick and spun into the air. Each time the wind made a complete circuit of the boat, it seemed to have grown a little stronger.

"What the hell!" Mills' face was drained of color, the web of broken blood vessels on his cheeks showing like a bright red tattoo.

Sara's nails bit into Peter's arm, and he was overwhelmed by the knowledge that this wind was what he had been warned against. Panicked, he shook Sara off, scrambled to the back of the boat and tipped down the outboard motor.

"The nets . . ." Mills began.

"Fuck the nets! Let's get out of here!"

The wind was keening, and the entire surface of the aggregate was starting to heave. Crouched in the stern, Peter was again struck by its resemblance to a graveyard with bones sticking out of the earth, only now all the bones were wiggling, working themselves loose. Some of the Clorox bottles were rolling sluggishly along, bouncing high when they hit an obstruction. The sight froze him for a moment, but as Mills fired the engine he crawled back to his seat and pulled Sara down with him. Mills turned the boat toward Madaket. The slick glubbed and smacked against the hull, and brown flecks splashed onto the windshield and oozed sideways. With each passing second the wind grew stronger and louder, building to a howl that drowned out the motor. A fluorescent tube went twirling up beside them like a cheerleader's baton; bottles and cellophane and splatters of oil slick flew at them from every direction. Sara ducked her face into Peter's shoulder, and he held her tight, praying that the propeller wouldn't foul. Mills swerved the boat to avoid a piece of driftwood that sailed past the bow, and then they were into clear water, out of the wind— though they could still hear it raging—and running down the long slope of a swell.

Relieved, Peter stroked Sara's hair and let out a shuddering breath; but when he glanced behind them all his relief went glimmering. Thousands upon thousands of Clorox bottles and fluorescent tubes and other debris were spinning in mid-air above the aggregate—an insane mobile posed against the gray sky—and just beyond the edge narrow tracks of water were being lashed up, as if a windy knife were slicing back and forth across it, undecided whether or not to follow them home.

Hugh Weldon had been out in Madaket investigating the vandalism of the condominiums, and after receiving the radio call it had only taken him a few minutes to get to Peter's cottage. He sat beside Mills at the picnic table, listening to their story, and from the perspective of the sofa bunk, where Peter was sitting, his arm around Sara, the chief presented an angular, mantislike silhouette against the gray light from the window; the squabbling of the police radio outside seemed part of his persona, a radiation emanating from him. When they had finished he stood, walked to the wood stove, lifted the lid and spat inside it; the stove crackled and spat back a spark.

"If it was just you two," he said to Peter and Sara, "I'd run you in and find out what you been smokin'. But Mills here don't have the imagination for this kind of foolishness, so I guess I got to believe you." He set down the lid with a clank and squinted at Peter. "You said you wrote somethin' 'bout Ellen Borchard in your book. What?"

Peter leaned forward, resting his elbows on his knees. "She was down at Smith Point just after dark. She was angry at her parents, and she wanted to scare them. So she took off her blouse—she had extra clothes with her, because she was planning to run away—and was about to rip it up, to make them think she'd been murdered, when the wind killed her."

"Now how'd it do that?" asked Weldon.

"In the book the wind was a sort of elemental. Cruel, capricious. It played with her. Knocked her down, rolled her along the shingle. Then it would let her up and knock her down again. She was bleeding all over from the shell-cuts, and screaming. Finally it whirled her up and out to sea." Peter stared down at his hands; the inside of his head felt heavy, solid, as if his brains were made of mercury.

"Jesus Christ!" said Weldon. "What you got to say 'bout that, Mills?"

"It wasn't no normal wind," said Mills. "That's all I know."

"Jesus Christ!" repeated Weldon; he rubbed the back of his neck and peered at Peter. "I been twenty years at this job and I've heard some tall tales. But this . . . what did you say it was? An elemental?"

"Yeah, but I don't really know for sure. Maybe if I could handle those combs again, I could learn more about it."

"Peter." Sara put her hand on his arm; her brow was furrowed. "Why don't we let Hugh deal with it?"

Weldon was amused. "Naw, Sara. You let Mr. Ramey see what he can do." He chuckled. "Maybe he can tell me how the Red Sox are gonna do this year. Me and Mills can have another look at the mess off the point."

Mills' neck seemed to retract into his shoulders. "I ain't goin' back out there, Hugh. And if you want my opinion, you better keep clear of it yourself."

"Damn it, Mills." Weldon smacked his hand against his hip. "I ain't gonna beg, but you sure as hell could save me some trouble. It'll take me an hour to get the Coast Guard boys off their duffs. Wait a minute!" He turned to Peter. "Maybe you people were seein' things. There musta been all kinds of bad chemicals fumin' up from that mess. Could be you breathed somethin' in." Brakes squealed, a car door slammed, and seconds later the bedraggled figure of Sally McColl strode past the window and knocked on the door.

"What in God's name does she want?" said Weldon.

Peter opened the door, and Sally gave him a gap-toothed grin. "Mornin', Peter," she said. She was wearing a stained raincoat over her usual assortment of dresses and sweaters, and a gaily-colored man's necktie for a scarf. "Is that skinny ol' fart Hugh Weldon inside?"

"I ain't got time for your crap today, Sally," called Weldon.

Sally pushed past Peter. "Mornin', Sara. Mills."

"Hear one of your dogs just had a litter," said Mills.

"Yep. Six snarly little bastards." Sally wiped her nose with the back of her hand and checked it to see what had rubbed off. "You in the market?"

"I might drop 'round and take a look," said Mills. "Dobermans or Shepherds?"

"Dobermans. Gonna be fierce."

"What's on your mind, Sally?" said Weldon, stepping between them.

"Got a confession to make."

Weldon chuckled. "What'd you do now? You sure as hell didn't burglarize no dress shop."

A frown etched the wrinkles deeper on Sally's face. "You stupid son of a bitch," she said flatly. "I swear, God musta been runnin' short of everything but horseshit when He made you."

"Listen, you ol' . . ."

"Musta ground up your balls and used 'em for brains," Sally went on. "Musta . . ."

"Sally!" Peter pushed them apart and took the old woman by the shoulders. A glaze faded from her eyes as she looked at him. At last she shrugged free of his grasp and patted down her hair: a peculiarly feminine gesture for someone so shapeless and careworn.

"I shoulda told you sooner," she said to Weldon. "But I was sick of you laughin' at me. Then I decided it might be important and I'd have to risk listenin' to your jackass bray. So I'm tellin' you." She looked out the window. "I know what done them condominiums. It was the wind." She snapped a hateful glance at Weldon. "And I ain't crazy, neither!"

Peter felt weak in the knees. They were surrounded by trouble; it was in the air as it had been off Smith Point, yet stronger, as if he were becoming sensitized to the feeling.

"The wind," said Weldon, acting dazed.

"That's right," said Sally defiantly. "It punched holes in them damn buildin's and was whistlin' through 'em like it was playin' music." She glared at him. "Don't you believe me?"

"He believes you," said Peter. "We think the wind killed Ellen Borchard."

"Now don't be spreadin' that around! We ain't sure!" Weldon said it desperately, clinging to disbelief.

Sally crossed the room to Peter. "It's true 'bout the Borchard girl, ain't it?"

"I think so," he said.

"And that thing what killed her, it's here in Madaket. You feel it, don'tcha?"

He nodded. "Yeah."

Sally headed for the door.

"Where you goin'?" asked Weldon. She mumbled and went outside; Peter saw her pacing back and forth in the yard. "Crazy ol' bat," said Weldon.

"Mebbe she is," said Mills. "But you ought not to be treatin' her so harsh after all she's done."

"What's she done?" asked Peter.

"Sally used to live up in Madaket," said Mills. "And whenever a ship would run up on Dry Shoals or one of the others, she'd make for the wreck in that ol' lobster boat of hers. Most times she'd beat the Coast Guard to 'em. Musta saved fifty or sixty souls over the years, sailin' out in the worst kind of weather."

"Mills!" said Weldon emphatically. "Run me out to that garbage dump of yours."

Mills stood and hitched up his pants. "Ain't you been listenin', Hugh? Peter and Sally say that thing's 'round here somewhere."

Weldon was a frustrated man. He sucked at his teeth, and his face worked. He picked up the container holding the combs, glanced at Peter, then set the container down.

"You want me to see what I can learn from those?" asked Peter.

Weldon shrugged. "Can't hurt nothin', I guess." He stared out the window, as if unconcerned with the issue.

Peter took the container and sat down next to Sara. "Wait," she said. "I don't understand. If this thing is nearby, shouldn't we get away from here?" Nobody answered.

The plastic container was cold, and when Peter pried off the lid the cold welled out at him. Intense, aching cold, as if he had opened the door to a meat locker.

Sally burst into the room and pointed at the container. "What's that?"

"Some old combs," said Peter. "They didn't feel like this when I found them. Not as strong."

"Feel like what?" asked Weldon; every new mystery seemed to be unnerving him further, and Peter suspected that if the mysteries weren't cleared up soon, the chief would start disbelieving them on purely practical grounds.

Sally came over to Peter and looked into the container. "Gimme one," she said, extending a grimy hand. Weldon and Mills moved up behind her, like two old soldiers flanking their mad queen.

Reluctantly, Peter picked up one of the combs. Its coldness flowed into his arm, his head, and for a moment he was in the midst of a storm-tossed sea, terrified, waves crashing over the bows of a fishing boat and the wind singing around him. He dropped the comb. His hands were trembling, and his heart was doing a jig against his chest wall.

"Oh, shit," he said to no one in particular. "I don't know if I want to do this."

Sara gave Sally her seat beside Peter, and as they handled the combs, setting them down every minute or so to report what they had learned, she chewed her nails and fretted. She could relate to Hugh Weldon's frustration; it was awful just to sit and watch. Each time Peter and Sally handled the combs their respiration grew shallow and their eyes rolled back, and when they laid them aside they appeared drained and frightened.

"Gabriela Pascual was from Miami," said Peter. "I can't tell exactly when all this happened, but it was years ago . . . because in my image of her, her clothes look a little old-fashioned. Maybe ten or fifteen years back. Something like that. Anyway, there was trouble for her on shore, some emotional entanglement, and her brother didn't want to leave her alone, so he took her along on a fishing voyage. He was a commercial fisherman."

"She had the gift," Sally chimed in. "That's why there's so much of her in the combs. That, and because she killed herself and died holdin' em."

"Why'd she kill herself?" asked Weldon.

"Fear," said Peter. "Loneliness. Crazy as it sounds, the wind was holding her prisoner. I think she cracked up from being alone on a drifting boat with only this thing—the elemental—for company."

"Alone?" said Weldon. "What happened to her brother?"

"He died." Sally's voice was shaky. "The wind came down and killed 'em all 'cept this Gabriela. It wanted her."

As the story unfolded, gusts of wind began to shudder the cottage and Sara tried to remain unconcerned as to whether or not they were natural phenomena. She turned her eyes from the window, away from the heaving trees and bushes, and concentrated on what was being said; but that in itself was so eerie that she couldn't keep from jumping whenever the panes rattled. Gabriela Pascual, said Peter, had been frequently seasick during the cruise; she had been frightened of the crew, most of whom considered her bad luck, and possessed by a feeling of imminent disaster. And, Sally added, that premonition had been borne out. One cloudless, calm day the elemental had swept down and killed everyone. Everyone except Gabriela. It had whirled the crew and her brother into the air, smashed them against bulkheads, dropped them onto the decks. She had expected to die as well, but it had seemed interested in her. It had caressed her and played with her, knocking her down and rolling her about; and at night it had poured through the passageways and broken windows, making a chilling music that—as the days passed and the ship drifted north—she came to half-understand.

"She didn't think of it as a spirit," said Peter. "There wasn't anything mystical about it to her mind. It struck her as being kind of a . . ."

"An animal," interrupted Sally. "A big, stupid animal. Vicious, it was. But not evil. 'Least it didn't feel evil to her."

Gabriela, Peter went on, had never been sure what it wanted of her—perhaps her presence had been all. Most of the time it had left her alone. Then, suddenly, it would spring up out of a calm to juggle splinters of glass or chase her about. Once the ship had drifted near to shore, and when she had attempted to jump over the side, the elemental had battered her and driven her belowdecks. Though at first it had controlled the drift of the ship, gradually it lost interest in her and on several occasions the ship almost foundered. Finally, no longer caring to prolong the inevitable, she had cut her wrists and died clutching the container holding her most valued possessions, her grandmother's silver combs, with the wind howling in her ears.

Peter leaned back against the wall, his eyes shut, and Sally sighed and patted her breast. For a long moment no one spoke.

"Wonder why it's hangin' 'round that garbage out there," said Mills.

"Maybe no reason," said Peter dully. "Or maybe it's attracted to slack points in the tides, to some condition of the air."

"I don't get it," said Weldon. "What the hell is it? It can't be no animal."

"Why not?" Peter stood, swayed, then righted himself. "What's wind, anyway? Charged ions, vacating air masses. Who's to say that some stable form of ions couldn't approximate a life? Could be there's one of these at the heart of every storm, and they've always been mistaken for spirits, given an anthropomorphic character. Like Ariel." He laughed disconsolately. "It's no breezy sprite, that's for sure."

Sally's eyes looked unnaturally bright, like watery jewels lodged in her weathered face. "The sea breeds 'em," she said firmly, as if that were explanation enough of anything strange.

"Peter's book was right," said Sara. "It's an elemental. That's what you're describing, anyway. A violent, inhuman creature, part spirit and part animal." She laughed, and the laugh edged a bit high, bordering on the hysteric. "It's hard to believe."

"Right!" said Weldon. "Damned hard! I got an ol' crazy woman and a man I don't know from Adam tellin' me . . ."

"Listen!" said Mills; he walked to the door and swung it open.

It took Sara a second to fix on the sound, but then she realized that the wind had died, had gone from heavy gusts to trifling breezes in an instant, and further away, coming from the sea, or nearer, maybe as close as Tennessee Avenue, she heard a roaring.

5

A few moments earlier Jerry Highsmith had been both earning his living and looking forward to a night of exotic pleasures in the arms of Ginger McCurdy. He was standing in front of one of the houses on Tennessee Avenue, its quarterboard reading AHAB-ITAT, and a collection of old harpoons and whalebones mounted on either side of the door; his bicycle leaned against a rail fence behind him, and ranged around him, straddling their bikes, dolled up in pastel-hued jogging suits and sweat clothes, were twenty-six members of the Peach State Ramblers Bicycle Club. Ten men, sixteen women. The women were all in good shape, but most were in their thirties, a bit long in the tooth for Jerry's taste. Ginger, on the other hand, was prime. Twenty-three or twenty-four, with red hair down to her ass and a body that wouldn't quit. She had peeled off her sweats and was blooming out a halter and shorts cut so high that each time she dismounted you could see right up to the Pearly Gates. And she knew what she was doing: every jiggle of those twin jaloobies was aimed at his crotch. She had pressed to the front of the group and was attending to his spiel about the bullshit whaling days. Oh, yeah! Ginger was ready. A couple of lobsters, a little wine, a stroll along the waterfront, and then by God he'd pump her so full of the Nantucket Experience that she'd breach like a snow-white hill.

Thar she fuckin' blows!

"Now, y'all . . ." he began.

They tittered; they liked him mocking their accent.

He grinned abashedly as if he hadn't known what he was doing. "Must be catchin'," he said. "Now you people probably haven't had a chance to visit the Whaling Museum, have you?"

A chorus of Nos.

"Well then, I'll give you a course in harpoonin'." He pointed at the wall of the AHAB-ITAT. "That top one with the single barb stickin' off the side, that's the kind most commonly used during the whalin' era. The shaft's of ash. That was the preferred wood. It stands up to the weather"—he stared pointedly at Ginger—"and it won't bend under pressure." Ginger tried to constrain a smile. "Now that one," he continued, keeping an eye on her, "the one with the arrow point and no barbs, that was favored by some whalers. They said it allowed for deeper penetration."

"What about the one with two barbs?" asked someone.

Jerry peered over heads and saw that the questioner was his second choice. Ms. Selena Persons. A nice thirtyish brunette, flat-chested, but with killer legs. Despite the fact that he was obviously after Ginger, she hadn't lost interest. Who knows? A double-header might be a possibility.

"That was used toward the end of the whalin' era," he said. "But generally two-barbed harpoons weren't considered as effective as single-barbed ones. I don't know why, exactly. Might have just been stubbornness on the whalers' part. Resistance to change. They knew the ol' single-barb could give satisfaction."

Ms. Persons met his gaze with a glimmer of a smile.

"'Course," Jerry continued, addressing all the Ramblers, "now the shaft's tipped with a charge that explodes inside the whale." He winked at Ginger and added *sotto voce*, "Must be a rush."

She covered her mouth with her hand.

"Okay, folks!" Jerry swung his bike away from the fence. "Mount up and we'll be off to the next thrillin' attraction."

Laughing and chattering, the Ramblers started to mount, but just then a powerful gust of wind swept down Tennessee Avenue, causing squeals and blowing away hats. Several of the riders overbalanced and fell, and several more nearly did. Ginger stumbled forward and clung to Jerry, giving him chest-to-chest massage. "Nice catch," she said, doing a little writhe as she stepped away.

"Nice toss," he replied.

She smiled, but the smile faded and was replaced by a bewildered look. "What's that?"

Jerry turned. About twenty yards away a column of whirling leaves had formed above the blacktop; it was slender, only a few feet high, and though he had never seen anything similar it alarmed him no more than had the freakish gust of wind. Within seconds, however, the column had grown to a height of fifteen feet; twigs and gravel and branches were being sucked into it, and it sounded like a miniature tornado. Someone screamed. Ginger clung to him in genuine fright. There was a rank smell in the air, and a pressure was building in Jerry's ears. He couldn't be sure, because the column was spinning so rapidly, but it seemed to be assuming a roughly human shape, a dark green figure made of plant litter and stones. His mouth had gone dry, and he restrained an urge to throw Ginger aside and run.

"Come on!" he shouted.

A couple of the Ramblers managed to mount their bicycles, but the wind had grown stronger, roaring, and it sent them wobbling and crashing into the weeds. The rest huddled together, their hair whipping about, and stared at the great Druid thing that was taking shape and swaying above them, as tall as the treetops. Shingles were popping off the sides of the houses, sailing up and being absorbed by the figure; and as Jerry tried to outvoice the wind, yelling at the Ramblers to lie flat, he saw the whalebones and harpoons ripped from the wall of the AHAB-ITAT. The windows of the house exploded outward. One man clutched the bloody flap of his cheek, which had been sliced open by a shard of glass; a woman grabbed the back of her knee and crumpled. Jerry shouted a final warning and pulled Ginger down with him into the roadside ditch. She squirmed and struggled, in a panic, but he forced her head down and held tight. The figure had risen much higher than the trees, and though it was still swaying, its form had stabilized somewhat. It had a face now: a graveyard smile of gray shingles and two circular patches of stones for eyes: a terrible blank gaze that seemed responsible for the increasing air pressure. Jerry's heart boomed in his inner ear, and his blood felt like sludge. The figure kept swelling, up and up; the roar was resolving into an oscillating hum that shivered the ground. Stones and leaves were beginning to spray out of it. Jerry knew, *knew*, what was going to happen, and he couldn't keep from watching. Amid a flurry of leaves he saw one of the harpoons flit through the air, impaling a woman who had been trying to stand. The force of the blow drove her out of Jerry's field of vision. Then the great figure exploded. Jerry squeezed his eyes shut. Twigs and balls of dirt and gravel stung him. Ginger leaped sideways and collapsed atop him, clawing at his hip. He waited for something worse to happen, but nothing did. "You okay?" he asked, pushing Ginger away by the shoulders.

She wasn't okay.

A splintered inch of whalebone stuck out from the center of her forehead. Shrieking with revulsion, Jerry wriggled from beneath her and came to his hands and knees. A moan. One of the men was crawling toward him, his face a mask of blood, a ragged hole where his right eye had been; his good eye looked glazed like a doll's. Horrified, not knowing what to do, Jerry scrambled to his feet and backed away. All the harpoons, he saw, had found targets. Most of the Ramblers lay unmoving, their blood smeared over the blacktop; the rest were sitting up, dazed and bleeding. Jerry's heel struck something, and he spun about. The quarterboard of the AHAB-ITAT had nailed Ms. Selena Persons vampire-style to the roadside dirt; the board had been driven so deep into the ground that only the letter A was showing above the mired ruin of her jogging suit, as if she were an exhibit. Jerry began to tremble, and tears started from his eyes.

A breeze ruffled his hair.

Somebody wailed, shocking him from his daze. He should call the hospital, the police. But where was a phone? Most of the houses were empty, waiting for summer tenants, and the phones wouldn't be working. Somebody must have seen what had happened, though. He should just do what he could until help arrived. Gathering himself, he walked toward the man whose eye was missing; but before he had gone more than a few paces a fierce gust of wind struck him in the back and knocked him flat.

This time the roaring was all around him, the pressure so intense that it seemed a white-hot needle had pierced him from ear-to-ear.

He shut his eyes and clamped both hands to his ears, trying to smother the pain. Then he felt himself lifted. He couldn't believe it at first. Even when he opened his eyes and saw that he was being borne aloft, revolving in a slow circle, it made no sense. He couldn't hear, and the quiet added to his sense of unreality; further adding to it, a riderless bicycle pedaled past. The air was full of sticks and leaves and pebbles, a threadbare curtain between him and the world, and he imagined himself rising in the gorge of that hideous dark figure. Ginger McCurdy was flying about twenty feet overhead, her red hair streaming, arms floating languidly as if in a dance. She was revolving faster than he, and he realized that his rate of spin was increasing as he rose. He saw what was going to happen: you went higher and higher, faster and faster, until you were spewed out, shot out over the village. His mind rebelled at the prospect of death, and he tried to swim back down the wind, flailing, kicking, bursting with fear. But as he whirled higher, twisting and turning, it became hard to breathe, to think, and he was too dizzy to be afraid any longer. Another woman sailed by a few feet away. Her mouth was open, her face contorted; blood dripped from her scalp. She clawed at him, and he reached out to her, not knowing why he bothered. Their hands just missed touching. Thoughts were coming one at a time. Maybe he'd land in the water. Miraculous Survivor Of Freak Tornado. Maybe he'd fly across the island and settle gently in a Nantucket treetop. A broken leg, a bruise or two. They'd set up drinks for him in the Atlantic Cafe. Maybe Connie Keating would finally come across, would finally recognize the miraculous potential of Jerry Highsmith. Maybe. He was tumbling now, limbs jerking about, and he gave up thinking. Flash glimpses of the gapped houses below, of the other dancers on the wind, moving with spasmodic abandon. Suddenly, as he was bent backwards by a violent updraft, there was a wrenching pain inside him, a grating, then a vital dislocation that delivered him from pain. Oh Christ Jesus! Oh God! Dazzles exploded behind his eyes. Something bright blue flipped past him, and he died.

6

After the column of leaves and branches looming up from Tennessee Avenue had vanished, after the roaring had died, Hugh Weldon sprinted for his squad car with Peter and Sara at his heels. He frowned as they piled in but made no objection, and this, Peter thought, was probably a sign that he had stopped trying to rationalize events, that he accepted the wind as a force to which normal procedures did not apply. He switched on the siren, and they sped off. But less that fifty yards from the cottage he slammed on the brakes. A woman was hanging in a hawthorn tree beside the road, an old-fashioned harpoon plunged through her chest. There was no point in checking to see if she was alive. All her major bones were quite obviously broken, and she was painted with blood head to foot, making her look like a horrid African doll set out as a warning to trespassers.

Weldon got on the radio. "Body out in Madaket," he said. "Send a wagon."

"You might need more than one," said Sara; she pointed to three dabs of color further up the road. She was very pale, and she squeezed Peter's hand so hard that she left white imprints on his skin.

Over the next twenty-five minutes they found eighteen bodies: broken, mutilated, several pierced by harpoons or fragments of bone. Peter would not have believed that the human form could be reduced to such grotesque statements, and though he was horrified, nauseated, he became increasingly numbed by what he saw. Odd thoughts flocked to his brain, most persistent among them being that the violence had been done partly for his benefit. It was a sick, nasty idea, and he tried to dismiss it; but after a while he began to consider it in light of other thoughts that had lately been striking him out of the blue. The manuscript of *How The Wind Spoke At Madaket,* for instance. As improbable as it sounded, it was hard to escape the conclusion that the wind had been seeding all this in his brain. He didn't want to believe it, yet there it was, as believable as anything else that had happened. And given that, was his latest thought any less believable? He was beginning to understand the progression of events, to understand it with the same sudden clarity that had helped him solve the problems of his book, and he wished very much that he could have obeyed his premonition and not touched the combs. Until then the elemental had not been sure of him; it had been nosing around him like—as Sally had described it—a big, stupid animal, sensing something familiar about him but unable to remember what. And when he had found the combs, when he had opened the container, there must have been some kind of circuit closed, a flashpoint sparked between his power and Gabriela Pascual's, and the elemental had made the connection. He recalled how excited it had seemed, darting back and forth beyond the borders of the aggregate.

As they turned back onto Tennessee Avenue, where a small group of townsfolk were covering bodies with blankets, Weldon got on the radio again, interrupting Peter's chain of logic. "Where the hell are them ambulances?" he snapped.

"Sent 'em a half hour ago," came the reply. "Shoulda been there by now."

Weldon cast a grim look at Peter and Sara. "Try 'em on the radio," he told the operator.

A few minutes later the report came that none of the ambulances were answering their radios. Weldon told his people to stay put, that he'd check it out himself. As they turned off Tennessee Avenue onto the Nantucket road, the sun broke through the overcast, flooding the landscape in a thin yellow light and warming the interior of the car. The light seemed to be illuminating Peter's weaknesses, making him realize how tense he was, how his muscles ached with the poisons of adrenaline and fatigue. Sara leaned against him, her eyes closed, and the pressure of her body acted to shore him up, to give him a burst of vitality.

Weldon kept the speed at thirty, glancing left and right, but nothing was out of the ordinary. Deserted streets, houses with blank-looking windows. Many of the homes in Madaket were vacant, and the occupants of many of the rest were away at work or off on errands. About two miles out of town, as they crested a low rise just beyond the dump, they spotted the ambulances. Weldon pulled onto the shoulder, letting the engine idle, and stared at the sight. Four ambulances were strewn across the blacktop, forming an effective roadblock a hundred feet away. One had been flipped over on its roof like a dead white bug; another had crashed into a light pole and was swathed in electrical lines whose broken ends were sticking in through the driver's window, humping and writhing and sparking. The other two had been smashed together and were burning; transparent licks of flame warped the air above their blackened husks. But the wrecked ambulances were not the reason that Weldon had stopped so far away, why they sat silent and hopeless. To the right of the road was a field of bleached weeds and grasses, an Andrew Wyeth field glowing yellow in the pale sun, figured by a few stunted oaks and extending to a hill overlooking the sea, where three gray houses were posed against a faded blue sky. Though only fitful breezes played about the squad car, the field was registering the passage of heavy winds; the grasses were rippling, eddying, bending and swaying in contrary directions, as if thousands of low-slung animals were scampering through them to and fro, and this rippling was so constant, so furious, it seemed that the shadows of the clouds passing overhead were standing still and the land was flowing away. The sound of the wind was a mournful, whistling rush. Peter was entranced. The scene had a fey power that weighed upon him, and he had trouble catching his breath.

"Let's go," said Sara tremulously. "Let's . . ." She stared past Peter, a look of fearful comprehension forming on her face.

The wind had begun to roar. Less than thirty feet away a patch of grass had been flattened, and a man wearing an orderly's uniform was being lifted into the air, revolving slowly. His head flopped at a ridiculous straw-man angle, and the front of his tunic was drenched with blood. The car shuddered in the turbulence.

Sara shrieked and clutched at Peter. Weldon tried to jam the gearshift into reverse, missed, and the car stalled. He twisted the key in the ignition. The engine sputtered, dieseled and went dead. The orderly continued to rise, assuming a vertical position. He spun faster and faster, blurring like an ice skater doing a fancy finish, and at the same time drifted closer to the car. Sara was screaming, and Peter wished he could scream, could do something to release the tightness in his chest. The engine caught. But before Weldon could put the car in gear, the wind subsided and the orderly fell onto the hood. Drops of blood sprinkled the windshield. He lay spreadeagled for a moment, his dead eyes staring at them. Then, with the obscene sluggishness of a snail retracting its foot, he slumped down onto the road, leaving a red smear across the white metal.

Weldon rested his head on the wheel, taking deep breaths. Peter cradled Sara in his arms. After a second Weldon leaned back, picked up the radio mike and thumbed the switch open. "Jack," he said. "This is Hugh. You copy?"

"Loud and clear, chief."

"We got us a problem out in Madaket." Weldon swallowed hard

and gave a little twitch of his head. "I want you to set up a roadblock 'bout five miles from town. No closer. And don't let nobody through, y'understand?"

"What's happenin' out there, chief? Alice Cuddy called in and said somethin' 'bout a freak wind, but the phone went dead and I couldn't get her back."

"Yeah, we had us some wind." Weldon exchanged a glance with Peter. "But the main problem's a chemical spill. It's under control for now, but you keep everybody away. Madaket's in quarantine."

"You need some help?"

"I need you to do what I told you! Get on the horn and call everyone livin' 'tween the roadblock and Madaket. Tell 'em to head for Nantucket as quick as they can. Put the word on the radio, too."

"What 'bout folks coming' from Madaket? Do I let 'em through?"

"Won't be nobody comin' that way," said Weldon.

Silence. "Chief, you okay?"

"Hell, yes!" Weldon switched off.

"Why didn't you tell them?" asked Peter.

"Don't want 'em thinkin' I'm crazy and comin' out to check on me," said Weldon. "Ain't no point in them dyin', too." He shifted into reverse. "I'm gonna tell everyone to get in their cellars and wait this damn thing out. Maybe we can figure out somethin' to do. But first I'll take you home and let Sara get some rest."

"I'm all right," she said, lifting her head from Peter's chest.

"You'll feel better after a rest," he said, forcing her head back down: it was an act of tenderness, but also he did not want her to catch sight of the field. Dappled with cloud shadow; glowing palely; some quality of light different from that which shone upon the squad car; it seemed at a strange distance from the road, a view into an alternate universe where things were familiar yet not quite the same. The grasses were rippling more furiously than ever, and every so often a column of yellow stalks would whirl high into the air and scatter, as if an enormous child were running through the field, ripping up handfuls of them to celebrate his exuberance.

"I'm not sleepy," Sara complained; she still hadn't regained her color, and one of her eyelids had developed a tic.

Peter sat beside her on the bed. "There's nothing you can do, so why not rest?"

"What are you going to do?"

"I thought I'd have another go at the combs."

The idea distressed her. He started to explain why he had to, but instead bent and kissed her on the forehead. "I love you," he said. The words slipped out so easily that he was amazed. It had been a very long time since he had spoken them to anyone other than a memory.

"You don't have to tell me that just because things look bad," she said, frowning.

"Maybe that's why I'm telling you now," he said. "But I don't believe it's a lie."

She gave a dispirited laugh. "You don't sound very confident."

He thought it over. "I was in love with someone once," he said, "and that relationship colored my view of love. I guess I believed that it always had to happen the same way. A nuclear strike. But I'm beginning to understand it can be different, that you can build toward the sound and the fury."

"It's nice to hear," she said, and then, after a pause, "but you're still in love with her, aren't you?"

"I still think about her, but . . ." He shook his head. "I'm trying to put it behind me, and maybe I'm succeeding. I had a dream about her this morning."

She arched an eyebrow. "Oh?"

"It wasn't a sweet dream," he said. "She was telling me how she'd cemented over her feelings for me. 'All that's left,' she said, 'is this little hard place on my breast.' And she told me that sometimes it moved around, twitched, and she showed me. I could see the damn thing jumping underneath her blouse, and when I touched it—she wanted me to—it was unbelievably hard. Like a pebble lodged beneath her skin. A heart stone. That was all that was left of us. Just this piece of hardness. It pissed me off so much that I threw her on the floor. Then I woke up." He scratched his beard, embarrassed by confession. "It was the first time I've ever had a violent thought about her."

Sara stared at him expressionless.

"I don't know if it's meaningful," he said lamely. "But it seemed so."

She remained silent. Her stare made him feel guilty for having had the dream, sorry that he had mentioned it.

"I don't dream about her very much," he said.

"It's not important," she said.

"Well." He stood. "Try and get some sleep, okay?"

She reached for his hand. "Peter?"

"Yeah?"

"I love you. But you knew that, right?"

It hurt him to see how hesitantly she said it, because he knew that he was to blame for her hesitancy. He bent down and kissed her again. "Sleep," he said. "We'll talk about it later."

He closed the door behind him gently. Mills was sitting at the table, gazing out at 'Sconset Sally, who was pacing the yard, her lips moving, waving her arms, as if arguing with an invisible playmate. "That ol' gal sure's gone down these last years," said Mills. "Used to be sharp as a tack, but she's actin' pretty crazy now."

"Can't blame her," said Peter, sitting down across from Mills. "I'm feeling pretty crazy myself."

"So." Mills tamped tobacco into the bowl of his pipe. "You got a line on what this thing is?"

"Maybe it's the Devil." Peter leaned against the wall. "I don't really know, but I'm starting to think that Gabriela Pascual was right about it being an animal."

Mills chomped on the stem of his pipe and fished in his pocket for a lighter. "How's that?"

"Like I said, I don't really know for sure, but I've been getting more and more sensitized to it ever since I found the combs. At least it seems that way. As if the connection between us were growing stronger." Peter spotted a book of matches tucked under his sugar bowl and slid them across to Mills. "I'm beginning to have insights about it. When we were out on the road just now, I felt that it was exhibiting an animal trait. Staking out territory. Protecting it from invaders. Look who it's attacked. Ambulances, bicyclists. People who were entering its territory. It attacked us when we visited the aggregate."

"But it didn't kill us," said Mills.

The logical response to Mills' statement surfaced from Peter's thoughts, but he didn't want to admit to it and shunted it aside. "Maybe I'm wrong," he said.

"Well, if it is an animal, then it can take a hook. All we got to do is find its mouth." Mills grunted laughter, lit his pipe and puffed bluish smoke. "After you been out on the water a coupla weeks, you can feel when something strange is hard by . . . even if you can't see it. I ain't no psychic, but seems to me I brushed past this thing once or twice."

Peter glanced up at him. Though Mills was a typical bar-room creature, an old salt with a supply of exotic tales, every now and then Peter could sense a kind of specific gravity about him, the kind that accrues to those who have spent time in the solitudes. "You don't seem afraid," he said.

"Oh, don't I?" Mills chuckled. "I'm afraid. I'm just too old to be runnin' 'round in circles 'bout it."

The door flew open, and Sally came in. "Hot in here," she said; she went to the stove and laid a finger against it. "Hmph! Must be all this shit I'm wearin'." She plumped herself down beside Mills, squirmed into a comfortable position and squinted at Peter. "Goddamn wind won't have me," she said. "It wants you."

Peter was startled. "What do you mean?"

Sally pursed her lips as if she had tasted something sour. "It would take me if you wasn't here, but you're too strong. I can't figure a way 'round that."

"Leave the boy alone," said Mills.

"Can't." Sally glowered at him. "He's got to do it."

"You know what she's talkin' 'bout?" asked Mills.

"Hell, yes! He knows! And if he don't, all he's got to do is go talk to it. You understand me, boy. It wants *you*."

An icy fluid squirted down Peter's spine. "Like Gabriela," he said. "Is that what you mean?"

"Go on," said Sally. "Talk to it." She pointed a bony finger at the door. "Just take a stand out there, and it'll come to you."

Behind the cottage, walled off by the spread of two Japanese pines and a tool shed, was a field that the previous tenant had used for a garden. Peter had let it go to seed, and the entire plot was choked with weeds and litter: gas cans, rusty nails, a plastic toy truck, the decaying hide of a softball, cardboard scraps, this and more resting upon a matte of dessicated vines. It reminded him of the aggregate and thus seemed an appropriate place to stand and commune with the wind . . . if such a communion weren't the product of 'Sconset Sally's imagination. Which Peter hoped it was. The afternoon was waning, and it had grown colder. Silver blares of wintery sunlight edged the blackish-gray clouds scudding overhead, and the wind was a steady pour off the sea. He could detect no presence in it, and he was beginning to feel foolish, thinking about going back inside, when a bitter-smelling breeze rippled across his face. He stiffened. Again he felt it: it was acting independent of the off-shore wind, touching delicate fingers to his lips, his eyes, fondling him the way a blind man would in trying to know your shape in his brain. It feathered his hair and pried under the pocket flaps of his army jacket like a pet mouse searching for cheese; it frittered with his shoelaces and stroked him between the legs, shriveling his groin and sending a chill washing through his body.

He did not quite understand how the wind spoke to him, yet he had an image of the process as being similar to how a cat will rub against your hand and transmit a static charge. The charge was actual, a mild stinging and popping. Somehow it was translated into knowledge, doubtless by means of his gift. The knowledge was personified, and he was aware that his conceptions were human renderings of inhuman impulses; but at the same time he was certain that they were basically accurate. Most of all it was lonely. It was the only one of its kind, or, if there were others, it had never encountered them. Peter felt no sympathy for its loneliness, because it felt no sympathy for him. It wanted him not as a friend or companion but as a witness to its power. It would enjoy preening for him, showing off, rubbing against his sensitivity to it and deriving some unfathomable pleasure. It was very powerful. Though its touch was light, its vitality was undeniable, and it was even stronger over water. The land weakened it, and it was eager to return to the sea with Peter in tow. Gliding together through the wild canyons of the waves, into a chaos of booming darkness and salt spray, traveling the most profound of all deserts—the sky above the sea—and testing its strength against the lesser powers of the storms, seizing flying fish and juggling them like silver blades, gathering nests of floating treasures and playing for weeks with the bodies of the drowned. Always at play. Or perhaps "play" was not the right word. Always employed in expressing the capricious violence that was its essential quality. Gabriela Pascual might not have been exact in calling it an animal, but what else could you call it? It was of nature, not of some netherworld. It was ego without thought, power without morality, and it looked upon Peter as a man might look upon a clever toy: something to be cherished for a while, then neglected, then forgotten.

Then lost.

Sara waked at twilight from a dream of suffocation. She sat bolt upright, covered with sweat, her chest heaving. After a moment she calmed herself and swung her legs onto the floor and sat staring into space. In the half-light the dark grain of the boards looked like a pattern of animal faces emerging from the wall; out the window she could see shivering bushes and banks of running clouds. Still feeling sluggish, she went into the front room, intending to wash her face; but the bathroom door was locked and 'Sconset Sally cawed at her from inside. Mills was snoozing on the sofa bunk, and Hugh Weldon was sitting at the table, sipping a cup of coffee; a cigarette smouldered in the saucer, and that struck her as funny: she had known Hugh all her life and had never seen him smoke.

"Where's Peter?" she asked.

"Out back," he said moodily. "Buncha damn foolishness if you ask me."

"What is?"

He gave a snort of laughter. "Sally says he's talkin' to the goddamn wind."

Sara felt as if her heart had constricted. "What do you mean?"

"Beats the hell outta me," said Weldon. "Just more of Sally's nonsense." But when their eyes met she could sense his hopelessness and fear.

She broke for the door. Weldon grabbed at her arm, but she shook free and headed for the Japanese pines back of the cottage. She brushed aside the branches and stopped short, suddenly afraid. The bending and swaying of the weeds revealed a slow circular passage of wind, as if the belly of a great beast were dragging across them, and at the center of the field stood Peter. His eyes were closed, his mouth open, and strands of hair were floating above his head like the hair of a drowned man. The sight stabbed into her, and forgetting her fear, she ran toward him, calling his name. She had covered half the distance between them when a blast of wind smashed her to the ground.

Stunned and disoriented, she tried to get to her feet, but the wind smacked her flat again, pressing her into the damp earth. As had happened out on the aggregate, garbage was rising from the weeds. Scraps of plastic, rusty nails, a yellowed newspaper, rags, and, directly overhead, a large chunk of kindling. She was still dazed, yet she saw with peculiar clarity how the bottom of the chunk was splintered and flecked with whitish mold. It was quivering, as if the hand that held it were barely able to restrain its fury. And then, as she realized it was about to plunge down, to jab out her eyes and pulp her skull, Peter dived on top of her. His weight knocked the breath out of her, but she heard the piece of kindling *thunk* against the back of his head; she sucked in air and pushed at him, rolling him away, and came to her knees. He was dead-pale.

"Is he all right?"

It was Mills, lumbering across the field. Behind him, Weldon had hold of 'Sconset Sally, who was struggling to escape. Mills had come perhaps a third of the way when the garbage, which had fallen back into the weeds, once more was lifted into the air, swirling, jiggling, and—as the wind produced one of its powerful gusts—hurtling toward him. For a second he was surrounded by a storm of cardboard and plastic; then this fell away, and he took a staggering step forward. A number of dark dots speckled his face. Sara thought at first they were clots of dirt. Then blood seeped out around them. They were rusty nailheads. Piercing his brow, his cheeks, pinning his upper lip to his gum. He gave no cry. His eyes bulged, his knees buckled, he did an ungainly pirouette and pitched into the weeds.

Sara watched dully as the wind fluttered about Hugh Weldon and Sally, belling their clothes; it passed beyond them, lashing the pine boughs and vanishing. She spotted the hump of Mills' belly through the weeds. A tear seemed to be carving a cold groove in her cheek. She hiccuped, and thought what a pathetic reaction to death that was. Another hiccup, and another. She couldn't stop. Each successive spasm made her weaker, more unsteady, as if she were spitting up tiny fragments of her soul.

7

As darkness fell, the wind poured through the streets of the village, playing its tricks with the living, the inanimate, and the dead. It was indiscriminate, the ultimate free spirit doing its thing, and yet one might have ascribed a touch of frustration to its actions. Over

Warren's Landing it crumpled a seagull into a bloody rag, and near the mouth of Hither Creek it scattered field mice into the air. It sent a spare tire rolling down the middle of Tennessee Avenue and skied shingles from the roof of the AHAB-ITAT. For a while it flowed about aimlessly; then, increasing to tornado-force, it uprooted a Japanese pine, just yanked it from the ground, dangling huge black root balls, and chucked it like a spear through the side of a house across the street. It repeated the process with two oaks and a hawthorn. Finally it began to blast holes in the walls of the houses and snatch the wriggling creatures inside. It blew off old Julia Stackpole's cellar door and sailed it down into the shelves full of preserves behind which she was hiding; it gathered the broken glass into a hurricane of knives that slashed her arms, her face, and—most pertinently—her throat. It found even older George Coffin (who wasn't about to hide, because in his opinion Hugh Weldon was a damned fool) standing in his kitchen, having just stepped back in after lighting his barbecue; it swept up the coals and hurled them at him with uncanny accuracy. Over the space of a half-hour it killed twenty-one people and flung their bodies onto their lawns, leaving them to bleed pale in the accumulating dusk. Its fury apparently abated, it dissipated to a breeze and—zipping through shrubs and pine boughs—it fled back to the cottage, where something it now wanted was waiting in the yard.

8

'Sconset Sally sat on the woodpile, sucking at a bottle of beer that she'd taken from Peter's refrigerator. She was as mad as a wet hen, because she had a plan—a good plan—and that brainless wonder Hugh Weldon wouldn't hear it, wouldn't listen to a damn word she said. Stuck on being a hero, he was.

The sky had deepened to indigo, and a big lopsided silver moon was leering at her from over the roof of the cottage. She didn't like its eye on her and she spat toward it. The elemental caught the gob of spit and spun it around high in the air, making it glisten oysterlike. Fool thing! Half monster, half a walloping, invisible dog. It reminded her of that outsized old male of hers, Rommel. One second he'd be going for the mailman's throat, and the next he'd be on his back and waggling his paws, begging for a treat. She screwed her bottle into the grass so it wouldn't spill and picked up a stick of kindling. "Here," she said, and shied the stick. "Fetch." The elemental caught the stick and juggled it for a few seconds, then let it fall at her feet. Sally chuckled. "Me'n you might get along," she told the air. "'Cause neither one of us gives a shit!" The beer bottle lifted from the grass. She made a grab for it and missed. "Goddamn it!" she yelled. "Bring that back!" The bottle sailed to a height of about twenty feet and tipped over; the beer spilled out, collected in half a dozen large drops that—one by one—exploded into spray, showering her. Sputtering, she jumped to her feet and started to wipe her face; but the elemental knocked her back down. A trickle of fear welled up inside her. The bottle still hovered above her; after a second it plopped into the grass, and the elemental curled around her, fidgeting with her hair, her collar, slithering inside her raincoat; then, abruptly, as if something else had attracted its attention, it was gone. She saw the grass flatten as it passed over, moving toward the street. She propped herself against the woodpile and finished wiping her face; she spotted Hugh Weldon through the window, pacing, and her anger was rekindled. Thought he was so goddamn masterful, did he? He didn't know piss about the elemental, and there he was, laughing at her plan.

Well, screw him!

He'd find out soon enough that his plan wouldn't work, that hers was the reasonable one, the surefire one.

A little scary, maybe, but surefire all the same.

9

It had come full dark by the time Peter regained consciousness. He moved his head, and the throbbing nearly caused him to black out. He lay still, getting his bearings. Moonlight spilled through the bedroom window, and Sara was leaning beside it, her blouse glowing a phosphorescent white. From the tilt of her head he judged that she was listening to something, and he soon distinguished an unusual pattern to the wind: five notes followed by a glissando, which led to a repetition of the passage. It was a heavy, angry music, an ominous hook that might have been intended to signal the approach of a villain. Shortly thereafter the pattern broke into a thousand skirling notes, as if the wind were being forced through the open stops of a chorus of flutes. Then another passage, this of seven notes, more rapid but equally ominous. A chill, helpless feeling stole over Peter, like the drawing of a morgue sheet. That breathy music was being played for him. It was swelling in volume, as if—and he was certain this was the case—the elemental was heralding his awakening, was once again sure of his presence. It was impatient, and it would not wait for him much longer. Each note drilled that message home. The thought of being alone with it on the open sea terrified him. Yet he had no choice. There was no way to fight it, and it would simply keep on killing until he obeyed. If it weren't for the others he would refuse to go; he would rather die here than submit to that harrowing, unnatural relationship. Or was it unnatural? It occurred to him that the history of the wind and Gabriela Pascual had a great deal in common with the histories of many human relationships. Desiring; obtaining; neglecting; forgetting. It might be that the elemental was some sort of core existence, that at the heart of every relationship lay a howling emptiness, a chaotic music.

"Sara," he said, wanting to deny it.

The moonlight seemed to wrap around her as she turned. She came to sit beside him. "How are you feeling?"

"Woozy." He gestured toward the window. "How long's that been going on?"

"It just started," she said. "It's punched holes in a lot of the houses. Hugh and Sally were out a while ago. More people are dead." She brushed a lock of hair from his forehead. "But . . ."

"But what?"

"We have a plan."

The wind was playing eerie triplets, an agitated whistling that set Peter's teeth on edge. "It better be a doozy," he said.

"Actually, it's Hugh's plan," she said. "He noticed something out in the field. The instant you touched me, the wind withdrew from us. If it hadn't, if it had hurled that piece of wood at you instead of letting it drop, you would have died. And it didn't want that . . . at least that's what Sally says."

"She's right. Did she tell you what it does want?"

"Yes." She looked away, and her eyes caught the moonlight; they were teary. "Anyway, we think it was confused, that when we're close together it can't tell us apart. And since it doesn't want to hurt you or Sally, Hugh and I are safe as long as we maintain proximity. If Mills had just stayed where he was . . ."

"Mills?"

She told him.

After a moment, still seeing Mills' nail-studded face in his mind's eye, he asked, "What's the plan?"

"I'm going to ride in the jeep with Sally, and you're going with Hugh. We'll drive toward Nantucket, and when we reach the dump . . . you know that dirt road there that leads off into the moors?"

"The one that leads to Altar Rock? Yeah."

"At that point you'll jump into the jeep with us, and we'll head for Altar Rock. Hugh will keep going toward Nantucket. Since it seems to be trying to isolate this end of the island, he figures it'll come after him and we might be able to get beyond its range, and with both of us heading in different directions, we might be able to confuse it enough so that it won't react quickly, and he'll be able to escape, too." She said all this in a rush that reminded Peter of the way a teenager would try to convince her parents to let her stay out late, blurting out the good reasons before they had time to raise any objections.

"You might be right about it not being able to tell us apart when we're close to each other," he said. "God knows how it senses things, and that seems plausible. But the rest is stupid. We don't know whether its territoriality is limited to this end of the island. And what if it does lose track of me and Sally? What's it going to do then? Just blow away? Somehow I doubt it. It might head for Nantucket and do what it's done here."

"Sally says she has a back-up plan."

"Christ, Sara!" Gingerly, he eased up into a sitting position. "Sally's nuts. She doesn't have a clue."

"Well, what choice do we have?" Her voice broke. "You can't go with it."

"You think I want to? Jesus!"

The bedroom door opened, and Weldon appeared silhouetted in a blur of orange light that hurt Peter's eyes. "Ready to travel?" said Weldon. 'Sconset Sally was at his rear, muttering, humming, producing a human static.

Peter swung his legs off the bed. "This is nuts, Weldon." He stood and steadied himself on Sara's shoulder. "You're just going to get killed." He gestured toward the window and the constant music of the wind. "Do you think you can outrun that in a squad car?"

"Mebbe this plan ain't worth a shit . . ." Weldon began.

"You got that right!" said Peter. "If you want to confuse the elemental, why not split me and Sally up? One goes with you, the other with Sara. That way at least there's some logic to this."

"Way I figure it," said Weldon, hitching up his pants, "it ain't your job to be riskin' yourself. It's mine. If Sally, say, goes with me, you're right, that'd confuse it. But so might this. Seems to me it's as eager to keep us normal people in line as it is to run off with freaks like you'n Sally."

"What . . ."

"Shut up!" Weldon eased a step closer. "Now if my way don't work, you try it yours. And if *that* don't do it, then you can go for a cruise with the damn thing. But we don't have no guarantees it's gonna let anybody live no matter what you do."

"No, but . . ."

"No buts about it! This is my bailiwick, and we're gonna do what I say. If it don't work, well, then you can do what you have to. But 'til that happens . . ."

"'Til that happens you're going to keep on making an ass of yourself," said Peter. "Right? Man, all day you've been looking for a way to assert your fucking authority! You don't have any authority in this situation. Don't you understand?"

Weldon went jaw to jaw with him. "Okay," he said. "You go on out there, Mr. Ramey. Go ahead. Just march on out there. You can use Mills' boat, or if you want something bigger, how 'bout Sally's." He snapped a glance back at Sally. "That okay with you, Sally?" She continued muttering, humming, and nodded her head. "See!" Weldon turned to Peter. "She don't mind. So you go ahead. You draw that son of a bitch away from us if you can." He hitched up his pants and exhaled; his breath smelled like a coffee cup full of cigarette butts. "But if it was me, I'd be 'bout ready to try anything else."

Peter's legs felt rooted to the floor. He realized that he had been using anger to muffle fear, and he did not know if he could muster up the courage to take a walk out into the wind, to sail away into the terror and nothingness that Gabriela Pascual had faced.

Sara slipped her hand through his arm. "Please, Peter," she said. "It can't hurt to try."

Weldon backed off a step. "Nobody's blamin' you for bein' scared, Mr. Ramey," he said. "I'm scared myself. But this is the only way I can figure to do my job."

"You're going to die." Peter had trouble swallowing. "I can't let you do that."

"You ain't got nothin' to say 'bout it," said Weldon. "'Cause you got no more authority than me. 'Less you can tell that thing to leave us be. Can you?"

Sara's fingers tightened on Peter's arm, but relaxed when he said, "No."

"Then we'll do 'er my way." Weldon rubbed his hands together in what seemed to Peter hearty anticipation. "Got your keys, Sally?"

"Yeah," she said, exasperated; she moved close to Peter and put a birdclaw hand on his wrist. "Don't worry, Peter. This don't work, I got somethin' up my sleeve. We'll pull a fast one on that devil." She cackled and gave a little whistle, like a parrot chortling over a piece of fruit.

As they drove slowly along the streets of Madaket, the wind sang through the ruined houses, playing passages that sounded mournful and questioning, as if it were puzzled by the movements of the jeep and the squad car. The light of a three-quarter moon illuminated the destruction: gaping holes in the walls, denuded bushes, toppled trees. One of the houses had been given a surprised look, an O of a mouth where the door had been, flanked by two shattered windows. Litter covered the lawns. Flapping paperbacks, clothing, furniture, food, toys. And bodies. In the silvery light their flesh was as pale as Swiss cheese, the wounds dark. They didn't seem real; they might have been a part of a gruesome environment created by an avant-garde sculptor. A carving knife skittered along the blacktop, and for a moment Peter thought it would jump into the air and hurtle toward him. He glanced over at Weldon to see how he was taking it all. Wooden Indian profile, eyes on the road. Peter envied him his pose of duty; he wished he had such a role to play, something that would brace him up, because every shift in the wind made him feel frail and rattled.

They turned onto the Nantucket road, and Weldon straightened in his seat. He checked the rear view mirror, keeping an eye on Sally and Sara, and held the speed at twenty-five. "Okay," he said as they neared the dump and the road to Altar Rock. "I ain't gonna come to a full stop, so when I give the word you move it."

"All right," said Peter; he took hold of the door handle and let out a calming breath. "Good luck."

"Yeah." Weldon sucked at his teeth. "Same to you."

The speed indicator dropped to fifteen, to ten, to five, and the moonlit landscape inched past.

"Go!" shouted Weldon.

Peter went. He heard the squad car squeal off as he sprinted toward the jeep; Sara helped haul him into the back, and then they were veering onto the dirt road. Peter grabbed the frame of Sara's seat, bouncing up and down. The thickets that covered the moors grew close to the road, and branches whipped the sides of the jeep. Sally was hunched over the wheel, driving like a maniac; she sent them skipping over potholes, swerving around tight corners, grinding up the little hills. There was no time to think, only to hold on and be afraid, to await the inevitable appearance of the elemental. Fear was a metallic taste in Peter's mouth; it was in the white gleam of Sara's eyes as she glanced back at him and the smears of moonlight that coursed along the hood; it was in every breath he took, every trembling shadow he saw. But by the time they reached Altar Rock, after fifteen minutes or so, he had begun to hope, to half-believe, that Weldon's plan had worked.

The rock was almost dead-center of the island, its highest point. It was a barren hill atop which stood a stone where the Indians had once conducted human sacrifices—a bit of history that did no good whatsoever for Peter's nerves. From the crest you could see for miles over the moors, and the rumpled pattern of depressions and small hills had the look of a sea that had been magically transformed to leaves during a moment of fury. The thickets—bayberry and such— were dusted to a silvery-green by the moonlight, and the wind blew steadily, giving no evidence of unnatural forces.

Sara and Peter climbed from the jeep, followed after a second by Sally. Peter's legs were shaky and he leaned against the hood; Sara leaned back beside him, her hip touching his. He caught the scent of her hair. Sally peered toward Madaket. She was still muttering, and Peter made out some of the words:

"Stupid . . . never would listen to me . . . never would . . . son of a bitch . . . keep it to my goddamn self . . ."

Sara nudged him. "What do you think?"

"All we can do is wait," he said.

"We're going to be all right," she said firmly; she rubbed the heel of her right hand against the knuckles of her left. It seemed the kind of childish gesture intended to insure good luck, and it inspired him to tenderness. He pulled her into an embrace. Standing there, gazing past her head over the moors, he had an image of them as being the standard lovers on the cover of a paperback, clinging together on a lonely hill, with all probability spread out around them. A corny way of looking at things, yet he felt the truth of it, the dizzying immersion that a paperback lover was supposed to feel. It was not as clear a feeling as he had once had, but perhaps clarity was no longer possible for him. Perhaps all his past clarity had simply been an instance of faulty perception, a flash of immaturity, an adolescent misunderstanding of what was possible. But whether or not that was the case, self-analysis would not solve his confusion. That sort of thinking blinded you to the world, made you disinclined to take risks. It was similar to what happened to academics, how they became so committed to their theories that they began to reject facts to the contrary, to grow conservative in their judgments and deny the inexplicable, the magical. If there was magic in the world—and he knew there was— you could only approach it by abandoning the constraints of logic and lessons learned. For more than a year he had forgotten this and had constructed defenses against magic; now in a single night they had been blasted away, and at a terrible cost he had been made capable of risking himself again, of hoping.

Then he noticed something that wasted hope.

Another voice had been added to the natural flow of wind from the ocean, and in every direction, as far as the eye could see, the moon-silvered thickets were rippling, betraying the presence of far more wind than was evident atop the hill. He pushed Sara away. She followed his gaze and put a hand to her mouth. The immensity of the elemental stunned Peter. They might have been standing on a crag in the midst of a troubled sea, one that receded into an interstellar dark. For the first time, despite his fear, he had an apprehension of the elemental's beauty, of the precision and intricacy of its power. One moment it could be a tendril of breeze, capable of delicate manipulations, and the next it could become an entity the size of a city. Leaves and branches—like flecks of black space—were streaming up from the thickets, forming into columns. Six of them, at regular intervals about Altar Rock, maybe a hundred yards away. The sound of the wind evolved into a roar as they thickened and grew higher. And they grew swiftly. Within seconds the tops of the columns were lost in darkness. They did not have the squat, conical shapes of tornadoes, nor did they twist and jab down their tails; they merely swayed, slender and graceful and menacing. In the moonlight their whirling was almost undetectable and they looked to be made of shining ebony, like six enormous savages poised to attack. They began moving toward the hill. Splintered bushes exploded upward from their bases, and the roaring swelled into a dissonant chord: the sound of a hundred harmonicas being blown at once. Only much, much louder.

The sight of 'Sconset Sally scuttling for the jeep waked Peter from his daze; he pushed Sara into the rear seat and climbed in beside Sally. Though the engine was running, it was drowned out by the wind. Sally drove even less cautiously than before; the island was criss-crossed by narrow dirt roads, and it seemed to Peter that they almost crashed on every one of them. Skidding sideways through a flurry of bushes, flying over the crests of hills, diving down steep slopes. The thickets grew too high in most places for him to see much, but the fury of the wind was all around them and once, as they passed a place where the bushes had been burned off, he caught a glimpse of an ebony column about fifty yards away. It was traveling alongside them, he realized. Harrowing them, running them to and fro. Peter lost track of where they were, and he could not believe that Sally had any better idea. She was trying to do the impossible, to drive out of the wind, which was everywhere, and her lips were drawn back in a grimace of fear. Suddenly—they had just turned east—she slammed on the brakes. Sara flew halfway into the front seat, and if Peter had not been braced he might have gone through the windshield. Further along the road one of the columns had taken a stand, blocking their path. It looked like God, he thought. An ebony tower reaching from the earth to the sky, spraying clouds of dust and plant litter from its bottom. And it was moving toward them. Slowly. A few feet per second. But definitely on the move. The jeep was shaking, and the roar seemed to be coming from the ground beneath them, from the air, from Peter's body, as if the atoms of things were all grinding together. Frozen-faced, Sally wrangled with the gearshift. Sara screamed, and Peter, too, screamed as the windshield was sucked out of its frame and whirled off. He braced himself against the dash, but his arms were weak and with a rush of shame he felt his bladder go. The column was less than a hundred feet away, a great spinning pillar of darkness. He could see how the material inside it aligned itself into tightly packed rings like the segments of a worm. The air was syrupy, hard to breathe. And then, miraculously, they were swerving away from it, away from the roaring, backing along the road. They turned a corner, and Sally got the jeep going forward; she sent them grinding up a largish hill . . . and braked. And let her head drop into the steering wheel in an attitude of despair. They were once again at Altar Rock.

And Hugh Weldon was waiting for them.

He was sitting with his head propped against the boulder that gave the place its name. His eyes were filled with shadows. His mouth was open, and his chest rose and fell. Labored breathing, as if he had just run a long way. There was no sign of the squad car. Peter tried to call to him, but his tongue was stuck to his palate and all that came out was a strangled grunt. He tried again.

"Weldon!"

Sara started to sob, and Sally gasped. Peter didn't know what had frightened them and didn't care; for him the process of thought had been thinned down to following one track at a time. He climbed from the jeep and went over to the chief. "Weldon," he said again.

Weldon sighed.

"What happened?" Peter knelt beside him and put a hand on his shoulder; he heard a hiss and felt a tremor pass through the body.

Weldon's right eye began to bulge. Peter lost his balance and sat back hard. Then the eye popped out and dropped into the dust. With a high-pitched whistling, wind and blood sprayed from the empty socket. Peter fell backwards, scrabbling at the dirt in an effort to put distance between himself and Weldon. The corpse toppled onto its side, its head vibrating as the wind continued to pour out, boiling up dust beneath the socket. There was a dark smear marking the spot on the boulder where the head had rested.

Until his heart rate slowed, Peter lay staring at the moon, as bright and distant as a wish. He heard the roaring of the wind from all sides and realized that it was growing louder, but he didn't want to admit to it. Finally, though, he got to his feet and gazed across the moors.

It was as if he were standing at the center of an unimaginably large temple, one forested with dozens upon dozens of shiny black pillars rising from a dark green floor. The nearest of them were about a hundred yards away, and those were unmoving; but as Peter watched, others farther off began to slew back and forth, gliding in and out of the stationary ones, like dancing cobras. There was a fever in the air, a pulse of heat and energy, and this as much as the alienness of the sight was what transfixed him and held him immobile. He found that he had gone beyond fear. You could no more hide from the elemental than you could from God. It would lead him onto the sea to die, and its power was so compelling that he almost acknowledged its right to do this. He climbed into the jeep. Sara looked beaten. Sally touched his leg with a palsied hand.

"You can use my boat," she said.

On the way back to Madaket. Sara sat with her hands clasped in her lap, outwardly calm but inwardly turbulent. Thoughts fired across her brain so quickly that they left only partial impressions, and those were seared away by lightning strokes of terror. She wanted to say something to Peter, but words seemed inadequate to all she was feeling. At one point she decided to go with him, but the decision sparked a sudden resentment. He didn't love her! Why should she sacrifice herself for him? Then, realizing that he was sacrificing himself for her, that he did love her or that at least this was an act of love, she decided that if she went it would make his act meaningless. That decision caused her to question whether or not she was using his sacrifice to obscure her true reason for staying behind: her fear. And what about the quality of her feelings for him? Were they so uncertain that fear could undermine them? In a blaze of irrationality she saw that he was pressuring her to go with him, to prove her love, something she had never asked him to do. What right did he have? With half her mind she understood the unreasonableness of these thoughts, yet she couldn't stop thinking them. She felt all her emotions winnowing, leaving her hollow . . . like Hugh Weldon, with only the wind inside him, propping him up, giving him the semblance of life. The grotesqueness of the image caused her to shrink further inside herself, and she just sat there, growing dim and empty, saying nothing.

"Buck up," said Sally out of the blue, and patted Peter's leg. "We got one thing left to try." And then, with what seemed to Sara an irrational good cheer, she added: "But if that don't work the boat's got fishin' tackle and a coupla cases of cherry brandy on board. I was too damn drunk to unload 'em yesterday. Cherry brandy be better'n water for where you're headed."

Peter gave no reply.

As they entered the village, the elemental chased beside them, whirling up debris, scattering leaves, tossing things high into the air. Playing, thought Sara. It was playing. Frisking along like a happy pup, like a petulant child who'd gotten his way and now was all smiles. She was overwhelmed with hatred for it and she dug her nails into the seat cushion, wishing she had a way to hurt it. Then, as they passed Julia Stackpole's house, the corpse of Julia Stackpole sat up. Its bloody head hung down, its frail arms flapping. The entire body appeared to be vibrating, and with a horrid disjointed motion, amid a swirling of papers and trash, it went rolling over and over and came to rest against a broken chair. Sara shrank back into a corner of the seat, her breath ragged and shallow. A thin cloud swept free of the moon and the light measurably brightened, making the gray of the houses seem gauzy and immaterial; the holes in their sides looked real enough—black, cavernous—as if the walls and doors and windows had only been a facade concealing emptiness.

Sally parked next to a boathouse a couple of hundred yards north of Smith Point: a rickety wooden structure the size of a garage. Beyond it a stretch of calm black water was figured by a blaze of moonlight. "You gonna have to row out to the boat," Sally told Peter. "Oars are in here." She unlocked the door and flicked on a light. The inside of the place was as dilapidated as Sally herself. Raw boards, spiderwebs spanning between paint cans and busted lobster traps; a jumble of two-by-fours. Sally went stumping around, mumbling and kicking things, searching for the oars; her footsteps set the light bulb dangling from the roof to swaying, and the light slopped back and forth over the walls like dirty yellow water. Sara's legs were leaden. It was hard to move, and she thought maybe this was because there weren't any moves left. Peter took a few steps toward the center of the boathouse and stopped, looking lost. His hands twitched at his sides. She had the idea that his expression mirrored her own: slack, spiritless, with bruised crescents under his eyes. She moved, then. The dam that had been holding back her emotions burst, and her arms were around him, and she was telling him that she couldn't let him go alone, telling him half-sentences, phrases that didn't connect.

"Sara," he said. "Jesus." He held her very tightly. The next second, though, she heard a dull *thonk* and he sagged against her, almost knocking her down, and slumped to the floor. Brandishing a two-by-four, Sally bent to him and struck again.

"What are you doing?" Sara screamed it and began to wrestle with Sally. Their arms locked, they waltzed around and around for a matter of seconds, the light bulb jiggling madly. Sally sputtered and fumed; spittle glistened on her lips. Finally, with a snarl, she shoved Sara away. Sara staggered back, tripped over Peter and fell sprawling beside him.

"Listen!" Sally cocked her head and pointed to the roof with the two-by-four. "Goddamn it! It's workin'!"

Sara came warily to her feet. "What are you talking about?"

Sally picked up her fisherman's hat, which had fallen off during the struggle, and squashed it down onto her head. "The wind, goddamn it! I told that stupid son of a bitch Hugh Weldon, but oh, no! He never listened to nobody."

The wind was rising and fading in volume, doing so with such a regular rhythm that Sara had the impression of a creature made of wind running frantically back and forth. Something splintered in the distance.

"I don't understand," said Sara.

"Unconscious is like dead to it," said Sally; she gestured at Peter with the board. "I knew it was so, 'cause after it did for Mills it came for me. It touched me up all over, and I could tell it'd have me, then. But that stupid bastard wouldn't listen. Had to do things his goddamn way!"

"It would have you?" Sara glanced down at Peter, who was unstirring, bleeding from the scalp. "You mean instead of Peter?"

"'Course that's what I mean." Sally frowned. "Don't make no sense him goin'. Young man with all his future ahead. Now me . . ." She yanked at the lapel of her raincoat as if intending to throw herself away. "What I got to lose? A coupla years of bein' alone. I ain't eager for it, y'understand. But it don't make sense any other way. Tried to tell Hugh that, but he was stuck on bein' a goddamn hero."

Her bird-bright eyes glittered in the webbed flesh, and Sara had a perception of her that she had not had since childhood: the zany old spirit, half-mad but with one eye fixed on some corner of creation that nobody else could see. She remembered all the stories. Sally trying to signal the moon with a hurricane lamp; Sally rowing through a nor'easter to pluck six sailors off Whale Shoals; Sally passing out dead-drunk at the ceremony the Coast Guard had given in her honor; Sally loosing her dogs on the then-junior senator from Massachusetts when he had come to present her a medal. Crazy Sally. She suddenly seemed valuable to Sara.

"You can't . . ." she began, but broke off and stared at Peter.

"Can't not," said Sally, and clucked her tongue. "You see somebody looks after my dogs."

Sara nodded.

"And you better check on Peter," said Sally. "See if I hit him too hard."

Sara started to comply but was struck by a thought. "Won't it know better this time? Peter was knocked out before. Won't it have learned?"

"I suppose it can learn," said Sally. "But it's real stupid, and I don't think it's figured this out." She gestured at Peter. "Go ahead. See if he's all right."

The hairs on Sara's neck prickled as she knelt beside Peter, and she was later to reflect that in the back of her mind she had known what was about to happen. But even so she was startled by the blow.

10

It wasn't until late the next afternoon that the doctors allowed Peter to have visitors other than the police. He was still suffering from dizziness and blurred vision, and mentally speaking he alternated between periods of relief and depression. Seeing in his mind's eye the mutilated bodies, the whirling black pillars. Tensing as the wind prowled along the hospital walls. In general he felt walled off from emotion, but when Sara came into the room those walls crumbled. He drew her down beside him and buried his face in her hair. They lay for a long time without speaking, and it was Sara who finally broke the silence.

"Do they believe you?" she asked. "I don't think they believe me."

"They don't have much choice," he said. "I just think they don't want to believe it."

After a moment she said, "Are you going away?"

He pulled back from her. She had never looked more beautiful. Her eyes were wide, her mouth drawn thin, and the strain of all that had happened to them seemed to have carved an unnecessary ounce of fullness from her face. "That depends on whether or not you'll go with me," he said. "I don't want to stay. Whenever the wind changes pitch every nerve in my body signals an air raid. But I won't leave you. I want to marry you."

Her reaction was not what he had expected. She closed her eyes and kissed him on the forehead—a motherly, understanding kiss; then she settled back on the pillow, gazing calmly at him.

"That was a proposal," he said. "Didn't you catch it?"

"Marriage?" She seemed perplexed by the idea.

"Why not? We're qualified." He grinned. "We both have concussions."

"I don't know," she said. "I love you, Peter, but . . ."

"But you don't trust me?"

"Maybe that's part of it," she said, annoyed. "I don't know."

"Look." He smoothed down her hair. "Do you know what really happened in the boathouse last night?"

"I'm not sure what you mean."

"I'll tell you. What happened was that an old woman gave her life so you and I could have a chance at something." She started to speak but he cut her off. "That's the bones of it. I admit the reality's a bit more murky. God knows why Sally did what she did. Maybe saving lives was a reflex of her madness, maybe she was tired of living. Maybe it just seemed a good idea at the time. And as for us, we haven't exactly been Romeo and Juliet. I've been confused, and I've confused you. And aside from whatever problems we might have as a couple, we have a lot to forget. Until you came in I was feeling shell-shocked, and that's a feeling that's probably going to last for a while. But like I said, the heart of the matter is that Sally died to give us a chance. No matter what her motives, what our circumstance, that's what happened. And we'd be fools to let that chance slip away." He traced the line of her cheekbone with a finger. "I love you. I've loved you for a long time and tried to deny it, to hold onto a dead issue. But that's all over."

"We can't make this sort of decision now," she murmured.

"Why not?"

"You said it yourself. You're shell-shocked. So am I. And I don't know how I feel about . . . everything."

"Everything? You mean me?"

She made a non-committal noise, closed her eyes, and after a moment she said, "I need time to think."

In Peter's experience when women said they needed time to think nothing good ever came of it. "Jesus!" he said angrily. "Is this how it has to be between people? One approaches, the other avoids, and then they switch roles. Like insects whose mating instincts have been screwed up by pollution." He registered what he had said and had a flash-feeling of horror. "Come on, Sara! We're past that kind of dance, aren't we? It doesn't have to be marriage, but let's commit to something. Maybe we'll make a mess of it, maybe we'll end up boring each other. But let's try. It might not be any effort at all." He put his arms around her, brought her tight against him, and was immersed in a cocoon of heat and weakness. He loved her, he realized, with an intensity that he had not believed he could recapture. His mouth had been smarter than his brain for once—either that or he had talked himself into it. The reasons didn't matter.

"For Christ's sake, Sara!" he said. "Marry me. Live with me. Do something with me!"

She was silent; her left hand moved gently over his hair. Light, distracted touches. Tucking a curl behind his ear, toying with his beard, smoothing his mustache. As if she were making him presentable. He remembered how that other long-ago woman had become increasingly silent and distracted and gentle in the days before she had dumped him.

"Damn it!" he said with a growing sense of helplessness. "Answer me!"

11

On the second night out 'Sconset Sally caught sight of a winking red light off her port bow. Some ship's riding light. It brought a tear to her eye, making her think of home. But she wiped the tear away with the back of her hand and had another slug of cherry brandy. The cramped wheelhouse of the lobster boat was cozy and relatively warm; beyond, the moonlit plain of the sea was rising in light swells. Even if you didn't have nowhere good to go, she thought, wheels and keels and wings gave a boost to your spirit. She laughed. Especially if you had a supply of cherry brandy. She had another slug. A breeze curled around her arm and tugged at the neck of the bottle. "Goddamn it!" she squawked. "Get away!" She batted at the air as if she could shoo away the elemental, and hugged the bottle to her breast. Wind uncoiled a length of rope on the deck behind her, and then she could hear it moaning about the hull. She staggered to the wheelhouse door. "Whoo-oo-ooh!" she sang, mocking it. "Don't be making your godawful noises at me, you sorry bastard! Go kill another goddamn fish if you want somethin' to do. Just leave me alone to my drinkin'."

Waves surged up on the port side. Big ones, like black teeth. Sally almost dropped the bottle in her surprise. Then she saw they weren't really waves but shapes of water made by the elemental. "You're losin' your touch, asshole!" she shouted. "I seen better'n that in the movies!" She slumped down beside the door, clutching the bottle. The word "movies" conjured flashes of old films she'd seen, and she started singing songs from them. She did "Singin' In The Rain" and "Blue Moon" and "Love Me Tender." She knocked back swallows of brandy in between the verses, and when she felt primed enough she launched into her favorite. "The sound that you hear," she bawled, "is the sound of Sally! A joy to be heard for a thousand years." She belched. "The hills are alive with the sound of Sally . . ." She couldn't recall the next line, and that ended the concert.

The wind built to a howl around her, and her thoughts sank into a place where there were only dim urges and nerves fizzling and blood whining in her ears. Gradually she surfaced from it and found that her mood had become one of regret. Not about anything specific. Just general regrets. General Regrets. She pictured him as an old fogey with a white walrus mustache and a Gilbert-and-Sullivan uniform. Epaulets the size of skateboards. She couldn't get the picture out of her head and she wondered if it stood for something important. If it did she couldn't make it come clear. Like that line of her favorite song, it had leaked out through one of her cracks. Life had leaked out the same way, and all she could remember of it was a muddle of lonely nights and sick dogs and scallop shells and half-drowned sailors. Nothing important sticking up from the muddle. No monument to accomplishment or romance. Hah! She'd never met the man who could do what men said they could. The most reasonable men she'd known were those shipwrecked sailors, and their eyes big and dark as if they'd seen into some terrible bottomland that had sheared away their pride and stupidity. Her mind began to whirl, trying to get a fix on life, to pin it down like a dead butterfly and know its patterns, and soon she realized that she was literally whirling. Slowly, but getting faster and faster. She hauled herself up and clung to the wheelhouse door and peered over the side. The lobster boat was spinning around and around on the lip of a bowl of black water several hundred yards across. A whirlpool. Moonlight struck a glaze down its slopes but didn't reach the bottom. Its roaring, heart-stopping power scared her, made her giddy and faint. But after a moment she banished fear. So this was death. It just opened up and swallowed you whole. All right. That was fine by her. She slumped against the wheelhouse and drank deeply of the cherry brandy, listening to the wind and the singing of her blood as she went down not giving a damn. It sure beat puking up life a gob at a time in some hospital room. She kept slurping away at the brandy, guzzling it, wanting to be as looped as possible when the time came. But the time didn't come, and before too long she noticed that the boat had stopped spinning. The wind had quieted and the sea was calm.

A breeze coiled about her neck, slithered down her breast and began curling around her legs, flipping the hem of her dress. "You bastard," she said suddenly, too drunk to move. The elemental swirled around her knees, belling the dress, and touched her between the legs. It tickled, and she swatted at it ineffectually, as if it were one of the dogs snooting at her. But a second later it prodded her there again, a little harder than before, rubbing back and forth, and she felt a quiver of arousal. It startled her so that she went rolling across the deck, somehow keeping her bottle upright. That quiver stuck with her, though, and for an instant a red craving dominated the broken mosaic of her thoughts. Cackling and scratching herself, she staggered to her feet and leaned on the rail. The elemental was about fifty yards off the port bow, shaping itself a waterspout, a moonstruck column of blackness, from the placid surface of the sea.

"Hey!" she shouted, wobbling along the rail. "You come on back here! *I'll* teach you a new trick!"

The waterspout grew higher, a glistening black serpent that *whooshed* and sucked the boat toward it; but it didn't bother Sally. A devilish joy was in her, and her mind crackled with lightnings of pure craziness. She thought she had figured out something. Maybe nobody had ever taken a real interest in the elemental, and maybe that was why it eventually lost interest in them. Wellsir! She had an interest in it. Damn thing couldn't be any more stupid than some of her Dobermans. Snooted like one, for sure. She'd teach it to roll over and beg and who knows what else. Fetch me that fish, she'd tell it. Blow me over to Hyannis and smash the liquor store window and bring me six bottles of brandy. She'd show it who was boss. And could be one day she'd sail into the harbor at Nantucket with the thing on a leash. 'Sconset Sally and her pet storm, Scourge of the Seven Seas.

The boat was beginning to tip and slew sideways in the pull of the waterspout, but Sally scarcely noticed. "Hey!" she shouted again, and chuckled. "Maybe we can work things out! Maybe we're meant for each other!" She tripped over a warp in the planking, and the arm holding the bottle flailed above her head. Moonlight seemed to stream down into the bottle, igniting the brandy so that it glowed like a magic elixir, a dark red ruby flashing in her hand. Her maniacal laugh went skyhigh.

"You come on back here!" she screeched at the elemental, exulting in the wild frequencies of her life, at the thought of herself in league with this idiot god, and unmindful of her true circumstance, of the thundering around her and the tiny boat slipping toward the foaming base of the waterspout. "Come back here, damn it! We're two of a kind! We're birds of a feather! I'll sing you to sleep each night! You'll serve me my supper! I'll be your old, cracked bride, and we'll have a hell of a honeymoon while it lasts!"

The Black Cat

EDGAR ALLAN POE

For the most wild yet most homely narrative which I am about to pen, I neither expect nor solicit belief. Mad indeed would I be to expect it, in a case where my very senses reject their own evidence. Yet, mad am I not—and very surely do I not dream. But to-morrow I die, and to-day I would unburthen my soul. My immediate purpose is to place before the world, plainly, succinctly, and without comment, a series of mere household events. In their consequences, these events have terrified—have tortured—have destroyed me. Yet I will not attempt to expound them. To me, they have presented little but horror—to many they will seem less terrible than *baroques*. Hereafter, perhaps, some intellect may be found which will reduce my phantasm to the common-place—some intellect more calm, more logical, and far less excitable than my own, which will perceive, in the circumstances I detail with awe, nothing more than an ordinary succession of very natural causes and effects.

From my infancy I was noted for the docility and humanity of my disposition. My tenderness of heart was even so conspicuous as to make me the jest of my companions. I was especially fond of animals, and was indulged by my parents with a great variety of pets. With these I spent most of my time, and never was so happy as when feeding and caressing them. This peculiarity of character grew with my growth, and, in my manhood, I derived from it one of my principal sources of pleasure. To those who have cherished an affection for a faithful and sagacious dog, I need hardly be at the trouble of explaining the nature or the intensity of the gratification thus derivable. There is something in the unselfish and self-sacrificing love of a brute, which goes directly to the heart of him who has had frequent occasion to test the paltry friendship and gossamer fidelity of mere *Man*.

I married early, and was happy to find in my wife a disposition not uncongenial with my own. Observing my partiality for domestic pets, she lost no opportunity of procuring those of the most agreeable kind. We had birds, gold fish, a fine dog, rabbits, a small monkey, and a *cat*.

This latter was a remarkably large and beautiful animal, entirely black, and sagacious to an astonishing degree. In speaking of his intelligence, my wife, who at heart was not a little tinctured with superstition, made frequent allusion to the ancient popular notion, which regarded all black cats as witches in disguise. Not that she was ever *serious* upon this point—and I mention the matter at all for no better reason than that it happens, just now, to be remembered.

Pluto—this was the cat's name—was my favorite pet and play-mate. I alone fed him, and he attended me wherever I went about the house. It was even with difficulty that I could prevent him from following me through the streets.

Our friendship lasted, in this manner, for several years, during which my general temperament and character—through the instru-mentality of the Fiend Intemperance—had (I blush to confess it) experienced a radical alteration for the worse. I grew, day by day, more moody, more irritable, more regardless of the feelings of others. I suffered myself to use intemperate language to my wife. At length, I even offered her personal violence. My pets, of course, were made to feel the change in my disposition. I not only neglected, but ill-used them. For Pluto, however, I still retained sufficient regard to restrain me from maltreating him, as I made no scruple of maltreating the rabbits, the monkey, or even the dog, when by accident, or through affection, they came in my way. But my disease grew upon me—for what disease is like Alcohol!—and at length even Pluto, who was now becoming old, and consequently somewhat peevish—even Pluto began to experience the effects of my ill temper.

One night, returning home, much intoxicated, from one of my haunts about town, I fancied that the cat avoided my presence. I seized him; when, in his fright at my violence, he inflicted a slight wound upon my hand with his teeth. The fury of a demon instantly possessed me. I knew myself no longer. My original soul seemed, at once, to take its flight from my body; and a more than fiendish malevolence, gin-nurtured, thrilled every fibre of my frame. I took from my waistcoat-pocket a penknife, opened it, grasped the poor beast by the throat, and deliberately cut one of its eyes from the socket! I blush, I burn, I shudder, while I pen the damnable atrocity.

When reason returned with the morning—when I had slept off the fumes of the night's debauch—I experienced a sentiment half of horror, half of remorse, for the crime of which I had been guilty; but it was, at best, a feeble and equivocal feeling, and the soul remained untouched. I again plunged into excess, and soon drowned in wine all memory of the deed.

In the meantime the cat slowly recovered. The socket of the lost eye presented, it is true, a frightful appearance, but he no longer appeared to suffer any pain. He went about the house as usual, but, as might be expected, fled in extreme terror at my approach. I had so much of my old heart left, as to be at first grieved by this evident dislike on the part of a creature which had once so loved me. But this feeling soon gave place to irritation. And then came, as if to my final and irrevocable overthrow, the spirt of Perverseness. Of this spirit philosophy takes no account. Yet I am not more sure that my soul lives, than I am that perverseness is one of the primitive impulses of the human heart—one of the indivisible primary faculties, or sentiments, which give direction to the character of Man. Who has not, a hundred times, found himself committing a vile or a silly action, for no other reason than because he knows he should *not*? Have we not a perpetual inclination, in the teeth of our best judgment, to violate that which is *Law*, merely because we understand it to be such? This spirit of perverseness, I say, came to my final overthrow. It was this unfathomable longing of the soul *to vex itself*—to offer violence to its own nature—to do wrong for the wrong's sake only—that urged me to continue and finally to consummate the injury I had inflicted upon the unoffending brute. One morning, in cool blood, I slipped a noose about its neck and hung it to the limb of a tree;—hung it with the tears streaming from my eyes, and with the bitterest remorse at my heart;—hung it *because* I knew that it had loved me, and *because* I felt it had given me no reason of offence;—hung it *because* I knew that in so doing I was committing a sin—a deadly sin that would so jeopardize my immortal soul as to place it—if such a thing were possible—even beyond the reach of the infinite mercy of the Most Merciful and Most Terrible God.

On the night of the day on which this cruel deed was done, I was aroused from sleep by the cry of fire. The curtains of my bed were in flames. The whole house was blazing. It was with great difficulty that my wife, a servant, and myself, made our escape from the conflagration. The destruction was complete. My entire worldly wealth was swallowed up, and I resigned myself thenceforward to despair.

I am above the weakness of seeking to establish a sequence of cause and effect, between the disaster and the atrocity. But I am detailing a chain of facts—and wish not to leave even a possible link imperfect. On the day succeeding the fire, I visited the ruins. The walls, with one exception, had fallen in. This exception was found in a compartment wall, not very thick, which stood about the middle of the house, and against which had rested the head of my bed. The plastering had here, in great measure, resisted the action of the fire— a fact which I attributed to its having been recently spread. About this wall a dense crowd were collected, and many persons seemed to be examining a particular portion of it with very minute and eager attention. The words "strange!" "singular!" and other similar expressions, excited my curiosity. I approached and saw, as if graven in *bas relief* upon the white surface, the figure of a gigantic *cat*. The impression was given with an accuracy truly marvellous. There was a rope about the animal's neck.

When I first beheld this apparition—for I could scarcely regard it as less—my wonder and my terror were extreme. But at length reflection came to my aid. The cat, I remembered, had been hung in a garden adjacent to the house. Upon the alarm of fire, this garden had been immediately filled by the crowd—by some one of whom the animal must have been cut from the tree and thrown, through an open window, into my chamber. This had probably been done with the view of arousing me from sleep. The falling of other walls had compressed the victim of my cruelty into the substance of the freshly-spread plaster; the lime of which, with the flames, and the *ammonia* from the carcass, had then accomplished the portraiture as I saw it.

Although I thus readily accounted to my reason, if not altogether to my conscience, for the startling fact just detailed, it did not the less fail to make a deep impression upon my fancy. For months I could not rid myself of the phantasm of the cat; and, during this period, there came back into my spirit a half-sentiment that seemed, but was not, remorse. I went so far as to regret the loss of the animal, and to look about me, among the vile haunts which I now habitually frequented, for another pet of the same species, and of somewhat similar appearance, with which to supply its place.

One night as I sat, half stupefied, in a den of more than infamy, my attention was suddenly drawn to some black object, reposing upon the head of one of the immense hogsheads of Gin, or of Rum, which constituted the chief furniture of the apartment. I had been looking steadily at the top of this hogshead for some minutes, and what now caused me surprise was the fact that I had not sooner perceived the object thereupon. I approached it, and touched it with my hand. It was a black cat—a very large one—fully as large as Pluto, and closely resembling him in every respect but one. Pluto had not a white hair upon any portion of his body; but this cat had a large, although indefinite splotch of white, covering nearly the whole region of the breast.

Upon my touching him, he immediately arose, purred loudly, rubbed against my hand, and appeared delighted with my notice. This, then, was the very creature of which I was in search. I at once offered to purchase it of the landlord; but this person made no claim to it—knew nothing of it—had never seen it before.

I continued my caresses, and, when I prepared to go home, the animal evinced a disposition to accompany me. I permitted it to do so; occasionally stooping and patting it as I proceeded. When it reached the house it domesticated itself at once, and became immediately a great favorite with my wife.

For my own part, I soon found a dislike to it arising within me. This was just the reverse of what I had anticipated; but I know not how or why it was—its evident fondness for myself rather disgusted and annoyed me. By slow degrees, these feelings of disgust and annoyance rose into the bitterness of hatred. I avoided the creature; a certain sense of shame, and the remembrance of my former deed of cruelty, preventing me from physically abusing it. I did not, for some weeks, strike, or otherwise violently ill use it; but gradually—very gradually—I came to look upon it with unutterable loathing, and to flee silently from its odious presence, as from the breath of a pestilence.

What added, no doubt, to my hatred of the beast, was the discovery, on the morning after I brought it home, that, like Pluto, it also had been deprived of one of its eyes. This circumstance, however, only endeared it to my wife, who, as I have already said, possessed, in a high degree, that humanity of feeling which had once been my distinguishing trait, and the source of many of my simplest and purest pleasures.

With my aversion to this cat, however, its partiality for myself seemed to increase. It followed my footsteps with a pertinacity which it would be difficult to make the reader comprehend. Whenever I sat, it would crouch beneath my chair, or spring upon my knees, covering me with its loathsome caresses. If I arose to walk it would get between my feet and thus nearly throw me down, or, fastening its long and sharp claws in my dress, clamber, in this manner, to my breast. At such times, although I longed to destroy it with a blow, I was yet withheld from so doing, partly by a memory of my former crime, but chiefly—let me confess it at once—by absolute *dread* of the beast.

This dread was not exactly a dread of physical evil—and yet I should be at a loss how otherwise to define it. I am almost ashamed to own—yes, even in this felon's cell, I am almost ashamed to own—that the terror and horror with which the animal inspired me, had been heightened by one of the merest chimæras it would be possible to conceive. My wife had called my attention, more than once, to the character of the mark of white hair, of which I have spoken, and which constituted the sole visible difference between the strange beast and the one I had destroyed. The reader will remember that this mark, although large, had been originally very indefinite; but, by slow degrees—degrees nearly imperceptible, and which for a long time my Reason struggled to reject as fanciful—it had, at length, assumed a rigorous distinctness of outline. It was now the representation of an object that I shudder to name—and for this, above all, I loathed, and dreaded, and would have rid myself of the monster *had I dared*—it was now, I say, the image of a hideous—of a ghastly thing—of the GALLOWS!—oh, mournful and terrible engine of Horror and of Crime—of Agony and of Death!

And now was I indeed wretched beyond the wretchedness of mere Humanity. And *a brute beast*—whose fellow I had contemptuously destroyed—*a brute beast* to work out for *me*—for me a man, fashioned in the image of the High God—so much of insufferable woe! Alas! neither by day nor by night knew I the blessing of Rest any more! During the former the creature left me no moment alone; and, in the latter, I started, hourly, from dreams of unutterable fear, to find the hot breath of *the thing* upon my face, and its vast weight—an incarnate Night-Mare that I had no power to shake off—incumbent eternally upon my *heart*!

Beneath the pressure of torments such as these, the feeble remnant of the good within me succumbed. Evil thoughts became my sole intimates—the darkest and most evil of thoughts. The moodiness of my usual temper increased to hatred of all things and of all mankind; while, from the sudden, frequent, and ungovernable outbursts of a fury to which I now blindly abandoned myself, my uncomplaining wife, alas! was the most usual and the most patient of sufferers.

One day she accompanied me, upon some household errand, into the cellar of the old building which our poverty compelled us to inhabit. The cat followed me down the steep stairs, and, nearly throwing me headlong, exasperated me to madness. Uplifting an axe, and forgetting, in my wrath, the childish dread which had hitherto stayed my hand, I aimed a blow at the animal which, of course, would have proved instantly fatal had it descended as I wished. But this blow was arrested by the hand of my wife. Goaded by the interference into a rage more than demoniacal, I withdrew my arm from her grasp and buried the axe in her brain. She fell dead upon the spot, without a groan.

This hideous murder accomplished, I set myself forthwith, and with entire deliberation, to the task of concealing the body. I knew that I could not remove it from the house, either by day or by night, without the risk of being observed by the neighbors. Many projects entered my mind. At one period I thought of cutting the corpse into minute fragments, and destroying them by fire. At another, I resolved to dig a grave for it in the floor of the cellar. Again, I deliberated about casting it in the well in the yard—about packing it in a box, as if merchandize, with the usual arrangements, and so getting a porter to take it from the house. Finally I hit upon what I considered a far better expedient than either of these. I determined to wall it up in the cellar—as the monks of the middle ages are recorded to have walled up their victims.

For a purpose such as this the cellar was well adapted. Its walls were loosely constructed, and had lately been plastered throughout with a rough plaster, which the dampness of the atmosphere had prevented from hardening. Moreover, in one of the walls was a projection, caused by a false chimney, or fireplace, that had been filled up and made to resemble the rest of the cellar. I made no doubt that I could readily displace the bricks at this point, insert the corpse, and wall the whole up as before, so that no eye could detect anything suspicious.

And in this calculation I was not deceived. By means of a crow-bar I easily dislodged the bricks, and, having carefully deposited the body against the inner wall, I propped it in that position, while, with little trouble, I re-laid the whole structure as it originally stood. Having procured mortar, sand, and hair, with every possible precaution, I prepared a plaster which could not be distinguished from the old, and with this I very carefully went over the new brick-work. When I had finished, I felt satisfied that all was right. The wall did not present the slightest appearance of having been disturbed. The rubbish on the floor was picked up with the minutest care. I looked around triumphantly, and said to myself—"Here at least, then, my labor has not been in vain."

My next step was to look for the beast which had been the cause of so much wretchedness; for I had, at length, firmly resolved to put it to death. Had I been able to meet with it, at the moment, there could have been no doubt of its fate; but it appeared that the crafty animal had been alarmed at the violence of my previous anger, and forebore to present itself in my present mood. It is impossible to describe, or to imagine, the deep, the blissful sense of relief which the absence of the detested creature occasioned in my bosom. It did not make its appearance during the night—and thus for one night at least, since its introduction into the house, I soundly and tranquilly slept; aye, *slept* even with the burden of murder upon my soul!

The second and the third day passed, and still my tormentor came not. Once again I breathed as a freeman. The monster, in terror, had fled the premises forever! I should behold it no more! My happiness was supreme! The guilt of my dark deed disturbed me but little. Some few inquiries had been made, but these had been readily answered. Even a search had been instituted—but of course nothing was to be discovered. I looked upon my future felicity as secured.

Upon the fourth day of the assassination, a party of the police came, very unexpectedly, into the house, and proceeded again to make rigorous investigation of the premises. Secure, however, in the inscrutability of my place of concealment, I felt no embarrassment whatever. The officers bade me accompany them in their search. They left no nook or corner unexplored. At length, for the third or fourth time, they descended into the cellar. I quivered not in a muscle. My heart beat calmly as that of one who slumbers in innocence. I walked the cellar from end to end. I folded my arms upon my bosom, and roamed easily to and fro. The police were thoroughly satisfied and prepared to depart. The glee at my heart was too strong to be restrained. I burned to say if but one word, by way of triumph, and to render doubly sure their assurance of my guiltlessness.

"Gentlemen," I said at last, as the party ascended the steps, "I delight to have allayed your suspicions. I wish you all health, and a little more courtesy. By the bye, gentlemen, this—this is a very well constructed house," (in the rabid desire to say something easily, I scarcely knew what I uttered at all),—"I may say an *excellently* well constructed house. These walls—are you going, gentlemen?—these walls are solidly put together"; and here, through the mere phrenzy of bravado, I rapped heavily, with a cane which I held in my hand, upon that very portion of the brick-work behind which stood the corpse of the wife of my bosom.

But may God shield and deliver me from the fangs of the Arch-Fiend! No sooner had the reverberation of my blows sunk into silence, than I was answered by a voice from within the tomb!—by a cry, at first muffled and broken, like the sobbing of a child, and then quickly swelling into one long, loud, and continuous scream, utterly anomalous and inhuman—a howl!—a wailing shriek, half of horror and half of triumph, such as might have arisen only out of hell, conjointly from the throats of the damned in their agony and of the demons that exult in the damnation.

Of my own thoughts it is folly to speak. Swooning, I staggered to the opposite wall. For one instant the party upon the stairs remained motionless, through extremity of terror and of awe. In the next, a dozen stout arms were toiling at the wall. It fell bodily. The corpse, already greatly decayed and clotted with gore, stood erect before the eyes of the spectators. Upon its head, with red extended mouth and solitary eye of fire, sat the hideous beast whose craft had seduced me into murder, and whose informing voice had consigned me to the hangman. I had walled the monster up within the tomb!

The Dive People

AVRAM DAVIDSON

Edward Peterson moved restlessly in the bed, troubled by bad dreams, fatigue, and swift-approaching wakefulness. His mind insisted on his recognizing certain things he would sooner forget: that he had left Jinny to take up with Bran and left Bran to take up with Pauli. And with this last of the names coming up bubble-like and bursting at the surface of his mind, his body straightened out with a single convulsive kick and all at once he was awake and sitting up, sweating and trembling and sickened with fright. He knew now what he had done. It was no dream after all.

What Peterson had done was to take the sharp knife in his hand, reach out for the soft throat of someone he knew well, and draw the knife across from ear to ear.

He knew that he had done this and that it was a hideous thing and that it could not be happening to him though he knew it was.

They had been living in a fetid tenement to the south of Cooper Union, not one that still had a faint flavor of an honored past, but one that had been built to be a tenement, a five-story hovel which could never attain to dignity if it endured a thousand years. Of course, it was a question now if it would endure a thousand days, if it would not collapse inside its own filthy integument before the cannibal city fell upon it and destroyed it.

"Chili con carne for supper," Pauli said. As if he couldn't smell it, along with every other meal ever cooked on that greasy stove. Peterson looked around the single room of the place, feeling his feet burning in the shoes, wondering vaguely where he could sit down. Even the broken chair was piled high—his old shirts, torn ones which the Chinese laundryman had said wouldn't process; Pauli was going to mend them so they could be washed and he could have some clean spares. She wouldn't wash them, no, but she would mend them. One of these days—As for the sofa, it had been weeks since that had been available for sitting.

Pauli passed into the kitchen, took the lid off the pot. He wrinkled his nose, opened his mouth. What was the use?

Q. That's not your chili con carne, is it?

A. Oh, you know mine is no good.

That was quite true. Nothing she cooked was any good, because she never took any pains. But bad as her chili was, it was still better than the horrid cheap stuff she got in cans; and he had told her so. Again and again and *again*. So why do it now? Once or twice he had asked, wearily, why she didn't just boil a pot of potatoes. "You can boil them in their jackets," he said, "you don't even have to peel them." And she said, Yes, but she'd have to wash them.

"Is there any vermouth, Pauli?"

"No. But that's all right, there's no gin, either."

"I've got a half pint here."

"Where can you get half pints of gin in New York State?"

"It's lemon-flavored—that makes it legal, for some ungodly reason. Mixer?"

"There's *nothing*. Except that Chianti."

"Gimme."

"Oh, Ed, it'll taste awful."

"Who the hell cares about the taste? Where's the Chianti?"

But, of course, she didn't know where it was, nor—once he'd found it (in the closet, concealed by a pile of her things so carelessly hung up that they'd fallen down)—did she know where there was a clean glass. It turned out that there wasn't any clean glass. He washed one and she appropriated it while he was opening the gin, so he washed another for himself.

The Chianti did taste awful.

He had been on his feet all that afternoon, saving taxifare, delivery service, postage, literary agent's fees. At least he *said* he was saving the agent's ten per cent, but he knew he'd simply run through all the worthwhile literary agents in town and there was no one left who would advance him a cent until he paid back all the advances of the past year and a half. And one, Tom Thompson, wanted to know when Ed was "going to show some signs of straightening himself out." As if the mere fact that Ed was on his feet, seeing people, writing again—as if that wasn't the best sign of all that he had straightened himself out.

As compared to the too-long stretch when he was rarely sober, dunning for advances or loans and, when not getting them, living on Pauli's meager alimony. That is, not exactly alimony: a sum of money sent regularly by a Petty Officer Second Class who believed he was the father of Pauli's little girl. Pauli, who knew better, had told her mother she'd been married to the sailor, and had sent the kid to her.

And then, even harder to bear—because it was so near the truth—the agent said, "I don't call *this* writing, Ed. It's a scissors and paste job. They all are. What you've got here, you're cannibalizing your old material. No good market would take it, and I don't bother with the others."

Well, so the hell with Tom Thompson.

The whole afternoon had resulted only in a $30 sale to that crook, Joe Mulgar, who gave $5 in cash and the promise to pay the rest sometime after publication. Hence the pint of gin (lemon-flavored). The piece had netted Ed $300 the first time he sold it, five years ago.

Five years ago was just before he had married Jinny. Had he started his drinking and loafing and playing around because Jinny was the way she was, or was Jinny the way she was because of his drinking and loafing and carrying on? It was hard to say; Ed just didn't know. She had never cheated, like Lynn (Lynn was before Jinny), he was sure of that. Nor would she ever fight back the way Bran had, nor yield the way Pauli yielded. Jinny had always stayed so calm and cool. It was infuriating. She never tried to conquer him, she never even tried to conquer him.

"I'm leaving." That was all he had said to Jinny.

"I'll be here when you come back." That was all Jinny had said. Not even "if." "When." Well, he never would go back. Why had she said it? What did she want with him, if she could go on without him? Pauli, with all her faults—

Pauli!

Ed swung his feet over the side of the bed, cracking his heels on the floor. It wasn't a bed, actually but a pad, a mattress set up on box springs. He'd been on and off a thousand of them. Only it had been a regular bed, not a pad, in their apartment.

And now he realized that he'd known from the first moment of his awakening that he wasn't in their apartment. His eyes hurt and his head throbbed and he felt his heart beating in terror. Beside the pad was an up-ended orange crate, its top encrusted with dirty cigarette butts. The pad was in an alcove blocked off by a torn screen, and somewhere someone was taking a shower and whistling off-key. On the floor alongside was a pile of clothes. His.

Hangovers are funny only to those who have never really suffered from them. As he bent, half fainting, half retching, over his clothes, it was nothing so slight as a splitting headache that Ed Peterson felt, but a condition in which every cell in his body seemed at war with every other cell, and all his parts seemed loathsome to him. Closing his eyes, feeling that they would otherwise burst from their sockets, he got into his clothes. He had to get out of the apartment before whoever-it-was got out of the shower.

He had killed a human being—instinctively he raised his hands: there was no blood, unless that dark whatever-it-was, half on and half under the rough loose cuticle of one finger . . . And on his clothes? Was that spot there—and the one next to it—were they blood? Or the Chianti of the night before? Ed didn't know. He had no memory of the latter part of last evening.

In the subway station, sitting on the hard wooden bench (first he'd tried to thrust a nickel into the turnstile, then—recalling vaguely that the fare had been raised—he had found a dime and pressed that into the slot, and finally took both coins to the change booth and been given a token) he remembered that he did not even recall the location of the house he had just left. So far as he knew, he had never been in the place before, but he knew well enough what sort of a place it was: a dive.

Who was it that had been so scornful of "dive people"? Jinny? No, Jinny was never scornful of anyone—at least, not openly. Pauli? (Ah, God, Pauli!) They had met in a dive—"Riverside Dive" it had been called—a huge apartment tenanted jointly (or so it seemed) by several hundred harmless young men, mostly science-fiction fans, with half a dozen bathrooms and two score beds.

Yes, Pauli, curling her over-red lips and saying, "*Dive* people!" Pauli. Few of the dives, to be sure, were on the level of the one overlooking the River. Some were converted (or unconverted) lofts, some out-and-out slums; some made a faltering effort at achieving the more abundant life via the co-op method, with typewritten menus and duty rosters on the kitchen bulletin board (*WEDNESDAY: Breakfast: Doreen and Jack. Cleanup: Dickie*), and a membership of students or artists or other pursuers of beautiful dreams. And other dives were sort of pipeless opium dens, not—to be sure—scenes of orgies, but places for the restless and roaming to fall back on for a pad and a pancake if there weren't any orgies going for the moment. But they all had something in common—the same air of insubstantiality, of wary waitfulness, the presence of those who had turned their backs upon the past and their faces half away from the future— the unsuccessfully educated, the believers in nothing . . .

Not even looking to see where the train was going, Ed crept in and sank down in a corner. The man nearest him finished his *Daily News* and tossed it on the seat, thus by subway law making it public domain; Ed picked it up. Gory auto wreck on page one, European infamy on page two, society scandal on page three, page four the latest teenage gang fight, page five and further on the "news" dwindled to tiny paragraphs buried in advertising and syndication. Nothing there that meant anything to him. It was a late edition. If the body hadn't been found by press time it couldn't be in any well-frequented place. Or—was it true that the police sometimes didn't announce the finding right away? Waiting for the killer to—

To what? *What* killer? Edward Peterson? Absurd, he was no killer. He'd been no cuckold, either, but he had been cuckolded nonetheless by Lynn, his wife-before-Jinny. Strange, it hadn't occurred to him to kill then, although custom almost licensed it. Why had he killed this time?

The empty space next to him was suddenly filled and a pamphlet was thrust into his slack hands. "Brother, you look like an intelligent man," said a stranger (who didn't) to him. "Leave me tell you of something which you won't find it in no newspapers. Booze they'll advertise, yes, and filthy tobacco, and motion pitchers dealing with murder, sex, and other dreadful subjecks; the churches are all a them c'rupt, brother—" Ed got up abruptly and walked into the next car.

Booze . . . murder, sex . . . corrupt . . . He and Pauli had finished the gin and this had loosened her sufficiently to admit she had some money stashed away somewhere (but none of it had been forthcoming for him when he had set out on his rounds earlier in the day) and they had bought some more liquor and listened to the radio and smoked and talked and danced a while . . . nothing that should have ended in murder. But then nothing should ever end in murder . . . He leaned his head on his arm and tried to think. What had happened after that?

They had danced . . . had they gone out anywhere? Bought more to drink? He couldn't think. All that came to him was the sound of her breathing in the dark. He felt the softness of her throat, felt the pulse beating, took up the sharp knife—

The knife! *What* knife? Where had he found it? There wasn't a sharp knife in the apartment; bread came ready-sliced and they ate so much out of cans that only seldom did the lack of a knife occur to them, and nothing was ever done about it. Had he picked up a sharp knife somewhere else? Had they wound up in someone else's place? If the last, it must have been an apartment where the regular tenants were away, or—No, it didn't follow. The regular tenant (he? she? they?) may have gone out, leaving them to sleep. That would mean a separate room. And whom did they know well enough to descend on suddenly—people who had a separate room? Could there have been another room, temporarily vacant, in the dive in which he'd awakened? A dive with which Pauli was familiar and he was not? Would he have gone to sleep in the same place he'd committed murder? If he was drunk enough to kill—

The train stopped more abruptly than usual. 86th Street. Automatically he got off, then tried to remember why. Who lived near this station? There was only one person near here they knew. Margaret Thorpe. Massive Maggie, with her short-cut hair and her tailored suits and (it was said, but not to her face, her rack of briar pipes and her bar-bells). *She* had a guest room; they might have come up to *her* place, because Mag was known to be a good supplier of whiskey . . . Halfway up the stairs out of the station, Ed stopped. Yes, and suppose they *had* gone there? And suppose it *had* happened there?

Should he call Maggie and try to read her voice for guarded nuances, try to discern the men in uniform, the men in plain clothes, behind the subdued roughness of her voice? No, he didn't dare, any more than he dared return to their own apartment. Because if he did—and if he did find Pauli there on the bed with her throat cut from ear to ear—he knew he would run out, screaming his terror aloud.

What would he do then? Run for it? Where? And with what?

Still standing on the subway steps, he groped in his pockets. Two one-dollar bills and some change. He might run as far as East Orange on that. The only thing to do was for the condemned man to eat a hearty breakfast and then seek out the executioners.

Ed Peterson started up the steps.

Why had he done it?

Q. Why did you murder her?

A. I don't know.

Q. You must have had some reason.

A. Each man kills the thing he loves.

Q. But, did you really love her?

A. Yes—I—no. No, I hated her. She was a slut and a slattern and the misery of my daily life and I now see that I blamed her for all my misery.

Q. Why was that?

A. If she had given me the right kind of love I might have been strong enough, instead of weak.

Q. Where did you run to while I was taking a shower?

What? "Yes, you, Ed—snap out of the daydream! I came out of the shower and no Ed. Why—"

Somewhere, he knew, he had met the young man in the open shirt, some time before last night (and when and where last night? and why the invitation to skip out in the dive?) he had met this young man with the bulldog pipe.

"Well, never mind," said Bulldog, "Where are you headed for? The Great Dicie Taylor Exhibit, I suppose." And not waiting for an answer, (after a ritual gurgle of his pipe) he swept on. "Yep, Dicie's Mama has come out of the West and is treating Daughter to an art show as an act of contrition for not wanting her to leave La Harpe, Illinois. Everybody's there! And why not? Free drinks, free eats—oh, Mama's doing it up in real style—who knows how many years' interest on corn-and-hog mortgages are going into this show? Come on, let's fly!" He had taken Ed by the arm.

Where had he met Bulldog? At what coffee-and-crackers fest in Chelsea? Or in what *casa de cappucino* in the Village? Perhaps in another dive than the one he had awakened in, or at some antic conventicle of the Libertarian League, perhaps in cruising for women between Bran and Pauli, not caring in the least if the state never withered away . . . Now he felt weak and hungry; thirsty, too. Food and drink, yes . . .

He had let Bulldog pull him along without protest or comment.

The din and smoke finally made an impression on him after a few canapés and a few drinks. If he turned his head he might see Dicie Taylor (whoever *she* was) and her American Gothic mother, but he had no interest in doing so. He stood there, gazing with a dull look at a green nude in whose pelvic structure lay strange mysteries, though of real interest only to an anatomist. And then he heard a laugh—

"Ah, Pauli, Pauli," said a deep, male voice. Slowly, very slowly, Ed Peterson turned his head. There was Pauli, holding hands with a giant of a young man: fresh country face and coal-black hair. She saw Ed and raised her eyebrows.

"Well, I don't know where *you* went after we parted last night. *I* went up to Massive Maggie's—and guess who I met coming in, lives in the same house? Freddy, here. Never did get to Maggie's," she murmured; and then, as if anything were needed to make her meaning clear, she lifted her new friend's huge hand to her over-red lips and kissed it. Freddy, with an air of awkward ceremony, brushed his mouth against her hair, looking at Peterson with a mixture of wariness, defiance, excitement, and delight.

The smoke grew into a mist and the din to a roar. Then all came into focus again. It *had* only been a drunken dream, a nightmare out of Poe!

"I'm glad, Pauli!" Ed had said, and he had meant it.

"That's not very gallant of you," she pouted. "But thanks for not making any fuss. Of course, you know the apartment's in *my* name . . ."

"That's all right."

She frowned slightly. "But where will you go?"

For only a breath he hesitated. "Why, I think I'll go back to Jinny," he had said.

"Jinny? Well—yes, she said she'd be waiting for you, didn't she?"

Freddy, determined to do the right thing but wanting at the same time to make the new *status* definitely *quo*, said, "Have a drink before you leave."

"Thanks, but I don't think I'll have any more." No more boozing, no more catting, no more scissors-and-paste. An end to decay and dishonor!

She blew him a kiss. "Bye-bye."

All but singing aloud, he left the gallery on dancing feet and hailed a taxi to take him to his wife—to his faithful, patient wife, his only love. He gave all the money to the driver and ran into the outer hall, his finger finding the bell at once, his ear rejoicing in the sound of the buzzer. An elderly woman came down the hall, known to him by sight only, a tenant of the building; and she stopped short as Ed Peterson stepped into the elevator.

They were there in the apartment, waiting for him, not excited but mildly expectant, mildly gratified. "Here's Mr. Peterson now," one of them said. And took him by the arm a trifle diffidently and led him to the bedroom where Jinny was waiting for him as she had promised, calm and cool as always, lying on the bed with her throat cut from ear to ear.

Graffiti

STANLEY ELLIN

Up to that exchange with Veszto in the Faculty Club dining room, Halas had never really given much thought to the subject of graffiti. After all, these testimonies to marker-pens and spray-can paints smeared over walls, monuments, buses, subway cars—especially those subway cars—were a fact of life in New York City. A bit of an eyesore perhaps, but one easily outweighed by all the glories of this spectacular city itself. Halas, who knew a good many of the world's cities at first hand, adored New York City.

Of course, to give Veszto his due in that heated exchange at lunch, the man obviously could not help having been born a cheapskate, *ein Geizhals, un avare*—observe there the root of "avaricious"—so the knowledge that those graffiti recently applied to the hood of his almost brand-new Buick could only be erased at great expense had to strike him through the heart like a javelin. And, of course, by some regrettable genetic twist, he was one of your darkly brooding Hungarians with no capacity to take life's little jokes with a touch of humor, no *joie de vivre* in him at all. In spirit at least, thought Halas, who overflowed with *joie de vivre*, the man was hardly what you could even call a Hungarian.

And getting down to the nitty-gritty, Veszto was afflicted with a consuming envy. Granted that he was a brilliant physicist, a consultant in the national space program, a full professor at the university which, as it added more and more to its vast properties around Washington Square, was also moved to lure to its roster such shining stars as this Doctor Bela Veszto.

But, as sourpuss Veszto was well aware, where he was a star in this firmament Janos Halas was undeniably a superstar. Janos Halas himself, that mesmerizing savant, lecturer, author, that master of comparative philology, who almost singlehanded had overturned clumsy Nineteenth Century German scholarship in philology and had come up with the common basis of all human language. The Halas Linguistics, no less.

No mere professor either, but Distinguished Professor of Linguistics, with a secretary and an office for life.

Oh, yes. Enter any academic gathering in the world, never mind how prestigious its attenders, and observe that when Doctor Janos Halas was announced he was the one they all craned their heads to see, the one they all murmured over in awe. A pet of *The New York Times* itself, judging from the amount of print it now and again bestowed on him.

An especially bitter pill for that viperish cheapskate Veszto to swallow every time it happened. Viperish in his insults, calculatingly cheap in the way he had wrathfully stalked out of the dining room overlooking his bill for lunch—what a convenient oversight—thus sticking Halas with the bill.

"Sick with envy," Halas told his wise and wonderful Klara that evening, recounting the tale of the stormy lunch. "But this time he was at his absolute worst. Do you know what he had the temerity to say to my face?"

"What?" asked Klara, who, after thirty years of marriage to her adored Janos, was well rehearsed in her lines.

"That my opinion on any subject is irrelevant, because I am not a scientist but a fantasist. Because linguistics is not a science but only a stewpot of unverifiable theories."

"And then?"

"And then I pointed out to him that my flawless mastery of two dozen languages certainly suggested more than a talent for cooking up unverifiable theories and he said yes, it did suggest I might do very well teaching at Berlitz."

"And all this because of the graffiti?" said Klara.

"Because I didn't sympathize with him in his agony over that miserable automobile. You should have heard him carry on about the horrors of this city. Obviously, it is an abomination operated only for the benefit of *Lumpenproletariat* who go around marking up people's Buicks. So much for the most magnificent metropolis ever conceived by flawed humanity. In my judgment, a real worm's-eye view of it."

"And naturally you presented this judgment to him."

"Naturally."

Klara sighed. "Janos, why do you sit with him at lunch? There are other tables in that dining room, aren't there?"

"Why?" said Halas. "But, darling, Bela Veszto is my oldest friend. You know we played together in the streets of Budapest as children. That he was my schoolmate in the university at Prague. And if he's envious of me to the point of sometimes being insulting—"

"Yes?"

"Well, I can't be small-minded. I understand his feelings, and I forgive him for them."

No need to mention then and there that Veszto would have to suffer a little for venting those feelings so nastily. Would have to be stirred up a little by some mischievous baiting before the sun had set again.

So Halas was in a benignly mischievous mood when he left the house next morning to walk the mile downtown to the university. The October weather was crisp and clear; nowhere in the world was there more satisfying, more inspiring weather than this marvelous city offered during autumn. And the street itself made a pleasant prospect, a tree-shaded street in the East Thirties—the Murray Hill section—with facing rows of handsome old brownstones and graystones. The Halas residence was a four-storied graystone, one of the perquisites the grateful university, its owner, had provided at a nominal rental, and it offered all that could be desired for civilized living.

Which, come to think of it, was something that dried-up Veszto refused to appreciate. The joy of strolling among the endless variety of humanity in these streets. Of savoring the theaters, the concert halls, the museums and galleries, the exotic restaurants laid on in such profusion for the truly civilized. All wasted on a Veszto who fled the city in panic at every opportunity to take solitary refuge in his rustic hideout in Connecticut where he could sit and watch the grass grow. A scientist? A monk who had found the wrong vocation, that's what he was.

Well, that misplaced monk would have an interesting time of it at lunch today.

Graffiti, of all things. How the devil could anyone get so emotional about it?

Halas, about to cross the street, stopped short. Then he changed course and headed for the subway station on Park Avenue.

He let a couple of trains go by while he strolled the length of the platform studying the marker-pen and spray-can work adorning its walls. He missed another, so caught up was he by his examination of its gaudily spray-painted exterior as it unloaded and loaded passengers. Interesting. Really interesting. As any subject was when one put his mind to it. And the interior of the car he finally did enter was most rewarding of all, its walls, ceilings, even windows so thick with glossy black, illegible marker-pen messages that it made for an almost dizzying effect.

Dizzying. And inspiring.

In his office, at ease behind his desk, Halas considered how best to apply this inspiration to the forthcoming lunch. Across the room, Mrs. Gerard, his appointed secretary, attended to his mail, which arrived each morning by the bushel. It was her job to answer whatever of it she could and to then deliver the remainder to Klara who, in her study next to his on the third floor of the graystone, not only dealt with it, but copyread his manuscripts, saw to his accounts, arranged his travel itineraries, and kept house, contracting for whatever help was needed. The perfect wife. Not that she would altogether approve the entertainment he planned for Veszto. She had this unfortunate instinct for peacemaking. And if, God forbid, that instinct ever became prevalent among mankind, what a dreary world this would be.

At lunchtime, Halas delayed his arrival in the dining room so that Veszto would already be at the table and in no position to avoid unwanted company. Sure enough, there was Veszto well into his bargain-basement entrée—he always ordered the lowest-priced item on the menu—and, happy sight, there was Weissenfels of the psychology department deep in conversation with him. For all his many honors, Weissenfels remained *echt* Viennese, a roly-poly little man with deceptively innocent eyes behind those thick glasses and with a fondness for a good joke. His presence here and now, Halas felt, could only have been provided by a kindly and approving heaven.

Weissenfels greeted Halas warmly. Veszto looked for an instant as if he were ready to pack it in on the spot, but most likely because this would mean a waste of good money he decided to remain where he was, finishing his meal in stony silence. Weissenfels took all this in at a glance and, without actually doing so, gave the impression that he was settling back to enjoy whatever was forthcoming. Unlike dear Klara, Weissenfels had no unhealthy peacemaking instinct.

Halas concentrated on his menu, ordered luxuriously, then turned to Weissenfels. "My old friend Bela and I had a little contretemps yesterday. You see, his car—"

"Yes," said Weissenfels. "He was telling me about the car. And the contretemps."

"Then will you kindly inform him now that I regret the episode? That I apologize for what I had to say and the way I said it?"

Weissenfels looked disappointed that the curtain was apparently coming down before the action on stage had even warmed up. He said to Veszto, "You heard that, of course?"

"Heard it," said Veszto coldly, "and don't believe a word of it."

"In that case," Halas told him, "I withdraw the apology."

Veszto's lip curled. "That's more like it."

"At the same time, Bela," Halas said with intense sincerity, "get it into that thick head that I am truly grateful to you. Yesterday, without intending to, you led me to an absolute revelation. One of the most amazing insights into linguistics that anyone has ever known. And no matter what you think of it, linguistics does happen to be my discipline, my life's work, my *raison d'être*."

Veszto frowned. "What the devil are you talking about?"

"What do you think?" Halas said impatiently. "Graffiti, my friend. Graffiti. The subject you got into such a sweat about yesterday."

"Ah, yes. Your favorite art form."

"Art? Art has nothing to do with it, Bela. Those spray-can decorations I've been examining are an offense to the eye."

Veszto raised an eyebrow. "Oh?"

"I acknowledge it. Idiot swoops and swirls in the most atrocious colors. Infantile, electronic-age Art Nouveau. Pathetic."

Weissenfels regarded Halas with honest curiosity. "You mean you've been studying graffiti? Seriously?"

Halas turned to him and gave him a broad and meaningful wink. "Very seriously, Doctor. Last evening and this morning. In subway cars."

Weissenfels caught on at once. He managed to conceal a smile. "That's the place for it," he said.

"It is. And let us dismiss that spray-can foolishness. Forget it. But"—Halas held up a commanding forefinger—"in the marker-pen script we have a different story. A most meaningful and exciting one."

Weissenfels, definitely sent by heaven, put on an expression of intense interest. Veszto glowered.

"Script?" he snarled. "You call those scrawls by some slobbering vandal a script?"

"Yes, Bela. And the marvelous discovery I made by close examination—the discovery I owe to you—is that this script appears to be the simulation of a written language. Try to read it, and you find you can't. Those dashing loops and lines seem meaningless."

Veszto snorted. "And have you considered," he demanded scathingly, "that this is because they are the hopeless efforts of illiterates to shape letters they can vaguely recognize but cannot duplicate?"

"That was my original hypothesis, Bela. It doesn't hold water."

"Nonsense."

"Bela," Halas said in a tone of stern reproof, "keep in mind that you're in my province now. My department. I don't give you lessons in physics. Please do not give me lessons in linguistics."

"I see. And graffiti is now in that department?"

"It well may be. Now try to keep an open mind while I explain." Halas pressed his hand to his chest. "Will you do me that small favor?"

Veszto shrugged broadly. "Sure. Go right ahead, maestro. Consider my mind wide open." He returned to the chicken leg on his plate, carefully prying off the last bits of meat from it with his knife.

Halas leaned forward and lowered his voice. "Very well, now listen carefully. Those apparently meaningless scrawls are not meaningless. I traveled a considerable distance back and forth examining samples of them closely. It suddenly struck me, Bela—a veritable thunderclap—that I was looking at a fine and flowing calligraphy, highly sophisticated, with breaks and rhythms indicating that what we had here was an authentic language."

Veszto's fork, on its way to his mouth, remained poised in the air. "A language? What language?"

The waitress brought Halas his soup and Weissenfels his coffee. Halas dipped into the soup, grateful for the chance to recharge imagination. A fantasist, was he? All right, Bela, let's see just how good a fantasist. He shook his head at Veszto. "At this point, my dear Bela, a language unknown to me. Incomprehensible to me."

"Oh? Well, in that case, my dear Janos—"

"No, no. Think, Bela, think. No matter how incomprehensible a script may be to you—Chinese, Arabic, Cyrillic, whatever—when you see it you know it represents a language, don't you?"

"Well—"

"For that matter, if you, as a superb physicist, are faced by some mathematical formula which uses totally unfamiliar symbols, you would still know at once that this is a mathematical formula. Admit it."

"Well, yes," Veszto said unwillingly, "but—" and then seemed lost in troubled thought. Ready to sound the retreat, Halas surmised. Beautiful. The danger now was that Weissenfels, his round face unnaturally scarlet, was obviously struggling against open laughter. Halas narrowed his eyes at him warningly and returned to the shaken Veszto.

"Those graffiti are a language, Bela. In fact, tomorrow I am taking my camera into the subway—"

"Wait, Janos. A language? A sophisticated calligraphy? Produced by juvenile delinquents?"

"Of course not. I told you to forget that element with their spray-cans of disgusting colors. I am talking about a different element entirely. One capable of writing those lines of script. Of communicating with each other through those lines." He shrugged regretfully. "One would like to think that those are passages of magnificent poetry, but that would be, well, an indulgence in fantasy. No, I must accept the cold reality that those are probably messages."

"Messages," Veszto echoed.

"Yes, Bela. And unpleasant messages at that. You know how often you've catalogued for me the disasters that afflict this city. Those wildfires devastating whole blocks. Floodwaters suddenly erupting from broken pipes under the pavements. Cornices of buildings suddenly tumbling on people's heads. God knows how many other calamities each day. And my response to you, my dismissal of all this, was wrong, Bela. Unjust. Unscientific. Because the evidence now in hand convinces me that these endless disasters are no accidents."

"The evidence." Veszto squinted at Halas's solemn face. "Those lines of graffiti?"

"Exactly. Messages, plans, instructions exchanged by an invisible force among us conspiring to destroy this city by first destroying its population's morale. Agents of some galactic power out there whose designated prey we are. You see, Bela—"

Weissenfels could contain himself no longer. He sputtered help-lessly, choking with laughter, pounding a fist on the table. Veszto gaped at him, then suddenly released from the spell, he glared at Halas. "Buffoon!"

"Now, Bela—"

"*Szamár!*" snarled Veszto, his face drained of all color. "*Disznó!*" He stood up so violently that his chair almost went over backwards. Every face in the dining room turned his way as he plunged through the door. Then, as Halas glanced around, eyebrows raised, all faces politely turned away. And, Halas saw, there on the table was Veszto's lunch bill. So he had gotten away with it again, bad temper evidently becoming a profitable way of life. Halas picked up the bill, but Weissenfels, now under fair control, plucked it from his hand.

"No, I insist," Weissenfels said. He wiped the tears of mirth from his eyes. "I owe you this much at least for the entertainment. But you know, of course, that you really are a monster."

"Am I? Well, answer this question, Doctor. Did our friend ever inform you that your discipline—the field of psychology—was nonsense? That you yourself were no scientist at all but a spinner of fantastic and unprovable theories?"

"As a matter of fact, yes. But since he also charged Freud, Jung, and Adler with the same sin, I couldn't be too offended."

"Very generous of you."

"And very politic. After all, I work with him on the Faculty Coordinating Committee, and he could make life there difficult. Which," said Weissenfels, "reminds me that the committee meets tomorrow morning. I have a feeling a little soothing syrup in advance is prescribed. Too bad. I'd love to tell this story around, but he'd be let to know at once who it came from." Weissenfels shook his head in wonder. "Oh, Lord. Invisible invaders from outer space. Astral linguistics. And the way he sat there with his mouth open—"

"Being spoonfed the fantasy he so detests—"

"Yes, indeed. Of course," said Weissenfels, straight-faced, "I can only hope it is fantasy, Doctor. Otherwise, you must realize the dreadful danger you're in. I mean, once those invaders know you're onto their precious secret—"

"And shared it with you and our humorless colleague—"

"True. That makes three of us. Well, I suppose all we can do is bear up bravely under the strain."

"I'm sure we'll manage to," said Halas.

That evening, despite a powerful temptation to do so, he refrained from telling dear Klara about his triumph. He had the feeling that this time—especially since an outsider had witnessed the scene—he might have gone a bit too far in his teasing, and if he had that feeling Klara would have it even more acutely. She, angelic but deluded creature, somehow managed to find Bela Veszto pathetic. So next thing—it had happened before—there might be a surprise dinner party announced, a large and extravagant peacemaking dinner party, at which Doctor Bela Veszto would turn up as one of the guests and would sit there stuffing himself with expensive viands and treating his host, who had paid for them, with icy indifference.

And yet, what good friend had advised Veszto not to park that car on the streets overnight but to rent space in a garage, never mind the expense? Naturally, none other than the foresighted Janos Halas.

And how had Veszto responded to this wisdom? "But how generous you are with other people's money, aren't you, Halas?"

The devil with him. This time there would be no peacemaking dinner party, because Klara was not going to be given any reason for one.

Case closed.

So when Klara, with unclouded brow and affectionate good humor, woke him next morning he felt distinctly pleased with himself that he had not confided in her, had exercised an almost noble self-restraint. And, thought Halas, since there's no sense depending on virtue to be its own reward, he'd make sure of that reward tonight by taking himself and Klara to a supremely good restaurant for dinner and then to a show. Something frivolous.

Altogether a promising day. The weather was again crisp and clear, the seminar scheduled for the afternoon would bring around the table a dozen of his most fervent acolytes—including two of the prettiest graduate students in the university—and then would come that gormandizing dinner and a lighthearted entertainment. Altogether promising.

Until, after bidding dear Klara a loving farewell, he stepped through the outside door of the house and closed it behind him.

Graffiti.

Disgusting glossy black scrawls made by marker-pen fouling the stone wall beside the door. Several feet of that hitherto pristine gray wall—a lovely soft-toned Wedgwood gray—defaced by those loops and lines and cross-strokes. Halas backed up to get the whole view, and indeed the further he backed up, the more horrid the view. He took notice that people walking by glanced at it with distaste. An aristocratic-looking woman with a small aristocratic-looking dog on a leash slowed down to shake her head at the sight. It was that kind of block, after all.

Halas looked up and down the street. As far as he could see, it was still that kind of block, no trace of any such vandalism marring any other building in sight. Only this one. As if the home of Doctor Janos Halas had been singled out for desecration by some drooling delinquent.

Singled out?

But, of course, thought Halas, stunned by sudden enlightenment. And if he had gone a little too far in his teasing of Veszto, well, dear Bela had gone the whole distance in this vindictive and sophomoric response. On the other hand, it did make a comic picture: a man of Veszto's years and academic stature prowling around in the dark hours to filthy this wall. And probably foaming at the mouth with rage as he did so.

And the sweetest revenge now, Halas told himself, would be to react as Veszto would never expect him to. Overlook all this. Be blind to it. The wall should be promptly cleaned—it was just a matter of phoning Mrs. Gerard, the faithful secretary, to have the university put a maintenance man on it—and then, when meeting Veszto, to wear a bland and untroubled face. Make no complaint, no accusation, don't mention this business at all, it never happened. While all Veszto could do was grind his teeth in frustration.

Dear Bela. Some people never learned not to play games with really clever opponents.

Halas walked back into the house, and from high above Klara called, "Janos? Did you forget something?"

"Just a phone call, darling."

Not bothering to take off hat or coat, Halas used the phone in the hallway near the foot of the staircase. Mrs. Gerard, who was rarely made breathless by anything, answered his greeting breathlessly.

"Yes, Doctor. I was expecting you'd call as soon as you heard. Isn't it awful? I was just talking to Doctor Weissenfels's assistant, and he practically—"

"Mrs. Gerard?"

"Yes, Doctor?"

"What the devil is this all about?"

"Then you don't know? Oh, it's awful. It seems that last night Doctor Weissenfels got together with Doctor Veszto for a drink at some café near where Doctor Veszto lives. I mean, lived."

"Lived?"

"Yes. Because there was this terrible explosion—the police think it was a gas leak in the kitchen there—and they were both killed. Some other people were hurt, but they were killed. Both of them."

"Veszto and Weissenfels are dead?"

"Isn't it horrible? It was on the television news this morning. And Doctor Weissenfels's assistant was just telling me all—Doctor? Are you there, Doctor Halas?"

Halas put down the phone. His heart was hammering furiously, a cold sweat was enveloping him. So it wasn't poor Bela coming around to do mischief in the dark. How stupid, how unkind, to even suspect it might have been.

But Bela had been at that lunch table yesterday. And Weissenfels. How Weissenfels had laughed. How quickly both of them had been wiped out just like that. And Janos Halas, the third one at that table? Given a few hours dispensation? Thank God at least that he hadn't repeated to Klara one word of the story he had told at the table. Otherwise, she could walk out of the house on her way to do her shopping and suddenly—

What is this, Halas asked himself in astonishment. He pulled out his handkerchief and mopped his dripping forehead. Grotesque, the direction his thoughts were taking. Next thing he'd be reporting flying saucers to the police. All because of a thundering coincidence.

So he had told that story to Bela and Weissenfels. So, poor souls, they had suddenly died in an accident, the kind that could happen to anyone. A coincidence.

To believe for even one instant that invisible and malevolent beings were closing in because he had given their secret away was ridiculous.

But those fresh graffiti marking that wall outside?

"A coincidence!" Halas cried out, and when Klara called down, "What is it, dear?" he shouted back angrily, "It's nothing! Nothing at all! Absolutely nothing!"

Passionately shouting it out, he knew, like an exorcism.

The Dim Rumble

ISAAC ASIMOV

I try hard not to believe what my friend George tells me. How can I possibly believe a man who tells me he has access to a two-centimeter-tall demon he calls Azazel, a demon who is really an extraterrestrial personage of extraordinary—but strictly limited—powers?

And yet George does have this ability to gaze at me unblinkingly out of his blue eyes and make me believe him temporarily—while he's talking. It's the Ancient Mariner effect, I suppose.

I once told him that I thought his little demon had given him the gift of verbal hypnosis, but George sighed and said, "Not at all! If he has given me anything, it is a curse for attracting confidences—except that that has been my bane since long before I ever encountered Azazel. The most extraordinary people insist on burdening me with their tales of woe. And sometimes—"

He shook his head in deep dejection. "Sometimes," he said, "the load I must bear as a result is more than human flesh and blood should be called upon to endure. Once, for instance, I met a man named Hannibal West . . .

I noticed him first [said George] in the lounge of a hotel at which I was staying. I noticed him chiefly because he encumbered my view of a statuesque waitress who was most becomingly and insufficiently dressed. I presume he thought I was looking at him, something I would certainly not willingly have done, and he took it as an overture of friendship.

He came to my table, bringing his drink with him, and seated himself without a by-your-leave. I am, by nature, a courteous man, and so I greeted him with a friendly grunt and glare, which he accepted in a calm way. He had sandy hair, plastered down across his scalp; pale eyes and an equally pale face; and the concentrated gaze of a fanatic, though I admit I didn't notice that until later on.

"My name," he said, "is Hannibal West, and I am a professor of geology. My particular field of interest is speleology. You wouldn't, by any chance, be a speleologist yourself?"

I knew at once he was under the impression he had recognized a kindred soul. My gorge rose at the possibility, but I remained courteous. "I am interested in all strange words," I said. "What is speleology?"

"Caves," he said. "The study and exploration of caves. That is my hobby, sir. I have explored caves on every continent except Antarctica. I know more about caves than anyone in the world."

"Very pleasant," I said, "and impressive." Feeling that I had in this way concluded a most unsatisfactory encounter, I signalled for the waitress to renew my drink and watched, in scientific absorption, her undulating progress across the room.

Hannibal West did not recognize that our conversation had been concluded, however. "Yes," he said, nodding vigorously, "you do well to say it is impressive. I have explored caves that are unknown to the world. I have entered underground grottoes that have never felt the footsteps of a human being. I am one of the few people alive today who has gone where no man, or woman, for that matter, has ever gone before. I have breathed air undisturbed, till then, by the lungs of a human being, and have seen sights and heard sounds no one else has ever seen or heard—and lived." He shuddered.

My drink had arrived, and I took it gratefully, admiring the grace with which the waitress bent low to place it on the table before me. I said, my mind not really on what I was saying, "You are a fortunate man."

"That I am not," said West. "I am a miserable sinner called upon by the Lord to avenge the sins of humanity."

Now at last I looked at him sharply, and noted the glare of fanaticism that nearly pinned me to the wall. "In caves?" I asked.

"In caves," he said, solemnly. "Believe me. As a professor of geology, I know what I am talking about."

I had met numerous professors in my lifetime who had known no such thing, but I forebore mentioning the fact.

Perhaps West read my opinion in my expressive eyes, for he fished a newspaper clipping out of a briefcase at his feet and passed it over to me. "Here!" he said, "Just look at that!"

I cannot say that it much rewarded close study. It was a three-paragraph item from some local newspaper. The headline read "A Dim Rumble" and the dateline was East Fishkill, New York. It was an account to the effect that local residents had complained to the police department of a dim rumble that left them uneasy and caused much disturbance among the cat and dog population of the town. The police had dismissed it as the sound of a distant thunderstorm, though the weather department heatedly denied that there had been any that day anywhere in the region.

"What do you think of *that*?" asked West.

"Might it have been a mass epidemic of indigestion?"

He sneered as though the suggestion were beneath contempt, though no one who has ever experienced indigestion would consider it that. Beneath the diaphragm, perhaps.

He said, "I have similar news items from papers in Liverpool, England; Bogota, Colombia; Milan, Italy; Rangoon, Burma; and perhaps half a hundred other places the world over. I collected them. All speak of a pervasive dim rumble that created fear and uneasiness and drove animals frantic, and all were reported within a two-day period."

"A single world-wide event," I said.

"Exactly! Indigestion, indeed." He frowned at me, sipped at his drink, then tapped his chest. "The Lord has placed a weapon in my hand, and I must learn to use it."

"What weapon is this?" I asked.

He didn't answer directly. "I found the cave quite by accident," he said, "something I welcome, for any cave whose opening advertises itself too openly is common property and has been host to thousands. Show me an opening narrow and hidden, one that is overgrown with vegetation, obscured by fallen rocks, veiled by a waterfall, precariously placed in an all but inaccessible spot, and I will show you a virgin cave worthy of inspection. You say you know nothing of speleology?"

"I have been in caves, of course," I said. "The Luray caverns in Virginia—"

"Commercial!" said West, screwing up his face and looking about for a convenient spot on the floor upon which to spit. Fortunately, he didn't find one.

"Since you know nothing about the divine joys of spelunking," he went on, swallowing instead, "I will not bore you with any account of where I found it, and how I explored it. It is, of course, not always safe to explore new caves without companions, but I perform solo explorations readily. After all, there is no one who can match me in this sort of expertise, to say nothing of the fact that I am as bold as a lion.

"In this case, it was indeed fortunate I was alone, for it would not have done for any other human being to discover what I discovered. I had been exploring for several hours when I entered a large and silent room with stalactites above and stalagmites below in gorgeous profusion. I skirted about the stalagmites, trailing my unwinding twine behind me, since I am not fond of losing my way, and then I came across what must have been a thick stalagmite that had broken off at some natural plane of cleavage. There was a litter of limestone to one side of it. What had caused the break I cannot say—perhaps some large animal, fleeing into the cave under pursuit, had blundered into the stalagmite in the dark; or else a mild earthquake had found this one stalagmite weaker than the others.

"In any case, the stump of the stalagmite was now topped by a smooth flatness just moist enough to glisten in my electric light. It was roughly round and strongly resembled a drum. So strongly did it resemble one that I automatically reached out and tapped it with my right forefinger."

He gulped down the rest of his drink and said, "It *was* a drum; or at least it was a structure that set up a vibration when tapped. As soon as I touched it, a dim rumble filled the room, a vague sound just at the threshold of hearing and all but subsonic. Indeed, as I was able to determine later on, the portion of the sound that was high enough in pitch to be heard was a tiny fraction of the whole. Almost all the sound expressed itself in mighty vibrations far too long-wave to affect the ear, though it shook the body itself. That unheard reverberation gave me the most unpleasantly uneasy feeling you can imagine.

"I had never encountered such a phenomenon before. The energy of my touch had been minute. How could it have been converted into such a mighty vibration? I have never managed to understand that completely. To be sure, there are powerful energy sources underground. There could be a way of tapping the heat of the magma, converting a small portion of it to sound. The initial tap could serve to liberate additional sound energy—a kind of sonic laser, or, if we substitute 'sound' for 'light' in the acronym, we can call it 'saser.'"

I said, austerely, "I've never heard of such a thing."

"No," said West, with an unpleasant sneer, "I dare say you haven't. It is nothing anyone has heard of. Some combination of geologic arrangements has produced a natural saser. It is something that would not happen, by accident, oftener than once in a million years, perhaps, and even then in only one spot on the planet. It may be the most unusual phenomenon on Earth."

"That's a great deal," I said, "to deduce from one tap of a forefinger."

"As a scientist, sir, I assure you I was not satisfied with a single tap of a forefinger. I proceeded to experiment. I tried harder taps and quickly realized that I could be seriously damaged by the reverberations in the enclosure. I set up a system whereby I could drop pebbles of various sizes on the saser, while I was outside the cave, by means of a makeshift long-distance apparatus. I discovered that the sound could be heard surprising distances outside the cave. Using a simple seismometer, I found that I could get distinct vibrations at distances of several miles. Eventually, I dropped a series of pebbles one after the other, and the effect was cumulative."

I said, "Was that the day when dim rumbles were heard all over the world?"

"Exactly," he said. "You are by no means as mentally deprived as you appear. The whole planet rang like a bell."

"I've heard that particularly strong earthquakes do that."

"Yes, but this saser can produce a vibration more intense than that of any earthquake and can do so at particular wavelengths; at a wavelength, for instance, that can shake apart the contents of cells— the nucleic acids of the chromosomes, for instance."

I considered that, thoughtfully. "That would kill the cell."

"It certainly would. That may be what killed the dinosaurs."

"I've heard it was done by the collision of an asteroid with the Earth."

"Yes, but in order to have that done by ordinary collision, the asteroid postulated must be huge—ten kilometers across. And one must suppose dust in the stratosphere, a three-year winter, and some way of explaining why some species died out and others didn't in a most illogical fashion. Suppose, instead, that it was a much smaller asteroid that struck a saser and that it disrupted cells with its sound vibration. Perhaps ninety percent of the cells in the world would be destroyed in a matter of minutes with no enormous effect on the planetary environment at all. Some species would manage to survive—some would not. It would be entirely a matter of the intimate details of comparative nucleic acid structure."

"And that," I said, with a most unpleasant feeling that this fanatic was serious, "is the weapon the Lord has placed into your hands?"

"Exactly," he said, "I have worked out the exact wavelengths of sound produced by various manners of tapping the saser and I am trying now to determine which wavelength would specifically disrupt human nucleic acids."

"Why human?" I demanded.

"Why not human?" demanded he, in his turn. "What species is crowding the planet, destroying the environment, eradicating other species, filling the biosphere with chemical pollutants? What species will destroy the Earth and render it totally non-viable in a matter of decades, perhaps? Surely not some other than *Homo sapiens*? If I can find the right sonic wavelength, I can strike my saser in the proper manner, and with the proper force, to bathe the Earth in sonic vibrations that will, in a matter of a day or so, for it takes time for sound to travel, wipe out humanity, while scarcely touching other life-forms with nucleic acids of differing intimate structure."

I said, "You are prepared to destroy billions of human beings?"

"The Lord did it by means of the Flood—"

"Surely you don't believe the Biblical tale of the Flood?"

West said austerely, "I am a creationist geologist, sir."

I understood everything. "Ah," I said. "The Lord promised he would never again send a Flood upon the Earth, but he didn't say anything about sound waves."

"Exactly! The billions of dead will fertilize and fructify the Earth, serve as food for other forms of life who have suffered much at the hands of humanity and who deserve compensation. What's more, a remnant of humanity shall undoubtedly survive. There are bound to be a few human beings who will have nucleic acids of a type that will not be sensitive to the sonic vibrations. That remnant, blessed by the Lord, can begin anew, and will perhaps have learned a lesson as to the evil of Evil, so to speak."

I said, "Why are you telling me all this?" And indeed, it had occurred to me that it was strange that he was doing so.

He leaned toward me and seized me by the lapel of my jacket—a most unpleasant experience, for his breath was rather overpowering—and said, "I have the inner certainty that you can help me in my work."

"I?" I said. "I assure you that I haven't any knowledge whatsoever concerning wavelengths, nucleic acids, and—" But then, bethinking myself rapidly, I said, "Yet come to think of it, I may have just the thing for you." And in a more formal voice, with the stately courtesy so characteristic of me, I said, "Would you do me the honor, sir, of waiting for me for perhaps fifteen minutes?"

"Certainly, sir," he answered, with equal formality. "I will occupy myself with further abstruse mathematical calculations."

As I hastened out of the lounge, I passed a ten-dollar bill to the bartender with a whispered, "See that that gentleman, if I may speak loosely, does not leave until I return. Feed him drinks and put it on my tab, if absolutely necessary."

I never fail to carry with me those simple ingredients I use to call up Azazel and, in a very few minutes, he was sitting on the bed lamp in my room, suffused with his usual tiny pink glow.

He said, censoriously, in his piping little voice, "You interrupted me when I was in the midst of constructing a papparatso with which I fully expected to win the heart of a lovely samini."

"I regret that, Azazel," I said, hoping he would not delay me by describing the nature of the papparatso or the charms of the samini, for neither of which I cared the paring of a fingernail, "but I have here a possible emergency of the most extreme sort."

"You always say that," he said, discontentedly.

Hastily, I outlined the situation, and I must say he grasped it at once. He is very good that way, never requiring long explanations. My own belief is that he peeks at my mind, although he always assures me that he considers my thoughts inviolable. Still, how far can you trust a two-centimeter extraterrestrial who, by his own admission, is constantly trying to overreach lovely saminis, whatever they are, by the most dishonorable ruses? Besides, I'm not sure whether he says he considers my thoughts inviolable or insufferable; but that is neither here nor there.

"Where is this human being you speak of?" he squeaked.

"In the lounge. It is located—"

"Don't bother. I shall follow the aura of moral decay. I think I have it. How do I identify the human being?"

"Sandy hair, pale eyes—"

"No, no. His mind."

"A fanatic."

"Ah, you might have said so at once. I have him—and I see I shall require a thorough steam-bath when I return home. He is worse than you are."

"Never mind that. Is he telling the truth?"

"About the saser? Which, by the way, is a clever conceit."

"Yes."

"Well, that is a difficult question. As I often say to a friend of mine who considers himself a great spiritual leader: What is truth? I'll tell you this; he considers it the truth. He believes it. What a human being believes, however, no matter with what ardor, is not necessarily objective truth. You have probably caught a hint of this in the course of your life."

"I have. But is there no way you can distinguish between belief that stems from objective truth and belief that does not?"

"In intelligent entities, certainly. In human beings, no. But apparently you consider this man an enormous danger. I can rearrange some of the molecules of his brain, and he will then be dead."

"No, no," I said. It may be a silly weakness on my part, but I do object to murder. "Couldn't you rearrange molecules in such a way that he will lose all memory of the saser?"

Azazel sighed in a thin, wheezing way. "That is really much more difficult. Those molecules are heavy and they stick together. Really, why not a clean disruption—"

"I insist," I said.

"Oh, very well," said Azazel, sullenly, and then he went through a whole litany of puffing and panting designed to show me how hard he was working. Finally, he said, "It's done."

"Good. Wait here, please. I just want to check it out, and then I'll be right back."

I rushed down hastily, and Hannibal West was still sitting where I had left him. The bartender winked at me as I passed. "No drinks necessary, sir," said that worthy person, and I gave him five dollars more.

West looked up cheerfully. "There you are."

"Yes, indeed," I said. "Very penetrating of you to notice that. I have the solution to the problem of the saser."

"The problem of the what?" he asked, clearly puzzled.

"That object you discovered in the course of your speleological explorations."

"What are speleological explorations?"

"Your investigations of caves."

"Sir," said West, frowning, "I have never been in a cave in my life. Are you mad?"

"No, but I have just remembered an important meeting. Farewell, sir. Probably, we shall never meet again."

I hastened back to the room, panting a little, and found Azazel humming to himself some tune favored by the entities of his world. Really, their taste in what they call music is atrocious.

"His memory is gone," I said, "and, I hope, permanently."

"Of course," said Azazel. "The next step, now, is to consider the saser itself. Its structure must be very neatly and precisely organized if it can actually magnify sound at the expense of Earth's internal heat. No doubt, a tiny disruption at some key point—something that may be within my mighty powers—could wipe out all saser activity. Exactly where is it located?"

I stared at him thunderstruck. "How should I know?" I said.

He stared at me, probably thunderstruck also, but I can never make out the expressions on his tiny face. "Do you mean to say you had me wipe out his memory *before* you obtained that vital piece of information?"

"It never occurred to me," I said.

"But if the saser exists, if his belief was based on objective truth, someone else may stumble upon it, or a large animal might, or a meteorite might strike it—and at any moment, day or night, all life on Earth may be destroyed."

"Good Lord!" I muttered.

Apparently my distress moved him, for he said, "Come, come, my friend, look at the bright side. The worst that can happen is that human beings will all be wiped out. Just human beings. It's not as though they're *people*!"

Having completed his tale, George said, despondently, "And there you are. I have to live with the knowledge that the world may come to an end at any moment."

"Nonsense," I said, heartily, "Even if you've told me the truth about this Hannibal West, which, if you will pardon me, is by no means assured, he may have been having a sick fantasy."

George looked haughtily down his nose at me for a moment, then said, "I would not have your unlovely tendency toward skepticism for all the loveliest saminis on Azazel's native world. How do you explain this?"

He withdrew a small clipping from his wallet. It was from yesterday's New York *Times* and was headed "A Dim Rumble." It told of a dim rumble that was perturbing the inhabitants of Grenoble, France.

"One explanation, George," I said, "is that you saw this article and made up the whole story to suit."

For a moment, George looked as though he would explode with indignation, but when I picked up the rather substantial check that the waitress had placed between us, softer feelings overcame him, and we shook hands on parting, amiably enough.

And yet I must admit I haven't slept well since. I keep sitting up at about 2:30 A.M., listening for the dim rumble I could swear had roused me from sleep.

The Leather Funnel

ARTHUR CONAN DOYLE

My friend, Lionel Dacre, lived in the Avenue de Wagram, Paris. His house was that small one, with the iron railings and grass plot in front of it, on the left-hand side as you pass down from the Arc de Triomphe. I fancy that it had been there long before the avenue was constructed, for the grey tiles were stained with lichens, and the walls were mildewed and discoloured with age. It looked a small house from the street, five windows in front, if I remember right, but it deepened into a single long chamber at the back. It was here that Dacre had that singular library of occult literature, and the fantastic curiosities which served as a hobby for himself, and an amusement for his friends. A wealthy man of refined and eccentric tastes, he had spent much of his life and fortune in gathering together what was said to be a unique private collection of Talmudic, cabalistic, and magical works, many of them of great rarity and value. His tastes leaned toward the marvellous and the monstrous, and I have heard that his experiments in the direction of the unknown have passed all the bounds of civilization and of decorum. To his English friends he never alluded to such matters, and took the tone of the student and *virtuoso*; but a Frenchman whose tastes were of the same nature has assured me that the worst excesses of the black mass have been perpetrated in that large and lofty hall, which is lined with the shelves of his books, and the cases of his museum.

Dacre's appearance was enough to show that his deep interest in these psychic matters was intellectual rather than spiritual. There was no trace of asceticism upon his heavy face, but there was much mental force in his huge, dome-like skull, which curved upward from among his thinning locks, like a snow peak above its fringe of fir trees. His knowledge was far greater than his wisdom, and his powers were far superior to his character. The small bright eyes, buried deeply in his fleshy face, twinkled with intelligence and an unabated curiosity of life, but they were the eyes of a sensualist and an egotist. Enough of the man, for he is dead now, poor devil, dead at the very time that he had made sure that he had at last discovered the elixir of life. It is not with his complex character that I have to deal, but with the very strange and inexplicable incident which had its rise in my visit to him in the early spring of the year '82.

I had known Dacre in England, for my researches in the Assyrian Room of the British Museum had been conducted at the time when he was endeavouring to establish a mystic and esoteric meaning in the Babylonian tablets, and this community of interests had brought us together. Chance remarks had led to daily conversation, and that to something verging upon friendship. I had promised him that on my next visit to Paris I would call upon him. At the time when I was able to fulfill my compact I was living in a cottage at Fontainebleau, and as the evening trains were inconvenient, he asked me to spend the night in his house.

"I have only one spare couch," said he, pointing to a broad sofa in his large salon; "I hope that you will manage to be comfortable there."

It was a singular bedroom, with its high walls of brown volumes, but there could be no more agreeable furniture to a bookworm such as myself, and there is no scent as pleasant to my nostrils as that faint, subtle reek which comes from an ancient book. I assured him that I could desire no more charming chamber, and no more congenial surroundings.

"If the fittings are neither convenient nor conventional, they are at least costly," said he, looking round at his shelves. "I have expended nearly a quarter of a million of money upon these objects which surround you. Books, weapons, gems, carvings, tapestries, images— there is hardly a thing here which has not its history, and it is generally one worth telling."

He was seated as he spoke at one side of the open fireplace, and I at the other. His reading-table was on his right, and the strong lamp above it ringed it with a very vivid circle of golden light. A half-rolled palimpsest lay in the centre, and around it were many quaint articles of bric-à-brac. One of these was a large funnel, such as is used for filling wine casks. It appeared to be made of black wood, and to be rimmed with discolored brass.

"That is a curious thing," I remarked. "What is the history of that?"

"Ah!" said he, "it is the very question which I have had occasion to ask myself. I would give a good deal to know. Take it in your hands and examine it."

I did so, and found that what I had imagined to be wood was in reality leather, though age had dried it into an extreme hardness. It was a large funnel, and might hold a quart when full. The brass rim encircled the wide end, but the narrow was also tipped with metal.

"What do you make of it?" asked Dacre.

"I should imagine that it belonged to some vintner or maltster in the Middle Ages," said I. "I have seen in England leathern drinking flagons of the seventeenth century—'black jacks' as they were called—which were of the same colour and hardness as this filler."

"I dare say the date would be about the same," said Dacre, "and, no doubt, also, it was used for filling a vessel with liquid. If my suspicions are correct, however, it was a queer vintner who used it, and a very singular cask which was filled. Do you observe nothing strange at the spout end of the funnel?"

As I held it to the light I observed that at a spot some five inches above the brass tip the narrow neck of the leather funnel was all haggled and scored, as if someone had notched it round with a blunt knife. Only at that point was there any roughening of the dead black surface.

"Someone has tried to cut off the neck."

"Would you call it a cut?"

"It is torn and lacerated. It must have taken some strength to leave these marks on such tough material, whatever the instrument may have been. But what do you think of it? I can tell that you know more than you say."

Dacre smiled and his little eyes twinkled with knowledge.

"Have you included the psychology of dreams among your learned studies?" he asked.

"I did not even know that there was such a psychology."

"My dear sir, that shelf above the gem case is filled with volumes, from Albertus Magnus onward, which deal with no other subject. It is a science in itself."

"A science of charlatans."

"The charlatan is always the pioneer. From the astrologer came the astronomer, from the alchemist the chemist, from the mesmerist the experimental psychologist. The quack of yesterday is the professor of tomorrow. Even such subtle and elusive things as dreams will in time be reduced to system and order. When that time comes the researches of our friends on the bookshelf yonder will no longer be the amusement of the mystic, but the foundations of a science."

"Supposing that is so, what has the science of dreams to do with a large, black, brass-rimmed funnel?"

"I will tell you. You know that I have an agent who is always on the look-out for rarities and curiosities for my collection. Some days ago he heard a dealer upon one of the Quais who had acquired some old rubbish found in a cupboard in an ancient house at the back of the Rue Mathurin, in the Quartier Latin. The dining-room of this old house is decorated with a coat of arms, chevrons, and bars rouge upon a field argent, which prove, upon inquiry, to be the shield of Nicholas de la Reynie, a high official of King Louis XIV. There can be no doubt that the other articles in the cupboard date back to the early days of that king. The inference is, therefore, that they were all the property of this Nicholas de la Reynie, who was, as I understand, the gentleman specially concerned with the maintenance and execution of the Draconic laws of that epoch."

"What then?"

"I would ask you now to take the funnel into your hands once more and to examine the upper brass rim. Can you make out any lettering upon it?"

There were certainly some scratches upon it, almost obliterated by time. The general effect was of several letters, the last of which bore some resemblance to a B.

"You make it a B?"

"Yes, I do."

"So do I. In fact, I have no doubt whatever that it is a B."

"But the nobleman you mentioned would have had R for his initial."

"Exactly! That's the beauty of it. He owned this curious object, and yet he had someone else's initials upon it. Why did he do this?"

"I can't imagine; can you?"

"Well, I might, perhaps, guess. Do you observe something drawn a little farther along the rim?"

"I should say it was a crown."

"It is undoubtedly a crown; but if you examine it in a good light, you will convince yourself that it is not an ordinary crown. It is a heraldic crown—a badge of rank, and it consists of an alternation of four pearls and strawberry leaves, the proper badge of a marquis. We may infer, therefore, that the person whose initials end in B was entitled to wear the coronet."

"Then this common leather filler belonged to a marquis?"

Dacre gave a peculiar smile.

"Or to some member of the family of a marquis," said he. "So much we have clearly gathered from this engraved rim."

"But what has all this to do with dreams?" I do not know whether it was from a look upon Dacre's face, or from some subtle suggestion in his manner, but a feeling of repulsion, of unreasoning horror, came upon me as I looked at the gnarled old lump of leather.

"I have more than once received important information through my dreams," said my companion in the didactic manner which he loved to affect. "I make it a rule now when I am in doubt upon any material point to place the article in question beside me as I sleep, and to hope for some enlightenment. The process does not seem to me to be very obscure, though it has not yet received the blessing of orthodox science. According to my theory, any object which has been intimately associated with any supreme paroxysm of human emotion, whether it be joy or pain, will retain a certain atmosphere or association which it is capable of communicating to a sensitive mind. By a sensitive mind I do not mean an abnormal one, but such a trained and educated mind as you or I possess."

"You mean, for example, that if I slept beside that old sword upon the wall, I might dream of some bloody incident in which that very sword took part?"

"An excellent example, for as a matter of fact, that sword was used in that fashion by me, and I saw in my sleep the death of its owner, who perished in a brisk skirmish, which I have been unable to identify, but which occurred at the time of the wars of the Frondists. If you think of it, some of our popular observances show that the fact has already been recognized by our ancestors, although we, in our wisdom, have classed it among superstitions."

"For example?"

"Well, the placing of the bride's cake beneath the pillow in order that the sleeper may have pleasant dreams. That is one of several instances which you will find set forth in a small *brochure* which I am myself writing upon the subject. But to come back to the point, I slept one night with the funnel beside me, and I had a dream which certainly throws a curious light upon its use and origin."

"What did you dream?"

"I dreamed—" He paused, and an intent look of interest came over his massive face. "By Jove, that's well thought of," said he. "This really will be an exceedingly interesting experiment. You are yourself a psychic subject—with nerves which respond readily to any impression."

"I have never tested myself in that direction."

"Then we shall test you tonight. Might I ask you as a very great favour, when you occupy that couch tonight, to sleep with this old funnel placed by the side of your pillow?"

The request seemed to me a grotesque one; but I have myself, in my complex nature, a hunger after all which is bizarre and fantastic. I had not the faintest belief in Dacre's theory, nor any hopes for success in such an experiment; yet it amused me that the experiment should be made. Dacre, with great gravity, drew a small stand to the head of my settee, and placed the funnel upon it. Then, after a short conversation, he wished me good night and left me.

I sat for some time smoking by the smouldering fire, and turning over in my mind the curious incident which had occurred, and the strange experience which might lie before me. Sceptical as I was, there was something impressive in the assurance of Dacre's manner, and my extraordinary surroundings, the huge room with the strange and often sinister objects which were hung round it, struck solemnity into my soul. Finally I undressed, and turning out the lamp, I lay down. After long tossing I fell asleep. Let me try to describe as accurately as I can the scene which came to me in my dreams. It stands out now in my memory more clearly than anything which I have seen with my waking eyes.

There was a room which bore the appearance of a vault. Four spandrels from the corners ran up to join a sharp, cup-shaped roof. The architecture was rough, but very strong. It was evidently part of a great building.

Three men in black, with curious, top-heavy, black velvet hats, sat in a line upon a red-carpeted dais. Their faces were very solemn and sad. On the left stood two long-gowned men with portfolios in their hands, which seemed to be stuffed with papers. Upon the right, looking toward me, was a small woman with blonde hair and singular, light-blue eyes—the eyes of a child. She was past her first youth, but could not yet be called middle-aged. Her figure was inclined to stoutness and her bearing was proud and confident. Her face was pale, but serene. It was a curious face, comely and yet feline, with a subtle suggestion of cruelty about the straight, strong little mouth and chubby jaw. She was draped in some sort of loose, white gown. Beside her stood a thin, eager priest, who whispered in her ear, and continually raised a crucifix before her eyes. She turned her head and looked fixedly past the crucifix at the three men in black, who were, I felt, her judges.

As I gazed the three men stood up and said something, but I could distinguish no words, though I was aware that it was the central one who was speaking. Then they swept out of the room, followed by the two men with the papers. At the same instant several rough-looking fellows in stout jerkins came bustling in and removed first the red carpet, and then the boards which formed the dais, so as to entirely clear the room. When this screen was removed I saw some singular articles of furniture behind it. One looked like a bed with wooden rollers at each end, and a winch handle to regulate its length. Another was a wooden horse. There were several other curious objects, and a number of swinging cords which played over pulleys. It was not unlike a modern gymnasium.

When the room had been cleared there appeared a new figure upon the scene. This was a tall, thin person clad in black, with a gaunt and austere face. The aspect of the man made me shudder. His clothes were all shining with grease and mottled with stains. He bore himself with a slow and impressive dignity, as if he took command of all things from the instant of his entrance. In spite of his rude appearance and sordid dress, it was now *his* business, *his* room, his to command. He carried a coil of light ropes over his left forearm. The lady looked him up and down with a searching glance, but her expression was unchanged. It was confident—even defiant. But it was very different with the priest. His face was ghastly white, and I saw the moisture glisten and run on his high, sloping forehead. He threw up his hands in prayer and he stooped continually to mutter frantic words in the lady's ear.

The man in black now advanced, and taking one of the cords from his left arm, he bound the woman's hands together. She held them meekly toward him as he did so. Then he took her arm with a rough grip and led her to the wooden horse, which was a little higher than her waist. Onto this she was lifted and laid, with her back upon it, and her face to the ceiling, while the priest, quivering with horror, had rushed out of the room. The woman's lips were moving rapidly, and though I could hear nothing I knew that she was praying. Her feet hung down on either side of the horse, and I saw that the rough varlets in attendance had fastened cords to her ankles and secured the other ends to iron rings in the stone floor.

My heart sank within me as I saw these ominous preparations, and yet I was held by the fascination of horror, and I could not take my eyes from the strange spectacle. A man had entered the room with a bucket of water in either hand. Another followed with a third bucket. They were laid beside the wooden horse. The second man had a wooden dipper—a bowl with a straight handle—in his other hand. This he gave to the man in black. At the same moment one of the varlets approached with a dark object in his hand, which even in my dream filled me with a vague feeling of familiarity. It was a leathern filler. With horrible energy he thrust it—but I could stand no more. My hair stood on end with horror. I writhed, I struggled, I broke through the bonds of sleep, and I burst with a shriek into my own life, and found myself shivering with terror in the huge library, with the moonlight flooding through the window and throwing strange silver and black traceries upon the other wall. Oh, what a blessed relief to feel that I was back in the nineteenth century—back out of that medieval vault into a world where men had human hearts within their bosoms. I sat up on my couch, trembling in every limb, my mind divided between thankfulness and horror. To think that such things were ever done—that they *could* be done without God striking the villains dead. Was it all a fantasy, or did it really stand for something which had happened in the black, cruel days of the world's history? I sank my throbbing head upon my shaking hands. And then, suddenly, my heart seemed to stand still in my bosom, and I could not even scream, so great was my terror. Something was advancing toward me through the darkness of my room.

It is a horror coming upon a horror which breaks a man's spirit. I could not reason, I could not pray; I could only sit like a frozen image, and glare at the dark figure which was coming down the great room. And then it moved out into the white lane of moonlight, and I breathed once more. It was Dacre, and his face showed that he was as frightened as myself.

"Was that you? For God's sake what's the matter?" he asked in a husky voice.

"Oh, Dacre, I am glad to see you! I have been down into hell. It was dreadful."

"Then it was you who screamed?"

"I dare say it was."

"It rang through the house. The servants are all terrified." He struck a match and lit the lamp. "I think we may get the fire to burn up again," he added, throwing some logs upon the embers. "Good God, my dear chap, how white you are! You look as if you had seen a ghost."

"So I have—several ghosts."

"The leather funnel has acted, then?"

"I wouldn't sleep near the infernal thing again for all the money you could offer me."

Dacre chuckled.

"I expected that you would have a lively night of it," said he. "You took it out of me in return, for that scream of yours wasn't a very pleasant sound at two in the morning. I suppose from what you say that you have seen the whole dreadful business."

"What dreadful business?"

"The torture of the water—the 'Extraordinary Question,' as it was called in the genial days of 'Le Roi Soleil.' Did you stand it out to the end?"

"No, thank God, I awoke before it really began."

"Ah! it is just as well for you. I held out till the third bucket. Well, it is an old story, and they are all in their graves now, anyhow, so what does it matter how they got there? I suppose that you have no idea what it was that you have seen?"

"The torture of some criminal. She must have been a terrible malefactor indeed if her crimes are in proportion to her penalty."

"Well, we have that small consolation," said Dacre, wrapping his dressing-gown round him and crouching closer to the fire. "They *were* in proportion to her penalty. That is to say, if I am correct in the lady's identity."

"How could you possibly know her identity?"

For answer Dacre took down an old vellum-covered volume from the shelf.

"Just listen to this," said he; "it is the French of the seventeenth century, but I will give a rough translation as I go. You will judge for yourself whether I have solved the riddle or not.

"'The prisoner was brought before the Grand Chambers and Tournelles of Parliament, sitting as a court of justice, charged with the murder of Master Dreux d'Aubray, her father, and of her two brothers, MM. d'Aubray, one being civil lieutenant, and the other a counsellor of Parliament. In person it seemed hard to believe that she had really done such wicked deeds, for she was of a mild appearance, and of short stature, with a fair skin and blue eyes. Yet the Court, having found her guilty, condemned her to the ordinary and the extraordinary question in order that she might be forced to name her accomplices, after which she should be carried in a cart to the Place de Grève, there to have her head cut off, her body being afterwards burned and her ashes scattered to the winds.'

"The date of this entry is July 16, 1676."

"It is interesting," said I, "but not convincing. How do you prove the two women to be the same?"

"I am coming to that. The narrative goes on to tell of the woman's behaviour when questioned. 'When the executioner approached her she recognized him by the cords which he held in his hands, and she at once held out her own hands to him, looking at him from head to foot without uttering a word.' How's that?"

"Yes, it was so."

"'She gazed without wincing upon the wooden horse and rings which had twisted so many limbs and caused so many shrieks of agony. When her eyes fell upon the three pails of water, which were all ready for her, she said with a smile, "All that water must have been brought here for the purpose of drowning me, Monsieur. You have no idea, I trust, of making a person of my small stature swallow it all."' Shall I read the details of the torture?"

"No, for Heaven's sake, don't."

"Here is a sentence which must surely show you that what is here recorded is the very scene which you have gazed upon tonight: 'The good Abbé Pirot, unable to contemplate the agonies which were suffered by his penitent, had hurried from the room.' Does that convince you?"

"It does entirely. There can be no question that it is indeed the same event. But who, then, is this lady whose appearance was so attractive and whose end was so horrible?"

For answer Dacre came across to me, and placed the small lamp upon the table which stood by my bed. Lifting up the ill-omened filler, he turned the brass rim so that the light fell full upon it. Seen in this way the engraving seemed clearer than on the night before.

"We have already agreed that this is the badge of a marquise," said he. "We have also settled that the last letter is B."

"It is undoubtedly so."

"I now suggest to you that the other letters from left to right are, M, M, a small d, A, a small d, and then the final B."

"Yes, I am quite sure that you are right. I can make out the two small d's quite plainly."

"What I have read to you tonight," said Dacre, "is the official record of the trial of Marie Madeleine d'Aubray, Marquise de Brin-villiers, one of the most famous poisoners and murderers of all time."

I sat in silence, overwhelmed at the extraordinary nature of the incident, and at the completeness of the proof with which Dacre had exposed its real meaning. In a vague way I remembered some details of the woman's career, her unbridled debauchery, the cold-blooded and protracted torture of her sick father, the murder of her brothers for motives of petty gain. I recollected also that the bravery of her end had done something to atone for the horror of her life, and that all Paris had sympathized with her last moments and blessed her as a martyr within a few days of the time when they had cursed her as a murderess. One objection, and one only, occurred to my mind.

"How come her initials and her badge of rank upon the filler? Surely they did not carry their mediaeval homage to the nobility to the point of decorating instruments of torture with their titles?"

"I was puzzled with the same point," said Dacre, "but it admits of a simple explanation. The case excited extraordinary interest at the time, and nothing could be more natural than that La Reynie, the head of the police, should retain this filler as a grim souvenir. It was not often that a marchioness of France underwent the extraordinary question. That he should engrave her initials upon it for the information of others was surely a very ordinary proceeding upon his part."

"And this ?" I asked, pointing to the marks upon the leathern neck.

"She was a cruel tigress," said Dacre, as he turned away. "I think it is evident that like other tigresses her teeth were both strong and sharp."

Trinity

NANCY KRESS

"Lord, I believe; help Thou mine unbelief!"

—Mark 9:24

At first I didn't recognize Devrie.

Devrie—I didn't recognize *Devrie*. Astonished at myself, I studied the wasted figure standing in the middle of the bare reception room: arms like wires, clavicle sharply outlined, head shaved, dressed in that ugly long tent of light-weight gray. God knew what her legs looked like under it. Then she smiled, and it was Devrie.

"You look like shit."

"Hello, Seena. Come on in."

"I am in."

"Barely. It's not catching, you know."

"Stupidity fortunately isn't," I said and closed the door behind me. The small room was too hot; Devrie would need the heat, of course, with almost no fat left to insulate her bones and organs. Next to her I felt huge, although I am not. Huge, hairy, sloppy-breasted.

"Thank you for not wearing bright colors. They do affect me."

"Anything for a sister," I said, mocking the old childhood formula, the old sentiment. But Devrie was too quick to think it was only mockery; in that, at least, she had not changed. She clutched my arm and her fingers felt like chains, or talons.

"You found him. Seena, you found him."

"I found him."

"Tell me," she whispered.

"Sit down first, before you fall over. God, Devrie, don't you eat at all?"

"*Tell me*," she said. So I did.

Devrie Caroline Konig had admitted herself to the Institute of the Biological Hope on the Caribbean island of Dominica eleven months ago, in late November of 2017, when her age was 23 years and

431

4 months. I am precise about this because it is all I can be sure of. I need the precision. The Institute of the Biological Hope is not precise; it is a mongrel, part research laboratory in brain sciences, part monastery, part school for training in the discipline of the mind. That made my baby sister guinea pig, postulant, freshman. She had always been those things, but, until now, sequentially. Apparently so had many other people, for when eccentric Nobel Prize winner James Arthur Bohentin had founded his Institute, he had been able to fund it, although precariously. But in that it did not differ from most private scientific research centers.

Or most monasteries.

I wanted Devrie out of the Institute of the Biological Hope.

"It's located on Dominica," I had said sensibly—what an ass I had been—to an unwasted Devrie a year ago, "because the research procedures there fall outside United States laws concerning the safety of research subjects. Doesn't that *tell* you something, Devrie? Doesn't that at least give you pause? In New York, it would be illegal to do to anyone what Bohentin does to his people."

"Do you know him?" she had asked.

"I have met him. Once."

"What is he like?"

"Like stone."

Devrie shrugged, and smiled. "All the participants in the Institute are willing. Eager."

"That doesn't make it ethical for Bohentin to destroy them. Ethical or legal."

"It's legal on Dominica. And in thinking you know better than the participants what they should risk their own lives for, aren't you playing God?"

"Better me than some untrained fanatic who offers himself up like an exalted Viking hero, expecting Valhalla."

"You're an intellectual snob, Seena."

"I never denied it."

"Are you sure you aren't really objecting not to the Institute's dangers but to its purpose? Isn't the 'Hope' part what really bothers you?"

"I don't think scientific method and pseudo-religious mush mix, no. I never did. I don't think it leads to a perception of God."

"The holotank tapes indicate it leads to a perception of *something* the brain hasn't encountered before," Devrie said, and for a moment I was silent.

I was once, almost, a biologist. I was aware of the legitimate studies that formed the basis for Bohentin's megalomania: the brain wave changes that accompany anorexia nervosa, sensory deprivation, biological feedback, and neurotransmitter stimulants. I have read the historical accounts, some merely pathetic but some disturbingly not, of the Christian mythics who achieved rapture through the mortification of the flesh and the Eastern mystics who achieved anesthesia through the control of the mind, of the faith healers who succeeded, of the carcinomas shrunk through trained will. I knew of the research of focused clairvoyance during orgasm, and of what happens when neurotransmitter number and speed are increased chemically.

And I knew all that was known about the twin trance.

Fifteen years earlier, as a doctoral student in biology, I had spent one summer replicating Sunderwirth's pioneering study of drug-enhanced telepathy in identical twins. My results were positive, except that within six months all eight of my research subjects had died. So had Sunderwirth's. Twin-trance research became the cloning controversy of the new decade, with the same panicky cycle of public outcry, legal restrictions, religious misunderstandings, fear, and demagoguery. When I received the phone call that the last of my subjects was dead—cardiac arrest, no history of heart disease, forty-three Goddamn years old—I locked myself in my apartment, with the lights off and my father's papers clutched in my hand, for three days. Then I resigned from the neurology department and became an entomologist. There is no pain in classifying dead insects.

"There is something *there*," Devrie had repeated. She was holding the letter sent to our father, whom someone at the Institute had not heard was dead. "It says the holotank tapes—"

"So there's something there," I said. "So the tanks are picking up some strange radiation. Why call it 'God'?"

"Why not call it God?"

"Why not call it Rover? Even if I grant you that the tape pattern looks like a presence—which I don't—you have no way of knowing that Bohentin's phantom isn't, say, some totally ungodlike alien being."

"But neither do I know that it *is*."

"Devrie—"

She had smiled and put her hands on my shoulders. She had—has, has always had—a very sweet smile. "Seena. *Think*. If the Institute can prove rationally that God exists—can prove it to the intellectual mind, the doubting Thomases who need something concrete to study . . . faith that doesn't need to be taken on faith . . ."

She wore her mystical face, a glowing softness that made me want to shake the silliness out of her. Instead I made some clever riposte, some sarcasm I no longer remember, and reached out to ruffle her hair. Big-sisterly, patronizing, thinking I could deflate her rapturous interest with the pin-prick of ridicule. God, I was an ass. It hurts to remember how big an ass I was.

A month and a half later Devrie committed herself and half her considerable inheritance to the Institute of the Biological Hope.

"Tell me," Devrie whispered. The Institute had no windows; outside I had seen grass, palm trees, butterflies floating in the sunshine, but inside here in the bare gray room there was nowhere to look but at her face.

"He's a student in a Master's program at a third-rate college in New Hampshire. He was adopted when he was two, nearly three, in March of 1997. Before that he was in a government-run children's home. In Boston, of course. The adopting family, as far as I can discover, never was told he was anything but one more toddler given up by somebody for adoption."

"Wait a minute," Devrie said. "I need . . . a minute."

She had turned paler, and her hands trembled. I had recited the information as if it were no more than an exhibit listing at my museum. Of course she was rattled. I wanted her rattled. I wanted her out.

Lowering herself to the floor, Devrie sat cross-legged and closed her eyes. Concentration spread over her face, but a concentration so serene it barely deserved that name. Her breathing slowed, her color freshened, and when she opened her eyes, they had the rested energy of a person who has just slept eight hours in mountain air. Her face even looked plumper, and an EEG, I guessed, would show damn near alpha waves. In her year at the Institute she must have mastered quite an array of biofeedback techniques to do that, so fast and with such a malnourished body.

"Very impressive," I said sourly.

"Seena—have you seen him?"

"No. All this is from sealed records."

"How did you get into the records?"

"Medical and governmental friends."

"Who?"

"What do you care, as long as I found out what you wanted to know?"

She was silent. I knew she would never ask me if I had obtained her information legally or illegally; it would not occur to her to ask. Devrie, being Devrie, would assume it had all been generously offered by my modest museum connections and our dead father's immodest research connections. She would be wrong.

"How old is he now?"

"Twenty-four years last month. They must have used your two-month tissue sample."

"Do you think Daddy knew where the . . . baby went?"

"Yes. Look at the timing—the child was normal and healthy, yet he wasn't adopted until he was nearly three. The researchers kept track of him, all right; they kept all six clones in a government-controlled home where they could monitor their development as long as humanely possible. The same-sex clones were released for adoption after a year, but they hung onto the cross-sex ones until they reached an age where they would become harder to adopt. They undoubtedly wanted to study *them* as long as they could. And even after the kids were released for adoption, the researchers held off publishing until all six were placed and the records sealed. Dad's group didn't publish until April, 1998, remember. By the time the storm broke, the babies were out of its path, and anonymous."

"And the last," Devrie said.

"And the last," I agreed, although of course the researchers hadn't foreseen *that*. So few in the scientific community had foreseen that. Offense against God and man, Satan's work, natter natter. Watching my father's suddenly stooped shoulders and stricken eyes, I had thought how ugly public revulsion could be and had nobly resolved—how had I thought of it then? So long ago—resolved to snatch the banner of pure science from my fallen father's hand. Another time that I had been an ass. Five years later, when it had been my turn to feel the ugly scorching of public revulsion, I had broken, left neurological research, and fled down the road that led to the Museum of Natural History, where I was the curator of ants fossilized in amber and moths pinned securely under permaplex.

"The other four clones," Devrie said, "the ones from that university in California that published almost simultaneously with Daddy—"

"I don't know. I didn't even try to ask. It was hard enough in Cambridge."

"Me," Devrie said wonderingly. "He's *me*."

"Oh, for—Devrie, he's your twin. No more than that. No—actually less than that. He shares your genetic material exactly as an identical twin would, except for the Y chromosome, but he shares none of the congenital or environmental influences that shaped your personality. There's no mystical replication of spirit in cloning. He's merely a twin who got born eleven months late!"

She looked at me with luminous amusement. I didn't like the look. On that fleshless face, the skin stretched so taut that the delicate bones beneath were as visible as the veins of a moth wing, her amusement looked ironic. Yet Devrie was never ironic. Gentle, passionate, trusting, a little stupid, she was not capable of irony. It was beyond her, just as it was beyond her to wonder why I, who had fought her entering the Institute of the Biological Hope, had brought her this information now. Her amusement was one-layered, and trusting.

God's fools, the Middle Ages had called them.

"Devrie," I said, and heard my own voice unexpectedly break, "leave here. It's physically not safe. What are you down to, ten percent body fat? Eight? Look at yourself, you can't hold body heat, your palms are dry, you can't move quickly without getting dizzy. Hypotension. What's your heartbeat? Do you still menstruate? It's insane."

She went on smiling at me. God's fools don't need menstruation. "Come with me, Seena. I want to show you the Institute."

"I don't want to see it."

"Yes. This visit you should see it."

"Why this visit?"

"Because you *are* going to help me get my clone to come here, aren't you? Or else why did you go to all the trouble of locating him?"

I didn't answer. She still didn't see it.

Devrie said, "'Anything for a sister.' But you were always more like a mother to me than a sister." She took my hand and pulled herself off the floor. So had I pulled her up to take her first steps, the day after our mother died in a plane crash at Orly. Now Devrie's hand felt cold. I imprisoned it and counted the pulse.

"Bradycardia."

But she wasn't listening.

The Institute was a shock. I had anticipated the laboratories: monotonous gray walls, dim light, heavy soundproofing, minimal fixtures in the ones used for sensory dampening; high-contrast textures and colors, strobe lights quite good sound equipment in those for sensory arousal. There was much that Devrie, as subject rather than researcher, didn't have authority to show me, but I deduced much from what I did see. The dormitories, divided by sex, were on the sensory-dampening side. The subjects slept in small cells, ascetic and chaste, that reminded me of an abandoned Carmelite convent I had once toured in Belgium. That was the shock: the physical plant felt scientific, but the atmosphere did not.

There hung in the gray corridors a wordless peace, a feeling so palpable I could feel it clogging my lungs. No. "Peace" was the wrong word. Say "peace" and the picture is pastoral, lazy sunshine and dreaming woods. This was not like that at all. The research subjects—students? postulants?—lounged in the corridors outside closed labs, waiting for the next step in their routine. Both men and women were anorectic, both wore gray bodysuits or caftans, both were fined down to an otherworldly ethereality when seen from a distance and a malnourished asexuality when seen up close. They talked among themselves in low voices, sitting with backs against the wall or stretched full-length on the carpeted floor, and on all their faces I saw the same luminous patience, the same certainty of being very near to something exciting that they nonetheless could wait for calmly, as long as necessary.

"They look," I said to Devrie, "as if they're waiting to take an exam they already know they'll ace."

She smiled. "Do you think so? I always think of us as travelers waiting for a plane, boarding passes stamped for Eternity."

She was actually serious. But she didn't in fact wear the same expression as the others; hers was far more intense. If they were travelers, she wanted to pilot.

The lab door opened and the students brought themselves to their feet. Despite their languid movements, they looked sharp: sharp protruding clavicles, bony chins, angular unpadded elbows that could chisel stone.

"This is my hour for biofeedback manipulation of drug effects," Devrie said. "Please come watch."

"I'd sooner watch you whip yourself in a twelfth-century monastery."

Devrie's eyes widened, then again lightened with that luminous amusement. "It's for the same end, isn't it? But they had such unsystematic means. Poor struggling God-searchers. I wonder how many of them made it."

I wanted to strike her. "*Devrie—*"

"If not biofeedback, what would you like to see?"

"You out of here."

"What else?"

There was only one thing: the holotanks. I struggled with the temptation, and lost. The two tanks stood in the middle of a roomy lab carpeted with thick gray matting and completely enclosed in a Faraday cage. That Devrie had a key to the lab was my first clue that my errand for her had been known, and discussed, by someone higher in the Institute. Research subjects do not carry keys to the most delicate brain-perception equipment in the world. For this equipment Bohentin had received his Nobel.

The two tanks, independent systems, stood as high as my shoulder. The ones I had used fifteen years ago had been smaller. Each of these was a cube, opaque on its bottom half, which held the sensing apparatus, computerized simulators, and recording equipment; clear on its top half, which was filled with the transparent fluid out of whose molecules the simulations would form. A separate sim would form for each subject, as the machine sorted and mapped all the electromagnetic radiation received and processed by each brain. *All* that each brain perceived, not only the visuals; the holograph equipment was capable of picking up all wavelengths that the brain did, and of displaying their brain-processed analogues as three-dimensional images floating in a clear womb. When all other possible sources of radiation were filtered out except for the emanations from the two subjects themselves, what the sims showed was what kinds of activity were coming from—and hence going on in—the other's brain. That was why it worked best with identical twins in twin trance: no structural brain differences to adjust for. In a rawer version of this holotank, a rawer version of myself had pioneered the recording of twin trances. The UCIC, we had called it then: What you see, I see.

What I had seen was eight autopsy reports.

"We're so *close*," Devrie said. "Mona and Marlene—"she waved a hand toward the corridor but Mona and Marlene, whichever two they had been, had gone—"had taken KX3, that's the drug that—"

"I know what it is," I said, too harshly. KX3 reacts with one of the hormones overproduced in an anorectic body. The combination is readily absorbed by body fat, but in a body without fat, much of it is absorbed by the brain.

Devrie continued, her hand tight on my arm. "Mona and Marlene were controlling the neural reactions with biofeedback, pushing the twin trance higher and higher, working it. Dr. Bohentin was monitoring the holotanks. The sims were incredibly detailed—everything each twin perceived in the perceptions of the other, in all wavelengths. Mona and Marlene forced their neurotransmission level even higher and then, in the tanks—" Devrie's face glowed, the mystic-rapture look—"a completely third sim formed. Completely separate. A third *presence*."

I stared at her.

"It was recorded in *both* tanks. It was shadowy, yes, but it was *there*. A third presence that can't be perceived except through another human's electromagnetic presence, and then only with every drug and trained reaction and arousal mode and the twin trance all pushing the brain into a supraheightened state. A third presence!"

"Isotropic radiation. Bohentin fluffed the pre-screening program and the computer hadn't cleared the background microradiation—" I said, but even as I spoke I knew how stupid that was. Bohentin didn't make mistakes like that, and isotropic radiation simulates nowhere close to the way a presence does. Devrie didn't even bother to answer me.

This, then, was what the rumors had been about, the rumors leaking for the last year out of the Institute and through the scientific community, mostly still scoffed at, not yet picked up by the popular press. This. A verifiable, replicable third presence being picked up by holography. Against all reason, a long shiver went over me from neck to that cold place at the base of the spine.

"There's more," Devrie said feverishly. "They *felt* it. Mona and Marlene. Both said afterwards that they could feel it, a huge presence filled with light, but they couldn't quite reach it. Damn—they couldn't reach it, Seena! They weren't playing off each other enough, weren't close enough. Weren't, despite the twin trance, *melded* enough."

"Sex," I said.

"They tried it. The subjects are all basically heterosexual. They inhibit."

"So go find some homosexual God-yearning anorectic incestuous twins!"

Devrie looked at me straight. "I need him. Here. He *is* me."

I exploded, right there in the holotank lab. No one came running in to find out if the shouting was dangerous to the tanks, which was my second clue that the Institute knew very well why Devrie had brought me there. "Damn it to hell, he's a human being, not some chemical you can just order up because you need it for an experiment! You don't have the right to expect him to come here, you didn't even have the right to tell anyone that he exists, but that didn't stop you, did it? There are still anti-bioengineering groups out there in the real world, religious split-brains who—how *dare* you put him in any danger? How dare you even presume he'd be interested in this insane mush?"

"He'll come," Devrie said. She had not changed expression.

"How the hell do you know?"

"He's me. And I want God. He will, too."

I scowled at her. A fragment of one of her poems, a thing she had written when she was fifteen, came to me: "Two human species/ Never one—/One aching for God/One never." But she had been fifteen then. I had assumed that the sentiment, as adolescent as the poetry, would pass.

I said, "What does Bohentin think of this idea of importing your clone?"

For the first time she hesitated. Bohentin, then, was dubious. "He thinks it's rather a long shot."

"You could phrase it that way."

"But *I* know he'll want to come. Some things you just know,

Seena, beyond rationality. And besides—" she hesitated again, and then went on, "I have half my inheritance from Daddy, and the income on the trust from Mummy."

"Devrie. God, Devrie—you'd *buy* him?"

For the first time she looked angry. "The money would be just to get him here, to see what is involved. Once he sees, he'll want this as much as I do, at any price! What price can you put on God? I'm not 'buying' his life—I'm offering him the way to *find* life. What good is breathing, existing, if there's no purpose to it? Don't you realize how many centuries, in how many ways, people have looked for that light-filled presence and never been able to be *sure*? And now we're almost there, Seena, I've seen it for myself—*almost there*. With verifiable, scientifically-controlled means. Not subjective faith this time—scientific data, the same as for any other actual phenomenon. This research stands now where research into the atom stood fifty years ago. Can you touch a quark? But it's there! And my clone can be a part of it, can *be* it, how can you talk about the money buying him under circumstances like that!"

I said slowly, "How do you know that whatever you're so close to is God?" But that was sophomoric, of course, and she was ready for it. She smiled warmly.

"What does it matter what we call it? Pick another label if it will make you more comfortable."

I took a piece of paper from my pocket. "His name is Keith Torellen. He lives in Indian Falls, New Hampshire. Address and mailnet number here. Good luck, Devrie." I turned to go.

"Seena! *I* can't go!"

She couldn't, of course. That was the point. She barely had the strength in that starved, drug-battered body to get through the day, let alone to New Hampshire. She needed the sensory-controlled environment, the artificial heat, the chemical monitoring. "Then send someone from the Institute. Perhaps Bohentin will go."

"*Bohen*tin!" she said, and I knew that was impossible; Bohentin had to remain officially ignorant of this sort of recruiting. Too many U.S. laws were involved. In addition, Bohentin had no persuasive skills; people as persons and not neurologies did not interest him. They were too far above chemicals and too far below God.

Devrie looked at me with a kind of level fury. "This is really why you found him, isn't it? So I would have to stop the drug program long enough to leave here and go get him. You think that once I've gone back out into the world either the build-up effects in the brain will be interrupted or else the spell will be broken and I'll have doubts about coming back here!"

"Will you listen to yourself? 'Out into the world.' You sound like some archaic nun in a cloistered order!"

"You always did ridicule anything you couldn't understand," Devrie said icily, turned her back on me, and stared at the empty holotanks. She didn't turn when I left the lab, closing the door behind me. She was still facing the tanks, her spiny back rigid, the piece of paper with Keith Torellen's address clutched in fingers delicate as glass.

In New York the museum simmered with excitement. An unexpected endowment had enabled us to buy the contents of a small, very old museum located in a part of Madagascar not completely destroyed by the African Horror. Crate after crate of moths began arriving in New York, some of them collected in the days when naturalists-gentlemen shot jungle moths from the trees using dust shot. Some species had been extinct since the Horror and thus were rare; some were the brief mutations from the bad years afterward and thus were even rarer. The museum staff uncrated and exclaimed.

"Look at this one," said a young man, holding it out to me. Not on my own staff, he was one of the specialists on loan to us—DeFabio or DeFazio, something like that. He was very handsome. I looked at the moth he showed me, all pale wings outstretched and pinned to black silk. "A perfect Thysania Africana. *Perfect*."

"Yes."

"You'll have to loan us the whole exhibit, in a few years."

"Yes," I said again. He heard the tone in my voice and glanced up quickly. But not quickly enough—my face was all professional interest when his gaze reached it. Still, the professional interest had not fooled him; he had heard the perfunctory note. Frowning, he turned back to the moths.

By day I directed the museum efficiently enough. But in the evenings, home alone in my apartment, I found myself wandering from room to room, touching objects, unable to settle to work at the oversize teak desk that had been my father's, to the reports and journals that had not. His had dealt with the living, mine with the ancient dead—but I had known that for years. The fogginess of my evenings bothered me.

"Faith should not mean fogginess."

Who had said that? Father, of course, to Devrie, when she had joined the dying Catholic Church. She had been thirteen years old. Skinny, defiant, she had stood clutching a black rosary from God knows where, daring him from sacred dark eyes to forbid her. Of course he had not, thinking, I suppose, that Heaven, like any other childhood fever, was best left alone to burn out its course.

Devrie had been received into the Church in an overdecorated chapel, wearing an overdecorated dress of white lace and carrying a candle. Three years later she had left, dressed in a magenta body suit and holding the keys to Father's safe, which his executor had left unlocked after the funeral. The will had, of course, made me Devrie's guardian. In the three years Devrie had been going to Mass, I had discovered that I was sterile, divorced my second husband, finished my work in entomology, accepted my first position with a museum, and entered a drastically premature menopause.

That is not a flip nor random list.

After the funeral, I sat in the dark in my father's study, in his maroon leather chair and at his teak desk. Both felt oversize. All the lights were off. Outside it rained; I heard the steady beat of water on the window, and the wind. The dark room was cold. In my palm I held one of my father's research awards, a small abstract sculpture of a double helix, done by Harold Landau himself. It was very heavy. I couldn't think what Landau had used, to make it so heavy. I couldn't think, with all the noise from the rain. My father was dead, and I would never bear a child.

Devrie came into the room, leaving the lights off but bringing with her an incandescent rectangle from the doorway. At sixteen she was lovely, with long brown hair in the masses of curls again newly fashionable. She sat on a low stool beside me, all that hair falling around her, her face white in the gloom. She had been crying.

"He's gone. He's really gone. I don't believe it yet."

"No."

She peered at me. Something in my face, or my voice, must have alerted her; when she spoke again it was in that voice people use when they think your grief is understandably greater than theirs. A smooth dark voice, like a wave.

"You still have me, Seena. We still have each other."

I said nothing.

"I've always thought of you more as my mother than my sister, anyway. You took the place of Mother. You've been a mother to at least *me*."

She smiled and squeezed my hand. I looked at her face—so young, so pretty—and I wanted to hit her. I didn't want to be her mother; I wanted to be her. All her choices lay ahead of her, and it seemed to me that self-indulgent night as if mine were finished. I could have struck her.

"Seena—"

"Leave me alone! Can't you ever leave me alone? All my life you've been dragging behind me; why don't *you* die and finally leave me alone!"

We make ourselves pay for small sins more than large ones. The more trivial the thrust, the longer we're haunted by memory of the wound.

I believe that.

Indian Falls was out of another time: slow, quiet, safe. The Avis counter at the airport rented not personal guards but cars, and the only shiny store on Main Street sold wilderness equipment. I suspected that the small state college, like the town, traded mostly on trees and trails. That Keith Torellen was trying to take an academic degree *here* told me more about his adopting family than if I had hired a professional information service.

The house where he lived was shabby, paint peeling and steps none too sturdy. I climbed them slowly, thinking once again what I wanted to find out.

Devrie would answer none of my messages on the mailnet. Nor would she accept my phone calls. She was shutting me out, in retaliation for my refusing to fetch Torellen for her. But Devrie would discover that she could not shut me out as easily as that; we were sisters. I wanted to know if she had contacted Torellen herself, or had sent someone from the Institute to do so.

If neither, then my visit here would be brief and anonymous; I would leave Keith Torellen to his protected ignorance and shabby town. But if he *had* seen Devrie, I wanted to discover if and what he had agreed to do for her. It might even be possible that he could be of use in convincing Devrie of the stupidity of what she was doing. If he could be used for that, I would use him.

Something else: I was curious. This boy was my brother—nephew? no, brother—as well as the result of my father's rational mind. Curiosity prickled over me. I rang the bell.

It was answered by the landlady, who said that Keith was not home, would not be home until late, was "in rehearsal."

"Rehearsal?"

"Over to the college. He's a student and they're putting on a play."

I said nothing, thinking.

"I don't remember the name of the play," the landlady said. She was a large woman in a faded garment, dress or robe. "But Keith says it's going to be real good. It starts this weekend." She laughed. "But you probably already know all that! George, my husband George, he says I'm forever telling people things they already know."

"How would I know?"

She winked at me. "Don't you think I got eyes? Sister, or cousin? No, let me guess—older sister. Too much alike for cousins."

"Thank you," I said. "You've been very helpful."

"Not sister!" She clapped her hand over her mouth, her eyes shiny with amusement. "You're checking up on him, ain't you? You're his mother! I should of seen it right off!"

I turned to negotiate the porch steps.

"They rehearse in the new building, Mrs. Torellen," she called after me. "Just ask anybody you see to point you in the right direction."

"Thank you," I said carefully.

Rehearsal was nearly over. Evidently it was a dress rehearsal; the actors were in period costume and the director did not interrupt. I did not recognize the period or the play. Devrie had been interested in theater: I was not. Quietly I took a seat in the darkened back row and waited for the pretending to end.

Despite wig and greasepaint, I had no trouble picking out Keith Torellen. He moved like Devrie: quick, light movements, slightly pigeontoed. He had her height and, given the differences of a male body, her slenderness. Sitting a theater's length away, I might have been seeing a male Devrie.

But seen up close, his face was mine.

Despite the landlady, it was a shock. He came towards me across the theater lobby, from where I had sent for him, and I saw the moment he too struck the resemblance. He stopped dead, and we stared at each other. Take Devrie's genes, spread them over a face with the greater bone surface, larger features, and coarser skin texture of a man—and the result was my face. Keith had scrubbed off his make-up and removed his wig, exposing brown curly hair the same shade Devrie's had been. But his face was mine.

A strange emotion, unnamed and hot, seared through me.

"Who are *you*? Who the hell *are* you?"

So no one had come from the Institute after all. Not Devrie, not any one.

"You're one of them, aren't you?" he said; it was almost a whisper. "One of my real family?"

Still gripped by the unexpected force of emotion, still dumb, I said nothing. Keith took one step toward me. Suspicion played over his face—Devrie would not have been suspicious—and vanished, replaced by a slow painful flush of color.

"You are. You *are* one. Are you . . . are you my mother?"

I put out a hand against a stone post. The lobby was all stone and glass. Why were all theater lobbies stone and glass? Architects had so little damn imagination, so little sense of the bizarre.

"No! I am not your mother!"

He touched my arm. "Hey, are you okay? You don't look good. Do you need to sit down?"

His concern was unexpected, and touching. I thought that he shared Devrie's genetic personality and that Devrie had always been hypersensitive to the body. But this was not Devrie. His hand on my arm was stronger, firmer, warmer than Devrie's. I felt giddy, disoriented. This was not Devrie.

"A mistake," I said unsteadily. "This was a mistake. I should not have come. I'm sorry. My name is Dr. Seena Konig and I am a . . . relative of yours, but I think this now is a mistake. I have your address and I promise that I'll write you about your family, but now I think I should go." Write some benign lie, leave him in ignorance. This was a mistake.

But he looked stricken, and his hand tightened on my arm. "You can't! I've been searching for my biological family for two years! You can't just go!"

We were beginning to attract attention in the theater lobby. Hurry-

ing students eyed us sideways. I thought irrelevantly how different
they looked from the "students" at the Institute, and with that
thought regained my composure. This was a student, a boy—"you
can't!" a boyish protest, and boyish panic in his voice—and not the
man-Devrie-me he had seemed a foolish moment ago. He was nearly
twenty years my junior. I smiled at him and removed his hand from
my arm.

"Is there somewhere we can have coffee?"

"Yes, Dr. . . ."

"Seena," I said. "Call me Seena."

Over coffee, I made him talk first. He watched me anxiously over
the rim of his cup, as if I might vanish, and I listened to the words
behind the words. His adopting family was the kind that hoped to
visit the Grand Canyon but not Europe, go to movies but not opera,
aspire to college but not to graduate work, buy wilderness equipment
but not wilderness. Ordinary people. Not religious, not rich, not
unusual. Keith was the only child. He loved them.

"But at the same time I never really felt I belonged," he said, and
looked away from me. It was the most personal thing he had know-
ingly revealed, and I saw that he regretted it. Devrie would not have.
More private, then, and less trusting. And I sensed in him a grittiness,
a tougher awareness of the world's hardness, than Devrie had ever
had—or needed to have. I made my decision. Having disturbed him
thus far, I owed him truth—but not the whole truth.

"Now you tell me," Keith said, pushing away his cup. "Who were
my parents? Our parents? Are you my sister?"

"Yes."

"Our parents?"

"Both are dead. Our father was Dr. Richard Konig. He was a
scientist. He—" But Keith had recognized the name. His readings in
biology or history must have been more extensive than I would have
expected. His eyes widened, and I suddenly wished I had been more
oblique.

"Richard Konig. He's one of those scientists that were involved in
the bioengineering scandal—"

"How did you learn about that? It's all over and done with. Years
ago."

"Journalism class. We studied how the press handled it, especially
the sensationalism surrounding the cloning thing twenty years—"

I saw the moment it hit him. He groped for his coffee cup, clutched the handle, didn't raise it. It was empty anyway. And then what I said next shocked me as much as anything I have ever done.

"It was Devrie," I said, and heard my own vicious pleasure, "*Devrie* was the one who wanted me to tell you!"

But of course he didn't know who Devrie was. He went on staring at me, panic in his young eyes, and I sat frozen. That tone I heard in my own voice when I said "Devrie," that vicious pleasure that it was she and not I who was hurting him . . .

"Cloning," Keith said. "Konig was in trouble for claiming to have done illegal cloning. Of humans." His voice held so much dread that I fought off my own dread and tried to hold myself steady to his need.

"It's illegal now, but not then. And the public badly misunderstood. All that sensationalism—you were right to use that word, Keith—covered up the fact that there is nothing abnormal about producing a fetus from another diploid cell. In the womb, identical twins—"

"Am I a clone?"

"Keith—"

"*Am I a clone?*"

Carefully I studied him. This was not what I had intended, but although the fear was still in his eyes, the panic had gone. And curiosity—Devrie's curiosity, and her eagerness—they were there as well. This boy would not strike me, nor stalk out of the restaurant, nor go into psychic shock.

"Yes. You are."

He sat quietly, his gaze turned inward. A long moment passed in silence.

"Your cell?"

"No. My—our sister's. Our sister Devrie."

Another long silence. He did not panic. Then he said softly, "Tell me."

Devrie's phrase.

"There isn't much to tell, Keith. If you've seen the media accounts, you know the story, and also what was made of it. The issue then becomes how you feel about what you saw. Do you believe that cloning is meddling with things man should best leave alone?"

"No. I don't."

I let out my breath, although I hadn't known I'd been holding it. "It's actually no more than delayed twinning, followed by surrogate implantation. A zygote—"

"I know all that," he said with some harshness, and held up his hand to silence me. I didn't think he knew that he did it. The harshness did not sound like Devrie. To my ears, it sounded like myself. He sat thinking, remote and troubled, and I did not try to touch him.

Finally he said, "Do my parents know?"

He meant his adoptive parents. "No."

"Why are you telling me now? Why did you come?"

"Devrie asked me to."

"She needs something, right? A kidney? Something like that?"

I had not foreseen that question. He did not move in a class where spare organs were easily purchasable. "No. Not a kidney, not any kind of biological donation." A voice in my mind jeered at that, but I was not going to give him any clues that would lead to Devrie. "She just wanted me to find you."

"Why didn't she find me herself? She's my age, right?"

"Yes. She's ill just now and couldn't come."

"Is she dying?"

"No!"

Again he sat quietly, finally saying, "No one could tell me anything. For two years I've been searching for my mother, and not one of the adoptee-search agencies could find a single trace. Not one. Now I see why. Who covered the trail so well?"

"My father."

"I want to meet Devrie."

I said evenly, "That might not be possible."

"Why not?"

"She's in a foreign hospital. Out of the country. I'm sorry."

"When does she come home?"

"No one is sure."

"What disease does she have?"

She's sick for God, I thought, but aloud I said, not thinking it through, "A brain disease."

Instantly I saw my own cruelty. Keith paled, and I cried, "No, no, nothing you could have as well! Truly, Keith, it's not—she took a bad fall. From her hunter."

"Her hunter," he said. For the first time, his gaze flickered over my clothing and jewelry. But would he even recognize how expensive they were? I doubted it. He wore a synthetic, deep-pile jacket with a tear at one shoulder and a cheap wool hat, dark blue, shapeless with age. From long experience I recognized his gaze: uneasy, furtive, the expression of a man glimpsing the financial gulf between what he had assumed were equals. But it wouldn't matter. Adopted children have no legal claim on the estates of their biological parents. I had checked.

Keith said uneasily. "Do you have a picture of Devrie?"

"No," I lied.

"Why did she want you to find me? You still haven't said."

I shrugged. "The same reason, I suppose, that you looked for your biological family. The pull of blood."

"Then she wants me to write to her."

"Write to me instead."

He frowned. "Why? Why not to Devrie?"

What to say to that? I hadn't bargained on so much intensity from him. "Write in care of me, and I'll forward it to Devrie."

"Why not to her directly?"

"Her doctors might not think it advisable," I said coldly, and he backed off—either from the mention of doctors or from the coldness.

"Then give me your address, Seena. Please."

I did. I could see no harm in his writing me. It might even be pleasant. Coming home from the museum, another wintry day among the exhibits, to find on the mailnet a letter I could answer when and how I chose, without being taken by surprise. I liked the idea.

But no more difficult questions now. I stood. "I have to leave, Keith."

He looked alarmed. "So soon?"

"Yes."

"But why?"

"I have to return to work."

He stood, too. He was taller than Devrie. "Seena," he said, all earnestness, "just a few more questions. How did you find me?"

"Medical connections."

"Yours?"

"Our father's. I'm not a scientist." Evidently his journalism class had not studied twin-trance sensationalism.

"What do you do?"

"Museum curator. Arthropods."

"What does Devrie do?"

"She's too ill to work. I must go, Keith."

"One more. Do I look like Devrie as well as you?"

"It would be wise, Keith, if you were careful whom you spoke with about all of this. I hadn't intended to say so much."

"I'm not going to tell my parents. Not about being—not about all of it."

"I think that's best, yes."

"Do I look like Devrie as well as you?"

A little of my first, strange emotion returned with his intensity. "A little, yes. But more like me. Sex variance is a tricky thing."

Unexpectedly, he held my coat for me. As I slipped into it, he said from behind, "Thank you, Seena," and let his hands rest on my shoulders.

I did not turn around. I felt my face flame, and self-disgust flooded through me, followed by a desire to laugh. It was all so transparent. This man was an attractive stranger, was Devrie, was youth, was myself, was the work not of my father's loins but of his mind. Of course I was aroused by him. Freud outlasts cloning: a note for a research study, I told myself grimly, and inwardly I did laugh.

But that didn't help either.

In New York, winter came early. Cold winds whipped whitecaps on harbor and river, and the trees in the Park stood bare even before October had ended. The crumbling outer boroughs of the shrinking city crumbled a little more and talked of the days when New York had been important. Manhattan battened down for snow, hired the seasonal increases in personal guards, and talked of Albuquerque. Each night museum security hunted up and evicted the drifters trying to sleep behind exhibits, drifters as chilled and pale as the moths under permaplex, and, it seemed to me, as detached from the blood of their own age. All of New York seemed detached to me that October, and cold. Often I stood in front of the cases of Noctuidae, staring at them for so long that my staff began to glance at each other covertly. I would catch their glances when I jerked free of my trance. No one asked me about it.

Still no message came from Devrie. When I contacted the Institute on the mailnet, she did not call back.

No letter came from Keith Torellen.

Then one night, after I had worked late and was hurrying through the chilly gloom towards my building, he was there, bulking from the shadows so quickly that the guard I had taken for the walk from the museum sprang forward in attack position.

"No! It's all right! I know him."

The guard retreated, without expression. Keith stared after him, and then at me, his face unreadable.

"Keith, what are you doing here? Come inside!"

He followed me into the lobby without a word. Nor did he say anything during the metal scanning and ID procedure. I took him up to my apartment, studying him in the elevator. He wore the same jacket and cheap wool hat as in Indian Falls, his hair wanted cutting, and the tip of his nose was red from waiting in the cold. How long had he waited there? He badly needed a shave.

In the apartment he scanned the rugs, the paintings, my grandmother's ridiculously ornate, ugly silver, and turned his back on them to face me.

"Seena. I want to know where Devrie is."

"Why? Keith, what has happened?"

"Nothing has happened," he said, removing his jacket but not laying it anywhere. "Only that I've left school and spent two days hitching here. It's no good, Seena. To say that cloning is just like twinning: it's no good. I want to see Devrie."

His voice was hard. Bulking in my living room, unshaven, that hat pulled down over his ears, he looked older and less malleable than the last time I had seen him. Alarm—not physical fear, I was not afraid of him, but a subtler and deeper fear—sounded through me.

"Why do you want to see Devrie?"

"Because she cheated me."

"Of *what*, for God's sake?"

"Can I have a drink? Or a smoke?"

I poured him a Scotch. If he drank, he might talk. I had to know what he wanted, why such a desperate air clung to him, how to keep him from Devrie. I had never seen *her* like this. She was strong-willed, but always with a blitheness, a trust that eventually her will would prevail. Desperate forcefulness of the sort in Keith's manner was not her style. But of course Devrie had always had silent money to back her will; perhaps money could buy trust as well as style.

Keith drank off his Scotch and held out his glass for another. "It was freezing out there. They wouldn't let me in the lobby to wait for you."

"Of course not."

"You didn't tell me your family was rich."

I was a little taken aback at his bluntness, but at the same time it pleased me; I don't know why.

"You didn't ask."

"That's shit, Seena."

"Keith. Why are you here?"

"I told you. I want to see Devrie."

"What is it you've decided she cheated you of? Money?"

He looked so honestly surprised that again I was startled, this time by his resemblance to Devrie. She too would not have thought of financial considerations first, if there were emotional ones possible. One moment Keith was Devrie, one moment he was not. Now he scowled with sudden anger.

"Is that what you think—that fortune hunting brought me hitching from New Hampshire? God, Seena, I didn't know how much you had until this very—I still don't know!"

I said levelly, "Then what is it you're feeling so cheated of?"

Now he was rattled. Again that quick, half-furtive scan of my apartment, pausing a millisecond too long at the Caravaggio, subtly lit by its frame. When his gaze returned to mine it was troubled, a little defensive. Ready to justify. Of course I had put him on the defensive deliberately, but the calculation of my trick did not prepare me for the staggering naivete of his explanation. Once more it was Devrie complete, reducing the impersonal greatness of science to a personal and emotional loss.

"Ever since I knew I was adopted, at five or six years old, I wondered about my biological family. Nothing strange in that—I think all adoptees do. I used to make up stories, kid stuff, about how they were really royalty, or lunar colonists, or survivors of the African Horror. Exotic things. I thought especially about my mother, imagining this whole scene of her holding me once before she released me for adoption, crying over me, loving me so much she could barely let me go but had to for some reason. Sentimental shit." He laughed, trying to make light of what was not, and drank off his Scotch to avoid my gaze.

"But Devrie—the fact of her—destroyed all that. I never had a mother who hated to give me up. I never had a mother at all. What I had was a cell cut from Devrie's fingertip or someplace, something discardable, and she doesn't even know what I look like. But she's damn well going to."

"Why?" I said evenly. "What could you expect to gain from her knowing what you look like?"

But he didn't answer me directly. "That first moment I saw you, Seena, in the theater at school, I thought *you* were my mother."

"I know you did."

"And you hated the idea. Why?"

I thought of the child I would never bear, the marriage, like so many other things of sweet promise, gone sour. But self-pity is a fool's game. "None of your business."

"Isn't it? Didn't you hate the idea because of the way I was made? Coldly. An experiment. Weren't you a little bit insulted at being called the mother of a discardable cell from Devrie's fingertip?"

"What the hell have you been reading? An experiment—what is any child but an experiment? A random egg, a random sperm. Don't talk like one of those anti-science religious split-brains!"

He studied me levelly. Then he said, "Is Devrie religious? Is that why you're so afraid of her?"

I got to my feet, and pointed at the sideboard. "Help yourself to another drink if you wish. I want to wash my hands. I've been handling specimens all afternoon." Stupid, clumsy lie—nobody would believe such a lie.

In the bathroom I leaned against the closed door, shut my eyes, and willed myself to calm. Why should I be so disturbed by the angry lashing-out of a confused boy? I was handy to lash out against; my father, whom Keith was really angry at, was not. It was all so predictable, so earnestly adolescent, that even over the hurting in my chest I smiled. But the smile, which should have reduced Keith's ranting to the tantrum of a child—there, there, when you grow up you'll find out that no one really knows who he is—did not diminish Keith. His losses were real—mother, father, natural place in the natural sequence of life and birth. And suddenly, with a clutch at the pit of my stomach, I knew why I had told him all that I had about his origins. It was not from any ethic of fidelity to "the truth." I had told him he was a clone because I, too, had had real losses—research, marriage, motherhood—and Devrie could never have shared them with me. Luminous, mystical Devrie, too occupied with God to be much hurt by man. *Leave me alone! Can't you ever leave me alone! All my life you've been dragging behind me—why don't you die and finally leave me alone!* And Devrie had smiled tolerantly, patted my head, and left me alone, closing the door softly so as not to disturb my grief. My words had not hurt her. I could not hurt her.

But I could hurt Keith—the other Devrie—and I had. That was why he disturbed me all out of proportion. That was the bond. My face, my pain, my fault.

Through my fault, through my fault, through my most grievous fault. But what nonsense. I was not a believer, and the comforts of superstitious absolution could not touch me. What shit. Like all nonbelievers, I stood alone.

It came to me then that there was something absurd in thinking all this while leaning against a bathroom door. Grimly absurd, but absurd. The toilet as confessional. I ran the cold water, splashed some on my face, and left. How long had I left Keith alone in the living room?

When I returned, he was standing by the mailnet. He had punched in the command to replay my outgoing postal messages, and displayed on the monitor was Devrie's address at the Institute of the Biological Hope.

"What is it?" Keith said. "A hospital?"

I didn't answer him.

"I can find out, Seena. Knowing this much, I can find out. Tell me."

Tell me. "Not a hospital. It's a research laboratory. Devrie is a voluntary subject."

"Research on what? I will find out, Seena."

"Brain perception."

"Perception of what?"

"Perception of *God*," I said, torn among weariness, anger, and a sudden gritty exasperation, irritating as sand. Why not just leave him to Devrie's persuasions, and her to mystic starvation? But I knew I would not. I still, despite all of it, wanted her out of there.

Keith frowned. "What do you mean, 'perception of God'?"

I told him. I made it sound as ridiculous as possible, and as dangerous. I described the anorexia, the massive use of largely untested drugs that would have made the Institute illegal in the United States, the skepticism of most of the scientific community, the psychoses and death that had followed twin-trance research fifteen years earlier. Keith did not remember that—he had been eight years old—and I did not tell him that I had been one of the researchers. I did not tell him about the tapes of the shadowy third presence in Bohentin's holotanks. In every way I could, with every verbal subtlety at my use, I made the Institute sound crackpot, and dangerous, and ugly. As I spoke, I watched Keith's face, and sometimes it was mine, and sometimes the expression altered it into Devrie's. I saw bewilderment at her having chosen to enter the Institute, but not what I had hoped to see. Not scorn, not disgust.

When I had finished, he said, "But why did she think that *I* might want to enter such a place as a twin subject?"

I had saved this for last. "Money. She'd buy you."

His hand, holding his third Scotch, went rigid. "Buy me."

"It's the most accurate way to put it."

"What the hell made her think—" he mastered himself, not without effort. Not all the discussion of bodily risk had affected him as much as this mention of Devrie's money. He had a poor man's touchy pride. "She thinks of me as something to be *bought*."

I was carefully quiet.

"Damn her," he said. "*Damn* her." Then, roughly, "And I was actually considering—"

I caught my breath. "Considering the Institute? After what I've just told you? How in hell could you? And you said, I remember, that your background was not religious!"

"It's not. But I . . . I've wondered." And in the sudden turn of his head away from me so that I wouldn't see the sudden rapt hopelessness in his eyes, in the defiant set of his shoulders, I read more than in his banal words, and more than he could know. Devrie's look, Devrie's wishfulness, feeding on air. The weariness and anger, checked before, flooded me again and I lashed out at him.

"Then go ahead and fly to Dominica to enter the Institute yourself!"

He said nothing. But from something—his expression as he stared into his glass, the shifting of his body—I suddenly knew that he could not afford the trip.

I said, "So you fancy yourself as a believer?"

"No. A believer manqué." From the way he said it, I knew that he had said it before, perhaps often, and that the phrase stirred some hidden place in his imagination.

"What is wrong with you," I said, "with people like you, that the human world is not enough?"

"What is wrong with people like you, that it is?" he said, and this time he laughed and raised his eyebrows in a little mockery that shut me out from this place beyond reason, this glittering escape. I knew then that somehow or other, sometime or other, despite all I had said, Keith would go to Dominica.

I poured him another Scotch. As deftly as I could, I led the conversation into other, lighter directions. I asked about his childhood. At first stiffly, then more easily as time and Scotch loosened him, he talked about growing up in the Berkshire Hills. He became more light-hearted, and under my interest turned both shrewd and funny, with a keen sense of humor. His thick brown hair fell over his forehead. I laughed with him, and broke out a bottle of good sport. He talked about amateur plays he had acted in; his enthusiasm increased as his coherence decreased. Enthusiasm, humor, thick brown hair. I smoothed the hair back from his forehead. Far into the night I pulled the drapes back from the window and we stood together and looked at the lights of the dying city ten stories below. Fog rolled in from the sea. Keith insisted we open the doors and stand on the balcony; he had never smelled fog tinged with the ocean. We smelled the night, and drank some more, and talked, and laughed.

And then I led him again to the sofa.

"Seena?" Keith said. He covered my hand, laid upon his thigh, with his own, and turned his head to look at me questioningly. I leaned forward and touched my lips to his, barely in contact, for a long moment. He drew back, and his hand tried to lift mine. I tightened my fingers.

"Seena, no . . ."

"Why not?" I put my mouth back on his, very lightly. He had to draw back to answer, and I could feel that he did not want to draw back. Under my lips he frowned slightly; still, despite his drunkenness—so much more than mine—he groped for the word.

"Incest . . ."

"No. We two have never shared a womb."

He frowned again, under my mouth. I drew back to smile at him, and shifted my hand. "It doesn't matter any more, Keith. Not in New York. But even if it did—I am not your sister, not really. You said so yourself—remember? Not a family. Just . . . here."

"Not family," he repeated, and I saw in his eyes the second before he closed them the flash of pain, the greed of a young man's desire, and even the crafty evasions of the good sport. Then his arms closed around me.

He was very strong, and more than a little violent. I guessed from what confusions the violence flowed but still I enjoyed it, that overwhelming rush from that beautiful male-Devrie body. I wanted him to be violent with me, as long as I knew there was no real danger. No real danger, no real brother, no real child. Keith was not my child but Devrie was my child-sister, and I had to stop her from destroying herself, no matter how . . . didn't I? "The pull of blood." But this was necessary, was justified . . . was a necessary gamble. For Devrie.

So I told myself. Then I stopped telling myself anything at all, and surrendered to the warm tides of pleasure.

But at dawn I woke and thought—with Keith sleeping heavily across me and the sky cold at the window—*what the hell am I doing?*

When I came out of the shower, Keith was sitting rigidly against the pillows. Sitting next to him on the very edge of the bed, I pulled a sheet around my nakedness and reached for his hand. He snatched it away.

"Keith. It's all right. Truly it is."

"You're my sister."

"But nothing will come of it. No child, no repetitions. It's not all that uncommon, dear heart."

"It is where I come from."

"Yes. I know. But not here."

He didn't answer, his face troubled.

"Do you want breakfast?"

"No. No, thank you."

I could feel his need to get away from me; it was almost palpable. Snatching my bodysuit off the floor, I went into the kitchen, which was chilly. The servant would not arrive for another hour. I turned up the heat, pulled on my bodysuit—standing on the cold floor first on one foot and then on the other, like some extinct species of water fowl— and made coffee. Through the handle of one cup I stuck two folded large bills. He came into the kitchen, dressed even to the torn jacket.

"Coffee."

"Thanks."

His fingers closed on the handle of the cup, and his eyes widened. Pure, naked shock, uncushioned by any defenses whatsoever: the whole soul, betrayed, pinned in the eyes.

"Oh, God, no, Keith—how can you even think so? It's for the trip back to Indian Falls! A gift!"

An endless pause, while we stared at each other. Then he said, very low, "I'm sorry. I should have . . . seen what it's for." But his cup trembled in his hand, and a few drops sloshed onto the floor. It was those few drops that undid me, flooding me with shame. Keith had a right to his shock, and to the anguish in his/my/Devrie's face. She wanted him for her mystic purposes, I for their prevention. Fanatic and saboteur, we were both better defended against each other than Keith, without money nor religion nor years, was against either of us. If I could have seen any other way than the gamble I had taken . . . but I could not. Nonetheless, I was ashamed.

"Keith. I'm sorry."

"Why did we? Why *did* we?"

I could have said: *we* didn't; I did. But that might have made it worse for him. He was male, and so young.

Impulsively I blurted, "Don't go to Dominica!" But of course he was beyond listening to me now. His face closed. He set down the coffee cup and looked at me from eyes much harder than they had been a minute ago. Was he thinking that because of our night together I expected to influence him directly? *I* was not that young. He could not foresee that I was trying to guess much farther ahead than that, for which I could not blame him. I could not blame him for anything. But I did regret how clumsily I had handled the money. That had been stupid.

Nonetheless, when he left a few moments later, the handle of the coffee cup was bare. He had taken the money.

The Madagascar exhibits were complete. They opened to much press interest, and there were both favorable reviews and celebrations. I could not bring myself to feel that it mattered. Ten times a day I went through the deadening exercise of willing an interest that had deserted me, and when I looked at the moths, ashy white wings outstretched forever, I could feel my body recoil in a way I could not name.

The image of the moths went home with me. One night in November I actually thought I heard wings beating against the window where I had stood with Keith. I yanked open the drapes and then the doors, but of course there was nothing there. For a long time I stared at the nothingness, smelling the fog, before typing yet another message, urgent-priority personal, to Devrie. The mailnet did not bring any answer.

I contacted the mailnet computer at the college at Indian Falls. My fingers trembled as they typed a request to leave an urgent-priority personal message for a student, Keith Torellen. The mailnet typed back:

TORELLEN, KEITH ROBERT. 64830016. ON MEDICAL LEAVE OF ABSENCE. TIME OF LEAVE: INDEFINITE. NO FORWARDING MAILNET NUMBER. END.

The sound came again at the window. Whirling, I scanned the dark glass, but there was nothing there, no moths, no wings, just the lights of the decaying city flung randomly across the blackness and the sound, faint and very far away, of a siren wailing out somebody else's disaster.

I shivered. Putting on a sweater and turning up the heat made me no warmer. Then the mail slot chimed softly and I turned in time to see the letter fall from the pneumatic tube from the lobby, the apartment house sticker clearly visible, assuring me that it had been processed and found free of both poison and explosives. Also visible was the envelope's logo: INSTITUTE OF THE BIOLOGICAL HOPE, all the O's radiant golden suns. But Devrie never wrote paper mail. She preferred the mailnet.

The note was from Keith, not Devrie. A short note, scrawled on a torn scrap of paper in nearly indecipherable handwriting. I had seen Keith's handwriting in Indian Falls, across his student notebooks;

this was a wildly out-of-control version of it, almost psychotic in the variations of spacing and letter formation that signal identity. I guessed that he had written the note under the influence of a drug, or several drugs, his mind racing much faster than he could write. There was neither punctuation nor paragraphing.

> Dear Seena Im going to do it I have to know my parents are angry but I have to know I have to all the confusion is gone Seena Keith

There was a word crossed out between "gone" and "Seena," scratched out with erratic lines of ink. I held the paper up to the light, tilting it this way and that. The crossed-out word was "mother."

all the confusion is gone mother

Mother.

Slowly I let out the breath I had not known I was holding. The first emotion was pity, for Keith, even though I had intended this. We had done a job on him, Devrie and I. Mother, sister, self. And when he and Devrie artificially drove upward the number and speed of the neurotransmitters in the brain, generated the twin trance, and then Keith's pre-cloning Freudian-still mind reached for Devrie to add sexual energy to all the other brain energies fueling Bohentin's holo-tanks—

Mother. Sister. Self.

All was fair in love and war. A voice inside my head jeered: And which is this? But I was ready for the voice. This was both. I didn't think it would be long before Devrie left the Institute to storm to New York.

It was nearly another month, in which the snow began to fall and the city to deck itself in the tired gilt fallacies of Christmas. I felt fine. Humming, I catalogued the Madagascar moths, remounting the best specimens in exhibit cases and sealing them under permaplex, where their fragile wings and delicate antennae could lie safe. The mutant strains had the thinnest wings, unnaturally tenuous and up to twenty-five centimeters each, all of pale ivory, as if a ghostly delicacy were the natural evolutionary response to the glowing landscape of nuclear genocide. I catalogued each carefully.

"Why?" Devrie said. "*Why?*"

"You look like hell."

"Why?"

"I think you already know," I said. She sagged on my white velvet sofa, alone, the PGs that I suspected acted as much as nurses as guards, dismissed from the apartment. Tears of anger and exhaustion collected in her sunken eye sockets but did not fall. Only with effort was she keeping herself in a sitting position, and the effort was costing her energy she did not have. Her skin, except for two red spots of fury high on each cheekbone, was the color of old eggs. Looking at her, I had to keep my hands twisted in my lap to keep myself from weeping.

"Are you telling me you *planned* it, Seena? Are you telling me you located Keith and slept with him because you knew that would make him impotent with me?"

"Of course not. I know sexuality isn't that simple. So do you."

"But you gambled on it. You gambled that it would be one way to ruin the experiment."

"I gambled that it would . . . complicate Keith's responses."

"Complicate them past the point where he knew who the hell he was with!"

"He'd be able to know if you weren't making him glow out of his mind with neurotransmitter kickers! He's not stupid. But he's not ready for whatever mystic hoops you've tried to make him jump through—if anybody ever *can* be said to be ready for that!—and no, I'm not surprised that he can't handle libidinal energies on top of all the other artificial energies you're racing through his brain. Something was bound to snap."

"You caused it, Seena. As cold-bloodedly as that."

A sudden shiver of memory brought the feel of Keith's hands on my breasts. No, not as cold-bloodedly as that. No. But I could not say so to Devrie.

"I trusted you," she said. "'Anything for a sister'—God!"

"You were right to trust me. To trust me to get you out of that place before you're dead."

"Listen to yourself! Smug, all-knowing, self-righteous . . . do you know how *close* we were at the Institute? Do you have any idea what you've destroyed?"

I laughed coldly. I couldn't help it. "If contact with God can be destroyed because one confused kid can't get it up, what does that say about God?"

Devrie stared at me. A long moment passed, and in the moment the two red spots on her cheeks faded and her eyes narrowed. "Why, Seena?"

"I told you. I wanted you safe, out of there. And you are."

"No. No. There's something else, something more going on here. Going on with you."

"Don't make it more complicated than it is, Devrie. You're my sister, and my only family. Is it so odd that I would try to protect you?"

"Keith is your brother."

"Well then, protect both of you. Whatever derails that experiment protects Keith, too."

She said softly, "Did you want him so much?"

We stared at each other across the living room, sisters, I standing by the mailnet and she supported by the sofa, needing its support, weak and implacable as any legendary martyr to the faith. Her weakness hurt me in some nameless place; as a child Devrie's body had been so strong. The hurt twisted in me, so that I answered her with truth. "Not so much. Not at first, not until we . . . no, that's not true. I wanted him. But that was not the reason, Devrie—it was not a rationalization for lust, nor any lapse in self-control."

She went on staring at me, until I turned to the sideboard and poured myself a Scotch. My hand trembled.

Behind me Devrie said, "Not lust. And not protection either. Something else, Seena. You're afraid."

I turned, smiling tightly. "Of you?"

"No. No, I don't think so."

"What then?"

"I don't know. Do you?"

"This is your theory, not mine."

She closed her eyes. The tears, shining all this time over her anger, finally fell. Head flung back against the pale sofa, arms limp at her side, she looked the picture of desolation, and so weak that I was frightened. I brought her a glass of milk from the kitchen and held it to her mouth, and I was a little surprised when she drank it off without protest.

"Devrie. You can't go on like this. In this physical state."

"No," she agreed, in a voice so firm and prompt that I was startled further. It was the voice of decision, not surrender. She straightened herself on the sofa. "Even Bohentin says I can't go on like this. I weigh less than he wants, and I'm right at the edge of not having the physical resources to control the twin trance. I'm having racking withdrawal symptoms even being on this trip, and at this very minute there is a doctor sitting at Father's desk in your study, in case I need him. Also, I've had my lawyers make over most of my remaining inheritance to Keith. I don't think you knew that. What's left has all been transferred to a bank on Dominica, and if I die it goes to the Institute. You won't be able to touch it, nor touch Keith's portion either, not even if I die. And I will die, Seena, soon, if I don't start eating and stop taking the program's drugs. I'll just burn out body and brain both. You've guessed that I'm close to that, but you haven't guessed how close. Now I'm telling you. I can't handle the stresses of the twin trance much longer."

I just went on holding her glass, arm extended, unable to move.

"You gambled that you could destroy one component in the claim of my experiment at the Institute by confusing my twin sexually. Well, you won. Now *I'm* making a gamble. I'm gambling my life that you can undo what you did with Keith, and without his knowing that I made you. You said he's not stupid and his impotency comes from being unable to handle the drug program; perhaps you're partly right. But he is me—*me*, Seena—and I know you've thought I was stupid all my life, because I wanted things you don't understand. Now Keith wants them, too—it was inevitable that he would—and you're going to undo whatever is standing in his way. I had to fight myself free all my life of your bullying, but Keith doesn't have that kind of time. Because if you don't undo what you caused, I'm going to go ahead with the twin trance anyway—the *twin trance*, Seena— without the sexual component and without letting Bohentin know just how much greater the strain is in trance than he thinks it is. He doesn't know, he doesn't have a twin, and neither do the doctors. But I know, and if I push it much farther I'm going to eventually die at it. *Soon* eventually. When I do, all your scheming to get me out of there really will have failed and you'll be alone with whatever it is you're so afraid of. But I don't think you'll let that happen.

"I think that instead you'll undo what you did to Keith, so that the experiment can have one last real chance. And in return, after that one chance, I'll agree to come home, to Boston or here to New York, for one year.

"That's my gamble."

She was looking at me from eyes empty of all tears, a Devrie I had not ever seen before. She meant it, every demented word, and she would do it. I wanted to scream at her, to scream a jumble of suicide and moral blackmail and warped perceptions and outrage, but the words that came out of my mouth came out in a whisper.

"What in God's name is worth *that*?"

Shockingly, she laughed, a laugh of more power than her wasted frame could have contained. Her face glowed, and the glow looked both exalted and insane. "You said it, Seena—in God's name. To finally know. To *know*, beyond the fogginess of faith, that we're not alone in the universe. . . . Faith should not mean fogginess." She laughed again, this time defensively, as if she knew how she sounded to me. "You'll do it, Seena." It was not a question. She took my hand.

"You would *kill* yourself?"

"No. I would die trying to reach God. It's not the same thing."

"I never bullied you, Devrie."

She dropped my hand. "All my life, Seena. And on into now. But all of your bullying and your scorn would look rather stupid, wouldn't it, if there really can be proved to exist a rational basis for what you laughed at all those years!"

We looked at each other, sisters, across the abyss of the pale sofa, and then suddenly away. Neither of us dared to speak.

My plane landed on Dominica by night. Devrie had gone two days before me, returning with her doctor and guards on the same day she had left, as I had on my previous visit. I had never seen the island at night. The tropical greenery, lush with that faintly menacing suggestion of plant life gone wild, seemed to close in on me. The velvety darkness seemed to smell of ginger, and flowers, and the sea—all too strong, too blandly sensual, like an overdone perfume ad. At the hotel it was better; my room was on the second floor, above the dark foliage, and did not face the sea. Nonetheless, I stayed inside all that evening, all that darkness, until I could go the next day to the Institute of the Biological Hope.

"Hello, Seena."

"Keith. You look—"

"Rotten," he finished, and waited. He did not smile. Although he had lost some weight, he was nowhere near as skeletal as Devrie, and it gave me a pang I did not analyze to see his still-healthy body in the small gray room where last I had seen hers. His head was shaved, and without the curling brown hair he looked sterner, prematurely middle-aged. That, too, gave me a strange emotion, although it was not why he looked rotten. The worst was his eyes. Red-veined, watery, the sockets already a little sunken, they held the sheen of a man who was not forgiving somebody for something. Me? Himself? Devrie? I had lain awake all night, schooling myself for this insane interview, and still I did not know what to say. What does one say to persuade a man to sexual potency with one's sister so that her life might be saved? I felt ridiculous, and frightened, and—I suddenly realized the name of my strange emotion—humiliated. How could I even start to slog towards what I was supposed to reach?

"How goes the Great Experiment?"

"Not as you described it," he said, and we were there already. I looked at him evenly.

"You can't understand why I presented the Institute in the worst possible light."

"I can understand that."

"Then you can't understand why I bedded you, knowing about Bohentin's experiment."

"I can also understand that."

Something was wrong. Keith answered me easily, without restraint, but with conflict gritty beneath his voice, like sand beneath blowing grass. I stepped closer, and he flinched. But his expression did not change.

"Keith. What is this about? What am I doing here? Devrie said you couldn't . . . that you were impotent with her, confused enough about who and what . . ." I trailed off. He still had not changed expression.

I said quietly, "It was a simplistic idea in the first place. Only someone as simplistic as Devrie . . ." Only someone as simplistic as Devrie would think you could straighten out impotency by talking about it for a few hours. I turned to go, and I had gotten as far as laying my hand on the doorknob before Keith grasped my arm. Back to him, I squeezed my eyes shut. What in God would I have *done* if he had not stopped me?

"It's not what Devrie thinks!" With my back to him, not able to see his middle-aged baldness but only to hear the anguish in his voice, he again seemed young, uncertain, the boy I bought coffee for in Indian Falls. I kept my back to him, and my voice carefully toneless.

"What is it, then, Keith? If not what Devrie thinks?"

"I don't know!"

"But you do know what it's not? It's not being confused about who is your sister and who your mother and who you're willing to have sex with in front of a room full of researchers?"

"No." His voice had gone hard again, but his hand stayed on my arm. "At first, yes. The first time. But, Seena—I *felt* it. *Almost.* I almost felt the presence, and then all the rest of the confusion—it didn't seem as important anymore. Not the confusion between you and Devrie."

I whirled to face him. "You mean God doesn't care whom you fuck if it gets you closer to fucking with Him."

He looked at me hard then—at me, not at his own self-absorption. His reddened eyes widened a little. "Why, Seena—*you* care. You told me the brother-sister thing didn't matter anymore—but *you* care."

Did I? I didn't even know anymore. I said, "But, then, I'm not deluding myself that it's all for the old Kingdom and the Glory."

"Glory," he repeated musingly, and finally let go of my arm. I couldn't tell what he was thinking.

"Keith. This isn't getting us anywhere."

"Where do you want to get?" he said in the same musing tone. "Where did any of you, starting with your father, want to get with me? Glory . . . glory."

Standing this close to him, seeing close up the pupils of his eyes and smelling close up the odor of his sweat, I finally realized what I should have seen all along: he was glowing. He was of course constantly on Bohentin's program of neurotransmitter manipulation, but the same chemicals that made the experiments possible also raised the threshold of both frankness and suggestibility. I guessed it must be a little like the looseness of being drunk, and I wondered if perhaps Bohentin might have deliberately raised the dosage before letting this interview take place. But no, Bohentin wouldn't be aware of the bargain Devrie and I had struck; she would not have told him. The whole bizarre situation was hers alone, and Keith's drugged musings a fortunate side-effect I would have to capitalize on.

"Where do you think my father wanted to get with you?" I asked him gently.

"Immortality. Godhead. The man who created Adam without Eve."

He was becoming maudlin. "Hardly 'the man,'" I pointed out. "My father was only one of a team of researchers. And the same results were being obtained independently in California."

"Results. I am a 'result.' What do *you* think he wanted, Seena?"

"Scientific knowledge of cell development. An objective truth."

"That's all Devrie wants."

"To compare bioengineering to some mystic quest—"

"Ah, but if the mystic quest is given a laboratory answer? Then it, too, becomes a scientific truth. You really hate that idea, don't you, Seena? You hate science validating anything you define as non-science."

I said stiffly, "That's rather an oversimplification."

"Then what do you hate?"

"I hate the risk to human bodies and human minds. To Devrie. To you."

"How nice of you to include me," he said, smiling. "And what do you think Devrie wants?"

"Sensation. Romantic religious emotion. To be all roiled up inside with delicious esoterica."

He considered this. "Maybe."

"And is that what you want as well, Keith? You've asked what everyone else wants. What do you want?"

"I want to feel at home in the universe. As if I belonged in it. And I never have."

He said this simply, without self-consciousness, and the words themselves were predictable enough for his age—even banal. There was nothing in the words that could account for my eyes suddenly filling with tears. "And 'scientifically' reaching God would do that for you?"

"How do I know until I try it? Don't cry, Seena."

"I'm not!"

"All right," he agreed softly. "You're not crying." Then he added, without changing tone, "I am more like you than like Devrie."

"How so?"

"I think that Devrie has always felt that she belongs in the universe. She only wants to find the . . . the coziest corner of it to curl up in. Like a cat. The coziest corner to curl up in is God's lap. Aren't you surprised that I should be more like you than like the person I was cloned from?"

"No," I said. "Harder upbringing than Devrie's. I told you that first day: cloning is only delayed twinning."

He threw back his head and laughed, a sound that chilled my spine. Whatever his conflict was, we were moving closer.

"Oh no, Seena. You're so wrong. It's more than delayed twinning, all right. You can't buy a real twin. You either have one or you don't. But you can buy yourself a clone. Bought, paid for, kept on the books along with all the rest of the glassware and holotanks and electron microscopes. You said so yourself, in your apartment, when you first told me about Devrie and the Institute. 'Money. She'd buy you.' And you were right, of course. Your father bought me, and she did, and you did. But of course you two women couldn't have bought if I hadn't been selling."

He was smiling still. Stupid—we had both been stupid, Devrie and I, we had both been looking in the wrong place, misled by our separate blinders-on training in the laboratory brain. My training had been scientific, hers humanistic, and so I looked at Freud and she looked at Oedipus, and we were equally stupid. How did the world look to a man who did not deal in laboratory brains, a man raised in a grittier world in which limits were not what the mind was capable of but what the bank book would stand? 'Your genes are too expensive for you to claim except as a beggar; your sisters are too expensive for you to claim except as a beggar; God is too expensive for you to claim except as a beggar.' To a less romantic man it would not have mattered, but a less romantic man would not have come to the Institute. What dark humiliations and resentments did Keith feel when he looked at Devrie, the self who was buyer and not bought?

Change the light you shine onto a mind, and you see different neural patterns, different corridors, different forests of trees grown in soil you could not have imagined. Run that soil through your fingers and you discover different pebbles, different sand, different leaf mold from the decay of old growths. Devrie and I had been hacking through the wrong forest.

Not Oedipus, but Marx.

Quick lines of attack came to me. Say: Keith it's a job like any other with high-hazard pay why can't you look at it like that a very dangerous and well-paid job for which you've been hired by just one more eccentric member of the monied class. Say: You're entitled to the wealth you're our biological brother damn it consider it rationally as a kinship entitlement. Say: Don't be so nicey-nice it's a tough world out there and if Devrie's giving it away take it don't be an impractical chump.

I said none of that. Instead I heard myself saying, coolly and with a calm cruelty, "You're quite right. You were bought by Devrie, and she is now using her own purchase for her own ends. You're a piece of equipment bought and paid for. Unfortunately, there's no money in the account. It has all been a grand sham."

Keith jerked me to face him with such violence that my neck cracked. "What are you saying?"

The words came as smoothly, as plausibly, as if I had rehearsed them. I didn't even consciously plan them: how can you plan a lie you do not know you will need? I slashed through this forest blind, but the ground held under my feet.

"Devrie told me that she has signed over most of her inheritance to you. What she didn't know, because I haven't told her, is that she doesn't have control of her inheritance any longer. It's not hers. I control it. I had her declared mentally incompetent on the grounds of violent suicidal tendencies and had myself made her legal guardian. She no longer has the legal right to control her fortune. A doctor observed her when she came to visit me in New York. So the transfer of her fortune to you is invalid."

"The lawyers who gave me the papers to sign—"

"Will learn about the New York action this week," I said smoothly. How much inheritance law did Keith know? Probably very little. Neither did I, and I invented furiously; it only needed to *sound* plausible. "The New York courts only handed down their decision recently, and Dominican judicial machinery, like everything else in the tropics, moves slowly. But the ruling will hold, Keith. Devrie does not control her own money, and you're a pauper again. But *I* have something for you. Here. An airline ticket back to Indian Falls. You're a free man. Poor, but free. The ticket is in your name, and there's a check inside it—that's from me. You've earned it, for at least trying to aid poor Devrie. But now you're going to have to leave her to me. I'm now her legal guardian."

I held the ticket out to him. It was wrapped in its airline folder; my own name as passenger was hidden. Keith stared at it, and then at me.

I said softly, "I'm sorry you were cheated. Devrie didn't mean to. But she has no money, now, to offer you. You can go. Devrie's my burden now."

His voice sounded strangled. "To remove from the Institute?"

"I never made any secret of wanting her out. Although the legal papers for that will take a little time to filter through the Dominican courts. She wouldn't go except by force, so force is what I'll get. Here."

I thrust the ticket folder at him. He made no move to take it, and I saw from the hardening of his face—my face, Devrie's face—the moment when Devrie shifted forests in his mind. Now she was without money, without legal control of her life, about to be torn from the passion she loved most. The helpless underdog. The orphaned woman, poor and cast out, in need of protection from the powerful who had seized her fortune.

Not Marx, but Cervantes.

"You would do that? To your own sister?"

Anything for a sister. I said bitterly, "Of course I would."

"She's not mentally incompetent."

"Isn't she?"

"No!"

I shrugged. "The courts say she is."

Keith studied me, resolve hardening around him. I thought of certain shining crystals, that will harden around any stray piece of grit. Now that I was succeeding in convincing him, my lies hurt—or perhaps what hurt was how easily he believed them.

"Are you sure, Seena," he said, "that *you* aren't just trying a grab for Devrie's fortune?"

I shrugged again, and tried to make my voice toneless. "I want her out of here. I don't want her to die."

"Die? What makes you think she would die?"

"She looks—"

"She's nowhere near dying," Keith said angrily—his anger a release, so much that it hardly mattered at what. "Don't you think I can tell in twin trance what her exact physical state is? And don't you know how much control the trance gives each twin over the bodily processes of the other? Don't you even know that? Devrie isn't anywhere near dying. And I'd pull her out of trance if she were." He paused, looking hard at me. "Keep your ticket, Seena."

I repeated mechanically, "You can leave now. There's no money." *Devrie had lied to me.*

"That wouldn't leave her with any protection at all, would it?" he said levelly. When he grasped the door knob to leave, the tendons in his wrist stood out clearly, strong and taut. I did not try to stop his going.

Devrie had lied to me. With her lie, she had blackmailed me into yet another lie to Keith. The twin trance granted control, in some unspecified way, to each twin's body; the trance I had pioneered might have resulted in eight deaths unknowingly inflicted on each other out of who knows what dark forests in eight fumbling minds. Lies, blackmail, death, more lies.

Out of these lies they were going to make scientific truth. Through these forests they were going to search for God.

"Final clearance check of holotanks," an assistant said formally. "Faraday cage?"

"Optimum."

"External radiation?"

"Cleared," said the man seated at the console of the first tank.

"Cleared," said the woman seated at the console of the second.

"Microradiation?"

"Cleared."

"Cleared."

"Personnel radiation, Class A?"

"Cleared."

"Cleared."

On it went, the whole tedious and crucial procedure, until both tanks had been cleared and focused, the fluid adjusted, tested, adjusted again, tested again. Bohentin listened patiently, without expression, but I, standing to the side of him and behind the tanks, saw the nerve at the base of his neck and just below the hairline pulse in some irregular rhythm of its own. Each time the nerve pulsed, the skin rose slightly from under his collar. I kept my eyes on that syncopated crawling of flesh, and felt tension prickle over my own skin like heat.

Three-quarters of the lab, the portion where the holotanks and other machinery stood, was softly dark, lit mostly from the glow of console dials and the indirect track lighting focused on the tanks. Standing in the gloom were Bohentin, five other scientists, two medical doctors—and me. Bohentin had fought my being allowed there, but in the end he had had to give in. I had known too many threatening words not in generalities but in specifics: reporters' names, drug names, cloning details, twin trance tragedy, anorexia symptoms, bioengineering amendment. He was not a man who much noticed either public opinion or relatives' threats, but no one else outside his Institute knew so many so specific words—some people knew some of the words, but only I had them all. In the end he had focused on me his cold, brilliant eyes, and given permission for me to witness the experiment that involved my sister.

I was going to hold Devrie to her bargain. I was not going to believe anything she told me without witnessing it for myself.

Half the morning passed in technical preparation. Somewhere Devrie and Keith, the human components of this costly detection circuit, were separately being brought to the apex of brain activity. Drugs, biofeedback, tactile and auditory and kinaesthetic stimulation—all carefully calculated for the maximum increase of both the number of neurotransmitters firing signals through the synapses of the brain and of the speed at which the signals raced. The more rapid the transmission through certain pathways, the more intense both perception and feeling. Some neurotransmitters, under this pressure, would alter molecular structure into natural hallucinogens; that reaction had to be controlled. Meanwhile other drugs, other biofeedback techniques, would depress the body's natural enzymes designed to either reabsorb excess transmitters or to reduce the rate at which they fired. The number and speed of neurotransmitters in Keith's and Devrie's brains would mount, and mount, and mount, all natural chemical barriers removed. The two of them would enter the lab with their whole brains—rational cortex, emotional limbic, right and left brain functions—simultaneously aroused to an unimaginable degree. *Simultaneously.* They would be feeling as great a "rush" as a falling skydiver, as great a glow as a cocaine user, as great a mental clarity and receptivity as a da Vinci whose brush is guided by all the integrated visions of his unconscious mind. They would be white-hot.

Then they would hit each other with the twin trance.

The quarter of the lab which Keith and Devrie would use was

softly and indirectly lit, though brighter than the rest. It consisted of a raised, luxuriantly padded platform, walls and textured pillows in a pink whose component wavelengths had been carefully calculated, temperature in a complex gradient producing precise convection flows over the skin. The man and woman in that womb-colored, flesh-stimulating environment would be able to see us observers standing in the gloom behind the holotanks only as vague shapes. When the two doors opened and Devrie and Keith moved onto the platform, I knew that they would not even try to distinguish who stood in the lab. Looking at their faces, that looked only at each other, I felt my heart clutch.

They were naked except for the soft helmets that both attached hundreds of needles to nerve clumps just below the skin and also held the earphones through which Bohentin controlled the music that swelled the cathedrals of their skulls. "Cathedrals"—from their faces, transfigured to the ravished ecstasy found in paintings of medieval saints, that was the right word. But here the ecstasy was controlled, understood, and I saw with a sudden rush of pain at old memories that I could recognize the exact moment when Keith and Devrie locked onto each other with the twin trance. I recognized it, with my own more bitter hyperclarity, in their eyes, as I recognized the cast of concentration that came over their features, and the intensity of their absorption. The twin trance. They clutched each other's hands, faces inches apart, and suddenly I had to look away.

Each holotank held two whorls of shifting colors, the outlines clearer and the textures more sharply delineated than any previous holographs in the history of science. Keith's and Devrie's perceptions of each other's presence. The whorls went on clarifying themselves, separating into distinct and mappable layers, as on the platform Keith and Devrie remained frozen, all their energies focused on the telepathic trance. Seconds passed, and then minutes. And still, despite the clarity of the holographs in the tank, a clarity that fifteen years earlier I would have given my right hand for, I sensed that Keith and Devrie were holding back, were deliberately confining their unimaginable perceptiveness to each other's radiant energy, in the same way that water is confined behind a dam to build power.

But how could *I* be sensing that? From a subliminal "reading" of the mapped perceptions in the holotanks? Or from something else?

More minutes passed. Keith and Devrie stayed frozen, facing each

other, and over her skeletal body and his stronger one a flush began
to spread, rosy and slow, like heat tide rising.

"Jesus H. Christ," said one of the medical doctors, so low that only
I, standing directly behind her, could have heard. It was not a curse,
nor a prayer, but some third possibility, unnameable.

Keith put one hand on Devrie's thigh. She shuddered. He drew her
down to the cushions on the platform and they began to caress each
other, not frenzied, not in the exploring way of lovers but with a
deliberation I have never experienced outside a research lab, a slow
care that implied that worlds of interpretation hung on each movement. Yet the effect was not of coldness nor detachment but of
intense involvement, of tremendous energy joyously used, of creating
each other's bodies right then, there under each other's hands. They
were *working*, and oblivious to all but their work. But if it was a kind
of creative work, it was also a kind of primal innocent eroticism, and,
watching, I felt my own heat begin to rise. "Innocent"—but if innocence is unknowingness, there was nothing innocent about it at all.
Keith and Devrie knew and controlled each heartbeat, and I felt the
exact moment when they let their sexual energies, added to all the
other neural energies, burst the dam and flood outward in wave after
wave, expanding the scope of each brain's perceptions, inundating
the artificially-walled world.

A third whorl formed in each holotank.

It formed suddenly: one second nothing, the next brightness. But
then it wavered, faded a bit. After a few moments it brightened
slightly, a diffused golden haze, before again fading. On the platform
Keith gasped, and I guessed he was having to shift his attention
between perceiving the third source of radiation and keeping up the
erotic version of the twin trance. His biofeedback techniques were
less experienced than Devrie's, and the male erection more fragile.
But then he caught the rhythm, and the holograph brightened.

It seemed to me that the room brightened as well, although no
additional lights came on and the consoles glowed no brighter. Sweat
poured off the researchers. Bohentin leaned forward, his neck muscle
tautening toward the platform as if it were his will and not Keith/
Devrie's that strained to perceive that third presence recorded in the
tank. I thought, stupidly, of mythical intermediaries: Merlyn never
made king, Moses never reaching the Promised Land. Intermediaries—and then it became impossible to think of anything at all.

Devrie shuddered and cried out. Keith's orgasm came a moment later, and with it a final roil of neural activity so strong the two primary whorls in each holotank swelled to fill the tank and inundate the third. At the moment of breakthrough Keith screamed, and in memory it seems as if the scream was what tore through the last curtain—that is nonsense. How loud would microbes have to scream to attract the attention of giants? How loud does a knock on the door have to be to pull a sleeper from the alien world of dreams?

The doctor beside me fell to her knees. The third presence—or some part of it—swirled all around us, racing along our own unprepared synapses and neurons, and what swirled and raced was astonishment. A golden, majestic astonishment. We had finally attracted Its attention, finally knocked with enough neural force to be just barely heard—and It was astonished that we could, or did, exist. The slow rise of that powerful astonishment within the shielded lab was like the slow swinging around of the head of a great beast to regard some butterfly it has barely glimpsed from the corner of one eye. But this was no beast. As Its attention swung towards us, pain exploded in my skull—the pain of sound too loud, lights too bright, charge too high. My brain was burning on overload. There came one more flash of insight—wordless, pattern without end—and the sound of screaming. Then, abruptly, the energy vanished.

Bohentin, on all fours, crawled toward the holotanks. The doctor lay slumped on the floor; the other doctor had already reached the platform and its two crumpled figures. Someone was crying, someone else shouting. I rose, fell, dragged myself to the side of the platform and then could not climb it. I could not climb the platform. Hanging with two hands on the edge, hearing the voice crying as my own, I watched the doctor bend shakily to Keith, roll him off Devrie to bend over her, turn back to Keith.

Bohentin cried, "The tapes are intact!"

"Oh God oh God oh God oh God oh God," someone moaned, until abruptly she stopped. I grasped the flesh-colored padding on top of the platform and pulled myself up onto it.

Devrie lay unconscious, pulse erratic, face cast in perfect bliss. The doctor breathed into Keith's mouth—what strength could the doctor himself have left?—and pushed on the naked chest. Breathe, push, breathe, push. The whole length of Keith's body shuddered; the doctor rocked back on his heels; Keith breathed.

"It's all on tape!" Bohentin cried. "It's all *on tape!*"

"God damn you to hell," I whispered to Devrie's blissful face. "It didn't even know we were there!"

Her eyes opened. I had to lean close to hear her answer.

"But now . . . we know He . . . is there."

She was too weak to smile. I looked away from her, away from that face, out into the tumultuous emptiness of the lab, anywhere.

They will try again.

Devrie has been asleep, fed by glucose solution through an IV, for fourteen hours. I sit near her bed, frowned at by the nurse, who can see my expression as I stare at my sister. Somewhere in another bed Keith is sleeping yet again. His rest is more fitful than Devrie's; she sinks into sleep as into warm water, but he cannot. Like me, he is afraid of drowning.

An hour ago he came into Devrie's room and grasped my hand. "How could It—He—It not have been aware that we existed? Not even have *known*?"

I didn't answer him.

"You felt it too, Seena, didn't you? The others say they could, so you must have too. It . . . created us in some way. No, that's wrong. How could It create us and not *know*?"

I said wearily, "Do *we* always know what we've created?" and Keith glanced at me sharply. But I had not been referring to my father's work in cloning.

"Keith. What's a Thysania Africana?"

"A what?"

"Think of us," I said, "as just one more biological side-effect. One type of being acts, and another type of being comes into existence. Man stages something like the African Horror, and in doing so he creates whole new species of moths and doesn't even discover they exist until long afterward. If man can do it, why not God? And why should He be any more aware of it than we are?"

Keith didn't like that. He scowled at me, and then looked at Devrie's sleeping face: Devrie's sleeping bliss.

"Because she is a fool," I said savagely, "and so are you. You won't leave it alone, will you? Having been noticed by It once, you'll try to be noticed by It again. Even though she promised me otherwise, and even if it kills you both."

Keith looked at me a long time, seeing clearly—finally—the nature of the abyss between us, and its dimensions. But I already knew neither of us could cross. When at last he spoke, his voice held so much compassion that I hated him. "Seena. Seena, love. There's no more doubt now, don't you see? Now rational belief is no harder than rational doubt. Why are you so afraid to even believe?"

I left the room. In the corridor I leaned against the wall, palms spread flat against the tile, and closed my eyes. It seemed to me that I could hear wings, pale and fragile, beating against the glass.

They will try again. For the sake of sure knowledge that the universe is not empty, Keith and Devrie and all the others like their type of being will go on pushing their human brains beyond what the human brain has evolved to do, go on fluttering their wings against that biological window. For the sake of sure knowledge: belief founded on experiment and not on faith. And the Other: being/alien/God? It, too, may choose to initiate contact, if It can and now that It knows we are here. Perhaps It will seek to know *us*, and even beyond the laboratory Devrie and Keith may find any moment of heightened arousal subtly invaded by a shadowy Third. Will they sense It, hovering just beyond consciousness, if they argue fiercely or race a sailboat in rough water or make love? How much arousal will it take, now, for them to sense those huge wings beating on the *other* side of the window?

And windows can be broken.

Tomorrow I will fly back to New York. To my museum, to my exhibits, to my moths under permaplex, to my empty apartment, where I will keep the heavy drapes drawn tightly across the glass.

For—oh God—all the rest of my life.

Island Man

R. A. WILSON

Had he been forced to give it a figure, the old man probably would have said that his life described a perfect arc; like a rainbow, or like a projectile obeying a basic law of ballistics. Like a rainbow, it was composed of many colors melting one into another. Like a projectile, it seemed destined to succumb to gravity.

"My life," he would say to himself as he sat through the evening hours on his front stoop, "has been a brief soaring above the dust." The darkness made the old man grow both lonely and philosophical, so that he would comfort himself with long monologues on difficult subjects. "Now, the arc that I have striven to complete by my living is near its end. And how different, in such a symmetrical thing as an arc, can the end be from the beginning? Yes," he smiled, fond of the image, "I have risen from the golden haze of my childhood only to descend again into the yellow fog of my dotage."

Ironically, just as he had spent his childhood among them, so he now lived his golden years surrounded by children. They came from where they played upon the river bank to sit around the old man's stoop. They were daubed with mud from the water which, as they listened to the old man, dried into a yellow dust. Despite the dirt, their good health and youthful vigor shone through, causing the old man to breathe an occasional, envious sigh.

"No," he would say to himself in one of his nocturnal monologues, "I do not envy them. Rather, I am drawn to them as though their golden haze exerts a magnetism upon my yellow fog. Is this something inevitable? Does this joining of the end of my arc with the beginning of theirs constitute a circle then?"

Soon, the old man would lose himself in a muddled and mystical exploration of rebirth and extinction; for it was dark and he was lonely and growing philosophical. In the daylight, he would forget such somber thoughts. When among the children, it was impossible for him to feel lonely. In the face of so much rambunctious life, even philosophy faltered.

The children came to hear the stories that he told of the old days
and the old city. Their common belief, caught from their parents, was
that the old city was haunted. So, for them, the stories took on
somewhat the flavor of ghost tales. The old man did not mean them
to be such. He meant, through the stories, to preserve some fragment
of an earlier time, a time when men had been like gods. He was not
displeased, however, when a flicker of his own childhood returned to
him during a story, bridging the chasm between him and the children.

That also was why he told the stories.

Usually, he would relate to them an incident from his own childhood, embellishing it with descriptions of the casual wonders that
had existed in those days when men had been like gods. Certainly
some of what he told them was exaggerated (childhood memories
magnified by the lens of eighty summers) and some of it mistaken
(childhood misconceptions never put right), for the old man had left
the city at an early age and perhaps he did not completely understand
the place himself.

His actual name was Geof Talmund, though no one ever called
him that. The children, exercising a polite formality, addressed him
with a reverential 'sir.' While the adults, having shed much of their
reverence with their baby fat, referred to him simply as the old man.
What did he call himself? Well, he scarcely ever talked about himself—except in the stories and in those he always called himself
'Young Geof.'

Each new generation of children learned of the exploits of Young
Geof, while hardly realizing that the old man was speaking of himself. Not a child passed into adulthood without receiving the old
man's gentle, almost accidental tutelage. All of them shared this
golden experience of sitting on the tall grass by the old man's front
stoop—with small knees drawn up or kneeling, but always with
expressions rapt—listening to Geof Talmund's stories of an earlier,
miraculous time.

His white hair was kindled by the midsummer sun. His face, too,
seemed to glow, as though its weathered surfaces gathered and rera-
diated the ample energies of the sun. Fortunately, a persistent breeze,
generated by cool sea air from the west, tousled the children's hair
and riffled through the soft linen of the old man's tunic. Without the

breeze and the bit of shadow thrown by the elm on the wide front yard, the day would have been oppressively warm.

With calm brown eyes, Geof Talmund gazed down the strip of umber road (just a cartpath really) to see what the child had pointed to. Halfway down the hill, a group of men labored toward them. Rising from the dark path, the warm air shimmered in front of them as they came, making recognition difficult—especially for the old man, whose eyesight was not what it once had been.

"The Council, sir!" said the sharp-eyed boy who had pointed. "The Council is coming to visit you!"

"Is it?" said Geof Talmund as he squinted down the hill. "Oh yes, Joshua. I think you are right."

After a moment of watching, the old man turned again to the children. His eyes were watery, perhaps from the sun. When he spoke, there was a perceptible tremor to his voice that the children had never heard before.

"Time has come, I suppose," he said to himself. Then to the children he said, "You will have to go. The Council's business is not your business. Not yet."

"But you haven't finished the story, sir."

"I will finish it in the afternoon, perhaps, or tomorrow." He nodded at one of the girls. "Wanda, you will be responsible for remembering where I left off."

He turned away from them to gaze down the hill at the approaching delegation. As he watched through the rising, troubled air, they appeared like things reflected in turbulent water: some of them foreshortened and squat, almost ugly, others pulled out vertically like strings of taffy. The very air they lived in had, by warming, turned them into changeable, malleable figures.

Like the children are malleable, thought the old man.

"Sir?"

He turned to find that one of the children had not left, the one he had appointed to remember the story.

"Yes?"

"My name is Wendy, sir."

"Of course it is, dear."

The girl's eyes were downcast as she worked one bashful toe into the grass.

"But you called me Wanda."

"Did I?" The old man raised a startled eyebrow. "Then I am sorry, Wendy. From now on I shall remember your name as carefully as you remember the story I was telling."

The girl took that as a test of sorts. She said, "And I *do* remember, sir. You were telling about the wagons that run on sunlight—the way that sailboats run on the wind."

"Yes. And where did I leave off?"

"Young Geof had just boarded the magic wagon. The door would not open, so he climbed in through the window. Then he . . ."

"That is enough, Wendy. Thank you. You remember very well."

"Thank *you*, sir." She turned to catch up with her playmates.

"Ah, Wendy?"

At the sound of his voice, the girl stopped and turned back. She had gone as far as the elm's shadow. The part of her that remained in sunlight seemed, to the old man's vision, incredibly illuminated. Her ashen hair shimmered in the light. Her skin shone so pale and freckled and smooth that he ached to reach out and touch her cheek. Her soiled jumper—just two pieces of poor cloth stitched casually together—seemed somehow better for hanging upon such a graceful creature. But a part of her had entered the shadow, where the old man's failing vision could make out only a misty and indistinct form. He felt—it was foolish, he knew—but he felt that he had stopped her on the brink of oblivion, where she hung now, suspended between the sunlit present and the shadowy future.

"Sir?" The shy warble of her voice brought him back.

He rubbed his eyes, trying to clear his vision.

"Yes, dear," he said after a moment. "But there *is* someone in your group named Wanda, isn't there?"

"No, sir." Though she tried to contain it, her face fairly blossomed into a grin.

"But you *do* know someone named Wanda?" suggested the old man.

"Yes, sir." The grin had changed to a strange, wise smile. "My mother's name is Wanda." Then she tripped into the shadow laughing, and was gone.

Geof Talmund gazed at the place where the girl had stood. He supposed she would tell her mother about the old man's mistake. If she did, then he knew at least one household this night, besides his own, that would lie awake to the passing of the years.

The old man shook his head once, almost resentfully.

"Perhaps they are right," he said, looking at the Council which was negotiating the last few meters of the path. "Perhaps I *should* stop telling the stories. I grow too old for it."

The men fanned out upon the wide front lawn around the stoop where the old man sat. They wore stern visages all of them, as though theirs was a mission of high dignity and seriousness. Geof Talmund had known them all as children and, in many ways, he thought of them as children still. He found himself smiling gently at their stiff postures and sober faces. And he wondered if he mightn't look a little sappy to them: an old man sitting with the sun in his face, grinning.

"Well, it has happened at last," he declared. "The high elders of the community have come to stop the crazy old man from filling their children's heads with notions."

With the sun in his face, the old man could not see the consternation that appeared suddenly on many faces, nor the puzzled glances they exchanged.

"High time, too," he said with sadness and resignation mingled in his voice. "I grow too old for it. I have become like an old house with weathered shingles and dusty cobwebs festooning the rafters." He grinned at them with the sunlight streaming in his face. "Or maybe I'm an old copper kettle that's worn so thin it won't survive another polishing."

"—But the stories must not end," blurted Hugh Clure, who was the first among the delegation to find his voice. There remained within each of them a certain reticence in the old man's presence, a reluctance to interrupt him as he spoke that was carried over from childhood.

Geof Talmund squinted up at the man.

"Who is this?" he said. "Is it Hugh Clure? I remember you. You were something of a bully as I recall."

Hugh glanced quickly at a couple of his nearest companions, but there was no embarrassment in his voice when he spoke.

"You taught us, old man, that childhood is merely one part of a process. Had I been perfect as a child, there would have been no need to grow into a man."

"You are right, of course," said Geof, smiling proudly at a lesson well taught. "But you say that the stories must not end? I conclude that your errand with me is much different from the one I had feared."

"Our *errand*," announced Hink Bardo, as he shouldered himself to Hugh's side, "is to guarantee the survival of the stories of Young Geof."

The old man shaded his eyes briefly as he looked up at the riverman, Captain Bardo.

He said, "I do not know if I desire to stay and tell stories forever, but I think I have no choice in the matter. For several years now a succession of veils has been interposed between the world and myself. First, my eyes obtained a gauzy dimness and no longer penetrate the mysteries of shadows. Now, my sinews fail me; sometimes they refuse to lift me from my bed. My tongue no longer detects the nuances of food. And my memory returns me only fleeting images. The stories crumble and die even as I die."

"—Then you must take an apprentice," said Hink Bardo, "and soon."

"An apprentice Storyteller?" said Geof, seemingly surprised. But he spoke inwardly also, saying, *Or an apprentice Old Man? No. You are all of you already apprentices with that guild, though you may not know it.*

"We implore you," said Hugh Clure. "Take one of us as your apprentice so that our grandchildren may hear the stories as we have heard them, and as our parents heard them before us. Beside the river, the stories are what make us a people. They are a part of our common heritage. We are afraid to lose them. We fear our descendants will be much poorer without them."

Of course, the old man felt gratified that the river people took his stories so seriously. As he gazed at the crowd of men, some of them standing in the shadow of the elm, some of them in sunlight, he reflected on how childlike they remained even after so many years. But for their size, they might be children still, arrayed before him on the grass, awaiting a story. Blessed Sol lent the scene the same eerie brilliance and acute detail that Geof had witnessed with the girl, Wendy.

Or Wanda? The old man chuckled softly. *Perhaps I should take an apprentice,* he thought. *Perhaps Wendy's children would prefer a storyteller who doesn't bungle names.*

Again Hink Bardo put himself forward, saying, "You should choose a riverman to learn the stories. During long trips to the sea, our men have little to amuse themselves with, so they tell stories. Many of them, I've found, have a natural aptitude for the spinning of yarns."

"For sure," said someone in the crowd. "They're born liars."

Nature itself seemed to pause. The breeze sucked down to nothing. The sun hung brazen and still above as the men greeted a dangerous moment with cautious silence.

It was with extreme difficulty that Hink Bardo, who was a choleric individual at best, restrained himself from whirling about on the man who had spoken. Old Geof watched with alarm as an angry tic began below one of the Captain's eyes. Only when that nervous affliction had subsided (soothed by one of the calming mental exercises that they all practiced), did Geof dare to speak again. As was usual in such cases, he spoke gently.

"Do they provoke you often, Captain Bardo?"

"No, not often," said Hink, his voice still choked with feeling. "Not since I was a child."

"Ah, I remember," said Geof. "As I recall, you, Hugh Clure, were one of the worst offenders in those days."

Hugh Clure, a large, raw-boned man, averted his eyes from Geof's in mute acceptance of the charge.

"I have grown since then," he said after a moment.

"Some of you have not," said Geof, pointing with his eyes at the man who had cast an aspersion on rivermen. "Respect me with this much," he said, "and raise no quarrels today. I am an old man with no wish to see any of my children gasping and writhing like sad, dying fish on the ground."

They were all silent then, chastened and suddenly reminded that they were, indeed, this old man's children—just as their parents before them had been his children. As they stood there upon the hill by the elm tree, each man experienced a warmth and a light that had nothing to do with the noontime sun. This quiet mood abided many minutes as the breeze fingered the clothing of the grownup children and soughed the heavy branches of the elm.

Reluctantly, Geof broke the silence, directing his words at Captain Bardo.

"I am sure," he said, "that all your sailors are fine men, but my apprentice must be a man who has worked for years shaping things with his hands. I myself was a metal worker before I took up this peculiar profession of telling tales, but a mason, I suppose, would do the job as well—or a carpenter."

"—Or a potter?" suggested one man who, from the clayey stains upon his trousers and tunic, was himself of that profession.

Old Geof laughed out loud at the eagerness in the man's voice. "Yes," he said, "a potter certainly shapes things." He grinned happily at all of them. "Bring me an assortment of candidates chosen from among your shapers and I will select one to be your storyteller."

Only a small, chiding voice, buried deeply in Geof's mind, reminded him that the end was now in sight. Strangely, that notion did not trouble him. Enough, he told himself, was enough. Eighty summers was more than enough.

Myriad images, superimposed one upon another, crowded the old man's wide front yard. The past and the present vied within Geof's mind, like ocean tides pushing and pulling upon the mother water. In the bright sunlight, he could see the forms of men, but his memory— worn as it was—provided him with the faces of children, children who seemed somehow realer to him than these adults. But the past had always seemed more real to the old man. Perhaps that was truly why he told the stories—to preserve this higher reality of his own.

Geof Talmund looked away from the Council and gazed across the broad river valley. He could see the tiny houses below on the opposite bank, and the patchwork fields beyond them, and above that the broad brow of Riverbend Hill, shielding the horizon. In the foreground, the river itself shone only in flashes of sunlight reflected through the waving branches of the trees. He could not see the children for the trees, but he could hear them playing on the near riverbank.

He nodded his head approvingly, thinking that much good had been accomplished in eighty summers. He shaded his eyes for a moment with the palm of one hand and squinted, trying to see the valley as it had appeared those many years ago. There had been no corn fields then, only sumac and groundsedge and a few willowy saplings. Where a rutted dirt path now marked the traffic of the village, there had once been a hard asphalt road that snaked along beside the river for miles and miles. The last remnants of the highway were vanished long ago, absorbed by the vegetable world. Gone too was the old automobile—yes, it had been old even then—that had brought Geof here from the city. It had been among the first things to go as Geof cannibalized it for the tools its metal parts could provide.

The old man allowed his vision to return to the present scene. He looked at the men before him. They seemed slightly embarrassed, as though reluctant to interrupt Geof's reverie, yet anxious to have their business with him finished.

He squinted at the noontime sun, then at them.

"It is hot," he said, "and you have had a long hike up the hill. You should sit down here and rest before you leave."

Uneasy glances were traded among the councilmen.

"But we had thought to hurry back to the village," said Hugh Clure, "so that we may begin the selection of your apprentice."

"Do I look so unwell," laughed the old man, "that you must rush to find my replacement?" He paused and pretended to consider his own question for a moment. "No," he decided, mocking them gently, "I do not think I shall die today—nor even tomorrow. You have time to spend here with me. Or is your dignity so great that you dare not sit upon the grass as the children do?"

He made a downward gesture with his hands, indicating that they should sit. They hesitated, exchanging glances, then complied, each of them finding a place to settle in the tall green grass.

"I have a story for you."

"But the stories are for the children," protested one man.

"Some stories are not for children," said the storyteller.

"Is it a story of Young Geof?"

"Yes. It is the last story of Young Geof; for, after the time I will tell you of, Geof was never again young."

Sitting upon the familiar hillside, all of those men must have felt the long fingers of the past reaching for them, pulling them backward to their childhoods. Some few of them may even have found themselves enchanted by the drowsy midday heat and by the gentle cadences of the old man's voice so that they (via an easy sleight of mind) sloughed off the accumulation of the years and became again small boys listening to a wondrous story—as a sort of recess between stints of hard play on the riverbank.

But this was unlike any story they had heard before; less full of wonder than heartache. It began in turmoil and ended in grief.

*   *   *

The building survived.

But that was to be expected. Its prospectus had billed it and the other so-called 'Solo Structures' as islands of stability in a sea of change. No longer did a respected firm need endure the indignities of municipal service. The building's plumbing and sewage were self-contained. Its offices were 'modules of the future.' Its power came from an 'eye in the sky.' It stood aloof and unaware; independent of the city around it; independent of energy crunches and garbage strikes; independent of the people it contained.

Each morning at six thirty the lights in the groundfloor lobby (and vestibules, restrooms, hallways, info desks, etc.) came on like magic—or like clockwork, if you knew about the master chronometer that ticked away like the building's secret heart in a private room of an upper floor. Again like magic (or clockwork) the urinals all flushed twice an hour, so that many secretaries on many floors had once been able to prick up ears and hear the gentle, background *whooshing* sound that told them it was half past the hour. Such was the fearsome regularity of this flushing that it had not been uncommon once, near quitting time, to see a member of the steno pool with her head cocked curiously to one side and a far-off expression on her face as though she were listening to an inner music—an illusion that was ironically dissolved when the muffled gurgling of the urinals set her to putting pencils and paper clips away.

Still, twice an hour, the urinals throughout the building flushed. There were, however, no longer any secretaries to hear. Only Young Geof heard the *whooshing* and, though he quickly discovered the cause, he never understood that it signaled half-hour intervals. To him, who knew nothing of the master chronometer upstairs, it seemed like so much magic.

Geof had not thought to count the sequences of light and dark in the corridors of the building, so he was not certain how long he had been inside. It had been many days at least since he had sought shelter there from the storm of depravity outside. At first he had been wary, prowling the corridors, searching storerooms and ante-chambers for a sign of grownups. But it had been a weekend when the first outbreaks had occurred, which was a dead time for the office building. Its ordinary denizens had been away. Only in the basement did Geof find a hint of what had transpired elsewhere. Two security guards, their drab brown uniforms decorated with dark medallions of blood, lay crumpled in their little office. Though Geof did not feel threatened by them, he did not venture into the basement again.

Nor did he venture outside again. He feared that the streets, which seemed so quiet, might spring again into violent life, with running feet slapping on pavement and anguished cries ringing down the urban canyon.

The building was his new home, his haven. He explored it carefully. He took his meals in the restaurant on the top floor. He slept in corridors since, even at night, the lights in the offices and waiting rooms would flicker to life when he entered and stay stubbornly on until he left. At night, only the corridors offered the succor of darkness to a young boy who craved sleep.

And he would not sleep on the soft furniture of the ground-floor lobby, for the glass doors that looked out on the darkened street also looked in. Geof did not want any chance passerby to spot a small boy asleep on the couch.

Once or twice, he fell asleep in the penthouse restaurant, while watching the jagged silhouette of the city. Many of the buildings, like his own, maintained a pattern of illumination, lifting strange three-dimensional ghosts of themselves against the night sky. Below, a few senseless streetlamps survived. They lit random, meaningless sections of pavement. Scarcely visible above the buildings, Geof could see a few lines of smoke rising, like slack ropes of gray against the greater blackness. The fires had diminished considerably since those first few days when smoke had risen in every quarter. Many of the older buildings had actually been destroyed.

But the new, self-sufficient buildings, like Geof's, survived. Fed by invisible filaments of power from transceivers in geosynchronous orbit overhead, they automatically defended themselves from the arson that became practically epidemic as madness spread throughout the city. At the first hint of fire, the control of a given building passed from clockwork into computer mode. Doors in the affected areas received an electric impulse that magnetized their latches, pulling shut those that were open. This sealed the rooms off, while not preventing the escape of their inhabitants. Then, carbon dioxide gas was pumped into the burning rooms. Quietly, yet effectively, the offending flames were smothered.

Those men or women foolish enough or mad enough to set the fires in the first place were also unimpressed by the noise of the alarms. Unalert to the invisible, silent gas, they too were smothered.

It had been weeks, perhaps, since young Geof had seen humans. But that had been according to his own wishes. The last he had glimpsed had been vague figures running in the streets, chasing or being chased. Geof had been pursued himself, many times, but he had always eluded capture by hiding under automobiles or ducking down sidestreets. The constant fleeing had brought him at last to the downtown area, the area of the 'Solo Structures.' Since then he had seen nothing, as he watched from the windows of the penthouse restaurant, save for occasional, indefinable motions on the street below.

So, as he ate one morning in the rooftop restaurant, he was shocked to notice that one of the elevators was slowly climbing from the lobby below.

Reacting quickly after a moment of panic, Geof cleared the remnants of his meal from the window booth where he had been sitting and carried it through the swinging double doors to the kitchen. He shoved it, plate and all, into a disposal chute, then looked hurriedly around for any other signs of his presence that could be erased. Finding nothing, he darted back through the dining room to the foyer where the elevators opened out. He watched the digital readout above the door as the elevator climbed past floor after floor. He kept a hand on the call button for the other elevator. If the intruder rose above thirty-six—the floor below him—then Geof planned to head down in a hurry.

After several seemingly endless moments, the readout flashed the number thirty and counted no higher. Geof felt the muscles of his stomach unclench and realized that he had been holding his breath. Relieved, he sat down on the plush carpet of the foyer and watched the readout with a suspicious eye, making certain that it didn't wander from the thirtieth floor.

Gradually, it dawned on him that he was trapped—cornered in a penthouse restaurant thirty-seven stories above the street. Whoever, or whatever, now occupied the thirtieth held Geof prisoner unaware. Just as he had noticed the elevator bringing the intruder up, so the intruder would surely notice if Geof tried to ride the elevator to the lobby. And there was no stairway for him to escape down. As long as the stranger remained on the thirtieth floor, Geof could do nothing but watch the readout and wait.

As he maintained this vigil, he grew steadily more curious about what was happening on the thirtieth floor. There had been nothing tentative about the elevator's path. Without pause, it had gone to that floor and no other. Was this a sign that the long, unfathomable nightmare was over? Was this some man returning calmly to his work as though the extended and terrible weekend had never happened? Maybe Geof was making a mistake in hiding. Perhaps if he simply descended to the thirtieth floor he would find that his exile was over. Perhaps he could even be reunited with his parents.

That, of course, was childish, wishful thinking. Things could never be the same again. His mother was gone beyond recall. And his father? Well, Geof knew he could never feel comfortable with him again, could never call 'father' the man who had killed his mother.

Who had almost killed Geof.

But those ugly memories were already sheathed in protective tissue, were becoming gradually encysted like grains of sand in an oyster, becoming pearls. (Eighty years later, the memories would indeed resemble pearls; bright and round and smooth, ungraspable as actual events, but useful as shimmery symbols of something immense that had happened. Just so does Nature and Man's Mind decorate the ugliness of this world.)

Despite his curiosity, Geof was not seriously tempted to investigate what was happening on the thirtieth floor. The vividness had not yet worn off the dreadful images in his mind. For all he knew there was a storm of madness now raging seven stories below him. He could not bring himself to enter it willingly.

When the intruder finally did leave, Geof watched the digits of the readout diminish as the car descended through the lower levels. When it reached the ground floor, and remained there, Geof waited many minutes more before he was convinced that the stranger was gone for good. Then he stepped into the other elevator car and pushed the button for the thirtieth floor.

He knocked his elbow hard against the back wall of the elevator as he scrambled reflexively away from the doors. He barely noticed the pain though, being too intent upon the apparition that stood before him. Geof may have made a sound—perhaps a whimper, though he didn't remember it later—while his thoughts reeled around a pivot of terror. He had made a terrible, perhaps fatal mistake. Apparently, there had been more than one intruder. This one had stayed behind.

At first, Geof did not recognize it as a man. It was tall—twice his height—and entirely enveloped in a silvery fabric. Where a man's joints would be, the material was gathered into elastic bands, giving the creature a segmented, puffy appearance. The helmet was a creased silver shell with a window in the front. There were many other details to the outfit (such as the bulky tanks upon its back, and the elaborate, girdlelike appliance with dials and a speaker grill) but Geof was too stricken with fear to notice much more than the menacing outline as he cringed against the far wall of the elevator.

"Are you crazy too?" The man's voice was given a flutter by the simple transducer of his suit. He peered forward, bending slightly at the waist. He seemed as puzzled as Geof was frightened. He straightened and conked himself lightly on the helmet. "Damn," he said, "if that isn't a stupid question. If you *are* nuts, you certainly won't tell me." His silver-clad feet made scuffing noises as he entered the elevator to get Geof, who went rigid with horror as the slippery fabric of the man's gloves closed around his arms.

"Hey. Relax, fella. I'm not gonna hurt you."

The words, as spoken, were soothing, but the vinyl speaker element added a sinister-sounding burr edge to man's voice. Geof shrank further from his hands.

"Damn," said the man as he stood up and stepped back from Geof's huddled form. The boy had his slender arm folded around his head, anticipating a beating. "You sure must've had a rotten time of it," said the strangely dressed man. For a moment he watched the mute curve of the child's spine where it came through the torn fabric of his shirt, then he lifted his eyes to gaze at the wall of the elevator car as though seeing through it and through the rest of the building to the crypt-quiet city beyond. "Another stupid thing to say," he murmured. "*Everybody's* had a rotten time of it."

Not having received the expected pummelling, Geof relaxed a little. He turned his head just enough to peer out at the man from under one arm.

The lights in the corridor reflected off the window in the man's helmet, so that Geof could not see the grin that came to his lips.

"So? Have you decided that it's safe yet?"

With the unthinking honesty of a child, Geof shook his head slowly.

The man laughed.

"Believe me," he said. "You are safe."

It was then that the other elevator doors opened and a second suited figure joined the first.

"Well, I'll be damned," said the newcomer. "Blakely said it might not affect the children the same way."

"Oh? I didn't think he had it isolated yet."

"Doesn't. But he figures it'll turn out to be another acid virus with a jawbreaking name. If it is, then he says some of the children will adjust to it—absorb it, or something like that." He shrugged his shoulders, which caused the silvery fabric of his suit to rustle. "I don't pretend to understand it," he said. "Recombo's not my field."

"Sure glad it isn't mine," said the first man as they both looked down at Geof, who had risen into a low crouch.

"What's your name, son?"

"Geof," he said as he got his feet beneath him and came slowly erect.

"Geof," said the first man, pointing to himself, "my name is Bill and this is Jackson—but you can call him Jake if you want. We're friends. We want to help you."

"Sure," muttered the other. "A lot of good we can do him. We sure as hell can't take him back up with us."

"Why not?"

"Don't be dense. He's a carrier. You saw how quickly it spread here. Imagine how much faster it would move in our closed system."

The one called Bill thought about that for a moment.

"Yeah," he said, his speaker adding a painful flutter to his voice. "Still, we should do something to help him."

"Like what?"

"I don't know. I'll think of something while you're cutting into the cooler. Did you get the torch?"

The one called Jackson ducked back into the other elevator and returned hefting a device with hoses and nozzles attached to a cylindrical tank.

"So let's get to work," he said as he began lugging the apparatus down the corridor.

Bill knelt down, putting himself on a level with the boy.

"Geof," he said, "have you ever seen a cutting torch at work?"

Geof shook his head.

"Well, that thing Jake has is a torch. You want to come watch him use it?"

Appealing to his curiosity was perhaps the surest way of overcoming Geof's fears. That plus the fact that, with the lighted corridor behind him, Geof could now see through the window in the man's helmet to his face. Knowing that there was indeed a man inside that bulky, graceless costume provided a further reassurance. Geof craned his neck to peer along the corridor. Three doors down, Jake had entered an office. Geof looked back to the one called Bill.

"Yes, sir," he said. "I would like to watch."

"Well, come on then," said Bill. "We'll have to find you a pair of goggles in the lab."

Together they walked to the door that Jake had left ajar.

They didn't pause in the waiting room because there was nothing to see. It looked like every other waiting room in the building. (The literature had dubbed them 'reception modules.') Beyond that was the room that Bill had called the Lab. This was a place unlike any that Geof had yet explored. It had little in common with the other offices. It more nearly resembled the kitchen upstairs with its stainless steel sinks and metal cabinets. One side of the large room was sectioned off from the rest by man-high dividers made of opaque plastic panels. This was intended to give the effect of private office space. Above the dividers, Geof could see a black blossom of soot climbing the wall and spreading out upon the ceiling. Jake was standing beside a doorway, looking into one of the cubicles. He turned toward Bill.

"Better not let the kid see this," he said.

Bill motioned for Geof to stay put and went to join Jake. Geof could hear the men talking but he wasn't certain what it was about.

"What are those?" asked Bill. "Lab smocks?"

"Yeah. Looks like he soaked them in something. Maybe alcohol. I guess he meant to burn the whole place down."

"What stopped him?"

Jake pointed to rows of grillwork along the ceiling. "This building has one of those new computerized ventilation systems. It puts out fires with gas. Guess it must've put him out too."

"What's this stuff on the floor?" There was the sound of feet crunching on something brittle.

"Looks like pyrex. From the blood, I'd say he fell on something—like a beaker or a flask. What are you doing?"

"What does it look like? I'm covering him up."

"Terrific," Jake sneered. "I'm sure his family will thank you."

Bill didn't respond to that. He brushed by Jake as he left the cubicle, but he stopped before reaching Geof. He peered curiously at something on the wall. It looked to Geof like a squashed pie tin.

Following Bill, Jake picked up an object from the floor. It was a metal lab stand with a gleaming long rod screwed into a cast iron base. He came up beside Bill and placed the object's heavy base against the depression in the wall.

"Perfect fit," he said. "I believe I've discovered the murder weapon."

"Yes. But what was the victim?"

Jake looked closely. "It appears to be a speaker," he said, "or an alarm of some kind." He tossed the lab stand aside. "Its noise must've bothered him."

"That's crazy."

"Exactly the word I was thinking of," said Jake as he picked up his equipment and headed for the rear of the room. "Crazy."

The man called Bill shook his head sadly, then turned to a cabinet and rummaged through its drawers until he found a pair of dark-tinted glasses, which he handed to Geof.

"You have to wear them when you look at the torch. Otherwise the light will hurt your eyes."

They passed between tables like square columnar islands with sinks and gas fonts built into them. At the back of the room Jake was arranging his equipment in front of a glossy, stainless steel door. That reminded Geof of something he had seen in the kitchen upstairs.

"Is it a refrigerator?"

Bill looked at Geof as though surprised.

"—I mean, if it's food you're after, sir, there's a whole room upstairs—at least it looks like a room, but it's really a refrigerator and it's filled with food. It's not locked either."

"Hey, Jake. Did you hear that? He recognized it as a refrigerator."

"Yeah?" grumbled Jake. "So he's a bright kid. That doesn't change anything. We still can't help him."

"Maybe we can, Jake, if we just think the problem through." He turned toward Geof again. "Son, do you have any idea of what happened here?" He swung both arms wide in an all-encompassing gesture.

Geof regarded him silently for a moment, his eyes reflecting a haunted reminiscence. "You mean," he said quietly, "do I know what happened to make everyone angry?"

"Angry?"

"Acute paranoid schizophrenia," suggested Jake, "might look like a temper tantrum to the kid."

"Is that what they're calling it back home?"

"Yeah, but all they really know is that it's some sort of chemical imbalance." Jake chuckled sourly. "They don't even know *that* for sure. All they've got are theories."

"That's all they've ever had."

"Hell of a note, isn't it?" Jake gave a dry, short chuckle—more of a cough really than a sound of humor. "Epitaph for a Species: Lost Control of Late Model Theory at High Speed."

"Don't be so damned cynical. We haven't lost the whole species."

"So what's left? Us?" Again Jake made that humorless sound. "I suppose we've got a statistical chance of surviving—especially with the bone juice in here." He slapped the cooler door. "But still we're a mighty small gene pool to rebuild from."

"You're forgetting the kids," said Bill. "I know there are a lot of small bodies out there mixed in with the big, but there must have been quite a few, like Geof here, who avoided getting beaten or trampled to death."

"You said it yourself," answered Jake gloomily. "Think of all the *bodies*. There's gonna be plague to beat hell. That oughta take care of the rest of the kids."

Bill seemed deflated by the thought of the impending corruption on the streets outside. He leaned heavily against one of the tables.

"We're carrying our own air," he murmured, "so we couldn't tell. But it must already stink out there."

"—To high heaven," agreed Jake.

"God," Bill looked at Jake, "you seem almost *pleased* about it."

"Look, *partner*," Jake pointed a stiff finger at Bill, "I'm just trying to point out the plain facts for you. The kids don't have any more chance of surviving here than they would standing naked on Tranquility. This is now a hostile environment. Even if they survive whatever plagues that come, the damned en-ay-virus that killed their parents will eventually kill them too!"

"How can that be? I mean, if they're not dead from it yet?"

"If you'd been at the last overview session instead of playing house with what's-her-name, you'd *know* how that can be."

"Her name is Shansi, Jake, and we weren't playing house—"

"—I don't care what you were doing. *My partner* should have been there. Who do you think caught hell? Not you, you were having a fine time. It was *me*, good old Jake, who got his hide flayed by Ricker!"

"I'm sorry, Jake. But, dammit, we've had sessions every day for the past two weeks and we've just gone over and over the same stuff. I didn't think it could do any harm to skip the last one."

Jake made a disgusted sound. "Try telling that to Ricker when we get back."

"Yeah," said Bill with an uneasy laugh. "I guess I've got one coming, huh?"

"You and me both. I've got another one coming for helping smuggle you into the booster range at the last second."

"I wouldn't worry about it," Bill laughed archly. "The black marks don't show up on you the way they do on me, Jake."

"I'm not worried about black marks! I'm just getting tired of hauling your white ass out of trouble all the time!"

"Okay, okay, I said I'm sorry. Just tell me what happened at the last session that was so blasted important."

"They brought in three muckamucks from Biochem for a sort of question and answer period."

"Three? Blakely and Marenkov and who else?"

"Schaus—*Dok*tor Mildred Schaus."

"Never heard of her."

Jake shrugged. "She didn't have much to say. Blakely fielded most of the questions, of course."

"So what'd he have to say about the children?"

"That some of them *might* survive. And, if they did, they *might* develop a natural immunity to the virus—but that it wasn't very likely."

"Why not?"

"I'm not real sure, but it has something to do with an en-ay-virus being a *mimic*. It imitates the structure of genetic material."

"You mean, like the viceroy imitates the monarch?"

"What?"

"Butterflies, Jake. The monarch butterfly tastes awful bitter so the birds have learned to leave it alone. The viceroy imitates the colors of the monarch so the birds leave it alone too. They figure if it looks like a monarch, it must taste like one."

"Okay, country boy," Jake laughed. "I don't know about butterflies, but that sounds about right. What the virus does is imitate genetic material and insinuate itself into the chromosome."

"You mean it actually hooks up with the—"

"—It becomes *part* of the genetic message. The problem is that part of the message it makes up is bogus, false information."

Bill thought about that for a moment before saying, "Like a glitch?"

"Exactly. A glitch. It's like they all have this tremendous glitch in their genetic program."

"Is that what killed the adults?"

"Blakely doesn't think so. He thinks they all suffered from a massive immune reaction—or overreaction—that resulted in chemically induced psychosis, shock, coma, then death."

"You make it sound too clinical."

"There's no other way to deal with it."

"Maybe," said Bill, though he was plainly unconvinced.

Then, both of the strangely clad men looked at Geof as though scrutinizing him down to his genes. He had understood none of their conversation; nor did he understand the attention he was getting. He was content to wait there quietly. He had no impulse to flee. These two were different from the others. They behaved themselves as Geof thought grownups ought to. He did not feel threatened by them.

"You think Geof has a glitch?"

"According to Blakely, yes."

"Couldn't it be recessive or something?"

Jake shrugged his shoulders. "Why don't you face it, Bill. The boy doesn't have a chance. None of them do."

There was a pause, then, in the bleak conversation. Geof did not comprehend the bleakness or the pause. He knew only that these men were different.

"Are you gods?" he said.

A startled sound came from each of the men's speakers.

"My father said there are men who can do anything—like gods. You're not angry like the others so I wondered if you could be them."

The boy looked at them with a plea stamped on his face, wanting them to be gods. Jake and Bill had lost their voices to the childish question.

"I mean, if you're gods," said Geof, "then you can fix things, can't you? You can make them back like they used to be."

Jake, the first to recover his voice, spat out a bitter 'dammit' and turned to his torch, fussing silently with the gas nozzle.

Bill reached down and lifted Geof onto one of the tables, so that Geof's face was on a level with his own. Geof could see the man's face dimly through the window in his helmet. He did not understand why the eyes were sad. He did not want to understand.

"Geof," said the man, "we are not like the others because we are from a place far away where the disease could not reach. We are not gods. Even if we were, I do not think we could repair the damage that's been done. Things can never be like they used to be."

"No." Geof denied it.

"Yes! Too much has happened, Geof. Too many people have died. Your parents are dead. *Everyone's* parents are dead. They can't be brought back." Bill glanced briefly at his partner, then added grudgingly, "Even you, it seems, can never be the same again."

Bill reached his puffy, silver arms toward the boy, as if to console him. But Geof shrank from the slippery fabric.

"Noooo!" he said in a shrill, childish voice. "You're lying!"

Geof held both of his small fists clenched in front of him. He seemed ready to strike out at Bill. His lower jaw was protruding pugnaciously, perhaps to disguise the trembling of his lower lip.

Again, Bill stretched out his arms to the boy, saying, "Geof, believe me, I'm telling you the truth."

"You're lying!"

Suddenly, Bill had thirty kilograms of fury on his hands. He tried to close his arms around Geof's arms, to hold him still. But he squirmed free of the slippery fabric and rained surprisingly hard blows against his chest.

"Stop it!" he shouted, but the shouting overloaded his speaker. All that came out was a brittle static.

As abruptly as the attack began, it ceased. Bill felt the boy's body stiffen in his arms. Carefully, he settled him back upon the table. He muttered a curious "What the hell?" as the boy's breathing began coming in short, painful gasps. When Geof's eyes rolled slowly upward in their sockets, the battle began in earnest.

He clattered his head against the hard tabletop twice before Bill was able to surround his upper body with his arms, cushioning the skull from damage. But the torso and legs writhed and kicked uncontrollably.

"Jesus!" said Bill. "Give me a hand here, Jake. Grab his legs."

With a startled curse, Jake dropped what he was doing and parried a number of kicks before wrapping his arms securely around the boy's legs. Geof's shirt had worked its way up to his armpits, leaving his torso bare as it heaved and tossed between the two men.

"What the hell happened to him?" said Jake.

"Maybe this is his glitch." Bill's voice sounded a little ragged from the exertion of holding the boy.

"Maybe. Or maybe he's epileptic. Don't let him swallow his tongue."

With both hands needed to hold the boy's head and shoulders, Bill wasn't certain how he could prevent that. Even as he worried about it, though, the tremors that wracked Geof began to subside, slackening in frequency and severity until he hung limp and still between them.

"Is he alive?" asked Jake.

"Yeah, he's still breathing."

They both lifted the boy onto the tabletop.

"No," said Bill at once. "Let's put him on the floor. He looks too much like a specimen laid out on the table that way."

Jake muttered something indecent about people who worried over 'niceties.' But he helped his partner lower Geof to the floor.

"We need something to cushion his head," he said.

"No. I'll hold him," said Bill who had settled on the floor and was cradling the boy in one arm. "I think he's starting to come around. You finish with the torch, Jake. We're behind schedule already."

Bill uttered this last not urgently but absently, with his attention diverted entirely to Geof. Jake saw something disturbingly familiar in his partner's manner.

"Don't get carried away with those parental instincts," he growled. "We still have to leave him when we go."

"I know that."

"What happened to trigger the fit or whatever it was?"

"He got mad, I think." There was a note of amazement in Bill's voice. He looked up at Jake who was standing. "It was the strangest thing I ever saw, Jake. He just got mad and it was like a big fist grabbed him and started shaking."

"Yeah. I saw."

"You suppose this has any connection with the way the adults seemed to have temper tantrums before they died?"

"Maybe." Jake shrugged his shoulders. "Like I said, it's not my field."

"He's a *human being*, Jake!" It was as though a floodgate had finally rotted through, letting the anguish of the past few weeks rush into Bill's voice. "Or isn't *that* your field either?"

Jake whirled on Bill, proving that his floodgates, too, were weakening.

"—My *field*, and your field too, is inside that cooler! The only thing we have any right to worry about is the osteonase. There are two hundred and fifty people back home who have a fighting chance if we bring it to them. Here, there are only children who we can't help! Do you hear me, dammit? We can't help them!"

Bill had extended a second arm protectively around Geof, as if to shield him from the assault of Jake's words. It was an inadvertent gesture, but its significance was lost on neither man. Now, he withdrew that arm and cradled the boy only in his left. He tapped his helmet with a finger of his free hand.

"Up here, Jake, I know you're right. But I just can't be the cold fish that you are." He struck a blow with his hand on the tile floor. "I can't help thinking about all the other kids who must be hiding in these buildings. They must be scared and hungry and some of them sick. And there's nothing to do for them. It's like this is a second, unfair punchline to a joke that was awful the first time I heard it."

"Or," said Jake quietly, "it's like being awakened twice in one night by the same nightmare, finding yourself screaming the first time in terror, the second time in pity."

There was silence then. Geof stirred feebly against Bill's arm. The man glanced at the boy's face, then up at his partner.

"I didn't mean that you don't have feelings, Jake. It's just that you control them better than I do."

"I knew what you meant. It's okay," said Jake as he turned back to the cooler door. He started to work with grim efficiency, igniting the slim finger of flame with a sudden popping sound. The fire sizzled and bit into the bright metal, adding a glitter of actinic light to the cool fluorescence of the overhead fixtures.

Bill retrieved the pair of goggles from where they had fallen on the floor. He nudged Geof gently until his eyes opened and looked at him. They were bloodshot and seemed out of focus.

"How you feeling?"

"My head hurts," said Geof hoarsely.

"Here. Put these on." Bill fastened the goggles around the boy's head and adjusted the strap. "There, now you can watch the torch."

But Geof hardly seemed interested in the torch. He nodded weakly and was still.

"I think the boy's gonna be alright," said Bill. "He's just awful tired."

Jake didn't attempt to answer that above the snarling of the torch.

"You know the time I spent with Shansi, Jake, when I missed the last meeting?" Bill paused as though expecting a response from his partner. When none came, he continued anyway. "You know what she called that, Jake? She said, since I was going where there was so much death, that I needed a life inoculation. That's what she called it. Said she was inoculating me with life."

"An inoculation?" growled Jake. "First time I ever heard it called *that*."

"What?"

Jake pulled his torch away from the door and eased back on the flame. He looked at Bill. "Just who," he said, "was inoculating who?"

"Ah, you're a vulgar bastard. You know that?"

"Yeah, I know that." Jake chuckled as he turned up his torch again.

"Shansi's quite a girl, Jake." Bill raised his voice to be heard above the cutting sound. "You'd like her. We've got a bit of a problem though. At least we did before all this mess down here. She's with Colonel Purlman's section and they were scheduled to make a move over past the terminator in about a month. Maybe they won't go now. I mean, astronomy doesn't look like such a priority item any-more, does it?" There was no answer from Jake, only the steady crackling and snarling. "Lord, I hope they don't go. The way things are now, I couldn't stand not seeing her for a month at a time."

"Don't worry about it, kid," Jake raised his voice. "The calendar's been cleared for the next six months. Everything's on standby now. Purlman's group isn't going anywhere."

"Where'd you hear that?"

"I had time to scan the late graphics while I was waiting for you to show up at the terminal."

"Believe me, Jake. I *am* sorry about that. It won't happen again."

"Forget it, Billy. Never let it be said that Jackson Cays ever stood between a young man and his flu shots."

"Huh?"

"Your inoculation, dummy."

"Oh, yeah."

Jake sat back on his heels and turned off the torch for a rest.

"If you hadn't wasted all that time exercising your jaw," he said, "I'd have this done by now."

He had sliced out three sides of a fairly regular rectangle, measuring roughly one meter by a half. The steel was blackened where it had been cut.

Bill still sat with Geof, who seemed to be dozing.

"Can't you just bend that piece back," he said, "and get at the lock mechanisms from there?"

"No way," grumbled Jake. "The damned lock's buried in the wall. I'm going to have to pull out all this insulation and cut through the other side too." He stood up to relax his joints. "This gravity's killing me," he said. "How's the kid?"

"All that thrashing around he did must've wore him out. He's done nothing but sleep since."

Jake was performing a routine check of the girdle-like appliance at his waist. "Damn," he said. "Here's another one for maintenance. I can't get a readout for external oxygen. What's your belt say?"

Bill consulted a dial on his belt.

"I guess mine's busted too," he said.

"What!"

Quickly, Jake knelt down beside the boy. He pulled off the goggles and peered into his face. His lips were cyanotic, his cheeks sallow.

Jake slapped him sharply but there was no response. He peeled back one eyelid but he could read nothing in Geof's pupil.

"—Get him out into the corridor, Bill. See if you can revive him. Our meters aren't broken and he isn't asleep. He's been gassed. This whole damned room must be filled with CO_2."

Bill was stunned. "How in the hell—"

"—Get him out of here!"

Spurred to action, Bill moved toward the door with the boy in his arms.

Jake looked at the torch that he still carried and he looked at the cooler door with three quarters of a rectangle scorched into it. Then he gazed around himself at the walls of the room.

"Stupid building," he said. "Did you think I was trying to burn you down?"

With the fire presumably smothered by the gas, the building had cancelled its alert. The doors were no longer magnetized. They stood open where Bill had raced through the waiting room and out into the corridor. Jake could see his partner with the boy, a limp mass, kneeling on the hard floor. Jake took two steps forward so that he could see over a lab table.

"Any luck?" he asked.

Bill was too busy to answer. He was anxiously pressing both hands, thumbs together in the accepted fashion, against the boy's back, then tugging on his arms. He repeated this technique several times. Finally, he stopped and shouted something at Jake. His speaker translated most of this into static but Jake understood the desperation in the man's voice. He tossed down the torch that he held in a gesture of disgust.

"Leave him, Bill," he said. "He was as good as dead already. Maybe this is the easiest, kindest thing for him."

Then, there was a sudden burst of static from Jake's speaker as he too shouted something. Abruptly, he was straining to get around the lab table, trying to reach his partner in time. His movements were underwater slow in the unaccustomed gravity.

"Don't be a fool," he hissed. "The boy's poison."

But when he reached Bill it was already too late. The latches that held his helmet in place had been undogged and pulled apart. Bill had pushed the creased silver shell back from his face. It was trying to regain its proper position, slipping repeatedly down over his eyes and nose, creating a minor hindrance as Bill covered the boy's open mouth with his own. Jake stood stiffly in the doorway and looked down on them. His partner was now irrevocably exposed to the poisonous world. He could hear Bill's voice each time that he came up for air.

"Breathe," he was saying. "Damn you, *breathe*."

Jake watched silently for a moment. Perhaps he was too stunned to speak. But when he saw the boy's chest begin rising and falling on its own, he swore softly.

"You know what you've done, don't you?"

Bill looked up at him with his eyes unnaturally wide. The helmet had fallen again into its proper position. His face, seen through the window, seemed dimmed, as though already drained of life. He laughed nervously, trying to mask what was written plainly on his face.

"Yeah, Jake, I know." He looked down at Geof. The boy was not yet conscious, but he was breathing evenly. "He's the only living human we found down here." Bill shrugged his shoulders in a helpless gesture. "I couldn't just let him die."

"You fool," spat Jake. "You probably haven't done him a favor. Odds are he'll be dead in a week anyway." Jake paused, seemingly reluctant to state what was obvious to both of them. But he did. "And *your* odds aren't even that good."

"I know. I'm sorry, Jake."

"You're *sorry*?" Jake lifted his arms in exasperation, but dropped them in defeat. Anger was the only emotion that came easily to him then. He was angry at Bill for what he had done, at himself for not stopping it, at Geof for precipitating it, at the building for causing it, at the whole world for coming to such a dismal conclusion. When he spoke, his voice was tense with anger.

"I don't know what sort of incubation period the thing has, but you have to leave *now*. I can't take the risk that you'll go crazy and somehow keep me from getting home with the bone juice." He pointed toward the elevators. "Go on. You've got the whole damned, poisoned mess of a world to yourself. Get as far away from here as you can." He pointed at Geof. "And take the little murderer with you. You deserve each other. No discussion!" Bill had been about to say something before Jake cut him off. "I got this rule. I don't talk to fools or dead men. And you're both!"

Silently, Bill lifted Geof, who had begun to stir feebly, and turned toward the elevators. When he reached the doors, he turned again to look at his partner who was regarding them both sternly, his arms folded across his chest.

"Jake?" he said. "I gotta ask you a favor."

There was no response.

"When you get back up there, Jake, I know you gotta make a report to Ricker. And in *that* you gotta tell it the way it really happened."

Bill paused, as though expecting some reaction from Jake. There was none.

"But if Shansi comes around—and she might, Jake—please don't tell *her* how it really happened. I mean, tell her I tripped and tore my suit open or something like that. Okay? Just don't tell her how it really happened."

Jake looked at him mutely for many seconds. When at last he did speak it became obvious why he had not before. He hadn't wanted his partner to know that he was crying.

"Sure," he said, his voice breaking huskily. "I won't tell her."

"Thanks, Jake." Bill's voice was also fraught with emotion. He clutched Geof like something precious to his chest and stepped into the waiting elevator car.

A discarded newsheet, displaying the headlines of weeks before, pinwheeled along the curbing. It was caught in an early evening gust of contagion. The cloying, sick-sweet scent was intensified by the man's awareness of its source. For the first dozen or so blocks he had worn the bulky airtight suit to protect him from the smell. But he had grown warm, so very warm that his own body heat had seemed to accumulate, trapped within the silver fabric, until the suit itself appeared to swell. The buildings, too, seemed swollen, their upper stories bulging out above the street. Even the pavement underfoot had become inflated. It resembled the huge, humped back of an incredibly long snake. It glistened in the light of the occasional streetlamp.

He knew, in his head, that the street was not really swollen, nor the buildings, nor even the suit. And he was of the vague opinion that he wasn't really hot. The gauge on his belt assured him that his suit's air conditioner was working perfectly. He suspected that the gauge was right. It was he who was out of whack, not the air conditioner.

In a lucid moment, he discovered that the suit was gone. He was wearing only his blue short-sleeved jumpsuit. He looked behind him but could see nothing that glittered silver in the darkness. He concluded that he must have discarded it several blocks before.

And he discovered that the boy was still behind him.

"Go away!" He shouted and waved his arms. "I told you that you can't stay with me!"

Unlike the man, the boy stood off to one side, as though still obeying a parental injunction to stay out of the street. His dirty brown hair, long uncombed or cut, was tossed alternately over his eyes and away again by the wind. He seemed both attracted to and repelled by the man. One arm hugged the slim post of a streetlamp that no longer worked fully. Its argon bulb glowed dimly above, illuminating itself but nothing more. A wan, other light seemed to come and go with the breathing of the wind. That came from a lamp half a block away, and from the moon.

"I want to stay with you," said Geof.

"You can't! I'll be dangerous soon!"

An excess of energy, flowing into gesticulating hands and arms and a grimacing face, kept the man's body in constant motion. His feet moved in an irregular shuffle as though he found it difficult maintaining his balance on the snake's back.

"I told you what to do, Geof. You have to search the buildings. You have to find the other children. You have to take them out of the city."

"I don't know where to go," said the boy.

The man took two stiff steps in Geof's direction. "That way!" He stabbed one arm out in the direction from which he had come. "Go in the opposite direction to the way I go. Otherwise, you're liable to get hurt."

When the man had approached him, Geof had automatically put the lamp post between them. He seemed frightened and yet drawn to the man.

He said, "I want to stay with you."

As he took another menacing step forward, the snake's back—or the pavement—seemed to shudder beneath the man's feet, because he lurched abruptly sideways. One knee buckled. His arms gyrated like a doomed equilibrist's balancing pole. When the clumsy maneuver was completed, he was sitting flush against the curbing. Geof altered his position slightly to put the lamp post between them again. He peered around the slim column with a mystified look on his face.

"Are you alright?" he said.

"I'm *dying*," moaned the man. "I can't get less alright than that."

Geof pondered for a moment before saying, "You're like the others, aren't you?"

Bill glared at the boy with a face that looked like it had just taken a mouthful of sand.

"No," he muttered. "I'm not like the others. They're dead. *I'm* dying. There's a difference."

Geof seemed willing to accept that. He said, "Did you come from an island?"

"Huh?"

"When you said you were from a place where the sickness couldn't reach, I thought of an island."

Bill looked at Geof curiously, his head wobbling slightly on the stem of his neck.

"Yeah," he said, rubbing his eyes with the backs of his hands. "I guess you could say I come from an island." He laughed and glanced skyward, "Luan, you're a perfect island, aren't you?"

(Eighty years later, that was the mistaken name that old Geof would remember. *Luan*, island of the gods. That, too, was the name that he told the councilmen. It didn't really matter that he had it wrong. Places and things don't care what you call them.)

Curiosity had overcome caution, so Geof now stood beside the pole as he watched Bill. He said, "If it was safe, why did you leave Luan? I wouldn't have."

"Oh, Luan is far from safe," said the man as he stared at the palms of his hands. "By its nature it's a dangerous place for people. But we've tamed it mostly." He turned his hands over and stared at their backs for a moment. He seemed troubled. He glanced at Geof. "What if I said *Calcium Resorption*? Would that mean anything to you?"

Geof shook his head.

"What if I said *Osteoporosis*?"

Another shake of the head.

"What if I said a disease that saps the strength from a person's bones? Would that tell you more?"

Geof appeared to think a minute, then shrugged his shoulders.

"I'm not sure," he said.

Bill was rubbing his hands together nervously. "It's what happens to old people," he tried to explain, "except on Luan it happens much earlier. We have children there with old bones."

Geof looked at him out of a baffled face.

"It's true," he said defensively. "I'm not raving, if that's what you think. Not yet anyway."

"How will I know when you start?"

The man clapped his hands and laughed. "This all sounds like gibberish to you, doesn't it?"

"What's gibberish?"

"It's Crazy Talk!" Bill shouted and leaned his face so aggressively in the boy's direction that Geof prudently stepped behind the light pole again.

Bill passed a weary hand across his eyes as though brushing away cobwebs. "Don't worry," he said, "I'm not going to hurt you—unless you stick around too long. I'm just trying to explain why Jake and I came here. You see, our leaders up there on Luan hired the lab back here to synthesize—that means to make—a serum or medication of some sort that would fix the calcium resorption."

The man paused again and wiped a hand across his face. The dim light left bleak hollows around his eyes. His energy seemed to be slowly draining away—like a balloon with a slow leak.

"What the scientists told us was that we could only solve our problem by recombo—like what they did with those fish people in Sumatra."

"The frog men?" said Geof, evincing a sudden interest.

"Yeah, I guess that's what the papers called them. You've heard about them?"

"My father talked about them . . ." Geof hesitated. "That was when he talked about men who were like gods."

Bill made a face like there was a bad taste in his mouth.

"Yeah. I remember," he said. "Anyway, there was a large group on Luan who wanted to be self-sufficient. They didn't like the idea of sending our women away to give birth, then waiting while the children's bones developed in a heavy gravity. That group thought that any price—even recombo—was worth paying if we could raise our children on Luan. I guess I agreed with them, mostly because Shansi did.

"But there was another group that stood against recombo, saying that it would take us out of the species and isolate us even more than we already were. The argument between the two groups has been going on for over two years now, and still nothing's been decided. The lab down here came up with a temporary treatment, called osteonase, that we'd have to take like a diabetic takes insulin. It wouldn't really solve the problem, but it would give us more time to argue about the other, the recombo."

Bill sat staring at his hands. His voice had become a dreary monotone.

"But, before they could ship the stuff—what Jake calls the bone juice—to Luan, we got this strange report that Buenos Aires had gone crazy and died." Bill gave a short laugh. "That's all it said. There weren't any details. I guess they were tyring to keep it quiet until they could figure out what had happened. There were a lot of rumors—but there always are a lot of rumors running around Luan. None of us gave it much thought until two days later when the reports began coming in as regular as heart beats. First Buenos Aires, then Capetown and Rio and Kinshasa and Miami and Madrid." Bill still stared gloomily at his hands. "At first we thought it might be some new kind of war going on, but it became clear early that if it *was* a war, then humanity was losing. I guess some big shots down here thought it was war too, because they ordered us to deploy our tactical nukes. Luckily, our leaders ignored that. Instead, they slapped a quarantine around us, cancelling all shuttles, and we waited." Bill looked at Geof with elements of grief and guilt lighting his eyes dimly."What else could we do?" he asked. "We couldn't help anyone here. All we could do was save ourselves."

As he spoke, Bill had gradually reclined. Now he was nearly supine with his shoulders propped up by the curb. He held his hands before his eyes, examining them curiously. Then he let them drop wearily to his sides.

"The rest of it's simple," he said. "When the dying was over down here, seven teams came down to seven cities to pick up things that we didn't have on Luan—things we had to have to survive. Jake and I were the team that came down for the bone juice." He stopped, then added, seemingly as an afterthought, "We were all expendable personnel."

He seemed enormously tired. He barely had enough strength left in him to lift his hands and look at them. He frowned and turned on his side. He looked at Geof.

"Find the other children, Geof. Take them out of the city. It doesn't matter where—just away from here."

Then, Bill closed his eyes and nestled his cheek against the concrete curb as if it were as soft as any pillow. Geof thought he was asleep. But, after a moment, he roused himself and lifted up on one elbow.

"I don't want to hurt you," he said. "But if you're here when I wake I might, Geof. So don't stick around." He paused and looked at his hands again. "There's something I need to know before you leave." He raised his hands for Geof to see. "What color are they?"

This seemed no sillier than the other things Bill had said. Geof peered around the light pole at the man's hands.

"It's dark," he said. "I can't tell."

"You mean they don't look red to you?"

Geof looked again.

"Maybe a little."

"No, no," moaned Bill. "Not a little red. They're godawful red, aren't they? Like cherries or like red roses in sunlight?"

That scared Geof. He clutched the pole tightly with one arm.

"You don't see it?"

Geof shook his head.

"Oh my Jesus, it must be starting," he moaned as he curled into a semi-fetal position with his hands clenched before his face. "Go away," he said, pressing his cheek against the concrete. "Let me sleep. Let me die."

But Geof did not go away.

It was still dark. Geof's stomach complained that it had not been fed since morning. The wind hissed between the buildings, coming steadily out of the west. It seemed to bear toward them a change in the weather. The dawn would find the gutters filled with rain. Bill lay face down on the pavement, snarling.

Geof thought that the man was still asleep, but he could not know for certain. When delirium troubles the border between wakefulness and sleep, both nations suffer a loss of territory. In his fevered mind, Bill may have imagined himself a sharp-fanged lupine beast, prowling the edge of a piney forest. Or he may have been a frightened soldier at Verdun, preparing for a bayonet charge by raising a feral growling in his throat. Whatever it was, it was not a sane sound that Bill was making, nor was it pleasant.

When the snarling began, Geof had retreated considerably from his position behind the light pole. He was now many meters distant with his back propped against the bricks of a building. He would not sit down for fear that he would fall asleep. He wanted to make certain that he was awake and mobile when Bill revived.

Why did he stay? Of that he wasn't certain himself. It was a sort of clinging, a cleaving to this man who, only hours before, had represented normalcy to Geof. That he was now far from normal wasn't reason enough to abandon him. Also, there was a certain dreary fascination to Geof's watching. A melancholic, empathetic, humane circuit had been fired in the boy's mind. This watching, like a deathbed vigil, seemed a natural thing for him to do.

Words had begun to take form within Bill's snarling, though little of what he said carried meaning for Geof. Seldom were any two of these words arranged to make consecutive sense—and even then it may have been an accident, a random noun followed by a chance verb followed by a place—a monkey slapping out sentences on a typewriter. Or what he said may have followed his mental topography; if so, it was a rough terrain. He spat out gullies filled with curses. He moaned oceans of trembling sibilants. He shouted rivers of objectless verbs. He called out a forest of names (names meaningless to Geof, who could never know the people they described). He choked on syllables of hate and coughed up a thin string of bile onto the pavement.

As this verbal landscape was taking shape, an energy seemed to gather in Bill's body, manifesting itself at first by vague twitchings and slow writhing, but later by frantic swimming motions. Eventually, Bill reached a stage in his strange, psychotic exodus where he propped himself up with his left arm and seemed to stare angrily at a single spot on the pavement. With terrible suddenness, he began slugging that spot with his balled right fist.

Geof winced and turned his head away. He knew that the popping and cracking he heard was not the sound of the pavement breaking. Somehow the disease had disarmed his synapses. The message of agony was not reaching Bill's brain.

When the frightful sounds stopped, Geof turned quickly to see what was happening. What he saw made him wary and sick.

Bill was struggling to rise to his feet. Unaware of his own injury, however, he was relying on his right arm to lift himself. Each time that he tried, fractured bone and torn muscle would fail him and drop him to the bloody pavement. The sight might have been comical had it not been so grisly. His right elbow had been dislocated and the ulna was driven through the flesh. The front and side of his blue jumpsuit were stained dark where he had fallen and rolled in his own blood.

Geof made himself small against the building, feeling the smooth cold bricks against his back and arms. He prayed that the man would not notice him. For Geof, this was a grim reprise of the things he had witnessed weeks before. He flexed his knees, preparing them for flight. He kept his eyes on the dying man.

Somehow, Bill had managed to get his feet beneath him. He staggered up in the noxious air like some poor ravaged creature out of Goya. His right shoulder was lifted above the left. His ruined right arm hung at his side. He had wounded himself in many other places while thrashing around. In the darkness, all the blood appeared black. His left eye and cheek were black. His chin was black. There was a black smear across his forehead.

He was talking again. Now, however, his voice contained awareness and his words were comprehensible. In a way, this was more terrible than the gibberish he had spoken earlier. It was hateful to think that there was still a thinking human being suffering inside that distempered creature. It would have been more comfortable to believe that he had become a mere collection of tortured muscles and dying organs without consciousness. It would have been more comfortable, but it was not so.

Bill was still a member of *Homo sapiens*, albeit a dying member.

"Jake?" he said, his voice a frightened whisper as he looked around. His left eye was swollen shut and glued with blood. But the right was opened wide with terror. He turned slowly and awkwardly around and around, searching for something in the windows of the buildings.

"Jake?" he repeated in a louder voice so that the name echoed up and down the urban canyon. His chest was rising and falling erratically beneath the bloodstained fabric of his jumpsuit. He seemed to detect something in the shadow of a doorway. He took a step toward it.

"Shansi?"

He listened for a moment, but only the wind answered him. The air had grown cold and heavy. Clouds blotted out the stars above. An expression of excruciating pain distorted the man's mottled features. He stared suddenly and accusingly at the tops of the buildings.

"Jackson Cays!" he bellowed. "Get your black ass out here!" He looked straight above into the invisible clouds. "The joke's over!" he screamed. "I want to go home!"

This outburst ricocheted off the metal and glass surfaces around him, so that it was several seconds before the steady hiss of the wind could be heard again. The man turned around three times and listened. But there was nothing more to be heard. Then he cried out again and again until his throat was raw and his voice hoarse. When he could shout no more, he stood hunched over and gasping for air. He had not quite recovered his wind when he spotted Geof.

"*You*," said the creature in a sandpaper voice, fixing the boy with its one good eye. "*You* did this to me." Outraged, the monster that had once been Bill stared murderously at Geof as if it could harm him simply by staring. Then it started in Geof's direction, traveling in an unbalanced, shambling gait.

The boy seemed mesmerized by the creature's single, glittering eye. He stood as though riveted to the bricks of the building. The chill, wet wind stirred the hair on his head and rippled the torn cloth of his shirt, but it could not move his eyes away from the approaching apparition's face. Besmirched and contorted, it seemed like the face of Hell's own representative on earth. Death Incarnate, making a noise in its throat and showing its teeth, was closing on Geof and he could not move. He could not even breathe.

"Murderer," rasped the monster when at last it stood above him. It stank of blood and sweat and hate. The entire right side of its body began to convulse spasmodically. The ruined right arm swayed harmlessly. The mask of hate that it wore gave way to one of bewilderment. In the bleary, painless, half-dead world where the creature now dwelt, it imagined its right arm to be intact. Yet, try as it might, it could not manage to strike Geof with that fist. Baffled, the monster emitted a roar of frustration and loathing as it raised its left fist above Geof's head.

The berserker yell was enough to knock Geof from his trance. With a scrambling of small feet on pavement, he dashed away parallel to the buildings. He stumbled and fell. He rolled and came up running. He did not look back.

Behind him, the dying monster screamed.

"Murderer!"

The sound echoed down the concrete ravine.

Finally, the rain began to fall.

The old man had added a soft leather jerkin to his linen tunic. The sun had turned red and oblate as it dropped into the western horizon. The air was cooling rapidly. The old man imagined he heard a faint, faroff hissing sound as Sol met the western sea. He chuckled at his own whimsy. He knew the sun was a very distant thing that could never touch the water. He knew that it was a mammoth thing, larger than the earth, and that only its distance made it seem small. And he knew about Luan.

He had chuckled when Hink Bardo, the riverman, had vowed that his men and he would sail the vast ocean to find the island, Luan, wherever it might lie.

"Ah, little captain," said the old man to himself. "If the great madness could not reach Luan, how can you?"

All the other councilmen had been struck silent by the old man's story. They had always believed the old city to be haunted, but they had never known with what. They left, mumbling their thanks, returning to the rude village to find an apprentice storyteller. They did not leave with the same fervor for the task that they had shown when they arrived.

The old man had been right. It was not a story for children.

In the twilight, without the company of the children, Geof Talmund felt the cool loneliness of night creeping in. He grew philosophical, reflecting on his own life and on the lives of the river people.

"Yes," he murmured, "my life has been like a simple rainbow. A many-colored arc, falling as gently as it rose. And the children? Their golden haze meets my yellow fog and forms a . . . what? Not a circle." The old man shook his head. "For we can never come full circle. Instead, we must form a spiral." Old Geof made a corkscrew motion with an index finger, stabbing the air in front of him. He smiled. "Yes, our lives mingled form a spiral, winding down through the ages."

It did not occur to the old man to call that a helix.

He sat quietly for many minutes. The night had grown perfectly black. He felt a curious contentment as he listened to the river sounds that rose through the cool air from far below. There was the gurgle and plink of water as it made its way toward the sea and the gruff, self-satisfied *hur-mph* of a bull frog. Occasionally, a sound would reach him from the village. A door would open or close creakily. A mother would call out in a tiny, faroff voice, scolding a child, or a husband. As he listened, the old man imagined all the lives below him as rainbows taking shape and for a moment in his mind he saw the world as a circus of colliding colored light.

He closed his eyes then to improve his vision. When he opened them again, there was a shadowy, sylphlike creature moving noise-lessly on the path. It stepped into his yard and the old man heard the hiss of its feet brushing through the tall grass. By that sound, he knew that it was real and not a vision. It stopped a few meters from him. There was no moon yet to see clearly by, but the old man was familiar with the creature's size.

"You are out late, child. Do your parents know?"

"My parents weren't home to ask."

Geof recognized the musical voice of the girl, Wendy.

"Oh?" he said. "Where have they gone?"

"Up the big hill," she said and she might have pointed across the river toward Riverbend Hill though Geof could not be certain in the darkness. "Once a week they go up the hill at night. They come back in the morning."

Geof smiled, recognizing this as one solution to a young couple's problem when raising a small child in a one-room frame house. Some nights they must spend together, alone.

"They left no one to watch you?"

"Only grandmother. But she was sleeping, and I didn't want to wake her. She sleeps so poorly these days."

"What is so important," said Geof, "that you could not wait until morning to tell me?"

"I wanted you to know that I still remember the story from this morning."

The girl obviously had something more on her mind, but Geof was not one to press an issue.

He said, "I expected all of you back in the afternoon. I would have finished the story."

"We had to stay inside this afternoon."

"A punishment?"

"Yes. Rory and Joshua got into a fight and they both had the shaking sickness." There was a note of disapproval in her voice.

"Are they alright now?"

"I don't know." Her tone made it clear that she could not care less about the two roughnecks. "They had to stay inside like everybody else."

"Ah, poor Wendy," said the old man. "It has always been so. The innocent are punished along with the guilty."

"But it wasn't fair to make the rest of us stay inside too."

"Fairness," said the old man, though he had little hope that she would understand, "is not a principle of the universe. It is a principle peculiar to Man. And, like Man, it sometimes fails."

She worked on that silently for a moment as a chill breeze lifted the elm's branches. The moon had risen above the eastern hills and the west wind seemed to be working against it, trying to impede its progress across the sky. It threw clouds against it and shook the trees at it angrily.

"Why did the Council visit you?"

Geof thought about that for a moment as he watched the movements in the sky.

"They came to hear a story," he said.

"Which one?"

"It was one that you haven't heard," said Geof. "It was a story for grownups."

"You mean you won't tell it to us?"

The old man looked at the girl. The fragile moonlight gleamed on her cheek, illuminating a puzzled frown.

"No," he said, "*I* will not tell it to you. But when you have grown into a woman with children of your own, then you may hear it. There will be another storyteller then, a younger one. Ask him for the story of the island man. He will know which one you mean."

"The island man," said Wendy quietly. "I will remember."

"You better go home now, before your grandmother wakes to find you gone."

She turned to go, but took only two steps before turning back.

"Sir?"

"Yes, dear?"

The thin shift that the girl wore offered little protection from the night air. Wendy hugged her slender arms around herself and dug her toes into the grass, searching for the warm soil beneath.

She said, "I told my mother that you called me Wanda."

"And?"

"She cried."

"I'm sorry."

"Oh, she wasn't sad," the girl added quickly. "I think it was just the other way. I think it made her happy."

Geof nodded. He had experienced nostalgic tears before.

"In fact," the girl smiled mischievously, "I think *that* was the reason she and father climbed the hill tonight. I don't think they planned to go before I told her."

Geof grinned sheepishly, somewhat abashed at the consequences of his simple mistake. He lifted his eyes across the valley toward the broad dark mass of Riverbend Hill. It was somehow pleasing to know that a ritual as old as the species was taking place there now, even as he watched. He turned his eyes away, giving them back their privacy.

"Thank you, Wendy," he said. "Go home now, before you catch cold."

She left, moving noiselessly on the moonlit path, then disappearing into the shadow of the trees.

Geof Talmund sat for a while longer on his front stoop, watching the moon battle its way across the sky. The wind in the trees made a sound like distant surf. A seashell sound. The river continued its glide to the west. When it grew too cold, Geof clutched his kidsoft jerkin around him and went inside to his bed of straw.

An old man at the end of his rainbow.